P9-CKF-582

Kristen Britain's
exciting tale
of Karigan G'ladheon:

Green Rider
First Rider's Call
The High King's Tomb
Blackveil
Mirror Sight
Firebrand

KRISTEN BRITAIN

FIREBRAND

DAW BOOKS, INC.
DONALD A. WOLLHEIM, FOUNDER
375 Hudson Street, New York, NY 10014
ELIZABETH R. WOLLHEIM
SHEILA E. GILBERT
PUBLISHERS
www.dawbooks.com

Jacket art by Donato.

Jacket design by G-Force Design.

Book design by Stanley S. Drate/Folio Graphics Co., Inc.

DAW Books Collector's No. 1750.

Published by DAW Books, Inc.
375 Hudson Street, New York, NY 10014.

First Printing, March 2017
1 2 3 4 5 6 7 8 9

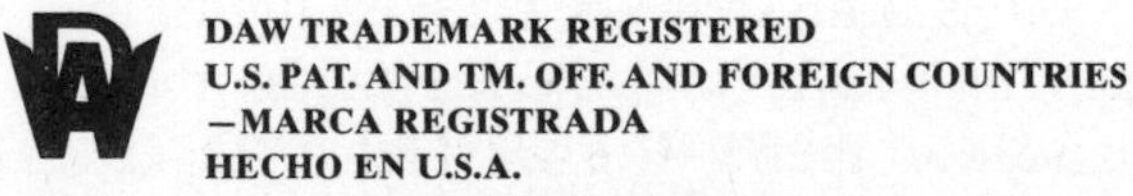

PRINTED IN THE U.S.A.

ACKNOWLEDGMENTS

The creation of a book is a journey, a dangerous quest through dark forests of malevolent story threads, steaming, stinking quagmires of grammatical conundrums, and toothy mountain ranges of authorial uncertainty. Opposing forces of all kinds (including procrastination orcs) attempt to thwart the goal of the quest. (That would be the book you now hold.) The author would not overcome such obstacles without helpers along the way. This is her (my) opportunity to thank them.

Any quest would be much more difficult and lonely without stalwart companions to help face the many perils encountered. Thank you to the Schoodic Peninsula Writers Group East (especially when I presented stacks of chapters for critique): Cynthia Thayer, Brian Dyer Stewart, Melinda Rice, and Bianca Lech.

Some quests require someone with an extraordinary skill to accomplish a task in order for the protagonist to achieve her goal. In a fantasy story, that might be a thief or swordfighter. In the production of this book, it was the sharp pen-wielding expertise of my copyeditor, Annaliese Jakimides. I thank her for her skillful and sensitive touch in making this book better. Yay style sheets!

If I am to take this analogy further, there has to be a wizard, and that title I give to my editor, Betsy Wollheim, who magically brings everything together, and whose story insight I value. Working with Betsy at DAW Books are co-wizard and co-editor, Sheila Gilbert, and their wizardlings: Josh Starr, Katie Hoffman, Briar Herrera-Ludwig, Sarah Guan, Peter Stampfel, and George. I thank them all for the benevolent use of their magic on my books. And actually, they sort of sound like a rock band.

There is often a mysterious, cloaked figure in a story who makes things happen behind the scenes. In my case, there are three. I thank my agents Russell Galen, Danny Baror, and Heather Baror-Shapiro for doing the mysterious things they do.

Thank you also to artist Donato Giancola who has cast a magical spell of his own with yet another beautiful cover painting, as well as to his counterpart in France, Alexandre Dainche.

I also thank wise woman Chris (Chrissy) Thompson for sitting with me in coffee shops to pursue some very odd conversations despite the concerned looks and raised eyebrows of other patrons directed our way.

And to my readers, thank you for giving the Green Rider books a try. You are, for a writer, journey's end. Now, where is the village tavern and its barkeep?

* * *

Ruth Stuart, I miss you, but I always see you in the shimmer of the stars at night.

For
Elizabeth Patton
and
Katharyn Howd Machan
and
all the educators
whose encouragement lifted me
like a leaf
upon a wisp
of a
breeze

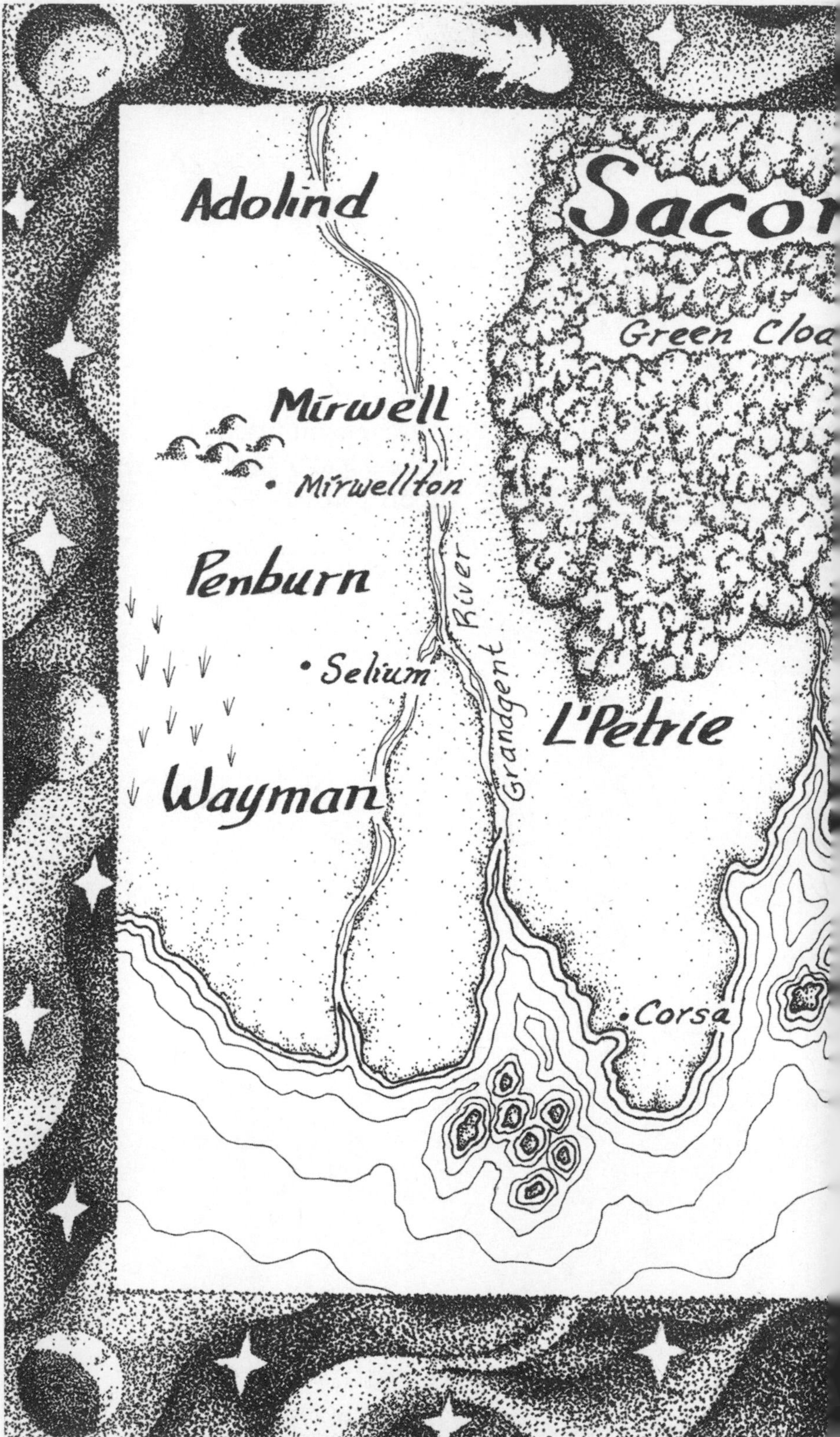

Adolind
Sacor
Green Cloa
Mirwell
Mirwellton
Penburn
Selium
Grandgent River
L'Petrie
Wayman
Corsa

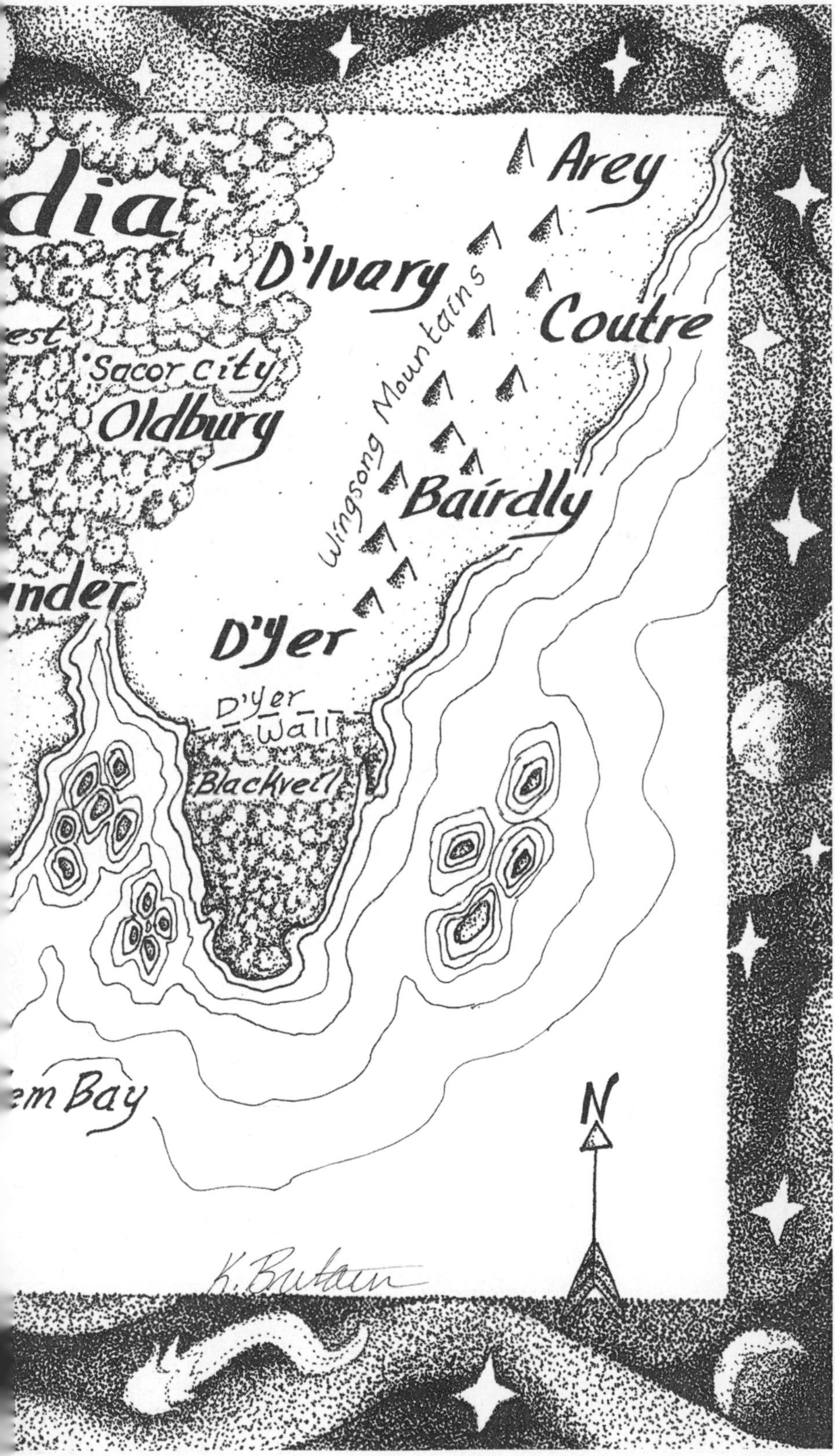

dia
est
Sacor city
Oldbury
D'Ivary
Arey
Coutre
Wingsong Mountains
Bairdly
nder
D'Yer
D'Yer Wall
Blackveil
em Bay
N
K. Butain

ARRIVALS

"I know you can do it." Mara placed her hands on Karigan's shoulders and squeezed.

"But—"

"You survived Blackveil and Mornhavon the Black. You've even been through time!"

"I don't know . . ." Karigan glanced uncertainly toward the open doors of the throne room. The guards posted there watched her with interest.

"*I* know." Mara turned her around and marched her toward the entrance.

This had to happen sooner or later, Karigan thought, but still she resisted. Mara just pushed harder until they stood on the threshold.

"Now be a good Green Rider and go on in there," Mara said.

"Easy for you to say. Aren't you coming?"

"Heavens no! You couldn't drag me."

"Coward." Karigan knew her friend meant well, but a little more support would not have been asking too much.

Mara simply smiled and gave her a gentle push. Karigan took a shaky breath and stepped across the threshold into the throne room.

"KARIGAN HELGADORF G'LADHEON!"

It thundered like a pronouncement of doom from the gods, and she pivoted as if to run back the way she had come, but Mara, arms crossed and shaking her head, blocked her escape.

"Helgadorf?" asked an amused voice. King Zachary.

Karigan winced, and warmth crept into her cheeks. Mara grinned at her.

"Named after her great grand aunt, Your Majesty," came a crusty reply. "A prickly old banshee no one particularly liked. Why Stevic would name her after—"

"Brini!" came a sharp warning.

Karigan slowly turned back around. There arrayed before the king's throne, with a frazzled-looking Captain Mapstone in their midst, were her aunts, all four of them, and standing aloof just off to the side, her father. When Mara had informed her of their arrival, she'd been caught off guard, for they'd sent no forewarning, and it was winter, when travel was difficult. Karigan, still struggling to adjust to ordinary life after her all-too-recent adventures, coupled with the accompanying darkness and sorrow, now faced a huge dose of "ordinary" in the form of her family, and it threatened to overwhelm her.

Her aunts could exasperate even the stoutest of souls at the best of times, and she was so very tired . . .

"Helgadorf was more a leader than anyone else on Black Island during her day," Aunt Stace said with a sniff. "She organized the island to repel pirates and raids from the Under Kingdoms."

"She was still a banshee," Aunt Brini muttered, and then whispered loud enough for all to hear, "and she still is."

Great Grand Aunt Helgadorf had been dead for forty years.

Ignoring her sister, Aunt Stace, with her hands on her hips, said, "Don't just stand there like a post without a fence, Kari girl, come here."

Karigan glanced over her shoulder. Mara had not lingered to witness the reunion. She considered making a run for it, but doing so would only prolong the inevitable. Best to face them now. She took a deep breath and started walking slowly down the runner like a swimmer reluctant to dive into icy water. It wasn't that she didn't want to see her family—she loved them more than anything—but she didn't want to face their questions about the expedition into Blackveil, about how she'd gone missing and was presumed dead. She didn't want to speak of the future and her experiences there because to do so was to relive the dark. And her memories of Cade? Those were hers, and hers alone, and not a casual topic of conversation. Knowing her aunts, however, they would pick and pry until they stripped the carcass to the bone.

When she had written them after her return just over a month ago, she'd been characteristically terse, reassuring them she was alive and well, but avoiding the painful details. Captain Mapstone had also written her father, but she had no idea what had been said. Her aunts' questions would come, she knew, from a place of love and concern, but she was not ready or willing to encourage them with additional fodder.

And then there was the subject of her eye, about which she had said nothing, and about which they were bound to make an issue. She touched the leather patch that covered it, her right eye, and took another determined breath and picked up her pace. When she reached her aunts, they swarmed her with crushing hugs and kisses and complaints.

"You are too skinny!"

"We were told you were dead!"

"Thank the gods you came back to us."

Aunt Gretta stared at her critically, her head canted to the side. "What is wrong with your eye?"

"Got something in it, is all," Karigan replied.

"Let me see." Aunt Gretta reached for her eyepatch.

"No!" Karigan backed away.

"I just want to see what's wrong with your eye," Aunt Gretta said in a stung voice.

Karigan covered it with her hand. *"No."*

"Removing the patch," Captain Mapstone said, "causes her eye pain."

That was very true, but it was so much more than that.

Because the captain had spoken up, all four aunts now turned on her demanding explanations. The captain must have known this would happen, and Karigan made a mental note to thank her at the next opportunity.

Her father, who had stood remote, used the distraction to finally reach for her, his arms wide open. She stepped into his embrace and hugged him hard. "We had to come and see you," he murmured. "Nothing could stop us. We thought we had lost you."

"I know," she said, "but I came back. I am too stubborn to be lost. Stubborn, like you."

When they parted, he rubbed his eyes. Karigan stared, astonished. Had she ever seen him cry before? He took a rattling breath and collected himself. "I would like the complete story of what happened to you. The captain," and now his voice tightened, "was vague on the subject, and your letter was, shall we say, rather lacking?"

"I, uh—"

At that moment, a hand rested on her sleeve. Startled, she looked up. The king. He had descended from his throne chair and approached from her blind side. She'd never get used to the loss of her peripheral vision in that eye.

"Your Majesty," she said a little breathlessly. She looked down, unable to meet his gaze, for it held so much that remained unresolved between them.

"I believe your captain requires rescuing."

She glanced at her besieged captain. All four aunts were still chivvying her about Karigan's appearance, and didn't she take better care of the people under her command? Thankfully, Karigan thought, they could not see her other scars, those of the flesh hidden by her uniform, as well as the invisible wounds within.

"Enough," she told them firmly. "Captain Mapstone is not to blame for anything." When this failed to quell their outrage, she added, "And do not forget you are in the king's presence."

That silenced them, and quite suddenly they each looked ashamed and started curtsying to the king and uttering chastened apologies. Captain Mapstone simply looked relieved.

"Sir Karigan," the king said, "*We* are releasing you from duty so you may spend a couple days with your family. We hope you will be able to satisfy their curiosity about your most recent exploits. And to your family, We say, know that Sir Karigan has Our highest esteem. She has served this realm well and courageously time and again. She should receive no reproach from her closest kin, only praise and honor."

Karigan stared at him in surprise. First, he had used the royal "we," which she had rarely, if ever, heard from him. Then there was the rest of his speech. Her aunts looked astonished and her father very proud. It wasn't as if they hadn't known the king regarded her highly; he had knighted her, after all, but it must have made more of an impression on them coming directly from his mouth. It certainly impressed Karigan.

Her father bowed. "Thank you, sire. I have always considered my daughter exceptional, and it pleases me she has served Your Majesty well. But we have been enough of a distraction to you, as you must have important matters of state to attend to."

As if his words had been prescient, there was a brief commotion at the throne room entrance, and a moment later, Neff, the herald, bolted down the length of the room and bowed before the king. "Your Majesty, visitors from—"

He didn't have to complete his sentence for them to know where the visitors were from. Three of them, cloaked in shimmering gray against the winter, entered the throne room. The dim afternoon light seemed to stretch through the tall windows for the singular purpose of brightening their presence. The trio glided down the runner with long, matched strides. Not too fast, not too slow.

Aunt Tory tugged on Karigan's sleeve. "Child, are those Elt? *Real* Elt?"

"Very real," she murmured on an exhalation. A sense of familiarity washed over her. Not as if she had experienced this scene before, but more as if there were a rightness to it, like a thread of time that had been realigned.

Also, because the Eletian leading his two companions was well known to her.

"Lhean."

He halted before her and nodded. "Galadheon."

Aunt Brini loudly whispered, "Why does he say our name like that?"

Karigan did not answer. Unable to restrain herself, she hugged Lhean. She had never hugged an Eletian before, and he stiffened in surprise, then relaxed and hugged her back, if tentatively. He smelled of the winter wind and fresh snow. They had been through much together, the two of them, first the journey into Blackveil, then being thrust into the future. He was Karigan's only living link to what had befallen her in the future, the only one, besides herself, who had known what it was really like there.

He studied her for a timeless moment, and what went on behind his clear blue eyes, she could not say. Eletians, their behaviors and expressions, were not always easy to interpret. Then he nodded to himself as if satisfied by his observation of her. "It is good to see you again."

He swiftly turned from her, and he and his companions bowed to King Zachary. The others were familiar to Karigan, as well. She had briefly met Enver and Idris upon her return from the future to the present.

Karigan's aunts watched the scene in wide-eyed enchantment. Her father, however, glowered. Karigan knew he distrusted all things magical, and Eletians embodied magic as no other beings did. She was sure he also resented them for any questionable influence they'd had over his late wife and daughter.

"We bring you greetings, Firebrand," Lhean told the king, "from our prince, Ari-matiel Jametari."

King Zachary stepped up to the dais and sat once more upon his throne chair. "And to what honor do I owe his greetings, brought in the midst of winter?"

Karigan knew she should be escorting her family out of the throne room so the king could conduct his business without an audience, but she couldn't help herself. A visit by Eletians was momentous, and besides, it was Lhean! What, she wondered, would he tell King Zachary?

His answer, however, was delayed, delayed by the arrival of yet another unexpected visitor.

FROSTBITE

A bedraggled figure stood uncertainly in the throne room entrance, wrapped in a bulky, hooded fur coat and trailing a scarf. Everyone watched as Neff spoke to and peered beneath the hood of the visitor, who tugged a flat object out of a satchel and showed it to him. He studied it for a moment, and then coming to some conclusion, turned and hastened down the runner.

When Neff reached the dais, he announced, "Your Majesty, Lady Estral Andovian, daughter and heir of Lord Fiori, the Golden Guardian of Selium, begs an audience."

"Estral?" Karigan hadn't realized she'd blurted her friend's name aloud until she noticed everyone's gaze on her.

"Of course," King Zachary told Neff. Then projecting his voice down the length of the room, he said, "Please approach, Lady Estral. You are ever welcome."

The Eletians, speaking softly to one another, intently watched Estral's advance. Their musical voices, however, were drowned out by the chatter of Karigan's aunts.

Estral's steps looked pained as she moved forward, and it was clear she was experiencing some difficulty. It was Karigan's father who leaped to her aid. He strode to her and placed his arm around her for support. Karigan, as if roused from a dream, shook herself and followed after him. As she neared Estral, it was easier to see the windblown tendrils of sandy hair sticking out from beneath her hood. White patches had formed in the middle of her ruddy cheeks.

Frostbite.

She did not spare Karigan a glance, but kept determinedly pushing forward, her gaze fixed on the king.

"Send for a mender," Karigan's father ordered. "I don't think she can feel her feet."

Karigan did not hesitate, but ran to the corridor just outside the throne room entrance where a couple of Green Foot runners stood on duty.

"We need a mender down here," she told one of them. "Get Rider-Mender Simeon *now*!"

"Yes, ma'am!" the boy said, and he set off down the corridor at top speed.

Karigan's step faltered as she turned back to the throne room. When in the name of the gods had she become a *ma'am*? It made her feel old. Maybe it had just been the tone of her voice that inspired the boy's response, or maybe to those young Green Foot runners she *was* old. Ancient, even.

She trotted back down the length of the throne room to find the king, the captain, her aunts and father, and the Eletians gathered around Estral, who was seated on the bottom step of the dais. Lhean knelt before her, helping her to sip from a flask.

"It is a warming cordial," Lhean explained.

After just a few sips, Estral's color looked better, but she did not speak, and then Karigan remembered that she could not. Mara, who had caught Karigan up on so much news upon her return, had told her Estral's voice had been stolen by a magical spell.

Aunt Stace held Estral's hands in her own to warm them. Aunt Gretta was removing her boots.

"She needs a lukewarm bath," Aunt Brini said.

Lhean continued to speak to Estral in a voice so quiet that Karigan could not hear his words. She wondered what he said. Captain Mapstone and the king, meanwhile, stood aside, shoulder to shoulder, gazing at the flat object Estral had carried with her—a slate—and spoke to one another in low voices.

What was that about?

Karigan's gaze swept beyond those who hovered over Estral to where Lhean's companions stood, and she caught Enver watching her. He quickly looked away. Since her arrival home, she'd caught people staring at her every now and then. Rumors had been circulating about her returning from the dead in spectacular fashion on Night of Aeryc. She really couldn't blame them for looking at her askance, and she wouldn't have given Enver a second thought, except that his averting his gaze struck her as not very Eletianlike. An Eletian, she believed, would not care if she caught him staring, but just as she thought when she had first met him, she suspected he was not a typical Eletian, or maybe not even a full Eletian, which was an interesting notion.

Fortunately, Ben Simeon and a trio of apprentice menders soon arrived. Ben knelt beside Estral, and he and his assistants helped her into a litter, then buried her beneath blankets. All the while, Karigan's aunts provided Ben with their unsolicited advice.

"Please, Aunt Tory," Karigan pleaded, tugging on her aunt's sleeve, "he doesn't need your recipe for hot toddies just now."

Ben cast her a grateful, harried glance.

"Do not spare the whiskey, young man," Aunt Tory exhorted. It was not a surprising suggestion, as she was rather fond of strong toddies herself.

Despite the "help" of Karigan's aunts, the menders worked efficiently.

"It will be all right," Karigan tried to reassure Estral, but if she heard, Karigan could not tell, and the menders lifted her away on her litter and whisked her from the throne room.

Karigan stood at a loss, feeling torn about which direction to go. She glanced from the Eletians, who were now conferring with the king, to her family, and then to the throne room entrance, through which Estral and her bearers disappeared.

Captain Mapstone joined Karigan and her father, the slate tucked beneath her arm. Aunt Gretta marched up to them and said, "Those menders best heed my advice. I have plenty of experience with frostbite."

"I am sure they've got all the expertise they need," Karigan's father replied.

Aunt Gretta made an indignant *hurrumphing* noise, standing square with her hands on her hips. "You have no appreciation for all I've ever done for *you*, Stevic, including caring for *your* bouts of frostbite."

"Gretta—"

Uh oh, Karigan thought.

"You remember the time Stevic went into the snow in only his smallclothes?" Aunt Gretta asked her sisters.

Aunt Brini snickered, and the others nodded.

"Gretta, *no*," he said in a strangled voice. "It is unseemly to—"

She jabbed her finger at his chest. "Who kept you from freezing, eh? All your little fingers and toes, your ears and cheeks, and your wee little—"

"Enough! That's—I was only four years old!"

A wicked gleam shone in Aunt Gretta's eyes. "Wouldn't be any Kari if I hadn't been there to thaw out your important bits."

Karigan's father looked mortified. Captain Mapstone had turned away with her hand over her mouth, either choking or laughing, or both. Karigan glanced toward the king and was relieved to find he was absorbed in conversation with his visitors and seemingly unaware of the familial squabbling occurring in his throne room.

Stevic G'ladheon restrained further outburst and straightened his shoulders as if to exude dignity, but he only looked pained. He took a deep breath, then a second, before speaking. "It is time to leave." He stared his sister down. "The menders have their hands full, and so does Karigan." He passed Aunt Stace a significant look.

Ordinarily, the sisters would heed Aunt Stace when they would not heed their brother, but before she could even open her mouth, Aunt Tory complained in a querulous voice, "He is always telling us what to do."

The others nodded in agreement and made no move to leave. Karigan was sure it was going to turn into a scene, one she'd rather avoid in the king's throne room. She gazed at the walls, where in sheltered alcoves, the king's Weapons stood watch. They were so silent, so still, their black uniforms blending in with the shadows, that it was easy to forget they were there, and that was how they liked it. She espied her friend

Donal, if a Weapon could be deemed a friend, and gestured frantically for his help.

At first Donal remained statue-still as if he had not seen Karigan, or chose to ignore her. As the voices of her aunts grew in pitch at their brother's attempt to shepherd them out of the throne room, Karigan despaired, but then Donal did move, and a second Weapon, Travis, fell in step with him, though Donal had given no discernible signal.

"Clever of you," a forgotten Captain Mapstone murmured beside her, humor alight in her hazel eyes.

The two Weapons halted in front of Karigan's aunts, who fell into a wary, and welcome, silence. Weapons were deadly warriors and forbidding in countenance. Most found it unnerving to fall under their stern gazes. Donal bowed, leaving all four aunts, it appeared, flabbergasted.

"As you are family of our esteemed Sir Karigan," Donal told them, "it would be our honor to escort you out."

It could have just as easily been a courteous offer to throw them out.

It sounded like Captain Mapstone was trying not to laugh again. Karigan's aunts remained speechless, clearly flummoxed by being confronted by two of the king's own Weapons up close with their warrior bearing and stony, solemn faces. Her aunts craned their necks to look up at Donal. He towered over them, all shoulders and black leather. Karigan had never seen her aunts so silent. Even in sleep they were not this quiet.

Then Donal did the inconceivable—he offered Aunt Stace his arm in a courtly manner. She tentatively took it, gazing up at him uncertainly. With little prompting, he and she started to walk down the runner toward the entryway of the throne room. Aunt Tory, Aunt Brini, and Aunt Gretta hastened after them. Travis brought up the rear.

"Breyan's gold," Karigan's father said in awe and relief. "I have never seen the like. I'd take one of these Weapons home with me, but I do not think it would be long before my sisters had him cowed like the rest of us."

"You are clearly of one family," Captain Mapstone remarked.

Karigan and her father glanced at the captain, who offered them an innocent smile and shrug.

"Hmm," Stevic G'ladheon said after a considered moment, his eyebrows drawn together as he regarded the captain with an enigmatic look. Abruptly he turned to Karigan. "I had better catch up before those Weapons return and decide to haul me out, too, but I wanted a hug and to tell you that I will see you again tomorrow. When your duties permit." As they embraced, he added, "I bet Estral could use a friend right now."

He then nodded to the captain and strode away. Karigan watched after him, one part relieved and one part sorry he was leaving already. But as he said, she would see him tomorrow. He was only going into the city. It was not as if he were departing for Corsa.

"I think your father is right," Captain Mapstone told her. "Lady Estral could use a friend right now, and probably *these*, too." She handed Karigan the slate and a piece of chalk.

Karigan stared blankly at the items, until she realized this was how Estral communicated. Scrawled across the slate in smudged chalk were the words: *Father still missing. Please help.* Her father, Mara had told Karigan, had been missing since the summer. The words were deceptively simple, for she could well guess the depth of sorrow and fear behind them.

"Don't worry about our visitors," Captain Mapstone said. "I will call on you if we need anything. On your way out, could you please send a runner after the king's other counselors?"

That was a dismissal if Karigan had ever heard one. She looked regretfully at Lhean, his back to her as he spoke with the king. Not only did she want to know what had brought the Eletians to Sacor City, but she wished to speak with Lhean. She wanted to ask him what he remembered of the future, to validate all that had happened to her there. Surely he would not leave without seeing her first, but one never knew with Eletians.

Her father and the captain were also right—Estral could use a friend right now, and that overrode Karigan's own needs. Reluctantly she left the throne room behind and, as requested, sent a Green Foot runner after the king's counselors, and received another "Yes, ma'am!" in return.

She headed to the mending wing, and once there, Ben greeted her with a smile. "Lady Estral is fine. I've thawed out her flesh, and there will be no permanent harm resulting from the frostbite. She is, however, very tired, so don't keep her awake if she wishes to sleep."

When Ben said he'd "thawed her flesh," he meant it literally. He had trained as a mender before hearing the Rider call, and the call had brought out his innate gift for true healing. His magic had healed Estral of her frostbite.

Karigan stared at the door, unsure of her welcome. She and Estral had not parted well on the morning of the spring equinox, the day Karigan had crossed over the D'Yer Wall and entered Blackveil Forest.

She had arrived at the wall, a sense of doom weighing on her at the prospect of entering beneath the shadowy eaves of the forest. She might not return. She might not see those whom she loved ever again. Despite being among friends, she felt alone and hoped that Alton would help assuage her fears, comfort her on the eve of her departure into who-knew-what dangers. Alton, with whom she had once been close. They might have had more, but for their erratic schedules and a certain reluctance on her part.

Despite the fact she had never told Alton one way or the other how she felt about him, even as he indicated he desired more, she had expected him to be there for her, to welcome her into his arms. She had expected him to wait for her. It never crossed her mind that he might fall for someone else.

And she certainly never expected him to fall for her best friend.

Estral had found her way to the wall well before Karigan arrived with the expedition, and she and Alton had fallen in love. Karigan clenched her hands recalling her feelings of betrayal with fresh intensity. She'd been a fool, reacted badly. Childishly. On the morning of the equinox, she had entered Blackveil, spurning her would-be lover and her best friend.

She might never have returned, might have gone to her grave without reconciling with either of them. But now time had passed and she had been through so very much, and her anger had faded long ago. The world, she thought, was too perilous and uncertain to throw away the bond of friendship over something she was not clear she had ever really wanted in the first place.

The question was, would Estral forgive her for her execrable behavior back at the wall?

There was only one way to find out, and she knocked on the door.

ASH GIRL

Karigan tentatively opened the door and peered into Estral's room. A lamp was set at low glow, but she made out her friend propped up on pillows, covered in extra blankets, and sipping a steaming liquid out of a mug. Broth, she guessed, unless Ben had followed Aunt Tory's instructions for a hot toddy.

"Do you mind having a visitor?" she asked.

Estral smiled and gestured that she should enter. Karigan crossed the room to the chair next to Estral's bed. Her friend looked much better, her cheeks a warm pink, but dark circles beneath her eyes revealed her exhaustion.

"I—I thought you might want these." Karigan held out the slate and chalk.

Estral set her mug aside on a small table and eagerly took the items, but before she could write a message, Karigan said, "I have something to say." Estral glanced up at her curiously. Karigan took a deep breath as she gathered her courage to say what she had to say. "I—I need to tell you I'm sorry. I'm sorry for my behavior when I last saw you. It was uncalled for. I was childish."

Her heart thrummed in fear as she waited to see how Estral would respond. After a moment, Estral reached over and squeezed her wrist and shook her head. Then she hastily wiped away the previous message on her slate and wrote, *I understand why you were upset. No apology needed. Afraid I'd lost you forever.* It was in her eyes, the grief, the despair.

Karigan's throat constricted and she fought back tears. "That is far better than I deserve."

Estral wrote, *It's called friendship.*

They hugged, cried, and laughed together, and agreed to forget any regrettable behavior of the past.

When once more they were settled, Estral took up her slate. The chalk tip-tap-tapped as she wrote, *So good to see you. Was worried—Blackveil, you dead.* She then pointed at her own eye to indicate Karigan's patch, her expression full of questions. She wrote, *Tell me everything. Got only pieces at wall.*

Estral may have lost her voice, but her curiosity remained intact.

"It's a very long story," Karigan said. Or was it? She remembered so very little, at least about her time in the future, just fragments from notes she had made after her return to the castle. There were some details and people she could picture quite clearly, thanks to drawings made for her by the ghost of Yates Cardell, but to give a linear tale of her adventures? The part about Blackveil, maybe, but not so much about what had come after.

As for her eye, with a shard of the looking mask lodged in it, it was its own long story.

"We can talk about that later," Karigan added. "Right now I'm more worried about you. Why in the bloody hells are you traveling in this weather?"

Estral wrote furiously on her slate. *Father missing too long. No word. Very worried.*

"The king has all his Riders keeping their eyes and ears open." Karigan glanced at the frosty window. Of course, few Riders had gotten out on errands between storms. "Word has also been passed from garrison to garrison. You don't think he's with your mother?" Estral's mother managed a lumber camp in the northern wilds.

Estral shook her head.

"So," Karigan said, "you decided to set out and look for him yourself."

Estral nodded, her expression fierce. She wrote, *And to prod the king—more searchers.*

Karigan suppressed a smile at the idea of prodding the king—any king, for that matter. One just did not do that, but

Estral wasn't just anyone. Beneath her gentle demeanor was the heart of a catamount. As for searching, where and how would she even begin? First of all, this was Estral who disliked travel and leaving home. For all that she'd spent a good amount of time down by the D'Yer Wall, Karigan knew her friend was an avowed homebody. Second, it was a big world—Lord Fiori could be almost anywhere. Not to mention it was winter, and a fierce one at that. Estral had survived the journey to Sacor City from the wall, but by the look of it, just barely.

WELL? Estral demanded, underlining the word three times. *Aren't you going to tell me I'm stupid?*

"Of course not," Karigan replied. "If it was my father, I'd want to search, too." Just the idea of someone she loved going missing, however, gripped her so suddenly, so unexpectedly, she caught her breath. Grief surfaced sharp and raw, and a tremor daggered through her body. She fought to maintain her composure, to rein in a torrent of emotion.

Cade . . . Without him, she was but cold ashes.

Estral reached over and placed her hand on Karigan's, her eyes of sea green conveying her appreciation for Karigan's understanding and, perhaps, detecting her distress, concern.

Karigan took a trembling breath before she could speak again, hastening to move on from the grief that haunted her. "And what did Alton have to say about your plan to leave and search for your father?"

Estral shrugged, her expression inscrutable.

"You didn't tell him, did you?"

Estral wrote, *Left note.*

Karigan could only imagine how well that went over. The wall had changed Alton, he had grown more volatile, and she knew he'd be distraught by Estral's departure. It did not help that, at the moment, there was no direct contact between the castle and the wall, so there was no way to allay his fears. Rider-Lieutenant Connly, whose ability was to mentally communicate with another Rider who was stationed at the wall, was stranded by the weather in the west. She could only hope the storms would calm so Connly could make his way back and restore contact. If the weather settled down, they could also send a message by conventional means.

"I'll ask the captain to send Alton word of your arrival when we are able," Karigan said.

Estral once again touched her hand in gratitude and mouthed, *Thank you.* Then she yawned.

Karigan stood. "I was told you were very tired. I'd better go so you can rest."

Estral looked ready to protest, then seemed to reassess. She sagged against her pillows.

"We'll talk again when you are feeling better," Karigan assured her. "I'll look in on you tomorrow."

Estral held her arms open, and the two embraced, something Karigan had feared she'd never get to do again.

She stepped out into the corridor of the mending wing and softly shut Estral's door behind her, then paused, closing her eyes. It had turned into an eventful day, but even with all the surprise visitors, she was left feeling bereft, alone.

When she returned from the future to her present, she had been torn from Cade. He had been unable to cross through time with her. His loss cut through her gut—cold, steely, and excruciating, but she tried to cope with it by throwing herself into her duties—minding the Rider accounts, mucking stalls, cleaning tack, working with Arms Master Drent . . . She kept hoping time would give her distance, make each passing day a little easier, dull the pain. Some days she would begin to feel as if she were regaining her equilibrium, feel like her old self again, and then something—the sound of a voice that had a familiar texture to it, or even the scent of boiled cabbage, strangely enough—would bring it all back, remind her of those last moments when they were ripped from one another, leaving them separated by a gulf of almost two hundred years.

She constantly wondered what had become of him, or rather, what *would* become of him. Her return had to have altered the threads of time in some way, and there was no telling if he would even exist in the future now.

She set off, leaving the mending wing behind. The walls around her blurred as she walked, descended stairs, crossed through halls and corridors. She had been doing well for several days in a row now, but Estral's distress for her father had heightened Karigan's own sense of vulnerability, aroused her fear for all that could be lost, and her grief for what had been.

Lhean's presence also brought the pain back with a sharp, terrible immediacy. He had been in the future with her, had met Cade. He'd been there the very moment Cade had been torn from her. Lhean was her connection to memories of which she possessed only glimpses. She wanted to speak of Cade with Lhean. Doing so, she thought, would keep him alive, but would also hurt. Sometimes she wished she could forget so the pain would go away. Oblivion would be so much easier.

The castle appeared nearly empty. Most inhabitants would be at supper at this hour. The deserted corridors echoed the hollowness she felt within.

She shook her head thinking that only *she* could feel lonely when her father and aunts had come all the way from Corsa to visit her, and her best friend was also here.

She turned down the dim main corridor of the Rider wing, suddenly exhausted by it all. She would take advantage of the quiet, and sit and rest in the Rider common room. It was usually too noisy with boisterous young Riders made restive by being stuck indoors for so long, but with them all at supper, the common room beckoned.

Yes, she would sit for a while and think of Cade. She would try to remember.

Anna the ash girl was just exiting the Rider wing with full buckets when she espied Rider Sir Karigan's approach, her head bowed in a thoughtful manner. Possessed by some unknown urge, and before she could be seen, Anna scurried away and hid behind a bulky suit of armor standing at attention in the main corridor.

She watched Sir Karigan enter the Rider wing, continuing at her deliberate pace. Anna carefully set her buckets and brooms down, trusting they would remain unnoticed behind the armor, and crept back to the entrance of the Rider wing. The area had been abandoned by its occupants, who were off to supper. She'd been on her own there while cleaning the fireplaces and stoves that kept it warm, but she hadn't felt entirely alone. Certain sections of the castle, the really old parts like the Rider wing, often left her feeling spooked, like she was being watched by someone who was not there. She hated when she had to work in such places by herself, but was now inexorably drawn back by the presence of Sir Karigan.

She slipped into the dim, rough-hewn corridor of the Rider wing, making sure to keep her distance, clinging to the wall thinking she could dart into one of the arched doorways that led into the bed chambers, if need be.

What am I doing? Anna wondered. Her fellow servants often called her "Mousie" for being so timid and quiet, but for some reason, she could not help herself. She had always been intrigued by the Green Riders, their easygoing manner, the confidence with which they carried themselves. They rode into danger willingly, knowing they might never come back. Most of them were commoners like her.

Among them, Sir Karigan stood out.

They had said she was dead, but she had returned, and if rumor held truth, she had returned in a most unusual manner.

Spat right outta thin air, as Wallf the footman would say, reverting to his common burr, rather than the more refined speech he used when on duty in the presence of the highborn. He had been working in the king's great hall during the feasting on Night of Aeryc. *Spat right outta thin air and landed on the table of the nobles. What a mess! And Lord Mirwell howling like a cat in heat when the soup spilled and scorched his itty bits.*

Up ahead, Sir Karigan turned into the common room. After cleaning the spent ashes in the fireplace there, Anna had banked the coals. The chamber would still be warm. She increased her stride, hoping Sir Karigan didn't suddenly decide to turn around and discover she was being followed.

Anna slowed as she neared the common room, tiptoed to the doorway, and peered in. Sir Karigan left the lamp on the big table at low glow, but threw a log onto the coals. She stood there staring into the hearth.

Anna had heard, of course, about some of Sir Karigan's deeds, how she had helped save the king's throne from his usurper brother, and how she had helped rescue the queen from Mirwellian thugs, before the queen was the queen, that was. Then she'd been brave enough to go into Blackveil Forest. But Anna also heard rumors of magic and even greater deeds that were not openly discussed. Just whispered nuances she caught as she went about her duties sweeping away ashes. The Riders were careful not to speak of magic—she'd never overheard anything, anyway, but she believed there was a lot more going on than was apparent on the surface, and that Sir Karigan was involved in much of it. It was a shame the Rider could not receive proper acclaim for her accomplishments, but she guessed that was why the king had made her a knight when there had been none for a very long time. For Anna, it just made the Rider more of a mystery.

The log ignited, the hearth flaring with firelight. With a heartfelt sigh, Sir Karigan sank into a rocking chair. Slowly, the chair creaked back and forth. The Rider appeared to have a lot on her mind. If Anna were more brave, she'd ask what troubled her.

I shouldn't be spying, Anna chided herself. She was about to hurry back to work when the Rider spoke. Anna froze, fearing she'd been discovered. How would she explain? But she then saw the Rider had not shifted her attention and seemed to speak to the fire. She crossed her arms as if to hold herself.

"I miss you," Sir Karigan was saying. "I would give anything to have you here, or me to be there. To be with you."

Anna had no idea of whom Sir Karigan spoke. It was odd, she thought. Sir Karigan was regarded with admiration by important people, not least of all the king, and she was often surrounded by her friends and fellow Riders. She had to be strong to survive her many adventures. She'd accomplished heroic deeds. And so Anna thought she would be invulnerable to the difficulties more common folk suffered.

But now she saw how wrong she was. As Sir Karigan

murmured the name "Cade," she thought she had never heard such pain, seen so lonely a soul.

Anna hurried away, cheeks warm at having witnessed so raw a moment that was not meant to be seen. Even heroes, she learned, bore more sorrows, worse than any bodily wound, than she could have guessed.

THE WINTER WOOD

In the deepening dusk of the winter wood, Grandmother stared in disappointment at the remnants of the snowball on her mittened hand. It had simply crumbled apart, refusing to take form around the knotted yarn as the spell required. The weather had been too frigid to make packable snow.

She shook the snow off her yarn. The weather was too frigid period. Oh, how she yearned for summer. Despite all the hats, mittens, scarves, and socks she knitted for herself and others, no matter the number of furred hides she wrapped around herself, she just couldn't keep warm. She stamped her feet to force feeling back into them.

A crow cawed among the clacking branches of the winter wood, her only company. She'd needed to leave the encampment of her people, civilians and soldiers of Second Empire alike. She'd come alone because she needed silence and the ability to hear herself think. As Second Empire's apparent spiritual and practical leader, they constantly sought her counsel on the minutest of troubles, whether they needed her to mediate disputes over the ownership of chickens or help mend a child with the croup. She could not get a moment alone, but today she had even left her granddaughter, Lala, behind.

Yes, she had set off alone, but not without protest from those who looked up to her. The woods were not safe, they said, warning that she could run into a pack of starving groundmites on the hunt, or be tracked by assassins from the king. Why, the woods were filled with ferocious wolves.

"The cold will likely kill me first," she muttered.

She had shrugged their concerns away and come into the woods alone. If she wanted this spell to work, she needed silence.

Caaaaw!

Relative silence, anyway.

She examined her knots. To the untrained eye, they resembled nothing more than a lump of snarls, but she saw the spells she had instilled in them, full of her intention, potent with magic. There still existed in the natural world powers both small and great, which were the basis of elemental magic. It was possible to go even further and conjure spirits that were an embodiment of specific elements, cause them to manifest and do one's bidding. The calling of such an entity, however, was not easy, for the conditions would have to be perfect and the spell carried out without flaw. Further complicating the procedure was the fact that elementals were unpredictable. One could try to bind them for better control, but such a tactic could compel them to turn on the spellcaster in retaliation. So, she had been careful to weave into her knots goodwill, as well as what it was she wished to achieve.

An attack on the castle, she thought. She hoped the power she beckoned could accomplish in winter what an army could not.

The flapping of wings drew her attention back to the crow. It shot up through the trees and became a dark blot in the sky, sailing away on air currents.

Truly alone at last, Grandmother examined her knots once more and found them satisfactory. This time she removed her mittens, exposing her flesh to the bitter air, and scooped up more snow. She must use the snow, for it was an expression of the entity's essence that she called upon. She started molding it around the yarn. This time the heat of her bare hands caused the snow to adhere even as it froze her fingers. She tried to prevent her hatred for the cold from seeping into the spell—such an attitude would surely anger the one she called. She concentrated instead on the beauty of an unsullied field of snow, icicles glistening in pale sunlight, flurries muting the air, the bite and raw power of a blizzard.

She shunted her hatred toward King Zachary and all those

who served him into the spell, for Sacoridia was Second Empire's ancient enemy. The king hunted and persecuted them, and while her people suffered and perished in this harsh winter, the king stayed warm and well-fed in his grand castle. They needed a victory, Second Empire did, for there had been too few, and if this spell worked, it could bring Sacoridia to ruin. Oh, how she fantasized about what she might do if she could get her hands on the king. He was not invincible, but a man of flesh and blood, and she knew the ways to extract the utmost pain from one such.

"To Sacor City, I beseech you!" she cried, holding the snowball aloft. Better to beseech an elemental for its help than offend it by commanding it. The wind howled and rattled branches seemingly in approval. "To the castle! I call upon your winter fury."

She tossed the snowball as high as she could. It plummeted back to Earth and plopped into a drift between a pair of trees. She stood over it, blowing on her stinging hands to thaw them before pulling on her mittens.

Nothing happened. The snowball just sat in the crater it had created in the drift.

She waited some more. The crow, or one of its brethren, returned to a branch over her head and cackled. At *her*, she thought sullenly.

Still nothing.

She hopped up and down to get her blood flowing. She paced and pounded her hands together. It was freezing and she was exhausted by the casting of the spell, and she still had a long walk back to the encampment. The spell, if it had been correctly fashioned, should have worked by now. Standing around and turning into an icicle wasn't going to change anything.

A howl shattered the quiet of the wood, and was answered by others. Grandmother shivered, and not entirely from the cold. Wolves were on the hunt.

She gave the spell a little more time, but the howls came closer, and she dared not linger. She shook her head at the futility of it all and turned away. What had she expected? Some grand whirlwind of ice to rise up? A snow demon? A chorus of supernatural beings singing her praises? It was too much to hope that an elemental power would rise forth to aid Second Empire against the Sacoridians, and she wondered what she had done to so displease God.

Her boots squeaked in the snow as she walked away. She decided to forget about elementals and their complicated spells. She would instead focus on simple magic that would restore feeling to her fingertips and toes.

As the old human trudged away and faded into the woods, the crow turned his keen gaze to a shimmer that grew from the snowball she had discarded. It coalesced into an icy sphere that rose above the snowdrift and hovered, pulsating with life. The crow cocked his head as he watched. He liked the shiny, but was clever enough to know that this was no treasure for him, that he must stay away, for the sphere emanated ancient power like the force of a blizzard, and predatory intent. He shook his feathers, and then settled to keep watch on it.

When the sphere rushed suddenly up into the branches, the crow squawked and, flailing its wings, leaped out of the way. He croaked his displeasure as the sphere sped off through the branches and around tree trunks in a silver streak, and set a course southward.

GHOSTS

Somewhere in the twilight between sleep and awakening, the spirits of the Rider wing gathered around her bed. Smoky figures whispered, their forms flickering and rustling in spectral currents. They fingered her hair and patted her body as she lay curled beneath her blankets. They left cold touches upon her cheek and neck.

She flailed out with a hand as if to knock away the filament of a spider web. Dreams. These were dreams. But still the incessant whispers filled her mind as ghosts told her their stories, stories of battles lost and won, of unruly children and handsome courtiers. They told her of loveless marriages and the loss of true heart mates, the latter causing her to cry in her sleep.

There were triumphs and judgments, complaints and boredom, stories of never-ending tasks lacking fulfillment, that nevertheless repeated themselves over and over. Their stories came in snatches, one crowding out the other.

From the bed beside his sleeping human, Ghost Kitty hissed and swatted at the apparitions if they annoyed him too much, shredding swaths of revenant translucence with living claws.

Under the onslaught, his human twisted and turned and murmured. Undeterred, the ghosts kept coming, drawn to the one who could hear them.

RIDER CROTCHETY

In the morning, Karigan sat alone hunched over a steaming cup of kauv in the dining hall, her head propped on her hand, oblivious to the comings and goings of others around her. Mara slipped onto the bench across the table from her with a bowl of porridge.

"You look terrible," Mara said.

"Good morning to you, too," Karigan grumbled, her voice scratchy.

"My, aren't we all sunshine and kittens. Your aunts keep you up all night, Helgadorf?" Karigan stuck her tongue out at her, and Mara laughed as she dipped her spoon into her porridge. "Seriously, you look like you are on the wrong end of a full night's carousing at the Cock and Hen."

Karigan could only wish she'd been indulging in the Cock and Hen's ale to make her feel so miserable. "No. If you must know, I just haven't been sleeping well."

"Is that why you're drinking kauv? I thought you despised the stuff."

"I do." Kauv was as bitter as all five hells, but it was a stronger stimulant than tea, especially with all the sugar she dumped in it to make it palatable. It used to be difficult, or at least expensive, to acquire kauv beans, but that had all changed with a trade agreement between Sacoridia and the Cloud Islands that had gone into effect while she was away. Several of her fellow Riders seemed unable to function without it now, even though they'd never needed it before.

"Makes my hair curl," Mara said with distaste, tugging on a springy ringlet, "and more curling isn't what it needs."

Karigan sipped from her mug and grimaced, and observed Mara watching her intently. Much too intently. *"What?"*

"I was going to ask, Rider Crotchety, why you haven't been able to sleep."

"I am not crotchety."

"Really?"

Karigan glared at her.

"Well?" Mara pressed, undeterred. "Why can't you sleep?"

"Dreams, or something." Karigan shrugged.

Mara sobered at this. "Not surprising considering all you've been through. Do you . . ." She lowered her voice. "Do you dream about where you were? About . . . ?"

Karigan knew she was about to ask if she dreamed of Cade. Mara was one of the few who knew much about her experiences in the future. She'd been present when Karigan had reported all she could remember to King Zachary and Captain Mapstone. Karigan had not explicitly told anyone what Cade meant to her, but it was clear Mara had been able to guess.

She shook her head. "No, none of that." The jumbled dreams, the scattered narratives were blurry and difficult to recall. Of what she remembered, they seemed to have little to do with her own life, as if a thousand strangers crowded into her mind every night to tell her *their* stories.

They sat in silence until Mara said, "Weather's changing," as if to engage her in conversation. "Clouds moving in."

Karigan shrugged, not really interested. It was the same old story of their winter.

Mara shook her head and sighed in what sounded like resignation. Karigan knew her attitude wasn't the best, and she gave her friend credit for knowing when to back off and give her peace and silence to sip her kauv. It took her several seconds to realize it wasn't just Mara who'd grown quiet, however, but the entire dining hall. Servants, laborers, messengers, administrative staff, soldiers, all the commoners who worked in and around the castle and used the dining hall, were staring in one direction. She followed their gazes to the entryway. There stood not only a Weapon, whose clannish order possessed its own dining hall so its members did not have to associate with lesser mortals at meal times, but an Eletian, as well.

"What in the name of the gods?" Mara murmured, her spoon halfway to her mouth.

Everyone else appeared to be wondering the same thing, so transfixed were they by the unexpected visitors. Eletians were still enough of a novelty in the land that they attracted attention no matter where they appeared. That one of those magical folk now stood in the castle's common dining hall was almost too extraordinary a vision to apprehend, but there he was.

At first, Karigan's hopes surged that maybe Lhean had come looking for her, then plummeted when she realized it was just his companion, Enver. Enver, for his part, searched the room with his gaze, and when it alighted upon Karigan, he brightened. "Galadheon!"

Everyone else in the room shifted their gazes to stare at *her.* Bad enough people looked strangely at her from time to time after her "return from the dead." She didn't need Enver adding to the whispers she sometimes heard behind her back.

As Enver, and the Weapon, Ellen, picked their way toward her table, she muttered, "Five hells. What does *he* want with me?"

"Be nice," Mara warned her. "I am sure King Zachary would not appreciate a diplomatic incident just because you are feeling crotchety."

"I am *not* crotchety."

"Are, too."

"Am not." Then Karigan groaned. "Why did I even bother to get out of bed today?"

"Because you couldn't sleep?"

Before Karigan could come up with an appropriate retort, Enver and Ellen halted at their table. Ellen said, "Master Enver wished to see a little of the castle, and visit with *you*, Sir Karigan."

"Good morning," Enver said with a slight bow.

"I leave him in your care, Riders." And Ellen turned on her heel and strode away. Enver regarded them expectantly.

Mara recovered first. "Good morning, Enver. We were never properly introduced. I am Mara Brennyn, Chief Rider."

Enver extended his hand to shake hers. Just as Karigan had been disconcerted by his manner the first time she'd been introduced to him, so now was Mara.

"How do you do?" he asked.

"I am well, thank you," Mara replied.

Instead of releasing her hand, however, Enver pulled it closer to inspect it. Mara cast a sideways glance at Karigan and mouthed, *Is this normal*?

For an Eletian, she meant. Karigan shrugged. She had probably been around Eletians more than anyone, but they still defied expectation.

"You've missing fingers," Enver observed. "And many deep burn scars." He released Mara's hand and bent close to study her face. She leaned as far back on her bench as she could without tipping over. "Very deep," he murmured.

Karigan cleared her throat. "Enver . . ." His examination wasn't making just Mara uncomfortable.

"Beautiful," he said, raising his hand as if to touch her cheek.

"Enver," Karigan said more sharply, half-rising from her bench.

He looked at her, startled. "Yes?"

A quick glance around revealed that others in the dining hall watched Enver with deep suspicion, which manifested in scowls and muttering over his presumption. His own expression was ingenuous. He had no idea, she realized, he had transgressed the boundaries of appropriate conduct, of appropriate *human* conduct. She took a deep breath to calm her own irritation, but needed to act quickly before anyone decided to "teach" him manners.

"Enver, please have a seat." She patted the bench next to her.

"Have I done something wrong?"

So, he wasn't entirely witless. "Please, sit." When he slid onto the bench, she explained, "The attention you gave to Mara's scars is considered . . . unseemly."

He looked from Karigan to Mara and bowed his head. "My pardon, Chief Rider Brennyn. I did not mean to cause offense. I have some learning in the healing arts, and what I saw in you was a triumph of healing, and thus beautiful. It seems I need to learn more of your ways so I may express myself correctly."

Karigan thought it strange that the Eletians would send to the castle one who was not versed in the customs and etiquette of its people, but then again, were any of them? They were *other*, and in Karigan's experience, diplomacy did not seem to be of overriding importance to them. At least the tension in the dining hall eased, with the watchers returning to their breakfasts and their own conversations.

"No offense taken," Mara said. "I had never thought of my scars in that way before . . . as beautiful. I think . . . I think I like it."

"The healing is not only of the flesh," Enver said, "but of the spirit, which shines through you. You are radiant."

Mara looked taken aback, unable to speak, maybe a little flustered. Enver's demeanor did not reveal whether he was intentionally flirting, or if this was another of the "ways" about Sacoridians he did not understand. If the latter, combined with his ethereal good looks, it could lead to a lot of painful misunderstandings.

"Thank you," Mara said finally. "Would you like some breakfast? Kauv? Tea?"

"I thank you, but I am sated for the time being."

Karigan sipped her tepid kauv as Mara questioned him about how his night had been. He and the others, he said, had passed the night outside the city for Lhean did not like sleeping upon the mortal dead. Mara's brow creased, and Karigan shook her head at the oblique reference to the royal tombs that catacombed the small mount that the castle and city sat upon.

Eletians, she thought in exasperation. She pushed her half-finished mug of kauv away and interrupted whatever Enver was about to say next. "Do you know where I might find Lhean?"

"He is meeting with your king."

Damnation. When would she get to see him? She tapped her fingers on the table in annoyance. Maybe it was the kauv, maybe it was Enver, but she was feeling twitchy. She suddenly needed to move, to get up and go, but without Enver underfoot. She stood abruptly and cast Mara a pleading look, hoping her friend would understand and help. After all, Enver had come looking for "the Galadheon."

Mara raised an eyebrow and seemed to grasp what she wanted all right if her expression of disapproval was any indication, but she did not argue. Karigan mouthed a "thank you" and Mara pursed her lips. She wondered what favor she would owe Mara as a result of this.

"It was very nice seeing you," she told Enver, "but I must . . . I must attend to my duties." Technically, the king had given her leave to spend time with her family, but wasn't seeing family a sort of duty?

"I will talk to you later," Mara said.

Karigan did not doubt she would. Enver looked a little confused, and when Karigan started to walk away, she heard the bench creak as he rose from his seat to follow.

"I wouldn't," Mara warned him, loud enough for her voice to carry. "She's a bit crotchety this morning."

Karigan winced. She deserved that.

A quick glance over her shoulder revealed Enver sitting back down and asking, "This crotchety—is it a malady? A disease?"

This morning, Karigan thought, it surely felt like it, and she hastened her steps to leave the dining hall behind, hoping Mara didn't mind too much being saddled with the curious Eletian.

"Er, not a disease," Mara told Enver, "but a matter of temperament." She watched Karigan disappear through the doorway. She would indeed speak to her later, but more out of concern than reproach. She rarely saw her friend so out of sorts, and even after all her experiences in Blackveil and the future, her loss of Cade and the oddity of her eye, she'd done a good job of maintaining outward equilibrium, but Mara could see through it, how a heaviness weighed on her, how she threw herself into her work, how she sought to be alone more often than not. She was not as quick to smile or laugh.

A patch covered Karigan's mirror eye, but in her other eye, Mara caught flashes of sorrow, and something else, a fathomless dark, like a well of the heavens. Thinking of it made her shudder.

Enver had watched after Karigan, as well, his gaze thoughtful. "I do not think she remembers me."

"From when she returned on Night of Aeryc? Of course she does."

He shook his head, his eyes growing distant. "It was nearly five of your years ago. Our tiendan was traveling the great wood that your people call the Green Cloak, and in the night we saw the light of a muna'riel. We sensed no others of our own kind nearby, and investigated."

"It was Karigan?"

"Yes. She had just slain a creature of Kanmorhan Vane and was fevered with its poison in her blood."

Mara realized he was speaking of when Karigan, a runaway schoolgirl and not yet officially a Green Rider, had carried a life-or-death message given her by the dying F'ryan Coblebay to King Zachary. One of her amazing feats along the way was slaying the monstrous creature and its numerous young.

"You were there?"

Enver nodded solemnly. "There were twelve of us. We danced and sang the healing while my father treated her wounds."

"Your father? Your father is—?"

"Somial, yes."

"Huh," was the only thing Mara could think to say. She wondered what Karigan would make of it.

"I ask that you do not speak to her of it for I do not think she is one who would wish to be reminded of a time when she was weakened and helpless, and at the mercy of strangers."

Mara reassessed Enver, his earnest demeanor, his desire for her to honor his request. His hands were folded on the table, and he waited for her response with a stillness she believed no mortal could attain. His artless conduct might lead to misunderstandings between his culture and hers, but his shrewd observation showed he had no trouble when it came to understanding Karigan G'ladheon.

A POET AND MEMORY

Thanks in no small part to Mara, Karigan was free of the dining hall, but not of other obligations. She went to the mending wing to check on Estral, but peeking through the cracked door revealed that her friend was still sound asleep. Truth be told, she was rather envious.

She meandered out of the mending wing, a little at a loss. Estral was asleep and Lhean unavailable. She'd been given leave to spend time with her family, but in the flurry of the previous night's events, she hadn't even thought to ask her father where he was staying, so she'd have to wait for him to find her, however long that would take.

As she stepped into the main hall of the castle, she was accosted by a Green Foot runner.

"There you are, Rider," the boy said, huffing and puffing. "Been all over looking for you."

"Is there some emergency?"

"No, ma'am. The queen requests that you attend her."

Karigan wanted to tell the boy she was not a "ma'am," but she just watched him trot off to his next task. Estora wanted her to visit? What a morning. It wasn't that she disliked Estora; on the contrary, they had been friends, but as to their relationship now? "Complicated" didn't even begin to describe it. Since her return, she'd made no effort to see the queen, which was rather easily accomplished since Estora was sequestered due to her pregnancy, a pregnancy made more perilous by the fact she was carrying twins. Master Mender Vanlynn was being adamant about her remaining confined for her safety and that of the babies. It was essential for the realm that she produce healthy offspring.

Karigan felt guilty she had been avoiding Estora, but seeing her as King Zachary's wife was just so very difficult. No matter how hard she tried to get past it all, the pain was ever-present. But now, Estora had requested to see her, and she had no real excuse not to. She did consider riding away somewhere to avoid everyone—the queen, Enver, her family—but she'd pretty much made herself give up running away. The adult thing was to face her challenges. Besides, a glance outside revealed more winter weather was on the way, which would make riding neither pleasant nor easy.

She continued into the royal section of the castle in the west wing, wondering why she had to face *so many* challenges.

The west wing was quiet, though guards and Weapons were present, and a couple of servants hurried along the main corridor, their footfalls silent on deep carpet. The Weapon Rory stood at the door of the queen's rooms.

"Ah, Sir Karigan," he said.

"Hello, Rory, I was told the queen wished to see me."

"She does. Are you, or have you been ill?"

"What?"

"Master Vanlynn does not want anyone who is sick to pass through this door."

Karigan understood. Winter, with everyone cooped up together, could be a time when illness spread readily. A few waves of colds and fever had already passed through both the castle and city populations. Karigan was one of the few who'd made it through relatively unscathed.

"I am not sick," she said, though she realized it would be an excellent excuse to avoid Estora. *No running away*, she reminded herself. "Just crotchety, apparently."

"Very well," Rory said, and he opened the door. "Come with me."

Karigan followed behind him into the queen's domain. She had never been in the royal apartments before, and found Estora's, as she walked through the entry, was as well appointed as one would expect, with hangings and coastal landscape paintings from Coutre Province on the walls.

Rory led her to a spacious sitting room, where Estora rested, propped on a sofa before the fire. She was absorbed in a book, lamplight glinting on her golden hair. Bundled beneath a blanket as she was, it was not obvious she was with child. Or, rather, *children.*

Being in Estora's presence often aroused a sense of inadequacy in Karigan, for Estora embodied graceful femininity and perfection. She wore no uniform nor had she acquired calloused hands from rough work. Her porcelain complexion was unmarred by scars, and a leather patch did not cover one of her long-lashed eyes. Not that Karigan would trade places with her, and not that she wasn't proud of her uniform and work, but Estora's simple existence had the power to show Karigan, in stark contrast, what she was not and never would be.

"My lady," Rory said, "Sir Karigan."

Estora looked up from her book. "Karigan!"

Karigan bowed. "You wished to see me, my lady?"

"Yes, yes. Please come sit with me, and don't be so terribly formal. This is not an official visit. I simply have seen so little of you since your return, and it is not as if I've been allowed to come to you. Master Vanlynn insists I repose in my rooms for the duration."

Karigan took an armchair beside the fire.

"Have you need of anything before I return to my post, my lady?" Rory asked.

"No, thank you, Rory." He nodded and retreated from the room. "I have been so terribly bored," Estora continued. "My ladies come to provide me with companionship, to do needlework and gossip, but it is so inane. I rarely get a chance for intelligent conversation, and Zachary is always so busy. But he did bring me this volume of poetry." She lifted the book so Karigan could see the blue-dyed leather cover. "Have you read the work of Lady Amalya Whitewren?"

"Lady Amalya Whitewren?" Karigan asked. "No, I don't think I've ever heard of her." But there was a niggling something about the name. Might she have heard of her and just forgotten?

"Oh, well, she is creating quite a sensation on Gryphon

Street, as I hear it, and no wonder for she is a divine poet." Estora was so enthusiastic about Lady Amalya Whitewren that she began reading some passages from the book. It was romantic poetry in the form of sonnets.

Karigan tried to conceal a yawn. Besides being short of sleep, she did not share Estora's enthusiasm for poetry. She liked a good yarn instead, a story she could follow with colorful characters and adventures, although possibly, after so many adventures of her own, she'd become less inclined to seek out such tales. As Estora read on, the warmth of the fire and the crackle of flames lulled her. Her surroundings grew hazy and she drifted.

"Who was Lady Amalya Whitewren?" Cade asked. His voice was suspicious, demanding. He was testing her, and she must prove she was who she said she was, a Green Rider from the past. His expression remained stern as he awaited her answer, his posture stiff. She saw him clearly, his dark hair and the open collar of his shirt. His eyes bored into her.

"I have no idea," Karigan replied.

Cade's brows narrowed, and there was a quirk to his lips. He'd poked a hole in her story. "She was only one of the most popular poets of your time."

Karigan could only shrug, but then another voice entered her dream, or was it memory?

"Cade," the professor said, "if I am not mistaken, Lady Amalya came into prominence after Karigan G'ladheon left for Blackveil."

Cade conceded this could be true, but he was eager to continue his questioning of her, his expression no longer stern, but curious, his eyes lively.

Background voices irritated her like the whine of flies around her ears. Her vision of Cade began to slip away.

"No," she mumbled, "don't go away."

"Karigan?"

She looked up to find Estora gazing at her, her book closed on her lap.

"Lady Amalya," Karigan said, trying to force herself to alertness. "She . . . she came to prominence after I left for Blackveil. Wait, I . . . when . . ." She shook her head trying to clear it. "It happened while I was gone. Her rise to prominence." Her dream, or memory, or whatever, was fast dissipating. She actually reached out as if to grasp Cade, to pull him back, to pull him to her as she had failed to do when she returned to her own time. *"Cade . . ."* It took a moment, and seeing her pain reflected in Estora's face, to realize she had spoken her anguish aloud.

"Karigan?"

This time it was not Estora who spoke. The voice was male, familiar. Not Cade, and here in the room with her. She looked around, and there beside her stood King Zachary gazing down at her.

"I am afraid we awoke you from some dream," he said.

Karigan scrambled to her feet to give a clumsy bow. "Excellency, my pardon. I—I don't know what came over me."

"It was the poetry," Estora said, her face lighting with amusement. "I'd say my reading of Lady Amalya's poetry put you to sleep."

"Forgive me. I—" Karigan looked about, as if a magic door of escape would suddenly materialize.

"The captain isn't working you too hard, is she?" the king asked.

"What? I mean, no, Your Majesty."

"Hmm. Well, you are supposed to be on leave so you may spend time with your family."

"Is she?" Estora asked. "I did not know they were here. Perhaps they should join us for tea."

The very idea horrified Karigan, but it was the king who spoke. "I don't think Vanlynn would approve. The G'ladheon contingent is quite . . ." He searched for the right word.

"Overwhelming," Karigan provided.

"I was thinking more along the lines of formidable, but

overwhelming is apt," he said. "Very passionate people, are G'ladheons. I am afraid they would exhaust even the most vigorous and determined of people."

"Perhaps I could tame them with readings of Lady Amalya's poetry," Estora replied.

"I do not think we would want our G'ladheons tamed."

Karigan glanced between the two of them, king and queen, observing the humor in their eyes and the ease they seemed to feel with one another. This should be a good thing. She wanted to be pleased for them, and one part of her was. The other part of her was ineffably sad. Sad for all she could not attain herself.

"With your leave, Your Majesties," she said almost too hastily, "I should probably go see about that family of mine. I don't know when to expect them, and they'd probably rouse the whole castle looking for me."

"So soon?" Estora said. "We haven't even had a chance to catch up—you must come see me again."

"Yes," Zachary said, "the queen could use the company. It would please us both."

Karigan tried not to read anything into his words and avoided looking at him. Would this tension between them always exist? She mumbled something polite, gave a cursory bow, and began to walk away. Suddenly she paused and turned around. "Your Majesty?"

"Yes, Karigan?"

She noticed he did not use her title. "With your leave, I would like to speak with the Eletian, Lhean."

"I am sorry," he said, his gaze softening. "I would gladly grant you, of all people, leave to see him, but the Eletians have already departed."

Karigan clenched her hands, willing herself not to scream or cry or break something. How could Lhean leave without seeing her first? *Eletian*, she thought, and that was all the answer she needed.

With constricted control, she bowed once more. "Thank you, Your Majesty." She turned on her heel and strode out, not wishing to see the pity on King Zachary's face.

Estora watched her husband as he gazed after Karigan. She knew his was not just the concern of a sovereign for his servant. He loved Karigan, and had for years. Had fate been different, had he not been a king, or Karigan not a commoner, Estora would not be his wife, but fate was what it was, and his wife *she* was. She had never expected to love anyone again after F'ryan Coblebay, and had resigned herself to her lot in life, a loveless marriage for a noble alliance and to produce children of royal lineage. But something happened during her betrothal to Zachary. She found herself enjoying his company, admired his acumen, and looked forward to discussing the realm's issues with him over tea. By the time they married, some ten months ago, she had come to love him. When she discovered his heart lay elsewhere, she wished, though she had been ashamed of it, that Karigan would not return from Blackveil.

He slowly turned back toward her, his expression troubled. Absently he sat in the chair so recently vacated by Karigan. When his schedule permitted, he took his midmorning tea with Estora, and they discussed the business of the realm. He made an effort to collect anecdotes about what was happening around the castle to entertain her in her confinement. They'd grown easier with one another and she knew he was fond of her, but he did not love her, not in the fashion she desired, and not in the way he loved Karigan.

"Do you know who this Cade is that she speaks of?" Estora asked.

He looked up, startled out of his own thoughts. "Someone she met in the future time. She has revealed little about him, except that he helped her there. Helped her return home, and for that I owe him my gratitude. We all do."

Estora knew there was more to this Cade, whether or not Karigan chose to say anything aloud. It was in the pain she carried silently and the story told by a sadness in her face. The yearning when she said his name. She was markedly different from the Karigan who had left for Blackveil last spring, no longer the youth innocent of life's wounds. The gods had used her harshly, and it displeased Estora to see such a bright spirit now clouded by sorrow and shadows.

How did her husband feel about the mysterious Cade? Truly grateful, she did not doubt, for helping Karigan return to her rightful time, to *him*. But was he also, perhaps, a little envious of whatever Cade might have had with her?

"Is Karigan ready to resume her duties? She seems . . . fragile." Estora did not think it was too severe a description for what she had just seen.

"She has been working very hard, but as you know, there have been few message errands to assign due to the weather. When spring comes, it will be Laren who will ultimately decide if she's ready."

Estora did not think he was aware that she knew how he felt about Karigan. After they'd married, when they'd made love for the first time, albeit under especially difficult circumstances—he still battling the poison of an arrow wound—he'd called out a name that had not been hers. She never enlightened him, and though it had never happened again, she knew, intimately, his true feelings.

"It must be very difficult for her with the injury to her eye," she said.

"I am to understand it is painful at times."

"Poor thing."

Upon Karigan's return, shards of the looking mask she had shattered in Blackveil had followed her across time, whether propelled by magic, the gods, or some force of nature, no one really knew. One shard impaled her eye and transformed it into a mirror and, like the looking mask, it contained the power to reveal visions of past and future, and who-knew-what.

The nature of her eye was not widely known, but a secret maintained by Zachary, Captain Mapstone, and a handful of others. Zachary had been reluctant to tell even Estora about it. He feared that common knowledge of Karigan's strange eye would place her in jeopardy from both those who hated magic, and those who might covet its power.

"Have you gazed into it?" Estora asked.

"Only Somial the Eletian has, and some menders by necessity. I would never ask that of her without good reason."

She understood why he was protective of Karigan, and understood well. She was joyful her friend had returned seemingly from the dead, and yet?

And yet.

She craved to be the recipient of her husband's most ardent regard.

She studied him as he gazed into the hearth, firelight playing across his features, shadows highlighting lines of care and a scar that scored his eyebrow. He'd received it in battle with Second Empire, and she shook a little just thinking of it. Someone else might hold his heart, but he was *hers*. They were bound by marriage, and she carried his heirs. As a man of honor and duty, she did not think he'd stray, but love was potent and one never knew.

There were other threats, as well. She had almost lost him to the assassin's arrow. Though his Weapons guarded him well, next time an assassin might prove successful, and there would be, she knew, a next time. It was the nature of his position. Then there was the conflict with Second Empire and his desire to lead his troops. Just as it had been her lot to marry a nobleman for alliance and not love, it was also her lot to see her husband ride off to war, never knowing if he would return, never knowing if her children would get to meet their father.

She caressed her belly and was a little startled to feel a flutter. "Oh!" she exclaimed.

"What is it?" Zachary asked.

She stretched her hand out to him. "Come sit with me. One of your children is kicking."

He sat beside her a little shyly, and she guided his hand to her belly. When the flutter came again, his expression turned to one of awe and delight.

She could not lose this man she had come to love. Perhaps she could not protect him on the field of battle or repel an assassin, but she could, and she would, make sure no one ever came between them. No matter what, no matter who.

ICE AND FIRE

Karigan's head started throbbing about the time she rushed out the door of Estora's rooms and past Rory. Her lack of sleep and breakfast was catching up with her, along with everything else. She still wanted to break something, or maybe even several somethings, but first she would bury her head in a pillow and rest.

How could Lhean leave without speaking to her? Her frustration only caused her headache to build. As she strode through castle corridors, anxious to reach that pillow, she heard others around her muttering about the weather, that a storm was brewing. Just what they needed during a winter that had already proven harsh.

She swung into the Rider wing and briefly greeted those she encountered. Daro Cooper caught her arm. "Karigan, wait."

"What is it?"

"Thought you might want to know that your family is waiting for you."

So much for her pillow. She thanked Daro for the warning and pushed on down the corridor, her head pounding ever more insistently. When she reached the far end, she paused to collect herself. No reason to burden her father and aunts with her sour mood. She took a deep breath and turned the corner into the ancient corridor she alone inhabited. Light filtered out the doorway of her chamber, clearly indicating they had let themselves in.

When she entered, she almost tripped over one of her old traveling chests. It had simply been deposited in the middle of the floor. The rest of the scene was not unexpected. Aunt Stace examined the gaudy gilt headboard of her bed, with unicorns and a young girl carved on it, that Garth had dug up gods-knew-where. Aunts Tory and Gretta were inspecting the contents of her wardrobe, which consisted of uniforms and not much more, and Aunt Brini sat at her massive desk, going through the drawers. Privacy had never been one of her aunts' strong points.

Her father, meanwhile, unaware of her arrival, waved his arms at his sisters and said, "I don't think she'd appreciate you going through her things. Brini, put that back! Stace, tell them."

Karigan cleared her throat and they all turned immediately and started asking questions, but it was Aunt Brini, at her desk holding a piece of paper, who claimed her full attention.

"Kari, who are the people in this picture? They are dressed very strangely."

Karigan stormed right up to Aunt Brini and snatched the paper out of her hand. It was the drawings the ghost of Yates had made of Cade and other people she had met in the future. It was her strongest connection to people that her memory and the contradictions of time tried very hard to erase.

"This," she said in so angry a voice she surprised even herself, "is none of your business." She gently settled the paper into its proper drawer and slammed it shut, making Aunt Brini flinch. "None of this," she told her aunts, gesturing at her chamber and unable to stop herself, "is any of your business. I am not a child anymore that you can just go searching through my things."

Her aunts raised their voices in protest.

The throb in Karigan's head intensified so much her vision rippled. "*No.* I won't have it. You intrude on me, on my life, without warning, and then start looking through *my* things? I would not do it to you, but you can't seem to show me the same respect. It never seems to matter what I've done here in the king's service. You just keep treating me like a child." She had never raised her voice to them like this before, and they stared at her in shock.

"Kari," Aunt Stace began.

"No! I don't want to hear it. I didn't invite you here. I just want to be left alone." She sagged against one of the stone pillars that supported the ceiling in her room, her headache now full blown. Between the pain and the venting of her anger, she thought she might throw up.

Aunt Stace opened her mouth again as if to speak, but Karigan's father placed his hand on his sister's arm. "She's right. We are remiss. We have presumed much."

Aunt Tory sniffled and dabbed at her eyes. Aunt Gretta looked like she was about to cry. Aunt Brini was so upset she rose and brushed past Karigan on her way out the door, sobbing.

Karigan was exhausted, her fury only partially spent, but now she was also engulfed by guilt. She hadn't wanted to make them cry. Her aunts and father were there because they loved her and needed to see her after she had seemingly come back from the dead.

Beyond the pain in her head and the emotion that suffused her chamber, she sensed a building pressure in the air. Her father was saying something, but it felt as if the very walls were crushing her. Her vision swam and she thought she might pass out, but a shriek from somewhere outside her room brought her back to herself.

What in five hells? Was it her imagination, or had the temperature cooled considerably?

"Karigan!" Daro Cooper appeared at her door, her face pale. "Something—something strange is going on!"

She could tell just by the tone of Daro's voice it had to be bad.

"Grab your sword," Daro said, and disappeared from the doorway.

She didn't have a sword. She had yet to replace the saber she'd lost in Blackveil, but she did have her bonewood staff. She bounded across her room to where it leaned against the wall next to her bed. The black lacquered fighting staff felt natural and good in her hands. Touching it seemed to knock her headache down a notch.

"You will close the door behind me," Karigan instructed

her father and aunts, "and lock it. Do not let anyone in till I return."

"Brini," Aunt Stace said.

"I'll find her." Karigan was astonished to see her breath fog the air as she spoke. "And stoke up the fire, try to keep warm." A tingle on the back of her neck told her the rapidly cooling temperature was not natural, that magic was at play. As she passed through the door, she turned once more and looked in. "Remember, lock the door!" Not, she reflected, that a locked door would necessarily be a defense against a magical attack, or any other.

She sprinted around the corner into the main Rider corridor, and was faced with a rush of frigid wind and a scene of which she could not quite make sense. A rime of frost coated the walls. Her fellow Riders spilled out of their rooms to hack and slash at what appeared to be . . . small whirlwinds? They were about as tall as her knees.

Another shriek caught her attention—*Aunt Brini!* She dashed down the corridor. Daro and Brandall shielded Aunt Brini from the whirlwinds, Daro stabbing into one, which burst in a *poof* of crystalline fragments, revealing its inner skeleton, child-sized with translucent bones of ice that were vaguely human in shape, but disturbingly *other.* It clenched an icicle dagger ready to puncture Daro's foot. Her sword swept down and cleaved through the creature's skull. Ice splintered and cracked, and scattered across the floor.

"Kari!" Aunt Brini cried.

"Stay back," Karigan said, joining Daro and Brandall to shield her.

More whirlwinds filled the space left by the one they'd destroyed, and the Riders faced them, their weapons glinting in the lamplight. Karigan swung her staff and smashed a creature against the wall.

"Well done!" Brandall shouted.

Karigan grinned mirthlessly and crushed another beneath the metal handle of her staff. It took at least two good whacks to stop one. When the cloak of swirling ice fragments fell away, the creatures always held a dagger ready to stab at the first opportunity.

"What are these things?"

"No idea," Daro replied, her gaze never leaving the creatures.

Down the corridor, other Riders put their special abilities to use: Ylaine lifted the creatures with her mind and smashed them into the wall. Carson had a new shielding talent to prevent himself from being stabbed, and young Gil summoned a wind in an attempt to push them back.

"Kari!" Aunt Brini cried in warning.

She pivoted just in time to smash a creature that had approached on her blind side. She was showered with ice as she destroyed it.

"Is it my imagination, or are they getting bigger?" Brandall asked between gritted teeth.

He was right. The whirlwinds were growing taller. They had started out knee-high, but now they were about hip-high.

"And faster!" Daro said before slicing through ice bones.

Karigan closed her mind to her aunt's half-hysterical sobbing behind her, and focused on what she needed to do. Fortunately, she'd been working with Arms Master Drent since her return and her condition was good, allowing her to keep up with the onslaught of growing, faster whirlwinds.

Daro cried out beside her, an icicle dagger jammed into her thigh. The jaw of the creature opened revealing jagged sharp teeth and clamped on Daro's leg. Her cries of pain mingled with Aunt Brini's screams. Karigan hammered the ice skull with her staff, and shards of it flew in all directions. Brandall turned to catch Daro, but she did not fall. Her bleeding wounds crystallized, turned to ice that spread rapidly, freezing her wounded leg, then creeping upward to her hip.

"Daro!" Brandall cried, but he, like Karigan, had to fend off attackers lest they, too, get stabbed and bitten.

"So cold," Daro moaned. Though she struggled, the ice continued to creep up her torso, and her movements became slow, labored. She could not move her lower body at all.

Karigan watched helplessly and in horror, not knowing how to help Daro as she stopped moving altogether, her hair frosted over, her face frozen in an expression of pain. Her cries turned to silence, and her sword slipped from her stiff hand. The ice continued to thicken over her in layers. Karigan slammed away another creature, her attention and Brandall's divided between their attackers and Daro, but there was little they could do for her. The ice had turned her into a frozen statue.

Fire flared down the corridor. Balls of it flew through the air—Mara! The din of battle died as she progressed toward them. Flame grew from her hand, the one with the missing fingers, and she molded it into roiling balls and splashed them into the creatures. Bones of ice melted into slushy puddles.

Brandall smashed the last of the whirlwinds, and the corridor was filled with the panting of tired Green Riders. Mara made her way to them, her face wet with sweat, her eyes feverish.

"Thank the gods," Karigan said. She turned to put her arm around her aunt's trembling shoulders to comfort her.

"They are everywhere throughout the castle," Mara said.

"What about Daro?" Brandall asked, reaching to touch the hand of their friend.

"Don't," Mara said. "If you accidently push her over, she will shatter on the floor."

They all took a step away from Daro.

"But, is she still alive?" Karigan asked.

"I don't know."

A moment of horrified silence passed among them.

"Couldn't you just thaw her with your ability?" Brandall asked Mara.

"I don't dare risk it. I don't know the nature of this magic, and I could too easily burn her."

"The king . . ." Karigan began.

"Yes," Mara replied, "we need to reach the king. We need to organize, sweep the castle, and wipe these things out. *If* it is possible."

"If?" Brandall asked.

"They are magical and anything is possible." Mara called to the other exhausted Riders to join them. "We need to regroup."

As Mara assembled the Riders, Karigan rushed her shocked aunt back to her chamber, making sure there were no other creatures along the way. She pounded on the door. "It's me! Me and Aunt Brini!"

Her father flung the door open, and Karigan thrust her aunt inside and into the arms of her anxious sisters.

"Karigan," he asked, "what is happening?"

"No time," she said. "I've got to go. Aunt Brini will tell you."

"I am coming with you."

"No! You need to look after my aunts. Here!" She thrust her staff into his hands. "Use this if you need to. Don't let anything in!"

"Any*thing*?"

She slammed the door shut in reply and ran to rejoin Mara and the others, who were making plans near the grotesque ice statue that was Daro Cooper. Karigan found Daro's sword and hefted it in her hand. It was lighter than what she had become accustomed to, but it would serve.

"I'll take good care of it," she promised Daro. "I'll bring it back to you."

As she moved in to hear Mara's instructions, she realized her headache had almost entirely dissipated. It seemed it took battle to balance her frame of mind.

There were a good thirty-five Riders present who had not been turned to ice. Who knew where the rest were and what they faced? Was the city also under siege, or just the castle? Regardless, their first duty was to the king and queen. Mara chose not to split them up, for their strength was in numbers, small as theirs were compared to that of the ice creatures.

"I saw the king and queen in the queen's sitting room not long ago," Karigan said, though she could not say for certain how much time had elapsed since then.

"Right," Mara said. "We'll head to the royal apartments. I'll take point."

"But—" Karigan protested.

Mara turned, her palm up and flame dancing on it. "Can you really argue with this, Sir Karigan?"

She was right, of course. Her ability was ideal, the best for destroying any of the creatures that got in their way, but Karigan was more concerned about what the constant use of the fire bringing would do to Mara. She did not dare speak of it, however, in front of the mostly young, untried Riders, their faces already full of fear.

"Torches," Karigan said instead. "So we can all have fire."

"Excellent idea." Mara ordered the Riders to grab any torches they could find in the corridor. The castle was largely lit by whale oil lamps and candles, but many of the old torches remained unused in their sconces.

While the Riders were busy, Karigan took the chance to grab Mara's arm. The heat of her radiated through her sleeve. "Don't you dare overdo it with your ability."

"I won't, thanks to your suggestion." Mara indicated the others collecting torches. A few trailed cobwebs. "And thank you for not mentioning it in front of the others." She paused, then added, "Do me a favor?"

"Anything."

"Keep an eye on the newest ones for me. Be the sweep." Karigan was about to argue, but Mara forestalled her. "It's an order, Rider. Plus, you said *anything*." She grinned, but it was without humor. "And don't think I am doing you any favors. Sweep will be as dangerous as point, and I need someone there who is experienced and capable."

Karigan nodded, but with misgiving, thinking she should be up front with Mara breaking through the attackers. The Riders found about a dozen torches that were still usable. Mara touched one and flame sprang to life, and was passed from torch to torch. Karigan did not take one, ensuring that the inexperienced Riders got them first. It would be their best defense.

Mara formed them into a wedge, and Karigan took her place at the rear. When this was over, there would be jokes. She hoped there would be, anyway.

HOT COALS AND A CHANDELIER

The Riders clattered through the corridor, destroying whirlwind creatures as they went, careful not to knock over their friends who had been turned to ice. When they reached the main castle hall, they halted in shock. People frozen in their tracks stood throughout, some trapped in time as they wielded weapons at unseen foes. Women lifted skirts, caught as they fled, their faces contorted in fear and pain. The floor, the walls, even the empty suits of armor that stood at attention along the walls, were frosted over and sparkled in the light. Flame gave life to shadows. It was silent.

"Remember," Mara said, even her quiet voice carrying, "try not to knock anyone over."

They trotted through the main hall, carefully weaving among courtiers, soldiers, and servants who'd been turned into statues of ice. Karigan recognized several though she tried not to look too closely. A few had already toppled and shattered across the floor, and she swallowed hard. She adjusted her grip on the hilt of her sword, her fingers stiff with the cold, and maintained her position as rear guard.

As for the king and queen, she told herself over and over that they would be stoutly protected by Weapons and the regular castle guard. They had a much better chance of remaining safe than these other folk. The king, a trained swordmaster, was very capable of defending himself and Estora, as well. These thoughts, however, failed to reassure her very much.

The sound of Rider boots echoed in the strangely quiet hall as they continued on. Movement down a side corridor caught Karigan's eye. She slowed at the odd sight of flame jabbing out of a wall at a whirlwind creature. Someone was clearly in distress. Her desire to reach the royal apartments, her desperate need to see her king safe, battled with her wish to help someone who had no Weapons, no guards, to protect him or her.

"Brandall," she called, "I'm going to check something out, and will catch up as soon as I can. You take sweep."

He nodded, and she darted down the side corridor. As she approached, she realized the flame was not coming out of the wall but from a large hearth in a seating alcove. Someone was attempting to fend off a creature with a bundle of burning kindling.

The whirlwind was considerably larger than the ones she had already fought. It was almost as tall as she, and as she neared it, she was whipped by wind that grabbed her breath. The whirlwind spewed needles of ice, and she raised her arm to protect her face. She thought maybe this side trip had not been such a good idea, after all, but a glance into the hearth revealed the ash girl who took care of the Rider wing. She must have been on her rounds when the magical attack struck. Her buckets of ash were strewn across the floor, and the fire in the hearth threatened to ignite her skirt, but it was helping to hold the whirlwind creature at bay. She looked frightened to bits as she thrust the burning kindling at it, but determined, as well.

The king would have Weapons, Karigan tried to remind herself. This girl had no one. No one, but her.

The whirlwind appeared to take notice of her, and she lunged. Alas, this one was not as easy to dispatch. It skated around her in erratic patterns, and the ice needles and wind made it difficult to see. She shielded her face with her hand—she did not want to lose her one good eye. The more the creature spun, the more ice that layered the floor and walls.

I have fought on ice before came the unbidden memory, but she hadn't the time to consider its source as she slipped and tried to maintain her footing with the whirlwind bearing down on her.

She hacked into it. The swirling funnel was wide enough

now that she buried the sword up to the guard, and ice particles shredded her knuckles. The blade struck the creature's skeleton, but it did not shatter like the smaller ones.

She withdrew the sword and hacked again with nearly the same result, but as she backed away, her feet slipped out from beneath her. One moment she was standing, and the next she was flat on her back. The creature roared toward her. She tried to rise to her feet, but could gain no traction. In a moment, it would have her. Would the frozen survive, or were they already dead?

The ash girl sprang into action and threw a shovelful of hot coals at the creature. It skittered aside, but as the coals hit the icy floor, steam rose and caused the creature to pause long enough for Karigan to climb to her feet. The coals melted through the ice layered on the floor and smoldered on the carpet beneath.

Karigan slid around the creature and stabbed into it. The hilt of her sword was slick with her own blood. Was it only wishful thinking, or was the whirl of ice thinning? Might it finally be weakening?

She thrust once more, and the wind, with all its spinning ice particles, dropped, unveiling the creature within. It clacked its jaw of jagged teeth at her. It carried no icicle dagger, but an ice sword, and when she crossed blades with it, its sword rang as though made of steel.

As the creature had been fast in its whirlwind form, so it was also fast with its sword work, and she had to use all the advanced moves Arms Master Drent had taught her. She slid and scrambled to keep up. As she tried to drive past its guard, it suddenly lurched and hopped, looking down at its boney feet, which were melting on the burning carpet. It roared like a windstorm, and then toppled over.

She hacked at its spine. When it still clacked its jaw at her, she stomped on the skull repeatedly until it cracked and shattered. She stood for a time, panting hard.

"Sir Karigan?" came a little voice.

She had almost forgotten the ash girl, who was just now stepping tentatively away from the hearth. "Anna, isn't it?"

The girl looked astonished Karigan knew her name. "I—I

have an extra handkerchief." She held the white cloth out like a flag of surrender. When Karigan just stared stupidly at it, she said, "For your hand."

Karigan looked down at her scored, bleeding hand. She'd barely noticed it before, but now it stung like the five hells.

"Here." The girl came forward hesitantly, as if warring with her own timidity, but when Karigan held her hand out for her, she bound it with assurance.

When she was done, Karigan flexed her fingers. "Thank you." The melting creature beside her appeared to be dousing the burning carpet. She stamped on singed fibers just to make sure.

"Anna, I need to reach the king. Do you—"

She was cut off by a new burst of wind as another creature appeared at the far end of the corridor. Anna looked like she might faint, and Karigan grabbed her arm and dragged her as fast as she could into the main hall. She paused to ensure they would not rush headlong into another whirlwind.

When she saw the way was clear, she said, "Ready to run, Anna?"

Anna nodded, her face pale.

"Good. Follow me and keep up best as you can."

The unnatural wind picked up as the creature skimmed its way toward them from the side corridor. It then paused, possibly to investigate the slushy remains of its comrade.

Karigan and Anna sprinted down the main hall past dozens of ice statues. Karigan glanced over her shoulder, and noting that Anna struggled to keep up, she moderated her pace. When she saw a whirlwind ahead coming down the main hall, she seized Anna's arm again and hauled her down another side corridor. They pressed their backs against the wall, their breaths ragged. Across from them was a frozen soldier, his arms thrown up defensively, his expression one of agony. Anna whimpered.

"It'll be all right," Karigan whispered. It had better be. Always in the back of her mind was her concern for her family and King Zachary.

"Anna," she whispered, "I have a certain ability—I can make us fade out so maybe that creature can't see us." Anna looked at her in bewilderment, but let Karigan take her hand. Karigan called on her fading ability, and her vision went gray as was usual. Anna gasped beside her.

The whirlwind passed by their corridor. She counted to ten and then dragged Anna out into the main hall once again. "Don't look back," Karigan admonished her. The first whirlwind still followed them, and the second was beginning to reverse its direction to also follow. It was clear they could sense her and Anna even when faded out, so she dropped the fading as they ran. Keeping it up was pointless and would only exhaust her.

They ran, passing beneath a chandelier, and once more she hauled Anna aside, this time stopping at the winch that hoisted and lowered the chandelier.

"They're getting close!" Anna cried. "And there are more coming!" She turned and hid her face as if this would make them vanish.

Anna was right—there were more, about a dozen appearing out of nothing, joining the others, and all rapidly advancing. Karigan removed the pin that secured the chandelier at its present position at the ceiling. The winch's hand crank started spinning, spinning out of control, letting out chain and lowering the chandelier. She made no attempt to control it even as it gained momentum. The flames of burning whale oil in their glass chimneys flared as the whole apparatus descended at an alarming rate. She did not wait to witness it crashing to the floor, to see if it crushed the whirlwinds, or if the splash of flaming oil melted them. She took Anna's hand and led her away at a run, just hoping she didn't burn down the castle.

AUREAS SLEE

They continued on into the west wing, where the royal apartments lay, finding more ice statues or their shattered remains along the way. To Karigan's dismay, she saw some of her fellow Riders frozen in various positions of fighting. Scorch marks on the wall, and singed tapestries, indicated Mara's handiwork.

They paused at the bottom of the stairs. There appeared to be no whirlwinds nearby, but there was more evidence of their passage, more frozen Riders and at least one Weapon. The distant din of fighting broke the eerie silence. She slicked sweat from her brow with her bloody, bandaged hand.

When she caught her breath, she asked Anna, "Are you all right?"

Anna looked to be in a perpetual state of shock, but nodded.

"Good," Karigan said. "You are doing well. We are going up these stairs to the wing that houses the royal apartments. I don't know what we'll find. Do you think you can stay with me?"

Anna nodded again, and Karigan gave her a reassuring smile. At least, she hoped it was reassuring.

They ran up the stairs, and Karigan was dismayed to find Mara sprawled on the top landing. She was not turned to ice. On the contrary, when Karigan knelt beside her she felt waves of heat rippling off her body. Her face was flushed and glistened with beads of sweat. She had used her ability to full capacity. The magical abilities of Riders exacted a price for their use, and Mara's was fever. Karigan had never heard of a Rider dying because of overuse of an ability, but that didn't mean it couldn't happen. Mara seemed to be breathing normally and Karigan prayed she'd be all right, but she could not linger to aid her friend, for there was fighting ahead.

Soon enough, she, with Anna shadowing her, came upon her fellow Riders, about a third of the complement they'd started out with, battling the ice creatures. There were a couple of guards in black and silver also fighting. Riders with torches swiped at their attackers, but the wild wind the creatures emanated blew the flames backward and snuffed some out.

Steel rose and fell, and the fury of the wind raised by the creatures ripped tapestries and paintings off the walls. Karigan ducked as a portrait of Queen Isen barreled toward her, the heavy wooden frame splintering when it hit the floor. The temperature was numbing.

"Stay close," Karigan told Anna.

She added her sword to the fight, trying to batter her way through the whirlwinds so she might reach Estora's rooms. She had started the day tired, and though her body felt the exertion of so much sword work, it was exhilarating to have an enemy to demolish, a clear-cut problem to solve. No traveling through time, no mirror eyes, no loss of memory, just creatures of ice to crush.

She went for the legs of the skeletal creatures to topple them, and left them for someone else to finish off. She booted skulls aside and into the wall. She helped others stab into the whirlwinds to eliminate the veil of churning ice, and then helped to chop apart the bones within. All the while, Anna managed to remain with her, not getting in the way, and not getting picked off by an errant sword or being frozen into an ice statue.

It surprised Karigan when she finally reached Estora's door. Turned to ice was Rory, caught in what looked like a shout of alarm to warn others of the attack. She ran inside, Anna on her heels, and when she reached Estora's sitting room, she found three Weapons at work attempting to dispatch several of the creatures. The king wielded a poker and bashed it into the skull of the nearest one. Estora was off her sofa with her back pressed against the wall beside the great hearth.

The fire was dying. "Anna," Karigan said, "you must build up the fire to help keep the queen safe. I will get you there."

Fighting the creatures became a mindless chore. Now well-versed in what to do to destroy them, her technique became methodical. She began to wonder, however, if more would simply reappear and fight until they all collapsed from exhaustion.

The Weapons, Fastion, Donal, and Ellen, were dervishes themselves, twisting and turning with blinding sword work to demolish one creature after the other in an explosion of ice. King Zachary was no less agile with his poker.

Finding a gap in the action, Karigan led Anna along the wall toward the fireplace, ducking as an ice skeleton cleaved its sword at her. She hacked off its sword arm, then its leg, and it clattered to the floor in a heap.

They maneuvered around furniture, Karigan keeping Anna between herself and the wall. The Weapons seemed to be keeping the creatures occupied, so they reached the hearth quickly.

"You concentrate on the fire," Karigan told Anna. "Make it too hot for the creatures to get near the queen. I'll make sure nothing bothers you."

Anna nodded and started selecting sticks of wood stashed in a niche next to the hearth.

"Karigan!" Estora cried. She'd gone white around the lips, her face showing strain, and her hand on her belly.

"Stay near the fire," Karigan told her, dodging an ice sword that swiped by her head. She returned her focus to the fight before her. The creatures were now taller than she was, and getting harder to kill. She dispatched one, and another was there to replace it. Where were they all coming from?

When she was on her third, she began to feel the heat of the fire against her back. Her opponent backed away. *Good.* The fire should help keep Anna and Estora safe and prevent the creatures from attacking from behind.

A trio of blurs leaped into the fray, and Karigan wondered what new threat these were until she realized they were Eletians. Lhean had returned! They made even the Weapons seem sluggish in comparison as their swords smashed through the creatures with ease. One by one, in quick succession, they destroyed the enemy until there were no more left to fight. Shards of ice bones lay melting on the floor. Karigan, like the others, leaned on her sword breathing hard.

King Zachary saluted the Eletians with his poker. "Thank you for your timely arrival."

Lhean nodded. "After we left the city, we sensed the unnatural weather gathering around your castle." He and Idris were protected by the strange pearlescent armor of the Eletians, prepared for battle. Curiously, Enver was not similarly armored. He wore only the travel clothing she'd seen him in before.

"We must ascertain if there are more of the creatures out—" King Zachary was cut off by a rending howl and a blast of wind so powerful that it forced Karigan back toward the hearth. She felt her limbs tightening, beginning to freeze, but the fire behind her kept her from turning to ice. The others in the chamber, even the Eletians, struggled to move.

"Sir Karigan!" a forgotten Anna cried, and Estora shrieked.

A towering figure of ice and snow loomed over Estora. It gave off a haze of frost so thick that it was impossible to make out its features. It reached for Estora. Neither the Weapons nor the king seemed able to move. Karigan, too, was numb, but not frozen. She leaped past the hearth, onto the sofa, and hacked off the thing's arm. It howled, and she was thrown to the floor by the force of the wind, a blizzard of snow and ice.

And then it receded. She sat up blinking as flurries alighted on her. Everyone in the room remained in a momentary stupor. King Zachary was the first to recover, and he helped his shocked wife to her sofa. He murmured softly to her and draped a blanket around her shoulders.

"Is everyone all right?" the king asked.

"Fine here, sire," Fastion said, and Ellen and Donal chorused they were fine, too, as they flexed their limbs.

"Karigan?" the king asked. "Are you all right?"

"Yes . . . Yes, Your Majesty, I think so." She rose to her feet and realized Daro's saber had shattered. Only the hilt remained with a small jagged fragment beyond the guard. The rest lay in pieces on the floor. So much for her promise of returning it in good condition. Lhean strode over to her and examined it. The king and his Weapons also came over to look.

"Do you know what happened here?" the king asked Lhean. "What attacked us?"

"Aureas slee," Lhean replied softly. "A major elemental of the north."

"An elemental?"

"Yes, Firebrand. A manifestation of nature. It would not have likely attacked on its own, however. It was probably summoned."

The king paced back to where Estora reclined on her sofa and placed his hand on her shoulder and gazed down at her. "We will try to understand this attack later, but now we must attend to our wounded. Can those who were frozen be thawed?"

"It is best," Lhean said, "to let them thaw naturally. To interfere with elemental magic may do more harm than good."

The king nodded. "We must figure out how we may protect ourselves from another attack. It came for the queen. If not for Sir Karigan . . ."

Karigan saw the gratitude in his eyes, and she glanced away.

"Elemental spirits are often attracted to beauty and power," Lhean said, nodding toward Estora. "When etherea was more powerful in the world, those such as the aureas slee were more present and delighted in the stealing of human and Eletian children alike to raise as their own, to make their own. They would find your queen and the young she bears irresistible."

FOLLOWING SIR KARIGAN

Anna tried to remain as inconspicuous as possible beside the hearth, but she was getting too hot. She took a few steps away, hoping no one noticed her. Never in her life would she have ever imagined tending a fire in the queen's sitting room, much less being there with not only the queen, but the king, Weapons, Eletians, and, of course, Sir Karigan. Why, there were special household staff who attended the king and queen and looked after their fires. Down in the servants quarters, they'd never believe what she'd seen and done today. Of course, she did not know if her fellow servants had survived the attack.

The Weapons moved out of the room, out toward the corridor, followed by the Eletians. Anna had never seen Elt so close up. One time, a bunch of them had camped outside the castle gates, and like so many city dwellers, she'd gone down to gaze upon their colorful tents billowing in the breeze. Up close, the Eletians seemed to shimmer with enchantment. When they left the room, the light dimmed, the world grew more mundane.

"Young lady?" the queen said.

Anna looked over her shoulder, searching for the young lady.

Sir Karigan nudged her. "She means you."

Me? Anna quailed. Sir Karigan propelled her toward the queen on her sofa. Anna could not meet her gaze.

"Curtsy," Sir Karigan whispered.

Anna obeyed, hardly breathing.

"What is your name?" the queen asked.

Anna was aware of the king standing behind the sofa, a large and forbidding presence. She lived and worked in the castle, but rarely saw the king and queen, and always at a distance and surrounded by Weapons, courtiers, and aides. Anna found she could not speak and just stood there slack-jawed.

"This is Anna," Sir Karigan said. "She takes care of the hearths and stoves in the Rider wing, as well as other parts of the castle, I imagine."

"You are very brave," the queen said, "and build a fine fire. It held those creatures at bay."

"Yes," the king added in a grave voice. "You helped protect the queen. We are very grateful."

Anna blushed furiously and could not believe she was the object of their words. They were expressing their gratitude to *her*, a nobody! The king continued to speak, but this time to Sir Karigan.

"And yet again you have prevented disaster," he was saying. "Where would we be if you hadn't come when you did?"

"Uh . . . ?" Sir Karigan shifted on her feet. So, it wasn't only Anna who got nervous under the attention of the king and queen. She had not expected it of Sir Karigan.

"You may refuse to give yourself credit," the queen said, "but we know better."

"I believe I need to have a look outside," King Zachary said, "to see the state of things. Fastion?" he called. "Would you please come stay with the queen?"

The Weapon returned and said, "Those who were frozen are thawing out, Your Majesty. There are some, however, who have not made it."

The king left them, and Sir Karigan bowed to the queen. "With your leave, I would like to help where I can, and check on my family. And I think Anna might be needed to help warm up the castle again."

"Of course, Karigan, and thank you."

It did not pass Anna's attention that the king and queen spoke to Sir Karigan familiarly, without title. Anna bobbed a curtsy once more to the queen, who smiled at her. Color had returned to her cheeks, but her face still looked drawn.

Sir Karigan tapped Anna on the shoulder and beckoned

her to follow. In the outer corridor, Weapons, soldiers, and Riders were stirring. They had been statues of ice, but now after the battle, the ice was all gone. Those who had been frozen were soggy and stiff, but they were coming around. Sir Karigan paused to help her Chief Rider sit up. She was still flushed beneath her burn scars, but conscious.

"Leave me be," Mara Brennyn said, slapping Sir Karigan's hands away. "I'm fine, I'm fine. Go check on the others. I'll find the captain."

Sir Karigan led Anna on, checking on people as she went. At one point, she abruptly blocked Anna's view by stepping in front of her. "You don't want to see this." She walked so that Anna's gaze remained blocked, though she could still see blood on the floor filling the cracks between flagstones. Sir Karigan did this more than once to spare her the sight of the people who had fallen and shattered, their remains now thawing. She was grateful, for she did not wish to see the carnage.

Smoke filled the area where Sir Karigan had dropped the chandelier, but others had put out the fire it had caused. Still, she looked chagrined. As they continued along, people clamored for answers. Sir Karigan told them the castle had been attacked, but all was well now and there would probably be more of an explanation later. Many people had been injured with bites from the creatures, and some also with stab wounds, but menders were beginning to emerge from the mending wing to provide aid.

When they reached the Rider wing at long last, Sir Karigan took a deep breath before they entered, seeming to steel herself, but everyone they found within appeared to be up and about, and greeted her with cheery voices. A Rider hopped down the corridor on one foot, a blood-stained bandage tied around the thigh of the leg she favored.

"Daro!" Sir Karigan said, relief in her voice. "You're all right."

"Mostly," the Rider said.

"Uh, here's your sword." Sir Karigan handed her what was left of the saber.

"Karigan G'ladheon, you broke my sword! Do you know what the quartermaster is going to say?"

Sir Karigan grimaced and said, "Actually, I have a pretty good idea. Sorry, but it couldn't be helped."

Anna knew that Daro's accusation had been good-natured. Green Riders seemed to have a lot of camaraderie, much better than among the servants, where there was a lot of petty gossip and people divided into factions.

Sir Karigan gave Daro and the other Riders a quick rundown of what happened, then suddenly said, "This is Anna. She takes care of our hearths and stoves, and she helped keep the queen safe."

"Hello, Anna," the Riders said.

Anna could only stare wide-eyed, but the Riders did not seem to mind.

Sir Karigan briefly described the scene in the queen's sitting room, then said, "And we should probably see what we can do to help, except you, Daro, and any others of you who've been injured."

"But—" Daro began.

"To bed, Rider. You aren't helping anyone if you fall over from blood loss."

"You owe me a sword," Daro said as she hopped away.

"Wish I had one of my own," Sir Karigan muttered. The Riders dispersed, and she turned to Anna. "I'm sorry, I should have asked, but do you have anyone you need to see to?"

Anna shook her head. She had no family, and really wasn't close to anyone in the servants quarters. She'd rather be with the Riders.

"You sure?" When Anna nodded, she continued, "Then I guess you should check the fires where you can, get the others you work with to do the same, and warm up this castle. The people who were frozen need it. And . . ." She looked past Anna into the distance, speaking as if to herself. "And fire was the best defense against those creatures. Should they come again . . ." She shook her head as if remembering herself. "No, they would not dare. Thank you for your help today. It is time I attended to my own duties." She gave Anna a final smile and squeeze of her shoulder, and strode down the corridor.

Anna watched after her at a loss. What a day! She had been acknowledged by the king and queen, and had even helped Sir Karigan. No, they would not believe it down in the servants quarters. She basked in the fact that Sir Karigan had not introduced her as "the ash girl," as most people called her, but knew her name and made her job sound important when it had always seemed just lowly drudge work. But today, it had actually helped, and even the king and queen said so.

She shook herself, remembering what Sir Karigan said about attending to duties, and it was time she emulated the Rider and returned to her own work.

AN ESCAPE

Ordinarily, prisoners were held in the block house, but with only a few cells, it was for temporary holding only, for minor infractions such as soldiers drunk on duty. More serious offenders were moved to the city jail, or even transferred to prisons in other provinces. The most serious crimes, of course, were punished with execution.

The old dungeons beneath the castle had been closed up for a century at least, until recent years when Second Empire came to the fore and the king needed to detain those who were captured. A portion of the dungeons had been cleaned up and repaired. They were currently occupied by only one man, and he had to admit that his accommodations were humane, with a clean bunk, fresh water, and decent food. No one beat him on a whim as he would have been in his home province. He was not chained to the wall and forced to sit in his own waste. He was brought reading materials, and the guards were more or less genial, telling him the news of the land and trading jests, even though he was a traitor.

Immerez, the one-handed, one-eyed former captain of the Mirwellian provincial militia, did not know why he still lived. Other traitors had been carted off to the gallows long ago. No one had questioned him since that Rider, the false Mirwellian, in Teligmar, except for the king when he first arrived. If his connection to Grandmother and Second Empire had not been enough to hang him, the part he had played in the coup attempt on King Zachary should have been. And yet, alive he remained. Was it possible the king had forgotten about him? If not, what were they waiting for?

A sudden shout from a guard down the passageway roused Immerez from his bunk. He crossed over to the cell door. The small barred window did not allow him to see much but the opposite wall. He heard footsteps running up stone stairs and more shouting. What in damnation had stirred up the guards?

He strained to listen for clues as to what was going on, but for a very long time he heard nothing. He crossed to the back of the cell where the grate opened at ground level to allow fresh air in, but there was nothing to see except a barrier of snow. He shrugged and sat once again on his bunk. There was no reason anyone would bother to inform him about what was happening, but next time a guard came by to check on him, he'd certainly inquire.

After a while, he began to wonder if a guard *would* come by. They checked on him at least once an hour, but it felt like much more than an hour had passed. A lot more. Had they finally decided his fate was to perish in his cell without food or water? Not likely. King Zachary was too fair a man to allow such suffering, a weakness to Immerez's way of thinking. Of course, he'd been trained in the Mirwellian provincial militia, where there was no sense of fairness, and weakness was an invitation for abuse.

When he stood to stretch and pace again, he heard boots pounding down the passageway. Before he could peer out the window, there was the *cling* of a key ring and the turning of the lock. The door swung open. The guard, Rogan, bustled into the cell. Immerez fell back in surprise.

"Here, put these on." Rogan threw a bundle of cloth at him and dropped a pair of boots at his feet. "Hurry!"

After a shocked moment, Immerez did not waste any time, and drew on a tunic of Sacoridian black and silver, and then a heavy winter cloak. The boots fit well.

"We've been waiting for the right opportunity to get you out," Rogan said, "and it finally came." He peered out the door and down the passageway, then beckoned Immerez to follow him.

"Who is 'we'? What's happening?" Immerez was not about to worry overmuch about the intentions of someone breaking him out of prison, but he was curious.

"Some sort of . . . I dunno," Rogan said. "A magical attack or something. But now we can get you outta here. We have horses down in the city."

Immerez followed his unexpected benefactor up the stairs and into the upper corridor.

"When we reach castle grounds, act just like a regular soldier, right? Everyone else is busy. They won't even notice us."

Immerez paused with Rogan at the end of the corridor at a heavy, ironbound door. "Yes, but who are you working with?"

Rogan grinned and pulled down his collar to reveal a tattoo of a dead tree just below his throat. Then he thrust the door open to the wintry world beyond. "Grandmother wants you back."

Immerez followed Rogan out into the snow and left his prison behind forever.

AN UNDERSTANDING

As soon as Karigan stepped into her chamber, she was surrounded by her anxious aunts and had the breath squeezed out of her with their hugs. Their kisses were wet with tears. Her father, as always, stood aside awaiting his turn. When it came, he returned the bonewood staff to her.

"Didn't need it," he said. "What happened out there? Your Aunt Brini was half-hysterical and didn't make any sense."

Karigan described the magical attack and ice creatures. Meanwhile, her sharp-eyed aunts spied her bloody hand and set to tending it.

"Ow!" she cried as Aunt Stace pulled off the crusty handkerchief that had been Anna's. She winced at the bite of cold water from her wash basin used to clean the wounds.

"Stop making faces, Kari girl," Aunt Stace said. "It's just cuts and scratches."

"But it stings."

Aunt Stace clucked her tongue.

"The creatures," her father persisted. "They attacked the king and queen?"

"They're fine," she replied. "They had good protection."

"That is a relief. I do not like this resurgence of magic we've been experiencing over the past few years or so." Karigan must have scowled, for he added, "I know what you are going to say."

"Oh?"

"Yes, that not all magic is bad, that it depends on the intent of the user."

Karigan smiled. That was exactly what she'd been about to tell him. And it would not have been the first time.

"Believe it or not," he continued, "I have come to the conclusion that magic can be good if it is in *you*."

His statement so surprised her she did not know what to say. This was a great concession from him, and so imbued with love. She reclaimed her re-bandaged hand from her aunts and flashed her father a smile. Then she took a second look at the bandage. It was high quality linen with fancy stitchwork. "Where did you get this?" she asked Aunt Stace.

"It's your father's fine neckerchief."

"Stace!" he sputtered.

"You wouldn't begrudge your daughter a bit of cloth to staunch her wounds? You can afford to buy a new one."

Deciding she'd better intervene, Karigan told her aunts, "I bet there are injured people who could use some help out there." She waved her arm to indicate the greater castle. "I am sure the menders would appreciate your assistance." She hoped Ben wouldn't kill her.

"Yes, that's a sound idea," Aunt Stace said.

Karigan held her hand up to forestall them. "There are remains out there," Karigan warned. "It's—it's grisly."

"Back on Black Island," Aunt Stace said, "we tended many a wounded fisherman. You would not believe the accidents they got themselves into. We will help as we can. Come, sisters."

"Gods," her father said after they had left. "Between you and my sisters, it's a wonder I haven't gone all gray."

"You are very lucky," Karigan replied, "just to have hair at your age."

He gazed at the ceiling as though to the heavens. "The gods preserve me."

Karigan, feeling tired once again now that the excitement of the battle with the ice creatures had worn off, dropped onto her bed. With her aunts gone, Ghost Kitty came out of hiding and leaped up beside her. He rubbed against her arm until she scratched him behind his ear.

"I am sorry I yelled at you this morning," she told her father. "I wasn't myself."

He leaned against her desk. "We know you have had a lot to contend with. And I assume we don't know even the half of it. We should have waited, given you time, but when we heard you were alive, we had to see you. And, you know your aunts, they are . . . unrestrained."

Karigan laughed, remembering her conversation with the king and queen earlier. "Overwhelming," she said.

"Yes, overwhelming. The thing is, you are right. We weren't really showing you respect, despite all you've done and been through, despite the obvious regard the king holds for you. We remember you as our little girl, and keep making the mistake that you are still she."

"I know."

"Do you? I doubt you will know till you have children of your own." He smiled to take the sting out of his words.

Children? He hadn't even managed to marry her off yet, despite his best efforts.

"I *would* like grandchildren one day," he said as if he knew her thoughts.

"I think I am busy enough without—" and she gestured curtly "—*children*."

"You see? Here I am, interfering again." He crossed over to the bed and sat beside her. Annoyed by his intrusion, Ghost Kitty whacked the mattress with his tail. "I will keep seeing you as *my* child, no matter your age or accomplishments. I will never stop worrying and making wishes for the future. I never imagined my daughter becoming a Green Rider. It is not a path I would have chosen for you, but the point is that it is not my place to choose, is it? I just want you to be happy on the path you've chosen, though I'll always wish you were doing something safer and giving me grandchildren."

Karigan ran her hand over Ghost Kitty's soft fur. He purred loudly. "Thank you," she said.

"I only fear," her father said, "that I don't know you very well, the grown you, the woman you've become."

It was, Karigan knew, her own fault, her reluctance to share everything about her life as a Green Rider with him. Doing so, she believed, would only cause him to fear for her all the more, but maybe he would have come to the conclusion about her adulthood much sooner, had she been more forthcoming. She still could not, she decided, bring herself to tell him much of her trials, but perhaps she could tell him enough to satisfy his curiosity.

She told him about her journey into Blackveil, focusing on the details of the forest environment, the members of the company that went in with her, but she left out certain details of the dangers she faced. She touched lightly on the horror of companions who had been lost. She did not speak of the Coutre forester who'd attempted to murder her and why. She did explain how she helped the Sleepers of Argenthyne cross into Eletia through a piece of time, but she skipped over how she had barely escaped an attack by tainted Sleepers and how she was tested by the mirror man.

Then there was the complicated tale of her crossing into the future. She glanced at her father. He looked like he was having a hard time digesting it all, and despite her circumspect telling, he looked a little pale.

"I think," she said, "I'm too tired to tell the whole thing right now." And she was. Very. "Also, I should check in with Captain Mapstone."

"No need," the captain said from the doorway.

"Captain!" Karigan stood, and Ghost Kitty rolled away with an irritated meow. How long had the captain been standing there?

"I have been checking on everyone myself and taking stock," the captain said. "We fared surprisingly well, considering. Your aunts have been making themselves useful."

"Good. I mean, that *is* good, isn't it?"

The captain smiled. "Yes, good. They are helping a great deal."

That was a relief. "You are . . . well?"

"Castle grounds were hit lightly. The attack was concentrated in the castle. Nothing, from what I've heard, down in the city."

Karigan's father stood beside her. "Then all is well? It's all over?"

"I would not say *all* is well," the captain replied. "There were casualties, and your daughter tried to burn down the castle."

"Um—" Karigan began. Her father glanced sharply at her.

"Little harm done," the captain said, "and done for a good cause. Your daughter probably did not tell you that she prevented the queen from being taken from us by an elemental spirit."

"No, she did not." He gave Karigan a reproachful look.

Karigan smiled faintly and shrugged.

"Yes," Captain Mapstone said, "the king told me about it himself." She went on to describe the scene with great flourishes.

Karigan tried to prepare herself for her father's response, but he did not overreact. He did not demand or plead with her to leave the messenger service, which he might have done at some earlier time. No, he tilted his chin up and said, "You are fortunate to have a G'ladheon on the job."

A pleased smile crossed the captain's face, and Karigan, both astonished and delighted, laughed.

"Is our queen in any further danger?" he asked. "I met her some time ago, before she was betrothed to the king. It was that night when Prince Amilton tried to take the throne. She stood strongly against him, and it pains me to think of her suffering."

"We do not know, of course," the captain replied, "but one of our Riders, Merla, had an awakening of her special ability during the attack. It seems she can create protective wards, and the Eletians are guiding her on how to set them around the royal apartments."

That was good news, Karigan thought. Her father had stiffened beside her when the captain mentioned Merla's special ability, but he surprised her again when he said, "I am pleased that the queen may be protected by those with such abilities against enemies who would cause her harm. It has taken me a while to learn the concept of magic being used for good, but now I understand."

"Glad to hear it," the captain said, "as the special abilities of my Riders may make the difference in any conflict to come."

Her words hung heavy in the silence, though Karigan swore she could hear whispers in the depths of the dark corridor beyond her chamber.

"Why does your Rider not use her ability to . . . *ward* the whole castle?"

"In time," the captain replied, "she may, but the use of any ability has its cost, and just warding the queen's sitting room gave Merla a case of the hives."

Karigan's father glanced at her, and she could see him wondering about her ability and what it cost her, but to his credit, he did not ask.

"If you like, merchant," the captain said, "I'd be happy to answer your questions about Rider abilities. They are not usually discussed outside our ranks, but as you already know as much as you do, and since we have benefitted so much from your generosity over the years, you are our trusted ally, and it seems acceptable to discuss it with you."

He nodded. "Yes, that would be interesting."

"I do not make the offer without motive," the captain said, a crafty gleam in her eye.

"I do not suppose you do."

Karigan glanced from one to the other, not sure what to make of the two of them, and quite certain she didn't want to think too deeply about it.

"Find me in the stables tomorrow morning around the ninth bell," the captain told him. "We have unfinished business."

"I am sure we do," he murmured.

The captain turned on her heel and struck off down the corridor.

Karigan's father gazed after the captain with a perplexed expression on his face. "I do not know whether to be pleased or afraid when that woman wants to see me. She always strikes me as being taller than she is."

Karigan could agree on the last, but didn't dare speculate on the former.

After a few moments, he turned to her. "You look very tired, and I shouldn't wonder why after all you've done today."

"I am."

"Why don't you rest, and I'll come back around at supper. Meanwhile, I'd best make sure your aunts do not take over the entire castle."

Karigan hugged him good-bye, and before she dropped into bed, she was drawn by curiosity to the traveling chest they'd deposited on her floor. Inside she found the items of hers that had been sent home after her "death," including a certain blue gown with silver threading that had been cleaned and repaired of the abuse it had once received. She laughed, wondering what her aunts had made of its condition, and hung the gown in her wardrobe. She also discovered a tin of Cook's ginger snaps in the trunk and ate two right away.

She kicked off her boots, took off her shortcoat, and lay in bed. She pulled her comforter to her chin, and with Ghost Kitty purring beside her, fell soundly asleep. She did not awaken hours later when her family tiptoed into her chamber to retrieve their cloaks. Her father did not rouse her for supper, but let her sleep in peace.

The ghosts came to tell her their stories, but even the most insistent among them failed to disturb her.

UNFINISHED BUSINESS

As the city bells rang nine hour, Laren Mapstone tended her horse, Bluebird, in the Rider stables. Despite the frigid weather, the warmth of all the horses made the old building bearable, even snug. The contented sounds of horses munching on hay, their snorts and whickers, comforted her and were so very normal after the previous day's magical incursion. When, she wondered, would the next attack come, and the one after that? Would they be able to fend off whatever came next? Even worse, she'd had word that a prisoner had escaped during the chaos, had walked right off castle grounds during the fighting. *Immerez.* A guard had gone missing with him, which meant, despite all the precautions, Second Empire's operatives were still infiltrating their ranks.

She worked a curry comb over Bluebird's fluffy winter coat. She never spent enough time with him for her schedule was fraught with meetings, and attending the king, and attacking all the administrative needs of the messenger service.

"Good morning."

Laren looked up from where she was currying Bluebird's belly, and had to look even higher for Stevic G'ladheon was tall. He stood on the other side of the stall door, his hands deep in the pockets of his long beaver fur coat. He wore no hat, and his cheeks were ruddy from being outside.

"Good morning," Laren replied, setting the curry comb aside and dusting her hands off.

Bluebird stuck his nose out to snuffle Stevic's shoulder. Stevic patted his forehead. "Hello, old fellow."

Unfortunately, "old fellow" was apt. Bluebird was up there

in years with more gray than ever speckling his blue roan hide.

"I'd have brought some kauv—" Stevic began. When she frowned, he tried again. "Tea?" At her nod, he continued, "Yes, well, I would have brought tea, but I fear it would have frozen solid before I got here."

"It was a nice thought," she replied.

An awkward silence fell between them. The stables were quiet, aside from the usual horsey sounds. Hep, who had recently been promoted to stable master, and his assistants were off securing a load of hay, and her Riders were engaged in training, or lessons, or other duties.

"You mentioned yesterday that we had unfinished business," Stevic said. "How might Clan G'ladheon be of service to the Green Riders?" He bowed, hand to heart.

Laren regretted his formality when once their relationship had been more genial, warm. He blamed her, she knew, for all the dangers his daughter had faced since becoming a Green Rider. It had been difficult enough to tell him Karigan had been sent into Blackveil, and then, months later, on a crisp autumn day, the sky a clear blue and the trees laden with apples, she appeared on his doorstep unbidden, and he seemed to know why. When she informed him Karigan had been declared dead, he had crumpled to his knees, his grief so profound she still trembled to think of it.

"Captain?" Stevic said. "You wished to see me, did you not? Is this regarding further supplies for your messengers?"

She willed the memories to vanish and forced herself to the present. "Yes, there is that." She removed the envelope sealed with the mark of the Green Riders from an inner pocket of her greatcoat and handed it to Stevic. "Mara and Elgin came up with a list."

"I trust the supplies have been satisfactory thus far?" The envelope disappeared into one of the voluminous pockets of his fur coat.

"Yes. Yes, of course. Excellent."

He bowed again. "It is my pleasure to serve. If that is all, I wish you a good day, Captain." He turned to leave.

"Hold, merchant."

He halted and turned back to her. Was that a gleam of amusement in his eye? *Infuriating man.*

"Is there something else?" he asked. "Anything else I can do to serve the captain of His Majesty's Messenger Service?"

Damn his formality. As if there hadn't been more between them. "I realize we have not been on the best of terms ever since Karigan went into Blackveil, which I admit I find . . ." What? Sorrowful? Aggravating? Distressing? She settled on, "Unfortunate."

He said nothing, just stood there waiting for her to go on. Of course, he would, just to see her flounder. She was sure of it. She took a deep breath and continued, "Those of us who serve the king have a range of duties to perform, and certainly some of those duties can be dangerous."

"It seems to me," Stevic replied, "that certain of those who serve the king go into danger more often than others."

"Certain of those who do go, do so because they are extremely capable. Others just seem to attract trouble. Karigan is both. She is one of my best Riders as her performance during yesterday's attack should make abundantly clear."

"Tell me, Captain," he said, "which are *you*?"

Bluebird appeared to watch them with his ears pricked as though viewing a sporting match. Wind whistled through the cracks of doors and shutters, stirring up a fine dust from the rafters.

"What is your answer, Captain?"

She pursed her lips, unsettled by his intensity. "All messengers face danger in the course of their duties."

"But not all go into Blackveil."

"No, but three did. One of them never came home. The king could have just sent soldiers, but he wanted his Riders to go because of their competence."

"Would you go into Blackveil if he asked?"

"Of course." She had, in fact, volunteered, but Zachary refused her.

Stevic studied her for a moment, and then something about his posture relaxed. His features became easier. "I know you have faced dangers of your own. Karigan has told me a little. I know, also, that because of your position you are often in the middle of political struggles, which cannot be easy."

"No, it is not," she murmured, recollecting how, after the assassination attempt on Zachary, she had opposed the schemers who wanted a "deathbed wedding" for their wounded, unconscious king. Moving up the wedding, they believed, would ensure a continuity of leadership, should Zachary die leaving no heirs of his blood, but doing so, she argued, violated king's law for it disregarded *his* choice of successor, whose name was sealed in the Royal Trust. When Laren threatened to expose them, they'd drugged her and placed her under house arrest. Her future had been uncertain, her very life in jeopardy.

"I have always assumed that this—" He reached across the stall door and traced the scar that began on her chin, the poorly healed brown scar that slashed down her neck and disappeared beneath her collar. She started at the warmth of his touch. "I have always assumed it happened in the course of your duties."

"Yes," she replied. "Brigands along the road." That was the short, less painful version.

He withdrew his hand and waited as if he expected more. What did he want? The whole bloody story and its nightmarish details? Instead, she said, "I was younger, a mere lieutenant during Queen Isen's reign. If I hadn't been with another Rider, I would have died." She had almost died anyway. "Is that what you were waiting to hear? That I, too, have experienced close calls?"

"In a way," he admitted. "It is a confirmation and a relief."

She was incredulous. "A relief? A relief I was nearly gutted and almost died but for the grace of the gods?"

"Gutted?"

Laren clenched her hands at her sides. Bluebird nickered as though to comfort her. "The scar doesn't stop at my throat."

He backed away as though struck. "I am sorry. I did not mean to overstep—to pry. I—" He cleared his throat. "What I mean, is that I am relieved that the one who sends my daughter into perilous situations knows those dangers first-hand and does not make such decisions lightly. I mean, I am sorry you've known those dangers, but . . ."

Laren decided to let *him* flounder this time.

"I cannot find the words," he said at last.

"So, the merchant's golden tongue has turned to tin?" She could not help herself but gloat a little.

He laughed. It was a full, hearty laugh that seemed to clear the last of the tension from the air. When he subsided, he said, "I apologize for my questioning. It is not easy to hear your only child is dead. Then the shock of her return . . ."

"I have had to inform too many families of the loss of their children during my time as captain. Far too many. And I know it was the same for my captain when I was a young Rider, and for his captain before him."

"It must be extremely difficult."

"It is. I care about each of my Riders, and the last thing I ever want to do is tell a parent they have lost a child."

Bluebird turned in the stall, presenting his rump as he lipped stray bits of hay from his bedding. Laren patted him and stepped out of the stall. She latched it soundly behind her and turned to face the merchant once more.

"Perhaps," she said, "I should tell you how capable your daughter is, and maybe that would make you easier about her work as a Green Rider. Knowing Karigan, she probably doesn't talk much about all she's done." Laren had overheard enough of Karigan's conversation with her father yesterday to know this was true.

"I would like that," he replied. "She does have a knack for leaving out details."

"She knows how much you worry, and admittedly, some of the things she's done are hair-raising, but it only further exemplifies her competence."

She gave him the details of stories of which he had heard only the basics, like those of Karigan's rescue of the then Lady Estora in the Teligmar Hills, and more of her experiences in Blackveil than she had told him the day before. Laren didn't tell him everything, certainly little about Cade Harlowe, whom Karigan had been so careful to keep to herself. Another subject she avoided? Karigan's mirror eye. Few knew of it for her own protection.

So many secrets.

Even as Laren attempted to enlighten Stevic about his daughter's adventures, she held back much. How calculating was the exclusion of details, how it could manipulate emotion and opinion, and make certain truths mislead. How she could soothe the worry of a father by emphasizing his daughter's cleverness.

"Not only is Karigan able to find her way out of insane situations," Laren concluded, "but she helps people along the way, like that ash girl yesterday. It was not only the queen she kept safe."

Stevic had bowed his head so that it was hard to know what he made of it all. She rubbed her lower back. The cold had crept up from the floor into her joints. The city bell rang ten hour.

Eventually he said, "She would have made an excellent merchant, but it is clear she was meant to serve the realm and its people, and not just one clan. I thank you for telling me what she would not, though I sense there are details even you are holding back."

She gave him a tight smile. "Greenie secrets."

"Hmm."

Bluebird rubbed his head on her shoulder, and she turned to pat him, only to find it wasn't Bluebird, but the horse in the neighboring stall. He was at least sixteen and a half hands high, and was white with a splattering of black spots.

"No nibbling, Loon," she told him in a stern voice. He stopped and shook his mane and blinked at her. She turned to speak to Stevic again, but paused and stood frozen for a moment.

"What is it?" Stevic asked.

She glanced back at Loon. He'd returned to his hayrack, paying her not a whit of attention. How was it she knew his name? He'd been brought by the horse trader, Damien Frost, last spring with all the other new horses. Loon must have partnered with one of the newer Riders and someone had told her his name, but she couldn't remember anything about it. She'd have to ask Elgin when she next saw him.

"Laren?" Stevic asked. "Something wrong?"

She noted his use of her name and smiled. "No, nothing is wrong."

He nodded, getting that intense look in his eyes again as he gazed down at her. "I believe our business is not quite complete."

Just then, a horse nose—she didn't know if it was Loon or Bluebird—shoved her so that she neatly stumbled into Stevic's arms.

"No," she said, looking up at him, "I guess it's not."

EMINENTLY SUITED

A full night's restful sleep did Karigan a world of good, and so far this morning there was no reappearance of the strange ice creatures that had terrorized the castle the previous day. At breakfast, however, she heard about the escape of Immerez.

"I thought you'd want to know," Mara said.

And with good reason. Karigan had been caught in his clutches more than once, the first time when she was carrying a desperate message to King Zachary before she was even officially a Green Rider, and the second time in the Teligmar Hills when she served as a decoy to draw away Immerez's henchmen to enable Estora's escape to safety. He had never forgiven Karigan for cutting off his sword hand.

"Thank you," Karigan replied, picking at her sausage, "I think."

"The king has soldiers out tracking him. I am sure they'll bring him back one way or the other."

Karigan decided she would not allow this piece of news to overshadow her day. Mara was right—the king's soldiers would bring Immerez back, and she felt too good after yesterday's exertions fighting the ice creatures and then having a full night's sleep, to get tied up in knots about it, though she suspected that some vestige of a shadow would follow her no matter how much she tried not to worry.

After breakfast, she sought out Lhean, but learned he was still helping Merla with the warding around Estora's apartments. Just after ten hour, she strode along the path to Rider stables to visit Condor, her breath fogging in the frigid air.

She wore a new pair of wool mittens, a scarf, and a cap knitted by Aunt Brini. They were Rider green, and the envy of several of her fellow Riders.

The large sliding doors to the stables were closed against the weather, so she entered through a side door. Like the Rider wing filling up with new Greenies who had heard the call, the stables were now quite filled with horses, and a new section that had not been used in decades was now occupied. It only made her happier to think about it.

She turned a corner to where Condor's stall was and halted. Down the aisle she saw her father, his height and beaver fur coat unmistakable. A Rider stood in his arms. Karigan squinted through the gloom and realized, with a start, that that wasn't just any Rider, but her captain.

What in the name of the gods . . . ? Clearly they were unaware of her arrival. They spoke to one another so quietly she could not hear their words. Her father placed his finger under the captain's chin and tilted her face up, and she grabbed handfuls of his coat and rose on her toes to meet him in a kiss. It was no simple, friendly peck, either, but the lingering, intense kiss of romantic partners.

Karigan blushed and did an about-face, and rushed from the stables, hoping the cold air would jolt her back to reality, maybe help her unsee the scene. Her father? And Captain Mapstone? She scrubbed her face and hurried back the way she had come.

She had sensed there was *something* going on between the two of them, but it still took her by surprise. She slipped on a patch of ice in her haste but saved herself from a fall. Her father, she knew, still mourned her mother, and there had never really been anyone else, at least that she knew of, unless one counted the madam of a brothel in Rivertown, and Karigan did not. Now that she thought about it, she wondered how many fellow merchants had tried to marry off their daughters to her widowed and very rich father for a beneficial alliance. He had gone his own way, however, successful enough he did not require a marriage alliance. At least not for himself. He could get one, he believed, through his daughter and had tried.

She wanted to be happy for him, but the *captain*? Not that there was anything wrong with the captain, except that she was her captain.

"Ugh." She was having a hard time trying to dislodge the image from her mind of their rather passionate kiss. It was fine for them to be intimate. She just didn't want to see it!

What in the hells did they even have in common? A few strides more and she thought, *Oh, gods, ME.* If not for her, it was unlikely they would have even met. Wind blew her hair into her face and lifted a fine powder of snow off the castle heights, which descended in a glittery cascade. Her father and the captain were at once an unlikely pair and at the same time eminently suited to one another. Both were strong-minded, which, she reflected, might make for an interesting spectacle. Her father would have to use all his charm to draw the captain out. She was not exactly an open book.

Obviously, her father *had* been using his charm already.

Ugh. Karigan continued on and stomped up the steps into the main castle entrance. The notion of her father and Captain Mapstone being together would take some getting used to.

She went in search of Estral. She needed someone to talk to about this latest wrinkle in her life. She found the mending wing full of wounded from the previous day's incursion, and a mender told her Estral had been moved to the diplomatic wing to make space. Karigan looked for her there, but she was not to be found. So, Karigan gave up and headed down to the Rider wing and, to her surprise, found Estral sitting in the common room with Mara in front of a crackling fire. Estral was writing in a journal with pen and ink, and Mara was saying, "—and the change is noticeable."

"What change?" Karigan asked.

They both looked up in surprise at her approach.

She sat on a bench beside Mara's rocking chair. To Estral, she said, "I've been looking all over for you."

Estral smiled in reply.

"What are you two up to?" Karigan asked.

"Estral here is taking notes," Mara replied.

"About what?"

Estral grabbed her slate and chalk and wrote out her response. *All the Rider things YOU never tell me about.*

"Oh." Karigan did have that problem with details, and she'd never been a good letter writer. She wondered what "all the Rider things" encompassed.

"Estral says she might write a book about more recent Rider history and how the Riders fit into the scheme of the realm."

Estral erased her slate with a rag and wrote, *Can't sing, but can write.*

Karigan knew she could. She had written numerous songs even before she'd been an apprentice minstrel. When they were in school together at Selium, she used to show Karigan all the songs she was working on. A history was a different matter altogether, but Estral was a good writer in general.

"Can I see?" Karigan asked, pointing at the journal.

Estral shook her head and hugged the journal to her chest. Then she jotted on her slate, *Not book yet. Just notes.*

"You'll let me read it when it's done?"

Estral nodded and mouthed, *Of course.* For some reason, there was a mischievous glint in her eye.

Hmm, Karigan thought. However, she had something else on her mind and glanced over her shoulder to make sure the three of them were alone in the common room. There were some voices out in the corridor, but no one who would overhear.

"Do you know," she asked Mara quietly, "if the captain is, er, seeing someone? Like . . . seriously?"

Mara stared blankly at her for a moment before recovering. "You mean, like a man?"

Karigan gave her an exasperated look. "What do you think I mean?"

"Well, you never know. I mean, the captain is pretty private about her personal life. Not that she has much of a life beyond the Green Riders. Why, do *you* know something?"

"N-no, not really," Karigan lied.

As Chief Rider, Mara spent the most time in the captain's company of any Rider. Karigan thought that if anyone had inside information, Mara would.

"Elgin," Mara mused, "has hinted there was someone many years ago and that there was some tragedy. When I tried to draw him out, he shut right up, told me it wasn't his place to talk about it if 'Red' wouldn't do so herself."

That was certainly interesting. Elgin, a retired Rider who'd served with the captain years ago, had returned to the castle to help with all the new Riders. Karigan was under the impression that he, too, was haunted by his own experiences. Both had fought against the notorious Darrow Raiders, in addition to surviving the usual perils of Rider life. She was certainly not the only one to suffer loss.

"In any case," Mara said, "if Captain Mapstone is seeing someone, it is well overdue. It's time she had something for herself." She added in a low, confidential voice, "I will keep an eye out now."

Estral had watched the exchange with some interest. She didn't miss much. Karigan would tell her about her father and the captain later, when they were alone. She did not need to start the Riders gossiping about their captain's love life, but then thought it might be too late now that she'd said something to Mara.

"Mara, don't—" she began. She was about to tell her friend not to bother keeping an eye on the captain, but just then a trio of visitors entered the common room, escorted by Merla. Her face looked mildly swollen from the hives, but it was the visitors who claimed Karigan's attention.

"Karigan," Merla said, "the king asked that I bring these folk to you."

Karigan was gratified he'd done this for her, that he'd remembered her request to see Lhean.

"In truth," Lhean said, "I was remiss in not seeking you out earlier, Galadheon, and Lady Estral, too."

Estral started in surprise, and Lhean gave his usual enigmatic smile. Both Merla and Mara excused themselves, Mara cryptically telling them she had to "go see what the captain was up to."

Hells. Karigan hoped the captain and her father were not still in the stable. The Eletians joined her and Estral, Enver looking curiously at all the games stacked on a shelf.

"Little cousin," Lhean said to Estral, "we are glad to see you looking well."

Estral bowed her head in response.

There was Eletian blood in Estral's ancestry, and Karigan was pleased they acknowledged it in so positive a manner. People could be ugly about those of mixed races.

"We are distressed by the theft of your voice," Idris said. It was a surprise to hear her speak, for she rarely did so that Karigan had ever observed.

"And your music," Lhean added. "Would you allow Idris to seek the root of this spell that is upon you?"

Estral nodded emphatically, but Karigan, knowing Eletians as she did, was suspicious. "Is there any danger to Estral?"

"You are wise to ask, Galadheon," Lhean said. "No harm shall come from Idris, but if the person who placed this spell left a . . . I believe you call it a *booby* trap? If such a thing is tied to the spell, both Idris and Lady Estral would be in danger. A strong enough trap could ensnare or even kill them. Idris, however, is very learned on how to avoid such traps."

"Are you sure you want to do this?" Karigan asked her friend.

Estral scribbled on her slate, and when she showed it to Karigan, *YES* was scrawled across it in large letters.

IDRIS' GIFT

"It is decided then," Lhean said. "Are you ready?"

Estral nodded, and Idris pulled her chair forward so that she was knee-to-knee with her.

"It will not cause pain," Idris told her. "You must place your hands in mine."

Estral reached forward and clasped Idris' hands with her long fingers. As if already in rapport, they both closed their eyes and became very still. To either side of Karigan, Lhean and Enver also closed their eyes and hummed. It was low, hardly discernible, but she felt it vibrating along her nerves.

She watched her friend closely, looking for signs of change or pain or danger, but Estral's expression remained relaxed. Time passed slowly. The fire looked like it could use another log thrown on it, but Karigan did not dare move lest she disrupt whatever connection the Eletians maintained with Estral.

Shadows shifted in the room as more time passed. Karigan yawned, almost missing the crease that furrowed Estral's brow.

Idris said, "There is a snake, and it has swallowed her voice, the soul of her music, and given it to another. I will—"

She was cut off by Estral coughing and then intensifying into choking, her hands going to her throat.

Karigan jumped up to go to her friend, but Idris was already on her feet, clasping Estral's shoulders. She leaned down to touch her forehead to Estral's, and Estral's choking subsided. Idris released her and returned to her chair. Estral's eyes fluttered open. She was breathing hard, but nothing worse.

"Are you all right?" Karigan asked.

Estral nodded.

"There was a trap," Idris said.

"You cannot overcome it?" Lhean asked.

"No. It is well done. To restore her voice and the soul of her music, she must extract it from the thief. Then the snake will die."

Estral's face fell in disappointment. She looked on the verge of tears.

"Do not despair," Idris said. "I can give you a key to retrieve it, though the finding of the thief may be difficult. I can only tell you that the thief is female, very strong, and young."

"Magically strong?" Karigan asked.

"Yes, the thief has a natural affinity for working with the etherea, and she has had training."

"What would you wager . . ." Karigan murmured. No one had heard anything about Grandmother, the leader of Second Empire, since Karigan and her companions had entered Blackveil. She could not help but think this had something to do with Grandmother, but she did not voice her thought because Idris was speaking to Estral.

"There is a gift I can give you in the meantime, for it pains us that you have not your voice."

Estral cocked her head curiously.

Idris simply held her hands out for her again. Karigan started to protest, but Lhean said, "Hold, Galadheon. This will not hurt your friend, but bring her joy."

Estral took Idris' hands, and both closed their eyes once more. Lhean and Enver hummed again. A pale golden light coalesced between Estral and Idris, intensifying and then diminishing until it was gone, and Karigan wondered if she'd actually seen it. Whatever was happening did not take long this time. The humming abruptly ended, and Idris let go of Estral's hands and watched her expectantly. Estral looked confused.

"Try speaking, little cousin," Lhean said.

Estral glanced at him with a flash of anger and reached for her slate.

"No," Lhean said, unperturbed. "Please try."

Estral opened her mouth. Closed it. Cleared her throat, and said, "I—" She clapped her hands to her mouth, eyes wide. Then she tried again. "I can't—I can't believe it—I have a voice again!"

"What did you do?" Karigan asked Idris.

Idris was smiling, but it was Lhean who spoke. "Idris has transferred her voice to Lady Estral. It will sound mostly like Lady Estral's voice, but with a little of Idris. But you must be aware the transfer will eventually fade. It could be a few months, or it could be many."

"This is remarkable." A tear streaked down Estral's cheek. It did indeed sound like her, but with an overtone reminiscent of Idris. Karigan was so pleased for her friend she felt tears in her own eyes. It was about time something went right.

"Your musicality may return, too," Lhean said, "but that is more difficult. You must nurture it."

"I will. Thank you. I mean, this goes beyond thanking. Is Idris without her voice? It is a sacrifice . . ."

Idris said, in a soft whisper, "It is not entirely gone, and any sacrifice is worth seeing your joy."

"Galadheon," Lhean said, "might we go someplace where there will be no interruption?"

She led him back to her chamber. She hoped her family would not suddenly show up, but there really wasn't any other place she could claim for privacy. She closed the door behind her and faced him. His gaze appeared to follow drafts upon the air. He reached out as if to touch them.

"This is a restless place," he said.

"I don't sleep well," she replied.

"It is no surprise. They are attracted to you."

"They? Do you mean the ghosts?"

His gaze became unfocused, his blue eyes like the turmoil of ocean waves. She'd seen a similar look in the gazes of other Eletians, and she wondered if he was on the verge of saying something prophetic, but his eyes focused on her once more, like a door closed. She shuddered despite herself.

"Yes," he said, "kings and queens, courtiers and servants, soldiers and laborers, all with tales to tell. Remember, you have the command of them."

"What do— "

Lhean raised his hand to silence her. "I know why you have been wishing to see me."

Karigan wavered with the abrupt change of topic. Conversing with Eletians could be like riding a wild horse, highly unpredictable. "You do?"

"Your heart is not difficult to read, Galadheon. Would you reveal your eye to me?"

"Is that necessary?" She crossed her arms. What did it have to do with anything?

"No," he replied.

"Then, why?"

"It may be useful."

Karigan could not hold back her irritation. "I wanted to know what you remembered about the future time—about Cade."

"Like you, alas, very little. The threads shifted when we returned. We cannot remember what has not yet happened."

She had heard this Eletian circularity before. "I know." It almost came out as a shout. "But it did happen, we were there."

"Yes."

"Please, don't you remember anything?"

"I saw but little of your Cade in the end. I recall that there was fighting, and that he was unable to come with us. But yes, Galadheon, he was there in that thread of the future, and your grief is not without foundation."

Lhean stepped forward, and she stood mesmerized as he, without asking, slipped the patch off her eye. She did not protest, did not stop him, and did not know why not. She could not see out of her mirror eye, for mirror it was, a final jest of the mirror man, a being of unknown origin and power. When in Blackveil, she had crossed into a place between the layers of the world where the mirror man had tested her, given her three masks from which to choose and wear, each representing some role. There'd been a queen's mask, very tempting for what she might have and could not otherwise claim; a black mask of malevolent power; and a green mask the hue of her Rider uniform.

She rejected them all. She did not wear masks, and she refused to be stuck in a role, even that of the green one, but the mirror man would not release her until she chose, so being clever, she pointed at the looking mask that he wore. He released her then.

She'd not been so clever after all. As it turned out, the mask had been left for her in the nexus of Castle Argenthyne, and she'd shattered it to keep its power out of the hands of Mornhavon the Black. The shattering sent her and Lhean into Sacoridia's dark future, where she met, and fell in love with, Cade. The shards of the looking mask, however, followed her through time, through the starry heavens and all the way back to her present where a piece had lodged in her eye, turning it into a mirror, a living looking mask.

Few had seen her eye, for it was disturbing, but those who had had seen things, she knew, but could not say what. The past? The future? Dreams and illusions? The original looking mask opened a window of the universe and the weaving of all the world's possible outcomes, and now her eye was a microcosm of it, painful, and one over which she had no control. Had she not smashed the looking mask, had she worn it, she would have been its servant as much as its master, rethreading futures, pasts, and presents. She had rejected the power, but the small remnant in her eye forced her to serve anyway.

Lhean placed his hand on her cheek, and though his touch was warm, she shivered. He gazed into her mirror eye, and as usual, she had no vision in it, just the dark infinite nothing. A minute, two minutes, three, or perhaps an hour elapsed, and they both stood motionless. The fire popped in the hearth on the other side of the room, so she knew the world still went on.

A streak of light slashed across her vision, and she cried with the sudden pain of it. Then there was another, and another. Threads of light, tails of falling stars, perhaps, demarked the weaving of the world. These were accompanied by an assault of images, which had never happened before. They came like an avalanche pummeling her so fast she could make no sense of them. Then they slowed so suddenly that she staggered. Lhean caught her so that she did not fall.

Impressions of the future time came to her. They were cloudy, unfocused. Dirty skies roiled across her vision, along with dreary brick buildings, carriage wheels bumping over cobble streets, a tiny metal man in an open timepiece. She saw people she recognized from Yates' drawings—Mirriam with her hands on her hips and a stern expression on her face, the professor sitting at a big table with a cup of kauv and a paper, Luke saddling Raven. *Raven* with his dark dappled bay coat.

And Cade. Cade trained with a practice sword, flowing through forms with grace and power, the ways in which he moved so familiar to her. The vision changed, and he smiled as he told her some story about buttons. *Buttons?* This, too, slipped away into yet another vision, but one that drew her in, made real as though she could feel his warmth as they lay entwined in the night. His heartbeat, his breaths, the taste of him. She quivered as his hand brushed across her skin. The elation of their joining.

She was thrust into another vision and saw Cade in the light of thousands of moonstones and the maelstrom of a world crumbling around him. She grasped his hand, trying to take him home with her, but he was anchored in the future, anchoring her, too. Lhean was also there pulling on her other arm, attempting to haul her back to their present. She was caught in between, being ripped in two. She would not go home without Cade, but he would not allow her to be trapped in the future, a dangerous future in which it was likely neither of them would survive. *Karigan*, he said, *I love you*, and he released her hand. Let her go so she could return home and live, and maybe change the course of history.

Torn apart.

"Nooo!" Karigan screamed. She found herself kneeling on the floor of her chamber, the cold flagstone eating into her knees, with Lhean beside her, supporting her. She screamed

again into his shoulder. He spoke softly to her in Eltish as to a child, and held her in his arms, gently rocking her.

"Why?" she cried. "Why didn't you let go of me so I could stay with him? *Why?*"

"This is your world, Galadheon," he said quietly, "and we cannot do without you."

A LEAF UPON THE BREEZE

Estral jumped up from her chair at the heart-rending screams that keened down the corridor and penetrated through stone walls, but the Eletians remained seated and serene. She dashed out of the common room and followed alarmed Riders to Karigan's chamber. The Riders clogged the doorway with swords drawn. Estral tried to see over their shoulders, but all she could make out was the top of Karigan's head. She must be kneeling on the floor.

"What's going on here?" Mara demanded from the front of the pack. "What have you done to her?"

The Riders tensed as they waited, which made Estral's anxiety rise even higher.

"Peace, Green Rider," came Lhean's calm voice. "It is but grief."

A silence fell, except for the sound of racking sobs.

Oh, Karigan, Estral thought, desperate to comfort her friend.

"Everyone out," Mara said.

The clot of Riders shifted and backed out, sheathed their swords, and at Mara's order, dispersed, muttering among themselves. Before Mara shut the door, Estral glimpsed Karigan bowed over on the floor, her hands over her face and Lhean beside her. When the door closed, she reached for the handle so she could go in and help, but one look from Mara warned her against doing so.

"I think this is between Karigan and the Eletian for now," Mara said.

Daro Cooper limped up to them. "Are you sure she's all right?"

"If you mean, is she in danger? No, I don't think so. Is she all right? That's a different question. A lot happened to her when she was in the future time." She then gave Daro a stern look. "And I thought Master Mender Vanlynn said you were to stay off that leg."

"But—"

"To bed, Rider."

Daro gave her an impudent salute. "Yes, ma'am." And limped away grumbling something about going mad with nothing to do.

"You might take a look at Rider payroll," Mara called sweetly after her.

Daro grumbled unintelligibly, and Mara snorted.

Estral instinctively looked at her hands as if expecting to find slate and chalk in them, before recalling she now had a voice.

"Earlier when we were talking," she said, "you never got to the part about what happened to Karigan in the future."

Mara glanced at her in surprise. "Your voice is back!"

As they walked back toward the common room, Estral explained the gift Idris had given her.

"That is quite a gift," Mara said, pausing in the corridor.

"Yes, it is, a miracle even, but about the future," Estral reminded her.

"That's a hard story to tell, because even Karigan can't remember much. Something about coming home messed up her memory. She tried to tell us what she could, but it's pretty garbled. The captain has a transcript of what Karigan told her and the king about it. I suspect she'd allow the heir of the Golden Guardian to see it."

Estral smiled. Her father was not only a master minstrel, but as Golden Guardian, he was a sort of lord-governor of Sacoridia's history, culture, and arts. He also oversaw the school at Selium, as well as the city itself, though others managed the day-to-day details. His status conveniently came with a few privileges for his heir.

"Thank you," she told Mara.

The Rider nodded. "I am glad you are here, frankly. I think Karigan can use all the friends she's got. She tries not to show how hard it's been, but you saw her in there. I'm not surprised she's finally broken down after trying to contain it all for so long."

High-pitched female voices could be heard at the entrance to the Rider wing. "Oh, dear," Mara murmured. "What she does *not* need right now is those aunts of hers barging in on her. I am going to have to sidetrack them." She licked her lips and tugged on her shortcoat as if girding herself, then took off in a determined stride. Estral wished her luck and proceeded to the common room. Enver and Idris still sat within, gazing into the fire.

Enver, perceiving her presence, said, "Little cousin, Idris and I are wondering if you would like to try singing."

Estral hesitated in the doorway. Karigan's obvious suffering had tempered her joy at being able to speak again. Even if she found she could sing, she didn't really feel it was right to do so under the circumstances. And if she couldn't sing? She was not sure she could face being incapable.

"I don't know," she told the Eletians. "I am worried about Karigan."

Enver looked grave. "Lhean has lanced her wound. She will not heal quickly, her path is long. But be comforted that she can begin healing. Come sit with us now. I will teach you some of our songs."

Karigan pointed an accusing finger at Lhean. "You should have released me. You should have let go of me in the end." She clambered to her feet and reeled away from him. It felt like jagged edges of glass were grinding inside her eye. In a twisted way, she was glad of the pain. It sharpened her focus. All the same, she covered her eye with her hand in an effort to ease it and prevent further visions.

"You would have been destroyed there," Lhean said, "the both of you."

She turned on him, tears cold on her cheeks. The cold

came from within. "Don't you understand? I don't care. All that matters is that I would have been there with *him*." Lhean remained serene in the face of her rage, and it only incensed her more. "This world . . . I don't care. You should have let me go." She murmured, "I am so tired." She wanted it all to go away, to sleep, for sleep was an escape from the pain. To sleep and never wake up.

She wanted Cade even more, his touch, his arms around her. A memory came unbidden of a sultry summer evening, she practicing swordfighting forms without the sword, and he wrapping his arms around her from behind, moving with her, his hands gliding down her body so that the forms became a sensuous dance. She cried out in pain as the memory faded, and grasped the corner post of her bed to hold herself up.

Cade . . .

"You can't do without me," she snapped at Lhean. "That's what you told me. What does it even mean? Has your prince made some new prophecy? You need me to fix everything? Why can't *you* fix things for once? Why must *I* sacrifice everything?" When Lhean did not answer, she continued, "I am sick and tired of being manipulated by gods and—and things like this." She pointed at her mirror eye. "And Eletians. For all I've ever done, all I get is punishment. What did I ever do to deserve it?"

"Galadheon," Lhean said, "would you forsake your home? Your family? Your friends? Yesterday, what if you had not been here?"

"The Weapons would have protected the king and queen."

"Are you so sure? And what of the young girl, Anna? And all the people you saved by destroying the spell of the aureas slee?"

"Do not put that on me; do not make me responsible!"

"It is true, is it not? There are those who are alive and safe this day because of your actions. Had your queen been taken with her unborn, would it not have bolstered the enemy and demoralized your countrymen? What would have become of your family, had you not been here?"

"Stop!" The tears flowed once more. He was being cruel, so terribly cruel.

Lhean stepped toward her. "Galadheon, your Cade let you go because he wanted you to live, and because he hoped you would create a better future."

Karigan slid back to the floor, the racking sobs overwhelming her once again. Her hands filled with tears tinted crimson.

Lhean gazed down at her for a moment, a flicker of emotion crossing his face. "Do not move," she thought she heard him say. "I am going to retrieve the true healer."

She was vaguely aware of him opening and closing her chamber door on his way out. She lay on her side on the cold, cold floor, her bloody tears pooling on the flagstone. Strains of a voice in song, song without words, permeated her pain. The harmony of it created peaceful images of a breeze in a spring-green wood, of a clear stream trickling over rounded cobbles. Leaves rustled, and bees buzzed on blossoms of shad and iris and cinqfoil.

Gone. Cade was gone, and she just wanted to die.

And yet, there was a clarity about her after releasing so much she had held within. Today she wanted to die of the unbearable pain, and probably tomorrow she would feel the same, but maybe, just maybe, as the song lifted her as a leaf upon the breeze, a day would come when she was ready to live again.

TOWER OF THE HEAVENS

"I put Karigan's aunts off by telling them she had duties to take care of for the king," Mara said, hands clasped behind her back, "and I expect they will relay that to her father."

Laren, sitting behind her worktable, rubbed her eyes. She had a mind to go shake those Eletians and demand to know what they thought they were doing. That they had given Lady Estral a voice did not appease her in the least. "What did Ben have to say?"

Mara shifted her stance. "He says that the hard weeping must have caused the shard to cut deeper inside her eye and that's what caused the bleeding. He said," and now she looked down at her feet, "that even if the shard came out without hurting her eye further, it's done enough damage that she probably won't see out of it again."

"Damnation," Laren said. She had held out some hope that Karigan would one day regain normal use of her eye, but now it appeared unlikely. "I trust Ben made her comfortable."

"Gave her a draught to control the pain and sleep. She took it without argument."

Laren frowned. Karigan accepting a draught without argument? That worried her more than the eye. "All right, we need to prevent the king from catching wind of this. He would be most . . . upset. Not that he'd do anything rash, but no need to stir him up unnecessarily."

Mara nodded as if she knew just why the king might be upset with Eletians causing a particular Rider pain.

"On the off chance the king decided to act on his displeasure," Laren continued, "it could sour an alliance with Eletia."

"If it helps," Mara said, "Lhean says he was trying to allow her to express her grief. He thought it would be very bad if she continued to keep it all inside."

Laren thought he was probably right, but her preference would have been for Karigan to come at it in her own time. The king would not be appreciative of Lhean's efforts if word got back to him, and Stevic G'ladheon would not be either. "I'll have to handle her father. I'd rather he not hear of it, either."

"If you don't mind my saying, Captain, but as soon as her family leaves, maybe we can keep her extra busy, keep her mind off things."

Laren nodded. They'd had to be inventive keeping the weather-stranded Riders busy over the winter with additional training, lessons, inventorying gear, working with the new horses, and so forth. "The weather seems to be breaking," she mused, "and no doubt the king will have a number of messages to go out. Spring will be upon us soon." Too soon, for battles with Second Empire would pick up where they left off.

"We will be busy then," Mara said.

"Yes. We'll see what we can do to keep Karigan occupied in the meantime. If anything changes with her condition, let me know. And make sure the Eletian's part in this does not spread beyond the Rider wing."

"I will, Captain."

"Good. Dismissed."

Cold air rushed into Laren's chamber as Mara let herself out, and papers fluttered on her table. Karigan was grieving, and that was all she needed to know to understand what her Rider was going through. Loss, sadly, was part of life, something everyone had to experience at some point. Sometimes that loss came much too early. Laren had been of an age with Karigan when she lost her Sam, who was savagely killed by the Darrow Raiders. She still felt the pain of it, but it was more like her scar, an old wound that hurt but was not as raw as when it was fresh.

There was a knock on her door, and Mara poked her head back in. "Thought you'd want to know," she said, "Connly just rode in."

Laren stood. Good news at last.

Alton D'Yer stared at the image of Trace Burns, which seemed to hover like a ghost amid a green glow. His hand rested on the smooth green of tourmaline that was the tempes stone in the center of Tower of the Heavens so he wouldn't lose his connection to her. She was miles and miles away in Tower of the Ice, but through the magic of the tempes stones—one in each of the ten towers of the D'Yer Wall—they were able to communicate in this way. Did his image look the same to Trace in her tower as hers did to him? Kind of floaty and ghostly?

"Connly says that Estral says you are not to worry," Trace told him.

At first when Alton heard Estral had reached Sacor City unscathed, he'd about dropped to his knees in relief. He'd been spending the last few weeks in a profound state of worry after she disappeared one day, leaving only a note in explanation. The weather had been terrible and Estral not the most experienced traveler. There were also many dangers along the road that didn't have anything to do with the winter. He'd wanted to ride after her, but the encampment's commander, and his fellow Riders, reminded him of his duty.

Garth volunteered to go in his stead, and though Alton felt guilty about sending him out in the weather, he could not help himself. He was sure Captain Mapstone would be unhappy. Garth was not his to command beyond business pertaining to the wall and its towers. He'd been assigned to stand watch at Tower of the Trees, not to go chasing after errant journeyman minstrels.

Now that Alton knew Estral was safe, he was angry, and it came out in his voice. "Not to worry? Not to worry she could have gotten herself killed? Lost a foot to frostbite? How am I not supposed to be worried?"

"Do you wish for me to convey your tone?" Trace asked, an eyebrow raised.

He passed his hand through his hair in an abrupt gesture. "Do as you see fit."

Trace nodded and closed her eyes as she mentally conferred with Connly back in Sacor City. Poor Connly, whom he'd made Trace harass daily for updates on his journey to the city in hopes he would find Estral there at the castle. It was bad luck he'd been caught in snowstorms out west. More than once Alton had wished he had the same rapport with Estral that Connly shared with Trace. He wondered what it would be like to be so intimately in one another's thoughts.

Trace's image wavered, and she opened her eyes. "Connly says that Estral asks you to forgive her, but that she was driven by fear for her father's well-being."

Alton knew that. She'd been worrying since the fall about Lord Fiori having gone missing, on top of what had happened to her voice. He could not blame her for deciding to take action, and in a way, it was a good sign because previously she'd been so despondent over the loss of her voice. He just wished she'd told him in person instead of leaving a note, and had waited for the weather to improve.

Of course, if she had told him, he would've done his damnedest to talk her out of it. Gods, he missed her.

"I will consider forgiving her, especially if she comes back."

Trace gave him a look.

"What? I miss her."

She shook her head and went into her rapport with Connly again. Eventually she told him, "Estral says that she intends to continue her search. She loves you and is sorry, but it is something she has to do."

Alton took a deep breath and expelled it. "Could Connly, or better yet, Karigan, talk some sense into her?" He remembered belatedly that Karigan and Estral might not even be on speaking terms. When last he'd seen her, Karigan had been so angry with them both.

Trace relayed his message, then said, "Connly says he'll speak to her about it, and that Karigan is currently indisposed."

"Indisposed? What does he mean by that?"

"Not sure," Trace replied. "Connly says he'll tell me later when he knows more."

Whatever it was, Alton was sure she was fine. She was resilient, Karigan was, and had a way of bouncing back from whatever challenges she faced. Knowing her, she was probably barely ruffled by her journey into Blackveil and the future. He dismissed her from his mind, rather more concerned about Estral.

"Connly also says . . ." Trace's expression showed surprise. "He says that Estral has a voice again."

"What? How? She has to come back now!" Estral's singing had been helping to mend the cracks in the D'Yer Wall. The incorporeal spirits that were the guardians within the wall had responded to her in a way they never had to Alton. She had also been working out a riddle of music crafted by an ancestor of hers that might be the key to fixing the wall in its entirety.

"Estral says that the voice is not really hers." Trace scrunched her brow as if trying to understand. "Somehow an Eletian has temporarily transferred the use of her voice to Estral. In order for Estral to regain her own voice, she must seek out the thief who stole it. She plans to do this while looking for her father."

It was a mix of emotions that assailed Alton, joy that Estral had a voice, however it came about, and frustration all over again. His frustration at being helpless to aid her made him want to break something. When he was done here, he would go chop more wood. He used to pound his fist against the wall when he felt angry and helpless, but had mostly learned to channel his anger into less self-destructive activities. The cooks loved it when he needed to split wood.

"I have to go up there," Alton said. "Talk sense into her."

Trace looked like she was growing weary of being in the middle of this long distance discussion, but she did not express her annoyance. Instead, she closed her eyes to confer with Connly again.

At last she said, "Captain Mapstone says that you are not to leave the wall."

"The captain is there?" Alton asked sheepishly.

"Indeed. The captain also says that Lady Estral has free will to do as she chooses, but the captain also wants you to know she will do her best to make Lady Estral aware of the dangers."

Well, that was something, he supposed. "I guess I should tell her about Garth."

"I already have," Trace replied. "The captain says that when you are next on castle grounds that you will receive a full and proper reprimand, and probably a week of laundry duty."

"Hells," Alton muttered. He'd always managed to keep out of trouble and never got assigned laundry duty before. Not that he foresaw himself returning to Sacor City anytime soon, so the point was moot.

Trace laughed. "The captain says she knows it may be a while before you return to Sacor City, but besides Connly being a witness, Mara is there, as well. The captain says that between the three of them, they won't forget your punishment."

"Great." Captain, lieutenant, and Chief Rider, were all ganging up on him.

Trace's expression grew troubled. "Connly is telling me about an attack on the castle. Our Riders are all right . . ." She went on to tell him the details as she received them.

"Gods," Alton muttered when she finished. "As if we don't have enough trouble waiting behind the wall."

"Speaking of which," Trace said, "the captain asks if you have anything to report."

Alton shook his head. "Nothing of note. The forest remains quiet, and the wall is neither improving nor worsening. The guardians do seem to miss Estral. Everyone here is well, but for a few brief bouts of illness. Supplies are coming regularly from Woodhaven."

Trace nodded as she relayed his words, then said, "I am to inform you to continue your watch, and that this communication is to end."

"Wait! I wanted to speak with Estral again!"

"Sorry, Alton, but the captain is reminding us that Connly and I are not your personal link to communicating with Lady Estral."

He was definitely going to chop wood. "Could you at least pass on that she is always forgiven?"

Trace nodded, closed her eyes. "It is done." When he said nothing else, she added in a wry tone, "You're welcome."

"Thank you," he replied absently.

Trace sighed. "I am going now."

"All right. I'll be in touch tomorrow." He lifted his hand off the tempes stone, and Trace and her spectral green glow vanished. Though he stood in the tower, it appeared he stood surrounded by plains of drifting snow. It was the magic of the tower that made it seem a vast landscape existed within. It wasn't exactly illusion for he could walk off into the snow, though he did not know how far, and yet it was not entirely real. Once he left the tempes stone and stepped between the columns that encircled it, the landscape would vanish and he'd be surrounded by the environs of the ordinary tower.

It was frustrating to not be allowed to go after Estral, to not be allowed to leave the wall. Before she had come into his life, he had thought of nothing but the wall. She had reawakened him to so much he'd put aside. He'd forgotten *why* he wanted to repair the wall. It was, of course, to maintain the protection of his homeland against Blackveil, but also the way of life of his fellow Sacoridians, and that included *his* way of life with all its joys. Estral had returned music to him, and laughter, all the things he'd forgotten in his obsession with trying to find a way to repair the wall.

He missed everything she had ignited in him. He knew she had a mind of her own and that if in her shoes, he too would go in search of his father and voice. He could not blame her for that, but it was all right to miss her and worry about her, wasn't it?

He was about to leave the tower when its irascible guardian materialized out of the air. Alton had ceased being startled by Merdigen's comings and goings. He still wasn't clear on exactly what Merdigen was, except that he described himself as a magical "projection of the great mage, Merdigen," and that some essence of him existed in the tempes stone.

"I have been thinking," Merdigen said without preamble.

Uh oh, Alton thought.

"I have been thinking about the dark Sleepers and how they are able to pass through the towers."

"Oh?" Alton had faced such a creature in Tower of the Earth and had almost perished. Sleepers were Eletians who had receded from life, as he understood it, inhabiting great trees. There were Sleepers that had been left behind in Argenthyne when Mornhavon the Black conquered it centuries ago and his touch corrupted the land into what was now Blackveil Forest, and everything within it, including the Sleepers. They were tainted Sleepers, Eletians twisted into something dark and very dangerous. No one, not even the Eletians, knew how many tainted Sleepers remained in Blackveil, but because Eletians could pass through the towers from one side of the wall to the other, so could the tainted Sleepers, which presented a serious threat, should they awaken.

"I think I have an idea about how we might protect the towers."

"You do?" Merdigen had Alton's full attention.

"Yes," Merdigen replied. "I think we need kittens."

MERDIGEN'S CAT

Alton stared incredulously at Merdigen. *Kittens?* Did he expect to purr the Sleepers to death?

"I was sitting with my cat," Merdigen said, "and thought maybe we were ready for kittens."

Had the mage gone mad? Actually, Merdigen had always been a bit mad, but this was more so than usual. Though he'd spoken of having one before, the "cat," as far as Alton could tell, was some figment of Merdigen's imagination.

"I don't have time for this." Alton took a few more steps toward the tower wall through which he could pass into the outer world.

"Here, kitty, kitty, kitty!" Merdigen called. "Come, my Whiskers!"

Alton turned back to Merdigen and opened his mouth to tell him a thing or two, but just then an orange-tabby shape hurtled from the shadows of the tower heights and landed neatly at Merdigen's feet. The ordinary-looking shorthair cat rubbed against Merdigen's legs with rumbling purrs. Alton remained unmoved for he had seen Merdigen produce plenty of illusions before.

"This is my cat," Merdigen said proudly. "He is a stray I took in. His name is Mister Whiskers."

"Five hells," Alton muttered. "I am going to go chop wood." And he walked right through the wall into the cold outer world and sanity.

He made the cooks very happy that day, his ax cleaving hunks of wood into sticks that would fuel their ovens. Even in the frigid air he needed to strip down to his shirt. Swinging the ax, feeling it bite into the wood, was far more satisfying than smashing his knuckles on the wall. If he needed pain, he only had to keep at it until he felt the strain in his muscles. His frustrations, over time, were keeping him fit, and he'd developed tough calluses on his palms.

He couldn't mend the wall. The ax blade split the chunk of wood in half. He tossed the sticks onto a growing pile and placed another log on the stump of an old white pine that served as his chopping block.

Estral was in Sacor City and did not intend to return to the encampment, to him. The ax arced down, and when the log did not split with the first blow, he raised the ax with the wood still lodged on the blade and battered it on the block until finally it split.

He went on for some time until suddenly he felt empty, and with frustration no longer fueling him, he just felt spent. Not to mention sore, which he noticed as he pulled his greatcoat back on.

The cooks knew better than to try to persuade him to rest or stop when he was in a mood, but now they fussed over him, coaxing him into the rough log building that had been built in the fall to replace the old dining tent. Besides dining, it also served as a common room for those stationed at the wall, with a cheery fireplace at one end. The cooks fed him a good, thick stew and pan bread, served with hot tea. He was more hungry than he thought and tucked in.

Besides Estral, he found himself missing Dale. He'd sent her to stay in Tower of the Trees during Garth's absence. He couldn't even use the tempes stone to reach her because that tower was on the other side of the breach. He missed their casual banter and having another Rider around in whom he could confide. Dale had a way of making sure he stopped feeling sorry for himself. Idly, he wondered how she was faring with Mad Leaf, that tower's mage. If Merdigen was a bit mad, Mad Leaf was an entirely different order of lunatic. Garth had seemed relieved to have a chance to escape to Sacor City for a while, no matter the weather.

Even as Alton thought of Dale, Captain Wallace, who oversaw the military operation at the wall, stepped inside and stomped snow off his boots. He and Dale had been a pair for some while, and now he was seeing a lot less of her due to her assignment to Tower of the Trees.

He sauntered over to Alton's table. "Mind if I join you?"

Alton nodded to indicate that he should. The kitchen staff brought out more stew, pan bread, and tea, and after the captain had a chance to warm up over the hot food, Alton said, "I am glad to see you. I have finally received word from Sacor City." The captain had been around the strangeness of the wall for some time now, working with the Riders. It had not escaped his attention, Alton knew, that the Riders had certain abilities with magic, no matter how closed-mouthed they were about them. So when Alton mentioned he had received word from Sacor City and there had been no messengers arriving into the encampment, the captain took it in stride. He simply looked up from his bowl of stew.

"You have?" he asked. "Is Lady Estral there?"

"Yes. There and safe."

"Thank the gods."

"Not only is she safe, but she has a voice." Alton related what he'd been told by Trace.

"Extraordinary," the captain murmured. "We live in strange times, with all the magic awakening."

"There is actually more along those lines." Alton told him about the attack on the castle.

The captain listened attentively, and when Alton finished, said, "The king and queen are safe, and for that I also thank the gods, but how do we defend against such enemies?"

That was the question, wasn't it? The wall was supposed to protect them from Blackveil, its dark magic and the monstrous creatures within. It would not protect them from enemies in the north.

"I wonder," Alton said, "if Merdigen would know anything about these ice creatures. After all, he must have seen just about everything in his day." Merdigen's "day" had been the time of the Long War when the lands were rife with magic. Inspired by the thought, Alton stood, deciding he would ask Merdigen right away. Wishing the captain a good day, he left the comparative warmth of the dining hall for the outdoors.

His shoulders and back stiffened in the cold after all his chopping of firewood. He followed a trail packed down in the snow by the passage of many boots. Paths branched off to the little cabins and tents in which he and the others attached to this secondary encampment lived. Smoke twisted into the sky from numerous campfires and stoves as personnel attempted to stave off the cold.

Ahead of him lay the wall, soaring imperiously into the sky as though all the way to the heavens. It was as if the Earth ended here, that there was nothing beyond, but he knew better. Embedded in the wall was the rounded contour of Tower of the Heavens, rising skyward like a spear shaft. Its exterior showed no door, no windows, no ornamentation. The wall and its tower were forbidding and seemingly impervious, but not far to the west lay the breach. A breach opened by an Eletian.

The wall was the single greatest achievement of his clan. Built in a time of turmoil, it had required the sacrifice of many who were now incorporeal spirits within the wall, its guardians.

When he reached the tower, he placed his hands on it and walked through the wall. It permitted Green Riders to pass and had once admitted wall keepers, but there had been no wall keepers for at least two centuries.

When he emerged into the tower chamber, he came face-to-face with a giant orange cat, as large as a horse. He splayed himself back against the wall and emitted a strangled cry. Gold eyes watched him, and the cat raised a paw with sharp, hooked claws as if to toy with him. Its purrs rumbled through the tower, and its tail knocked over the long table, which held piles of books, with a resounding crash.

"Whiskers!" Merdigen materialized between Alton and the cat. "Bad kitty. You are to reduce size immediately."

"Meep." It was a strange little mew from such a large cat.

"There will be no treats for you unless you obey."

"Prrrt." And the cat shrank to the size of a normal house cat.

Just an illusion. Alton wiped sweat off his brow with a trembling hand.

"He's a little more impressive when he is big," Merdigen said, "but I did not mean for him to startle you. I told him not to, but, well, he is a cat and has a mind of his own."

Merdigen and his illusions. If they made him feel like he was alive, fine, but it was annoying, Alton reflected, when they were inflicted on *him*.

He tried to push it aside, threw a stick of wood on the glowing embers in the big hearth, and set to righting the table and picking up the books that had gone over with it. Merdigen's cat zigzagged across the floor chasing a spider. When Alton picked up the last book, it occurred to him to wonder how the cat, if it were an illusion, had toppled the table with its tail. He shook his head. *No, it can only be some fluke of magic.*

He dropped into the nearest chair and gazed at Merdigen. "What do you know of something called an aureas slee?"

Merdigen's eyes widened, and he conjured a chair of his own. "That is Eltish for an ice elemental. How in the world do you know it?"

Alton explained about the attack on the castle. Merdigen listened avidly.

"Such excitement!" the tower mage exclaimed when Alton finished. "And of course I can't be there to witness it." He shook his head. "Ah, well. Good that there were so few casualties. Of course, the aureas slee could have been distracted enough by the queen in her gravid condition to limit its path of destruction. With the twins she carries, and if she is indeed as beautiful as I've heard, the aureas slee would have found her irresistible."

"So you believe it came for Queen Estora?"

"Doubtful. For an elemental to directly attack a fortified castle like that, it was most likely called by a very skilled user of magic."

Grandmother. Alton supposed Mornhavon the Black could have awakened and done it, but the forest had been quiet ever since Karigan had wounded him. He rubbed his nose. It was itchy. "So what are these elementals?"

Merdigen conjured a moth for his cat to chase. The cat leaped and flipped trying to reach it. "Elementals are embodiments of nature. Mostly they remain at rest in their own realms, unless driven by significant need, or if they are called by strong magic. They can use powers related to their aspect of nature, like the ice creatures of the aureas slee. I imagine over the span of time, many elemental beings have simply slumbered into nonexistence after the backlash against magic and its use that followed the Long War. With no magic users left to call them and the etherea at low ebb, it would be difficult for them."

"Do you think the queen is still in danger?"

"Unless the aureas slee was badly injured, it won't be able to forget her."

That was not good. Alton sneezed.

"Allergic to Mister Whiskers, are you, boy?" Merdigen asked.

"Allergic to an illusion? Not very likely."

The cat leaped onto the table and sat before Alton and gazed at him with feline regard. His tail thumped on the tabletop.

"You should scratch him beneath his chin," Merdigen said. "He'd like that."

"Illusion," Alton reminded him.

"He is no illusion, I assure you."

Alton searched Merdigen's face for any indication he was making a joke, but saw none. That was not necessarily a sure sign. With skepticism and a good amount of caution, he held his hand out to the cat. Mister Whiskers rubbed his cheek against his knuckles, purring loudly. His sleek fur certainly felt real. Alton jerked his hand away and stared at Merdigen.

"This is a cat!"

"I know," Merdigen replied.

"But—when? How?"

"He has been here with me since my internment in the tower. I found him, a stray wandering about, and I knew that should the magic haters find him, he'd be slain."

"You are telling me this living, breathing cat has been with you for a thousand years?"

"Just about. As far as I know, he is the last of his kind."

"There were more?"

"My boy," Merdigen said, "there were many creatures and beings that once walked these lands, like your aureas slee, and Whiskers, here, or even the p'ehdrose. They are more legend now for they were intelligent enough to avoid human beings."

A magical cat. Alton gazed at Mister Whiskers with new respect. "Why haven't I seen him before?"

"He, like I, slept while you people were off fighting wars and neglecting the wall for two hundred years, and after my own revival, it was difficult to coax him to stay awake for very long. Like most cats, he likes to nap. And I must admit, I didn't try very hard, for I feared how he'd be received by the outside world, to which you belong, but I've learned to trust you. Whiskers, why don't you show the boy how you sleep."

The cat twitched his ears, and before Alton's eyes, he transformed into stone in the shape of a gryphon of myth, with a long raptor's beak and eagle wings, and a catamount's body. As a stone gryphon, he was much larger, his claws far more prominent. The sturdy table bowed under the weight of him.

"Uh, why is he a stone gryphon?" Alton asked.

"That is his true form, boy. Or, at least the gryphon part is. Whiskers, wake up."

The stone texture melded into fur and feather. A hint of orange tabby shone through the tawny hide of the catamount. He had a magnificent ruff. Whiskers stared at Alton from above and down his beak. Alton felt the blood drain from his head.

"I presented him to you in his cat form," Merdigen said, "because I did not wish to startle you unduly."

Of his own volition, Whiskers shrank into his house cat form and licked his paw.

"What have you been feeding him?" Alton asked faintly.

"Well, you may have noticed the tower is rather free of rodents, so there is that, but as a magical creature, he can feed off of etherea, so I let him eat a little of me."

Alton stared aghast at Merdigen.

"Don't look so mortified, boy. I just share a little bit of my energy. He wouldn't mind some real meat for sure, but this has done fine for quite some time."

Alton found it all a little hard to take. Even as a magic user himself, it was not easy for him to imagine a world in which real gryphons once flew the skies. It seemed in the aftermath of the wall being breached, many things had begun to awaken: the Eletians, Mornhavon the Black, and the monsters of Blackveil, the elemental, and now a *gryphon.* A gryphon named Mister Whiskers, who was now in the shape of an orange house cat purring contentedly on his back with his paws in the air.

"Do you see why I said we need kittens?" Merdigen asked.

Alton had a flash of little orange kittens flying around the tower with eagle wings. "You want *kittens*?"

"To guard the towers, boy, against Sleepers. Though I admit, it would be fun to have little ones to play with."

"You think gryphons would guard against Sleepers?"

"I understand your skepticism," Merdigen replied. "The cat nature is strong in them and they are not like guard dogs, but I'm quite sure they would recognize the threat of the Sleepers."

Alton felt another sneeze coming on and tilted his head back, but it failed. He sniffed. He bet his eyes were swollen and red-rimmed. "I thought you said Whiskers was the last of his kind. Doesn't it take, um, two to make kittens?"

"It does," Merdigen replied. "I am not absolutely certain he's the last gryphon. I thought to release him and see if he can find a mate, or if a mate can find him. At the very least, he can hunt for some fresh meat."

The sneeze finally came and was so powerful that Whiskers flipped onto his feet and hissed. If nothing else, Alton thought, releasing Whiskers to the wild would relieve his allergies.

A PICNIC

Karigan slept through the night deeply and without dreams. Only as she gradually climbed out of the depths did she recall what had transpired the day before, and immediately she wished she could succumb to oblivion once more. She felt wrung out despite the rest and like the slightest thing—a wrong word, or a certain look—would set her off. Lhean had brought everything raw and to the surface.

But she also felt cleansed by having released so much that she had held inside, both her sorrow and her anger. Yes, Lhean had dragged her away from Cade and into the present, but it had been Cade who had let her go. Some part of her was unreasonably angry with him because of it, and another part knew he'd done it out of love.

She choked back a sob and tried to steady herself as she stared at the beams of the ceiling above. Her eye hurt like the fires of all five hells, as if the shard in it had shredded her inner eye. Ghost Kitty hopped on her belly, awakening her bladder. She hastened to get up and take care of business, and stoked the fire in her hearth. She splashed water on her face and then dabbed some of the numbing salve Ben had given her on her lower eyelid. She slipped the patch on and climbed back into bed, prepared to hide all day beneath her blankets, when a gentle knock came on her door and someone peered in.

"Oh, good," Estral said, "you're awake."

Karigan let go a deep breath. If it had been anyone else . . .

Estral hauled in a basket and a teapot. "Thought you might like something to eat. They serve very good food in the diplomatic wing, and I asked if I could have a picnic basket with my tea. The staff kind of looked at me funny, but they didn't ask questions." She set the basket on the big desk and unloaded cups and muffins, cheese, and little mince pies and meat rolls, and even a couple wrinkly apples brought out of winter stores.

"I assume I missed breakfast," Karigan said, watching in fascination as Estral unloaded yet more food from the basket.

"Actually, both breakfast and morning tea. It is now midday."

"Oh, gods. My father and aunts—"

Estral poured tea in both cups and handed one to Karigan. "Not to worry. Your father is spending midday with members of the merchants guild, and your aunts are shopping."

"Shopping," Karigan murmured. The local shopkeepers ought to love seeing them coming, especially at a time of year when commerce was slow.

"Yes." Estral now passed Karigan a nut muffin. "Something you said to them the other day made them decide it was best to give you some quiet time. Plus, the captain told them you were still on king's business."

"The king told them I had leave."

Estral smiled. "Things have a way of coming up, don't they?"

Karigan snorted and leaned back against her headboard.

"How does your eye feel?" Estral asked. "I know Mender Simeon—or is it Rider Simeon? Mender Rider Simeon? Anyway, I know he came down to check on you."

"A little sore," Karigan replied. Estral pursed her lips as if she knew it was an understatement. Karigan blew on her tea, and then asked, "What of Lhean?"

Estral sat on the foot of the bed with her tea and muffin. "The Eletians departed last evening. I guess their business here is done for now."

Karigan stared into her mug. "I suppose the whole castle knows about . . ."

"Just those of us who were in the Rider wing at the time. The captain ordered the Riders to respect your privacy and avoid gossip."

Karigan looked up. "She did?"

"I think," and Estral spoke carefully, "according to Mara, she did not want the king to become angry with the Eletians for upsetting you. In the event he decided to express his displeasure, she did not want any possibility of an alliance with the Eletians endangered."

Karigan sputtered on her tea and coughed.

"Easy there," Estral said.

Estral was the only person she had ever confided in about the feelings between her and King Zachary, how he had once expressed his love for her. And the captain knew? And Mara? The captain was his closest advisor and an old friend, but was this something he and she had discussed? And she thought that Lhean's actions would endanger a possible alliance with Eletia?

"Gods," Karigan muttered.

"You know men," Estral said airily, with a smile to show she was jesting. "So emotional. In fact, I happen to know one such myself, and we spoke yesterday. After a fashion."

"Alton?"

Estral nodded.

"How? Is he here?"

"No. Lieutenant Connly arrived sometime after you met with Lhean."

"Ah, of course," Karigan murmured. "That's good."

"Yes." Estral told her all about her conversation with Alton, including his punishment from Captain Mapstone.

"Laundry duty?" Karigan laughed, and the sound of it surprised her.

Estral nodded solemnly. "He can be very intense sometimes. I imagine he's been chopping wood to vent."

"He changed after he was pushed into Blackveil." Karigan remembered well how he had treated her afterward. The forest's poison had turned him against her, and the wall had turned against *him.* His inability to mend the wall made his anger and frustration all the worse.

"Who wouldn't?" Estral asked, gazing keenly at Karigan. "Over time, though, I saw that part of him diminish. The anger. But when my voice was taken, I—I was not well. I thought it was the end of the world. I did not want to live, and it affected him. He felt helpless that he could not make everything better, and he got angry again."

I thought it was the end of the world, Estral had said. *I did not want to live . . .* Karigan understood only too well.

As if perceiving her thoughts, Estral said, "I came to realize losing my voice was not everything, that it was not the end of the world. It hurt, still does, but I found another kind of voice."

"You mean what Idris gave you."

"Oh, it's a magnificent gift, but no. The voice I found was my own, in writing. That is when I started taking down the history of the Green Riders, and it helped Alton, too, because he saw my interest in life rekindled, and he liked that I asked him and Dale many questions. It brought him back, until I left. But look at me now, all chatty thanks to Idris."

"I'm glad," Karigan replied. "I thought I heard singing yesterday, or something like song."

"You did, but it was not me. I was not ready. It was Enver."

They sat in silence for a while, working their way through the feast Estral had brought in the basket. Karigan was surprised to find herself famished when so often since her return she had been indifferent to food.

Estral quartered an apple and shared it with Karigan before sitting again at the foot of the bed. Dim daylight filtered through the arrow-slit windows, but left much of the chamber in shadow, but for the glow of firelight that played across Estral's face. She was getting a certain look in her eye, one that was not unfamiliar to Karigan. It usually appeared when Estral had some subject to broach that was probably difficult or uncomfortable.

"I lost my voice," Estral said. "It was stolen from me, but there is a chance I can restore it, so it's not nearly as terrible as losing someone I love."

So, she was broaching *that* subject. "Your father," Karigan said, hoping to divert the conversation.

"My father is missing," Estral replied, "but like my voice, I have hope of finding him." Karigan opened her mouth to speak, but Estral shook her head. "I know you are trying to waylay me down a different path because the one I'm on is painful for you. I am not going to push you, but you know you only need ask if you ever want to talk about it."

Silence fell between them, and Karigan took a rattling breath. She stared at the chunk of apple on her palm and then looked up at Estral. "His name was Cade."

Perhaps it was the food, or perhaps it was the comfort of having her best friend there, but Karigan's recounting of her time in the future was not as painfully draining as she feared. Estral was an excellent and patient listener, not interrupting except when she required clarification. The story was halting due to whatever blocked Karigan's memory. When she told how she had been wrenched from Cade, it all came back vividly and painfully in the wake of Lhean having made her relive it. There were fresh tears, though not nearly as hard as those of the previous day.

"I am so sorry," Estral said.

Just Estral's presence comforted her. Maybe, she conceded, keeping Cade's memory all to herself was not for the best.

The fire died down as the two talked quietly, and when someone tapped on her door, she had no notion of how much time had passed. Her father peered into her chamber. Thanks to Estral, she felt balanced enough to face him and the outside world.

When he entered her chamber, he bore a large bundle wrapped in brown paper and string in his arms and peered over the top to take in the basket and Estral, and Karigan still in her nightgown.

"A picnic?" he asked.

"Actually, yes," Estral replied.

"I heard about your voice from Captain Mapstone," he said. "I am very glad the Eletian could give you such a gift."

"Me, too."

To Karigan he said, "It is just as well you are not dressed. I have something I wish for you to try on."

Karigan looked askance at the bundle in his arms. Was it another gown? Was he going to try to marry her off again?

"I want you to try it on," he said, "and then show us in the common room."

Us? Karigan wondered. Ghost Kitty sat at the foot of the bed watching him intently as if waiting to see what tricks the male human could do.

Her father placed the bundle next to the cat and said, "Don't keep us waiting." Before Karigan could ask any questions, he was out the door and closing it behind him.

"Well," Estral said, "Let's see what it is."

"If it's a gown, I'm never leaving my room again." Karigan untied the string, or tried to, with Ghost Kitty attacking it. As the paper fell away, she gazed down at the cloth in Rider green.

"That looks familiar," Estral said.

It was, and it was not. Karigan unfolded first a greatcoat. It was much the same as her regular greatcoat with its caped shoulders, but with a noticeable difference—the back was split for riding, with a brass button closure for the flaps when one was not on horseback. There were straps for buckling the flaps in place around one's legs, which would protect them from rain and cold while on horseback. In addition, there were more pockets of varying sizes concealed in the interior. Why, she wondered, had Green Rider coats not been tailored this way to begin with?

"There's more," Estral said.

Karigan pulled out a longcoat, and it too was split for riding and had additional inside pockets. The final item she unfolded was a pair of trousers. No, not trousers, but true breeches with leather reinforcement all along the inseam. A vast improvement.

She dressed while Estral picked up the detritus from their picnic and piled it into the basket.

When Karigan was all dressed, with the longcoat on, she asked, "What do you think?"

"Looks like it fits well."

"It does." Karigan moved her shoulders and bent her knees. "Very comfortable." There was an advantage to having a father who dealt in textiles. When he had begun outfitting the Green Riders five years ago, there had been a major improvement in materials, but he'd tweaked the design very little. The biggest change had been the waistcoat, altered from the usual Rider green to the blue-green plaid in honor of the First Rider. She tried to get a good look at herself in her hand mirror.

"You had better show your father," Estral said, "before he dies of anticipation."

Karigan smiled and picked up the greatcoat to take with her, Estral following behind. When she reached the common room, she was not expecting the crowd that greeted her.

THE FINGERS OF A HAND

The common room was filled with Riders, two of whom she had not seen in a while. First, Garth barreled over to her and lifted her off her feet in one of his customary bear hugs, and she laughed. The hug and laughing—it felt good. Then she saw Connly and received another hug, if not as gregarious as Garth's. Connly might be lieutenant, but the Green Riders didn't stand on formality the way the regular military did.

"Well, let us see the new design," her father said. "Stand on a chair so all can see."

Someone pulled out a chair, and she cried out in surprise when Garth lifted her onto it. Her father began pointing out and explaining the new features of the design, and Karigan obligingly revealed pockets and gussets and flaps. She saw that the captain stood next to him, arms folded, her expression unreadable. Of anyone in the room, it was the captain he had to impress, because it was she who had to approve the design. If the *oohs* and *aahs* of her Riders had any power to sway her, she would approve it on the spot.

When Karigan's father finished describing the advantages of the new design, he turned to the captain. "What do you think? Your own Riders suggested the changes."

The room fell silent as the captain appraised Karigan's uniform, her expression unmoved and unchanged. Years seemed to pass, and Karigan could see the lines of tension etched in her father's face.

"Well," the captain finally said, "it's about time our uniforms were properly designed for riding since that's what we do." The Riders cheered and clapped, but she held up her hand to quiet them. "I would like to see the materials before I make my final decision."

"You know I use only the best," Karigan's father said.

"Patience, merchant." There was the briefest exchange of smiles between the two that did not escape Karigan's attention.

Hmm, she thought. She hopped off the chair so the captain, and everyone else, could get a closer look at the uniform pieces.

"I believe the existing greatcoats and longcoats can be modified to be close to the new design," her father was telling the captain. "I can contract with the tailors here in the city and arrange for them to come to the castle and make the alterations for your Riders."

Karigan handed her greatcoat to the captain so she could examine the materials, which were virtually the same as the old. She then let her fellow Riders check out the longcoat she was wearing and examine the breeches.

"As long as it can all be made to fit me," Garth said, "I am fine with the changes." He was a rather large fellow.

The captain, Mara, and Connly stood aside looking over the greatcoat. As the Riders were satisfied and dispersed out into the corridor, Karigan's father joined her. "We are to meet your aunts down in the city for a meal. I asked your captain if she would accompany us, but she must attend the king. What of Estral?"

Karigan was relieved the captain had declined. It would have been awkward to sit down to supper with the two of them after having witnessed their ardent kiss in the stables. Estral, who was conversing with Garth, also declined.

"I'd love to," Estral said, "but I want to catch up with Garth and Connly."

About Alton, she was sure.

So, when it was time to head into the city, it was just Karigan and her father riding down the Winding Way in a hired cab beneath the late afternoon sun.

"Your aunts have the wagon," he explained. They were no doubt filling up its cargo space on their shopping expedition.

They fell into silence as the cab rumbled over cobblestones and through slush. Karigan rubbed absently around her mirror eye to relieve the ache. Ben's salve helped, but not entirely.

"Does it hurt much?" her father asked.

She started at his speaking. "Aches a little," she replied. More than a little, she thought, as a result of her meeting with Lhean.

"Kari," her father began, his expression clouded, "if you ever need to talk . . ."

She gazed out the window at shops and houses with icicles hanging off the eaves that glistened in the sunlight. "I know." She had already done enough talking to both Lhean and Estral. She did not have it in her to delve into such difficult territory again in so short a time.

Unbidden, she thought back to seeing her father and Captain Mapstone together in the stables, and considered her loss of Cade.

"You know," she told him, "I want you to be happy just as much as you have always wanted me to be happy."

He smiled tentatively. "That is good to hear. Don't worry, I am not going to try to match you with another merchant's son, and I've been discouraging your aunts, too. I have come to realize, along with your vocation, you will find your own path in that regard, as well. When someone does come into your life, I can always hope he is a merchant, or he wants to learn the trade."

Well, that was a relief. "Good. I hope you will find someone who makes you happy, too."

"You do?"

His surprise saddened her. "Yes, I do. It's been a long time since mother passed." They sat silently in the sway of the carriage for a moment. "I know you still grieve, but I don't think she would wish for you to be lonely and sad because of her, and I certainly don't." She would not bring up the captain unless he did first. She didn't want him to know she'd caught them in an intimate situation. If it turned out to be serious between the two of them, then he could come around to telling her himself.

He gave her an appraising look, like he'd never expected

this from her. "You have truly grown up." And then his gaze became more serious. "No, not just grown up, but I suspect your experiences as a Green Rider have made you wise beyond your years. I will not intrude on whatever it is you wish to keep private, but my offer to listen will always remain open, should you ever need to talk. It is the hardest thing on Earth to lose someone you love. I never believed I would survive after your mother died, but I had you. When I heard you'd been declared dead?" He shook his head and looked down at his hands. "It all came back. I—I kind of gave up for a while, let things go. Your aunts and Sevano did what they could to keep the business going, but they were hurting, too."

"I'm sorry."

"For what? It isn't your fault you disappeared. At least, not entirely. We will recover from any shortfalls in business, but I am not sure what would have happened had you not returned."

"I would have wanted you to go on," she replied, and suddenly she realized that it was what Cade would have wanted for her, too. He would want her to live and find happiness, however she could.

"Yes, but when you are in the midst of grief, the darkness, it is not so easy to see."

She knew. The sideways glance he gave her made her believe he sensed something of her own grief. She supposed it wasn't difficult for anyone around her to guess what Cade had meant to her, which her father confirmed by his next statement.

"Just as I had my sisters and Sevano to support me in so difficult a time, so do you have your friends in the Green Riders, and Estral, too. They are your second family, if I am not mistaken, and you can lean on them in times of trouble."

"I know," she replied. At least, she thought she knew, but she had that terrible habit of hiding her wounds.

"I will also always be there for you."

"You'd better be."

"It is settled then. I may require your support now and then, as well."

She smiled and gazed out once more at snowy roofs and pedestrians picking their way over the icy street. She was very lucky, luckier than she had ever imagined, for her family. Both families.

A short time later, a mischievous thought came into her mind and she turned to her father. "I feel that I should warn you about Captain Mapstone."

He stared blankly at her. "Warn me about her?"

Karigan nodded solemnly. "Since you are aware that Green Riders have magical abilities, I do not feel it amiss to warn you she can tell if you are ever lying."

He paled. "She—she can read my mind?"

Karigan smiled. "Just thought you'd find it useful to know in your *dealings* with her." His look of consternation was so comical she could barely suppress her laughter. "As long as you don't lie to her, you should be all right."

Perhaps it was not her place to tell him of the captain's ability, but seeing him squirm a little was priceless. Merchants, she knew very well, were prone to exaggerations, and her father was no exception. She wondered, in amusement, what sort of things he'd already told the captain.

In the days that followed, winter eased with sunnier skies and longer days, allowing some of the snow to melt, only to freeze into ice during the night. Karigan spent time with her father and aunts visiting museums, shopping, and sipping tea at a cafe on Gryphon Street. There were times when it was just she and her aunts, and she suspected besides "attending to business" as she was told, her father was actually visiting the captain.

Her family was more cautious with her, she noticed. They tread carefully, treated her as an adult, and were well-behaved in her chamber, not prying but respecting her privacy. As much as she had wished for that respect, it felt like a part of her childhood had died, and she thought maybe they were being a little too careful.

On the day of their departure, she stood on the front steps of the castle with her aunts, waiting for her father to appear. He had, her aunts said, some final "business" with Captain Mapstone.

I bet he does, Karigan thought.

"While, we're waiting . . ." Aunt Stace said, and she stepped down to their wagon and leaned into the cargo area. She pulled out what looked like a bulging canvas sail bag. "We have passed the winter knitting and thought your friends would like hats and mittens like yours."

"Oh, yes," Karigan said, accepting the bag and peering inside at the green wool yarn. "They've been threatening to steal mine!"

Her aunts beamed. "There is also a set in minstrel blue for Estral."

"Don't forget the other thing," Aunt Tory said.

Aunt Stace's lips became a narrow line; then she said, "Of course, Tory." She pulled a jug from the wagon bed that sloshed when she handed it to Karigan.

"Did you know that your friend, Lord Alton, has an aunt who distills whiskey?" Aunt Tory asked Karigan.

"Uh, no, I did not." Karigan held the jug in her arms, regarding it dubiously.

"Well, he does, and that is a fine sample of her work. Very good for toddies."

If Aunt Tory expected her to consume it all herself, it would take years. Good thing it wouldn't go bad. She noticed the guards at the castle entrance eyeing the jug wistfully. Maybe she could share it with some new friends.

Her father soon joined them, cutting across castle grounds, no doubt from officers quarters, rather than exiting the castle itself. He looked well pleased with himself. His "business" with the captain must have gone well.

Hmm.

"It was time we departed, I suppose," he said, "while the weather holds and the day is young." He hugged Karigan, jug of whiskey and all. "Remember, we are all so proud of you. I can't even express how happy I am you are back with us."

When he pulled away, she espied what might have been a glistening of tears in his eyes, but then he was entirely himself, chivvying his sisters to get moving. Her aunts gave her kisses and hugs. He then helped them step up onto the wagon.

"It looks to be a challenging year for trade," he told her,

"with the uncertainty of forthcoming conflict, but we are G'ladheons and we will forge on." He then climbed up onto the driving bench with Aunt Stace. "Do visit if you can, and please, *please,* stay out of trouble."

"No promises."

"I know," he said quietly. Without an actual good-bye, he clucked and whistled the drays on. The wagon lurched forward. Her aunts did call out their farewells and waved to her. She watched the wagon make its way down the drive all the way to the portcullis and out of sight.

Rather suddenly the world had gone quiet, and she felt very alone. As much as their arrival had posed some difficulty for her, she now felt bereft with their departure. Perhaps, she thought, adjusting the jug of whiskey in her arms, she should go hand out the hats and mittens her aunts had knitted, and make herself a toddy. A toddy strong enough to please Aunt Tory.

She smiled, and hefting the sail bag over her shoulder, entered the castle.

When Karigan returned to the Rider wing with her burdens, she found the corridor quiet and empty but for one Rider, Sophina. She came from minor nobility and had heard the call not long before Karigan had entered Blackveil. Sophina had not gotten on well at first, thinking herself above all the others and too good to be a messenger. That Alton D'Yer was a Rider *and* the heir of a province did nothing to sway her. Apparently her attitude had begun to change the day her ability manifested, the day that an assassin's arrow almost took King Zachary from them. She had "seen" it happen.

And now she stared at the ceiling with glassy eyes.

"Sophina?" Karigan asked quietly.

Sophina's gaze did not waver, and she extended her hand toward the ceiling as though to touch something that was not there. "The light reaches down like the fingers of a hand."

A NEW DUTY

Karigan glanced at the ceiling as if she, too, might see what Sophina saw, but there was nothing. Then Sophina's hand fell to her side, and she staggered backward. Karigan dropped her bag of knitted goods and hastily shifted her jug so she could help steady Sophina. Sophina shook her head as if to clear it.

"Are you all right?" Karigan asked.

Sophina looked around as if she didn't know where she was at first. "What happened?"

"Your ability just now," Karigan replied. If she'd heard right from Mara, this would be only the second time it had emerged. "Do you remember anything?"

"No. Did I say something?"

"The light reaches down like the fingers of a hand."

Sophina laughed derisively. "Is that all? Ridiculous."

"It could mean more than it seems. You need to report it to Captain Mapstone."

Sophina shrugged and went on her way. Karigan shrugged, too, and headed to the common room where she deposited the sail bag of mittens and hats for anyone who wanted them, but for one set she removed to give to the captain later.

"I brought you a hat and mittens my aunts knitted." Karigan passed them across the worktable to the captain.

She looked delighted as she tried on a mitten. "I must write to thank them. You saw them off?"

"Yes."

"Good-byes can be difficult."

Karigan wondered if she was thinking about her own parting with a certain merchant.

"And your eye?" the captain asked. "How is it feeling?"

"All right. It's been worse." Before the captain could dig deeper into the subject, or address what had caused her eye to hurt more recently, she asked, "Did Sophina come by?"

"Sophina? No. Why?"

Karigan described her encounter with the Rider.

"Light reaches down like the fingers of a hand." The captain sat back in her chair. "It appears the Eletians do not hold dominion over mysterious visions and pronouncements. I will share it with the king and his other advisors, and I will also speak to Sophina. Her attitude is much improved compared to what it used to be, but sometimes she has lapses. I'll drum it into her that she is to report any time she has a vision." Then she smiled. "Or maybe I'll have Mara do the drumming. She's good at it."

Yes, she was, Karigan thought.

"As for you . . ." The captain gazed appraisingly at her. "Since you are now off leave, besides your usual duties, I think I will assign you to help Elgin in the records room in his research of old Rider documents. Your hand is better than most, and there are old documents that need transcribing."

Karigan tried to conceal her lack of enthusiasm. Transcription reminded her too much of keeping the Rider accounts, but at least when she was doing that, she was actively solving problems.

"Appreciate the quiet time," the captain said, detecting her disappointment, "for spring will soon be upon us, and not only will there be many message errands going out, but conflict with Second Empire will reignite. We'll be looking back at this time with some longing."

She was right, of course, Karigan thought as she headed back to the castle with reports tucked under her arm that were to be delivered to the records room. It was just that she'd never been one for stillness, and even less so now. She'd rather be moving, keeping both mind and body active so she did not end up dwelling on loss. And not just loss, but all the changes wrought upon her by whatever forces sought to manipulate her. The gods, specifically Westrion and his steed Salvistar, seemed to have some claim on her. Then there was the mirror man and what had become of her eye. *Mirare,* Somial had called her. Who or what were the Mirari? Ghosts had also manipulated her from time to time, and the Eletians, as well. It just wasn't normal, her life, and she had no idea what to expect next, or how she would be *used.* It seemed no matter how much she fought it, fate led her on its own course.

When she reached the records room, she found not only Elgin Foxsmith sitting at a table full of scrolls, manuscripts, and ledgers, but Estral and Connly standing behind another table looking over a map. Everyone glanced up at her arrival and exchanged greetings.

"I was expecting Elgin to be here," Karigan said, "and maybe Dakrias, but what are you two doing here?"

Connly and Estral exchanged smiles.

"We're looking at old tax and landholder maps," Estral said.

Karigan stepped up to the table and gazed down at the large curling sheet showing Sacoridia in detail. She'd seen plenty of maps in her time as a Green Rider, and this was nothing new.

"What are you looking for?"

"My father," Estral replied. "When Connly stopped in Selium and talked to the dean and others, there was some agreement that my father intended to travel north."

"North" encompassed a lot of territory in Sacoridia and beyond. North was where a lot of the action against Second Empire had occurred. Eletia was also north and slightly west. Lord Fiori would be but a grain of sand on all the beaches of Sacoridia combined.

"We are looking at villages and towns that are north, in both Adolind and D'Ivary," Estral continued. "But I suppose much has changed since this map was last updated."

Elgin laughed, and they all looked at him. "That map's forty years old. Of course things have changed. Why, when the Raiders were running rampant, people abandoned their small villages and settlements to find safety in larger towns."

"It's the most recent map we've got showing smaller villages and settlements," Connly said.

Green Riders rarely delivered messages to small villages. Usually their errands took them to lord-governors and other nobility, and administrators of the larger towns and cities. Any villages they traveled through were on the way along major routes. Those located in the hinterlands rarely saw the passage of a king's messenger. With just a glance at the map, however, Karigan could see a few villages that no longer existed.

"Where will you start?" Karigan asked.

Estral looked glum. "I don't know. Maybe Lord Adolind will have some word of my father, but if my father was traveling anonymously, there may be no way of knowing if he passed that way."

"I'm sure he'll turn up," Karigan said. "He always has before, though I know this time it's been longer than usual."

"I hope you're right," Estral said, "that he'll turn up."

Karigan deposited the captain's reports in a basket on Dakrias' desk. It felt strange that he was not present, but as chief administrator, his duties must extract him from his beloved records room on occasion.

Out of habit, she glanced up into the dark regions overhead. Dakrias was not the only one who occupied the records room. It was haunted, and now and then Karigan heard whispers by her ear or felt ghostly touches on her shoulder or cheek. She'd heard that when she was finally declared dead last fall, the captain had held a memorial circle here beneath the great stained glass dome, currently hidden by shadows, and that the ghosts had caused quite a ruckus.

They appeared to be quiet now, and she was just as glad. She left Estral and Connly to mull over their map, and halted at Elgin's table. He was gazing at a yellowed manuscript through a lens to enlarge the torturous-looking script. He was not an official Green Rider, not anymore, but a veteran Chief Rider from the time of Queen Isen's reign. Before Karigan had left for Blackveil, the captain had asked him to come assist with all the new Riders who had answered the call. As the newer ones got trained up and winter brought in no new

Riders, the captain found other tasks for him to handle, such as researching old records for mention of Green Riders in time of war that might help the current generation prepare for what was to come.

He glanced up at her. "Something I can do for you, Rider?"

"The captain said I was to help you with transcription."

A smile broadened on his grizzled face. "Did she now? That is good to hear. The young ones she had me working with—too fidgety. Didn't have the patience for the work. Nor had they the clean hand you do."

He patted a chair next to his. "Have a seat. The documents and books I've gone through are here." He indicated a huge pile on one side of the table. "I've marked them with a strip of paper where there is mention of the Green Riders. I need you to transcribe the text, page, date, that sort of thing."

Karigan gazed at the mountain with trepidation. It looked like years of work.

"Don't faint, lass," Elgin said. "Not all of those are marked. References to the Green Riders are frustratingly scarce."

She sat next to him and unrolled the nearest scroll. It was fragile, cracked, and smelled of mold. She raised an eyebrow in consternation. "This is in Old Sacoridian, or something."

"Aye," he said. "I don't know what it says, but I've a key for certain words that might indicate Green Rider activity." He showed her a list. "There's a caretaker down in the tombs who is versed in the old tongue, and he made this for me. He'll also translate whatever it is we find." He tapped the beginning of the scroll. "This is the date from very early in Rider history. Amazing it survives. See here?" He pointed to a line of gibberish. "That is the name of the captain back then. Siris Kiltyre, best as I can guess. He'd be the third or fourth captain."

"Third," Karigan replied.

Elgin looked at her in surprise. "How d'ya know that, lass?"

"I—I don't know," she replied, blinking. Memories, or what she thought were memories, rose up unexpectedly now and then, like the dream-memory she had had in Estora's sitting room of the poet, Lady Amalya Whitewren. But how had she come by this particular piece of information? This certainty of its correctness? Had she learned it in the future?

"However it is that you know, I believe you," Elgin said in a solemn tone.

She decided not to worry about it and dipped a pen in ink to begin copying the strange combination of letters in their old stylings. The work turned out to be more engrossing than she expected, and she found herself trying to guess words and meanings, but didn't allow herself to become so distracted that she miscopied the material.

When she came to Siris Kiltyre's name, she passed her finger over it. There was a subtle thrum of her brooch, and in her mind came a flash of ancient Rider garb and a bow. As quickly as it came, it was gone. She repeated the motion of touching his name, but the sensation did not recur.

She sat back in her chair after a time, exhaled a sigh, and looked up, surprised to see Connly and Estral gone.

"They said good-bye," Elgin told her, "but you were too deep into that scroll." He looked over her copying. "That is good work. And maybe you've come to a good place to stop."

"Not quite," she said.

"Well, my old bones don't take kindly to a chair overlong. Time for me to look in on Killdeer and Bucket. Don't stay too long, or you're apt to make mistakes."

"All right," she said. She watched the old warrior limp his way out of the records room. She realized she was alone, the weight of the dark weighing down on her from above.

Alone, but for the ghostly presences who watched.

WEAPONS

Karigan was not sure how long she had been working when she finally set the pen down and shook sand onto her paper. She'd copied a fair bit of the scroll with no real idea of what it said.

She sat back and rubbed the nape of her neck. The records room had remained quiet, funereal, really. She'd been so focused on the work that she'd lost track of time, hadn't even heard the city bells. Maybe, when her brooch abandoned her, she could become a scribe. No, doing it occasionally was all right, but how she filled her whole day, every day? She'd go mad.

She stood and stretched, and hoped she had not missed supper. She extinguished the lamp on her table, but left the others burning for Dakrias' return. She strode from the records room, only to discover two Weapons waiting in the corridor. What were they doing here?

"Rider," said Brienne Quinn of the tombs, "you are to come with us."

"Where?"

"No questions," said Donal.

"What?" And before she knew it, he was blindfolding her. She could not rip it off for the Weapons gripped her arms on either side and started to drag her away. "What in the five hells are you—"

"Silence." Donal's deep voice resonated along stone walls, low and threatening. "You will remain silent."

Or what? she wondered. She did not voice her questions, but plenty streamed through her mind. What in the hells was going on? Why the blindfold? Where were they taking her? Was there some sort of coup going on? Were the Weapons overthrowing the king? In desperation she struggled against their steely grips, but she was nothing against the two of them.

"Peace, Rider," Brienne said. "It will go easier if you don't struggle."

"What are you? Traitors?" And she struggled even harder, kicking, trying to break their hold on her, but they gave no inch, and Donal—she thought it was Donal—twisted her arm behind her back and pinioned it hard enough that she gasped in pain and stopped fighting.

"One more word," Donal said in his low, threatening voice, "and we shall gag you, as well. Do you understand?"

She nodded.

"And, if you struggle, I will break your arm. Do you understand this, as well?"

She nodded again, wondering all over what in the hells was going on. Why were they doing this to her? She could only think nefarious thoughts, had not expected the Weapons to turn on their king.

Their footsteps rang through empty corridors. The records room, like the Rider wing, was located next to an abandoned section of the castle, and the lack of sound from others, and the hollowness she sensed around her, indicated they followed an unused corridor. She had traveled through the abandoned corridors before and preferred not to again, but it seemed she had little choice in the matter.

She thought to count their steps and remember the turnings, but she'd been so shocked she hadn't done so from the beginning, and there were so many turns she could not have remembered them all, anyway.

Donal and Brienne led her steadily, and firmly, their pace never slackening. Being blindfolded made her feel like she was falling into a great, black pit, but the Weapons did not let her stumble, nor did they shove or drag her. They assisted her up and down short sets of stairs. There were enough of these that she could not say whether they gained or lost elevation, or remained at the same level they'd started from.

Her thoughts circled back to dark conspiracies and coups,

but what had the Weapons to gain, and what did they want with *her*? Surely they didn't consider her a serious threat.

She strained her senses to get an idea of what was around her, and so noticed a change in the sounds of their footsteps. It felt like the walls abruptly fell away. The air was different. They had left the corridor behind and must have entered a chamber. Abruptly, they halted.

"Stay," Donal commanded.

"I am not a dog," she snapped.

No one replied, and it took a moment for her to realize they no longer held her arms. She whipped the blindfold off and blinked at a solitary lamp aglow at her feet, and absently rubbed the arm Donal had pinned behind her back. The light was suppressed by the heaviness of dark in this vaulted chamber. She could not even see the walls around her, just the nearby support columns. Where was she? Where had the Weapons gone, and why had they left her here?

She was reaching for the lamp so she could use it to help her find her way out when she heard the rapid approach of footsteps. She turned to see a shadow running at her with a bared sword. She squawked and flung herself out of the way.

What in damnation?

The swordsman pivoted. All in black was he, his face covered by a mask. Black, but not a Weapon's uniform.

"What do you want?" she demanded.

He answered her by stalking forward, light glancing on the sharpened edge of his longsword. She skittered behind a column just out of reach of the lamplight as the sword streaked after her. She called on her fading ability, but it wouldn't work.

What the hells?

There was little time to consider it for the swordsman was after her again, and as she desperately dodged behind another column, the faint glow of something metallic a few yards away on the floor caught her eye. She could not make out its form for it was beyond the halo of light, but she sprinted and dove after it even as the swordsman pounded behind her.

She came back up with a sword and immediately fended

off blows from her attacker. She was so desperate to save herself that she did not wonder how a sword happened to be lying there just when she needed it.

The clash of blades echoed through the room. Karigan was clumsy at first, so taken off guard had she been, and she held off the swordsman only by reflex, thanks to her training. But he was relentless, and she made herself focus, made her movements more intentional. Her opponent was not the hack and slash variety of swordsman, but used refined techniques, forms like those that had been drilled into her by Arms Master Drent.

As the swordsman went into Aspen Leaf, she knew the series of blocks to use. The same for Butcher's Block and Viper. She was too much on the defensive, she thought, and attempted some more offensive moves trying to reach through his guard.

It was impossible. His sword flashed against hers, and there was a beauty in the rhythm, their footwork weaving them in and out of the columns and light. She thanked the gods she had been training hard with Drent since her return, especially when the swordsman bent unexpectedly and scythed his sword at his legs. She leaped just in time.

To her further surprise, he scurried away and vanished into the dark. She stood there panting and wiped sweat off her brow with her sleeve, keeping alert for his return, but she detected movement from her blind side and whirled just in time to meet another blade.

Clang! Clang! Cling-clang!

Karigan's mind kept rhythm with the fight by reciting expletives that would have impressed the dock workers down in Corsa Harbor. This was an entirely different opponent—shorter, lighter, quicker, and clearly female for all that she, too, wore a mask.

The first swordsman had been relentless and this one was the same, but the woman's speed was lightning quick, and she nearly skewered Karigan more than once. She was also versed in the forms, but altered and combined them in unpredictable ways. Karigan had to respond with split-second thinking to defend herself, then went on the offensive in kind, turning a half Crayman's Circle into Aspen Leaf.

Hah! This is a test, she thought suddenly. *Some kind of a—*

The woman's blade slashed through Karigan's sleeve and into the flesh of her wrist. She cried out and fought to not drop her sword. Her hand turned icy and numb. Without feeling, she could not maintain her hold of the hilt. She darted behind a column to evade the woman's swift sword and switched hands. Previous injuries to her sword arm had forced her to learn how to fight left-handed, and though she did well, she didn't do as well as with her right.

When she re-emerged from behind the column, panting hard and blood soaking into her sleeve, she found the swordswoman had vanished. What game were they playing at? She hunted the shadows with her gaze. Just when she thought they might be done with her, heavy footsteps echoed through the chamber, and a huge form, again in black and masked, lumbered into the light.

Karigan knew that shape, and knew it well. "Flogger?" she demanded. Her old sparring partner who knew how to hold a grudge.

He just laughed, then fell upon her like an avalanche, the quickness of his blade belying his size. Each time their swords met, she felt the concussion through her entire body. Her arm, her elbow and shoulder, burned as he took her through some of the most complicated forms of her training, and at speed. She was so weary at this point that only adrenaline kept her moving.

She had no idea how long she'd been in this chamber fighting, but it felt like hours. Flogger had technique, but he also possessed brute force and he slammed her sword out of her hand. She backed away, one hand numb and useless, the other stinging, and then Flogger rushed her.

She dodged aside from his blade and then stepped in to trip him. He sprawled onto the floor, his sword sliding from his grip. Karigan turned to run . . . to run where? She could not see the doorway to this chamber. In her moment of indecision, Flogger scrambled to his feet and grabbed her around the neck from behind. She gave him the usual elbow to his gut, but it moved him little. Boots guarded his shins and feet. She twisted in his grip so she faced him and jammed her fingers through one of the eye holes of his mask.

He howled and let her go, clapping his hand to his eye. She kicked him behind the knee; it buckled, and he collapsed to the floor like a great tree felled. She found her sword and swept it round to take him out.

"Hold!" someone cried, and lamps flickered to life in a wide circle around her, and she could see that the chamber was indeed vast and round. Each of the lamps was held by a black-garbed, masked person, the angle of light turning their visages demonic. All of them were armed.

Karigan held the sword ready to plunge into Flogger's back. "What is this?" she demanded. "Tell me why I shouldn't kill him now?" She jabbed the tip of the blade into his back to make her point, and he grunted.

"Because," said a pleasant male voice, "we should hate to execute you for killing a brother-at-arms."

THE CHAMBER OF PROVING

"What in the hells are you saying?" she demanded, jabbing Flogger again.

One of the people in black walked forward, lamp in hand, and removed his mask. *Fastion?*

"Peace, Sir Karigan. This was but a test."

"What the hells kind of test?" She did not release Flogger.

Others came forward removing their masks—Brienne and Donal, Willis and Rory, and several others, and finally Arms Master Drent.

Drent's presence in this escapade did not endear him to her at all.

"Let Flogger go," Drent said. "This was your test for acquiring swordmaster status."

Karigan stared incredulously at him. "*This?* This is how you test? *This* is what you do to your initiates?"

"Every one of us," Fastion said, "has been through a similar challenge. Of course, this was for the first level. The tests become more interesting as you climb the levels."

Karigan was too angry to care about levels. "You abduct me and attack me, and don't let me know what in five hells is going on? With sharpened blades?"

"How could we truly test your ability to respond to a threat? If you knew what was going on without the element of fear, it would have been just another practice yard exercise."

"You bastards!" she spat. "You git of bloody fekking goats!" She loosed all the curses she had ever learned on the docks of Corsa Harbor, and flung them all at Drent and the encircling Weapons. They showed no reaction, which only incensed her more, and when she finally came to a sputtering end, a pall of silence fell over the chamber and no one moved.

"Well," someone said finally, "she has passed the test for swearing."

"She doesn't need a sword with that sharp tongue," another replied.

"Five hells." She tossed the sword aside. It clattered with a resounding echo onto the floor. Flogger took his opportunity to escape and scrambled away.

"That is not how a swordmaster treats a sword," Drent observed.

That set her off again, with more colorful language. Those assembled did not try to interrupt. They just waited patiently.

"And this?" she demanded, raising her bloody wrist with its numb hand. "*This* was part of the test?"

"Actually, yes," Brienne said. She removed the bracer from her right wrist and pulled up her sleeve to reveal a scar on the back of her wrist. The others did likewise.

"You idiots," Karigan said. "You stupid idiots. Does the king know you do this to your own people?"

"He is a swordmaster," Fastion replied simply, "of the third order."

Oh, gods. Karigan suddenly felt exhausted. She thrust her hand in Brienne's face. "So, what is wrong with my hand? It has no feeling—I can't wiggle my fingers."

"A numbing agent that was smeared on my blade before I engaged you," Brienne replied, "which will also ensure a scar forms. The loss of feeling will wear off in time. A few hours, perhaps."

"Perhaps?" Karigan had an urge to swear again, but she was spent.

Brienne just smiled as enigmatically as an Eletian.

"Does anyone," Drent began, addressing all who were assembled, "wish to speak against this Rider becoming a swordmaster of the first order?"

No one spoke.

Drent grunted. "So it is done."

"What is done?" Karigan demanded.

"Congratulations," he replied, "you passed the test."

She wanted to sit down, but managed to keep to her feet.

"We deemed you already a swordmaster," Fastion said, "for past deeds you have performed, most recently your work against the aureas slee. You very likely saved our queen. However, despite the fact we have bypassed previous tests, this final one was required for the sake of tradition, and to formalize your status."

Brienne produced a length of black silk. "For your sword."

Karigan took the silk, bemused. It was what marked one as a swordmaster. Besides the slash across the back of her wrist, she thought darkly. At the moment, she just wanted to wrap the silk around someone's neck and throttle them. Instead, she muttered, "I don't have a sword."

"As I recall," Drent said, "you tossed it on the floor."

Donal picked it up and handed it to her, hilt first. It did weigh nicely in her hand, but it was a longsword. "This is mine? But it's not a saber."

"Of course it's not a saber," Drent grumbled. "Sometimes you are very limited in your thinking. Most of us have more than one sword." He gave her his gargoyle grin. "Many more."

"Your First Rider," Brienne said, "had a greatsword and a saber."

That was all right then, Karigan supposed.

"Look at the etching on the blade."

Karigan found the sigil of the Weapons, a shield etched and blacked into the blade. She looked up questioningly.

"You have been to us a sister-at-arms," Fastion explained. "An honorary Weapon, and now we wish to formalize your honorary standing."

"There are these." Brienne held out a handful of patches. They were embroidered black shields. "For the sleeves of your uniforms."

Karigan guessed that once her hand returned to normal, she would be doing some sewing—not just the mending of the slash through her sleeve Brienne had made, but sewing patches. Not something she was particularly good at.

"The king," Brienne added, "approves of us formalizing your status, so no one should object to the addition to your uniform."

The king approved . . . She bet Captain Mapstone might have a thing or two to say about it, regardless.

"It has never really been explained to me," she said, "what it means to be an honorary Weapon."

"Perhaps we should remove to someplace else where we may have refreshment and celebrate your accomplishment," Brienne replied. "And there we can answer your questions."

As they prepared to leave, Drent produced a plain black scabbard, in which Karigan sheathed her new sword. They filed from the chamber, and as she passed through the doorway, she felt a warming of her brooch. She paused and turned.

"What is that room?" she asked Brienne.

"The Chamber of Proving, an ancient space from the days after the Long War."

"My ability . . . it didn't work in there."

"Yes, it has the power to diminish magic. It was used during the Scourge."

The Scourge, when those who hated magic attempted to eradicate magic users whether they were innocent of war crimes or not. Karigan touched her brooch protectively, and watched as Donal and Fastion closed the chamber's iron-bound doors and locked them.

"It was an ideal space to test you," Brienne said, "so you could demonstrate your sword work without reliance on your special ability. Come, we will answer more of your questions over food."

Their lamps showed the way through labyrinthine corridors. Even though Karigan was not blindfolded this time, she did not think she could ever find the Chamber of Proving again by herself. Along the way, she found out she was the first Green Rider since Gwyer Warhein to complete sword-master initiate training.

"It is terrible to say," Brienne told her, "but many Riders die before they complete their training, like F'ryan Coblebay, or are just too often away. It is not for lack of talent that there have been so few Green Rider swordmasters. Your captain might have been one, but her duties took her on another path."

Karigan hadn't known this about the captain. When they passed the records room, the doors were shut and undoubtedly locked. Karigan wondered what the time was. Past supper, certainly, if her stomach's growling was any indication. The main passages were also quiet with the few courtiers and servants present looking askance at all the black-clad warriors with a single weary Green Rider in their midst. Karigan recognized one of the onlookers with her buckets of ashes and smiled at her.

At various points, Drent and other Weapons peeled away to attend to other duties, or went wherever it was that Weapons went. Some had houses in the city when they were not required to be on duty in the castle.

When they reached the great dining hall of the Weapons, servants were sent scurrying for food and wine, and Karigan's wound was cleaned and bandaged. It cut across an older scar acquired during adventures down in the tombs. Happily, feeling began to tingle in her fingers. Perhaps her hand would soon be back to normal. She thought back to when Donal and Brienne had spirited her away from the records room.

"Donal," she said, "would you have really broken my arm if I kept struggling?"

"Best," he said, "that we did not have to find out, eh?"

Karigan glowered, feeling a surge of anger rise up again, then realized that perhaps he was joking. Then again, maybe he was not. It was hard to tell with Weapons.

While they awaited food, Fastion showed her how to tie the strip of black silk to her sword just beneath the guard. Each knot held a meaning, she learned.

"The first is for loyalty," Fastion said as he tied the knot. "The second is for honor. The third is for protection, and the fourth is for death."

"Death?"

He nodded. "This is, after all, a *sword*. Its purpose is to reap death."

"Am I going to have to say, 'death is honor'?"

He gave her a rare smile. "It is the motto of the Black Shields, and you are an honorary Black Shield."

Mutton, bread, and potatoes, and bowls of barley soup, were served, and Donal and Brienne sat with Karigan to eat. The rest of the Weapons took to other tables or stole quietly away.

"As an honorary Weapon," Brienne said, "you will receive less protest from Agemon, should you have to enter the tombs."

Karigan looked up from her soup. "I can go into the tombs? I mean, officially?"

"Agemon will not force you to be a caretaker, but entry to the tombs should not be undertaken unless there is need."

Karigan had no desire to enter the tombs anyway if she didn't have to. All those corpses down there . . . Agemon, the chief caretaker, and all his fellow caretakers lived in the tombs. Whole families did. Besides caretakers, only Weapons and royalty were allowed within. All other interlopers were forced to remain as caretakers, never to see the living sun again.

"Being an honorary Weapon means," Donal said, "that we may call upon you in need. We find you worthy, even though you have not gone through the training at the Forge."

The Forge was the academy located on Breaker Island where swordmasters were either "forged" into Weapons, or rejected if they fell short. All Weapons were swordmasters, but not all swordmasters were Weapons.

"Because of the Rider call," Donal continued, "you cannot attend the academy, but we have seen through your deeds that you have, shall we say, the spirit of a Weapon."

Karigan grimaced, not seeing herself in that light, as the stone-faced, black-clad, and silent warrior lurking in the shadows.

"Though you do not guard the king and queen, or the tombs, your actions in the past have helped save all three."

It was pleasant to receive acknowledgment for her deeds, but what sort of onus might this put on her? They would be calling on her at need? How often and under what circumstances? She was about to ask when Brienne raised her goblet of wine for a toast, and the others who remained in the hall raised theirs as well.

"Congratulations, Sir Karigan," Brienne said. "Yours is a unique accomplishment and position."

They clinked goblets together and drank.

"Have you any words?" Brienne asked.

No, Karigan thought, she didn't, but then she gave them a half-smile. "Death is honor?"

THE SWORDMASTER'S PATRON

"It is an intriguing thought," Laren said as she walked beside her king in a corridor of the royal wing. The gazes of portrait subjects looked out at them, though that of Queen Isen had been removed for repair. Did Zachary feel the weight of their watching eyes, the judgment of his ancestors whenever he walked these corridors? They strolled at a leisurely pace, two Hillander terriers cavorting around them, and the Weapon Ellen following at a discreet distance. Gone for the evening was Zachary's usual entourage of courtiers, advisors, and personnel. It was a rare moment for her to speak privately with him.

"I have my misgivings," he replied.

"Why? Imagine finding and having contact with a people thought long extinct. Imagine that they might ally themselves with us against Second Empire."

Zachary did not reply at first, but walked on. He looked a little tired to her. Not terribly, but she could see it around his eyes, as if he'd been keeping long nights. His movements, though, were as sure and steady as ever, showing no other signs of exhaustion.

"Why would the p'ehdrose align themselves with us after they have hidden themselves for so long?" he asked. "It strikes me as though they have no wish to be found."

It had come to their attention, during the restoration of the great stained glass dome that arched over the records room, that during the Long War, there had been more than just Eletians, Rhovans, and a smattering of the other known realms that had fought Mornhavon the Black and his Arcosians. The League had been represented as a three-fold leaf. Only, when the stained glass dome was cleaned, removing centuries of accumulated grime, they learned that it was actually a four-fold leaf, and one of the panels revealed that what they thought had been horsemen were actually the half-man, half-moose people that were the p'ehdrosians.

"You may have a point," Laren replied, "but we won't know until we ask, will we?"

They emerged onto a gallery that overlooked the main castle hall. Zachary leaned over the balustrade, watching his people, unaware of their king's presence, move freely about down below. His terriers sat at his feet.

"The Eletians promised a guide if we furnished one of our own people," he said.

"Just one?"

"Yes. They figured two people could move more quickly and inconspicuously than a larger group into the northlands and evade Second Empire."

"Makes sense," Laren replied.

He straightened and gazed hard at her. "Are you so ready to send a Rider on such a whimsical endeavor? Even the Eletians cannot say if the p'ehdrose truly still exist or, if so, exactly where."

"One of my Riders?"

"Their request," he said, "not my idea, though it does hold a certain logic."

"A messenger to carry your greetings and suggestion of an alliance."

"Yes," he replied, "to serve as an ambassador of sorts."

"And the Eletians requested a Green Rider?"

"Not just requested, but require. They have a specific one in mind."

"Karigan," she murmured.

"Who else?" His smile was sardonic.

Who else, indeed. It had been an easy guess, for of all the Sacoridians they could choose from, it was Karigan with whom they'd had the most contact. Aside from their wishes, she was a good choice anyway, a very able Rider who had seen and done much. Plus, her status as a knight of the realm would give her more weight in dealing with the p'ehdrose from a diplomatic standpoint.

"She said she saw p'ehdrose," Laren murmured, "in the future time, stuffed and on display in a museum."

"Yes, lending credence to their existence. The Eletians seem keen to seek out the p'ehdrose, and as our alliance with Eletia is still tentative, I'd prefer not to disappoint them."

Laren could not discern what he thought of Karigan going north with an Eletian guide in search of legendary p'ehdrosians, for he kept his expression schooled. Was he loath to send her away after she had only so recently returned? Returned from being presumed dead? Or, did he think it would be a means of keeping her safely out of the way as they engaged in conflict with Second Empire? Both, she thought.

At the sound of many boots hammering on flagstone below, they both peered down at a large group of Weapons crossing the main hall. There was one person in green in their midst who was, unmistakably, the subject of their conversation.

"What is that about?" she demanded.

There was a slight smile on Zachary's face. "The first Green Rider swordmaster since Gwyer Warhein, if our history is correct."

Laren stared at him. "Why didn't anyone tell me she had been made a swordmaster?"

"I did not know until just now. See the sword?"

Laren looked again just before Karigan and the Weapons disappeared from view. She carried a longsword.

"I did know they were testing her tonight, though I think we had already settled the question of whether or not she was swordmaster quality due to all she has done on behalf of the realm. The test, however, was needed to ensure we were correct about her skills, and to mark the occasion. You should also be made aware that the Weapons have chosen to formalize her status as an honorary Weapon."

Laren was aghast. "I would like to know why I was not informed. She is *my* Rider."

"As you have reminded me on various occasions," he replied, "*they* are *my* Riders, and that includes *you.*"

Laren was not amused to have her words flung back at her. "You know what I mean."

"Yes." He nodded with a gleam in his eye. "You are their commander. I am sorry, Laren, but Weapons have their own agendas, and while Karigan is still, on the whole, a Green Rider, her abilities have developed in such a way that to contain them to a single discipline would be a disservice to the realm."

Laren could only stare incredulously at him.

"Now that her status as an honorary Weapon has been formalized, there will be some additions to her uniform."

Laren threw her hands in the air, and then paced up and down the gallery in agitation in an attempt to check her anger. The terriers bounded after her as if it were a game. Would it have hurt to have simply told her this was coming? When she halted once more before Zachary, his expression was more sympathetic.

"Laren, you are my oldest and dearest friend," he said. "Truly, the elder sister I never had. I would never do anything to undermine your command or the integrity of the Green Riders. The acknowledgment of the Weapons is just that: an acknowledgment of deeds accomplished and the esteem in which they've held her for a while now. In dire need, they may call upon her, but otherwise, she won't be diverted from her regular duties. Isn't that right, Ellen?"

From her post by the wall, the Weapon replied, "Yes, sire."

Laren folded her arms. She had, of course, known Karigan was in swordmaster initiate training, which, if all went well, would lead to swordmaster status. She'd known the Weapons held her in some esteem. That they would formalize it did make her feel as if they were taking something of her Green Rider away, no matter what Zachary said. And would it have been so hard for them to say something ahead of time? Yes, Weapons had their own agenda, but it did not have to mean a lack of professional courtesy. She would have a word with Les Tallman, one of the king's advisors and the head of the Weapons. While she was at it, she would go after Drent, too.

"There may be other tests ahead for her," Zachary said.

"What do you mean?" She could not keep the suspicion from her voice.

"She is a swordmaster of the first order now. There are four levels, the fourth being when one becomes a Weapon."

"Are you expecting Karigan to become a full Weapon?"

"No. Not while she hears the Rider call."

"And what level are you?"

"Third. As high as I can go as king, since I can't be a Weapon, too."

Laren gazed down into the quiet main hall once again. Few people moved about, none in a hurry. Suddenly she felt very tired, her joints aching.

Zachary placed his hand on her shoulder. "I understand if you are angry with me," he said in a subdued voice. "None of this was meant as an offense to you. Having a Rider who is a swordmaster, that is a worthy honor to your leadership."

He could make nice all he wanted, she thought, but it did not alleviate the sting of her command being undermined. She narrowed her eyes at him. "The sword."

"What sword?"

"The one Karigan was carrying. Where did it come from?"

"One of the finest smiths in the land."

"That is not what I meant. A swordmaster either has a patron who buys the sword, or they must come up with the funds to purchase one themselves. I am guessing it was not her father who bought it for her. He probably has no idea his daughter is now a swordmaster." He was going to *love* that. "Does Karigan have a patron?"

"Yes."

"Oh, Moonling," she said. "Does she know it is from you?"

"No, and she will not. My orders are that she is not to be told. She didn't take well to the last gift I tried to give her."

The two of them, Zachary and Karigan . . . It was hopeless. At least from Zachary's end. Karigan, with her loss of Cade, was likely too involved in her grief to be thinking much about Zachary.

"You are only making it harder on yourself," she said.

"Perhaps. But please do not lecture me, Laren. I have a wife who is carrying our children. I know my duty."

"Does it have to be just duty?" Laren asked.

He grew quiet, his expression softening. "Estora is a remarkable woman. I am very fortunate. It is not just duty." Then his gaze sharpened. "But do not deny me the pleasure of bestowing a gift on one whom . . ." He faltered as if searching for the right words. Then, "It is a gift she can use to preserve her life, and I am glad to give it."

"I won't lecture you for all that you called me the elder sister you never had. It gladdens me that you see Estora as more than duty. I care deeply about you and have ever desired your happiness."

"I know."

"So," she said, "when do the Eletians want to send their guide north?" The sooner Karigan was sent away, she thought, the better for Zachary. And Estora.

"I have not said I've agreed to this mission," he replied, "though it seems a likely course. As soon as they sense winter breaking is all they told me."

Not exactly definitive, Laren thought, but there were ways to keep Karigan busy and out of Zachary's sight in the meantime.

THE FIRE WITHIN

Zachary Davriel Hillander, king of Sacoridia, swordmaster, husband to the lady of Coutre, and soon-to-be father, watched as his old friend walked away to retire for the night. He saw how stiffly she moved, and was aware, though she would never tell him herself, how the use of her ability in his service, combined with years of injuries and knocks and tumbles in the course of her work, caused her recurrent pain. He wondered if it would always be so, that those closest to him should suffer. According to the counselors he'd inherited from his father when he first assumed the throne, he was not, as king, supposed to concern himself with such matters. His only concern was supposed to be that those who served him did so well. They were his tools, he was told. When they wore out, they should be discarded and replaced.

He discarded those counselors instead, and replaced them with advisors of his own choosing. Laren, who had practically overseen the raising of him, was one such. She'd made captain on her own merit, but he ensured she stood by his side as one of his most important advisors. Not every king or queen before him had thought so much of their Green Rider captains to have done so, but he knew well they were more than just simple messengers.

He left the gallery behind and started down the corridor that led to the royal apartments. Finder the Second and Jasper trotted at his heels. Normally the dogs spent the night in the kennels, but ever since the aureas slee's attack, he'd kept them with him in the queen's apartments. They were good watchdogs and, if he or Estora were threatened, vicious defenders, despite their small size. His Weapons were excellent, and he knew the queen's apartments were now warded against further magical intrusions, but he was determined to protect his unborn children and their mother in every capacity possible.

When he reached the door to his own rooms, Ellen asked, "Will you be guarding the queen again tonight?"

He paused. "Do you object?"

"No, Your Majesty. We are pleased you've taken an active role in her safety."

He tried to fathom if there was more behind her words, but like all Weapons, she was well-trained in keeping a neutral expression. Sometimes he wished he could be a Weapon himself, for their duties were clear, black and white, and devoid of entanglements of the heart. It must be simpler, but was it really? For all their stoicism, their stony facades, they were still flesh and blood and surely not immune to human emotion. No, theirs was discipline, a mastery over their passions and desires, and in this he wished he could emulate them.

"I am just going to retrieve my sword," he said, "then will spend the duration in the queen's sitting room."

"Very good, sire. We will be outside if you require us."

We indicated Ellen and Willis immediately outside his and Estora's rooms, and whoever relieved them at third watch.

Inside, Jasper sniffed the edge of a bookcase and sneezed. Finder yawned, waiting to see what interesting thing was going to happen next. Zachary removed his longcoat and tossed it over his chair. He could hear his valet snoring in the parlor—he'd probably tried to wait up for his master, but failed. Zachary did not awaken him, but as he had since the attack of the aureas slee, he retrieved his sword from its display. On impulse, he also grabbed a plain, wooden chest that rested on a shelf. With these items in hand, he and his terriers crossed through the passage that led to the queen's sitting room.

Embers glowed in the fireplace, and a lamp dimly glowed on the table before the sofa, but Estora was nowhere to be seen. He glanced into her bed chamber and made out her sleeping form beneath her blankets, her steady breathing. He returned to the sitting room and set aside the game chest and sword to throw a fresh log on the fire and stir the embers. Shortly, flames greedily attacked the log. Pleased, he sat on the sofa and drew the blanket over his lap that Estora had been using during the day to keep warm. It smelled lightly of lavender, of her. He kept the sword bared at his side, and snapped his fingers at the dogs to lie down by the fire. It did not take much to convince them.

He thought to pick up Estora's book of sonnets to read, but love poems did not appeal to him. They were overwrought with sentiments that were . . . that were unobtainable. Instead, he stared into the fire. Ordinarily, if he was awake in the night, it was because he was working late in his study, going over petitions and correspondence, and more recently, examining maps of the north marking the known movements of Second Empire. He was always busy, always with some problem for him to solve. These nights he kept vigil in Estora's sitting room, however, were silent.

At first he'd brought his own books to read to keep his restless mind satisfied, but tonight he stared into the dance of flames too tired for much else. He'd resisted the silence because it permitted unpleasant memories to surface, memories of betrayal and violation, and tonight was no different.

Betrayal had become too familiar an unwanted companion since his ascension to the throne. There'd been his brother, of course, but there'd been little love between the two of them to begin with. No, Amilton's betrayal had not been the knife twisted in his back that had been the betrayal of advisors he had chosen and trusted.

He reached across the table and opened the wooden chest he'd brought, which contained his game of Intrigue. He laid out the board and started setting up the markers, which were crudely carved wooden figures in red and blue, the paint worn and chipped from use. He held the green in reserve. The set had belonged to his great grandfather and was passed down to him.

As he considered the markers in their starting positions

on the board, he acknowledged that time eased the pain, that the betrayal was not nearly as visceral as when it had happened, but he remained angry, angry that he lost three experienced, hardworking men because they had simply not trusted him the way he had trusted them. When his survival was in question after the assassin's arrow, they took matters into their own hands and violated royal law by forcing his marriage to Estora while he lay fevered and insensible.

He punished them for their transgressions. Master Mender Destarion had been reassigned to an outpost in the northern wilds where he must suffer hardship and privation. General Harborough had been stripped of his rank and sent to stand before a military tribunal, but unable to endure the dishonor, he ended his life prior to sentencing by hanging himself in his cell. Colin Dovekey had been sent to Breaker Island, home of the Black Shields and the academy, and was summarily executed for treason.

Three men who had simply wanted what was best for their country, a continuity of leadership, gone because they had not trusted that he would provide for succession in the event of his own premature death.

He raised his hand, trembling with suppressed fury, to slam the game pieces off the board, but he drew back, reined in his anger, reined it in as he always must. The fire sizzled and flared as though a manifestation of how he felt inside. As king, he could not afford the luxury of venting his fury. He must always show himself to be in control. It was almost laughable for his outward calm was a sham. Inside, he burned as hot as the fire, and there was little release.

Thank the gods, he thought, that he still had Laren, the one person who had stood by him and opposed the schemers. If she had been complicit in the conspiracy, he didn't know what he would have done. If only he could tell her all that raged in him, but admitting such vulnerability, he feared, would lessen his standing in even her estimation.

As for his wife, she was the last one he would tell, for she'd been a player in the entire debacle. There was only one person who he thought would hear him out without judgment, but she was beyond his reach. She was not his that he could tell her his innermost thoughts and feelings.

He closed his eyes, willing himself to calm the anger, and soon relaxed, breathing deeply.

The pop of the fire startled him, and he realized he'd drifted off. He'd been dreaming, something about rushing through the woods and pursuing someone or . . . something. A deer, he thought. An image came back to him of a doe bounding through the woods, her tail flagged in alert. Graceful, wild and free, she was, and he could not catch up. He—

"Zachary?" asked a quiet voice.

He started again, silently cursing himself for failing so spectacularly at guard duty.

Estora came round the sofa and looked down at him. She was dressed in only her sleeping gown, its drape accenting the roundness of her belly.

"What are you doing here?" she asked.

"Enjoying the fire," he said.

"Is that all?" She gazed at his sword. "No, I see that it is not. You are keeping watch. Have you been doing this since . . . ?"

"Yes." He glanced at the terriers who snoozed soundly by the fire. They hadn't alerted him to Estora's presence, but by now they knew she was not a threat, but one of their own. "You should be in bed resting."

"If you must know, I am weary of rest."

"Vanlynn says— "

"I am most tired of hearing what Vanlynn says."

She was so emphatic he almost smiled, but he knew better than to do so.

"Perhaps," she said more evenly, "you should come to my bed and keep me company."

"It would be difficult to keep watch if I am . . . keeping you company."

"That is actually what I am counting on. Oh, Zachary, I am pregnant, not sick or dying. I simply wish . . . I wish to be with my husband." Then she gazed thoughtfully into the fire. "And

I have been having the strangest craving for fermented cabbage and maple cream. Together."

He cocked an eyebrow. "Shall I send for some?"

She shook her head, her long, loosely braided gold hair shimmering. "No, my love. I would prefer you, with me." She extended her hand to him.

He hesitated.

Through no fault of her own, Estora was a constant reminder to him of the betrayal he'd suffered, of how he'd been used. Of how they'd *both* been used, by those who should have known better. The conspirators had led her to believe that a deathbed wedding was the only way to preserve the realm, should he die from his wound.

As if the wedding had not been enough, one of the conspirators, Estora's cousin, had insisted the rite of consummation, an ancient tradition that sealed the contract of marriage, be performed and witnessed. It usually took place on the wedding night, but Zachary had been near death and unable to take part, so the push for it to happen came later.

Estora had protested he was still in no condition to participate, but her cousin overruled her with threats to ruin her and her family. She could not refuse. Zachary, fevered and bereft of his senses, and unaware of the machinations going on around him, was dosed with an aphrodisiac to enhance his responsiveness. Apparently he'd been strong enough to successfully complete the rite, but he remembered little of it, just the shadow of a dream.

With another surge of anger, he thought of how they'd both been violated that night.

"Zachary?" Estora said. "Is something wrong?"

She was blameless, and she was his wife, no matter how it had all come to pass.

"No," he said, "nothing is wrong." He took her hand and kissed it. He could not let her see his anger. He would save it for the battlefield. He would show her only the kindness, the tenderness, she deserved.

He stood, pushing the blanket aside, and collected his sword to take with him.

"I hope that is not the only sword you are bringing with you," she said, and she squeezed his hand.

"I would not be concerned on that account." When Finder and Jasper stood to follow, he ordered them to stay.

Estora led him steadily through the dark and into her bed chamber.

GHOSTS

The spirits came as they always did, even when she was too sound asleep to sense them. They crowded around her bed, their whispery babble like the rustling of curtains in air currents. The tomb cat glared at them from the foot of the bed, his ears flat and whiskers erect.

Their stories made her restless this night, and she rolled over many times, burying her head in her pillow. The spirits became agitated when she would not listen, became more aggressive, prodding her through her blankets, and moaning. One used all its energy to move a book one inch on her desk before dissipating in a twist of smoke. The tomb cat growled.

Suddenly she sat up. *"Leave me,"* she commanded in a voice that was perhaps not entirely her own. The spirits obeyed and vanished, and the cat leaped away in fright. She sat dazed and puzzled for a moment before flopping back into her pillow with a sigh, and quickly fell into undisturbed sleep.

Though all the others fled, one ghost remained behind, but he did not tell Karigan G'ladheon stories. He did not prod her. They had met before, she and he, though the death god would have obscured her memory of it. He'd been her counterpart in a long ago time, a Green Rider. He had worn the brooch she now wore. As he had once been, she was an avatar of Westrion.

She had commanded the ghosts, and they obeyed.

The tomb cat came out of hiding from beneath the bed and sat on his haunches, watching the spirit with the particular disdain only cats could muster. The ghost of Siris Kiltyre laughed before he turned and vanished.

A SWORDMASTER TRAINS

The next morning, Karigan woke up stiff and sore from her exertions during the "test" the previous night, and strangely satisfied. Yes, she'd made it to swordmaster at last, but her sense of satisfaction was something more. Perhaps it was just that she had slept so well.

Before she attended to anything else, she swung her legs off the bed and reached for her new sword where it leaned against the wall next to her bonewood staff. She drew it out of its scabbard, and it gleamed coldly in the dull morning light that filtered in through her arrow slit windows. The silk band knotted beneath the guard seemed to bisect the blade from the wire-wrapped hilt. Fastion had explained that the silk absorbed the blood of enemies, that to have it stain the silk was an honor and imbued the blade with the enemy's strength. It enlivened the blade's thirst for blood.

While she was not particularly stirred by Fastion's words, she was by the quality of the sword. She admired its precise, deadly form, the sharp double edges. It was unadorned but for a plain wheel pommel that balanced it so well, and the etching of the black shield on the blade. She swallowed hard and glanced at her bandaged wrist. They had fought with true edged blades last night, not just wooden practice swords. It was a tribute to a swordmaster's skill and control that it was so.

On the side opposite the black shield etching was the maker's mark, and she recognized it as that of one of the royal smiths, one of the finest. The kingdom, she thought, did well by its swordmasters. Or, at least, those affiliated with the Weapons, even if only honorarily.

It was not the bejeweled, ornamented sword some would want, and she preferred it that way. She admired its austerity. There was beauty in its bare form, and no mistaking the purpose for which it had been forged.

She swept it through the air until Ghost Kitty batted her elbow. She smiled and petted the cat, then sheathed the sword, pleased the scabbard was just as plain. Then her smile faltered. She wished she could tell Cade. She thought he'd be proud of her. He'd wanted to be a Weapon. Ghost Kitty rubbed against her arm, and for a time she simply stroked him and hugged him. Then, with a rattling breath, she began preparing for the day.

At breakfast, she joined Mara in the dining hall, choosing tea this time instead of kauv, and ham and eggs. She was starving.

"Oh, good," Mara said when Karigan sat down. "You can tell me all about making swordmaster last night."

"You know?"

"Oh, yes. The captain is fuming that no one warned her it was going to happen, and I think Drent is in for it. Congratulations, by the way."

"Thank you." Karigan sawed into her ham steak.

"Now tell me everything."

"Sorry, but I'm not allowed to say anything specific about the, er, test."

"Typical," Mara muttered.

"Typical?"

"Typical you, typical Weapon secrecy."

"If I could, I'd tell you the whole thing." In fact, Karigan was dying to do just that, but she'd been strongly admonished, on her honor, not to speak of the test, or even of where it took place, to avoid ruining the element of surprise for future swordmasters. She had been assured that if she continued to climb the levels, however, that those tests would not be surprises, but "interesting" in their own way.

"Word has gotten around about you making swordmaster in any case," Mara said, stirring her porridge. "Arms Master Gresia has asked if the captain could spare you to help with the training of our green Greenies, and maybe others if you are available and willing."

That was quite gratifying, Karigan thought.

"The captain thinks it would be all right as your other duties allow." Mara stared keenly at her. "The captain also mentioned your new official honorary Weapon status."

Karigan recalled, before she left for Blackveil, how concerned Mara had been that she was being taken away from the Green Riders and turned into a Weapon.

"I am not a Weapon."

"You are evidently enough of a Weapon to be summoned to the tombs this afternoon."

Karigan dropped her knife and it clattered loudly on the table. "What?"

Mara nodded. "Apparently the chief caretaker wants a word with you."

Agemon. Well, that certainly put a different slant on her day.

"I am a Green Rider," Karigan repeated, but she wondered what Mara would think when the black shield insignia got sewn onto her uniforms. What would Mara think of her new sword?

"Next bell we are expecting those seamstresses and tailors your father promised us, to arrive and do the fittings and alterations."

"Good timing," Karigan murmured, still thinking of the insignia. She was terrible with thread and needle.

"What's that?" Mara asked.

"Huh? Oh, nothing." Karigan busied herself with her food, but Mara was not finished.

"At one hour, you are to report to Drent for training."

Karigan groaned. "So soon?"

"Yes, Rider Swordmaster Sir Karigan Helgadorf G'ladheon."

"At least I'm not Rider Crotchety today, and I guess that makes you Chief Rider Bossy Mara Brennyn."

"Not by far, my dear. Not by far . . ."

"The way things are going already this morning, I shouldn't be surprised to see an Eletian walk through the door." Karigan glanced over her shoulder toward the entrance and hoped that just mentioning it would not make it so. She was relieved there were no Eletians in sight.

But then Mara said, "As for that, you are to report directly to the captain after training with Drent."

"What do you mean, 'as for that'?"

"Best that the captain tell you what's on her mind."

"I'm apparently not the only one who keeps secrets."

Mara gave her a catlike smile. Karigan turned her attention back to breakfast. Sounded like she was going to be busy, so she'd better fill up while she could.

Karigan, along with her fellow Riders, spent much of her morning getting her uniforms fitted for the modified design. She also managed to wheedle a seamstress into sewing the pile of new patches onto the sleeves of her coats and shirts.

At one hour, she reported to the field house, which served as the winter weapons training area. It was a high-ceilinged building, with tall windows, and sawdust upon the floor. There were six rings in which bouts took place.

Three other trainees were present, one of whom was Flogger. She knew, with a sense of dread, that he would make her pay for having bested him last night. Arms Master Drent lumbered up to them, his expression its usual mask of disapproval as he looked them over. Most of it was reserved for Karigan.

"Where is your sword?" he demanded.

Karigan saw that the others wore theirs. "In my chamber."

"What good is it going to do you there?"

"I didn't realize—"

"You are a swordmaster now. You practice with steel, not wood."

"Yes, sir." She had known this, but for some reason she had it in her mind that like her initiate training, there would be practice swords for her to use.

When normally Drent would bellow at her, he simply said, "Next time, bring your sword. How else will you become accustomed to it? I'll see what I can dig up while you lot warm up."

While Karigan stretched and sprinted up and down the

length of the field house, she wondered if Drent behaving as a reasonable human being was the difference between a student who was a swordmaster and a student who was not. His usual haranguing of his trainees was intimidating, and there were those who could not endure it, much less the physical rigors of the actual training. He must, she reflected, figure that if students could not handle *him*, then they were not suited to the demands of being a swordmaster. A sort of test of its own, she decided.

She learned, after Drent returned with a battered longsword for her to use, that he was just as merciless as ever in his training, and could still bark if students made mistakes. And there were other ways he punished them in the name of learning: He set the other three trainees against just her. She flailed at the very real, edged swords they wielded and was "killed" numerous times over by the painful blows of the flats of their blades.

At one point, she lay facedown in the sawdust with the tips of three swords digging into her back. One particularly. She had no doubt it belonged to Flogger. The toes of Drent's boots stood just inches from her nose.

"You need to learn to fight multiple opponents," he told her. "Instead of panicking, use what you've already learned, and you might have a chance."

She had fought multiple opponents before, but they hadn't been swordmasters.

He then put her through exercises to show her how to approach combat when outnumbered. There were new forms to learn, and adaptations of the ones she already knew.

"Real battle is messy," he continued, "and the enemy will not be nice enough to supply you with only one opponent at a time."

After Drent deemed she had gotten the new forms to some acceptable level, he set the other three on her again. She lasted a little longer this time, but the bout ended much the same with her facedown on the floor. She spat sawdust as Drent stood over her, shaking his head with a look of hopelessness on his face.

"Get up," he ordered.

He set the three on her again, and again, and again. They thrashed her each time, and it got harder and harder to clamber back to her feet. So far no one had accidentally killed her with their sword. She still had her head and all her limbs. She looked for the positives where she could find them. The other three students knew what they were about, and she learned they'd been swordmasters for a few months now, which meant they had a decided advantage over her. Two of them aimed to become Weapons, but Molly, who served in the light cavalry, was undecided about whether or not she wanted to become a Weapon. In the meantime, she claimed she just enjoyed the challenge of the training.

When the session finally ended, Karigan remained spread-eagle on the floor gazing up at the ceiling. She breathed hard, feeling bruised and battered. She was not so keen on the whole swordmaster thing at the moment, and all she could think of was soaking in a tub of very hot water. However, that would require standing, and she was not sure that she could.

Molly offered her a hand up, but Karigan said, "Thank you, but I think I'll examine the ceiling for a few more minutes."

Molly smiled. "Don't worry. It'll get better. I thought I'd die in the first month."

Month? A whole month? Karigan's face must have betrayed her dismay, for Molly chuckled.

"It *will* get better," she said as she walked away. "You'll see."

"Right." Karigan stayed where she was, thinking that Cade would find this all very amusing.

THE SECOND SWORD

When Karigan finally gathered the courage to rise from the floor, she brushed sawdust off her uniform and headed to the weapons room to return the sword to Drent. The room, with its racks of swords, pikes, knives, daggers, and staves, smelled of leather, oil, and sweat.

"Bring your own sword next time," Drent said.

"I will."

"And I am to remind you to see your captain now." A haunted look crept into his features. "Then it is my turn."

"Your turn?"

He nodded. "The heavens save me, yes." He bent to work, honing a blade, and muttered to himself.

Thus dismissed, Karigan grabbed her greatcoat from a hook. It hurt her abused muscles just to pull it on. She trudged out into the cold, wishing she could clean up before reporting to the captain, but she was to go directly, sweat, sawdust, bruises, and all.

When she reached officers quarters and the captain called, "Come!" at her knock, she straightened her uniform best as she could and entered. The captain glanced up from the other side of her work table.

"Well," the captain said, giving her a long, hard look. "It appears you've been at sword training. Did they use you as a quintain?"

Karigan grimaced. "Actually, sort of."

The captain smiled. "Have a seat and rest while we talk."

Karigan pulled a stool up to the table and sat, trying not to cry out as her sore body protested every movement.

"I suppose congratulations are in order," the captain said, "or perhaps sympathy?"

"I am leaning toward sympathy at the moment."

"You know, if you prefer not to continue at that level of training, I can terminate your sessions when I speak to Drent later."

Oh, gods, yes, Karigan thought, but what came out of her mouth was, "Thank you, Captain, but I've come this far, so I'd like to continue."

The captain looked amused. "Very well. Let me know if you change your mind. Swordmaster training, after all, is not regular Rider duty."

Karigan nodded.

"I have also been informed—" and here a slight frown tugged at the corners of the captain's mouth, "—that the Weapons have formalized your honorary status with them. I suppose it could be useful, as you can now venture into the tombs when we might have business there, as you will later this afternoon. What the Weapons may have in mind for you is harder to ascertain, if even *they* know." She shrugged. "Your first duty, of course, is to serve the king as a Green Rider while you still hear the call."

"I understand."

"I know you do, but I felt it needed to be aired. No doubt about it, but your swordmaster status brings honor to the Green Riders." She leaned back into her chair, legs crossed at the ankles, and she gazed levelly at Karigan. "I did not ask you to see me, however, just to discuss swordmaster training."

Karigan straightened. Might her captain need a message to go out? It would do her good to get off castle grounds, out of the city.

"It seems," the captain continued, "the Eletians are interested in searching for the p'ehdrosians."

"What? Really?"

The captain nodded. "According to the king, they became very interested after we found the four-fold leaf in the stained glass and spotted the p'ehdrosians in the backdrop of one of the panels. They became even more interested—and I'll admit I did, too—after you and Lhean returned from the future time."

The stuffed specimens of p'ehdrose Karigan and Lhean had seen in the future were proof that they still existed, but where in the world did one begin looking for a people who had hidden themselves so well for a thousand years?

"Interestingly," the captain continued, "they are willing to provide a guide to go in search of the p'ehdrose if we send one of our own along, specifically you."

"What? Why me?"

The captain crooked an eyebrow.

Once Karigan got over her initial surprise, she said, "All right, I guess I know why. They've gotten used to me." It was, she thought, a dubious distinction.

"The king and I guess as much," the captain said. "But you know how they are; they never come out and directly state their intentions."

"No, they don't," Karigan murmured. "When do they plan to start the search?"

"You should know the king has not decided absolutely to go along with this, though he is leaning toward approving it. He is curious about the p'ehdrosians and wonders if they might be allies in the fight against Second Empire. So, if it does happen, you will be in a diplomatic role. Providing you actually find the p'ehdrosians, of course."

Karigan's eyes widened. "But I'm not . . ."

"Diplomatic?"

Karigan nodded.

The captain smiled again. "You've come a long way, and you have proven it by being the object of the Eletians' favor."

Karigan wondered how much favor remained after her confrontation with Lhean. Still, she was to them a known entity.

"Shouldn't someone like a lord-governor do the diplomatic part?"

"You mean, like Lady Penburn's delegation seeking Eletia a few years ago?"

"Yes."

"Under the best of circumstances that might be the way it would go, but that sort of delegation requires, as you know, a great many people, horses, and supplies. The lord-governors are busy gathering their vassals and preparing for war. Plus, the Eletians believe the p'ehdrose lie north, and right now the north is perilous. By sending just two of you, it reduces the chance of Second Empire noticing. Also," and now the captain folded her hands on her lap, "while you may not be the lady-governor of a province, you are a knight of the realm, which gives you weight in representing Sacoridia's interests.

"As for when, the Eletians were vague. They did not give us anything more specific like 'on the equinox' as they did for the Blackveil expedition. They told us 'when winter breaks.' In the meantime, while the king makes his decision, and while we await something more definitive from the Eletians, you should continue your regular duties."

Karigan frowned.

"Something wrong, Rider?"

"It's just . . . What about Second Empire? I mean the fighting. I thought I'd be here to help."

"Let us not buy trouble. Remember, if you are able to sway the p'ehdrose to our cause, and I do expect you to use your merchant's power of persuasion, you will be doing a great service for the realm, and I suspect that even if you are not successful, there will be more than enough opportunity for you to draw a sword against our adversaries. Speaking of which . . ."

The captain stood and went back to her shelves and picked up an oblong item wrapped in cloth. "The quartermaster delivered this to me today." She removed the cloth revealing a saber in a black scabbard. "It is, perhaps, not as fine as the sword you received last night, but it is as well made as any Rider blade. It weighs the same as the one you lost and, I am told, balances the same."

Karigan rose and took the sword. The scabbard was unblemished, as was the blade when she drew it, which was very unlike the saber she had inherited from F'ryan Coblebay. Wrapped just below the guard was the black silk of the swordmaster.

"Fastion knotted that for me," the captain said. "May the sword serve you well, though I also would wish you never have need of it."

"Thank you," Karigan said. She wondered what Daro would say now that she had *two* swords. "Er, you know that I broke Daro's, don't you?"

"Never fear, I know all about it, and rather think that it was the nature of the elemental that caused her blade to break. Daro will receive a new sword in time, as well." The captain clasped her hands behind her back. "That is all I have for you today, but if you learn anything of interest in the tombs, please let me know. And, if your meeting with Agemon doesn't take long, you can help Elgin in the records room after. He is most pleased with your work."

Karigan waited to be dismissed, but the captain grew thoughtful and seemed to have something else on her mind. "Do you happen to know," she asked, "which Rider Loon belongs to?"

"Who?"

"Tall gelding, white with black spots."

"I know that horse," Karigan replied, "but I didn't know he'd been named."

"So you don't know which Rider he's chosen?"

"No, Captain. As far as I know he hasn't chosen . . ." She stared at the captain. "Did he choose you?"

The captain dropped back into her chair and looked unsettled. "Elgin thought the same thing. He didn't think Loon had chosen any of our new Riders. Mara hadn't heard either, and she believes all Rider and horse pairings are otherwise accounted for. I am the only one who seems to know his name and . . ."

What the captain didn't finish saying, Karigan thought she could guess. There was a sense of bonding between the two of them.

"It appears," the captain said, "that whatever fate governs such things, it was determined I require a younger horse for whatever trials lie ahead." She did not look particularly happy. She was already the longest-serving Rider anyone had heard of, though considering the loss of recorded Rider history, there could have been others. As for the trials that lay ahead? One only had to consider Second Empire and Mornhavon the Black. In the same way new Riders seemed to hear the Rider call in response to impending conflict, it made sense the captain would attract a younger horse that could stand up to the demands of—of whatever was required.

"If you ask me," Karigan said, "I think Bluebird would be just as happy to retire, at least from anything challenging. He is the lord of the pasture, you know." And he was. Just as the captain oversaw her Riders, Bluebird took charge of all the Rider horses.

The captain smiled weakly. "I never expected to be doing this for so long that I required a new horse. I should be retiring like Bluebird, but the call won't release me."

"I, for one, am glad," Karigan said, though she thought her father wouldn't be. "We need you."

"Thank you for that. Sometimes I am so buried in paperwork and meetings I wonder if my Riders even know who I am."

"Of course we do," Karigan replied.

The captain nodded and said, "You had better get going so you are not late for your meeting with Agemon. You may be dismissed."

New sword in hand, Karigan left her bemused captain behind and hurried out into the cold, trying not to slip on the slick path. With any luck, she could fit in a hot bath, or at least change, before having to meet Agemon in the tombs at the appointed hour.

CAPTAIN AND ARMS MASTER

Laren had her own appointment to attend, and after Karigan left, she drew on her greatcoat, and the hat and mittens knitted by Stevic's sisters. Her shock over Loon diminished as she stepped out into the bright winter air. She stood blinking on her step for a moment before setting off in a purposeful stride down the path that led to the field house. She would visit her horses—the plural felt odd—later. First she needed to have a word with Drent.

She found him in the weapons room tidying up racks of practice swords. He turned when she entered, and when he saw who it was, a muscle spasmed in his cheek.

"Ah, Captain."

"Arms Master."

"What can I do for you?"

Now that she was here, she found her fire from the previous night had subsided. "Next time you decide to make one of my Riders a swordmaster, I'd very much appreciate the courtesy of a forewarning."

He weighed a couple of wooden practice swords in his hands. "I wouldn't worry."

"Why is that?"

"The only other Rider who has a chance of it is never around."

"Beryl Spencer."

"That's right. The king has her away all the time. She can't keep up on her skills, and at this rate she will never make swordmaster."

Beryl was often off on secret missions to which even Laren

was not privy. Her special ability was to assume a role, and Zachary and his spymasters had made good use of it. Even now Laren could not say where her Rider was.

"As for your other Riders," Drent continued, "even if they come along with their skills, their training isn't consistent enough. Always gone on errands. Here, hold these." He handed her the practice swords, then lumbered away toward the big room with its tall windows, where bouts and training took place. She strode after him.

"Your Rider G'ladheon," he continued, stepping into one of the bout rings, "was well trained during her school years in Selium by Rendle, as much as it pains me to admit it, so she had a good foundation. Has a knack for the sword. Plus, she has proven herself in other ways, so she is a swordmaster."

"That is fine and good," Laren said, "but I should have been informed she was receiving a status that may affect her duties."

Drent shrugged. "Should enhance her ability to perform her duties."

Laren's ire began to reignite. Talking to Drent was like talking to a stone wall. He was as big as a wall, actually. "She is *my* Rider."

"Possessive, are we? Hand me a sword. No, the other."

She passed him the heavier of the two, and he swept it through the air.

"Of course I'm possessive! I am responsible for the Riders and how they serve the king. I am responsible for their lives."

"The king told you what was going on, didn't he?"

"Only after the fact and her so-called honorary Weapon status was formalized."

He took her by the elbow and guided her into the ring, she stepping over one of the low planks that delineated it. "Stand here, please. I do think you are overreacting, Captain."

Laren wanted to tear out her hair. "If it was one of yours being given honorary Rider status— "

"Wouldn't happen," he replied implacably.

"What do you mean it wouldn't happen?"

Drent shrugged. "I just don't think any of my swordmasters or Weapons would be of a messenger bent."

"I am being theoretical," she almost shouted, her voice echoing in the expanse of the building, "about me stealing one of your swordmasters."

"Wouldn't happen. Now, instead of waving that sword around every time you have something to say, hold it like so." He moved her arms and wrist into a guard position.

"Drent?"

"Captain?"

"What are you doing?"

In response, he attacked. She jumped backward, scrambling to block an onslaught of blows, the sound of clacking wooden blades thundering in the high-ceilinged space. She was too shocked by the suddenness of his attack, his jabs and thrusts and cuts, to even protest.

Just as suddenly as it began, it stopped. Laren stood at the edge of the ring trying to catch her breath. "What in the hells was that for?" she demanded.

Drent gazed critically at her. "How often have you been training with Gresia?"

"What? Oh, I don't know." She shrugged. It had probably been years since she did any regular training.

"I heard you were quite good in your day."

"*In my day?* Now wait a—"

He raised his sword as if to strike once more. "Yes. In your day. But clearly you've not kept up your skills. You are rusty, Captain. How are you to lead your Riders in the field when your skills are not up to par, eh? What sort of example are you setting for them? Too much sitting around in your quarters, I'll warrant."

"How dare—"

He lunged and she tripped backward over the ring's border and fell. He stood over her with the tip of his sword to her neck.

"You're an easy kill, Captain." He leered down at her. "You are to report to Gresia three times a week with your lieutenant and Chief Rider. We can't have any of you growing lax and comfortable."

"Lax?" she sputtered. "Comfortable? I can't—"

"The king agrees."

"Zachary—?"

"Yes, Captain. You can ask him yourself." He reached out to help her to her feet.

"I don't have the time!"

"No excuses, Captain."

"It's not an excuse!"

"Make the time. Remember, it's the example you set. Plus, the king has ordered your schedule cleared for training at ten hour."

Laren was so flummoxed she didn't know what to do or say. She'd come to give Drent an upbraiding he wouldn't forget, and the next thing she knew he'd "killed" her in a bout of swordplay. How did they even get there? He was truly in trouble now, she thought, but he was walking away, back into the weapons room.

"Of all the . . ." She trotted after him. When she caught up, he took the practice sword from her.

"Remember, ten hour, Gresia, tomorrow."

"You are impossible."

"It is something oft said about you."

"Why you—you—" She was so outraged she could only sputter.

He turned his back to her to replace the practice swords on their rack, but not so fast that she didn't see his gruesome grin. Then he turned on her. "Face it, Captain, I won this round."

"I would not be so smug if I were you."

"No?" He crossed his arms over his barrel chest. More seriously, he said, "The king wants you ready for whatever may come, not just because he wants the Riders fit for battle, but because he cares about what happens to *you*. Furthermore, the workout might help you with your rheumatism."

"My . . . ?" How did he know?

"My job is to observe the bodies of my trainees day in and day out, as they hone their skills. I know when they are hurting, I know when they are injured. I can see it when you walk and how you hold yourself. Gresia is aware, too, so she will work with you appropriately. Vanlynn has also been notified."

Laren was so aghast that something she had kept to herself for so long was apparently common knowledge that she didn't know what to say, except, "Bloody hells."

"You," Drent said, "are dismissed, Captain."

"This isn't over, Drent," she replied, and she turned on her heel and headed for the door, reddening when his low, throaty chuckle followed her outside. She slammed the door shut behind her. How had he turned it all around on her? How had he gotten the upper hand?

It would not, she thought, happen again.

AN APPOINTMENT WITH AGEMON

As it turned out, Karigan did not have enough time to take a bath, but settled for splashing freezing water from her basin onto her face and changing into a dry, clean uniform. She considered taking one of her swords along to prove to Agemon she really was a swordmaster and approved by the Weapons, but she remembered how, when last he had seen her, she and the Weapons had deceived him into believing she was a Weapon by doing nearly the same thing. Brienne had garbed her in black and lent her a sword with its swordmaster's silk so she could enter the tombs without any complaint from Agemon. Having a sword along with her, with its black silk band, would not impress him this time around.

She started when a knock came upon the door. She was relieved to find Brienne without, as she had been wondering how she was supposed to find her way to Agemon.

"Ready for your appointment?" Brienne asked.

Karigan grabbed her longcoat and nodded.

"What? No sword?"

"We're just going into the tombs, aren't we?"

"Yes," Brienne said, "but you are a swordmaster and honorary Weapon now."

"Does that mean I have to carry my sword *all* the time?"

"Not all the time, but certainly when you are on duty."

That, Karigan thought, was going to get tedious. She glanced at both swords, wondering which to wear.

"You could carry both," Brienne said, following her gaze, "as the First Rider once did."

"I don't think so." People would assume she was overcompensating or something. She decided on her new saber. She'd had time with the longsword last night, and it would be good to get acquainted with the saber.

"How many swords do *you* have?" Karigan asked Brienne.

The Weapon started counting on her fingers and gave up. "Several. Some for practice only, or ceremonies. I have also collected a few antiques that are for display. There are several others that I actively use."

"I see."

With that, they were off. The weight of the new saber actually felt good and proper against her hip, much the same as her old one, but it hadn't the history, the heritage, nor had it been proven in battle. The new one had not belonged to someone else before, and she guessed she'd have to give it a history of its own.

Brienne led her to the royal wing.

"I thought we were going to the tombs."

"We are."

Damnation. When they'd entered the royal wing, Karigan had felt the slightest kernel of hope they would not be entering the tombs, after all. They made her skin crawl, all those halls of the dead. Alas, it seemed the more she wished to avoid the tombs, the more she was drawn into them. She could not escape them. And what in five hells did Agemon want with her, anyway?

Brienne led her down stairs, where they came to a wide arched door with bas relief carvings of the gods above it, most prominently Westrion riding his steed, Salvistar. Another Weapon stood on guard at the door.

"This is Scotty," Brienne said, "newly come to us from the Forge. Scotty, this is Sir Karigan."

The fresh-faced young man gave her a half-bow. "It is an honor," he said. "I have heard about your feats, Sir Karigan, and congratulate you on your swordmastery."

"Thank you."

"You are most welcome."

He was very formal, but Weapons tended to be, and perhaps because he was fresh from the Forge, he was even more so.

"Sir Karigan has an appointment with Agemon," Brienne said. "She has not entered the tombs through the royal chapel before."

So, Brienne had brought her to the royal chapel of the moon . . . She'd entered the tombs through other entrances, but not this one, though her first time in the tombs, she had *exited* from a commoner chapel within the castle.

"How many entrances are there?" Karigan asked.

"This has the same entrance as the commoner chapel," Brienne replied. She patted the wall behind her where the corridor ended. "It's just on the other side of this wall."

Karigan noticed the Weapon had evaded the question about the number of entrances. Her honorary status as a Weapon only went so far, apparently.

Scotty opened the door for them, and, inside, the chapel was quietly lit with candles. Like the commoner chapel, there was a coffin rest that also served as an altar, but that was where the similarity ended. Where the commoner chapel had been plain and furnished with only wooden benches, this one was carpeted with rich red pile. There were rows of plush chairs. The candlelight glinted on silver and gold vessels and metalwork. The walls were covered with tapestries, and the ceiling paintings depicted the gods in the heavens among the constellations.

"We rarely enter through the chapels if we can help it," Brienne said, "in case there are parishioners within. We do not wish to disturb them. However, I thought you might like to see this one."

On the opposite wall, there was a set of double doors. Brienne strode to them, knocked, and they opened into another chamber. When Karigan followed Brienne through the doorway, she remembered it with its big fireplace and the coffin rest. It was a sort of antechamber to the tombs.

"Ah, Sir Karigan," said the Weapon, Lennir, who had let them in. "Good to see you again."

"You, too." She did tend to see rather less of the tomb

guards than the Weapons who attended the king and queen. She turned around to face the way they had come in. Next to the doors of the royal chapel stood another set of doors. Those must lead into the commoner chapel.

"Do you remember this place?" Brienne asked.

"I do." It had been the night of Prince Amilton's coup attempt, and she, along with the king, Brienne, and others, had infiltrated the tombs via the Heroes Portal, passed through the avenues of the dead, to this chamber, and then exited through the chapel for commoners. The king had then led them through other secret ways to reach the throne room.

"It is a receiving room for the royal dead, a place where the family can mourn without their retinue watching on. Of course, most of the time it is a post for our Weapons. We take tea here, warm up by the fire. But come, Agemon will become agitated if we do not reach his office at the appointed time."

They bade Lennir farewell and passed from the receiving room into a rotunda from which three corridors spoked. The way was brightly lit in all directions, the air cool and dry, with no scent of decay or must. Fresh air currents circulated throughout the tombs. They had been well built to preserve those who slept within, and to make them habitable for the caretakers. Statues of stern kings and queens in white marble stared down at them. Along the corridors lay the sarcophagi of the royal dead.

Karigan pulled her longcoat tighter about her, chilled as much by the atmosphere as by the natural coolness of the tombs.

Brienne struck off across the rotunda and into the corridor that lay straight ahead. Karigan was hard on her heels, not wishing to be left behind and alone. The corridor was wide with lamps aglow on the walls. The sarcophagi were precisely spaced, but not all were alike. Lifelike effigies reclined on some of the lids, while others held no figures at all. The iconography was either of the gods, or showed scenes from that monarch's life. The small sarcophagi saddened Karigan, for they contained children. A wooden toy horse was placed atop the tomb of one small prince.

In other parts of the tombs there were burial chambers

that were much more extravagant. One queen lay in a reproduction of the bed chamber she'd slept in during her life, and was read to each night by a caretaker. There were chapels and libraries and sitting areas throughout that were rarely used, but nevertheless were well maintained for royals who had not wished to slumber through eternity without the comforts they had known in life, as well as for those who mourned them.

Brienne halted at one such sitting area, the stone walls covered by wood paneling and paintings of pleasant landscapes. A decanter of wine and goblets sat waiting on a table. Karigan supposed such spaces could be used by visiting family, but there were only Zachary and Estora in residence, and would they really visit all the dead, or just those they had known in life? She shuddered remembering there were already empty sarcophagi awaiting the king and queen.

To her surprise, Brienne stepped between a pair of chairs to reach the wood-paneled wall. She pressed something recessed into the ornate molding, and the wall opened inward into a narrower passage.

"What's in there?" Karigan asked in surprise.

"The offices and workshops of the caretakers."

Karigan thought it clever that the entrance was concealed within the wall. This way, the presence of the caretakers remained unobtrusive and allowed the tombs to retain their overwhelmingly sepulchral impact.

The corridor they entered was more utilitarian and not at all sepulchral. The doorways they passed opened into offices where people worked at desks doing who-knew-what. It reminded her very much of the administrative wing in the castle above. What in the tombs could require so much office work? She asked Brienne.

"The same as Green Riders, I would guess," the Weapon replied. "The ordering of supplies, the keeping of accounts, the scheduling and oversight of all aspects of caretaker life. The tombs are almost a city unto themselves."

It was so strangely ordinary, Karigan thought.

"Beyond the administrative area," Brienne continued, "are the workshops of artisans who create and repair many objects in the tombs, including sarcophagi and statues. Many of the burial goods are very old and require special care, particularly textiles."

The caretakers they encountered in the corridor gazed curiously at Karigan. "Have you brought us a new caretaker, Brienne?" a man asked.

Like all the caretakers Karigan had ever seen, his skin was smooth and pale from never having seen the sun, and he wore robes of muted gray.

"This is Sir Karigan," Brienne replied, "a Green Rider and honorary Weapon. She has freedom of passage."

The man bowed. "Welcome, Sir Karigan."

"Thank you."

As they continued on, Brienne said in a hushed voice, "A green uniform is a novelty down here, but most will know who you are and that you are not trespassing, and that this isn't your first time here. Ah, here we are."

They halted at a door, and Brienne knocked and entered. Agemon's office was not large for all that he was the chief caretaker, but it was crammed with books and scrolls of all sizes, and broken bits of sculpture. Paintings on the walls depicted ocean and forest scenes, almost as if they were windows into the outer world, one he had never seen.

Across his desk lay what appeared to be a schematic of the tombs. Karigan gazed curiously at it, but it looked very complex. He rolled it up before she could make sense of it.

"Greetings, Agemon," Brienne said. "I have brought Sir Karigan as you requested."

"You are late," he replied in the querulous voice Karigan remembered well. His specs slid down to the end of his nose. Though his long hair was gray, it was difficult to judge his age with his smooth skin. His manner, however, indicated someone in his elder years.

"Not by much," Brienne replied. "I'll wait outside."

"No, no you will not," Agemon said. "What I ask this—this *green* may be useful for your ears, as well. What is this world coming to that Black Shields are bringing *green* into the silent halls?"

"You know, Agemon, that Sir Karigan is our sister-at-arms."

"Yes, yes, but to me it has no meaning. You Black Shields are turning the world upside down. What is it coming to? 'Here, Agemon, translate this. Here, Agemon, translate that.' The Silverwood book, you remember? It left me in the ward of the death surgeons for an entire week. An entire week!"

"I remember," Brienne replied, "but it is the king who requested these things of you."

"Yes, yes, His Majesty. Then I am set to impossible tasks. Seek and find. Does he realize how great this domain of the sleeping is?"

"I think he has some idea." Brienne's tone was placating, and Karigan knew she had to deal frequently with him. "Can't you get anyone to help you?"

"I do have scholars assisting with the translations of the Green Rider material." He looked pointedly at Karigan. "But this . . . this cryptic thing, this dragonfly device I am to seek in the vastness of these halls . . . Do you know how many objects, how many artifacts lie hidden here?"

"Yes, Agemon," Brienne replied. "Why don't you tell us why you wished to see Sir Karigan."

He peered through his specs at Karigan. "You," he said. "You disrupt my tombs at every turn. You, you, *you*."

THE BIRDMAN'S VOICE

"Me?" Karigan said.

Agemon pointed a shaking finger at her. "Yes, yes. You take the great Ambrioth's sword; you turn my tombs into turmoil. You come as a false Black Shield. You take royal robes from the dead and stain priceless carpets with blood. *You.*"

"Agemon!" Brienne snapped. "You know it was the king who wanted Sir Karigan to have the use of the First Rider's sword back then, and you know it was returned unscathed. As for the other things, she saved your hide that night, and prevented the Silverwood book from falling into the hands of Second Empire."

Agemon glowered in response.

"May I remind you," Brienne said, "that you are the one who asked her to come here today?"

Karigan placed her hand on the Weapon's arm. "It's all right, Sergeant. It seems I am overdue to offer an apology." The tombs were Agemon's entire life, one of order and serenity, until she had come and disrupted it all. She imagined that before that first time she and the others had entered the tombs, there'd been almost no contact between the caretakers and the outside world and its problems, with the exception of the tomb Weapons doing their duty as they had for centuries. Now the outside world was interfering with Agemon's day-to-day routine by asking him to translate old documents and search for an artifact that may not even exist.

"Please accept my deepest apologies," she said, placing her hand over her heart, "for my transgressions." She bowed low.

"Well, now." Agemon pushed his specs onto the bridge of his nose. "That is tolerable. But I would like Sergeant Quinn's assurance that this highly suspect status of 'honorary Weapon' is not a sham."

"As a matter of fact," Brienne said, "I can give you that assurance." She pulled two letters from beneath her cloak. One held the king's seal, and the other a seal of black wax imprinted with a black shield.

Agemon took the letters.

"One," Brienne told him, "was personally written by the king ordering you to accept Sir Karigan's presence here, and to reassure you she is not breaking taboo. The other is from Counselor Tallman certifying Sir Karigan's status."

Karigan shifted her weight with a sense of unease. It seemed like people had gone to an awful lot of effort on behalf of her honorary Weaponhood. Now she couldn't back out of it even if she wanted to, and it felt like there were those who wanted to ensure she didn't.

When Agemon finished reading the letters, he said, "I suppose these are genuine."

"Oh, for the sake of the gods," Brienne said in exasperation. She was uncharacteristically expressive for a Weapon, but Agemon *was* enough to try the most patient of souls.

"It is quite unorthodox," he said. "There is no precedent."

At that moment, a light gray cat rubbed against the door frame, entered the office, and jumped onto his desk.

"What are you doing here, Lizzie?" Agemon demanded of the cat.

"Meow."

Stepping lightly over papers, books, and pens, the cat looked at Karigan and unceremoniously leaped into her arms and started to purr loudly. Karigan scratched her under her chin.

Agemon sat hard in his chair, looking confounded, or perhaps even betrayed. "Lizzie likes her."

"One of the others has claimed Sir Karigan," Brienne said with a smug expression. "She calls him Ghost Kitty."

Agemon shook his head mournfully. "I guess I must accept it, this green. Not because I want to, but because I cannot ignore the signs."

Karigan set Lizzie down on the floor. Letters from the king and the head of the Weapons had not convinced Agemon, but a cat did?

"There may be no precedent for this," Brienne said, "but Sir Karigan *is* the precedent. Shall we get on with business?"

"Yes, yes." He blinked at Karigan like a wizened owl. "The king tells me, 'Agemon, you must search for the dragonfly device.' And I say, 'Dragonfly device? I do not know what this is.' The king says, 'It may be in the tombs.' You—" and he pointed again at Karigan, "—you put this notion in his head."

Agemon's various accusations were wearying, but she took a deep breath. "Yes? What of it?"

"Do you realize the hundreds of thousands of artifacts down here? The time it would take? And what is this thing, this dragonfly device?"

"I don't . . ." She tried to remember. When she'd returned from the future, she'd attempted to tell the king and captain everything she could before her memory failed completely. Fortunately the captain had made a transcript. Karigan had written down her recollections, as well. It must have made sense at the time, but a certain amount was garbled nonsense, and trying to understand it was like trying to apply logic to a strange dream. Her memory of the dragonfly device was really what she recalled of what had been recorded in the transcript. "It's a . . . an object that is supposed to repel Mornhavon's great weapon. If found, we might be able to prevent the fall of Sacoridia."

"You were informed," Brienne told Agemon, "that Sir Karigan brought this information back from the future, that she knows what a defeated Sacoridia looks like."

"Yes, of course. There are many layers of the world." His dismissive tone was almost amusing. "But *what* kind of object is it? I do not know what we are looking for."

That was the question, wasn't it? Karigan had drawn a stick figure that appeared to be holding a shield and sword or spear. She could not remember the source. "Something about the Sealenders," she murmured. "Were you shown a drawing?"

Agemon sighed loudly. "Yes, yes. You know nothing more?"

"I'm sorry. Just that maybe the stick figure is holding something that is the dragonfly device."

"Waste of time."

Karigan clenched her hands at her sides. It was perhaps the single most important piece of information she'd brought back. She stepped up to his desk and looked down at him, no longer apologetic. A great cold fury overcame her and it was like frost drafted off her body. Darkness closed on the edge of her vision where stars shone searing and infinite. In a voice that wasn't quite her own and was layered over by the frozen depths of the heavens, she said, "So you prefer a world in which your country falls? In which Sacor City is destroyed and your countrymen oppressed and enslaved?"

Brienne gave her a sidelong glance, as if not sure what it was she was witnessing. "It is pointless, Sir Karigan. Agemon's world is here, and he has no connection to the outside except on the occasion of a royal death."

Karigan stared unwaveringly at Agemon. "If you believe you are safe here, you are mistaken. In the future I visited, the tombs remained and were attended by Weapons and caretakers, but they were soon to be breached and invaded by those who wanted the dragonfly device to eliminate its threat to the empire." She leaned over his desk in her intensity, and he quailed in his chair, his face paler than normal. Her voice took on added power and authority. She felt great wings beat the air about her. "Do you wish outsiders to invade your tombs? Godless invaders with no reverence for the dead? What do you think they would do to those you've cared for all these years, and all the artifacts? What would they do to the living? *Your* descendants?

"You have no idea," she continued in a harsh tone, "what was sacrificed so I could return to bring back this one hope that might save our people."

"Of—of course I do not wish this. Not upon my tombs or my people." Agemon fiddled with his specs. "Not upon my king or country."

"Good," Brienne said. "I, for one, am relieved to hear it. Frankly, I was beginning to wonder."

Karigan staggered back then, Brienne steadying her. She

felt drained, addled, unsure of what had come over her. Both Brienne and Agemon looked at her like they'd seen one of the tombs' corpses rise from the dead.

"Long day," she murmured.

"Hmm," Brienne said. "Well, I think this interview is over."

Agemon stood and rounded his desk. He looked up at Karigan with a contrite expression. "It is my turn to apologize, yes, yes. I did not mean to disregard your sacrifices, and I assure you, we will seek the dragonfly device until we find it, wherever, and whatever, it may be." Then he leaned toward her and whispered, "You speak with the voice of the Birdman, yes, yes. You are his, and you are welcome in the tombs."

Karigan stepped back, disturbed. The god of death? What was he talking about? The next thing she knew, he was ushering them out of his office, and he slammed the door behind them.

Brienne's expression was both inscrutable and annoyed as she stared back at the closed door, like she wanted to say something, but only training stayed her tongue. She turned and led Karigan back down the corridor with quick strides. When they emerged into the tombs, she carefully closed the secret door behind them.

Brienne gazed at her. "I do not know . . ."

"Know what?" Karigan asked.

"I do not know what happened back there." Brienne peered at her as if to divine something about her that lay beneath the surface. Apparently not seeing what she sought, she said, "Whatever it was, you got Agemon to come to his senses." She started walking again. Karigan hurried to catch up. "He is not a bad person, just very focused, short-sighted even, and often he forgets about the living. He takes a lot of patience to deal with."

"I noticed," Karigan said, keeping pace along the rows of sarcophagi.

"Yes, well, somehow I am the one who has been given the duty of liaising with him over the years. You did well, apologizing and bowing to him like you did. It disarmed him. And the rest?" Whatever else was on her mind, she did not speak it, but rapidly led Karigan out of the tombs and into the living world above.

By the time she reached the castle's main hall and heard the bell for five hour, all Karigan knew was that she was sore from her session with Drent, and maybe a hot bath would not only soothe her muscles, but tease out the chill that had overcome her in the tombs.

AUREAS SLEE

The aureas slee drifted as an ice vapor upon the arctic winds as it had since it lost the battle among the humans. Slee nursed its wound, where the female had hacked its limb off. The limb would re-form just as winter's snow replenished the great ice fields of the far north, but it was still grievous to be wounded, and even more so to suffer defeat.

Slee remembered, from long ago interactions with the humans, that they fought savagely to protect their own, especially in defense of their young. Slee should have been more subtle, but the compulsion, the calling for the attack, had been strong—a calling Slee resented, as it resented being ordered about by any mortal being.

Now that Slee had seen the irresistible prize that was the beautiful queen and her unborn children in the large dwelling of the humans, however, the desire to return was great. Yes, soon, soon, Slee would return to claim what was Slee's, and to seek vengeance. This time there would be no defeat.

TRAINEES

When Karigan arrived at the field house the next morning to assist Arms Master Gresia with sword training, she'd been expecting the trainees to be a group of the newer Riders, not her captain, lieutenant, and chief.

"Well," Captain Mapstone said, "isn't this interesting."

An understatement, Karigan thought.

"Are you here for remedial training, too?" Connly asked.

"She's a swordmaster," Mara said. "Drent beats up on her regularly."

"I know. I was trying to make a joke."

"Ah, very good," Arms Master Gresia said, emerging into the weapons room. "Everyone choose a practice sword and let's warm up. You, too, Sir Karigan."

Karigan picked out a wooden sword and followed the others out into the main training room and started stretching. One thing was certain, if she kept working with Gresia in addition to her own training with Drent, she was bound to be in better condition than ever. She was still stiff from her first training as a swordmaster, but already, with the stretching, she was loosening up.

When it came to running and other exercises, the captain lagged, which was not surprising since her work required that she spend so much time sitting. She also had a few years on the rest of them. Gresia ran with her, not pushing her, but encouraging her, and allowing her to stop before everyone else.

They did some basic exercises with the swords, Karigan demonstrating as necessary while Gresia explained the finer points of various defenses and offenses. She soon realized she had also been requested to assist so they could pair up for bouts; otherwise, one of the three would have to spend time just watching, which was not efficient.

She was relieved to be paired up with Mara. The idea of trying to fight her captain was rather intimidating—not because the captain would best her, but because the captain was the captain. Inevitably, they'd end up switching partners and they'd have to face one another at some point, which she did not look forward to.

Gresia had them go through more basic exercises, first slowly, then picking up momentum, the clack of wood sounding dull compared to the ring of steel Karigan recalled from her swordmaster training session.

As she and Mara worked, she caught movement in the corner of her eye. Three others had entered the training chamber. A quick glance told her one was Drent, and one a Weapon, and . . .

She focused on parrying a swift blow from Mara.

"Not bad," Karigan said, pushing her back with a quick exchange.

Mara grinned. "I practiced staff fighting with Donal while you were gone. Some of the moves and principles are similar."

It showed. Mara was quick and Karigan needed to pay attention, but now a bout had begun in one of the other practice rings with Drent overseeing the Weapon and the third person. She squinted and saw, with some surprise, that it was King Zachary. She supposed she shouldn't be too surprised because he was, after all, a swordmaster himself and must keep up on his training, and it certainly was not the first time she had encountered him working with Drent.

As he faced off with Fastion, Karigan tried to return her attention to her own bout, but as she thrust and parried, her gaze kept slipping away to the king. He was even more adroit with the sword than a poker, and his exchange of blows with Fastion was lightning quick. Their steel sang, counterpoint to the dull clatter of the wooden practice swords the Riders used. She could not help but admire how the king—

Whack! Mara swatted the side of Karigan's thigh.

"Ow!" She hopped about the ring while Mara looked on with her hand on her hip.

"Someone wasn't paying attention," Gresia said.

Karigan was about to protest when she hopped too far and tripped over one of the planks that bounded the practice ring. She spilled unceremoniously onto the floor. As she looked upward, she decided she was getting much too familiar with this view of the ceiling. She raised herself on her elbows to find Gresia, the captain, Connly, and Mara gazing down at her. Mara looked particularly smug. Then to Karigan's dismay, Drent stomped over to join them.

"What is this?" he demanded. "I thought I trained you to be a swordmaster. Pitiful." He glanced appraisingly at Mara. "Perhaps we chose the wrong Rider."

The captain, her arms folded with her practice sword tucked beneath her elbow, cast Drent a sour look.

As Mara gave Karigan a hand up, she murmured, "A little distracted, were we?"

Karigan glared at her and set to patting sawdust off herself, something else with which she was becoming too familiar. She thanked the gods when she saw that the king and Fastion had not broken off their bout to witness her folly. Yes, she'd been gawking, and had to tear her gaze away again.

"I am disappointed in you," Drent said.

"Arms Master," Gresia said, "shouldn't you be working with your own trainee? I think I can handle this."

Drent glanced at her and, with a nod, murmured, "Arms Master." He then stomped back to where the king and Fastion practiced.

"Now, Sir Karigan," Gresia said, "I don't know where your attention went, but that was a beginner's mistake. Perhaps these exercises are too basic to hold your attention?"

"I apologize, Arms Master. It won't happen again."

"It is," Gresia told the other Riders, "a good example of what *not* to do, and the consequences of not paying attention on the field of battle are far more lethal."

"Well, then," the captain said, "if this lesson is done—"

"Not even close," Gresia said.

The captain and the arms master stared at one another as though engaged in a battle of wills. It ended when both seemed to look away at the same time.

"Now," Gresia said, "Sir Karigan and I will demonstrate the next exercise for you. Watch carefully."

Karigan faced the arms master in the ring. She made sure to pay attention this time with three sets of Rider eyes watching, including that of her captain. She would not humiliate herself again in front of them.

Gresia started slowly with basic moves, then sped up in increments, introducing some simple forms. Karigan was surprised, because though the forms were simple, the techniques were for more advanced training.

Gresia moved faster, and Karigan was truly paying attention now. This was no longer just a demonstration. Gresia's sword cut relentlessly at her as she moved into more difficult forms, all the while striking faster and faster. Once Karigan was over her initial surprise, she allowed her training to take over. She had never engaged in advanced swordplay with Gresia before, and the arms master was a hawk with talons spread, capitalizing on any weakness she perceived in Karigan's technique, a fierce joy on her face.

Karigan spun, leaped, swiveled side to side, as the blows rained down. She lost track of time, forgot the watchers, and took pleasure in pure movement, of attacking and defending.

Gresia chopped down with a hard blow and Karigan raised her sword to block it, but when the wooden blades met, there was an enormous *c-r-r-rack* and half of Karigan's blade broke off. She shimmied out of the path of Gresia's sword just in time.

Gresia swiftly collected herself and stepped back. She wasn't even breathing hard. She grinned. "That was pleasant."

Pleasant? Karigan supposed it was as apt a description as any.

"Do we have to do that?" Connly asked with trepidation.

Gresia laughed. "Not today. That was swordmaster level work, and I wanted to give Karigan a chance to redeem herself."

"I had no doubts," the captain said.

Karigan warmed in pleasure at her approval.

Mara lightly punched her arm. "Good job, Helgadorf!"

Karigan glared at her, then glanced toward the ring where the king and Fastion had been working, but they, and Drent, were gone, and she felt let down. She tried to tell herself it was because she wanted Drent's approval, but she knew it wasn't his she sought.

The rest of the session was spent going through basic exercises again, this time Karigan, borrowing Gresia's practice sword, sparring with Connly. When they finished up, she walked back toward the castle with Mara.

"You know, he watched you and Gresia with great interest," Mara said.

"He who?" Karigan asked.

"You know who."

Karigan's cheeks warmed, and she gave Mara a sideways glance, but Mara simply watched the path ahead, betraying nothing. While it was possible "he" had meant Drent or Fastion, or even Connly, Karigan was pretty sure Mara had meant the king, and she said it as if she'd known there was something between them. Karigan resigned herself to the idea of Mara knowing. How many people knew or suspected, she didn't care to guess. There was no point to it, anyway. He was the king and he was married, end of story.

The next morning, as she left her chamber for her shift at the stable to muck out stalls, she was intercepted by a Green Foot runner.

"The queen requests your presence," the boy said.

"Was a reason given?"

"No, ma'am, just that you are to go soonest."

Karigan reentered her chamber to change. She could not present herself to the queen in her stable work clothes. As she pulled a fresh uniform out of her wardrobe, she wondered what Estora wanted. Maybe she was just in need of company again. Would the king be there?

She drew on her longcoat, grabbed her saber, and then with a cursory look in her hand mirror, left her chamber behind to attend the queen. When she reached the royal apartments, she felt a ripple of the wards Merla had set, very much like the sensation when she entered the warded area around Rider waystations. In Estora's sitting room, she found it little changed since the last time she'd been there, except for the absence of the ice creatures.

Estora reclined on her sofa beneath a blanket, working on some sewing, a Hillander terrier lying across her feet. He sat up at Karigan's arrival and barked.

"Quiet, Jasper!" Estora said.

The terrier leaped off the sofa to sniff Karigan's boots. Karigan bowed to Estora and snuck in a pat to Jasper's head.

"Zachary thinks he leaves this dog to guard me," Estora said, "but mainly Jasper just naps and wants scratches when anyone visits. But come, come and sit. I am glad you are here. I think your presence will be most helpful."

Helpful? Karigan sat in one of the armchairs beside the fire, wondering exactly what the queen had in mind.

ASH GIRL AND QUEEN

"There she is, the queen's little hero!" The pronouncement was followed by laughter.

Anna didn't pause at the door to the servants' common room to retort. She simply walked on, her empty ash buckets banging together. She'd been right, of course, that her fellow servants would not believe what she'd done and seen the day of the attack of the ice creatures, or that she'd been personally thanked by the king and queen for her help. They mocked instead of praised her. The servants quarters had not been hit hard by the ice creatures, so many of them had not seen what she had.

Worse still, the servants gossiped about Sir Karigan's "uncanniness." Some made the sign of the crescent moon when they spoke her name. She could speak to ghosts, they said, and travel through time. Anna did not know how true or false these claims were, but she had witnessed Sir Karigan using magic to *protect* the two of them during the attack, not use it for ill. Whether she had magic or not, she'd gone on to save the queen, and had treated Anna very nicely. She wasn't, to Anna's eyes, "uncanny," but a kind person. When, on impulse, she told the gossips to shut their mouths, it produced yet more uproarious laughter and ridicule.

When finally she arrived at the storage room to leave off her buckets, broom, and shovel, Master Scrum was there in his apron, looking over a list. He eyed her sourly.

"A little slow today, are we, Mousie? Been out saving the queen again, eh?"

She scowled at the nickname and set the buckets down with a clatter.

"Don't you get airs, girl. I'll give you extra shifts if I've a mind. That what you want?"

"No, Master Scrum."

He grunted and returned to his list. "Just you be back here at one hour, sharp."

"Yes, Master Scrum."

She stepped back out into the corridor feeling rather dispirited. She almost wished the ice creatures would attack again. Then she'd go help the Riders like before. Then see what everyone would say. They'd probably just continue to mock her. They couldn't see beyond the ends of their noses.

As Anna came abreast of the common room, a Green Foot runner trotted down the corridor. The runners weren't usually seen in the servants quarters. He must be looking for Master Scrum, but to her surprise, he halted in front of her.

"You're Anna, aren't you? The ash girl?"

Doubly surprised, she couldn't answer.

"That's Mousie," some wag in the common room quipped.

It loosened her tongue. "Yes, I'm *Anna*."

"Good. You are to report to the queen immediately."

The chatter among the servants ceased. Anna refused to look in to see their faces. Let them think what they wanted. She followed the boy down the corridor, but what in the world would the queen want with her? Suddenly her legs got shaky.

"Am—am I in trouble?" she asked the runner.

He shrugged. "I dunno, miss. I'm just supposed to escort you there."

Escort. It sounded serious. Had she done something wrong during the attack? Had they only just figured it out and now wanted to reprimand her? Then she looked down at her hands and her skirts—they were coated with ashes and soot. How could she go before the queen like this?

"I need to clean up!"

"You look fine to me," the boy said. "Best not to keep the queen waiting."

Anna despaired and tried the best she could to pat ash off

her hands and skirts as they went. It was probably in her hair and on her face, as well.

She meekly followed the boy into the royal wing, her mind filled with the direst of dire thoughts of all that she might have done to displease the queen. The stern faces of the Weapons she saw along the way did little to bolster her confidence.

When the runner halted, she was so absorbed in her own worries that she walked into him.

"I'm sorry!"

"It's all right, miss. No need to be so fretful. The queen is kind."

His words made her feel better until she saw they'd reached the queen's door and one of the tall broad-shouldered Weapons was gazing down at her.

"This is Anna," the boy said, "the one Queen Estora sent me to fetch."

"You may take her in, Rob." The Weapon's low voice was like the low roll of thunder. He opened the door.

Anna thought to run, but the boy, Rob, took her by the wrist and pulled her into the queen's apartments. She followed him all the way into the sitting room and was surprised to find not only Queen Estora on her sofa petting one of the king's little white dogs, but Sir Karigan sitting beside the fire. A tall woman with steel gray hair stood beside the queen's sofa. She was immaculately attired, and Anna thought she had seen her before, an important servant in the royal wing.

Rob bowed before the queen. "Here is Anna as you requested, my lady," he said.

"Thank you, Rob," Queen Estora replied. "You are dismissed."

He bowed as he backed away, and when he turned, flashed Anna a smile, then hastened out. Remembering herself, she bobbed a curtsy.

"Hello, Anna," Sir Karigan said with a friendly smile. "It's good to see you again, and this time without us being under attack."

"Yes, Sir Karigan. I mean, hello." Sir Karigan looked well, Anna thought. She'd only seen the Rider at a distance since the day of the attack, and one of those times she'd been surrounded by Weapons.

"Anna," the queen said, "I would like you to meet Mistress Evans. Mistress Evans is in charge of the servants in the royal wing."

Anna curtsied again before the forbidding woman.

"None of that," Mistress Evans said. "I haven't a speck of noble blood in me."

True or not, Anna thought, she certainly had a regal bearing.

"Now, let's have a look at you, lass."

Mistress Evans looked her over with a critical eye and she just wanted to hide. As if sensing her discomfort, Sir Karigan told her, "Anna, the queen says there is an opening on her personal household staff, and she thought maybe you'd like the position."

Anna stood there in shock. She'd come expecting some kind of scolding, but now the queen wanted her as part of her personal staff?

"Well," Mistress Evans said, "I can see you've been taking care of fireplaces and stoves." Anna's cheeks heated up as she thought of her ash- and soot-stained skirts. "Has Master Scrum given you other duties?"

"No'm, just taking out rubbish sometimes."

"Hmm. Have you family around?"

Anna considered how to answer, conscious of all three women awaiting her answer. "No'm. I mean, not as there is any who care."

"Explain."

"Anna," Sir Karigan said with a sharp look at Mistress Evans, "you don't have to answer if you don't want to."

Anna gazed at her feet. "It's all right, Sir Karigan. I've got sixteen brothers and sisters, you see." The queen raised her eyebrows and placed her hand on her belly at this. "Too many mouths to feed for my mum and da," Anna continued, "so they found me a job at the castle and left me."

Mistress Evans, on the other hand, looked relieved. "That was sensible of them, lass, to find you a place that would keep you safe, warm, and fed."

Anna knew it could have been much worse, but she'd never gotten over her sense of betrayal at having been abandoned.

"Can you read? Figure?"

Ashamed, Anna shook her head.

"We can do something about that, perhaps," the queen said gently.

"I suppose," Mistress Evans replied. "Well, she is polite enough and seems biddable. I think she'd do for hearth duty for the time being, certainly, and perhaps some other simple tasks, and then we can see how she develops."

"What do you think, Anna?" Queen Estora asked. "Would you like to work here?"

Anna's eyes widened, disbelieving her good fortune. The prospect of attending the queen both thrilled and terrified her. What if she made a mistake? And if she was here, she would no longer be able to tend the Rider wing, would she?

"The Riders," she blurted, then clapped her hands over her mouth.

Sir Karigan looked like she was trying not to laugh. Mistress Evans appeared confused.

"Riders? What about the Riders?"

"She has been doing a very expert job of tending the hearths in the Rider wing," Sir Karigan said, "and we'd be lost without her."

"Surely," Mistress Evans replied, "she'd not be that difficult to replace . . ."

Sir Karigan exchanged a meaningful look with the queen. The queen smiled. "Do you suppose, Mistress Evans, that in addition to serving here, she could continue to tend the Rider wing?"

Anna's hopes surged and she crossed her fingers behind her back.

"It is somewhat irregular," Mistress Evans replied. "I would have to work it out with Master Scrum, and it might take some creative scheduling, but if it is what you wish, it will be done."

"It is what I wish."

Mistress Evans bowed her head.

Anna almost danced she was so happy.

"Congratulations, Anna," Sir Karigan said. "It's nice that we'll still get to see you in the Rider wing."

"Now, lass," Mistress Evans said, "we'd better go break the news to Master Scrum, and move you to your new quarters."

Anna could not believe it and almost forgot to curtsy to the queen. Then she said, "Thank you, Sir Karigan!"

The Rider looked genuinely surprised. "It is nothing I did. It was all the queen's idea."

Anna curtsied to the queen once more, then followed Mistress Evans out. Sir Karigan had helped without knowing, not realizing she'd shown Anna that she could be proud to be an ash girl, and that if she worked hard, and she determined she was going to work very hard indeed, and please the queen as best she could, that almost anything was possible. Even becoming a Green Rider.

"That was very kind of you," Karigan told Estora.

"I found I could not get her out of my mind. She has a spark to her."

"Yes, I agree, and her being stuck in the general servants quarters much longer might have snuffed it out." Karigan started to rise, thinking Estora's need of her presence concluded.

"Won't you stay a while?" Estora asked. "Jaid will bring tea soon."

"My other duties—" Karigan began.

Estora tinkled a hand bell and said, "That can be rectified." Her maid answered her summons. "Jaid, see to it a runner is sent to Captain Mapstone informing her I have need of Sir Karigan for an hour or so." When Jaid hurried off to obey, Estora smiled and said, "I may be confined, but being queen still has a few privileges."

THE QUEEN'S REQUEST

Karigan shifted uncomfortably in her armchair, not especially pleased to have her schedule disrupted, but as Estora said, a queen had privileges and it was Karigan's place to do as she was asked.

Estora happily showed her the baby gown she was sewing. "I have to make two of everything. I do not know how I'd manage without my ladies."

The whole idea of babies was foreign to Karigan. She'd had no siblings and grew up an only child doted upon by her aunts. Even her extended family lived far off so she rarely experienced contact with younger cousins. Her aunts had often told her birthing children was the bravest act a woman could perform, for it was so very perilous. Numerous complications could, and did, occur, and as many mothers and infants did not survive the process as did. That Estora was bearing twins was of particular concern, but she did have the attention of the best menders in all Sacoridia, including Ben with his true healing gift.

Estora spoke of the improving weather and how she awaited word from her mother and sisters. Ty Newland had been sent off to Coutre Province before the winter had turned truly execrable to take word of her pregnancy to Clan Coutre. No doubt her mother would once again make the long, difficult journey to Sacor City.

Estora's thoughts were apparently not solely upon her forthcoming children. "Zachary tells me you have become a swordmaster at last. I whole-heartedly approve. I congratulate you."

"Thank you."

Estora went on to speak of various tidbits of news about her ladies and servants. Karigan found her attention drawn to the Intrigue game set up on the table between them. She'd noticed it when she first arrived, and recognized it as the set she and the king had used during one very uncomfortable game some five years ago. She gazed in interest at the odd formations of the blue and red pieces on the board.

"You are curious about the Intrigue board?" Estora asked.

Karigan felt her cheeks flush at having been caught not paying attention. "Yes. I have never seen the pieces arranged that way." Not that she liked Intrigue enough to know every formation that was possible.

"Ah. Zachary brought it over to amuse himself in the evenings, but one afternoon it turned into a discussion about Second Empire and where it is believed their forces are situated."

"Can you show me?" Karigan asked her.

"Of course. The positions may have changed since our latest intelligence in the fall, though it is not likely Second Empire has moved much over the winter." She pointed to bands of blue pieces that were arranged across the top of the board. "Zachary believes their forces have occupied small settlements and farmsteads just north of the border to endure the winter. He knows which ones, and showed me a map once." She named a few of the settlements.

"What are the red pieces to the . . . the north of them?" Karigan asked.

"Yes, that's even farther north, the Lone Forest. Zachary believes more of Second Empire, perhaps its civilians and leaders, have entrenched themselves there."

"The Lone Forest," Karigan murmured. Before the Long War a thousand years ago, the Sacor Clans may have ranged that far north, but with the clans diminished during the war, the border receded to present-day Sacoridia. Might Grandmother herself reside in the Lone Forest?

"Zachary is certain they have not moved from the Lone Forest," Estora said, "though the winter has been much too harsh to get anyone up there to take a look and make sure."

Karigan gazed at the board for some time until Jaid reappeared with tea and cakes, and poured. Jasper eyed the cakes with interest from where he lay at Estora's feet.

"You are excused, Jaid," Estora said, "for your own tea."

"Thank you, my lady." Jaid curtsied and left them.

At first they sat in silence sipping their tea; then Estora seemed to come to some decision. "I was wondering . . . I was wondering how it is with you? How your eye is doing?"

Karigan's hand went reflexively to the patch. "It—it is unchanged." That wasn't exactly true, she supposed, after her confrontation with Lhean.

"Do you . . ." Estora was hesitant, couldn't seem to look directly at Karigan. "Do you ever look into it? Its mirror nature?"

"No. It is not something I wish to see. It is disorienting."

"It is difficult to imagine," Estora said. "I have always enjoyed the antics of tumblers with looking masks at parties and festivals. I had never imagined them as having real power, except maybe the one at the masquerade ball we held before you went to Blackveil." She gazed into the distance, as if remembering.

Karigan remembered, too. She'd beheld visions of Grandmother, and of descending arrows, in the tumbler's mask. Was it the very same mask she had shattered in Castle Argenthyne? The shard of which had claimed her right eye?

"Karigan," Estora said carefully, "I would like to see your eye."

Karigan restrained the impulse to scream, *No!* Why would Estora ask such a thing of her?

"I wonder about the children," Estora said, "their future, if there is a way I can prepare for any possible complications . . ."

Her expression was imploring, and Karigan could well understand her anxiety, but to ask this of her? No, not ask. She requested, and as queen, she could not be refused. Karigan gazed into her teacup, which shook in her hands. After what she had experienced with Lhean, she was not sure she could endure it again.

"Are you sure you really want this, my lady? Others have found it disquieting."

"Yes." Estora's expression was eager, hopeful.

Karigan hesitated.

"Please," Estora said quietly, "please do not make me demand it of you. It would be . . . it would be in service to your realm."

Karigan loosed a shaky breath. Estora was using her royal prerogative. As much as Estora might go on about the two of them being friends, Karigan was her servant first, and that would always stand between them. She nodded in acquiescence and set her teacup aside. She rose and knelt beside Estora's sofa, and removed her eyepatch. Estora's sharp intake of breath revealed that even though she knew what it was that had happened to Karigan's eye, it was still a shock.

At first Karigan saw nothing through that eye, but there was the needling pain of exposing it to light and air, and then she glimpsed stars and threads of light streaking through her vision. Images blurred by so rapidly she could not grasp them.

A dagger pain stabbed through her eye, and she turned away with a cry, half-falling over. She caught herself on the table, which shifted beneath her weight. Books and game pieces spilled to the floor, and teacups rattled in their saucers. Jasper barked. Hastily she replaced the patch over her eye and the pain diminished to a dull throb. She sat on the floor panting.

When she returned her gaze to Estora, Estora remained sitting forward on the sofa, her gaze distant as if she were ensnared by visions.

"What is it?" Karigan asked. "What did you see?"

Estora sat up, once more in the present. Her expression was difficult to read, and when she smiled, it seemed a little sad. "My children will be happy. I am very sorry, dear Karigan, that I put you through that. Please forgive me."

Karigan climbed to her feet. "I'm . . . I'll be all right." The dull throb of her eye migrated to the whole of her head and she felt unbalanced. She saw the afterlight of stars in her mind. "If I may have your leave, I had better attend to my duties."

"Yes," Estora said absently.

What had she *really* seen? Karigan wondered.

THE FUTURE, GOOD OR BAD

Karigan staggered out of Estora's apartments in something of a daze, her head pounding. She swerved around a corner in the corridor, and did not see the king until she nearly plowed into him.

"Your Majesty," she murmured. She stepped back, and tried to bow, but vertigo made her lose her balance. He steadied her.

"Are you ill?" he asked, peering at her.

She thought, with embarrassment, she probably looked more inebriated than anything. "Fine. I'm fine."

"Perhaps you should sit down."

In fact, the world was shifting into better focus now, the throb in her head easing. She straightened her shoulders. "Truly, I am fine. Please, do not trouble yourself."

"No trouble," he said. "Not ever."

She could not meet his gaze, and it was some moments before he released her. It made her feel unsteady in other ways.

"Fastion," he said, "see that Sir Karigan reaches her quarters without incident and that she takes some time to rest."

"Yes, sire."

The king nodded to her in leave-taking, and continued down the corridor. She watched after him for a moment before turning back to Fastion. As a Weapon, he should have ensured the corridor was clear of any impediment to the king. Certainly he would have known she was coming, wouldn't he?

"Why did you let me bump into the king?" she asked him.

"It is only you, Sir Karigan."

It was only her? Did he mean he knew she was of no danger to the king? But still . . . She stepped around him and said, "I don't need an escort."

"The king has commanded it," he replied, and he fell in step beside her.

She walked fast, deciding to pay Fastion no heed, but of course he kept pace. When they reached the main hall, she turned to head toward the records room, but Fastion placed his hands on her shoulders and steered her in the opposite direction.

"What are you—"

"You are to return to your quarters," he said, "as the king wishes."

"But—"

"The Rider wing, Sir Karigan. All else is disobedience."

"Granite Face," she muttered. If he heard, he did not respond.

Grudgingly, she started toward the Rider wing when someone called out to her. She paused, and Estral strode up, gazing first at Fastion before asking her, "Are you in some kind of trouble?"

"Sir Karigan is always in trouble," Fastion said, his voice betraying no humor.

"I guess I know that," Estral said.

Karigan made an aggravated sigh and glared at Fastion. "I am *not* in trouble."

"Then you and Weapon Fastion are just out for a walk?"

"He is escorting me to my chamber."

Estral raised an eyebrow.

"It's not what you're thinking!"

"What do you think I'm thinking?"

Karigan scowled and Estral looked like she wanted to laugh.

"For the sake of the gods," Karigan said in exasperation. "It's by the king's order."

"Are you sure you're not in trouble, then?"

Karigan strode off. The sooner she reached her chamber, the sooner she'd be rid of her "escort."

"Do you have a few minutes to talk?" Estral asked, hurrying beside her.

"I don't know. You'll have to ask *him*." She jabbed her thumb in Fastion's direction.

"I'll permit it," he said.

"Weapons," Karigan muttered, as if it were an oath.

When finally they reached her chamber, she let Estral in, but closed the door in Fastion's face.

"Will you tell me what that was all about?" Estral asked.

Karigan explained her encounter with the king.

"But why did he think you were unwell?"

She explained that part, as well.

"You know he ordered you to your room because he cares about you, don't you?"

She knew. She looked down at her hands, at the healing slash across the back of her wrist. "It would almost be easier if he didn't."

Estral gazed at her sympathetically. "I don't think you mean that."

Karigan wasn't sure. She wanted it both ways. Sometimes she wished she had never come to Sacor City and met him.

"Did you tell him you revealed your eye to the queen?"

Karigan shook her head. "It didn't come up."

"The king hasn't asked for a look?"

"No." It pleased her that he had not, though he must find it a great temptation with such a tool at his disposal, a mirror that could reveal visions that could help him against Second Empire. Of course, no one knew how reliable those visions were. But if anything showed her he cared, it was this one thing. She headed over to the hearth to stoke the fire and decided to change the subject from such dangerous ground. "You said you wanted to talk."

Estral nodded and slid into the chair at Karigan's desk. "I have a request, but first I thought you'd want to hear about Alton's gryphon."

Karigan, poker in hand, looked back at her. "Alton's *what?*"

"Actually, it's more Merdigen's gryphon." She told Karigan how in her most recent communication with Alton, through

Connly and Trace, she learned about Merdigen revealing his cat to be a gryphon.

Karigan laid a log on the coals. "Are you sure Alton has not taken to drinking in your absence?" She glanced at her untouched jug of whiskey that had been distilled by his aunt. "Gryphons aren't real."

"They are, apparently, as real as p'ehdrose," Estral replied, "although Mister Whiskers may be the last of his kind."

Karigan sat hard on her bed. *"Mister Whiskers?"*

Estral nodded solemnly, then told her about the plan to send him out in search of a mate. "Merdigen thinks it possible there could be more out there, and if there are, Mister Whiskers will find them. He's hoping for kittens." She explained the idea about having the gryphons guard the towers.

Karigan tried to work her way through her disbelief. "I don't know. If they're like cats, they're apt to ignore any Sleepers that pass through the towers. Or, maybe just play with them."

Estral waved her hand through the air as though it were inconsequential. "Can you imagine? Gryphons roaming the wild again?"

Karigan was not sure she wanted to. The world had grown strange enough to her mind. Did it really need gryphons, as well? She was envisioning the sky filled with flocks of flying cats when Estral interrupted her thoughts.

"What I wanted to talk about was your mission to the north."

"How do you know about that?"

"I've been speaking with Captain Mapstone about my own plans to resume my search for my father, and of course look for the person who stole my voice. As you know, I was going to look north. I thought it would make sense for us to travel together, at least for a little while."

Karigan would not mind in the least having her friend along, however . . . "I don't know if the king is going to actually approve the mission."

"The captain seemed pretty confident he would, and she had no objection to my going along so long as you and whoever the Eletians send don't."

"Well, then," Karigan said, "this will be a first."

Estral smiled. "I promised the captain I wouldn't get in the way. In fact, I'm doing some weapons training with Arms Master Gresia. As you may recall, I was not one of Rendle's most adept students in Selium, so I thought it would be a good idea to brush up on my skills. I've also been studying maps and researching the north."

It could almost be, Karigan thought, a pleasant excursion with her best friend, but the north, she knew, contained plenty of danger.

"What do you mean you looked into her eye?" Zachary demanded.

Estora, from her place on the sofa, looked startled by his vehemence. "She consented."

Zachary stood at the hearth, staring into the fire as flames leaped and wavered. "You are her queen. *Of course* she consented." It was a position of power. It was the lot of those who served her, and who were ruled by her, to obey. It was in her rights to demand anything of her subjects and their compliance was required. The difference between a just monarch and an unjust monarch was where they drew the line. The unjust monarch abused his subjects. In Zachary's own rule, he was at pains to maintain the trust of those who served him. He preferred they served out of loyalty rather than fear, though fear had its place and had worked admirably for a few of his predecessors.

"You are displeased because it was Karigan," Estora said.

"I would be displeased if it were any of my subjects," he said, perhaps too quickly, his voice cold. "I told you that her eye caused her pain. She could hardly stand when I came upon her in the corridor."

Estora gazed down at her hands folded on her lap. "I am sorry," she said, her voice remorseful. "In my excitement over the children, I forgot myself, that Karigan and I are no longer simply friends, that I am also her queen. Even as just a friend, I should not have asked her. I am sorry."

"I am not the one to whom you should apologize."

"I know it. But . . ." She looked up at him with hungry eyes. "Do you not wish to know what I saw?"

"No." He left the hearth and headed toward the passage that led to his own rooms. Jasper jumped off the sofa and trotted behind him.

"Zachary!" Her voice came after him sounding desperate now. "I saw our children."

He paused in the passageway despite himself, but only for a moment. Before she could say more, he entered his apartments and closed the door behind him. He did not slam it, but closed it gently. He then sought his favorite chair and dropped into it. Jasper leaped onto his lap and he scratched the terrier beneath his collar.

Usually, Estora used good judgment, but he remembered how excited she'd been by the tumbler with the looking mask during the masquerade ball they'd thrown about a year ago. The tumbler had been, seemingly, more than a tumbler, for Zachary had seen visions of his own. Visions of arrows arcing across the sky. Estora had seen their child. She'd been tremendously excited. And now, of course, with her pregnant, she'd want to see what Karigan's mirror eye might reveal. In a way, he could not blame her, but as queen, she must exercise restraint.

Besides, how accurate were these visions? At the masquerade ball, she'd seen only one child, but now she carried twins. Why the discrepancy? Had the mask not revealed the whole story? Or had something more fundamental shifted in the weaving of the future?

Just because she carried twins did not mean both would survive. Perhaps neither would. The prospect clenched his gut, and Jasper licked his hand as if sensing his distress. Estora, however, had sounded as if she had seen something positive in Karigan's eye.

He refused to return to her sitting room to ask. It would invalidate his belief in how a monarch should conduct himself with his subjects. He did not wish to encourage her, and . . . he was not sure he wanted to know the future, good or bad.

A PRECURSOR TO TROUBLE

The days came and went, the sun lengthening its stay in small increments, the icy weather alternating with influxes of milder air. Karigan continued to receive batterings in swordmaster training, and helped Arms Master Gresia with her trainees. She saw nothing of King Zachary, which she deemed for the best, nor did Estora invite her to visit again. Garth departed for the wall, but Tegan returned from her personal leave after helping her sister with her newborn baby.

Karigan assisted Elgin daily in the records room. One afternoon as she entered, Dakrias Brown rose from his desk to greet her, and after an exchange of pleasantries, he squinted at her through his specs.

"Er, something wrong?" she asked him.

"Not precisely." He darted glances about the chamber. "It's just that . . ."

"Just what?"

He looked sheepish. "It's the ghosts." He spoke in an almost-whisper.

"What are they up to now?"

"I am not sure. You see, whenever you are here, pardon my saying, they seem to disappear."

It was on her tongue to remind him that disappearing was generally what ghosts did, but then she realized he was right. When she worked with Elgin, the records room felt strangely empty and quiet. There were no ghostly whispers in her ear, no barely perceived touches upon her arm, no odd air currents circulating overhead. Now that she thought about it, she no longer sensed the spirits around her bed chamber or in the ancient corridor it inhabited. *You have the command of them,* Lhean had told her. He had been speaking of the ghosts, but failed to explain further.

Were the ghosts for some reason now afraid of her? Such a ridiculous notion, it almost made her laugh. The idea of her having "the command of them" was also laughable, but it had been said by an Eletian, and that gave her pause.

"I don't know what to tell you, Dakrias." They had plagued him enough in the past that she thought he'd be happy they were gone. He returned to his desk looking troubled. Had he become attached to them?

She found Elgin at his usual location at the table with its piles of documents. He looked up at her from around a stack of ledgers.

"Ah, just in time to see what was delivered from the tombs."

If she hadn't known what he was talking about, her imagination might have conjured up all sorts of ghastly visions.

He showed her a thick sheaf of papers. "We need to go through these and see what's useful, then pass on the relevant pieces to Red."

These were Agemon's translations of the materials she had copied. Chances were they would find nothing useful describing the comportment of the Green Riders during times of war, but if there *was* something, the research would prove well worthwhile.

Karigan took her seat next to Elgin, and he split the stack in half with her. The handwriting, whether in Agemon's own hand, or that of one of his clerks, was quite ornate and rather old-fashioned with swirls and flourishes.

"Need someone to translate this fancy lettering," Elgin grumbled.

It wasn't completely illegible, but it would take some time to pick through it. As she began, it appeared she'd ended up with inventories of fodder for horses, and not during wartime. Dakrias found that sort of thing interesting, but the captain wouldn't. As she went on, she gradually grew accustomed to the handwriting style and was able to read through the pages more quickly.

There was an account of a Rider named Tannen, who'd broken his back in a fall from his horse. The description of how he'd both survived and was mended proved circumspect. There must have been a true healer among the Riders at the time—what? Four hundred years ago? Otherwise, a broken back was likely a death sentence in those days. They would not have spoken baldly of Rider abilities even back then. She set the piece aside thinking that although it had nothing to do with wartime, the captain would be interested anyway.

She went through more inventories until it felt like her eyes were crossing. Elgin appeared to be nodding off beside her, his chin dipping to his chest. She had only a few more pages left, so she rubbed her eyes and continued.

One page was from a very long time ago, from the years following the Long War, copied from one of the ancient scrolls. It appeared to be a report detailing the various errands Riders had been sent on in the month of Hannon:

On the second day of Hannon, Ornan to Lord Penburn with a message from the king.

On the third day of Hannon, Lendon to Lady Izel with a message from the king.

On the third day of Hannon, Ranson dispatched to Corsa to take ship, thence to Lord Arey with a message from the king.

On the fifth day of Hannon, Gerrim returned from Lord Adolind with a reply for the king.

Karigan found it interesting just to read the names of these Riders of old, her predecessors. She wished she could know more about them, who they were, what they looked like, what their daily lives were like. The lack of details about their errands was maddening and made their work seem simple, but she knew from experience that it could not have been so. The month of Hannon appeared to be a busy one with many Riders coming and going, but with no indication of what business the king's correspondence held. There would not be, of course, because the Rider's job was only to deliver the message. The contents were not the Rider's concern unless the king made it so.

She continued down the list until she came to a curious notation:

> *On the twenty-third day of Hannon, C. Siris Kiltyre to Ifel Aeon (???)* to secure the Aeon Iire.*

The question marks belonged to the copyist. *Ifel,* he or she noted, could mean a forest, a fort or keep, or a glade. *Aeon* could not be translated without more research, but might indicate a proper name. Even more curious was that Captain Kiltyre had been going to Ifel Aeon not to deliver a message, but to secure . . . *something. Secure the Aeon Iire.* The copyist suggested that *Iire* could refer to "stamp" or "medallion," or "shield," but these translations were followed with question marks, as well. Perhaps if they could figure out what *Aeon* meant, they could then figure out *Iire.* One or both, she thought, could be misspellings, as well.

What, she wondered, had Captain Kiltyre been up to? She was going to ask Elgin what he thought, but now he was snoring. She chuckled. A Green Foot runner trotted into the records room just then.

"Sir Karigan," the girl said, "you are requested to go to the throne room." And then she was off before Karigan could ask any questions. She shook Elgin awake to let him know that she had to go, then set off for the throne room, wondering why she had been summoned.

When she reached the throne room, she found not only the king awaiting her, but Captain Mapstone and, to her surprise, Enver the Eletian.

"Ah, Sir Karigan," the king said. He stood with his hands clasped behind his back, and she bowed.

"Greetings, Galadheon." Enver stuck out his hand to shake.

"Hello," she said, clasping his hand. Did this mean what she thought it meant, that it was time to go north? If so, it could be hard going as winter had not yet left them. Enver revealed nothing.

"I've asked Lady Estral to join us," the king said, "as I

understand she has some interest in an expedition northward."

So, this *was* about searching for the p'ehdrose. The king revealed little of what he thought either in his expression or posture.

"Enver has arrived earlier than we were expecting," the captain said.

A ponderous silence followed until Estral hastened into the throne room. Greetings were exchanged, and the king climbed up onto his throne and sat.

"Sir Karigan," he said, "Eletia has sent Enver as a guide in the search for the p'ehdrosians. Prince Jametari is keen that this search take place. I have come to the conclusion that it is in Sacoridia's interests, as well. I've had my diplomats in other realms attempting to secure alliances against Second Empire and the probable reemergence of Mornhavon. It is time to become reacquainted with the p'ehdrose and extend the hand of friendship to them, and I wish for you to do this on my behalf. I understand Captain Mapstone has spoken to you of this."

"Yes, sire." She remembered well the captain explaining that she would be playing the part of an emissary.

"Lady Estral has requested to travel with you, and so long as you and Enver have no objections, I approve."

"She is welcome, Firebrand," Enver said. "Three is a good omen."

"I have no objections." Karigan flashed Estral a smile.

"Then you must prepare," King Zachary said. "Enver says the p'ehdrose have hidden themselves well, but the Eletians have a sense of where they reside."

"It is not marked on any map," Enver said.

"As you will be in the north," the king continued, "you are to take caution against Second Empire. Captain Mapstone will show you their last known positions on maps. It is, of course, possible they have shifted since our last intelligence." He stared hard at Karigan. "Use utmost caution, Rider. Do you understand?"

"Yes, sire."

His gaze seared into her as if to indeed make sure she understood. "You are also to aid Lady Estral in her search as you can. Lord Fiori is of importance to the realm."

"Yes, sire."

"Enver," he continued, "wishes to depart in two days. You will use that time to prepare. Captain, you will see to the details."

"Yes, Your Majesty."

With that, he abruptly rose and descended the dais, and, without another word, strode for the side exit, accompanied by two Weapons.

"Two days, eh?" Estral said doubtfully.

Enver nodded. "It has been foreseen."

Foreseen. The Eletians, Karigan thought, might like their portents, but to her, they always seemed like a precursor to trouble.

TAKING FLIGHT

Alton sneezed as Mister Whiskers, in his house cat form, twined between his legs. He stood conversing with Merdigen in Tower of the Heavens, and the cat, seeming to know his sensitivity, inflicted heaps of affection upon him.

Alton was not happy to begin with, after having received a communication from Trace, and he was explaining why to Merdigen. "Winter isn't even over and they're going north."

"Perhaps it is not sensible," Merdigen said, "but I assume they are prepared."

"To look for p'ehdrose!" Alton nearly exploded. "Legendary, nonexistent creatures."

Merdigen cleared his throat and pointed at Mister Whiskers, who was engaged in licking his paw. "Have you forgotten what *he* is? The p'ehdrose existed, and the Eletians and your king have reason to believe the p'ehdrose are still out there. Would you second-guess your king?"

Yes, Alton thought, though he would never say so aloud. Doing so could be construed as impertinent at the very least, and disloyal at worst. What he hoped was that the king possessed more information about the existence of the p'ehdrose than he was privy to. And yes, in the king's favor, there was Mister Whiskers.

"You are just upset that Lady Estral is going with them," Merdigen said.

And there was that. "She shouldn't be going on this—this mission. It isn't safe."

"You would prefer she went looking for her father and the voice thief on her own?"

"No, of course not. I just wish she didn't feel she had to go."

Merdigen looked askance at him. "How does she put up with you, boy?"

Alton smiled feebly. "I haven't the slightest."

"Well, then. I guess there is no more delaying the inevitable. I will have a final word with Mister Whiskers, and you will go prepare your people."

Alton nodded, rubbed his itchy eyes, and walked through the tower wall into the outside world. He squinted though the sky was hazy with a ceiling of clouds. It had been spitting flurries all morning off and on. He called to the nearest soldier and sent him to collect all of the encampment's personnel to assemble before him at the tower. The encampment at the breach, and the smaller camps at each tower, had already been notified about Mister Whiskers and that they were not to loose arrows at him.

When all the soldiers, cooks, hostlers, menders, laborers, and smiths were arrayed before him, he said, "We live in interesting times, where legends once again walk the lands. It was not so long ago Eletians had fallen into myth, only to reappear after hundreds of years. And we all know what lurks beyond the wall. Now, I have spoken to you before of the gryphon that has been inhabiting the tower. Today we release him so perhaps he may find a mate and bring her back. Kittens could be raised to protect the towers from within."

He paused, taking in the skeptical expressions on the faces around him. "I know it sounds mad, but such are the times we live in. I want you to meet Mister Whiskers, er, the gryphon. I want you to see him so he can come to no *ah-ah-ah—*" He sneezed explosively. When he blew his nose, he noticed everyone was gazing at the ground near his feet.

"Meep."

There sat the fearsome Mister Whiskers in the snow, wearing his house cat form, his orange-striped tail wrapped around his feet. He looked at his incredulous audience with curiosity.

"Yes, this is, uh, the gryphon," Alton said. "Mister Whiskers, would you change so everyone can see your true form?"

The cat just stared back at him. Members of his audience started to snicker and laugh.

"Please?" Alton asked, wondering if the cat knew just how ridiculous this was making him look.

"Meep?"

Would he have to grovel?

"You don't want them to fill you with arrows when you return in your true form, do you? They won't know it's you."

The cat blinked, then before his eyes, enlarged, elongated, transformed. His snout turned into a beak, and feathers replaced the fur on his head. His orange coat grew more tawny and wings sprouted from his back. He flapped them, then tucked them to his sides. He was even more fearsome and large than Alton remembered. The crowd had stepped back murmuring in consternation. Yes, they had seen a few "things" while stationed at the wall, but this was certainly something new occurring right before their eyes. Alton did not blame them for their disquiet.

"This is Mister Whiskers' true form," he said. "You are not to target him, or any other gryphon that may return with him. Is this understood?"

There was a jumble of uncertain *Yes, m'lords* and *Aye, sirs*. Then, to his surprise, Leese, the encampment's chief mender, came forward for a closer look.

"Hello, Mister Whiskers," she said. "You are a magnificent creature, aren't you."

Whiskers curved his neck as though inviting closer inspection. She stepped up to him and started to scratch his neck where fur met feather. Thunderous purrs rumbled out of him and vibrated the ground.

"What a nice kitty, er, gryphon," Leese said, her expression one of delight. "You are handsome." The crowd watched in awe, and, if anything, the purrs only increased in intensity.

Alton cleared his throat. "Mister Whiskers has a mission, don't you, Mister Whiskers."

The gryphon glared at him with his sharp eagle's eyes. He was enjoying Leese's attention.

"Leese," Alton whispered, "mission."

"Oh, of course." She scratched Mister Whiskers beneath the chin, so close to his raptor's beak that Alton felt queasy; then she returned to her place with the rest of the crowd. "Good-bye, Mister Whiskers."

The gryphon ruffled his feathers, gave Alton another look, then spread his wings, which knocked Alton over into a snowdrift. By the time Alton had righted himself, Mister Whiskers had launched into the air, the downbeats of his amazing wings gusting hats off heads and tousling hair. His shadow glided over them. For all his size, he gracefully arrowed high into the sky and grew smaller and smaller. He circled once, then twice, before darting northwestward.

Alton had never thought to see the like. "And that is Mister Whiskers," he concluded lamely.

Soon the assembled began to disperse, but Leese joined him, still looking to the sky. "I wonder if they lay eggs, or have live births."

"I've no idea," Alton replied.

Leese smiled. "Maybe we'll find out if his mission is successful. Professional curiosity, of course, and I do love kittens."

In addition to caring for human patients, Leese often treated the four-legged variety, as well.

"Let's hope this all works."

Alton reentered the tower to find Merdigen dabbing his eyes with a handkerchief. Was the cantankerous great mage crying?

"So, it is done?" Merdigen asked.

Alton nodded.

"It is not a safe world out there," Merdigen said. "So many dangers. People kill what they do not understand."

It was true, of course. "If anyone attempts it, it won't be anyone from our encampments or the castle."

"There are a lot of people between here and there, and beyond."

"I think," Alton said, surprised to hear himself trying to comfort the mage, "that Mister Whiskers will use his best judgment as to whether or not he will approach within arrow range of human habitation."

"Yes, of course, I did explain it to him, but he hasn't been out in the world much."

Everyone had to go out into the world sometime, Alton thought, even if the ones who loved them wanted to keep them safely home.

FAREWELLS

For an ordinary message errand, two days of preparation time was an overabundance, but since this was not exactly a message errand, but a journey into wild country, two days seemed rather inadequate to acquire all the supplies necessary. It was still winter and the weather would be fickle as they continued toward spring, so Karigan erred on the side of caution packing extra layers of clothing. They'd have a pack pony with them, specially chosen by Hep. The pony would be burdened with their gear and food supplies.

Drent accused her of running away from swordmaster training even though he knew very well she was leaving by the king's command. "Waste of effort to train you Riders," he grumbled at her during her final session. She had ended up on the floor only three times, an improvement.

Elgin was mournful at the news that he was losing his able copyist. She recommended Daro for the job, though she wasn't sure Daro would appreciate it.

She was excused from her other regular duties as well, so she could run about the castle for supplies and pore over maps. Mara, in her role as Chief Rider, assisted, but it was Estral who needed more help in finding adequate travel gear.

Enver, for his part, roamed the castle, looking into its nooks and crannies, studying tapestries and statues, knocking on the breastplates of suits of armor that stood along the corridors. Unlike Lhean and the other Eletians, he chose to spend his nights in a guest room in the diplomatic wing.

When the day came to leave, Karigan threw her stuffed saddlebags over one shoulder, and the longsword over the other. Her saber she wore at her hip, and she carried her bonewood staff at cane length in a scabbard that could be worn on her back or strapped to her saddle. She gave Ghost Kitty, who was sprawled on her bed, a final pat on the head. He'd probably start staying with Mara again. She was about to stride from her room, but paused and turned around and went to her desk. Setting her staff aside, she opened a certain drawer and withdrew the paper that held the image of Cade.

"I'm going away for a while," she murmured, and she touched his cheek, but felt only the texture of the paper. She closed her eyes trying to retain the image of him in her mind. After a deep breath, she returned the paper to its drawer where it would remain safe and, grabbing her staff, left her chamber without looking back.

Most of the Riders were out and about, but she bade farewell to the few she encountered. She also found Anna lugging her ash buckets and tools toward the common room. She now wore the livery of the royal household, a gray chemise and skirts with a fresh white apron, an improvement over her old allotment.

"Hello, Anna," Karigan said.

"Oh, Sir Karigan, I heard you were leaving."

"Yes, I'll be gone for a little while. How is your new position?"

"It's wonderful. The queen is kind, and even Mistress Evans treats me well. She never screams at me or accuses me of shirking my duties."

Karigan frowned. Had Anna been so mistreated working with the general castle staff?

"I have a real bed chamber now," Anna continued, "and have to share it with only one other person! But . . ."

"But?"

Anna glanced over her shoulder as if gazing off into another world; then her shoulders sagged. "Nothing. I couldn't be happier."

If Karigan had the time, she'd try to pry out whatever it was Anna had on her mind, but she didn't. Fortunately, she had asked Mara to keep an eye on the girl. Something about having helped Anna during the attack on the castle had made Karigan feel responsible for her.

"I wish you didn't have to go," Anna said.

"I'll be back sooner than we think." Karigan said it with more force than she intended. There would be, she had promised herself, no traveling to another time. No crossing through the layers of the world. "If you need anything, look for Mara, or if she's not around, Tegan or Daro."

"Thank you," Anna said, but she still looked disappointed.

"I've got to go now. You take care."

"Good-bye, Sir Karigan."

Karigan went on with the hope that Anna would fare well. Estora, she knew, would be good to her, and the Riders would keep an eye on her as well.

Estral and Enver awaited her just inside the castle entrance, each with their own packs and weapons. Estral wore a longknife beneath her coat, and Enver his sword, knife, and bow and arrows.

"Greetings, Galadheon."

"Good morning. Are we ready?"

"Better be, I guess," Estral said. She looked a little nervous.

They stepped outside into the gray day, the clouds gravid with snow. Karigan wondered if Tegan's ability to know the weather was failing, for she'd predicted fair skies. Perhaps it would clear off. The captain and Mara awaited them on the drive with Condor, Estral's gelding, and the pony.

Karigan glanced at Enver. "Are you walking north?"

"Eletians do prefer the land beneath their feet," he replied, "but I will mount when we leave the city."

On *what?* she wondered. The wind?

When they reached the captain and Mara, the captain held a message satchel out for her. "The king's letter to the p'ehdrose and related documents," she said, "should you find them. And a box of Dragon Droppings for your journey."

Karigan smiled and took the satchel. She then busied herself strapping the longsword and saddlebags to Condor's saddle. She slung the bonewood across her back and took the reins from Mara.

"Leg up?" Mara offered.

"I would, but Enver is on foot."

"I will keep up with your horses," he said. "I do not mind if you ride. I will lead the pony."

"His name is Bane," Mara said.

"Well, that's ominous," Estral commented from atop her gelding.

Karigan glanced at the shaggy mountain pony with his rakish forelock, their supplies laden on his back. She hoped he did not live up to his name.

She accepted Mara's leg up. "Any final orders?" she asked the captain.

"The usual. Stay out of trouble and come home safely."

Mara laughed. "As if that ever happens."

Karigan made a face at her.

The captain remained serious. "You are a capable Rider, Karigan; otherwise, the king would not be sending you out on this mission as his voice to make contact with the p'ehdrose for the first time in a thousand years."

"I understand."

"Good. And I'd prefer to not have to report bad news to your father again."

Karigan gave her a sly smile. "*When* you see him next, tell him I send my love."

The captain squinted suspiciously at her in return but did not reply.

Flurries started to drift down in lazy spirals as they bade their final farewells, and departed. Karigan and Estral rode side by side, and Enver followed with Bane. Just before they crossed through the castle gates, Karigan turned in her saddle to wave good-bye to the captain and Mara, but they'd already reentered the castle. Enver, she noticed, was gazing at the castle heights. When she followed his gaze, she saw only the pennants fluttering listlessly in the breeze, a raven soaring overhead, and soldiers at guard on the battlements.

She turned her attention to the way ahead.

Zachary stood upon the battlements, a breeze playing through his hair as he observed the three prepare to depart for the north. It was not the first time he had watched Karigan ride away from him. Would it be the last? It wasn't the first time he'd entertained that thought, either. She had returned all those previous times, sometimes miraculously. He hoped this errand would prove less perilous than those others, but of course, one could never tell how things would turn out. His messengers often rode into danger; it was the nature of their job, but he was the one who made the decision that they must go. And Karigan was more than a messenger to him.

He could not hear what words were exchanged down below, nor see their expressions, but he watched Karigan mount, so easy in the saddle. He wished he could ride out with her, leave the problems of the realm in someone else's hands. A light flurry descended from the sky, and he imagined the snow alighting softly upon her hair and shoulders.

The horses started forward, with the Eletian on foot leading the pony. As they approached the gates, he noticed the Eletian looking his way. He met the Eletian's gaze, then stepped back from the battlements. A raven wheeled overhead, and he turned on his heel. He strode for the doorway that led back into the castle, Fastion following close behind.

He'd almost felt the intensity of the Eletian's gaze, almost as if Enver could see into him, beneath his skin. Although Zachary had been unable to see Enver's face clearly at such a distance, he knew Eletians possessed exceptional sight. As a guard tugged open the heavy iron door for him, he wondered just how *exceptional* Eletian sight was.

Did Enver see Zachary's desire for the freedom to do as he wished? The desire to be other than king? His longing for the one who must always ride away, even in his dreams?

As he trotted down the stairwell into the comparative warmth of the castle, cold currents stalked him until the door above clanged shut. A prison door it was, for all that he was king.

GRAY ON GRAY

Zachary moved through a day that was gray on gray, stone walls against cloudy skies. He met with his generals and examined maps and plans, his vision filled with lines and shading, black ink delineating borders and territories. Outside his window, the dance of flurries continued, turned into a squall, a shower of arrows. He shook his head, tried to pay attention but did not hear the words. Laren, he saw, watched him carefully, but silently.

He took his mid-morning tea with his wife. Their relationship had turned awkward since Estora revealed she had looked into Karigan's mirror eye. They avoided one another's gaze, and what little conversation passed between them came in stilted bursts.

In the gloom of the day, he strode the corridors; his retinue of officers, counselors, Weapons, courtiers, secretaries, and attendants hastened to keep pace. The clamor as they spoke to him—no, not *to* him, but *at* him—rolled off behind him into dust. How often had he made this walk day after day? It was the same motions over and over.

Petitioners, common folk and nobles alike, awaited him in the throne room. They bowed at his entrance. They'd all want something of him, some advantage, perhaps, justice or absolution. He paused a moment gazing at them bent to him in supplication, some peeking at him with hopeful expressions on their faces.

He climbed the steps of the dais and seated himself on his throne, the queen's chair vacant. Castellan Javien called out the petitioners one at a time, who came before him humbly, or jauntily, or filled with their own smug self-assurance to express what it was they wished of their king.

They do not see me. He might as well be a statue. Even those closest to him did not *see*. To them, he was a symbol, not a simple man of flesh and blood.

The petitions took on a familiar pattern, and he gazed out the tall windows at snow streaking down, the hail of arrows, as his counselors discussed each case among themselves. He rendered judgment as if a sleeper. The throne room could have been frozen in time for all it never changed, the same old walls, the same old pleas and arguments.

After the last petitioner was dismissed, his counselors talked at him until he dismissed them, as well. Silence fell like a pall, and he sat there feeling as if his flesh were turning to marble. He closed his eyes and exhaled.

"Zachary?" Laren's voice came to him through the haze. He looked down to see that she had stayed behind. "You are very pensive today, distant."

He glanced out the windows. No arrows, just flurries whirled past the glass. "What is," he asked, "the point of it all?"

"Zachary?"

"The motions we go through. What is the point of it? One day I'll be no more than a marble effigy for the few who care to remember. What is the point of this life?"

"Oh, Moonling," Laren murmured, "you are in a dark mood."

"I don't know what I am."

"You know what you are," she replied softly.

He stood and stretched his back, and stepped down the dais. "I still don't understand the point of it, the striving, the scheming, the battles, when everything ends anyway."

"I think we need to take a walk."

They walked the central courtyard gardens. The paths had not been shoveled since the morning, and the only other footprints they encountered belonged to squirrels and birds. Chickadees hopped among the branches of trees and shrubs bowed by the weight of snow. The flurries came slowly now, but the temperature was plunging again. The cold did help dissipate the haze Zachary had been mired in, though some leaden aspect of it weighed on him still.

For a long time, neither of them spoke, just ambled along caught in their own reveries, a pair of Weapons trailing some distance behind. Zachary enjoyed the silence. The gardens were a world unto themselves with only the noises of nature around them. They may as well have been miles away from the castle rather than surrounded by it.

"You have always been introspective," Laren said. "In a way, that's a good quality in a king. In another way, it just makes life harder on you."

"My thoughts I can keep for myself as I choose. The rest, everything that I am, I cannot."

"Such as the choice of the person with whom you may marry and spend your life?"

He did not reply. He had not expected to be so affected by Karigan's departure, especially since she was heading off on a mission that should not be as hazardous as entering Blackveil. But she was only so recently returned to them, and the belief that she had been lost in Blackveil was still raw. He used to look out upon his petitioners during her long absence and imagine he saw her face among them, but it was always only a dream.

What if she had stayed in the future with Cade?

He remembered how it had been when she came home, how she pleaded to return to a disastrous future so she could be with Cade, how she was willing to give up her own life in the present to be with him, to probably die with him. He could still hear her shouting, *"Let me go back! I must go back to him!"*

She'd tried to hide her grief, but he'd seen how desolate she looked in unguarded moments when she thought no one was watching. He wished *he* could be the object of her regard. He was thankful to Cade Harlowe for his part in letting her go so she could come home, but also found himself envious of a man who did not exist in this time, and who was probably dead in his own.

And had Karigan stayed in the future or otherwise failed

to return? Zachary would never have known her fate, and the loss and grief would be his.

"I blame myself sometimes," Laren said.

He looked at her in surprise. "For what?"

"For being so eager for you to put the realm before your personal happiness."

"You did not make that decision. I did, and it was the right one. The realm is stronger for it, the eastern provinces now bound more closely to Sacoridia's heart through Coutre. We need that strength to face troubled times."

"There are always troubled times," Laren said, "although I'll admit some are more troubling than others." She reached out and knocked a clump of snow off a low-hanging bough. It sprang up, trailing the fragrance of balsam. "After seeing you today, it occurs to me that a realm is only as happy as its king."

"You do not think I'm happy."

"Sometimes, yes. You try to hide what's inside, it's what you do, and it's a matter of survival for you as a king. But I know you, and you are not happy today. You were wondering what is the point of living."

"Don't you ever wonder those sorts of things?"

"Don't turn this around on me."

Sometimes he forgot how sharp her tongue could be, and he looked away to hide his smile. They meandered along a wayside path, and he could hear the trickle of water: King Jonaeus' Spring, hidden behind snow-covered shrubbery and boulders. It rarely froze.

"Zachary," Laren said in a hushed voice, "you came close to dying from your arrow wound, and you've been close to death in other ways. It is not unusual to explore the nature of life and its end."

"Laren, please, you are lecturing me."

"If I was lecturing, you would truly know it. My Riders certainly do." She subsided for a moment. "Perhaps I am just trying to make myself feel better. It hurts me when you are in pain."

"I am not in pain."

"You know better than to lie to *me*."

He smiled again, this time in chagrin. He'd gotten into enough trouble with her when he was a boy.

"After being as close to death as you were," she continued, "it makes you aware of how fleeting life is, of its futility, especially when you can't attain what makes you happiest."

He felt an angry retort building that she would presume to know how it felt, but then he recalled she spoke from experience, from her own close calls and losses.

"If I ever thought . . ." She shook her head. "If I'd considered your marriage in the way I am doing so now, perhaps we could have found another way. I am sorry for not seeing another way when it counted."

"I don't think any of us saw another way, and even now I certainly don't know what could have been done differently. We can't change the past, so there is no use in agonizing over possibilities that never existed."

The wings of a crow swept overhead. Flurries spiraled along the trailing edges of ebon feathers.

"Still," Laren murmured, "I am guilty of trying to keep you and Karigan apart."

"For good reason."

"You knew?"

"Not at first, but eventually I caught on."

"You aren't angry with me?"

"Not at the moment." He halted, and she stopped and gazed up at him. He placed his hand on her shoulder with its gold captain's knot. "Laren Mapstone, you must have no regrets. You were serving the realm. And look, we have what we wanted—the fidelity of the eastern provinces and heirs on the way. These things please me."

"But your heart is empty."

"Not with you here, my friend."

She looked at him askance. "My ability, remember? Look, I know a king must make sacrifices in service to his realm. A good king will, at any rate, and you are one of the best, but perhaps you are too good in some ways."

"Do you wish for me to become a despot?"

She gave him another look. "Of course not. I just wish there was a way for you to find happiness." The bells in the city rang out two hour. She stiffened. "Damnation."

"What is it?" he asked.

"Time for one of those infernal sword training sessions you are forcing on me. If I'm very late, Gresia will make me run extra laps."

"You had better go then."

"But—"

"It's an order. Dismissed, Captain."

"This conversation isn't over." She bowed and hurried away down the path.

He wondered, as he watched after her, what more there was to say. His life was what it was. Perhaps as the days continued on, they'd be less gray, but as he looked skyward, he was not so sure.

ELETIAN WAYS

"What do you mean we're leaving the road?" Karigan demanded. They'd stopped alongside a field that went off into the woods.

The flurries alighted gently on Enver's shoulders and hair. The pony, Bane, had gone gray with the snow clinging to his shaggy coat.

"There are other ways," Enver said simply, his expression betraying nothing as he looked up at her.

She shifted in her saddle. "I studied the maps. We're going to follow the Kingway to—"

Enver raised his hand in a placating gesture. "There are ways. Eletian paths where the land knows my kind. They require no map."

She pursed her lips. It was not what she planned, and she was leery of trusting to an unmarked, unmapped path, no matter how fine the guide. Estral glanced between the two of them but said nothing.

"You propose going across country? Don't you think that would be rather impossible for the horses?"

"These Eletian ways are perhaps more accommodating to horses than your roads. Your captain has traveled such."

"Hmm."

"We may travel more efficiently if we leave the roads," Enver said.

This from a member of the race that had designed the crazy spiraling roads of Argenthyne. She snorted.

"Perhaps Lady Estral, with her Eletian blood, can see," Enver said.

Estral looked at him in surprise. "See what?"

He held his hand out to her. "Come, and I will show you."

She dismounted and led her horse over to where Enver stood at the edge of the road.

"It is how the light falls." He pointed across the field to the fringe of the woods. "Do not look directly, but with your side vision. See how the light falls upon the land?"

Karigan crossed her arms, watching skeptically as Estral tilted her head and gazed into the distance. Condor stomped a hoof. Enver murmured instructions to Estral while Karigan's toes grew numb as she waited. The minutes passed by, snow mounding on her shoulders. She was about to tell Enver to give up when Estral's sharp intake of breath forestalled her.

"I see it," Estral said. She turned to Karigan, her face alight with wonder. "I see the path he speaks of."

Karigan had to concede that Eletians accessed sources from beyond human ken. They were magical beings, after all, but she was still wary.

"Perhaps," Enver said, "I could show you, too, Galadheon. After all, you are Mirare. If you remove the patch covering your eye—"

"No! I am *not* Mirare, and *never* ask me to uncover my eye again." She remembered all too painfully the last time her eyepatch had been removed in the presence of an Eletian.

Enver bowed. "My pardon. I meant no offense, only to show you the path."

"It's beautiful," Estral said.

"I would not lead you astray." Enver handed Bane's lead rope to Estral and stepped up to Karigan's stirrup. "I will not ask you to bare your special eye, but if you give me your hand and you use your ability, perhaps you will see."

Still skeptical, she glanced around to ensure no one else was on the road with them who would witness her using her ability. They were alone. She held her hand out and Enver clasped it between both of his. The heat of his touch was startling even through her mitten. She almost forgot to fade. When she did so, the already white and gray world turned even grayer, and it was almost as if time slowed the fall of each individual snowflake that flashed white as they tumbled down around her.

"Look, Galadheon," Enver said from somewhere far away. He pointed, seeming to shed a blur of energy from his hand that lanced across the field toward the woods. "Use your side vision, let go your focus."

She turned her head slightly, let her vision relax. The pattern of the falling snow mesmerized her. Snowflakes landed on her eyelashes, feathered her cheeks. She may be faded out, but she was still real and solid. Then she saw a flicker of light—she almost missed it for the flash of individual snowflakes. Then another, and another. She forced herself not to look dead on or focus. Soon there was a stream of tiny blue-white flames that flowed across the field, like the fairy lights in children's tales. All else might be gray in her vision, but this was not. The lights flared and fairly hummed.

And then vanished in a blink.

She dropped her fading and sat there lost in thought until Enver released her hand. She had almost forgotten he'd been holding it. A dull headache pounded in her temple. She glanced at Estral, who had turned ashen. It occurred to her that her friend had never seen her use her ability before.

"You were . . ." Estral began.

"Like a ghost," Karigan finished. She'd heard others describe her thus. In the daylight, she would not have faded out entirely.

Estral nodded vigorously, still pale. "I knew you could do that, but . . ."

"Seeing it is different."

Estral nodded again.

"The way appeared to you," Enver said, "did it not?"

"I saw something," Karigan admitted.

"You saw the way."

Enver was nothing if not persistent. She sighed. It would not be the first time she had followed Eletians without maps.

"You say this path of yours is more efficient and easier on the horses?"

"Yes, Galadheon. We will travel with more speed than using your roads and trails."

"Very well," she said, still with some misgiving, "we'll give it a try."

He nodded solemnly. "Then I must call to my mare so we can all ride." He turned to face the field and spoke in Eltish, using a normal tone. The breeze took the words from him and carried them away.

That was it? Karigan wondered. They sat but for a moment before Condor gave a deep-throated whicker. Estral's gelding, Coda, and Bane the pony both raised their heads and pricked their ears. A horse appeared cantering across the field where she'd seen the path. The jingle of harness came to them as the horse neared. She was silver-white in the gloom, her mane and tail streaming out behind her. She slowed to a trot, then a walk, and then halted before Enver. She was one of the most beautiful horses Karigan had ever seen, fine-limbed, her neck a graceful arc. She made Condor and Coda look plain and rangy. Oddly, she was already tacked. Enver stroked her neck and spoke softly to her in Eltish.

"Is she real?" Estral asked.

"Quite real," Enver replied. "The *terrial ada*, who have befriended the Eletian people, consent to bear us now and then."

"Terrial ada?" Karigan asked. "Is that a breed?"

"No, Galadheon, but a race of horsekind rare to these lands."

A *race* of horsekind? She had a feeling that if she asked Enver to explain further, his answer would prove even more esoteric. She decided to wait and see if the horse passed gold nuggets and moonbeams.

"She is called *Muna'reyes*. It is Moonmist in the common tongue."

The mare nickered and bobbed her head.

"You may call her Mist. She will allow it." With that, Enver mounted in one swift motion.

Mist's bridle bore no bit, and the leather of the reins and saddle was ornamented with twining tree and birch leaf patterns. Enver retrieved the lead rope to Bane, and the pony pranced right up beside Mist, arching his stubby neck as though to impress her. She bobbed her head, her mane wafting softly like threads of silk.

"I shall lead us along the path now. You have but to follow." Enver reined Mist off the road and into the field.

Karigan let Estral follow next, and took up the rear. Condor stepped off the road into the snowy field and proceeded in an energetic walk as if he were as anxious to follow Mist as Bane. As she rode, she was aware of nothing that differentiated the path from the surrounding countryside, except maybe they followed a long furrow between drifts that made it easier for the horses. Soon they entered the woods.

As the day wore on, the farther they got from the castle, the more the sky cleared and the flurries let up. The interlacing of the branches above them further minimized the snowfall. Karigan had to admit that with Enver's guidance, the going was smooth. There was little underbrush to hinder them, no low-hanging branches she had to duck beneath. Windfalls did not block their way, and the snow was not at all deep.

They rode in silence away from the signs of human habitation, encountering only a doe and yearling, chickadees and nuthatches, along the way. This was the Green Cloak Forest they had entered, and the country would get wilder still.

They rode until twilight when Enver halted at a natural clearing. Or, was it? Was it of some magical making as the path they followed? They set to caring for the horses, and she saw that just like any other horse, Mist was untacked, brushed, and blanketed, and that she drank ordinary water and ate grain. And, indeed, her droppings looked pretty normal, too, though Karigan did not inspect them close up. The main difference was that Enver did not halter or hobble Mist. Even so, she did not wander far. Perhaps she'd turn to smoke and drift away in the night, and return only when Enver called her.

They readied their camp, Enver drawing out a muna'riel to illuminate the clearing. They needed no additional light from the lanterns Karigan had brought along. She collected wood while Estral struggled with their tent. Soon, she had a cheery fire blazing, and put a kettle over it to boil water for tea. As they ate a simple meal, the clouds appeared to disperse altogether above the boney branches of the trees. The stars shone eye-piercingly sharp.

"Would you like to try singing?" Enver asked Estral.

"No. I am sorry. I am . . . I am afraid."

Enver bowed his head in acknowledgment.

"Will this path we're on," Karigan asked, "take us directly to the p'ehdrose?"

"No," Enver replied. "There are branching ways, and it may be my people have left none that lead to the p'ehdrose."

"You don't know where they are? How do you know how to find them?"

"Not all worlds share the same space as ours," he replied. "You, Galadheon, would know this better than most."

She began to get an idea of why the Eletians had requested her for this mission. It was not her they wanted so much as her ability to cross thresholds . . .

"Why did no one mention this before we began?"

"Lhean did not say?" Enver asked, looking genuinely surprised. "The habitation of the p'ehdrose will be sensed more than seen."

"Like the path," Estral murmured.

"In a way," Enver replied. "Your king knew as much. He is perceptive, for he comprehends that not all in the world follows the same rules when etherea comes into play. It is most likely, Galadheon, we will not need your ability to find the p'ehdrose."

With the way things usually went, Karigan doubted such would be the case.

"Look," Estral said. She pointed toward the sky.

They all looked up and through the trees where glowing waves of green stretched across the sky.

"The northern lights," Karigan murmured. "It is the first I've seen them this winter." It felt like an omen.

AUREAS SLEE

Slee was frustrated. The way to the Beautiful One and the young she carried was blocked with wards, and not just any wards, but Eletian spells alongside the lesser mortal ones. Slee thrashed at them as a gust of wind, only to be rebuffed. There had to be another way.

Slee backed off, floated down corridors as a barely visible haze. It drifted into chambers and wove among those who dwelled in the castle, its presence nothing more than a chill draft. There was little of interest to be found, and the corridors were endless. Slee slipped back outside and hovered among the low-lying clouds. It dropped snowflakes of perception among the flurries and found two humans strolling in the courtyard gardens.

As Slee's snowflakes alighted on their heads and shoulders and swirled around the pair, it listened to their conversation, for the man was the One of Power. The castle was his, and he ruled all that fell within the boundaries of his realm. The woman who walked with him commanded etherea, but it was negligible.

Slee touched them with snowflakes, learned the workings of their minds. The woman was of little concern except for how she was regarded by her king. While her red hair fascinated Slee, she'd too many years on her, was too scored by old wounds to be of much interest.

The One of Power, the king, however, was the mate of the Beautiful One, and the sire of the unborn. His mind was keen, but in turmoil. He bore the heart of a warrior, but preferred peace. Despite all the man possessed—a realm, an army at his command, and the radiant queen with her young—a gloom lay over him as thick as night. Slee looked deeper, listened to words and thoughts, and formulated a plan that would allow it to have the Beautiful One and her young, and all the king's power.

Yes, Slee would have it all.

THE FINGERS OF A HAND

The fresh air had done Zachary good, and when he returned to the castle, he found his gloom had lifted appreciably. When he sat in on a long meeting of the treasury, he was engaged as his administrators recounted the state of taxes collected and budgets allotted. It was critical that sufficient funds be available to feed, clothe, and arm his military for the conflict to come, though he wished, with regret, those funds could go to building and maintaining roads, and other projects that would help Sacoridia progress into the future. Alas, war was upon them, and it must be confronted. Should the gods grant them victory, then he could turn his attention to improvements to his realm.

Satisfied all was in order, he moved on to other meetings until darkness fell, and then returned to the royal wing to look in on Estora. Jasper and Finder came tearing to greet him before he even reached her sitting room. He laughed and patted them before proceeding. He found Estora in her customary place on the sofa, blanket drawn over her legs. She looked up from her book of poetry when he entered. Her thoughts practically rippled across her face—hope and eagerness balanced by wariness and resignation.

"How are you this evening?" he asked.

"Fine."

He stood awkwardly there for a moment. He would not apologize for speaking sharply to her after she'd made Karigan reveal her mirror eye. As for the rest? He felt guilty he could not devote the whole of his affections to her. She deserved better.

"Will you be dining with me tonight, my lord?" she asked.

Her formality stung. "I cannot. I will be hosting a banquet for my generals."

The disappointment on her face was plain. "Will your ladies not join you?" he asked.

"They are as weary of me as I am of them."

It appeared that the gloom that had so plagued him earlier in the day now plagued her.

"I am sorry," he said, "that I cannot dine with you, but in reparation, would you be amenable to me reading you some poetry after I finish with the generals?"

There was hope alight once more in her face, then tempered as if she did not believe he'd actually return.

"I promise not to be overlong," he said. "I'd rather be here with you than with those gruff old soldiers."

She smiled tentatively. "I'd like it if you would. I've a new volume of Lady Amalya Whitewren."

He bowed in a courtly manner. "It is settled then. I will return as soon as I can." For good measure, he kissed her, and he was rewarded with a smile that was not at all tentative.

He ordered the dogs to stay with her and took the passage to his own rooms. His valet, Horston, greeted him.

"Shall I dress you for supper, sire?"

"Give me a few minutes." Zachary moved to his desk and sat. His queen was lacking amusement, and he thought perhaps there was a way to make her happier during her confinement since he could not be with her every hour. The demands of his rule required him elsewhere so much of the time.

He pulled out his writing implements and penned two letters. The first was addressed to Lady Amalya Whitewren, requesting the poet come entertain the queen with a recitation of her verse, and the second to the dean of the school at Selium, requesting he send minstrels to entertain queen and court. Usually a number of them rotated through Sacor City and the castle, but the severe winter had curtailed their travel. Perhaps, he told the dean, it was time, as in the old days, to post a minstrel at the castle on a permanent basis. Traveling minstrels would still rotate through, but one should be available all the year round to represent Selium and perform as needed.

There had been minstrels in residence at the castle for centuries, except during the reign of Agates Sealender some two hundred years ago. Old Agates had barred them from the castle on pain of death, for the paranoid king believed them to be spies of his enemies. There was some truth to that. Zachary, himself, through Aaron Fiori, used them as his eyes and ears of the realm, though he feared the Golden Guardian may have gotten in too deep this time and that was why he was missing. He hoped Estral's quest to find her father proved successful.

After the Clan Wars, when Zachary's own clan took the crown, minstrels once again served in court until his grandmother, he recalled, in a fit of pique, expelled her court minstrel. He never learned the cause of her outrage, but since then, they'd been without a resident minstrel, and it was time for that to change.

He sat back in his chair considering the benefits. There would be entertainment for his wife, a music tutor for the castle children—not to mention for his own, and again, they'd be the eyes and ears of his court.

Satisfied, he dripped wax on each envelope and pressed it with the royal seal. With the improving weather, there should be no hindrance for Laren to send her Riders out.

"Horston," he said.

The gentleman came forward and bowed. "Yes, Your Majesty?"

"Please give these letters to a runner to take to Captain Mapstone. She is to send them out as she can."

Horston accepted the letters. "Anything else, sire?"

Zachary stood. "I think I'll go for some fresh air before supper. Then I'll dress."

Horston bowed again, and left with the letters. Zachary found his heavy greatcoat, a scarf, and gloves, and exited his rooms.

"Fetch your coat," he told the Weapon Willis, who stood by the door. "I need air."

* * *

The air atop the castle was indeed fresh, fresh and bracing. Arctic currents funneled across the castle rooftop. Guards huddled close to their braziers and stood out of the wind in warming huts. Fine snow whirled around his feet, reminding him, unsettlingly, of the ice creatures that had attacked the castle.

He moved into the lee of a crenel along the battlements to gaze at the stars. They pierced the cloudless sky with chill intensity. He picked out constellations until a green glow emerged, fingering across the sky. The northern lights. He smiled, pleased to glimpse the rare celestial show. The heavens always reminded him of how small a mortal he was, how petty much of the concerns of human beings were, and he made a point of coming out to gaze at the stars to remind him of his place in the universe. It helped that he was entranced by the natural beauty of the night sky.

The northern lights intensified, rolling in waves. A blast of wind howled around him and stole his breath. The leading edge of green reached down with long tendrils. Laren had mentioned that Rider's vision to him about the fingers of a hand reaching down.

"Sire," Willis said uncertainly, "I think—"

Zachary never heard what it was that Willis thought. An icy wind slammed into him with such force that the last thing he saw before everything went black was the northern lights descending on him like a gigantic claw.

Slee sent the One of Power to its domain. Slee had learned enough about him to transform itself and *become* him. The One of Power was called Zachary, and now Slee would assume that role, and become so very close to the Beautiful One. It would serve, for now. Slee feared that moving the Beautiful One to its domain, as it had the Zachary, could endanger the young because of the shock involved. It would wait until the young were birthed. The danger then would be less.

Slee stood tall, sensing its new form from head to toes,

from vision to scent. Above, the lights it had called upon receded.

"Sire," said the one in black, "that wind did not feel natural."

Slee, as the Zachary, smiled. "Let us return indoors then." The vibration of the voice in his throat was an interesting sensation, a little rough, and deep.

The one in black, *Willis*, Slee knew from having absorbed the thoughts and memories from the Zachary, led the way to the door and they entered the castle. That the Weapon did not note that it was Slee in his king's form meant the disguise was well done. As Slee followed the Weapon down stairs and along corridors, it ran its fingers through the bristly hairs along its jawline and chin to familiarize itself with the odd sensation. When they arrived in the area of the royal apartments, Slee's nostrils flared at the scent of *her*. She was close by.

The Weapon halted at a door. "Do you wish to change before you sup with your generals, sire?"

"My generals? What do I want with them? No, I will attend my wife."

The Weapon schooled his surprise. "Yes, sire." He opened the door.

The rooms beyond smelled predominantly of the Zachary, a masculine human scent mixed with the tang of leather and steel. As Slee walked inward, it found the steel and instinctively quailed from it. There was a rack of swords displayed on the wall of varying lengths and ornamentation. Just gazing at the angry gleam of the blades burned Slee's eyes.

Slee stumbled past it and came face-to-face with an older man of noble bearing and graying hair. Slee recognized him, through the Zachary's memories, as the valet.

"Would you like me to dress you for supper now, my lord?"

"No, I am going to go to my wife. But I do not need this." Slee slipped off the heavy coat. It was uncomfortably hot. Other layers came off until Slee was down to shirtsleeves.

"Er," Horston said, "wouldn't you at least like a longcoat to wear in the presence of your lady wife?"

"No," Slee replied. "She has seen me in less."

Horston coughed and looked to be struggling to retain his composure. When he turned away, Slee's keen hearing picked up suppressed laughter. Had Slee said something humorous? It would have to be careful in its interpretation of words and situations through the filter of the memories and thoughts of the Zachary.

Slee looked at its new hands. They were strong, calloused by using the steel weapons. A gold band encircled one finger. It bound the Zachary to the Beautiful One, and now it was Slee's. *She* was Slee's.

It used the Zachary's memories to find the passage that led to his queen's apartments, and met resistance. Resistance that bounced Slee back a couple paces. The wards. Slee must subdue its intrinsic self, to wholly become the Zachary in order to fool the wards.

Slee closed its eyes and breathed deeply, let the essence it had absorbed of the Zachary flow over it. *Him.* Opening *his* eyes once again, he squared his shoulders and strode forward with purpose. There was still resistance, but it gave. He drove his will into it, and the wards fell away, allowed him to pass, for all that they sizzled across his skin.

I am Zachary, I am king. I will not be kept from my wife.

When he emerged into the queen's sitting room, he took in the great hearth, and the sofa where she reclined, studying a book. He took in the glow of her golden hair, her porcelain skin. Her cheeks blossomed with pink health. He noted the graceful hands that held the book. He took halting steps forward until two furry white canines came bounding up to him. Abruptly, they halted, and eager tail wagging turned into low, threatening growls.

The Beautiful One sat up and turned, looking startled.

Slee could freeze the dogs, or with a gesture, slam them into a wall, but the Zachary would never do such a thing. *He* loved the nasty little curs.

"Finder! Jasper!" he snapped.

The growling quieted, but continued on a register too low to be perceived by ordinary human ears, but Slee heard it. The posture of the canines remained rigid, their ears laid back and their fur standing on end.

"Why did they growl at you?" the Beautiful One asked.

"I do not know," he replied. "Come," he told them in a sharp tone of command, and he strode from the sitting room and toward the entrance. He did not expect the dogs to obey, but he sensed they would follow him warily to keep an eye on him. They knew he was not exactly their master, and yet he was. They were confused.

He flung the door open to the corridor and told the Weapons on guard there, "See that these dogs are returned to their kennel and do not return. They were disturbing the queen."

Before they could answer, he shooed the dogs out with a stern command and swung the door shut. The dogs barked on the other side, the sound fading as he returned to the sitting room.

"What was that all about?" the Beautiful One asked.

"I do not know." He feasted his gaze on her. "They will not misbehave again."

"Perhaps," she said, "they were as startled as I am to see you. I thought you were going to dine with your generals."

"I changed my mind. I could not bear to be away from you and the children."

She set her book down and looked confounded. Slee knew there was strain between her and the Zachary, and that the Zachary did not love her as he loved another. Only a great idiot would be so blind to the radiance of the Beautiful One. The Zachary did not deserve her, but he did deserve all that was going to be taken away from him.

HIS COLD EYES

An inconspicuous presence, Mistress Evans had told Anna, was the hallmark of a dutiful servant, especially of one who tended the royal quarters. Anna already knew how servants were disregarded in the castle by more important folk going about their daily business, but there was an art, Mistress Evans had insisted, to making the life of a royal function as if without effort, for instance, bringing the king or queen tea before they'd even voiced the desire, and doing so unmarked.

It was not easy to be quiet and inconspicuous, Anna thought, with her clunky metal ash buckets, but she took Mistress Evans' words to heart as she crept through the servants' entrance into the queen's apartments. The big Weapon with the deep voice, Donal, she thought his name was, had let her in. She'd never get used to the king and queen's black-clad guardians. They unnerved her, but she tried to tell herself that they were *supposed* to be unnerving.

She let herself through another door from the utilitarian servants' passage into the queen's apartments. She passed pantries, and a nursery that was in the process of being renovated, and then the queen's dressing room. She entered the queen's bed chamber to clean the hearth and lay a fire down. As she swept ashes, she reflected how fortunate she was. Who would have ever imagined she would be working in the queen's own bed chamber with its great canopied bed and velvet upholstered furnishings? Queen Estora's dressing table contained brushes and a comb, and tiny crystal bottles that must contain fragrances. There were ornate silver boxes in a line that perhaps contained jewelry. She did not dare look too closely. It would not go well for her if she were caught going through the queen's things. Not that she would, but she was sure that just laying her eyes on them would be enough to get her in enormous trouble.

It was as she had told Sir Karigan earlier, that her new situation was better than the old. Even the servants of the royal wing were easier to get along with, and she thought that had to do with Mistress Evans, who was demanding of those she supervised but fair. It had not been that way with Master Scrum, who yelled at the slightest mishap and who took some amusement in pitting servants one against the other. She smiled to herself remembering the shock on the faces of those who had tormented her when they learned of her new duty station. Yes, everything was an improvement in the royal household, and yet . . .

She began to lay down a fire, for the queen was due to retire soon, and it would not do for her to have a cold room. She struck flint until the kindling caught, and she watched as the fire grew from a solitary flame. She blew on it to encourage it.

She did not wish to be ungrateful for her new position, but a part of her yearned to ride out into the world like Sir Karigan to see new places and people, to experience adventures. Seeing that she could do something different from what she had been doing only fed the fire, so to speak, of her desires. Another part of her, however, quailed in fear at the whole idea of riding off into the world, and she did not think she had the courage to face what the Green Riders faced. She saw their scars and heard some of their stories of dealing with thugs along the road, or braving the terrible weather with no shelter in sight, or facing terrible monsters of Mornhavon the Black's making.

I am not strong enough.

She added a log to the fire, and when that caught, she added a second, and a third. Master Scrum and those she used to work with had called her "Mousie," and she guessed it was apt. With a great sigh, she collected her buckets and tools and departed the queen's bed chamber, and headed for the sitting room.

She paused when she heard the voices of both the king

and queen coming from there. It was intimidating enough to do her duty in the presence of the queen, who was kindly, but the king? Although he had been kind to her the day of the attack of the ice creatures, he terrified her. He was the *king*, the most important person in all of Sacoridia.

Anna took a deep breath. She could not turn around for it was time to tend the queen's fire. She'd a duty to do. She stepped lightly as she walked toward the sitting room, determined to make Mistress Evans proud of how inconspicuous she could be.

As she approached the sofa from behind, she paused. It appeared that both king and queen sat together, she leaning against his chest and giggling. There were times when she was to leave if her presence intruded on the intimacy of the royal couple. This did not appear to be quite that moment, for the queen started reading some verse aloud.

Anna gathered herself, and keeping close to the wall, made her way to the hearth. A furtive glance revealed the queen indeed snugged up against her husband's chest, he with one arm around her, his other hand stroking her hair. He appeared fascinated by it.

Anna set her buckets down and started shoveling the spent ashes. Her shovel dinged against an andiron.

"Who's that?" the king demanded.

Anna froze in panic. Then, taking a deep breath, she turned around and curtsied. "My pardon, Your Majesty."

"Zachary," the queen said, "you remember Anna. She now tends my fire."

Anna dared gaze up. The king had gone rigid and glared at her. After a moment, he relaxed and smiled, and once more made a pillow of himself for his queen.

"Of course, I remember," he said. "Mind, do not build the fire too . . . large."

"Yes, Your Majesty." Anna bobbed and turned back to her work with trembling hands, sweat flowing down her temples, and not just from the heat of the fire. She worked extra carefully to make no sound with her tools, and when she'd cleaned the ashes, she put a log over the coals. Normally she'd place two or three, but the king had told her not to build the fire too big.

He had smiled at her, but the smile had not reached his eyes. His eyes . . . She hadn't remembered them being so cold. As she collected her tools and buckets, she did not even glance at the royal couple. The queen was still reading verse. As for the king, Anna swore she could feel those cold eyes burning into her back as she retreated from the sitting room.

When she reached the sanctuary of the servants' passage, she set everything down and wiped the sweat off her face with her sleeve. She nearly wilted to the floor. With any luck, the king would not be present when she made her next rounds.

She almost leaped out of her skin when she heard the approach of footsteps, but was relieved when she saw it was only the queen's personal maid.

"What is it, child?" Jaid asked. "You look as though you've seen a ghost."

"It's noth-nothing," Anna gulped. She hastily collected her buckets and tools and hurried down the passage.

Slee reminded itself that servants would come and go, and that the Zachary, if he noticed them at all, would not be sharp with them without good reason. Slee must remember who it was it was trying to be, and behave accordingly.

For now, Slee was content, if overwarm with the Beautiful One leaning against it—*him.* Her voice vibrated against his chest as she read the poetry, and he could not keep his fingers out of her hair. It made her giggle, which pleased him more. He touched her cheek and traced her jawline, her neck, but it made her shiver. He must be careful, for though he wore the form of the Zachary, his element was still ice and he did not give off the heat the humans did.

Soon, another servant arrived, this one an adult. Slee searched the Zachary's memories and found a name: *Jaid.*

"My lady," the servant said, "I have turned down your bed. It is the hour Master Mender Vanlynn has prescribed for your retirement."

Slee felt the Beautiful One sag in disappointment. "So soon," she murmured.

Slee thought to protest, but the Zachary's memory was full of dictates from this Vanlynn that had been put in place to help keep mother and young safe. Instead of protesting, he assisted the Beautiful One off the sofa. Though he was intoxicated by her nearness, it was a relief to have her heat removed from him.

"You could come to bed with me," she told him.

It would be glorious to do so, but Slee had something else to take care of, and again drawing on the memories of the Zachary, he said, "Perhaps another night. I have some business to attend to." At her look of disappointment, he added, "Not to worry, my dearest, we will have long days and nights together ahead of us." He kissed her brow.

He watched after her as she followed her maid toward the bed chamber. She glanced over her shoulder at him and smiled. When she disappeared from sight, he returned to the king's rooms. When the valet appeared, he said, "Take the night off, Horston."

Apparently this was not too unusual a request for the servant didn't argue. Instead, he bowed and left Slee alone. Slee went to the king's bed chamber. First he created an illusion of a sleeping person beneath the covers should anyone come seeking the king; then he threw a casement window open and breathed deeply of the wintry air. Yes, he had business to attend to. He turned insubstantial and let the currents of the night wind carry him away.

IN SLEE'S LAIR

Plink.
Plink.
Plink.

Zachary wiped water off his face.

Plink.

Plink.

Was it part of some dream, this dripping?

"Definitely male," said a lovely female voice.

He incorporated her words into the darkness of the dream.

"Oh, we haven't had a boy in so long." Another female voice, but more ordinary.

Plink.

Plink.

He shivered as more drops of icy water splattered on his face. They were much too real to be a dream. Darkness clung to his mind even as consciousness leaked in. He became aware of the hardness of the surface beneath him, the cold air. What happened? He remembered being up on the castle roof stargazing, and then . . . and then being *slammed.* His body hurt all over and he groaned.

"He's waking," the lovely voice said.

"Do you s'pose he's a gift? I mean a new mate? We never got a big boy before. He looks strong."

"Yes, Magged, he looks very strong."

"Where . . . ?" he whispered. He opened his eyes to slits just in time for another drop to thunk on the bridge of his nose. He blinked rapidly, but still he could not see clearly. All was a blur, and light scorched his vision.

"I hope he likes us."

"Hush now, Magged. Let him wake up."

Zachary gazed upward. Suspended over his head was a stalactite, and it was this that was dripping water onto his face. He shivered as he regained his senses, his flesh reacting to the cold air. He was naked. He sat up and someone squawked and jumped back. His mind darkened for a moment, then churned in a vortex of dizziness. He rolled to his side and retched up whatever remained of his midday meal. He sat there panting, and soon he found some equilibrium. The world stopped spinning and the scene around him resolved in his vision, and what he saw made no sense at first.

He was in a huge rounded chamber of a cavern. Stalactites hung from the ceiling high above like gleaming teeth, droplets clinging to their pointed tips. The surface beneath him was smooth and moist. Dripstone—travertine—appeared to coat all the walls and floor like melted wax. Stalagmites grew up from the floor as mirrors of the stalactites above, some meeting in the middle to create grotesque pillars.

A natural glow emanated from the pale stone illuminating the chamber in an eerie wet pearlescence. Adding to the dreamlike quality of it all were the statues and white marble sculptures set about the chamber. Mostly they were of beautiful nudes. One he recognized as in the style of the late Second Age, Sacoridian. Some appeared to have stood in the chamber long enough that they were in turn coated in layers of dripstone, their beautiful forms turned into nightmarish visions.

A chest overflowed with gold and silver, and gem-encrusted jewelry. Large paintings leaned against one of the walls, but they were largely ruined by the damp and covered in mold. At one end of the cavern, dripstone had formed what looked like a frozen waterfall with a throne carved into it. A stone gryphon reclined beside it as though sleeping.

Zachary's gaze finally settled on two women. One had the youthful look and perfect features of an Eletian. The other was human, perhaps a little older than Laren, with long gray hair. Both were pale in the manner of his tomb caretakers, but reedy in a pinched, starved way, and this was not the dry, well-appointed tombs made by the hand of man, but a rugged, naturally formed cave.

The women wore shapeless, undyed woolen shifts, and he remembered his own nakedness as they stared at him, but he figured that since they'd apparently gotten a good look at him already, there was no use in being modest now.

He stood unsteadily, leaning against a natural stone pillar as thick as a small tree. "Where am I?" he demanded of the women. "Who are you?"

The two exchanged glances, and then the Eletian stepped forward, the other woman clinging behind her.

"You are in the domain of the slee," she said in her hushed voice.

Slee, the aureas slee, the ice elemental. It had struck again, but why had it snatched *him* and not Estora? He'd been led to believe that Estora was the one it had wanted. Perhaps the wards had protected her and the aureas slee had taken him in retaliation.

A violent wind gusted into the cavern. The women scurried from the chamber, and he was lifted by icy hands and thrown against the wall. All went dark again. When he blinked his eyes open to light once more, he found he'd slid to the ground and that his head throbbed. To his surprise, Estora stood before him with her hands on her hips, a frosty mist swirling around her. Strangely, she was wearing his trousers and oversized shirt.

He clambered to his feet, leaning against the wall to support himself. "My lady," he said, "how is it that you've come to be here."

In three long strides she stood right before him and appraised him critically up and down. "I thought you'd be pleased to see me."

"Yes, yes, more than you know!"

"Only because you want me to take you home."

He was confused. Could she do this, or was she now a captive of the aureas slee?

She reached out and touched his cheek. Her hand was ice cold. "I do not think it's because you want me."

"That is not—" He yelped when she raked his face with her nails.

He touched his fingertips to his stinging cheek. They came

away bloody. Before he could demand what she meant by her action, she whirled away, and when she turned to face him again, she'd turned into Karigan. His heart skipped a beat. His shirt flowed off her shoulders and draped below her hips. No patch covered her eye. She was as he remembered, but for the coldness of her gaze, and her eyes an otherworldly winter blue. A nightmare this was.

"This is what you want, isn't it?" she asked.

"I don't know what magic this is, but I will not have it."

"No? You think speaking like a king will get you what you want?"

"Whoever or whatever you are," he growled, "you know nothing."

"I know everything about you." She stepped uncomfortably close to him, almost touching. Cold radiated off her.

He swallowed hard. This was not Karigan. This was not Karigan. This was not—

Her hand, as icy as Estora's, wrapped around the back of his neck and violently pulled him into a kiss, a crushing kiss, she pressing against him. He tried to pull away, but she was unnaturally strong. He had dreamed of such a moment, but with Karigan, the real Karigan, with her physical and personal warmth, her sometimes tentative smile, her more gentle touch . . . The cold of contact with this false Karigan seeped through his skin, sending icy daggers of pain into his head.

When she finally released him, he gasped for breath, and found himself nose-to-nose with *himself*. Repulsed, Zachary pressed back against the cavern wall.

His other self laughed in his own voice. "Neither of them are yours. The first is mine. The second? We shall see. You have treated the Beautiful One without the adoration she deserves, but no matter. I will adore her, and your seed, the young she bears, will be mine as well."

Zachary hurtled at his false self, and was easily thrown across the chamber. He crashed into one of the statues. It was solid. He groaned and shook his head, then climbed to his feet once more. He would be bruised, badly so.

"Your realm is now mine," the other said, "and all it contains. You do not deserve it."

It was, Zachary thought, like looking into a skewed mirror. He saw himself and heard his own voice, and yet, it was all wrong.

"You will have none of it," he said.

The other laughed. "You are but mortal and fragile."

A blast of wind hurled Zachary back into the statue and he found himself on the ground again. An inhalation proved painful and he wondered if he'd broken ribs.

"You do not understand," the other said. "You exist at my sufferance, as my slave only. You will die here, sooner or later. Meanwhile, I will enjoy making all that is yours mine."

There was another frigid breeze, and the other was gone. Zachary raised himself to a sitting position, grimacing at the pain in his ribs. So, the aureas slee could change its appearance. The Eletians had not mentioned this fact.

The two women emerged from hiding and approached him tentatively.

"That changeling creature," he said, "that was the aureas slee."

"Yes," the Eletian replied, and the one called Magged nodded behind her. "Slee is our master."

"It is *not* mine."

"Perhaps not, but Slee will see it differently, and accepting that will make it less difficult for you."

He nearly started to argue, but realized the futility of it, and the absurdity, for he still wore nothing but his own skin. He was starting to shiver from cold, and probably shock. The Eletian woman removed her shawl and draped it around his shoulders.

"Thank you," he said.

"Come with us where it is warmer."

Zachary followed behind the two, pressing his hand against his ribs and wincing. Cracked and bruised, he thought, not broken. They led him behind a dripstone curtain formation and down steps carved into stone. The natural glow of the rock became more spotty, more like veins of some mineral in the limestone. Magged shyly glanced over her shoulder at him as they went. Soon they emerged into another large chamber. Little of the glow was in the walls and the air felt dryer. There were almost no formations. Glowing stalagmites that looked like they'd been broken off from elsewhere, however, provided light in strategic places around the chamber. He seized upon the idea of how useful a glowing mineral could be to light homes and streets, how it could be mined and brought to Sacor City, how there could be trade in—

He stopped himself. He had no idea where this cave was located, and if it would even be feasible to get miners and equipment wherever this was. Not to mention he was a captive and needed to find a way to escape before he could even think of bringing miners to the site.

A slab of rock rested in the center of the room and appeared to make a natural table. There were hides and wool blankets in nooks for sleeping that must have been painstakingly chipped out over a long period of time. Rough-hewn chairs provided seating, and someone had fashioned shelves upon which sat fine silver and gold cups and platters, and eating utensils. He ran his fingers across the nearest wall, which was incised with words and drawings.

"This is our house," Magged said proudly. "How do you like it?"

"You live here? In this cave?"

"It is our prison," the Eletian said, "but it is home. Come, we will see what we can find for you to wear."

She led him across the chamber to a chest. It must have once looked magnificent, ornately carved and inlaid with ivory, but the carvings were blurred with mold, the ivory yellowed and cracked, and the hinges rusty. She lifted the lid and inside there was cloth. She started pulling out pieces of clothing—gowns and cloaks, and breeches and shirts, and, most disturbingly, the garb of children and infants.

"Where has this all come from?" he asked.

"Slee brings those it desires here," the Eletian said, "in whatever they are wearing. Eventually the mortals die and leave behind their belongings. We weave some of our own cloth, of course." She plucked at her homespun shift. "Slee will occasionally bring us a komara beast for the wool and meat."

The komara, Zachary knew, roamed the arctic wastes. "Are there others here, besides you and Magged?"

"No. Slee has not collected anyone new since before Magged passed adolescence, a young boy, but he was sickly and did not last long."

He frowned, and cast an eye toward Magged, who held a fancy gown of silk and brocade, at least two centuries out of date, up to her shoulders. Most of the items looked to be from previous eras.

The Eletian found him a linen shirt, yellowed from age, patched and mended, a velvet double-breasted waistcoat that may have once been green but had faded to grayish brown, and loose trousers and a belt that had not moldered too much. Rough woven socks and a sturdy pair of boots rounded out the ensemble.

"Let me look at your ribs," the Eletian said, "before you are all dressed."

He pulled on the trousers, and then let her probe his ribs. He flinched as she pressed.

"Cracked, it would seem," she murmured. "You will be sore for a time, but not much to be done for it. At least they are not broken. We've a hot spring you can soak in down below to ease the pain."

Zachary nodded his thanks and drew the shirt over his head. "What are you called?" he asked. There was great depth and age, he thought, in her stormy blue eyes. He'd seen the ocean that color off the coast of Hillander.

"Nari," she replied. "And should I call you 'Your Majesty'? Slee made you sound a king."

"My name is Zachary." Titles, he thought, were irrelevant here.

"Magged is what she called herself when she came here," Nari said. "I am not certain if that's what her parents called her, for she was but a toddler when Slee brought her."

Zachary glanced at the woman, who was now whirling and dancing with the gown in her arms.

"Slee doted on her at first, but then grew tired of her, as Slee does of all those it collects."

"She was just torn from her family?"

"All of us who have been brought here were."

"I am sorry," he said.

"Were you not taken from your family?" Nari asked.

"I don't—" He was about to say he had no family, but then realized it wasn't true. He had not only Estora, but Laren, too. In a sense, even his Weapons and the servants could be construed as family. He must return to them, especially Estora, for there was no telling what the aureas slee would do to her and his realm. He could not bear the thought of her being brought here to live with their children. And what of Karigan? Would the aureas slee hunt her down to punish him? He could not permit the elemental to harm any of his people, his family.

Nari went to a small pool of water. A rivulet trickled out of a crack in the wall into the pool. She returned with a cloth and a tarnished silver bowl full of water. She dipped the cloth in the water and dabbed at his scored cheek.

"How long have you been here?" he asked, grimacing at the sting.

"I do not know," she replied. "There is no time here, and nothing to gauge it by, except when Slee brings a mortal." She glanced at Magged, who now folded the gown and replaced it in the chest. "It is only through the growth and death of the mortals that I know time."

DEAD ENDS

Nari's words about the passage of time became more profound to Zachary the longer he remained in Slee's lair. There was no way of telling if it were day or night in the cavern. No natural daylight reached them; there was no place from which to view the sky. At least no place, he amended, he had yet found. He guessed a few days to a week had passed, but he could not say for sure. They slept when tired, and ate when hungry.

Not that what was available for them to eat sated their hunger. He learned the women subsisted mainly on a bread-like fungus that grew in certain sections of the cavern, in deeper levels that had no illumination from glowstone. They also ate pale, mute crickets with long legs like spiders. Sometimes, Nari told him, Magged used a fine net to catch the white eyeless fish that swam in the underground stream that flowed in the lowest level of the cavern, but they were small and boney, and had to be consumed raw for there was no wood to burn. Slee occasionally brought them fresh meat, such as the komara from which they spun wool to make clothes and blankets, but it was rare. Slee, apparently, did not think of them much at all.

Zachary wondered how they did not go insane as he looked over the writing inscribed in the walls of the cavern where they resided. He ran his fingers over what looked like the scribblings of children that could have been dim memories of animals and trees and families in the outer world. There was Eletian script, and some that was Old Sacoridian. Rhovan and Hura-deshian, and other writing styles he could not identify, also covered the walls. He found dates and names chipped into the rock from hundreds of years ago.

I want to go home, was one plaintive inscription written in the common tongue, *to be with my husband and children. Please, O Aeryc and Aeryon, help me.*

How many hundreds, how many thousands, had been abducted by the ice elemental? How could it be stopped? Slee was accustomed to taking what it wanted, and Zachary was certain it would not negotiate. He must stop it. But how did one stop the wind or the rain, the sun or the clouds?

He wondered what transpired in Sacor City, what mischief the aureas slee was getting into. Would his people recognize the imposter? Laren surely would. His worry for Estora and their children nearly drove him mad. He also worried about the state of his realm, and preparation for conflict. What if his cousin, Xandis Amberhill, was found? What if he wasn't? In the future time, Karigan had seen that he'd become one with Mornhavon, and had overthrown Sacoridia and led it into a very dark age. Zachary must escape the cave. He must protect Estora and his realm.

He glanced over his shoulder at Magged playing with rocks, piling them so they balanced. When they fell, she started over. He did not know if Magged had been born simple, or if her captivity in this place made her so. Then there was Nari staring trancelike into the pool of water. She had been Slee's captive, he sensed, for centuries. How could she stand it?

No, he would not allow Slee to imprison his wife and children here. Somehow it had to be stopped, and the first step was escape. On impulse, he stalked off to the passage that led into the upper chamber with the throne and all the natural dripstone formations. Magged looked up as he passed by. Nari awoke from her trance.

"Where are you going?" they asked him.

He walked on without answering and only paused once he reached the upper chamber. He'd already searched it and looked through all the art treasures Slee had collected, but he found nothing of use and no exit.

He removed his borrowed cloak and started piling glowstone pebbles into it. Magged helped as if it were a game. When he'd amassed a satisfactory quantity, he gathered up the cloak and hoisted it over his shoulder like a sack, hissing at the pain it caused his ribs. He then looked over the stalactites and found a likely one that was not too large, but produced an ample amount of glow. He broke it off the ceiling with a good hard yank. It was to be his torch.

"I do not understand," Nari said, "what it is you intend to do."

"I am going to find my way out." He strode off then, and headed down past their living chamber, down past the hot spring pools on the lower level. He heard Magged whispering worriedly to Nari as they followed.

"Others have tried this," Nari said, "but a way has never been found."

"Perhaps they missed something."

They soon entered parts of the cave where little or no glowstone shone, his stalactite the main source of light. If others had come this way before him, he saw no evidence.

"Zachary," Nari said sharply. She grabbed his arm before he took his next step.

"What?" he asked in surprise.

"You must take care," she said. "There are pits underfoot."

He lowered his stalactite and saw that he'd almost stepped into a gaping abyss. He swallowed hard. The shaft was deep enough that no light reached the bottom. He did find scrape marks along its lip.

"Thank you," he said finally, a quaver in his voice. "You knew it was here . . . ?"

"It is a grave," Nari explained. "The dead ones must go someplace."

The dead ones, Slee's victims. He had almost joined them. How many were down there? How many children and mothers? Fathers, brothers, and sisters? From how many lands and what peoples? He took a glowing rock from his cloak and set it on the rim of the pit.

"What is that for?" Magged asked.

"It's a marker," he replied, and he stepped around the opening and continued down the passage, careful to watch his footing. Every so often he set a pebble down to mark where they'd been.

Did Magged and Nari follow him out of curiosity? For a change in routine from their dreary existence? Perhaps for companionship?

"Zachary," Nari said, "how do you expect to find a way out?"

"There could be a change of air current," he replied, "and that underwater stream has to come from somewhere and go somewhere."

He poked his "torch" into side passages. Some were just nooks, while others went beyond the glow of his light. Some were so narrow that he'd have to crawl through them, and the thought of it made beads of sweat break out on his brow. He decided to keep on this main passage first, then systematically check the side passages.

The footing was often a fine silt, but there were places where they had to clamber over rocks that clattered beneath their feet. Despite the light he carried, Zachary found the dark of the cave oppressive as it bore down on them. He kept leaving pebbles along their route should he decide to turn from it. He glanced over his shoulder to ensure he could see them.

After what felt like hours, they paused to rest, sitting on boulders. Magged drew in the dirt with her finger and hummed to herself. She seemed completely at ease in this subterranean world. To Zachary, it was an unnatural place for a person to exist, with no sunlight, no contact with the outer world. There was no bird song, no wind in the branches of trees.

"How have you survived here so long?" he asked Nari.

"What is long?" she asked. "For me, Magged's arrival and her growth are but the blinking of an eye. Such as she have come and gone, but I have learned how mortals value time with their short lives running out. When I was taken from the world, it was long before the one called Mornhavon came upon these shores, and your folk were but tribes roaming the lands. I am to understand there has been much change in the world. Slee has deigned to tell me some of it, and those it has brought here have told me more. For me, it does not seem so very long, but yes, I know for mortals it would.

"Magged knows no other life. The cave is her home and always has been, as it has been for other children. They never get to know their families, so they never miss what they have never known."

"I want a family," Magged chirped.

Zachary gazed sadly at her.

"Magged did not know her family," Nari said, "but she understands the concept. I taught her to read the walls, and of course, she asked questions."

"It is wrong," Zachary said vehemently. "This is all wrong, what the aureas slee does."

"It is the nature of elementals to love that which they find beautiful."

"Are you defending it?"

"You misunderstand." Nari's eyes were dark, like midnight over the ocean, but for the glow of his light glimmering in them. "I wish to escape this place, to return to the ones I have left behind. But I am afraid, too. I am of Argenthyne, Zachary, and I have heard of its fall."

"That was a thousand years ago or more," Zachary said softly.

"Yes. I was told there were many who did not escape."

"Queen Laurelyn kept some of the Sleepers of Castle Argenthyne safe in a piece of time, and they were taken to Eletia."

Nari's gaze sharpened. "Truly? You must tell me how this happened."

It was strange recounting what was really Karigan's story, but to see the joy in Nari's face was more than worth it.

"Had you kin among the Sleepers?" he asked.

"I do not know who may have been asleep after the time of my taking. Some may have awakened before Mornhavon, and others fallen asleep. But to know that some of my people are safe in Eletia? It is the most precious piece of news I've heard since Slee brought me here."

"I am glad I could tell you. It would not have been possible without your queen's foresight and . . ."

"Your Karigan," Nari filled in. "I can see she is of some importance to you. Was she not one of the forms Slee took to taunt you?"

"Yes." He looked away.

"She is a remarkable person to do what she did for my people, and I am grateful to her for it."

Zachary knew Karigan was remarkable, had known from the moment they met. But if he were to succeed in escaping the aureas slee, he must not allow thoughts of her to distract him. He stood, ready to go on.

"Zachary," Nari said, "you now understand that I have been here a very long time, yes?"

He nodded.

"I have searched these caves thoroughly, myself. I have had the time to do so. I can tell you this passage ends in rubble, a dead end. All of them do, or they turn round and open into the same passage elsewhere. Even the crawlways. Slee has blocked all the openings so its pets cannot escape."

"I don't want you to leave," Magged suddenly burst out. "I want a family."

Zachary closed his eyes, trembled. He could see that Nari did not lie. He would not let it stop him, though. He could not. He could not give up.

"Your words about Argenthyne and the Sleepers," Nari told him, "have given me hope that I have not known since I became trapped here. I wonder if there is a way that we are not seeing."

"We can only keep looking." He took up his bundle of glowstones and his torch. As they walked on, he considered Nari's words about hope. Perhaps he was wrong to shunt away thoughts of Karigan. Perhaps, thinking of her and her impossible accomplishments was what he needed to escape the lair of the aureas slee.

JUST DESSERT

"Hmm," the innkeeper said, "had someone like that come through here a couple years ago. Wish he'd come back, too. Folks traveled from miles around just to hear him sing."

"Thank you," Estral said.

Karigan could tell she was trying to hide her disappointment. Along their journey, thus far, if they chanced across villages, Karigan and Estral asked at the local inn or tavern if a minstrel of Aaron Fiori's description had been seen there in recent months. Of the few inquiries they'd made, including this one at the sign of the Painted Turtle, they had no luck.

The innkeeper must have sensed Estral's distress, as well, for he invited them to sit for a cup of hot spiced apple cider and a wedge of butter cream pie with, of course, the ulterior motive of hearing the latest news from Sacor City. It was worth it, Karigan thought, and Enver was missing out. He had insisted upon waiting for them out in the woods. He must be communing with the trees, or whatever it was that Eletians did.

The village was off the beaten track and rarely received current news. It turned out that word of the queen's pregnancy had reached the village, but not that she was expecting twins. The village of Red Rock wasn't much. It boasted the inn, a chapel of the moon, and little else. The residents were far-flung, scratching crops out of rocky patches in the Green Cloak in the warm months, and doing small-scale lumbering in winter. Some harvested cranberries from nearby bogs.

"Now, that is something," the innkeeper said, and he

sipped from his own mug of cider. Custom was nonexistent at this hour, so he could give Karigan and Estral his full attention. Karigan could tell he was hankering to spread the news. "Never thought the king would get around to taking a wife, and when he finally does?" He chuckled. "Making up for lost time."

Karigan had become somewhat used to the speculation and comments about the intimate lives of the king and queen, some of which could be rather coarse. She'd learned to face it all with a forced smile, and tried not to think too deeply about it.

Estral remained silent as she picked at her pie. If she wouldn't eat it, Karigan would.

"Haven't seen a Green Rider out this way in years," the innkeeper said. "Which way you heading?"

"North," Karigan replied.

"Town of North?"

"No." At least Karigan hoped not. It wasn't the friendliest of towns for Green Riders.

"Maybe we should," Estral murmured. "Someone may have heard something there."

"I ask," the innkeeper said, "because folk traveling north of here have had run-ins with groundmites. Winter's been hard on 'em and they've been bold. Getting bolder every year, it seems. You should tell the king next time you see him."

"I will." Karigan frowned. He was right. The groundmites were getting bold—desperate—if they were traveling this far into Sacoridia's borders. Encountering a band of the beasts was something she would rather avoid.

When the innkeeper left them to attend to some chores, Karigan turned to Estral and pointed at her pie. "You should really eat that. It will give you energy against the cold."

Estral sighed and pushed the plate toward Karigan. "You have it."

Karigan did not argue. At least Estral drank her cider. "You know, just because the innkeeper hasn't seen your father doesn't mean anything. We don't even know for sure he's gone north."

"I know. It just seems so hopeless."

It was not that long ago that Estral had been the one with hope. Perhaps the fatigue of traveling in the cold had gotten to her.

"We will keep looking," Karigan said. "He'll turn up."

Estral nodded. "Thank you for helping with this. I don't think I could do it on my own."

"You," Karigan said, gazing at the last bite of pie on her fork, "are capable of a great deal more than you think." She was rewarded by a brief smile from Estral.

As they left, the innkeeper's wife, overjoyed by the news of royal twins forthcoming, gave them a gift of a dozen cranberry nut muffins still warm from the oven. Estral swiped the sack of muffins from Karigan's grasp.

"I won't eat them all," Karigan protested.

"I want to make sure there are some left for Enver," Estral replied.

They left the inn and mounted up, riding down the road a fair piece before turning off into the woods where Enver awaited them. If it weren't so early in the day with hours of daylight left in which to travel, Karigan and Estral might have chosen to spend the night at the inn, but it appeared they'd be sleeping beneath the stars again.

Bane, the pack pony, nickered in greeting as they approached. Enver stood beside him while Mist ranged nearby.

"We have brought cranberry nut muffins, courtesy of the innkeeper's wife," Estral announced.

Enver looked intrigued. When Estral produced one and handed it to him, he looked it over and sniffed it like a connoisseur. After a nibble, his eyebrows shot up. "Ah, it is good. Sweet and tart." Then he gazed at Estral. "There was no sign of Lord Fiori?"

She shook her head, and Karigan said, "It sounds as if he came this way a couple years ago, but nothing more recently."

"That is unfortunate." Enver had neatly finished his muffin and mounted Mist. "Shall we continue, then?"

Enver led on, Bane right alongside him, followed by Estral. Karigan took the rear. The brightness of the sky, the weak warmth of the sun, dispelled concern about groundmites and she simply enjoyed the woods, the fragrance of spruce and fir, the damp of melting snow. Nuthatches crept up and down the trunks of pines, and chickadees called out. Being immersed in the Green Cloak settled her in a way that being stuck in Sacor City could not. She left behind a certain darkness in the castle, shadows that dissipated beneath the open sky. She did not forget Cade; she could not, especially with the reopening of that part of her still so raw, but in the woods she could feel some peace. She wished he could be there with her and see his world before it became the hard brick cities of the future, before the Green Cloak turned into a forgotten memory. Wishing for it brought sorrow, but it did not break her down or drown her in grief as it might have mere weeks ago.

Condor liked the journey, as well, walking on with eager steps as they went. It helped that Enver followed his Eletian path where the footing was even and easy.

As the day wore on and hot spiced cider and butter cream pie became distant memories, and the white, gray, and green of the winter woods took on a sameness, Karigan fell into a sort of trance watching the hind end of Coda with his tail swishing back and forth in hypnotic fashion. The flutter of crow wings among the branches became indistinct whispers, constant murmurings.

Or, was it the sound of the stream they followed? But when their path diverted from the stream, the susurrations only increased in volume and breaths of wind came at her from odd angles. At times she felt as if insects were crawling over her skin, which was unlikely this time of year, but she still tried to brush them off.

Enver suddenly halted and Karigan reined Condor around Coda to him. "What is it?"

"Cairns of the dead," he said, pointing to some snow-covered mounds ahead. Leafless trees and brush grew out of them, and Karigan might not have even seen them if Enver had not called attention to them.

"Makes sense," Estral said. "There were some large battles of the Clan Wars out this way."

"They lie across our path," Enver said. "We must go around."

Now that the mounds had been pointed out, Karigan saw there were many. Too many. Who lay forgotten beneath the cairns?

I do, I do, I do . . . ghostly voices whispered to her.

She shuddered and hastened to follow Enver and Estral. Once they picked their way around and were again on the path, she felt compelled to pause and look back. All was still.

Until it was not. Her senses filled with the clash of arms, shouting, the blowing of horns, the beating of drums, the shrill screams of dying men and horses, the stench of viscera. Pennants streamed in the wind, blood soaked into the earth. A thousand voices filled her mind and she swayed in her saddle. A spectral wind gusted over her bringing the voices in a deafening surge into her mind, and she thought she'd lose herself in the cacophony. Lose herself and become one of them.

A mist clouded her sight. *You have the command of them,* came the memory of Lhean as he spoke to her back in the castle.

Taken over by a force she could not explain, she sat tall in her saddle, and commanded, *"Sleep."*

The clamor quieted, but did not silence. The voice of command welled up inside her once again, as if from the depths of the heavens. "You have earned your rest. *Sleep.*"

Then she found herself just sitting there, staring back the way they had come, the cairns all around her in the woods quiet, at peace.

"Galadheon?"

She jumped a little in her saddle. It was as if she had napped and dreamed of ghosts, but she suspected it had not been a dream at all, not the way her life tended to go.

"Do you wish to linger?" Enver asked with more curiosity than the question warranted. "Or, would you rather go on?"

"Let's go on."

Estral awaited them some distance through the woods. Apparently Karigan had been caught in her reverie, or whatever it was, for quite some time before they realized she was not with them.

"Everything all right?" Estral asked her.

"It will be if you give me one of those muffins."

Estral gazed askance at her, but dug into one of her saddlebags and produced a muffin for her. They rode on, Karigan nibbling at her muffin and thinking that yes, things were all right. As all right as they ever got for her.

That night, as they sat in camp, Karigan observed Estral writing in her journal, using the light of Enver's muna'riel to see by. She wondered just what Estral found to write about. Enver, meanwhile, was wandering out in the woods as was his custom.

For her part, Karigan engrossed herself in oiling her swords and longknife. Two swords still felt excessive to her when she was so used to just one, but she had to admit she liked having them both. By the time she was done and had sheathed them, she noticed that Estral had closed her journal and was staring into the fire. Enver emerged from the woods and into their campsite, his expression serene.

"Little cousin," he said, "would you like to try singing tonight?"

"No, I don't think so," Estral replied.

Enver nodded in acceptance. The silver light of the muna'riel cast him into a being of ethereal beauty, not uncommon for Eletians, but he had always seemed more earthly to Karigan, of a simpler, more common nature. He'd been inquisitive about his surroundings in the castle, but out in the woods he was more in his element, quieter, mysterious. Who was this Eletian in whom they'd placed so much trust? They had time to find out, Karigan supposed.

Remembering the box Captain Mapstone had given her, she asked, "Anyone want a Dragon Dropping?"

Enver turned toward her, looking concerned. "Galadheon, those should be saved for dire need."

Estral, who had apparently never witnessed an Eletian in the presence of chocolate before, looked surprised.

"Chocolate," Karigan said, "may have some restorative effect on Eletians, but for the rest of us, it's just dessert."

"Perhaps," Enver replied, "but I still think it may be wise to save it until there is dire need."

Leave it to an Eletian, Karigan thought, to turn eating chocolate into so grave an affair.

ELI CREEK STATION

The next day brought much of the same, the gray-green woods, the quiet, until the clouds thickened and sent down, first, rain, then sharp sleet. The sleet scratched at Karigan's hood, and she was thankful for the flaps of her new greatcoat that kept her legs dry. Clumps of wet snow dropped on them from boughs above. It made Coda and Bane uneasy, but Condor was resigned, his head hung low. Even Mist shook her mane as though disgruntled.

When the sleet turned back to rain, a fog rose up from the ground, billowing among the tree trunks. Enver's mare, Mist, so aptly named, faded into the vapor, Enver only slightly more visible. Even Estral, just ahead, grew indistinct behind the layers of gauzy veils of fog that fell between them.

At what Karigan guessed to be midday, they huddled beneath the shielding boughs of a white pine to rest the horses and eat dried rations.

"I knew there was a reason why I didn't like travel," Estral grumbled.

She looked miserable with a runny nose and damp tendrils of hair sticking to her cheeks. Karigan didn't imagine she looked much better. Enver, in contrast, was unperturbed and undisheveled.

"When I find my father," Estral continued, "I am returning to Selium and never leaving again."

Karigan wondered what Alton would think of that plan. She was about to ask when a chilling howl rose up somewhere nearby in the woods. It was answered by another from a different location. There was a third distinct howl from somewhere behind them.

"Wolves?" Estral asked.

"Groundmites," Karigan replied. Immediately she unbuckled her swordbelt with the saber and longknife and thrust it into Estral's hands.

"What—?"

"Put it on," Karigan said. "You told me you were doing some arms training. You may need a sword."

Estral looked terrified. She'd probably never even seen a groundmite before. "What about you?"

"I have my longsword and the bonewood."

"We must hasten," Enver said, and Mist came right to him, though Bane stamped nervously.

"Put it on," Karigan ordered Estral, and went to Condor to tighten his girth and mount. She'd the longsword strapped to her saddle. The bonewood was harnessed across her back.

Estral had difficulty mounting her skittish horse with a sword girded at her side, so Karigan sidled Condor along Coda so he wouldn't swing away. When finally she was up, Enver led them out, with arrow nocked to bow string, guiding Mist with only cues from his legs.

When the horses were once again warmed up, Enver increased their pace to a trot, hooves churning and splashing through slushy snow. Karigan pushed her hood off despite the sting of icy rain, so her hearing and the peripheral vision of her one good eye were not hampered. Periodically the yowling wailed through the woods, sometimes farther away, sometimes closer at hand, but always around them. They were being stalked.

Karigan clenched her teeth as ice water runneled off her hair and down her neck. She rubbed her eye clear and darted glances into the woods. Sometimes she thought she saw movement, but it could have been just the fog undulating among the branches and trunks and underbrush.

A cry came very close from her right side, and suddenly they were racing ahead in a full-on dash. Karigan and Condor were pelted by clods of snow from Coda's hooves ahead. She shielded her face, peering around her hand to make sure Estral was all right. Enver and Mist were dragging poor Bane along, his burdens bouncing on his back. They could not keep up this pace for long. The Eletian path might be easier than others, but the weather had made it slick, and the horses labored to keep upright.

It was not long before Enver pulled up and turned to speak to them. Karigan reined Condor alongside Coda. Estral's cheeks were red and her eyes wide. Her knuckles were white from clenching Coda's reins. Steam rose from all the horses.

"We may have to make a stand," Enver said.

As if to punctuate his statement, more howls chorused through the woods, carried eerily to them by the damp air. Estral visibly trembled, the color draining from her face.

"We need to choose the place," Karigan replied.

"It may be," Enver said, glancing over his shoulder, "there is a place. Maybe even a refuge. It is made conspicuous by its desire not to be noticed."

"A place made *what*?"

"We will try to reach it before we exhaust the horses," he said. He unclipped Bane's lead rope.

"What are you doing?" Karigan demanded.

"Mist will tell Bane what to do," Enver said. "Our hands will be too busy to—"

A projectile whizzed past Karigan's face and smashed into a nearby tree, followed by a second that skimmed over her head. In a motion almost faster than she could follow, Enver answered with a pair of his own arrows. An inhuman scream pierced the woods.

And then they were off again at a gallop. Poor Bane lagged with his short legs and heavy packs, but he followed. More arrows fell about them. One stuck in Karigan's message satchel. They careened through the trees, and suddenly Coda's feet flew out from beneath him, and he and Estral went down.

Damnation. Karigan hauled Condor to a halt and threw herself off his back. Coda staggered to his feet, but Estral sat dazed in the snow shaking her head. Mist turned on her haunches, and Enver loosed arrows into the woods.

Karigan knelt beside Estral. "Are you hurt?"

"I'm alive. Fell clear."

"Good. You need to—"

Hulking figures rushed out of the fog. Karigan's hand went to her hip before she remembered Estral had her saber and that her longsword was strapped to her saddle. She reached Condor's side and drew it just in time to block a blow from a rusty broadsword. Several groundmites circled them. They were almost human in shape, but were covered in patchy fur and possessed mobile, catlike ears. The groundmites looked emaciated beneath their rags and pelts. Hunger made them ferocious.

Karigan dispatched the first, and Condor kicked a second in the gut. She heard Enver clashing with another. She fought to keep herself between the groundmites and Estral.

One swung a stout branch at her. She ducked and slid her sword between its ribs. Another swiped at her with its claws and nothing else. She danced around it, slipping in the snow.

"Karigan!" Estral cried.

Karigan was grabbed around the chest from behind and lifted off her feet. She kicked out at a groundmite in front of her, and it stumbled backward. Fetid breath gusted wetly past her ear from the one that held her; then it screamed and dropped her. Karigan whirled to see Estral on her knees, longknife in her hand dripping blood. The groundmite hopped on one foot and mewled piteously. Karigan dispatched it with a quick thrust and spun in time to kill another.

Then she stopped, glanced around, breathing hard. Enver severed the head off a groundmite and there was silence.

"Quickly," Enver said, "there are more out there. Mount up. We must ride fast before they gather their courage."

Karigan caught Coda's reins. The horse was panicked and she had no idea why he hadn't run off. He half-reared and pulled away until Mist whinnied sharply. He then stood still, trembling, and tolerated Estral to mount.

By the time Karigan had her foot in the stirrup to swing up on Condor, more ululating howls and yips ripped through the woods. When she was in the saddle, they launched into another run, arrows flying after them. More groundmites leaped out of the woods at them, and Karigan and Enver cut them down. Condor trampled another. Poor Bane, once again lagging, kicked at one that grasped at him.

Enver turned in his saddle, arrow nocked and aimed. For a moment, Karigan thought he meant to impale her, but his arrow sailed a whisker's breadth past her shoulder and took out a groundmite that had appeared behind her.

The nightmarish scramble continued, Karigan not knowing how much the damp on her face was from rain and sleet or sweat. Enver suddenly reined Mist sharply from the course they'd been on, onto tougher terrain. Karigan hacked at another groundmite that jumped in front of Condor.

They drove through a thicket of close-growing spruce and fir, the horses plowing through the sharp-needled boughs until they emerged into a clearing. A tingling sensation flowed over Karigan, and she sat up in surprise. Enver pulled Mist to a halt.

"We have made it," he said.

Poor Bane came crashing through the woods up beside them moments later, his sides heaving.

The howling of the remaining groundmites still filled the woods.

"Made it where?" Estral asked. "They are still all around us."

"They will not bother us," Karigan said, smiling. She pointed across the clearing to where a dilapidated cabin stood with an adjoining paddock. Enver had found a Rider waystation.

When Estral dismounted, she fell to the ground and sat there looking dazed.

"Estral!" Karigan swung off Condor and went to her friend. "Are you hurt?"

"No. I don't think so."

She was trembling hard, though, and her eyes shone with tears. It was the shock of battle, Karigan thought. Estral was pretty tough, but she'd never faced battling groundmites before and running for her life. Karigan helped her up and led her toward the cabin. The top step was clear of snow and dry beneath the overhanging roof.

"Sit here and rest," Karigan told her. "Enver and I will take care of the horses."

"So this is what you do," Estral mused through chattering teeth. "Gallop through the woods being chased by groundmites . . ."

"Er, sometimes."

"What is this place?"

"Old Rider waystation, a decommissioned one. If I'm not mistaken, this is Eli Creek Station."

Rider waystations had been built along routes where there were no other accommodations, no villages or towns, in which Riders could overnight. As the numbers in the messenger service dwindled, and populations disappeared or were built up along different routes, several waystations were decommissioned, closed up, and no longer supplied, but the buildings remained.

"How are we safe from the groundmites here?"

"The station is warded." Just as the buildings remained, so did the magical wards set long ago by her predecessors who had possessed the ability, as Merla now did. "They will not find us."

Estral appeared to sag in relief.

"I've got to help with the horses," Karigan said.

"Wait." Estral produced the longknife, pinching the hilt between two fingers as if she held a dead mouse by the tail. The tip was stained with blood. She handed it to Karigan. "I felt it . . . I felt it scrape bone when I stabbed that groundmite's foot."

"You probably saved my life," Karigan said quietly.

"I—I don't know. You do pretty well by yourself. I've never seen what you could do before."

"Don't downplay what you did," Karigan replied. "You got that 'mite to let me go."

Estral unbuckled the swordbelt and handed that to Karigan, as well. "I'll leave the fighting to you. You leave the writing about it to me."

Karigan smiled and started to turn away.

"Karigan," Estral said.

"Yes?"

"Those groundmites, they were just hungry."

Karigan nodded, and went to help with the horses. Yes, the groundmites had attacked out of hunger. In a way, she could not blame them, but even if they were well-fed, she would not wish to stumble across a band of them, for they were more inclined to attack than let an innocent traveler go by. They may have once been peaceable creatures, but their natures had been perverted by Mornhavon the Black just like everything else he touched. No doubt the centuries of being hunted down by her people hadn't endeared humans to them, either.

She tried not to feel too sorry for them. Those of the band that had survived the clash would probably sleep content with full bellies. They would likely consume their dead comrades, whether they be friends or relations, a fate Karigan, Estral, and Enver had barely escaped.

THE SONG OF HADWYR AND NARIVANINE

By the time Karigan returned to the paddock to help Enver with the horses, she found he had already untacked them, and that Mist was nudging them around the clearing at a walk to cool them down after their arduous run. With no humans leading them, it was an unusual sight.

"When they have been walked out," Enver said, "I will check them for injuries. Bane has some claw marks on his rump, but I see no other obvious wounds."

Karigan followed the horses with her gaze. "We were lucky."

"It is not always luck, or even skill, that leads to good fortune," he said.

"Then what? The gods? Fate?"

"There are many forces at work in the world."

Eletians, she thought in both exasperation and amusement. She'd enough "forces" in her world to contend with and didn't need more.

"Perhaps, Galadheon," he said, "you can prepare the cabin. I will continue to look after the horses."

She found the door to the cabin wide open. With the wards in place, there was little reason to lock the doors of waystations. She climbed up the steps and found Estral just inside, staring into the gloom.

"The place could use some work," Estral muttered.

Karigan peered over her shoulder into the musty, dark interior. Water dripped into a puddle on the floor from a hole in the roof. The rest looked coated in years of dust and cobwebs.

"Let's open the shutters and see if we can't get some more light in here."

When they did so, it helped only a little, for the weather was gray and they were shaded by the woods, besides. The lanterns they'd brought, or Enver's moonstone, would light the interior well, but she wasn't sure she wanted to see it in too much detail.

She began to poke around, first righting an overturned chair next to a small table, and then finding a few mouse nests in corners. Unfortunately, the waystation's wards did not repel rodents. She backed away from an inhabited spider web and, with some trepidation, opened a cabinet. The scent of cedar wafted out. In an active station, it would have been stocked with spare uniform parts and bedding. It appeared to be empty.

She discovered a mouse-nibbled broom leaning against the wall and used it to dislodge soot, and what might have been years of bird and squirrel nests, from the chimney. She turned away coughing and sneezing at the dust.

Estral laughed at her.

"What? What's so funny?"

"The brave Green Rider, knight of the realm, swordmaster and honorary Weapon, and now chimney sweep . . ."

Karigan looked down at herself and realized she was coated in soot and ash. She tried to pat it off. "My job requires many skills, you know." Anna, she thought, would find her woefully inadequate for hearth duty.

Estral just laughed harder, and Karigan left her to it to continue her investigation of the cabin. She found kindling tucked in a niche beside the fireplace and piled it on the hearthstone. Then she retrieved her flint and steel from one of her bags and sparked a fire.

Once Estral took up the broom and started to raise dust with it, Karigan retreated outdoors to find more wood. The horses, it appeared, had settled nicely into the paddock, and Enver was rubbing down Coda. The wood box beside the paddock contained a cache of split firewood, but it was old and would burn fast, so she decided to search the forest for more.

She was careful not to stray beyond the wards, and found Eli Creek rushing along nearby, its banks brimming with rain and snowmelt, glassy water smoothing over rocks. As she looked for deadfall on top of the snow, she thought about the decommissioned waystations and how, like most other Riders, she had scrutinized old maps to see where they were located in the event she required safe haven. The abandoned stations might be away from the usual routes, but one never knew when they might come in handy, just as Eli Creek Station had this day for her and her companions.

As she continued to gather wood, she found remnants of the old Eli Creek Trail. It looked long forgotten, overgrown, and blocked by fallen trees. At one time there'd been a whole network of trails and rough roads through this part of the Green Cloak, but no more.

By the time she returned to the cabin with an armload of wood, she found Estral and Enver sitting inside in the golden glow of lantern light. She noticed that water was no longer dripping through the roof.

Estral followed her gaze. "Enver found one of the shingles in the paddock and wedged it in place up there. If the wind doesn't blow it away, we should stay dry."

Karigan was pleased. She dumped the wood on the hearth and placed a pot of water over the fire for tea. Estral, who sat at the table, removed her journal, pen, and ink from an oilskin satchel and prepared to work.

Enver was seated cross-legged on the floor, quiet, his eyes closed as if he were in a meditative state. Karigan sat before the hearth and drew her knees to her chest, and gazed into the fire trying to absorb its heat. After a long day out in the damp cold, and then battling the groundmites, the dance of flames and warmth eased the tension of her muscles and made her drowsy. In time, she started to nod off and imagined, or dreamed, there were others there with them, filmy figures in faded green moving about the cabin, standing by the hearth, sitting at the table next to Estral, peering out the window. Ghosts or a dream, or some legacy of memory, she did not know. One walked right through her, and the chill of its passage sent a shiver rattling through her body.

"How did you get chosen for this journey?" she heard Estral ask Enver, as though from a distance.

The answer seemed to take a long time to come. "I was chosen by my prince to be *tessari*."

"What is tessari?"

"A witness."

There was a pause before Estral asked, "What is it that you are supposed to be witnessing?"

Karigan must have drifted off for she heard no reply. She attempted to pull out of her drowse, but it was like trying to claw her way out of a deep, black grave. When she finally managed to shudder awake, Estral was pouring hot water into a mug. Enver was gone, and the windows had darkened.

She stretched and asked, "What is the answer?"

Estral glanced at her in surprise. "Answer to what?"

"What is Enver supposed to witness?"

"Oh, that? That conversation was ages ago. I thought you were asleep."

"I was dozing in and out, I think. So, what is the answer?"

Estral smiled and handed Karigan the mug. A glance and a sniff revealed it contained tea. "He wouldn't explain, said it was an Eletian matter, if you must know."

Karigan sighed at Eletians and their impenetrable ways. She would ask Enver herself sometime later. Estral returned to her writing, and Karigan relaxed with her tea. By the time she took her last sip, Enver returned looking unperturbed by the wet snow that had accumulated on his shoulders.

"The horses are well," he said. He removed his cloak and hung it on a peg by the door. "The groundmites have left the area and taken their dead with them."

"You went looking for them?" Karigan said.

"They took their dead?" Estral asked at the same time.

"To eat them," Karigan told her dismissively. Estral's eyes widened and she scribbled something in her journal.

Enver looked from one to the other. "Yes. You call it scouting? I scouted."

Karigan did not think *she'd* ever go looking for groundmites unless she was ordered to, but it was a relief to know they were gone.

They ate warm stew that night, and after, with all three sitting on the floor, Karigan passed around Dragon Droppings. She told Enver that they each deserved one after their encounter with the groundmites. He did not argue.

He did ask, "Is it customary for your folk, when biding by a fire, to tell stories?"

"Sometimes," Karigan said. "And sometimes there is singing."

"Would you tell me a tale of your people?" he asked.

"I am not very good at stories, but Estral is." She turned to her friend. "Would you mind?"

Estral looked like she might refuse as she had the singing on previous evenings, but she licked her lips and, after a moment's hesitation, said, "All right. I'll give it a try, though I'm rusty."

She began the tale of Bovian's Seven Secrets, the story of a poor farm boy—it was always a poor farm boy in these sorts of stories—who had to destroy a curse on his village cast by the evil mage, Bovian, by untangling the Seven Secrets. At first Estral was hesitant in the telling, but gradually her voice grew more assured, more powerful, the parts with dialog animated with distinct voices for each of the characters. While Karigan clearly heard Estral speaking, she detected an undertone of Idris.

Enver looked delighted as Estral told how the clever farm boy discovered each of Bovian's secrets, saved his village from the curse, and was rewarded with riches, a fair maiden, and a kingdom. It was more the way the story was told than the story itself that drew one in, and Estral told it masterfully.

When she finished, Enver said, "Ah, that is very well done, and different from the tales told by my people."

"How so?" Estral asked.

"Eletian stories are often in verse, or sung, and of real people and deeds."

"We have many like that, too. Would you tell us one of yours?"

Enver bent his head in thought, then looked up. "There is the song of Hadwyr and Narivanine, and of when the world was new. I have not the skill to translate the verse, but it is the story of their love."

Karigan found she did not have to understand the words to understand the story. The power and texture of Enver's voice carried all the emotion, the yearning of two lovers, the intensity of desire, and the joy of their bonding. She was lifted by the soaring melody until a dissonance pulled her back. The tone turned dark and desperate. Her anxiety built with Enver's increasingly sharp tempo, her breath ragged as the anguish in his voice sawed right into her chest.

"Narivanine, Narivanine," he sang, and Karigan knew it was Hadwyr crying out for his lover, and she gasped with the pain of it. Narivanine was . . . lost. Sorrow washed over Karigan, the sort of which was raw, too close. She wanted to scream, but she ran out into the snow instead.

She pressed her back against the cabin trying to control her breathing, to hold back the sobs, her hands clenched at her sides. She pivoted and pounded the log wall as hard as she could, exulting in the pain.

WITNESS

Suddenly, Estral was there, grabbing her wrist and encircling her in an embrace that trapped her arms to her sides. She sobbed into Estral's shoulder, and Estral made soothing sounds and rubbed her back. Soon the sobs came to a shuddering halt, and Karigan drew away, wiping her tears with the back of her hand.

"Think you'll be all right?" Estral asked.

"Sometimes . . . sometimes it just comes out of nowhere," Karigan replied.

"Oh, it came from *somewhere*," Estral said acerbically. Lantern light shone from the cabin's interior to the outside through the dusty window, and fell upon her hair, which was collecting snowflakes. "If you're ready, let's go back inside. It's freezing out here."

Karigan nodded and followed her into the cabin. Enver was pacing and he drew to a halt when she entered.

"Galadheon," he said, worry wrinkled across his forehead, "forgive me. I meant no harm. The song of Hadwyr and Narivanine is well known among my people and often sung, and I reached for it naturally."

"Did he ever find her?" she asked.

Enver stared blankly at her.

"Hadwyr. Did he ever find Narivanine?"

Enver shook his head. "No, he did not."

Drained of emotion and energy, Karigan went to her bedroll and sank to the floor. She stared at her hand and flexed her fingers, the pain an echo of that which was always within her.

Enver knelt beside her and took her hand, gently unfolding her fingers. "Not broken, at least. I have evaleoren salve, which should soothe the pain."

"It doesn't hurt."

"Karigan Helgadorf G'ladheon," Estral said, standing above her with her arms crossed. "Now don't give me that look. We're not stupid. Let Enver slather his salve on it. He'll feel better, your hand will feel better, which will make me feel better. Plus, I won't have to worry about whether or not you can use a sword next time we are attacked by groundmites."

"I have two hands," Karigan reminded her.

"What if something happens to the other? Then where will we be?"

Karigan didn't have an argument for that, so she allowed Enver to apply the salve. Evaleoren was aromatic, so even as it warmed and soothed the pain in her hand, the scent relaxed her, calmed the turbulence that had sent her pounding on the cabin wall.

Enver seemed to know just how to massage the muscles of her fingers and hand, how much pressure to apply, and where.

"You heard about Helgadorf?" she asked Estral. She had never shared her middle name with even her best friend.

There was a hint of a smile on her friend's lips. "I have my sources."

Mara? Maybe her aunts? Oh gods, had Estral talked with her aunts? What other embarrassing things might they have told her?

Enver paused his massage to examine the back of her wrist. "This is a recent wound," he said, indicating where Brienne had slashed her during her swordmaster "test." It was pink, turning into a scar as had been intended.

"It is the mark of a swordmaster," Karigan said, and not without some rancor.

"The ways of your people are strange to me."

"Sometimes they are to me, too."

Enver smiled slightly and released her hand. "I will leave the evaleoren salve out in case you have need of it in the night."

Karigan nodded her thanks, and she and Estral began readying their bedrolls to sleep. Enver went outside to, as he told them, take in the air.

Estral sat cross-legged on her blankets. "Are you going to be all right?"

"Sometimes, I guess," Karigan replied. "And I guess, sometimes not."

Estral stared at her. "I think that is one of the most honest statements you have ever made."

It was simple truth, Karigan thought. There were times when Cade was not foremost in her mind and life felt pretty normal, or at least as normal as hers got. There were other times when everything rose to the surface unexpectedly, like an arrow in her gut, as it had tonight.

She stood and crossed over to the lantern to shield it. As shadows grew in the cabin, she gazed out the window and saw Enver standing beneath the trees, his muna'riel cupped in his hands, its light illuminating his face and the snowflakes that fell around him in silver flashes.

Karigan fell into a dreamless slumber, but was gradually awakened by what she thought was the sound of mice chewing on her gear and scrabbling about the cabin. When she was more awake and aware of her surroundings, she realized that maybe she had been hearing mice, but what had roused her was Estral restless in her sleep, murmuring and twitching like she was trying to escape something.

Groundmites, perhaps?

Suddenly, Enver was there, kneeling beside Estral. He held his hand to his lips and blew. Sparkling motes of gold sprinkled over her.

Karigan sat up. "What are you doing?"

"Her dreams trouble her," he said. "I wish only to ease them."

Estral sighed and slumped, her breathing easier. She stopped murmuring and moving. Enver, silhouetted by the glow of the banked coals in the fireplace, watched over her for a time before nodding to himself. Then he rose, stepped around her, and sat beside Karigan.

"I wish to apologize again for the song," he said. "Lhean lanced your wound. You did not need me to undo the healing."

"It is not undone. And the song was beautiful. Beyond beautiful, really. I just wasn't ready for it."

"I know that now. I will learn the human way of things. That is what I wish."

Now Karigan didn't feel sleepy at all, just curious. "Why?"

His eyes gleamed in the fire glow as he gazed down at her. "Surely you see my nature, that I am only part Eletian."

Karigan nodded slowly. She *had* seen. "I noticed you were a little different from other Eletians."

"As much as I ever tried," he said, "I could not abandon the human part of my nature. I am half-human through my mother. You know my father, Somial."

"Really?" She had never thought of Somial in terms of being a father before. She didn't know why. It was a little disconcerting because he and Enver looked to be of an age, but it was difficult to judge the ages of eternally-lived Eletians.

"Your mother," Karigan said, "is she still with you?"

Enver shook his head.

"I'm sorry."

"She lived a long, happy life, as judged by mortals. Her memory beats in my heart."

Karigan had many questions about his family. Had they all lived in Eletia? Then she remembered his mother couldn't have, because she'd been told no mortals had set foot in Eletia since just after the Long War. That mortal had been her, crossing the threshold of time to lead the Sleepers of Argenthyne to Eletia.

Did the Eletians accept Enver? Lhean and Idris had seemed to, but what about Eletian society at large? She wanted to ask, but didn't know how to do so without offense. Before she could come up with a polite way to ask her questions, Enver stood.

"I will go out into the night again."

"Don't you need sleep?"

He smiled. "Not as much as a full human. I find respite in nature, serenity and restoration." He paused. "Perhaps you would, too, Galadheon. I could show you how to find stillness, to hear the voice of the world."

He gazed at her with the intensity that Eletians harnessed so well. "Your inner light burns fast and bright, but without balancing it with stillness, it will burn to ashes. You should walk with me. Perhaps you, too, will find connection with the world."

It sounded like a spiritual thing, and if so, she wasn't interested. She was already in too deep with forces beyond her control. The god of death had flung her across the threads of time and generally interfered with her life. Then there were the Mirari, whoever, or *whatever*, they were, exactly, and her silver eye. No, she had no wish to invite such forces into her life. Wasn't that what Enver was doing? Best not to find out. "No, thank you."

"Perhaps another time." His intense gaze left her as he took his cloak from the peg next to the door and threw it around his shoulders.

When he placed his hand on the door latch, she hastily asked, "Enver?"

He paused. "Yes?"

"Earlier you told Estral you were chosen to be our guide because you are a witness, but you wouldn't tell her what you are supposed to be witnessing. Would you tell me?"

He did not reply, just stood there staring at the door with his hand resting on the latch.

"Enver," she said, her voice rising with suspicion, "what is it you are supposed to be witnessing?"

He tilted his head back as though to inspect the lintel.

"Enver?"

"I should not have said anything."

"If we are to travel together as we are," Karigan said, "there needs to be trust, not secrets."

Again, the pained silence.

"Enver."

"Very well." He let out a breath. "You, Galadheon. It is you I am to witness." And then he was out the door and into the night.

THE MEDDLING OF ELETIANS

Enver, Karigan decided, was not going to get away with being mysterious. She crawled out of her blankets, slid on her boots, wrapped herself in her greatcoat, and ran out the door into a wall of freezing air. She could not see him; he was not using his muna'riel.

The snow had stopped falling, and the moon backlit the receding clouds. Stars glittered in the clear patches of sky. She heard the horses shifting in the paddock, the thud of a hoof, a sigh. The trees rustled in the breeze like breaths taken and exhaled, and the rush of Eli Creek was a constant, faint conversation between water and stone in the background. The woods were otherwise serene.

"Enver," she called, her own voice startling in the quiet. "What do you mean you're witnessing me?"

Silence. The clouds parted from the moon and the brightening light unveiled the clearing around the cabin. She shivered with the cold and was about to give up when his voice came to her from behind.

"I am here."

She whirled, heart thudding, and made out his form in the dark with the glint of moonlight in his eyes. "I wish you wouldn't sneak up on me like that."

"Apologies. For sneaking."

"Hmm." She took a deep breath and demanded, "What did you mean you are witnessing me?"

He did not answer immediately. Then, "Just as Lady Estral chronicles her observations in her journal, so do I also watch."

She did not like where this was going. She did not like the Eletians prying into her life. "Why? Why do you watch?"

"It is my designated role."

"What? Your role?" She perceived him nodding in affirmation more than saw it. "Why in the hells is this your—your *role*?"

He went silent again, and she thought he might not answer, but he said, "Those who are the wise among Eletians are, shall we say, baffled by you. You are unexpected for a mortal, and they wish to see what you will do next. That is all."

Karigan didn't even know what to say to this. She stood there gaping at him.

"I was not supposed to tell you," he said, "for how it might affect your natural behavior, but I can see that it is unfair not to."

Her *natural behavior*? "They want you to spy on me?" she demanded. Then she thought, bitterly, there had been Eletians who, in the past, had wanted to kill her. What was a little spying?

"'Spy' is perhaps too strong a word."

"Then what in the hells do you call it?" When he didn't answer, she continued, "So this whole journey to find the p'ehdrose is an excuse for you to *watch* me? You Eletians haven't meddled enough in my life? What I do is not your business."

He raised his hands in a placating gesture. "Galadheon—"

"And why in the name of the gods do you call me 'Galadheon'? My name is Karigan, or Rider G'ladheon." "Galadheon", which meant "betrayer" in the imperial tongue, was the origin of her name, but it had not been used in centuries; not until recently when the Eletians had begun addressing her that way.

Moonlight limned his shoulders when he shrugged. "It is what we call you."

"Eletians!" she sputtered. "I should have stayed in Sacor City."

"Do you wish to return?" he asked quietly.

"I'd like nothing better, but you convinced my king that this journey needed to be made. So you can spy on me."

"It was Lhean who did the convincing."

"You're all culpable."

"Galadheon," Enver said.

"What?"

"The journey was not devised just so we could spy on you. Our prince believes it important to seek the p'ehdrose, as does your king. To observe you was just a coincidental opportunity."

"That makes me feel so much better." She hoped her sarcasm was thick enough that even an Eletian could recognize it. If she ever saw Prince Jametari again, she would tell him a thing or two. "And why *you*? Why are you the one to watch me?"

"It was foreseen."

"Oh, good gods. Did your prince foresee you annoying me to death?"

"Galadheon—"

"I have had it with Eletians interfering in my life."

"I apologize," Enver said. "I cannot seem to do or say the right thing. How may I make amends?"

"Stay out of my way." She turned and headed for the cabin. Before she climbed the steps, she paused and told him, "And no spying."

She entered the cabin, and before she closed the door, she thought she heard a forlorn "very well" from outside.

She sighed and crawled back beneath her blankets. Sometimes she thought that if her brooch left her at that very moment, it wouldn't be too soon. Then she could go back to an ordinary life and never see another Eletian again.

Estral, Karigan noted the next morning, awoke cheerful and rested. Apparently she had slept peacefully through the night, oblivious to Karigan's confrontation with Enver. Karigan, on the other hand, could only glare at the day. She had not slept well. She wasn't surprised that Enver kept his distance.

When, over breakfast, Estral suggested they make way for the town of North, Karigan responded with a flat, "No."

"Why not?"

"North isn't safe."

"I know it's a rowdy backwater," Estral said, "but remember, I lived in a lumber camp before Selium."

"Well, *I* didn't."

Estral gave her a sideways glance. "My, my, someone rolled out of bed on the wrong side this morning."

Enver seemed to disappear into the wall.

"North is not friendly to representatives of the king," Karigan said, "like me."

"I know the story of what it was like when you traveled through North five years ago," Estral replied, "but this time you don't have brigands or Shawdell the Eletian pursuing you."

"We have *him.*" Karigan pointed accusingly at Enver. He looked ever more uncomfortable.

"He hasn't tried to kill you, has he?"

"Not yet," Karigan muttered.

"Now you're just being ridiculous." When Karigan didn't respond, Estral continued, "It's not like we have to stay. In fact, you won't even have to go into town with me. I just want to ask around to see if my father's been through there."

Karigan snorted and stood by the fireplace with her hands on her hips, no longer interested in her porridge. "As if the people of North like being questioned. You've never been there, so you don't know what it's like. You'd be prey by yourself."

"Maybe you could disguise yourself," Estral suggested. "Conceal that you're a Green Rider."

"I can't," Karigan said. "Not without good reason."

"But you did last time."

"I wasn't a Green Rider back then. Not that I knew of, in any case."

Estral's brightness looked to be waning. "Then I'll go alone."

"No."

"Sometimes you are just so pig-headed!"

"You're the one who brought the whole thing up."

"Look," Estral said, "I know there is usually a minstrel assigned to North. He or she might know something of my father."

Karigan, as much as she hated to admit it, knew Estral was right, for she'd met a Selium minstrel there herself, who had known what was going on in the town. She also hated that she felt so intimidated, but the experience of having a mob of angry townsfolk turn against her was not easily forgotten. The Anti-Monarchy Society had been quiet for years, so at least they would not be stirring the pot to boiling. Still, the townsfolk would not take kindly to her presence as a representative of the king.

"What does Enver think?" Estral asked.

He put up his hands as though to deflect her question. "I am not meddling."

Karigan laughed in dark amusement.

Estral raised an eyebrow at her. "Did I miss something last night?"

"Nothing. Nothing at all."

"Well, then," Estral said, "it is just between you and me."

Karigan frowned.

"North is not far from our path," Enver ventured.

"I thought you weren't meddling," Karigan shot back.

He shrugged. "I believed it was worth mentioning."

"If the king told you to go to North," Estral said, "would you hesitate?"

"You are not the king," Karigan replied.

"I know, but would you?"

"No, of course I would not hesitate. Not for my king. I can't refuse."

"If you were going at the king's behest, would you be afraid?"

Karigan clenched her teeth. "I wouldn't like it, but I would do it. Without question."

Estral sipped her tea, the intensity gone from her. "Karigan, I've got to go into North with or without you."

"You won't get far if I wrap you up in your bedroll and tie you to Coda's back."

"You're being ridiculous again."

"Am I?"

"Lady Estral," Enver said, "I'll go with you."

"You're meddling," Karigan accused.

"Not with *you*," Estral pointed out. "Enver and I will go into North while you sulk somewhere else."

Karigan treated them to a round of swearing, concluding they were the asses of donkeys, and worse, before stomping out of the cabin and slamming the door behind her. The sound echoed through the woods. Mara, were she there, would call her crotchety.

She also knew Estral was right. They needed to go to North to find out if Lord Fiori had passed that way. If there was in fact a Selium minstrel assigned to one of the inns there and Lord Fiori had traveled through, there was little question he'd have been marked by the minstrel.

As much as Karigan disliked the idea of going into North, she had been instructed to assist Estral as she could. *By the king.* So in a way, it was an order from him to go into North. She sighed in resignation. It wasn't like she didn't want Estral to find her father; she absolutely did. And she certainly would never allow her to go into North alone. Not even with Enver. She couldn't imagine the reception the folk of North would give an Eletian. She loosed another long, drawn-out sigh.

"Meep."

"What?" She looked around to see what creature had made so unexpected a noise.

"Prrrt."

Down at the bottom of the steps, an orange tabby cat sat on his haunches with his tail wrapped around his feet.

"Hello," Karigan said. "What are you doing out in these woods?"

The cat cocked his head as he stared at her. She crouched and put her hand out, and he climbed the steps to rub against it, purring loudly.

"Friendly," she murmured. "Do you live near here?"

The cat, of course, did not answer. He wended around her legs and scratched on the door. Surprised, she opened it. Inside she found Estral and Enver going over a map, no doubt planning their route into North. The cat immediately trotted to Estral, who occupied the chair, and jumped onto the table and the map spread upon it.

"What?" Estral said in surprise.

"Meep." The cat was nose-to-nose with her, and started sniffing her face.

Estral stroked his cheek. "Where did he come from?"

"I don't know," Karigan replied. "He was just suddenly there. He must live nearby."

Enver had an odd look in his eye as he gazed at the cat, but offered nothing, not even surprise.

"He sure seems to like you," Karigan told Estral.

"Well, what do you expect? He's a nice kitty with good taste," she said. "And he has majestic white whiskers. Yes, you do, you little sweetie."

"Prrrt."

For gods' sake, Karigan thought. She cleared her throat. "I've decided to accompany you to North."

Estral smiled as if she'd known all along that she would.

Karigan narrowed her eyes. "I am going so I can keep you two out of trouble." As if she were any good at keeping herself out of trouble. It would take several days for them to reach North. Maybe Estral would change her mind about going there in the meantime, but by the look of triumph on her face, she doubted it.

"Meep," the cat said.

GETTING BACK IN THE SADDLE

"You are as poor a patient as my predecessors made you out to be in their reports," said Master Mender Vanlynn.

This particular statement, Laren thought, in misery, was not helping. Her shoulder was back in its socket, the pain greatly diminished, but her whole body felt like it had been trampled by a herd of horses. She sat hunched on Vanlynn's exam table, her shoulder and arm tightly bound to her body to prevent the joint from shifting and causing additional tearing and pain.

Vanlynn shook her head; her eyes crinkled as she gazed at Laren. "This is not a first for you, either."

"No," Laren mumbled.

"Not surprising."

Laren glanced sharply at her and instantly regretted the move, for her neck was not feeling well either.

Vanlynn was not at all cowed by her patient's temper. "Captain, once you have dislocated your shoulder, it makes it more susceptible to recurrence."

"It was years ago, the first time."

Vanlynn shrugged. "Well, you have my instructions, the willowbark tea, and the ice. Your concussion is mild, but I recommend you rest for a few days."

That was not very likely, Laren thought.

Vanlynn, as if reading her mind, looked askance at her. "You are fortunate it's not worse. I'll send Ben to look in on you later. Do you need assistance to return to your quarters?"

"No, thank you." Laren slid off the table and Vanlynn

helped her into her coat, loosely draping the left side over her injured shoulder.

Laren tottered out of the mending wing, thinking maybe she'd been a little too hasty to decline help. It was not so very long ago she'd blacked out and vomited with the pain after the fall, and she had only made it to Vanlynn's exam room because Hep and his assistant had half-carried her. But, Zachary was scheduled for his public audience today, and she was determined to be at his side as usual.

As she slowly descended the stairs, willing the vertigo to go away, she figured Vanlynn was right, that she could have been much worse off. Yes, she had broken fence rails when she went flying off Loon, but snowdrifts had buffered her fall. She could have broken bones, even her neck. She could have gotten a more severe concussion.

Luckily, she injured her left shoulder and not her right. She'd be able to write and do the things she had always done with her right hand. Or, maybe that was not so lucky, considering the number of reports that needed writing. She smiled a little thinking that she'd get out of Gresia's arms training sessions.

When finally she reached the main hall, she paused to rest and gather herself for the trudge to the throne room. She wouldn't be late. The hurrying to-and-fro motion of the people in the main hall, however, did not help her vertigo and she fought to keep her stomach down. Cold sweat beaded on her forehead.

"Ah, Captain, there you are."

Les Tallman, one of the king's chief advisors and the head of the Weapons, strode up to her. He peered appraisingly at her.

"What happened to you?" he asked.

"It's nothing. Just a riding mishap."

To his credit, he did not dispute her claim of it being "nothing," but by his skeptical expression, she could tell he'd formed a contrary opinion on the matter.

"Are you on your way to audience?" she asked.

"Yes, I was hoping to intercept you to advise you that the king will not be present."

"What?" He'd been choosing not to attend meetings of late, but he never missed public audiences.

"He has ordered us to oversee the audience, and has commended to us his authority to make judgments in the cases presented to us."

There was nothing especially egregious about this, except that Zachary was very hands-on and his subjects were accustomed to seeing him on audience day. It was important for the citizens of Sacoridia to actually see the man who ruled over them and tell him their concerns.

"Did he give you a reason?" Laren asked.

"The same as before. He wants to be with his queen."

Laren was pleased Zachary had suddenly become so devoted to Estora, but he hadn't left her side in days.

"My mother," Les Tallman said, "was a midwife, and she used to say that there were some expectant fathers who'd start nesting during a pregnancy. Perhaps our king is doing just that."

"Perhaps," Laren mumbled. She didn't know what to think of Zachary's behavior. Perhaps he would return to his duties when he needed a break from his "nesting."

"Captain, if you don't mind my saying, you should probably sit this audience out. You're looking rather peaked. Castellan Javien and I can handle it."

She was about to protest, but thought better of it. She *was* feeling rather "peaked," and she had something else in mind that she needed to do before too much time elapsed. If she hadn't been in such pain and blacking out earlier, she would have attended to it immediately.

"Thank you," she said. "I believe I will take the opportunity to finish a *project*."

He raised an eyebrow, but went on his way toward the throne room.

When she reached Rider stables, she faced the stalls of Bluebird and Loon. They stared back at her, then seemed to exchange some comment between them with whickers and shakes of their heads.

"Two peas in a pod, aren't you," she muttered.

They both looked away as if ashamed. Loon was clearly more nervous, tossing his head, and as well he should be. Messenger horses were more apt to protect their Riders than allow them to get hurt, but Loon was young and inexperienced, just as Bluebird had once been.

"Best we get on with this."

Anna had tossed and turned during the night, trying to come to a decision, trying to screw up her courage. When she finally rose in the morning, she was resolved. She wanted to be more than just an ash girl, even more than an ash girl who served the queen.

Her resolve got her through breakfast, through her morning duties, and out of the castle. However, as she walked across castle grounds, her skirts skimming snow, her step faltered. Who did she think she was? She had no courage. She'd never been anywhere. She'd always been a servant. Why did she think she could be anything else?

Doggedly, she put one foot in front of the other and pushed forward against the invisible force that wanted her to turn back, to give up.

It would be easier to speak to Rider Mara, Rider Daro, or any of the others, but no, she had decided she needed to go right to the captain. As she approached officers quarters, her heart pummeled the inside of her chest and her legs shook. She could just forget this whole idea, just turn around and go back. Who did she think she was? But she had come *this* far.

She stepped up to the captain's door and raised her hand to knock when someone cleared his throat. She whirled as if she'd been caught filching a tart from the kitchens.

"Looking for Captain Mapstone?" It was Lieutenant Connly striding by on the path.

"Yes." She squeaked the word.

He did not appear to be fazed by her presence there, and he actually smiled. "You might try Rider stables. I saw her heading in that direction a short while ago."

"Thank you," Anna said, but he was already on his way

toward the castle. She thought maybe she ought to follow him, but worked up her courage to walk over to Rider stables.

When she stepped inside and smelled the sweet hay and felt the warmth of the stable filled with horses, she quailed once more. She was trespassing. She had no business here. This time she really was going to retreat, but one of the stablehands caught sight of her as he pitched manure from a stall into a wheelbarrow.

"You lookin' for someone?" he asked.

"No—no. Sorry." She was about to run off when the object of her search, and terror, appeared from another part of the stables.

"Hep," said Captain Mapstone, "could you give me a hand with Loon?" Then, espying Anna hovering in the doorway, she said, "Hello."

Anna's throat was too dry to respond. Perhaps it was the captain's importance, or maybe her serious demeanor—at least she always looked serious to Anna—or maybe it was her red hair, but she was terribly daunting.

Captain Mapstone gazed at her, head tilted as if trying to see her clearly in the gloom, a look of interest on her face. "Are you looking for me?"

How did she know? Anna, her voice still betraying her, nodded.

"Do you hear hoofbeats? In your mind? Like all you can think about is finding a horse and riding?"

No, Anna thought. She hadn't experienced anything like that. She shook her head.

Disappointment flashed across the captain's face, then recognition. "You're the ash girl Karigan helped, aren't you."

Finally finding her voice, Anna blurted, "Yes'm!"

The captain looked into the distance as though she was trying to remember something. "Rinnah? Hannah? . . . Anna?"

"Yes'm. It's Anna."

"So, Anna," the captain said, "why don't you come and give me a hand while you tell me what you need. Then Hep can finish his chores without interruption."

"Yes'm," Anna said with apprehension.

"You sure, Cap'n?" the stableman asked.

"Yes," she replied. "Don't forget you have a fence to fix."

He grunted in response and murmured under his breath something about the daftness of Green Riders.

Anna followed meekly behind the captain down the aisle, with horses in the stalls to either side. Some watched her; others ignored her existence. They were *big.* People like her didn't have horses. They walked. What in the world had she been thinking by coming here?

The captain led her into another section of the stables where a spotted horse stood with his halter hooked to cross ties in the center aisle. He was taller than many of the other horses. She halted uncertainly some distance away.

"I need help with getting this saddle on his back," the captain said. "The rest I think I can manage."

Only then did Anna register that the captain's arm was strapped to her body. Between being so nervous and the drape of the captain's coat, Anna had completely missed it. She stepped forward hesitantly.

"The saddle isn't too heavy," the captain said, "just awkward one-handed."

With directions from the captain, Anna helped her lift it into place on the horse's back. All the while, the horse bowed his neck around to look at what they were doing.

"So what brings you to see me?" the captain asked as she reached under the horse's belly for the girth.

The words tumbled out all at once: "IwanttobeaGreen-Rider." Anna clapped her hands over her mouth.

The captain turned to her in surprise, one end of the girth in her hand. "Did you just say you want to be a Green Rider?"

Anna nodded.

"Well." The captain turned back to the horse, worked the leather tongues through buckles, and tightened the girth. When she finished, she faced Anna once more and rested her hand on the horse's shoulder. "It is commendable that you wish to serve our king and queen. Are you sure you didn't hear hoofbeats?"

"Yes'm."

"Hmm. I can't think of anyone who has voluntarily asked

to join in many years," the captain murmured. "May I ask why you wish to join us?"

"Yes'm." Anna then gabbled about Sir Karigan, about doing important work, and about traveling and seeing the country.

"I see," the captain replied. "Don't you serve the queen now? That's important work, too."

"Yes'm, but it's not the same." Anna hoped she did not come across as ungrateful.

The horse blew through his nostrils as if bored by the whole proceedings.

"Hush, you," the captain told him. Then to Anna, she said, "I would like nothing more than to welcome you into our ranks, but there is a . . . a certain prerequisite Riders must meet, and it's not exactly something someone obtains. It is inherent."

"Magic?"

The captain looked surprised, then nodded as if to herself. "The day of the attack, Karigan told me she'd used her ability in front of you. Yes, Anna, Riders answer a call to serve, a magical calling, one that has been in place for as long as there have been Green Riders, but it is one we don't talk about."

Anna looked at her feet. She had no magic. She was just an ash girl. She couldn't be a Green Rider. "I understand."

"I'm sorry, Anna."

Anna curtsied to the captain and rushed out of the stables. She stood in the snow breathing hard. After all her trepidation, after all it had cost her to gather her courage and seek out the captain, she was not worthy. She'd never been worthy and never would be.

She trudged on a few paces, then paused to glance at the paddock, and saw that the captain had brought her horse out and had somehow managed to mount him with the use of only one arm. The two seemed to be having some kind of disagreement near the broken fence, the captain reining him around, and he circling and bobbing his head in agitation.

Hep suddenly appeared beside her, pushing his full wheelbarrow. "You're better off not being one of them," he told her. "Sensible. Look at the captain. See that broken fence rail?"

He pointed at the paddock. "She broke it this morning with her shoulder when the horse got all squirrely and threw her. Shoulder is dislocated, she got a concussion. So, what does she do instead of going to bed? Drags herself back over here to give the horse a teaching, that's what. Getting back in the saddle, she says. Lucky she didn't break her head. *Daft.* They all are."

He then rumbled off with his wheelbarrow, and she watched the captain ride the recalcitrant horse around the paddock. Repeatedly he shied where the fence was broken.

Hep, Anna thought, was likely right that she was better off not being a Rider, that the lot of them were most likely daft. But as daft as they might be, a part of her couldn't help but admire the captain's grit. Maybe there was some lesson for her in "getting back in the saddle," but it was too hard to see it through the tears of disappointment that blurred her vision.

THE INTERESTING PROBLEM OF ANNA THE ASH GIRL

A dislocated shoulder, Laren learned the next day, did not get her out of arms training. Granted, Gresia went easier on her than Connly and Mara, but had called Laren's injury an "excellent learning experience." She was forced to fight with her right arm only, whether with a sword, a knife, a staff, or her bare hand. Her balance was off because of how she had to carry her injured arm, so Gresia made her work on a balance beam while parrying attacks. The training was reminiscent, she thought with chagrin, of what she and Drent had made Karigan do after sustaining an elbow injury. Laren found it all very ironic, as if it were some sort of divine retribution.

The exercises she engaged in were made to jostle her shoulder as little as possible, but she was still shaking and in pain by the time she was done. Her "mild" concussion also kept her out of sorts with an achy head and unsettled stomach. It was a great relief when the session ended, but short-lived for Drent entered the practice chamber just then and detained her. Mara glanced back in concern at her as she and Connly headed for the weapons room.

"Yes?" Laren asked Drent.

For a moment he just stared at her, then said, "It looks like the horse won."

Laren scowled. "Maybe the battle, but not the war."

"I heard it's not the first time you've done battle." His laugh was like sandpaper.

Laren rubbed her shoulder. No, it hadn't been, and she really wondered if Bluebird had told Loon stories about his younger days. Did horses do that? Tell each other stories?

"I'd really like to get on with my day," she said. "Is there something you wished to say to me?"

Drent glanced around, but they were alone. "The boy has refused to attend his usual training sessions."

By "boy," she knew he meant Zachary. "He's been declining to do many things." Like attend a public audience, she recalled.

"What's going through his head?" Drent demanded. "This is no time to shirk his duty."

She shrugged and winced. She supposed Drent was asking her because he knew she and Zachary were close. "Les Tallman thinks Zachary is nesting, that it is not unusual for an expectant father."

"Mmpf. I wouldn't know anything about that. My father could've cared less about his family. He just liked the act of planting his seed." Reflectively, he added, "It's because of him I learned to fight. Got tired of getting knocked around."

Laren knew next to nothing of Drent's history, but thought sadly that the little bit he shared probably was not uncommon. "I would guess men react in different ways to impending fatherhood. I am pleased Zachary has taken such an interest in his family, though I admit it's unlike him to not maintain his schedule."

"The boy's gone soft."

"If by soft you mean being an attentive husband and father, perhaps. We could use more like him."

"Mmpf."

"Was there anything else?" Laren asked.

"Next time you see him, prod him, will you? Won't take long for him to lose his edge if he doesn't train."

"I am not his keeper, but I'll let him know."

Drent nodded. "Good enough."

She left him for the weapons room. She did not know when she'd see Zachary next. He had not summoned her, and if he was in this nesting mood, then he might not appear at meetings for some time. However, he'd have to rouse himself sooner or later. His counselors might be able to keep the kingdom running for a while, but the king was its heart, and he was especially needed in the face of hostilities with Second Empire.

She was pleased to find that Mara and Connly had waited for her, for she'd had something else on her mind to talk to them about ever since the ash girl, Anna, had come to see her the day before.

Connly helped her with her coat. "You look like you could use a day off, Captain," he said.

And a dose of something to kill the pain, Laren thought. *Oh, and a hot bath.*

When they stepped outside, she shivered, still damp with sweat from her session. There had been fair skies, but it still remained cold on castle grounds. Some of her Riders had mentioned it felt warmer just stepping across the moat into the city.

As they walked, she asked, "Do you two know Anna, the ash girl?"

Mara answered that she did, and Connly said he'd seen a girl tending the hearths in the Rider wing, but didn't know her name. Laren told them about her encounter with Anna the day before.

"That would have taken her a great deal of courage," Mara said, sounding impressed. "Do you know what the other servants called her before she moved to the west wing?" When Laren shook her head, Mara said, "Mousie."

"She must have a bit of hidden steel in her, then," Laren replied, "to overcome any fear she might have had to seek me out."

"Truly," Connly said. "You can be intimidating."

"What? I can?"

"Well, you are the captain," he said. "You can be very intense and serious sometimes."

"Intense and serious?"

"Yes," her Riders chorused.

Well, she thought, one learned something new every day.

"It's a wonder," Mara reflected, "that she didn't come to me or Daro. She felt strongly enough that she had to go to our scary captain."

"Scary! I am not—"

"Terrifying," Connly said. He grinned.

"Damnation, but it does bring me to the point. Here is someone who, without being called to serve in the conventional manner, at least the conventional Green Rider manner, came to me out of her own desire to be a Green Rider, who wished to be one enough that she overcame her own apprehension to face me. It's a calling of its own, and it seems a shame to turn away someone who seems eager and willing just because she lacks a special ability."

Mara shrugged beside her. "Not much that can be done about it if she doesn't have one."

"And so it has been through the centuries, though frankly it's rare that anyone tries to *volunteer* to be a Green Rider." Her own daughter, Melry, might have been one for she was desperate to join, to become a Green Rider, but she also knew about the Rider call and what it meant that she hadn't heard it. Laren, knowing the perils of the job, secretly hoped Melry never heard the call and found some other, safer, calling that drew her. What she said next, however, would be something Melry would jump at. "I have never seen any regulation requiring that a king's messenger have a special ability."

Connly stumbled. "Captain, are you suggesting that we open the messenger service to—to anyone?"

"Why not?" At his stricken expression, she added, "All right, we wouldn't take just anyone. But people who have the same sense of duty and independent spirit that all Riders do. Look, when Lil Ambrioth formed the Green Riders, it was during a time of war. The brooches were created to call people with innate abilities to the king's service, abilities so minor they were useless without a device to augment them. You could say the original Riders were misfits—too minor in ability to be of any consequence to those with real power, and yet unable to fit in with those who were mundane. Their formation as a unit was out of desperation during a time of war. Might the messenger service have looked different if it was formed during a time of peace? You don't have to have a special ability to ride a horse and deliver a message. Much of what we do in the course of our duties does not require the use of magic."

They halted by her door at officers quarters.

"It is difficult to know exactly what Lil Ambrioth intended when she formed the Green Riders," Connly said. "That was a long time ago."

"Yes, it was," Laren agreed. "And do we know for sure there weren't Riders of mundane origin among their ranks?"

"I can see the attraction of increasing our force," Mara said, "but what would that do to our cohesiveness as a unit? Our abilities, the brooches we wear, bind us together, make us strong. Would bringing in outsiders weaken us?"

"If we regard them as outsiders," Laren replied, "yes. I am not suggesting we suddenly start recruiting and accepting people without magical abilities into our ranks, but I think it is worth thinking about and discussing. We'll talk about it again, but I'd like the two of you to ruminate on it for a while. Then, if we decide it is worth pursuing, I'll present it to the king. He is the one who would make the final decision, after all."

Mara and Connly exchanged uneasy glances. The idea of allowing people without abilities into the Green Riders was a radical one. She had not expected their enthusiastic endorsement, but it was good to get them thinking it over.

She dismissed them and entered her quarters, sighing at the relative warmth within. She would make some willow-bark tea and rest, but afterward, she must throw herself back into the world of endless meetings and reports. She did not think, however, with even those distractions, that she'd get the interesting problem of Anna the ash girl out of her mind.

THE POET'S VISIT

Slee disliked the intrusion, but tolerated it because it filled the Beautiful One with delight, and when she was delighted, her radiance was nearly blinding. The poet sat in the chair opposite them sipping tea, and wrapped in her cloak for she said the room felt chilly. Slee felt the opposite, but he ensured the Beautiful One was wrapped in blankets so that she was comfortable.

Slee did not see much in the person of the poet. She was round with ordinary brown eyes and faded hair, and in her middle years, but when she read her poems, Slee learned that words could be music the way they sounded together, and the images they rendered in the mind as fine as any painting by a master. It was song without music. Slee was not sure how to capture the beauty to add to his collection, for the words were ephemeral, drifting in the air, vanishing before him after providing the most intoxicating visions. The words were laid down in a book, but seeing them printed on the page seemed so prosaic. He was not sure he could recreate the magic of having the words read to him.

"From where do you get your inspiration?" the Beautiful One asked.

"Many places, Your Majesty," Lady Amalya replied. "From couples who have had lengthy marriages, to young lovers like yourselves, if I may be so bold. One hears of how cold and loveless royal marriages can be."

The Beautiful One's smile almost melted Slee. He had his arm around her shoulders and was really beginning to think of himself as the Zachary. He kept meaning to return to his lair to contend with the real Zachary, but he could not tear himself from the Beautiful One's side.

"In fact," Lady Amalya was saying, "just seeing the two of you together makes me eager for pen and paper."

"Perhaps," the Beautiful One said, "it is your words that have inspired *us*. We have been reading them to one another, haven't we, dearest."

Slee nodded. "Yes."

"You are the perfect portrait," Lady Amalya said, "of love, the strong warrior king and his lady, the enchanting queen. Would it be permissible for me to use you as inspiration? To immortalize you in verse?"

"What do you think?" the Beautiful One asked. "Should we be immortalized in the poetry of Lady Amalya Whitewren?"

Her eyes hypnotized him. "Yes, my love."

"That is wonderful," Lady Amalya said. "You are very gracious to a humble poet."

When the Beautiful One's gaze left him, the light dimmed in Slee's vision just a tiny bit.

"Will you write it in a sonnet?" she asked the poet.

Lady Amalya leaned forward as if to tell a secret. "It may seem scandalous, but I've been experimenting with—" and here she whispered, "free verse."

The Beautiful One brightened once more. "Truly? That is very daring of you."

"Art, my lady, should be daring. For too long the old graybeards of the literary world have held sway in their judgments of what is art and what is not. It is time to break the mold, so to speak."

The two carried on an animated discussion that Slee was content to just watch. It was not out of character for the Zachary to sit back and be remote, to listen thoughtfully and speak only when he had something useful to say. So Slee mainly watched his Beautiful One, the light in her eyes, the curve of her neck, the way she smiled.

Before long, the visit came to a conclusion. Lady Amalya left them signed copies of her latest works, and curtsied with promises to visit again. Her presence had not been unpleasant, but Slee was only too glad to have his Beautiful One back to himself, alone.

"Thank you so much for asking her to come," she said. "It was a wonderful surprise, and Lady Amalya is a delight."

"Anything for you, my love." It had been a surprise to him, too.

"Oh!" she exclaimed suddenly. "Your children must have liked her, too, for they are all stirred up."

She let him slide his hand over her belly to feel tiny feet kicking. What was it like inside the womb? How did they look in there? Slee had stolen enough infants to know what they looked like after they'd been birthed. This was the first time he'd really gotten to know some while they were inside. They would be innocent and as glorious as their mother. They were *his*.

"Sire?"

Slee had placed his face against her belly to feel the movement of the babies against his cheek. Now he sat up, displeased to find one of the black-garbed guardians standing before him.

"What is it?"

"An envoy from Rhovanny has arrived."

Slee searched the thoughts of the Zachary. This was an important development, but he did not wish to leave his queen's side.

"Tallman and Javien can handle it."

The Weapon shifted uncomfortably. "Sire, it may be considered an aspersion if you do not honor the envoy with your presence."

Slee was about to argue, but the Beautiful One placed her graceful hand on his arm. "Zachary, you must go. You have been waiting for this for a very long time."

"But—"

"I will be fine, and will await your return."

Slee struggled with himself, but nodded. It would not do to arouse their suspicions. He would go and play king for a while, and yes, she would be here when he returned.

"Come," Laren said in response to the knock on her door. She was struggling with her longcoat when, to her surprise, the Weapon, Fastion, and not a Green Foot runner, stepped inside her quarters.

"Fastion? I heard the envoy from Rhovanny has finally appeared. Have you come to fetch me?"

"Not to see the envoy."

He stepped around her work table to assist her with the coat, and then helped her buckle on her swordbelt. It was disconcerting, to say the least. She felt like a child needing help to get dressed, and that that help was a warrior in black . . . ?

"Doesn't the king need me?" she asked.

After a considered moment, he replied, "Most likely, but it is the queen who wishes to see you. She asked me personally to bring you to her."

"The queen? Whatever for?"

"I do not know."

It was something that he looked uncertain, almost as if he wanted to speak his mind, but discipline stayed him. In their walk over to the castle, he revealed nothing.

The castle entrance was clogged with the envoy's entourage and attendants, in addition to castle servants coming forward to aid them. Laren was rather astonished by the number of people and horses, and wondered what dignitary of Rhovanny had made the journey to see Zachary. To avoid the crowd, Fastion took her through the servants entrance and through the back corridors until finally they reached the west wing and the queen's apartments. She found Estora standing before the hearth, her hand pressed against the small of her back. She looked plump and rosy.

"Your Majesty," Fastion said, "Captain Mapstone is here to see you."

"Thank you, Fastion. Please see that we are not disturbed."

He bowed and left them, and Estora turned to Laren. "Good heavens, Captain, what happened to you?"

Apparently word of the mishap with Loon and the fence had not reached this far. "An argument with a horse, my lady."

"I am so sorry. Please, sit down. Should you even be out of bed?"

Laren took one of the chairs across from the sofa and smiled, thinking she'd done everything *but* rest in bed. "I ache, but I am well enough."

Estora seated herself on her sofa, and drew a blanket over her lap. "Usually I think of Green Rider danger occurring out in the world, and not from their own horses."

"I am ashamed to admit it happened in the paddock outside Rider stables." Laren smiled briefly. "You wished to see me, Your Majesty?"

"Yes, Captain. I don't quite know where to begin . . ."

"Is it about Zachary?"

Estora nodded. "Yes. It is rare he is away from my side, so with the envoy distracting him, I thought this a good opportunity to have you here. In fact, he is so attentive that I admit to feeling a little smothered."

"I was wondering. He's declined to attend his public audience and meetings."

"I once wished for such attention," Estora replied. "There were times when he was distant and I ached to have him close with me. Now he is the opposite."

"Les Tallman says he is nesting."

Estora smiled. "Vanlynn said something similar, and perhaps I should relax and revel in his attention while I have it. But it's a little like he's besotted."

"Seeing you in bloom as the mother of his children may have moved something in him. He may not seem it, but he is quite sensitive."

"Yes, but, Captain . . . Let us not mince words. He did not marry me out of love, but duty. He has been fond of me, yes, but not in the same sense as he loves Karigan."

Said so bluntly, it took Laren by surprise, especially to hear it from Estora. "People change. Perhaps he has seen what is really before him."

"I do not know, Captain. It does feel hypocritical to complain about that which I once desired, but it—*he* feels . . . *wrong*. I had wondered if you noticed him acting differently."

"I haven't seen him in days to notice."

"Because he has been with me," Estora murmured. "If you

do notice anything, please tell me. You have been close to him for a very long time and would notice anything unusual."

Laren could not even begin to fathom what could possibly be off, except this whole nesting business, but who was she to know anything about the behavior of expectant fathers? Estora's sense of wrongness, however, was enough to concern her.

"I will seek him out later and see how he seems," she said.

"That is all I ask," Estora replied.

Laren paused a moment before taking her leave of the queen.

"Is there something else, Captain?"

"I was going to speak with Mistress Evans," Laren replied, "but since I am here, I thought I might address it with you directly." She told Estora about the visit she had had from Anna, and the girl's request.

"She is so quiet," Estora said, "that I would not have guessed she had so adventurous a soul."

"Unless she hears the Rider call, I cannot bring her into the messenger service, but I was thinking, if you and Mistress Evans approve, that perhaps she could join in on some Rider training. I hate to crush the ambitions of one so eager."

"What training do you have in mind?" Estora asked.

"Beginning riding, basic arms. I know she is receiving lessons in reading and figuring, but if it can be worked into the schedule, there are lessons in geography, history, and etiquette, as well."

"It sounds," Estora said quietly, "as if you wish to turn her into a Green Rider even if she can't be one."

"Does it?" Laren asked, trying to sound innocent. "It may turn out that none of it appeals to her after all, and she will become more content as a servant, perhaps eventually meet a young man, and carry on a more or less traditional life. Or, if this interest of hers is real, she may come to serve her king and queen in some more useful capacity."

Estora smiled. "More useful than tending my hearth?"

Laren smiled back.

"Very well," Estora said. "I will speak to Mistress Evans, and I will see what can be arranged."

"Thank you," Laren replied.

They spoke for a while longer, then Laren excused herself. As she walked through the corridors of the royal wing, she found herself pleased with how receptive Estora had been to the idea of allowing Anna to participate in Rider training, but disquieted by her words about Zachary. Was he simply nesting as Vanlynn suggested, or was something more at play? Perhaps it was nothing and the arrival of the Rhovans would stir his intrinsic sense of duty and motivate him to return to more usual patterns. If not, Laren would get to the bottom of it. After all, war was upon them and it was no time for him to indulge in capricious behavior no matter his fatherly impulses. It would neither impress their allies nor instill confidence in him as Sacoridia's king.

As she descended stairs to the lower level, she was certain Zachary would snap out of it, whatever *it* was, and continue to guide the realm with a steady hand. If he did not, they were in trouble.

NORTH

Unfortunately, to Karigan's line of thinking, Estral had not changed her mind about going to North, and as they drew closer, the dense elder woods of the Green Cloak with its grand pines gave way to newer, spindly growth bare of leaves, and thence to an open expanse of stumps and scrub half buried by wet snow where the forest had been clear-cut.

They worked carefully around the broken branches of snags that poked out of the snow like the ribs of a skeleton, and avoided pits where trees had been removed by the roots. Every time Karigan glimpsed Enver's face beneath his hood, he looked more and more disturbed. She couldn't blame him, for it was a desolate scene, and it did not help that the low dark clouds were unloading a torrent of rain. Mist rose from the snow-clotted land like ghosts awakening.

She shivered. Even her excellent greatcoat wasn't keeping the damp out. It was saturated. The horses looked as dank and miserable as she felt. Perhaps the only one who wasn't sodden and gloomy was the cat, who rode beneath Estral's coat. He poked his nose out now and then with a twitch of his whiskers, but quickly retreated into his warm and dry refuge.

Karigan had expected to leave the cat behind when they departed Eli Creek Station, that he would surely return to his owner, but as they left, he leaped right onto the packs that burdened Bane. He'd ridden there until the rain. What Bane had thought of his unexpected passenger, he did not say.

The only thing that kept Karigan's spirits at a reasonable level was the thought that after they took care of business in town, they could head for the waystation and dry out. Unlike Eli Creek, the North waystation was active and kept well stocked.

But first, town. When the hooves of their horses splashed into the half-frozen river of mud that was the North Road, she resigned herself to the inevitable. They plodded westward along the road that would lead them over the River Terrygood and into the town itself.

The horses slogged through the main thoroughfare in North, their legs and bellies caked in mud. Except Mist who, even with her white coat, remained nearly pristine as if she magically repelled all dirt. Few townsfolk were out in the downpour, and those who were hurried along beneath the overhangs in front of shops. Karigan guessed that few took any notice whatsoever of three drenched and bedraggled travelers.

Karigan took the lead, riding past brothels and noisy pubs, searching for the sign of the Fallen Tree Inn. The present seemed to merge with the past as she remembered riding down this very street five years ago, albeit in the opposite direction, and not in the rain. She had encountered a horse cart that first time, with the body of a dead Green Rider, Joy Overway, in the back. Karigan remembered the scene well, Joy's hand flung out, fingers slightly curled, the glint of light from a nearby inn shining on her hair. Two black-shafted arrows protruded from her chest. The arrows were soul-stealers used by the Eletian Shawdell to control the spirits of the dead.

Karigan had recovered Joy's brooch and given it to Captain Mapstone. It was most likely the same one Trace now wore, for she shared the same ability as Joy, to communicate with the mind. Connly was the other with the ability, and he and Joy had been very close. While Karigan had resumed her schooling in Selium after her first Green Rider adventure, Connly had traveled to North in what must have been a heart-rending mission to claim Joy's remains and take her home to Oldbury Province, where she was interred in her family plot. He'd found no sign of the black arrows, however, and Karigan felt a sense of a story left unfinished. Did Joy's spirit still suffer with the arrows left unbroken? Or, had the defeat of Shawdell dissolved the spell of the arrows?

Pain, a breath of air seemed to whisper.

She shook herself and focused on finding the inn. It was where she had stayed during her first journey through North, for it was known as more orderly, less raucous, than other establishments in town. It was also where she'd found a minstrel of Selium named Gowen. When they finally came upon the inn, she reined Condor into the courtyard and was met by a stableboy.

Karigan dismounted and told him, "We won't be staying long, but see to the comfort of the horses. Get them dry and warm." She produced a couple coppers for him.

"Yes, ma'am," he said.

Ma'am again, she thought in bad humor.

Before he could lead Condor and the others away, she removed her longsword from the saddle and slung it over her shoulder. She was not going to let any of her weapons out of reach. As Estral and Enver joined her, she watched the strange sight of the cat riding on Coda's saddle into the stable. Maybe the cat would like it there and become a mouser. She couldn't see him joining them on their journey to find the p'ehdrose.

She headed for the inn's main entrance and said, "I think you should keep your hood up, Enver."

"Why?"

"I don't know how the people here would react to an Eletian."

"Why don't you worry about how *I* might react to *them?*" he asked.

Estral laughed.

"They outnumber you," Karigan replied, "and this is not Sacor City, but *North*, which is not particularly civilized."

Enver shrugged, the rain rolling off his shoulders, but he kept his hood up when they stepped into the inn. It was a relief to escape the constant pound of rain. The inn's common room was shadowed, but warm with a cheery fire in the hearth. Many people, mostly men, huddled about it, drinking from tankards. A good many of the tables were full.

The innkeeper approached them, and Karigan remembered him, the spindly man with his thinning red hair. Even more thin now, she reflected. Wiles was his name, she recalled. He looked them up and down as if to assess their character.

"King's messenger?" he said in surprise.

"Yes."

"There are no rooms available tonight."

"We are not looking for rooms."

"Then you may sit at a table if that is what you are here for. We take only currency, no credits from the king."

Karigan nodded curtly, and Estral was already heading for one of the tables. "Innkeeper," she asked before he could get away, "do you have a minstrel who performs here?"

"He is on break. He'll be back soon. Is there something you need with him, Rider?"

"I was just wondering." She left him for the table Estral had chosen. There was no reason why Innkeeper Wiles should know their business.

When a server came to take their order, Karigan asked for whatever was hot, which turned out to be chicken in a thick gravy with dumplings, and a pot of tea. With a warm, full belly, and her uniform starting to dry, she began to relax a little. A few patrons gave her dark looks, but most, on the whole, ignored her. She espied a tall, muscular fellow watching the common room from against the far wall, his meaty arms folded across his chest. Karigan guessed he was the innkeeper's enforcer, who kept order over rowdy patrons.

When Estral's attention shifted from her food, Karigan followed her gaze. A man entered the common room with a lute and sat on a stool by the fire.

"Do you know him?" Karigan asked her.

"Yes," Estral said. "Barris Griggs. He made master a few years ago."

The minstrel tuned up, then launched into some rousing folk tunes, the sort of which were often sung in common rooms, and which were so well-known the audience could sing along. Estral's lips moved to the words though she uttered no sound that Karigan could hear. Enver watched and listened with great interest. If he wished to learn the fireside customs of Sacoridians, he was now witnessing them in full form.

Karigan, content with her meal and the warmth, yawned. She might have dozed off, but something scratched at the edge of her mind, an irritation. She had no idea what it was, but it was there, something trying to attract her attention, the faintest whisper beneath the music and murmur of patrons. Then it was gone.

The server brought squares of gingerbread slathered in clotted cream out to them, and Karigan nearly forgot the irritation as she dug in. They listened to Barris as he played mostly jaunty tunes. When he paused for a break, Estral crossed the room to intercept him and Karigan watched, but could not hear their lively exchange.

"You are getting a good look at everyday Sacoridians in an ordinary setting," Karigan told Enver. "What do you think?"

"Illuminating," he replied. "Especially the music. I wish to learn it."

Karigan smiled at the thought of an Eletian singing a song that was all about praising the attributes of common ale.

Estral brought Barris over for introductions.

"I have heard a fair bit about you, Sir Karigan," he said, and then smiled, "including your days as a student in Selium. It is an honor."

"Thank you," Karigan murmured. It was a mixed compliment at best, considering the notoriety of her school years.

Barris chuckled at her discomfiture. He was a dark-bearded fellow with a wide girth, and wore nothing to openly indicate he was a master minstrel of Selium. He turned to Enver. "And an honor to meet you, sir." Very softly he added, "One does not see Eletians in this benighted town."

"I should like to learn your music one day," Enver said. "It is quite entertaining."

Barris looked tickled. "I would be happy to teach you, but Estral says you are not staying long."

"No," Karigan said, "we are not."

"Things here are not quite as bad for the king's folk as they used to be," Barris said, "but I don't blame you."

"Have a seat," Estral told him. "Barris says my father did travel through here several months ago."

"It was a brief meeting," Barris warned her, "and he never came back through that I'm aware of."

"Did he say where he was going?"

"He talked about a lumber camp north of here. There are a number of those, of course." Barris grimaced. "I hate to tell you this, but while he wouldn't say exactly what his aims were, I'm under the impression he was trying to get near the Lone Forest to see what Second Empire was up to. It's rumored there is a base up that way."

Rumored? Karigan thought. More than rumored. Captain Mapstone had ensured she knew the latest intelligence on Second Empire's positions. A glance at Estral showed how disturbed she was by this information.

"The Lone Forest was once united with this forest you call the Green Cloak," Enver said.

And was once the northern limit of the lands of the Sacor Clans, Karigan thought. Given that it was likely under Second Empire's control, they would be avoiding that region as if it were a plague town.

As Barris and Estral continued to discuss Lord Fiori's whereabouts and news of Selium, Karigan found herself distracted once again by the irritation. It was like stirrup leathers chafing her calves when she wasn't wearing boots. And there were the whispers, and now a cool touch on the back of her hand. Perhaps it was just an air current, but she knew better.

The voices of the inn's patrons, the clink of dishware, the laughter, and hurrying steps of servers, all washed away to a dull murmur and Karigan stood. Estral and Barris, deep into their discussion, did not pay her attention, but she was aware of Enver's gaze on her.

She observed a flicker of filmy movement by the bottom of the staircase that led to the inn's rooms above. Without another thought, she headed for the stairs, disregarding the displeasure of those she bumped into.

"Watch it, ye bloody Greenie."

She barely perceived their words. They did not touch her. Nor did she see the inn's watchful enforcer leave his post by the wall to follow her.

BLACK ARROWS

Karigan climbed the stairs to the inn's upper level as though she knew where it was she needed to go. *Had* to go. At the landing, the compulsion led her unerringly down the hall past the doors of guest rooms. She rounded a corner into another hall of doors, carried along as though she were a leaf borne upon the currents of a strong-flowing stream.

A transparent figure walked through one of the doors. Karigan strode to it and tried the knob, but it was locked. Driven by an impulse that was not her own, she kicked at the door until wood splintered in the frame and then used her shoulder to force it open. That this was not acceptable behavior for a representative of the king was not foremost in her mind.

The room was unkempt, with blankets strewn about the bed and clothes piled on the floor. It smelled stale. An entire collection of weapons hung on the walls—knives, cudgels, a throwing ax, and even a shortsword.

"Here now, what ya doin'?" a man bellowed from behind her.

She turned and saw the enforcer. She took in, without emotion, the knife he carried, and promptly dismissed his existence. She moved across the room as though in a dream, pulled toward that which irritated her. She felt the presence of Westrion hovering, his great wings beating frigid downdrafts from the depths of the heavens.

"Get outta my room!"

She turned once more to face the man. He blanched and backed off.

"What the hells are you?" he whispered.

She gazed past him and sensed another presence in the shadows of the corridor, the Eletian, her witness.

The whispering drew her to one of the walls where a trophy of sorts was displayed, two arrows, each black and inscribed with dark ruins. One was splintered not quite in half. They burned in her vision. She removed them from their mount. They were loathsome to the touch, stung her hand, sought flesh and spirit. The arrowheads were encrusted with old blood.

"Those are mine!" the man protested from the doorway, but he seemed afraid to cross the threshold of his own room.

Karigan ignored him and broke the arrows over her knee. There was a release, an easing, and all else seemed to vanish from existence, the noise from downstairs, the yelling man, the unkempt room. The filmy figure of a Green Rider appeared before her. It was Joy Overway. Karigan had never known her in life.

You have freed me, Joy said. Her hair floated about her shoulders in the downdraft of the great wings. *Thank you, Avatar.* She faded away and then all was normal once again.

Karigan shook herself as though awakening from a dream. She stared at the broken arrows in her hand, not clear on how she'd ended up in this room with them. The only thing she did know was that she wanted to be rid of them, but the inn's enforcer blocked the doorway.

"I paid lots for those," he said, holding his knife in a threatening manner. Yet, his eyes flicked nervously. He almost looked scared.

There were any number of actions Karigan might have taken. She could have impressed him with her status as a swordmaster and honorary Weapon by drawing her saber to reveal the knotted silk on the blade, or she might have allowed him to attack. The first might have only served as provocation, and the second would certainly end in spilled blood. Both would have drawn Enver into a situation that would unmask him and cause even more trouble. As a representative of the king, starting a fight if it could be avoided would reflect poorly on the Green Riders and King Zachary, especially in a town such as this. Instead of drawing her sword, she reached into her pocket and tossed four silvers, an exorbitant amount, at the man's feet.

"Sorry," she said, and slipped past.

He'd pressed against the door frame so as not to touch her. "You *will* be sorry," he said, "if I see you around here again. Unnatural bitch."

Enver shadowed her back down the stairs. She eased her way between patrons to the hearth and threw the broken arrows into the fire. It flared and she fancied she could see a demonic face form in the flames, which was gone as quickly as it had appeared. She glanced at her hands. They were unscathed, but a sense of uncleanliness lingered. The people warming themselves at the fire regarded her curiously and with some suspicion.

She hurried to where Estral still sat talking with Barris. A glance over her shoulder revealed the enforcer stomping down the stairs, still unhappy, but his confidence back and looking ready for a fight. She dropped more coins on the table, grabbed her longsword, and said to Estral, "We are leaving. *Now.*"

"What? Barris and I were—"

Karigan grabbed Estral's arm. *"Now."*

Estral uttered farewells as Karigan dragged her out of the common room and into the wet courtyard, Enver close behind. The rain made the dusk even darker and the day feel even later than it was.

Estral wrenched her arm out of Karigan's grasp. "What was that for? Barris and I were catching up."

"We've overstayed our welcome." She and Enver hastened to help the stable boys tack the horses and reload Bane with their gear. When all were ready, Karigan did not pause, but rode out of the courtyard. A quick glance over her shoulder revealed the enforcer watching them from the doorway of the inn. To her credit, she kept Condor at a walk and did not run, but it was a fast walk.

Estral nosed Coda alongside Condor. The cat poked his face from beneath Estral's coat into the rain, and quickly hid himself again. "What was that all about?"

"Avoiding trouble," Karigan replied.

"Trouble? What did you do this time?"

Karigan looked at her askance. She supposed it *was* her fault, though she did not know exactly how she'd sensed the arrows and been drawn right to them. She shuddered, recalling how they had felt in her hands, how they'd wanted to feed on her soul. She had done that enforcer a favor, really, by destroying them. Not that the arrows would have impaled themselves in him of their own volition, but their mere presence in his room, with the malevolence they emanated, might have affected him in some way. How he obtained the arrows in the first place she did not wish to know. She had last seen them impaled in Joy's body, and he'd displayed them as prized possessions. He said he'd paid for them and she could only guess at what sort of person would sell arrows removed from a corpse. She tried to not let dark thoughts cloud what she had accomplished, the release of the spirit of Joy at long last.

"The Galadheon," Enver told Estral, "diffused a difficult situation."

Karigan glanced at him wondering how much he had witnessed. A good deal of it was unclear to her. She could not see his face for he still wore his hood.

"*What* difficult situation?" Estral demanded.

"I was taking care of unfinished business," Karigan replied. "It angered the inn's enforcer."

"What are you talking about? What unfinished business?"

Apparently Estral was not going to be satisfied until she explained. They were now outside the town and no one appeared to be following, so she told her about the arrows.

"Oh, gods," Estral murmured. "I remember the arrows. Captain Mapstone came looking for my father with the pair that had killed F'ryan Coblebay. They were . . . dark. As I recall, you broke the ones you found after the Battle of the Lost Lake."

"Yes, and later, the ones that killed F'ryan." The battle had not been long after Karigan's first passage through North. Shawdell had set up an ambush to kill King Zachary, and many nobles with him. When they fought Shawdell off, she had broken all the soul-stealing arrows she could find to release the spirits he'd enthralled.

"There were many I could not help," Karigan said, "and I never expected to find the pair that had taken Joy."

"If not for you," Estral said, "none would have been helped at all."

"Perhaps."

Traveling through North was a reminder of how it had all begun for her, a runaway schoolgirl who promised a dying messenger she encountered along the road that she would complete his mission. His brooch accepted her, and she learned very soon that it augmented a weak magical ability she had not known she possessed, an ability to fade out. More time passed before she learned that she was in fact not just fading out, but crossing thresholds in the layers of the world.

On that first momentous journey, she'd begun interacting with ghosts, and since then, had even seen and dealt with Salvistar, the steed of the god of death. It was not something she wanted, but it came with her brooch and being a Green Rider. Fortunately, it did not dominate her life, and once in a while, something good came of it, such as being able to break the arrows that had trapped Joy's spirit.

They had ridden a few miles when Enver halted Mist.

"What is it?" Karigan asked.

"Our path lies off the road here," he said.

"But we haven't reached the waystation."

"That is still hours down the road, is it not? We would have to backtrack. The path is here."

"I want to dry out," Karigan grumbled.

"The rain is slackening. It will be clear tomorrow."

"Karigan," Estral said, "I would like to be dry, too, but I would just as soon not lose time backtracking. I am also not interested in riding all night."

"We will ride for only a little while," Enver said, "then set up camp. There is a way I can spare you some of the damp."

Karigan wondered at that.

"Please," Estral said, "the farther north we go, the closer I may be getting to my father."

"We are *not* going to the Lone Forest." Karigan realized, unamused, that that was what she had said about North.

"This path does not lead to the Lone Forest," Enver said, "but it does lead north."

Estral fell uncharacteristically quiet.

Karigan contemplated the shadowy forms of her companions in the dark, rain dripping off the rim of her hood. She'd been looking forward to a roof over her head, the warmth and dryness of the waystation, and perhaps seeing the forester who was guardian in that area, but this was no leisure jaunt through the woods. The waystation was almost a day's ride from North and it would be well after midnight when they reached it. Then, if Enver was right about the path, they'd have to turn around and ride all the way back.

The cat poked his nose out from beneath Estral's coat again and sniffed the air. "Meep," he said.

"You say you can keep us dry?" Karigan asked Enver.

"Yes, Galadheon."

He must, she thought, have some sort of Eletian magic at hand. She let out a mournful sigh. "All right. We'll take the path."

CAT-MONSTER-THING

They did not ride long before Enver found a place for them to camp for the night in a patch of older woods that had not yet been harvested by the lumber merchants. The boughs of tall pines offered some protection from the rain.

"You will have to care for the horses," Enver told Karigan and Estral, "if I am to give us dryness."

Karigan thought that if he could work some magic, she was fine with that. Her fingers were stiff and cold as she tried to undo buckles of tack and harness. Enver, meanwhile, had drawn out his muna'riel and stood gazing into its depths. She glanced over her shoulder as she worked to see him moving his hand over the muna'riel, almost as if he were sculpting light.

Another time when she looked, it was much the same, but the rain did not seem to fall where there was light. The cat sat at Enver's feet, long whiskers rigid as he watched the Eletian's every move.

When the horses were taken care of, Karigan realized it wasn't raining on her even though she was outside the range of the light. The horses would be dry, too. She stretched her palm out to make sure, but no rain fell on it. She could hear it falling elsewhere. She carried their gear closer to where Enver sat cross-legged on his cloak, his head bowed and the muna'riel cupped in his hand. The cat lay stretched out beside him.

"Are you all right?" Karigan asked.

"I am well," he replied, "but using etherea has its cost, especially for one who is only half Eletian."

Karigan and Estral exchanged glances and continued to

set up camp. Enver may have created a dry area for them, but they were not going to find dry wood. Karigan was just as glad she'd had a hot meal in North.

"Do you want us to set up your tent for you?" Estral asked Enver.

"No. It takes persuasion."

Persuasion? Karigan wondered. *Eletians.*

After a time, he left the muna'riel nested on a pile of pine needles and rose to set up his tent. Karigan lit a lantern even with the light of the muna'riel, thinking it could at least be reminiscent of a fire. Then she and Estral collected wood and brought it into the light of the muna'riel. Perhaps it would dry enough overnight that they could have a fire in the morning.

When Enver emerged from his tent having, apparently, persuaded it to be set up, Estral asked, "Is there anything we can do for you?"

"Yes," he said, giving her a penetrating gaze. "You can teach me the song about the ale."

They sat around the lantern, and Estral did teach him, hesitantly at first, uncertain of the gift Idris had given her, then more strongly as her confidence grew. Karigan found herself amused by Enver, with his melodious Eletian voice, singing such a common song, especially the parts about belching ale bubbles. Whatever magic he had used to shield their campsite from the rain, it not only kept them dry, but seemed to warm them as well. Karigan's mood lightened, and any tension she'd felt since leaving North was vanquished.

When the song ended, Enver said, "You see, Lady Estral, you can sing. Your voice will not fail you."

"Yes," she said quietly, "but one day it *will* leave me, as it is borrowed. I don't know if I can face being silenced again."

"You'll get your own voice back," Karigan told her. "We'll find the thief and get it back."

Estral smiled wanly. "Thank you for your confidence. You seem to have it when mine fails."

Karigan thought that was what friendship was about.

They retired to their tent for the night, the cat choosing to sleep on Estral's face. She lifted him off, spitting out orange hair, and placed him between her and Karigan.

"I think he needs a name," Estral said. "Something other than 'Cat.'"

Karigan yawned, pulling her blankets to her chin. "Let me know when you come up with one."

The cat was actually an asset in their small tent, giving off more heat than one would think a creature of his size capable. He was better than a hot warming stone, and softer. The vibration of his resonant purrs was like a massage to the small of her back.

The dome of dryness and warmth Enver had placed around their camp had been so effective that it was a shock when Karigan crawled out of her tent and discovered the world outside the dome was coated in ice. Morning light shone golden across the glazed landscape. Ice sheathed the branches of trees and shrubs, which chimed in the breeze. An enchanted fairy world it looked. It was also perceptibly colder, and Karigan wrapped her arms about herself.

Enver stood looking outward. "Winter still has some strength in it." His breath fogged the air. "I do not think we should remove ourselves from this place until perhaps tomorrow."

Karigan mourned the waystation anew. So they were going to be delayed after all, but at least at the waystation they would have had four walls, a roof, and a fireplace. Enver's shielding spell was nice, but it did not have the solidity of log walls. He was right, though, that they should stay put. The slippery and sharp ice would be treacherous to the horses. Overhanging limbs could crash down on them beneath all that weight.

"It looks like a realm for the aureas slee," Karigan said.

She had meant it lightly, but Enver's response was serious. "I do not think the aureas slee was behind this. It feels . . . unmanipulated."

Unmanipulated. The idea that some elemental could purposely create such a scene? She did not want to think about it. Instead, she set to building a fire, grateful she'd collected wood the night before. It was relatively dry, and soon she had smoky flames crackling.

Estral and the cat emerged from the tent, both stretching and yawning. The cat then trotted over to the fire. When Estral's eyes popped open, she gazed in wonder at their surroundings.

It had been a sound decision not to continue the journey. Even as they sat by the fire, all around them trees creaked and the snap and crash of ice-laden branches reverberated through the otherwise still forest. The cat meowed in protest and hid his head beneath the tails of Estral's coat, and the horses snorted in alarm, except for Mist who nuzzled the others in an attempt to calm them.

Karigan thought she could use some calming herself. This was not her first ice storm, but every time a limb crashed in the woods and ice shattered on the ground like a thousand glass bottles, her frayed nerves caused her to jump and her heart to pound. Perspiration broke out on her forehead. The noise bared memories from across layers of time, of a chamber of ice, a horse screaming . . .

Bam! Another stout limb snapped and she wanted to scream. A vision rushed into her mind of a metal device in a man's hand, its explosive report and the smoke it emitted, Raven going down in the throne room of the emperor. She cried out.

"Karigan, are you all right?" Estral said.

She covered her ears as another ice-laden branch smashed to the ground. Estral put her hand on her shoulder. Karigan bent over with a gasp. *"Raven, Raven, Raven . . . "* she murmured, her cheeks moist and vision blurred. There was muffled conversation between Estral and Enver, and then, she did not know how much later, Enver took her hand from her ear and pressed into it a mug of a hot, herby-scented tea, with a hint of tangy spice.

"This will make it easier for you," he said.

She eyed him suspiciously, but when another tree cracked and fell and she almost dropped the mug, she took a sip. It did relax her, but her heart still thudded with every fallen branch.

"The noise reminds you of something in the future time?" Estral asked her.

Karigan shuddered and nodded, but would say no more.

As the day wore on and the explosive noises in the woods became less frequent, Karigan was further calmed, and entertained, by Estral teaching Enver drinking songs. She wondered what his people would make of it when he brought those songs back to Eletia. It was dusk when she noticed the horses growing nervous, and it was not from snapping branches this time, for the forest had quieted. Mist gave a shrill whinny, and the cat stood with his ears back and fur on end. His growl was so menacing that Karigan had to take a second look to make sure he had not turned into a catamount.

Enver stood fluidly. "Predators." He reached for his bow.

"Groundmites?" Estral asked, barely above a whisper.

"No. Wolves."

As if to confirm his words, howls filled the woods. If winter had been hard on groundmites, Karigan thought, it certainly had been hard on other creatures, as well. Wolves would not ordinarily attack people at a campsite, but if they were as desperate as the groundmites had been? She reached for her longsword and handed her saber to Estral, who accepted it without comment.

The howls came again, chillingly closer. Karigan saw movement in the nearby brush.

"They desire the horses," Enver said.

Just then, a gray-brindle wolf darted toward the horses. Mist, who was not hobbled, turned on her haunches and thrust her front hooves at it. Even as Enver nocked an arrow to his bowstring, and even as Karigan set foot toward the horses, sword in hand, the cat, still growling and snarling, pelted by her and leaped. He looked bigger in his fury, and then she realized he *was* bigger and growing as he flew through the air, and so shocked was she that she halted in her tracks as their sweet orange tabby cat morphed into a large cat-monster-thing with wings.

He went after the wolves snarling, leaping, flying, lunging. The wolves yipped as they ran off.

"We will not be seeing them again," Enver said in satisfaction, his bowstring now slack.

"What in the name of the gods?" Karigan said, still trying to work out what had become of their little tabby.

The cat-monster-thing padded back to camp. He paused by the horses, who were not afraid of him, and rubbed his face against Bane's neck and flank. Then he approached them, ruffled his eagle wings, and sat in front of them.

"Mister Whiskers?" Estral asked.

"Meep," came the little voice.

"What . . . ?" Karigan could barely squeak the word out.

"A gryphon, Galadheon," Enver said, "the likes of which have not been seen in a millennium."

Karigan, who had seen so much in her life that was strange and wondrous, found that she kind of wanted to faint.

Estral walked right up to the creature and started scratching him under his chin.

"Estral!" Karigan said in alarm.

"It's Mister Whiskers, the gryphon that Alton released from Tower of the Heavens. Who's a good kitty now?"

"Good gods," Karigan murmured, watching her friend pet and speak baby talk to the monster. "I have seen everything now."

"Everything?" Enver asked. "There is much in this world to see."

Mister Whiskers preened with the attention, then spread his wings. Estral retreated several paces to give him room. He flapped his wings with great downbeats creating a wind that rippled their tents and sent debris flying. He recoiled on his hind end, then launched into the air, circling a few times overhead, then flew off in a northwesterly direction. It was an unusual sight to see the giant cat-thing airborne.

"I guess he is off to seek a mate," Estral said.

Karigan wished him well, but wondered what the world would be like if gryphons once again ruled the sky.

THE STRANGE BEHAVIOR OF ZACHARY

Laren saw little of Zachary, and only at a distance, as he conducted the dance that was the ceremonial welcoming of a royal prince of Rhovanny. Tuandre was the seventh son of seven sons, and therefore the least of King Thergood's progeny, which in itself revealed that Thergood was little interested in Sacoridia's problem with Second Empire, and was not taking the threat of Mornhavon the Black very seriously. Most of these issues were occurring within Sacoridia's borders, after all, and not Rhovanny. Still, if Thergood hadn't some interest, he would have sent some lesser envoy than one of his own sons.

So, there was the formal welcome, the public greeting, the shared chalice of wine representing the blood between cousins, for they were related. Rhovanny had had many blood ties with Sacoridian royalty over the generations. If Thergood had had a daughter, she would have been a strong contender to become Zachary's wife.

There were feasting and other stuffy formalities that accompanied a royal visit. The king and the prince would get down to business soon enough, and Zachary would have to convince Tuandre of the seriousness of the threat from their ancient enemy. Laren's presence was not required for the ceremonial aspects of the visit, but she was certain Zachary would summon her when formal talks began.

In the meantime, she had not been able to see Zachary on a more informal basis as Estora had wished, and as she strode through the chill air across castle grounds, she was not sure when she'd get the opportunity. Zachary was, of course, tied up with the prince's visit, and when he was not with the prince, he was with Estora.

Laren, in turn, was kept busy overseeing her Riders being sent out to convey messages and invitations to nobles and others of importance for functions involving the prince. She did take a moment one afternoon to visit Loon and Bluebird, though she did not ride. Vanlynn had heard about how she'd ridden Loon after having been patched up, and gave her a stern upbraiding. She was ordered not to ride until she was declared fit. When it came to injuries and sickness, the master mender outranked generals, much less mere captains.

Bluebird gently nuzzled her shoulder as if he knew exactly how it had been hurt, while Loon continued to look rather abashed. They had had words, of course, but now she stroked the spotted horse's nose.

"I don't hold a grudge," she told him, "and you are still young. You'll learn."

His ears seemed to relax at her words.

"Ah, Captain, good to see you about and visiting your boys."

Laren turned to find Horse Master Riggs approaching. She was a compact woman of middling years and came from a family of hostlers from Hillander Province. Her father had served Zachary's family estate, as her brother did now, and she came to Sacor City to train both horses and riders. Laren had seen her handle the most high-strung of stallions and the shyest of foals with a sure and kind hand, and she had a knack for teaching riders of all abilities. Laren was glad that Riggs was there to oversee the training of Green Riders and their horses.

"You're right about Loon," Riggs said. "He'll learn. How's the shoulder?"

"Not bad." She'd been following Vanlynn's instructions exactly, and Ben had given her tiny bits of his true healing touch to encourage her shoulder to mend, but it was a secret between the two of them, for after the assassination attempt on Zachary last spring, Vanlynn decreed that Ben's ability was to be reserved for dire need only. His ability had its limits and was not to be exhausted on illnesses and injuries that would mend fine on their own. Laren agreed, especially with the queen expecting, but her shoulder had become a hindrance in accomplishing her duties, and Ben had wanted to help. He said that he could make her shoulder less likely to dislocate again. Who was she to argue?

"Glad to hear it." Riggs rubbed her elbow as if remembering an old injury of her own. "I'm waiting for your young lady to appear for her lesson."

"My young lady?" Laren stared blankly at her.

"Anna? One of the queen's servants?"

"Of course. It's been arranged then?"

"Yes, through Mistress Evans. Going to put the girl on Mallard."

Mallard was an unclaimed Rider horse with an easygoing disposition, more likely to nap in the sun than run away with a novice rider. Laren couldn't think of a better mount for Anna's first lesson.

"Ah, this must be her now," Riggs said.

The girl stood uncertainly at the far end of the building.

"Hello, Anna," Laren said, hoping to put her at ease. "Come meet Horse Master Riggs."

After introductions, Riggs looked Anna over with a critical, but not unkind, eye.

"We won't be doing side saddle."

Anna was wearing a skirt.

"Have you no trousers?" Riggs asked. "Boots?"

Anna shook her head.

"Mistress Evans won't thank me if your livery is soiled."

"Hmm," Laren said. "I could probably track down something secondhand that one of my Riders can't use anymore." Rider uniform parts did begin to look shabby after a while and had to be put out of service, even if they weren't worn out, because the king's messengers must look polished.

Riggs nodded. "Good. Then we'll just begin with the basics of getting to know a horse."

Laren patted Loon and Bluebird one last time and nodded farewell as Riggs led Anna down the aisle toward Mallard's stall. Laren did not want to be a distraction—the girl already looked nervous enough. Undoubtedly, she would be introduced to the horse, get to pet and brush him, and learn to put a halter on him and lead him around. It would be a good, gentle start. Laren, meanwhile, would find Mara and ask her to track down some likely pairs of trousers and boots.

Later that day, Laren was going over Rider accounts with Daro in officers quarters when a Green Foot runner came to her door with a message.

"From Counselor Tallman, ma'am."

Laren thanked the boy and unfolded the paper awkwardly with her good hand. According to Les, there was a meeting transpiring with Prince Tuandre on substantive issues, and that perhaps she would like to be present. Why hadn't Zachary summoned her? This was most unusual.

Her dismay must have been plain for Daro asked, "What is it, Captain?"

"A meeting underway without me. Would you help me with my dress longcoat and sash?" The visit of a dignitary like Prince Tuandre required her formal uniform, and with Daro's help, she was properly attired, though the coat had to be draped over her bad shoulder. There was nothing else for it, though, and she set off for the castle.

When she reached the meeting room, Willis opened the door so she could slip in. Zachary sat slumped in a small version of his throne chair at the head of the table, and the prince at the opposite end in a comfortable chair of his own. Along the sides sat advisors and courtiers of both Rhovanny and Sacoridia. Laren kept against the wall near Fastion, for there were no empty chairs, and she did not wish to disrupt the proceedings by requesting one, or even by moving to stand near Zachary. She tried to catch his eye, but his attention seemed concentrated inward, his attitude withdrawn.

The meeting focused on issues of trade, and with Rhovanny as one of Sacoridia's primary trade partners, it was certainly important. As the prince's people negotiated with the king's over tariffs, it brought to mind a customer and a merchant haggling on market day. Rhovanny's most important export was wine, and the Rhovans were eager to find relief from taxes, just as Sacoridia's merchants would likewise desire relief.

Laren watched Zachary more than the negotiators. Normally he'd join in on such talks, but she did not think he was paying any attention whatsoever. Was he sick? He looked healthy enough. It was clear to her he did not wish to be present. To be fair, Prince Tuandre spoke little, but at least he made the occasional remark and seemed otherwise engaged. This must be quite the education for him, for he was but eighteen or nineteen. He'd a bevy of counselors with him, however, to speak for Rhovanny's interests.

When the session ended at the tolling of four hour, Laren sighed in relief. It was a long time standing and she ached all over. She stood aside as the assembled dispersed, with the intention of speaking with Zachary, but he left in haste and spoke to no one, not even Prince Tuandre. She couldn't even ask Fastion if he had any idea what was going on with Zachary because he had to rush out of the chamber to keep up with the king.

She found herself standing alone in the chamber, mystified. Zachary hadn't even glanced her way when normally there would have been at least some acknowledgment of her existence. His excessive attention to Estora had been odd enough, though she'd taken to heart what Les Tallman had said about "nesting." Even if Estora had not already asked her to look into it, she would have anyway based on the behavior that she had just witnessed.

Laren decided there was no time like the present to go talk to Zachary and see for herself the cause of his behavior. By the time she reached his door, however, he was already closed away in his apartments, with Weapons on guard outside.

"Fastion," she said, "I'd like to see the king."

"I'm sorry, Captain," he replied, "but he has ordered no disturbances. Perhaps if you made an appointment with his secretary?"

Laren had never required an appointment to see Zachary before, though she had also never infringed on his desire for privacy.

"I would like to see the queen, then."

"I'm sorry, Captain, but the king is with the queen."

She wondered how much Estora wished not to be disturbed, or if it was just Zachary imposing his wishes upon her.

"Could you just please tell the king I am here? I'm sure he'd see me."

Fastion's expression remained stony, and he did not move an inch. "I'm sorry, Captain, but his orders were explicit."

If he said "I'm sorry" one more time . . . She stared at him. He was as immoveable as a statue. She glanced at Willis, and he was much the same. It would be of no use to wheedle and cajole. She'd just have to catch Zachary while he was out and about, or try later. Thing was, if he wasn't even sending for her to attend him at meetings, it would be difficult to know when these times were, and she could not camp outside his door. It would be unseemly, and she had enough of her own work to attend to.

She turned on her heel and strode brusquely down the corridor only to encounter a familiar figure burdened with ash buckets and the other implements of her vocation.

"Anna," she said, "how did your time with Master Riggs go today?"

"Fine, ma'am." Anna looked rattled to be suddenly confronted by her. Her buckets were full, so she must have just come from the royal apartments by way of the servants corridor.

"Did you like Mallard?"

"Oh, yes'm. He is so big, but gentle. He let me pet his nose and everything."

Laren was relieved. The girl was nervous as a hare and it wouldn't take much to scare her off, and yet there was the steely aspect to her.

"Anna," she said, "were you just with the king and queen?"

"The queen, ma'am. I made sure I got out of there before the king returned."

"Made sure?"

"Yes'm. I don't think he likes me in there when he's with the queen, and when I am . . ." She shuddered.

"When you are, what?"

"His eyes. I should not say this about our king, but his eyes get all hard and I can feel him watching me until I leave."

That, Laren thought, was not like the Zachary she knew. She glanced about to make sure there wasn't anyone in hearing range. "Anna, if you would, let me know if you observe anything unusual where the king is concerned."

"Unusual?"

"Er, if something just doesn't seem right to you."

Anna looked thoughtful. "He likes his rooms cold, never wants a fire. But then he is usually with the queen anyway."

That was somewhat odd, Laren thought, but Zachary was generally practical, and if he was spending his time in Estora's quarters? "Anything like that," she said, "bring it to me. And also, if you are alone with the queen, tell her that if she ever needs anything from me, that she is to send you to me immediately."

"Yes'm."

There were questions in Anna's eyes, but she did not ask them.

"Thank you, Anna. You may carry on with your duties."

"Yes'm."

Laren watched thoughtfully after the girl carrying her buckets down the corridor. Having an ash girl keep watch on Zachary was perhaps not the most reliable way of finding out the cause of his behavior, but it was certainly better than nothing, and who would suspect an ash girl?

It was the best she could do for the moment, until an opportunity to confront Zachary directly presented itself.

WHAT SIR KARIGAN WOULD DO

The next morning, Anna woke up nervous, for today she would actually ride Mallard. Mara had found her some old but serviceable boots to wear, and green trousers that were no longer suitable for a Rider to wear on King's business. They fit well, and she had gazed at herself for so long in the mirror that her roommate could only roll her eyes.

After breakfast, she hurried to Rider stables. She couldn't believe her luck, really. First she'd been transferred to working in the royal quarters, and then she started having new lessons to learn history and such, and with Green Riders even. Best of all, despite the fact she couldn't be a Green Rider herself, she was going to learn to ride. Not so long ago she could not have conceived of coming to Captain Mapstone's attention, much less the queen's. She, of course, couldn't forget Sir Karigan. If not for her, none of this would have happened. Anna would not have met the queen and captain, and, this part made her shiver, she might very well be dead. Sir Karigan had saved her from the ice creatures, after all.

The stables were warm compared to the outdoors, and she waited by Mallard's stall in anticipation for Horse Master Riggs to arrive. When she did, Anna was told to groom Mallard the way she had learned the previous day. Then she learned to tack him and was instructed to lead him out to the paddock where the lesson began in earnest. Anna had been on horses only a few times before, always riding behind someone else, and they'd been burly farm beasts. Mallard was sleek in comparison. It was strange being up in the saddle all by herself, but Master Riggs went slowly to make sure she was not scared. She learned how to use the reins and her legs, and how to sit and maintain her center of balance, but they did little more than move at a walk.

Afterward, Anna learned how to untack Mallard, and she brushed him down. She then had to hurry back to the castle for her shift.

As Anna lugged her implements down the servants quarters to the queen's apartments, she could feel the ache in her legs. Sitting on a horse took a lot more muscle than she thought. It always looked like the horse was doing all the work and the rider just sat there, but now she was learning there was much more to it.

She cleaned the ashes out of the queen's bed chamber hearth, and by the time she reached the queen's sitting room, she was pleased to discover the king was not present. He must be meeting with the Rhovan prince, and she was glad. King Zachary's hard eyes and cold manner disturbed her.

The queen reclined on her sofa and looked to be napping. Anna went to work at the hearth as silently as possible, but her presence did not go unmarked.

"Hello, Anna," the queen said.

Startled, Anna whirled and made a clumsy curtsy. The queen was not asleep after all.

"How are you?" the queen asked. "Are you enjoying your new lessons?"

"Yes, Your Majesty. It's wonderful."

The queen smiled, but it was a tired smile. Anna remembered then what Captain Mapstone had asked her to do the day before. "Your Majesty?"

"Yes, Anna?"

"Captain Mapstone asked me to tell you that if you ever need anything from her, to send me immediately."

The queen smiled again. "A crafty woman, is our Captain Mapstone. She's turning you into a regular messenger." The city bells started ringing out the noon hour. The queen frowned, and when the last bell faded, she said, "Anna, please tell the captain to meet me here this time tomorrow."

"Yes, Your Majesty."

Anna returned to work, and as she finished up, she heard a door open and close, and there was a curious inrush of cold air. A quick glance over her shoulder confirmed that the king had arrived. She hefted her buckets and tools and scuttled from the sitting room.

She heard the king say, "I am returned, my dearest. Now we can sit together."

"So soon?" the queen asked. She did not sound particularly pleased.

Anna entered the servants' corridor and their voices fell away as she left the queen's apartments behind.

The following day, Anna had no lessons, but as always, she attended to her rounds. It was one of the days she took care of the Rider wing and she had found that she'd gone from unnoticed to known, for many of the Riders she happened to encounter in the course of her work now knew her name and greeted her. Her life had changed so dramatically she could hardly believe it. Tomorrow she would begin basic arms training, and the idea was both thrilling and even more frightening than riding a horse. The Riders reassured her that Arms Master Gresia was a good instructor and that it wouldn't be frightening at all.

Buoyed by their words, she headed back to the west wing to tend Queen Estora's rooms. As she worked in the queen's bed chamber, she heard the queen speaking to someone out in the sitting room, and then remembered it was the time that the queen had requested Captain Mapstone to see her. When Anna had delivered the message to the captain, the captain had sat back in her chair deep in thought, looking concerned. Anna didn't know what was going on, but she sensed the queen was unhappy. Snippets of their conversation drifted back to her.

"—and the prince and his counselors are right to be offended," the captain said. "His lack of interest has been rude. He was the one, after all, who requested the Rhovans to come. It's entirely unlike him."

The queen said something Anna could not hear.

"No," Captain Mapstone replied. "I have not. He has not let me near him, and he does not summon me to attend him. I find out about meetings if Les Tallman remembers to send me a message."

The frustration was, to Anna's ear, clear in the captain's voice. She crept toward the sitting room trying to remain as inconspicuous as possible, but the two women were so deep into their conversation that they did not appear to notice her.

"It is troubling," the queen said. "He will not even allow his dogs near him."

"That is extremely unusual," the captain replied.

When Anna reached the hearth, she chanced a backward glance. The captain stood, seeming to gaze off into the distance, her left arm still bound to her. The queen sat on her sofa, seeming to have sunk into her own thoughts.

"I cannot believe I am saying this," the queen told the captain, "but I prefer the old Zachary. He did not smother me, and he let me see other people."

"What? What do you mean? He doesn't let you see other people now?"

"Not even my ladies. He barely lets the servants do their work. Jaid is almost afraid to come tend me. That is why I had you come now, because I knew he'd be meeting with the Rhovans."

"That . . . that is not Zachary. Something is very wrong." The captain's boots tapped the floor as she paced. Then she paused. "It's almost as if he's bespelled, and I wouldn't put such a thing past Second Empire."

Anna dumped a panful of ashes into one of her buckets. She was working slowly, too slowly, but the conversation was very interesting. She knew she shouldn't even be paying attention, but she couldn't help herself. She shook her head. *I need to—*

Her thought was cut off by the opening and closing of a door, and that curious inrush of cold air made the flames leap and crackle. She hunched down, not wishing to be spotted by the king.

"I am returned, my—" He stopped short, the air and attitude of the room turning decidedly frosty. "Laren, what brings you here?" His tone was almost one of menace.

"I requested that she come," the queen said. "Surely you would not begrudge a visit from your old friend."

Silence. Then, "You are not to expose yourself to outsiders who may be carrying sickness."

"Laren is not an outsider," she countered, "and though you are my king and husband, I resent your telling me who I may and may not see. I am not your prisoner."

Anna glanced over her shoulder again. The king looked furious, and the captain, who had remained quiet during the exchange, peered oddly at him, almost as if she were searching his soul.

"You have not been yourself," the queen told him.

The room chilled considerably.

"All I wish to do is cherish you," he said, "to honor you and our children."

"You are right," the captain told the queen, "he is not himself."

Anna held her breath.

"In fact," the captain said, "I would venture to say it is not even him."

"What do you mean?" the queen asked.

"You know I have the ability to read a person's honesty? I cannot read *him*. I am blocked by a wall of ice. I know Zachary's mind and he has no ability to block me like this. Whoever this is, his mind is . . . alien. This is not Zachary." The captain unsheathed her saber and cried, "FASTION!"

The king flung his hand out, and the captain was hurled across the room, her sword ringing when it hit the floor. She did not rise. The queen stood aghast, and there was pounding on the doors, voices shouting outside, Weapons trying to enter.

Terrified, Anna crouched down low to stay out of sight, not believing what her eyes and ears were telling her. The room was so cold no matter she was beside the fire.

"Who are you?" the queen demanded, fear quavering in her voice.

"I am more powerful than any king in the world. I am the north wind and the ice that bites in winter and thaws in spring. I am the maelstrom of a blizzard and the tranquility of a snow-covered field. The Eletians name me aureas slee. I am ice."

As he spoke, the room grew colder and colder. Anna wrapped her arms around herself not wanting chattering teeth to give her away.

"Leave me," the queen said. "Don't touch me."

"I must take you away from here. I will take you to my domain."

"No!"

"I admit it is risky for your offspring, but I must have you."

"Let me go!"

Anna turned and peered around the end of the sofa. The king, or whoever he was, held the queen's wrists. She was trying to break away. It sounded like he planned to take her somewhere against her will. The Weapons battered the doors. They should have broken them down by now, but there must be magic at work holding them at bay. The captain couldn't help, for she lay unmoving on the floor. The only one left to help was Anna.

But I am no one.

She was "no one" with a fire burning beside her. She took a breath to collect herself and gazed into flame.

"You are hurting me," the queen protested.

"Calmly, my love. Being distressed will not be good for the children. We will be there in but a blinking."

The sound of scuffling and the queen's throttled scream came from behind. There was no time for Anna to worry if she was brave enough. She had to act. She thrust a bundle of kindling into the fire.

"Let me go!" the queen cried.

"Do not resist. You do not wish to harm the children, do you?"

The flames ate at the ends of the kindling. It seemed to take forever. In a flash, Anna remembered Sir Karigan dropping the chandelier on the ice creatures and by doing so almost setting the castle on fire. It was an extreme emergency and damage to the queen's chambers was less important than helping the queen herself.

Anna grabbed her shovel and filled it with live coals. All at once she stood and turned and flung the coals toward the aureas slee. Most landed on the sofa, and flames flared up. The aureas slee was so surprised he let the queen go. He must have also been hit because he roared in pain. Anna ducked down and grabbed her bundle of kindling, the ends now ablaze. She tried not to think, to not let worries trip her up. She sprinted around the sofa and jabbed the burning kindling into the face of the aureas slee. He fell back, threw his arm up to protect his face. She kept pressing.

This is what Sir Karigan would do, she thought. Well, actually, Sir Karigan would probably use her sword, or maybe her staff, but if she had kindling, this is what Sir Karigan would do.

The sleeve of the elemental's coat caught fire. He shrieked. His face began to lose shape, took on an icy translucence. He stumbled back into a chair and sent a great wind howling through the room. Tapestries and drapes ripped off the walls. Vases crashed to the floor. It tore the breath from Anna and nearly bowled her over, and it bent the flames of her kindling back at her.

The aureas slee must have been losing control for suddenly the doors crashed open and Weapons poured in. They bore down on the creature like furious hornets. It was now more than clear that the aureas slee was *not* the king for he'd lost all the king's features, was a figure of clear ice, with eyes like hailstones. Its arm melted off with the heat of the flames. Its wail pierced through Anna's chest, then failed as swords hacked into it.

There was another enormous blast of wind that blew out her kindling, and then nothing. The aureas slee was gone. It left behind only a pile of the king's clothes that it had been wearing, and a puddle that had been its arm. All grew quiet, the wailing had ceased, the air stilled. For a breath, no one moved, but for a breath only.

"See to the queen," one of the Weapons ordered the others. "Get Vanlynn and Rider Simeon, *now*!"

"Captain Mapstone is down," another Weapon shouted from near her crumpled body.

Anna stood where she was as the Weapons swarmed about the room and around her. She still held the smoking bundle of kindling like an extinguished torch. Beside her the sofa smoldered, and in her peripheral vision, she saw a Weapon lift the queen into his arms and carry her away toward her bed chamber.

It was as good a time as any, Anna thought, to faint.

BENEATH THE OPEN SKY

Zachary dreamed once more of the deer fleeing before him, bounding this time not through the woods, but through tall grasses. He pursued her, but he could never run fast enough. He was always trying to catch up, his bow in hand. The grasses whipped his legs as he ran, the distance ever widening between him and his quarry. He would never have her. He . . .

He lost the dream as he awakened, awakened not to a lush green grassland, but a cave with all its hues of gray and brown, the constant low light of the glowstones. Was it day or night in the outside world? Was it still caught in the grip of winter, or had the thaw begun? He did not know if he'd been a prisoner here for days, or weeks. It felt like years.

What was happening in his kingdom? What damage had the aureas slee wrought on all his people? Was Estora all right? Surely she could tell the elemental was not him. Laren ought to be able to tell right away. If they were able to detect and overcome the elemental, how would he ever know? Surely they'd never find him. He could be anywhere in the world.

He groaned and rolled over in his sleeping alcove only to jolt to full wakefulness when he came face-to-face with Magged, who knelt beside him.

"You move and mumble in your sleep," she said.

How long had she been watching him?

"Slee brought us a deer once," she told him. "We butchered and ate it. It was delicious." She licked her cracked lips, her gaze distant in memory.

Zachary swung his legs out of the alcove and stood in an attempt to get some distance from her. His ribs, at least, no longer twinged every time he moved, though the bruises were slow to fade.

"It was a lady deer," Magged continued. "I can tell the difference, you know."

She followed him as he strode across the cavern. Nari was nowhere to be seen. Magged was on his heels as he descended to the lower cavern. Midway down, he halted and turned. She practically walked into him.

"I would like some privacy," he said.

"Oh, are you going to make water?"

"Yes."

"It doesn't bother me to watch."

He tried to suppress his mounting irritation. "It bothers *me*."

Magged gave him a look like she thought he was being silly, but she sat on a rock. "I will wait here, then."

Zachary took a deep breath and continued on. He was accustomed to the constant presence of others around him, but even the Weapons allowed him to urinate in private. When he finished, he found the hotspring and splashed water on his face. He'd take a full bath, but he suspected Magged would come looking for him. In fact, when he rose from the pool, he turned to find her standing there. He was so startled he almost stepped backward into it.

"Magged!" he said sharply. "Please don't sneak up on me."

She tilted her head as she looked up at him, then pulled her shift over her head and stood naked before him.

"Magged," he said, this time more subdued, and he averted his gaze from her pale body. "Please cover yourself."

"Don't you want me?"

"No." There was no kinder way to say it that she would hear.

"Why?" she asked plaintively, reaching out to him. He stepped away. "Do you like Nari better?"

His cheeks burned. Nari was undeniably lovely in the Eletian way, and what man would not think in those terms? "I am married," he said. "I have a wife."

"You will never see her again. I can be your wife."

"No, Magged. I'm sorry." Keeping his gaze averted, he walked around her and away. A quick glance over his shoulder revealed her staring into the pool. He felt easier knowing that she was not following. He wondered not for the first time from where Magged had been taken. She'd been raised and taught by Nari, so there was no clue from accent or mannerism. She'd been too young when abducted by the aureas slee to have developed the ways of her homeland. Could she be one of his own subjects?

If he found a way out of this cave, how would Magged adapt to the outside world? It would all be new to her, completely foreign. The cave was her home, all she had ever known. Could she survive outside?

He supposed, as he paused in the cavern where they slept and ate, it wasn't worth worrying about since he'd failed thus far to discover an exit. There was no sign of Nari, so he continued up the steps to the upper cavern with all the dripstone formations. Nari, he guessed, was off collecting the fungus they survived on. His stomach rumbled at the thought of food, no matter how unsatisfying and bland.

He was holding up rather well, he thought, despite the absence of regular, hearty meals, and of the hundreds of servants who saw to his comfort. He would have guessed he'd feel more adrift without a secretary organizing his days, but there was no need for a schedule in the cave. He did not feel exposed without his Weapons, for the cave was a quiet, contained environment, though he'd surely wish for them if the aureas slee returned. There was no one constantly vying for his attention, no political intrigue, no real demands. It was, in fact, something of a relief. But then he'd remember his predicament and the danger to his wife and realm and start searching once more for a way out.

When he reached the upper cavern, he was so surprised by the sight that greeted him, he thought he must be hallucinating.

"Meep," said the orange tabby cat. It sat on the stone gryphon.

A cat was not something Zachary would usually consider

eating, but his stomach rumbled at the thought of fresh meat. His initial thought of food then transformed into shock that there was a cat sitting right there before him. Where had it come from? If it had gotten in, then surely there had to be a way of getting out. Then he remembered both Nari and Magged mentioning that the elemental brought them food occasionally. But why would it bring a cat? It wasn't much of a meal for three people.

"Where did you come from, little one?" Zachary asked. It just rubbed its cheek against the back of the gryphon's head. He stepped toward the cat. It did not flee. With another step, it paused its rubbing and stared at him. He halted. Was this some trick of the aureas slee? But the cat rolled over and wriggled its back against the gryphon and purred madly.

Zachary began to search the chamber anew, hunting for a possible exit that he might have overlooked before. He searched feverishly, crawling into crevices, feeling into cracks with his hands, even areas he'd combed before.

"How did you get in?" he demanded of the cat, but it just lay on the stone gryphon with its paws in the air, purring blissfully as though gorged on catnip. There was a reason, Zachary thought, that he gravitated toward dogs.

Nari entered the chamber and stared first at Zachary, and then at the cat. She spoke softly in Eletian, stepped closer to gaze at the cat.

"I have not seen," she finally said, "one of these creatures in so very long."

"I have been trying to figure out how it entered."

She gazed at him with wide eyes, eyes filled with hope. "To feel the sun on my face again," she said. "To smell of the earth and green of living things."

"Will you help me look?"

"Yes," she replied, "though the creature could have squeezed through a very narrow opening."

"Could the elemental have put it here?"

"I do not think so. I did not feel Slee's presence."

They started working along the walls, examining the barest cracks, and gazing up at the ceiling.

"You can feel the aureas slee's presence?" Zachary asked.

"It is very cold."

"So, where could the cat have come from?"

"Almost anywhere," she replied. "We do not know where we are, after all."

That was true and Zachary considered the possibility they were near civilization, but he had a hard time believing it. If they were somewhere in the wilderness, how had an ordinary house cat found them? He glanced back at the cat many times to ensure it did not slink off and disappear on them.

"Maybe we should get Magged to help," he suggested.

"She is sulking." Nari gave him an accusing look.

"Because I rebuffed her?" He peered behind a thick stalagmite.

"Yes. It is the way of your race. She desires family. I have tried my best to be a companion to her, but I cannot provide for all her needs, particularly those which only a male can gratify."

"I am afraid I cannot fulfill that need for her either," he replied. "One cannot always have what one desires. I am committed to another. I've a wife, with children on the way."

"I understand," Nari replied, "and I have gleaned you are the king of the Sacor Clans. You feel great responsibility toward your people."

"I do, very much so."

"That is honorable. For Magged, whose whole world is the cave, what is outside is meaningless. She cannot comprehend the weight of your responsibilities. I tried to explain, but all she feels right now is the pain of rejection."

Zachary looked behind a boulder. "I did not wish to hurt her. If we can find a way out, perhaps there will be someone with whom she can have that family."

Nari paused her search. "I do not know if she would survive the outside world for long. I do not know that she would wish to leave."

Zachary sat on the boulder to rest. He could not imagine wanting to stay in this hole in the ground, but he had not spent his whole life there. "What about you, Nari? Would you leave?"

"Yes," she said without hesitation. "There is one who . . ."

"Someone from whom you were taken?"

"Yes. I would search for him, see if he still awaits me, or if he was lost in Argenthyne."

She spoke as though only a few years had passed, not centuries, and in Eletian terms, he supposed it was. He'd been so intent on exploring and trying to find a route of escape from his prison that he hadn't thought to ask her what the world had been like before she was abducted by the aureas slee. What had Argenthyne been like? Might she have had contact with his ancestors? These questions and more now came to him. In his role as king, there'd been little propriety for casual conversation with the Eletians who had presented themselves to him. But now? He was no king here.

No king.

He was about to ask Nari his questions when he noticed the cat standing with its fur on end. It growled. The cave amplified the growl until it expanded into every nook of the cavern and sent sonorous vibrations along the dripstone formations.

Magged emerged from the passage that led to the lower cavern. "What is—?" she began.

Zachary never heard the rest of her question because freezing air shrieked through the cavern and slammed into him. He was blown back and ice crystals raked his skin. He leaned into the maelstrom and shielded his face with his hands and tried to see what was happening. Nari jumped behind a large stalagmite to shield herself from the tempest. Magged huddled against the cavern wall.

The wind eased and a translucent form, like a glazed man, appeared before him, and he realized it was of his own approximate shape and features, had he been made of ice. The elemental's body, if it could be called such, was crisscrossed with deep scores as though from sword blades and was missing one of its arms. Zachary broke off a large stalagmite and held it like a club.

"So," he said, "you have been ousted." Wind gusted into him.

"You!" the elemental shouted, its voice the oscillating

howl of the winter wind. "You will exact the price. All I wanted was to treasure her."

"Treasure, or imprison?" Zachary demanded, but he did not await an answer and launched at the aureas slee, brandishing the stalagmite. He pounded it into the glassy form, but it was the limestone that shattered into thousands of glowing pieces, not the ice.

The creature laughed. "Did you not know that ice shatters rock?"

It then swung its one arm and Zachary flew across the cavern. He skidded across the floor and must have blacked out for a moment, for the aureas slee loomed over him, reached for him.

"Slee!" Nari cried, leaping out from behind cover and shouting in Eletian.

The aureas slee turned and advanced on her. Zachary climbed unsteadily to his feet and leaped on its back, gripping it around its chest. It shook him off as though he were no more than a flea, then turned and knocked him over again. Zachary peered up through a haze, his consciousness wavering, his whole body screaming. The aureas slee reached down and grabbed him by the neck and lifted him with monstrous strength.

Zachary pried at ice fingers that crushed his throat, his legs dangling, the world growing ever more dim. He gasped for air. Vaguely he heard Nari shouting and a roar filled his ears. Was it the wind that roared, or some great beast? There was an impact, and an impression of tawny fur and giant wings. The aureas slee released him and he dropped to the cavern floor. He closed his eyes, and when he opened them again, Nari was there kneeling beside him, her hand on his chest.

"Zachary . . ." She glanced over her shoulder. There was a great din, the sound of snarling and crashing. "There are two of them."

Two of what? he wanted to ask, but he didn't seem to have the energy to speak.

A translucent hand of ice swept Nari away and grasped

Zachary's wrist and lifted him like a doll. The rest he was never sure of, whether it was real or a nightmare. A pair of gryphons—one tawny and one black—had sprung to life as if from ancient tapestries, and attacked the elemental. Dripstone formations shattered as the aureas slee hurled the gryphons off itself, all the while keeping hold of Zachary. A portion of ceiling came crashing down revealing the daylit sky overhead, freshening the air, but Magged disappeared beneath the rubble. He could not see Nari through the dust.

The gryphons flew through the cloud of dust and dug their scimitar claws into the aureas slee, and lifted it with great wingbeats. Slee still clutched Zachary's wrist even as it was carried away. Up and up and up into the sky they went, and then dropping to skim the tips of evergreens. The gryphons tossed the aureas slee between them, toying with it like it was a mouse, jerking the dangling Zachary back and forth. He thought his arm would surely be torn from his shoulder.

The aureas slee howled at its tormentors, sent sputtering winds at their wings, but its efforts were fruitless. "I am done with you," it hissed at Zachary, then it flung him away, away through the unbearable cold and into darkness.

Nari wiped grit out of her eyes and filled her lungs with the sweetest air she had breathed in centuries. It was laden with fir and spruce, the scent of damp, fecund earth. The vision of gryphons carrying Slee away, Slee in turn lifting Zachary away, played in her mind. Did Zachary still live? Mortals were such fragile beings.

Magged.

Nari gazed where she had last seen the woman. It was all rubble. She clambered over fallen rock, unwieldy stone clacking underfoot, only her Eletian sense of balance keeping her upright.

"Magged?" she called. She pulled away rock and debris. "Magged, can you hear me?"

There was a muffled sound from nearby. She worked even faster, tearing away the debris, and soon found Magged's face plastered in a mask of dust. The rest of her was buried beneath more rubble and gigantic slabs of rock that had once been the cavern's ceiling.

"Nari?" Magged whispered. Blood traced through the dust on her face from her nose and mouth, and from a gouge on her temple. She seemed unable to see. Nari sensed the life leaving her.

"I am here, Magged." Nari lightly touched the woman's cheek.

"I—I am sorry," Magged said. "I wanted him to be family."

"What do you have to be sorry for?"

Magged's breaths were ragged and wet. "I know the way out."

"What?" Nari spoke more sharply than she intended.

"A hole . . . hidden beneath the throne. A passage to the outer world. Knew it since I was little."

"Oh, Magged," Nari whispered.

"Wanted family . . . We are family, aren't we?"

"Yes, Magged, *m'shea*. We are family."

When Magged said no more, her harsh breaths silent, Nari closed her staring eyes. For a time, Nari just knelt there. In but a moment, her world had changed, just as it had when Slee stole her from the forests of Argenthyne and brought her to the cave. She gazed up at the brilliant sunshine that showered down through the opening, and sang for Magged, sang for Magged into the blue sky, for Magged who would never experience freedom and that outer world, and who had only wanted a family. To Nari, she had indeed been family. Nari had raised her, as she had raised so many other children Slee had brought. Some had lived for as many years as Magged. Others had failed quickly, and she sang for them all. It was a song of mourning. Though Eletians lived eternally, they could die, and so yes, her people knew songs of mourning.

When she finished, she stood. She left Magged's face uncovered so she could lie beneath the freedom of the open sky. Nari gazed at the gold columns of sunlight that poured through the collapsed ceiling of the cave. Long had she held an essence of the outer world within her, a piece of Argenthyne, the scent of the forest, the moss beneath her feet, shade and fern and birdsong. It was all that allowed her to endure years of captivity. Now was her rebirth into the world. She could leave and discover how much had changed during her captivity, seek her lost love. And she would hunt the aureas slee.

She left Magged and started to climb her way out.

INTERCEPTED

The days were growing longer and, at times, milder. Freezing nights were followed by days with more direct sunlight that penetrated the forest canopy and provided warmth. Karigan willed it to wash over her and dreamed of being a cat curled up in a patch of sunshine that beamed through a window.

But, it was only a dream, for she could not remember being thoroughly warm and dry. Condor's hooves sucked in slushy mud—the Eletian ways were apparently not immune to mud—and the trees constantly unloaded collected rain or clumps of wet snow on her. At night, the shield Enver created over their campsites with his muna'riel helped some, but never entirely. They would have to cease even that protection soon so the intense light of the muna'riel did not attract the attention of any scouts of Second Empire.

Estral sat slumped on Coda ahead. She was bearing up well, but Karigan could tell the journey was taking its toll. At least it would bring a certain veracity to what she was writing about Green Riders. The soggy cold was taking a toll on Karigan, as well, despite all her experience. Her nose constantly ran and her weathered knuckles cracked and bled. Old injuries, especially her wrist that had been broken last spring in Blackveil, ached. Even Enver did not appear unfazed by their travel conditions. He was quieter than usual and looked a little haggard, which was something she'd never seen before with an Eletian. Not even among her companions in Blackveil. It must be, she thought, his human blood that, well, made him more human.

They'd been traveling together long enough that there was little left to say, or little they had the energy to say, and each knew his or her tasks when it came to setting up and taking down camp. No one spoke while they rode, and few words passed among them when they paused for breaks. They were just too dead tired to sing or tell stories even when they rested by the campfire, though, in the evenings, Enver would still often leave camp to roam the woods, to listen to the voice of the world, as he put it. He would return with a peaceful expression on his face and a light in his eyes. Maybe, Karigan thought, she'd follow him sometime to see exactly how it was he attained "stillness." She had to admit she was curious.

When Enver halted up ahead, Karigan looked about in surprise, but saw no reason for him to stop. He stood in his stirrups and peered through the dense evergreen growth into the forest, then motioned for Karigan to come forward.

When she brought Condor up beside him, she said, "What is it?"

"I sense others."

"Groundmites?" Estral asked sharply from behind them.

When Karigan glanced back, she saw her fearful expression.

"Not groundmites," Enver replied.

"Second Empire?" Karigan asked.

"I cannot tell."

"How close? Do they know we are here?"

"I sense we are being watched."

"Damnation."

There was nothing else for them to do but keep slogging forward, but now Karigan did not lose herself in daydreams of napping in a beam of sunlight, but strained her senses to discern others in the forest with them. She turned at every crackling, at every chitter of a squirrel, at every branch bending beneath the weight of a blue jay, but she detected no human presence other than her own, and that of her companions.

She continued to keep her senses heightened as they went on, but was still surprised when a man stepped out of the woods beside them and ordered them to halt. Enver swiftly nocked an arrow to his bow, and Karigan drew her saber.

"Put your weapons away," the man ordered. "There are a dozen arrows trained on you."

He was attired in woodsman's clothes, dyed in greens and browns and grays to blend in with the forest. Karigan glanced about her and now, knowing what to look for, espied three archers camouflaged in the woods. If there were more as the man claimed, she could not see them. Neither she nor Enver put their weapons away, but neither did they make any threatening moves. Three archers were enough to kill them.

"I said," the man told them, "put your weapons away."

When Karigan and Enver did not obey, an arrow *thwacked* into Karigan's saddle right beside her thigh. She fought to control her wildly beating heart as Condor whinnied and sidestepped.

"The next arrow," the man told her, "will cripple your leg. Put your weapons aside. I am not asking you to disarm."

True enough, Karigan thought, though she could not quite tear her gaze from the arrow impaled in her saddle. She shook herself and nodded to Enver. He lowered his bow, and she sent her saber home into its scabbard.

"Who are you?" she demanded of the man.

He took his time walking around them to look them over. When he stopped by her stirrup, he gave her an especially hard look. He had a winter's growth of beard, which almost disguised his youth. The authority he exhibited was what made him appear older than his years.

"Green Rider, eh?" he said.

"I am Rider Sir Karigan G'ladheon, king's messenger. Now do me the courtesy of telling me who *you* are."

"Thought so," he murmured. He gave her something of a mocking smile. "We can talk later. First you will follow me." He turned to enter the woods, obviously expecting them to fall in behind him.

Karigan held her hand up to stay Enver and Estral. Estral gazed anxiously at her. They were not going anywhere until the man identified himself and his companions.

"Halt," she commanded him.

He turned in surprise. "You are not the one giving orders here."

"I will not take orders from someone who just appears out of the woods, threatens us with arrows, and refuses to identify himself."

"The north woods are perilous," he said. "I need to take you to have a conversation with my captain."

"We are not going anywhere until you tell us who you are."

"I have heard how stubborn you Greenies can be," he said, "even with the threat of arrows trained on them, and trust me, Greenie, my archers have not let down their guard."

Karigan just waited.

The man made a sound of annoyance. "If it eases your mind," he said, "you've been found by a patrol of Sacoridia's River Unit. I am Lieutenant Miles Rennard, at your service." Again, the mocking smile, this time as if to challenge her to dispute his claim.

She accepted. "Prove to me you are Sacoridian and not Second Empire."

"You are a smart girl, Rider Karigan."

"That's Rider G'ladheon to you, Lieutenant. *If* you are a lieutenant."

He yanked his longknife out of its sheath and she tensed, but he just showed her the blade with its maker's mark. It was that of one of the smiths who created arms for Sacoridia's military. It was, in fact, by the same smith who had forged her saber.

"You could have picked that up anywhere," she told him.

He threw his cloak back to show her his sleeve with its insignia of the River Unit and Sacoridia's firebrand and crescent moon above it. "I suppose you are going to say I could have gotten this anywhere, as well."

"Did you?"

"No. It was issued to me by the same quartermaster who issues you Greenies your gear." He drew out a silver chain from beneath his collar and from it dangled a pendant of the crescent moon, and another of the sun. "Do you think you'd catch a Second Empire rat wearing the sign of Aeryc and Aeryon?"

"Yes, if that rat was trying to pass himself off."

Lieutenant Rennard bristled. "And do you suppose we were waiting here in the woods just for a Green Rider and—and whoever these other two are to pass by?"

Karigan shrugged. "I have seen Second Empire do all manner of things."

"I know you have, Rider G'ladheon, for I've heard something of your deeds. Apparently you've survived Blackveil, and however you did must make for a fascinating tale. As for me, I am who I say I am. We are on routine patrol here, and as a courtesy, I request that you return to camp with us to speak with Captain Treman. I am sure he would wish to have some word from the city."

Karigan yanked the arrow out of her saddle. The arrowhead's sharp, broad blades, she observed, *could* cripple a leg, and do much worse. She handed it to the lieutenant. "If only you had said so to begin with."

"You believe me, then?"

"Mostly."

He laughed. "This way, then."

Karigan and her companions ended up dismounting as the terrain grew more difficult than the Eletian way, with too many low-hanging branches making sitting atop a horse annoying at best, and hazardous at worst.

"Are you sure about this?" Estral whispered to her.

"As sure as just about anything else." Karigan did not know Captain Treman personally, but she had heard Captain Mapstone and Mara speak highly of him, and he was a decorated warrior. Even if this was some elaborate ruse perpetrated by Second Empire, there would have been no escaping the arrows of Lieutenant Rennard's archers.

She watched their surroundings as they traveled over the bump and swale of the forest floor and splashed through gullies. They were good, the soldiers of the River Unit. She could only pick out two or three that kept apace of them in the distance.

Enver, who seemed to know what she was looking for, said, "There are twenty of them, Galadheon."

Twenty! They *were* good. But so was Enver to have spotted and counted them.

After about an hour of walking, she caught a whiff of wood smoke. A guard stepped out from hiding and challenged Lieutenant Rennard, then let them through. After another half hour or so, they stepped into the encampment guarded by soldiers watching their every movement. The encampment appeared to occupy the grounds and buildings of an old lumber camp. Tents were pitched in precise rows, and there were numerous campfires and soldiers occupied with various tasks, fixing gear, fetching and carrying, honing weapons. Lieutenant Rennard's scouts suddenly appeared and filed into the encampment behind them. Enver's count had been accurate.

"Larson!" Rennard shouted. "Tend these horses."

A soldier trotted up to them and gathered reins and Bane's lead rope. When she reached for Mist, Enver said, "She will follow. You need not lead her." And then, "Be wary of the pony. He is quick to bite."

"Thank you for the warning, m'lord." Her eyes were large as she took in both Enver and the always elegant Mist.

Karigan made sure to grab her longsword from her saddle before Condor was taken away, and slung it over her shoulder. Rennard led them toward a long, low building that was blessedly warm and dry within. It clearly served as a common room and dining hall for the encampment, with many long tables set up. There was a fireplace on either end, and through the dark gloom, Karigan espied officers seated at the far end deep in discussion. She started forward, and then to her astonishment, a man emerged from the shadows and hastened to her side.

"Rider G'ladheon!" he exclaimed. "Am I ever glad to see you!"

INTUITION

"Master Destarion?" Karigan said in surprise. She had known he'd been reassigned to some rugged post in the north, but she had not expected to ever see him again. He was not a young man, and life with the River Unit had graven new lines into his face, and he had lost considerable weight.

"You made it!" he said.

"Made it?" Had he been expecting her?

"Out of Blackveil, dear woman."

"Oh, uh, yes." She noticed that everyone in the building was watching her and Destarion.

"You must tell me all about it," Destarion said, and then more quietly added, "and how the king is getting on."

"Of—of course."

Destarion receded back into the shadows, and Karigan and her companions continued forward and halted before the table of the officers.

"So, Rennard," said the man in the middle, "what have you dragged in today?"

"A Greenie and her friends, Captain," the lieutenant said.

"Interesting-looking friends," the captain said, his keen gaze falling on Estral and Enver.

Karigan stepped forward. "I presume you are Captain Treman?"

"Yes, indeed. And according to Destarion, you'd be Rider G'ladheon. Or do you prefer Sir Karigan?"

"Rider G'ladheon is fine. Please allow me to introduce Lady Estral Andovian, heir of the Golden Guardian, and Enver of Eletia."

The officers gawked. Finally, the captain said, "What in the name of the gods are a Green Rider, a noble lady, and an Eletian doing here in my woods?"

"King's business," Karigan replied. She had no reason to explain, and Treman would know that an explanation was not required.

"Even the Eletian?"

Karigan glanced at Enver. "Er, joint business between our realms."

"Truly, strange days have come upon us."

Estral now stepped forward. "Sir, my own business has little to do with the king's. It was just convenient to travel with Rider G'ladheon and Enver."

"And what business might that be?"

"I am searching for my father."

"Lord Fiori? I'd heard he passed through a lumber camp north of here some months ago."

Estral leaned over the table. "Please, if there is anything you can tell me . . ."

"I don't believe so, Lady Estral, but I'll think on it. Why don't you three sit with me by the fire and maybe we can get something warm in your bellies."

They drew chairs by the fire while Captain Treman issued orders for food and finished up with his officers. Sitting before a fire, Karigan thought, with a roof overhead, had never felt so good. She nodded off, only to be awakened, in what felt like mere moments later, by a soldier wanting to hand her a mug of hot tea.

"Thank you," she murmured, and she wrapped her hands around it.

Another soldier brought them meat pasties, still hot from the oven, the dough blackened on the corners. There were also cups of steaming savory broth in which to dip the pasties or sip.

"The lumber camp has a good kitchen," the captain told them. He dragged a chair over so he could sit with them. "And fortunately, my unit has some good cooks."

He told them about the encampment while they ate, about the quiet winter with no direct encounters with Second Empire. "One group of them, mainly civilians, are holed up for the winter in the Lone Forest. We've seen sign of them a little north of here, but they've not dared come this far south in months."

When Karigan finished eating and was sipping her second cup of tea, the captain asked her about news back in Sacor City. Apparently, little had reached the River Unit since autumn, including the fact that the queen was expecting twins. Out of the corner of her eye, she saw Destarion listening to every word.

"That will cheer my people to hear," the captain said. "But tell me, Rider, about Blackveil. I had heard a contingent had entered, and I see you survived, but did everyone make it back?"

"No." And so began the painful process of telling the captain about Blackveil and those who perished. She kept it as short as possible, not going into any great depth about her experiences there, and certainly nothing about her travel into the future. Her brief explanation appeared to satisfy him.

"I know you are travel-weary," he said, "so I appreciate your willingness to indulge my curiosity. I also understand how difficult it can be to describe a campaign to someone who wasn't there, so no worries about that. But if I might ask one more question . . ." He pointed at her right shoulder. "Why do you wear the Black Shield insignia?"

"I am . . ." Karigan began. "I have been made an honorary Weapon. Officially."

Did he look at her with some new respect? "You are not the usual Green Rider."

What was the "usual" Green Rider? she wondered. They were all different and accomplished in their own ways.

"We like her anyway," Estral said, bringing some levity to the conversation.

Much to Karigan's relief, the captain turned his questions to Estral. They discussed her missing father, and though Treman reacted with concern, he seemed to have little useful to offer.

Karigan stood with her back to the fire. She saw Destarion sitting at a table with jars and herbs arrayed before him.

Currently he was grinding dried leaves with mortar and pestle. It was awkward seeing him here. She'd always liked the master mender and had been under his care more than once, which was difficult to reconcile with the part he'd played in the scheme to ensure the king's marriage to Estora. He'd gone so far as to dose Captain Mapstone so she would not interfere with the plans of the conspirators. Destarion was, in effect, a traitor, and his reassignment to the north was his sentence.

She was torn between asking him how he was holding up, and demanding what in the hells he had thought he was doing when he took part in the scheme.

He looked up and saw her gazing at him, and his expression became beseeching. She could not pretend she didn't see him. Taking a breath to prepare herself, she excused herself and made her way to Destarion's table.

"Please, please sit, Rider."

"How have you been?" she asked, sliding onto the bench.

He smiled sadly. "I am not as young as I used to be, but I am all right here, though when hostilities start up again, it may be a different story. I miss my family terribly, but I understand why I am here and will serve my penance without complaint."

Karigan was tempted to ask if he regretted his past decisions and actions, or would he do the same all over again if given the chance, but she decided she did not wish to know.

"It gladdens me to hear of the twins," he continued. "All I have ever wanted was what was best for the king. It sounds as if Vanlynn is doing well by him."

Karigan nodded.

"She was my mentor, you know. She trained me. There is no finer mender in all of Sacoridia. And Ben? How is Ben doing?"

"He is well," Karigan replied.

"I am very glad you made it back from Blackveil. I was listening to what you told Captain Treman. I hope you don't mind. I am sorry about Rider Cardell. He was a mischievous young man, but had a good heart."

This was a different Destarion than Karigan had known.

The old Destarion had been the top mender in all the land who commanded a large complement of menders just at the castle. He'd wielded his authority with calm assurance. This Destarion had folded in on himself. He moved his hands nervously and spoke in apologetic tones.

"Do you mind my asking," he said, "what happened to your eye?"

She lightly touched the patch. "A shard . . . It was injured. After Blackveil."

"No doubt Vanlynn has taken good care of it," he said, "but if you might let me have a look at it, I—"

Karigan stiffened. "No."

He gazed down at the tabletop. "I am sorry. I shouldn't have. I understand that you wouldn't want *me* to—"

"It's not that," she said. "Even Ben couldn't fix it." She, of course, would not tell him the real reason why she wouldn't let him see her eye.

"Ben couldn't fix it? Then certainly I couldn't, but if it bothers you, I might be able to provide you with something to ease it."

"Thank you," she said. She requested nothing for she'd been well-supplied by Ben for the journey, but Destarion looked so eager to help. "I do have an aching wrist, however."

He brightened. "Let me have a look then." He noted the fresh scar on the back of her wrist from Brienne's blade. "You've made swordmaster."

"Yes," she said.

"I've seen the mark before, had one or two that festered."

He probed her wrist, and she explained that it had been broken.

"I have a rub that might ease it," he said, "and a good soak in warm water would provide some relief from the pain. I will brew a cup of willowbark tea for you, as well." He busied himself organizing supplies, and appeared much more cheerful. At the idea of him making her tea, she thought unpleasantly of what he'd done to Captain Mapstone.

She returned to the fireplace just in time to hear Captain Treman tell Estral, "I would not recommend it."

"Not recommend what?" Karigan asked.

"Going to the lumber camp where he thinks my father was last seen," Estral said.

Captain Treman looked uneasy. "It is very near territory Second Empire has claimed for itself. The camp itself has been closed up for winter. No one there. If your father did pass through the camp, it would seem he has a penchant for living dangerously."

"I'm afraid he does," Estral muttered. "It's the only clue I've gotten at this point."

"The captain said it's closed up," Karigan told her, "and we aren't going anywhere near Second Empire."

"*You* aren't," Estral said, "but I can go where I please."

Karigan wasn't about to let her friend hare off into danger like that, even though Estral's reason for joining in on the journey was for her own purposes. "Actually, I was thinking you could bide your time here while Enver and I continue north and—"

"It is not your decision," Estral told her with surprising heat. "I am not yours to command, no matter what titles have been bestowed upon you."

Karigan schooled herself before responding with her own heat. "True enough, but to ignore the advice and warning of Captain Treman, who has been in this region for some time fighting Second Empire, would not be wise." Before Estral could reply, she continued, "Do not stay here if that is what you wish. Come with Enver and me, and perhaps we'll find more clues. But please, don't go walking into danger."

"As if you don't?"

Karigan felt her cheeks warm. "If I do, it's because of duty. If you do and something happens to you, then I'm the one who must contend with Alton, and he would *not* be happy with me."

Humor returned to Estral's eyes. "That might just make it worthwhile."

"Oh, dear gods," Karigan muttered. She noted Enver looked curiously uncomfortable, and she learned the reason why a little while later while she soaked her wrist in the pan of warm water Destarion had prepared for her.

"Galadheon," he said when he came to her.

"What is it?"

"About our travel . . ."

"Is there a problem?"

He looked uncharacteristically abashed. "Our path. It lies close to the Lone Forest."

"What?" Water sloshed over the rim of the bowl with her reaction. Others in the room looked over at them. In a low voice she said, "Why didn't you mention this before? Like a long time ago?"

"I did not know."

"What do you mean you didn't know? *You're* the guide."

"The way is, as you were told, found on no map. It is, as I explained long ago, a matter of intuition."

Intuition. It was like some kind of terrible Eletian joke.

"If it helps, Galadheon, Eletian intuition is stronger than that of humans."

Yes, but he was half *human*, she thought with rancor. Was his intuition only half as good as a full Eletian's? The gods, she decided, hated her. Wayfinding by intuition? What was next? Finding the p'ehdrose through dreams?

Eletians.

RENNARD OF THE RIVER UNIT

Enver no doubt sensed Karigan's displeasure and so moved off to once more sit by the fire next to Estral. Yes, she was sure the gods were laughing at her. Well, she'd have to make sure that when they neared the Lone Forest they were very careful. She would have continued to stew over it all, but Lieutenant Rennard sat down across the table from her. *Now what?* she wondered.

"Hurt yourself?" he asked.

"Broke my wrist last spring. The damp cold makes it ache."

"I have a knee like that," he replied. "Tramping out in the woods all day like we do doesn't help much, but Destarion is good with the remedies. Don't know how we got so lucky to get him, but he's the best mender we've ever had. When we were posted by the Terrygood, settlers and lumbermen would come from miles around to see him. You'd think he worked miracles."

Karigan swirled her hand around in the now tepid bowl of water. Of course Rennard would not know why Destarion had been assigned to the River Unit. The whole affair around the assassination attempt on the king, and the circumstances surrounding his precipitate wedding, had been kept quiet.

"I'm glad Master Destarion has been useful to your unit." She removed her wrist from the water and dried it off with a towel.

They sat in silence for a few moments before Rennard finally said, "I am sorry I was disrespectful when we met in the woods."

She was surprised by his apology. "I know that soldiers often think of messengers as lesser."

"I am afraid that's true," he replied, "but I also think that perception is changing. It's just that when we're posted out here in the wilds, we are more coarse, rougher. Part of it is the danger; part of it is the nature of a group of soldiers living closely together and sharing that danger. Anyway, I had heard a little about you, but I guess I hadn't believed it until we met out in the woods and you held your ground." He laughed as though to himself. "Had I known you were a swordmaster and honorary Weapon, I would not have turned my back on you. And, of course, I should not have been so rude regardless. I apologize for the way we received you."

"Hmm. Can't say I'm happy about the hole your archer punched in my saddle, but apology accepted."

He inclined his head. "I am much relieved."

"Perhaps," she said, "from now on you will treat my fellow Riders with courtesy. We are all on the same side, after all, and since messengers don't necessarily trumpet all that they endure during the course of an errand, it is deceptive to assume they are less than capable and do not regularly face danger."

"I will endeavor to do better," he replied. "I promise." He glanced over his shoulder to see who might be observing them, then he leaned in close as if to let her in on a secret. "There *is* something I would like to ask you."

"Yes?"

His eyes shifted nervously. "I wanted to ask something—something personal."

Karigan waited. Surely he hadn't been flirting with her, had he? He wasn't going to express interest in courting her, was he?

"Can you tell me . . ." He was blushing.

Uh-oh, she thought. "Yes?"

"Can you tell me," he began again, "if your friend is married or otherwise attached?"

She almost burst out laughing. No, he had not been flirting. Not with *her.* No wonder he was making nice. She managed to contain herself, and feeling fiendish, she asked, "Enver or Estral?"

His blush intensified. "Estral."

"Well, she *is* seeing someone," Karigan replied, "but I

wouldn't let that stop you. You never know, but she might be open to another suitor."

He looked thoughtful. "Thank you." He rose from the bench, straightened his uniform, and sauntered toward where Estral sat before the fire. He pulled up a chair of his own and straddled it so he could face her.

Cocky lad, Karigan thought in amusement. Apparently Rennard was not intimidated by Estral's noble status. Flirting with the lover of the future lord-governor of D'Yer Province? Poor Rennard hadn't a chance, and Estral would be annoyed with her for sending him over, but to Karigan's line of thinking, it would be worth it.

Captain Treman invited them to stay the night. Relieved to be dry and warm, Karigan was only too glad to accept. At supper, the building filled up with the members of the River Unit and became noisy with the raucous sounds of hungry, chattering people and the clatter of dishware. The cooks had produced a savory moose stew. The soldiers supplemented their stores with hunting.

Karigan sat with the captain, Enver seated beside her and listening gravely to their discussion about the terrain in the vicinity of the Lone Forest. Out of the corner of her eye, Karigan espied Estral being occupied by Rennard's advances. She chuckled to herself.

"They will have patrols well outside the forest," the captain was warning her. "I would really caution you against going anywhere near there."

"I do not wish to," she replied, "but according to my guide—" and she gave Enver a stern look, "—the object of our search may lie in that vicinity." She had wondered more than once if finding the p'ehdrose was worth it. She hoped so.

She dipped a wedge of pan bread into the hot stew, and continued to listen attentively while Treman, with interjections from his officers, detailed the lay of the land and warned her there would be traps in the forest.

"Traps like to snare animals," Lieutenant Dannyn said, "but made to snare people. We've lost a few of our own to them."

This revelation did not alleviate Karigan's trepidation

about traveling near the Lone Forest, but the grim talk soon faded and gave way to entertainment after the meal. Word had gotten out that Estral was of Selium, and she was requested to lead the singing. She had only sung with Enver at their campsites and looked nervous, but once she began a cheerful tune about a soldier and his sweetheart, her voice was steady and strong. Soldiers on fiddle and pipe accompanied her. Rennard, Karigan observed, watched her raptly as one besotted. Good thing they weren't staying long.

Most of the songs Estral chose were upbeat, the sorts that could be heard in any tavern, and well-known to her audience. Many sang the choruses with her. She inserted a couple of wistful ballads, but nothing morose. Soldiers away from home, Karigan reflected, did not need morose.

"I must rest my throat," Estral said after another rollicking tune. The audience met her announcement with disappointment. "But maybe Enver would sing for us."

This was greeted with uneasy silence, but to Karigan's surprise, Enver looked pleased. He stood and joined Estral by the fireplace.

"I would like to sing about the ale," he said.

Looks of disbelief and murmuring spread through the audience, but once Enver launched into the song that Estral had taught them after their time in North, it was clear his beautiful voice and spirited rendition captured their astonished attention. Most would not have ever seen an Eletian before, and to hear one sing a simple tune about ale? When he finished, there was silence.

"Did I sing it wrong?" he asked uncertainly.

"Hells, no!" someone shouted, and the audience broke out in enthusiastic applause and calls for more. Enver smiled tentatively, and then sang a couple more of the tunes Estral had taught him.

Estral edged her way to where Karigan sat, Rennard's gaze following her all the way. She leaned down and whispered, "You are in big trouble."

Karigan pretended she could not hear and clapped to the beat of Enver's song along with everyone else. She was darkly satisfied.

When the time came for those not on duty to turn in, Captain Treman gave profuse thanks to Estral and Enver for providing the night's entertainment.

"It's been a hard winter," he explained, "and this has raised everyone's spirits."

They were invited to sleep on pallets in the dining hall before the fire. It might be the last dry, warm night of their journey, and Karigan planned to take full advantage of it. Enver, conversely, chose to wander the woods within the perimeter.

She and Estral shared the dining hall with the cooks. Before they turned in for the night, they sat on the edges of their pallets, whispering to one another.

"What on Earth were you thinking when you sent Rennard after me?" Estral demanded. "Now he won't leave me alone."

"Sorry," Karigan lied. "You've told him about Alton, haven't you?"

"Of course I have."

"Well, we'll be gone tomorrow." Karigan folded aside the top blanket of her bedroll. "You probably won't see him again."

"He's not really a bad sort, just persistent."

Karigan tried to smother a smile. Estral squinted at her.

"This is really about the Lone Forest, isn't it," Estral said. "You're just mad because we're going near it."

"I'm not happy about it, if that's what you mean."

"I'd rather not go that way either, truth be told, but if it leads to my father?"

Karigan sobered. "I know."

She lay down and pulled her blanket to her chin. From the dark around her came the deep breaths and snoring of sleeping cooks. She could only hope to sleep just as well as they, but with thoughts of the next leg of their journey on her mind, she was not so sure that she would.

From the vicinity of Estral's pallet came the whispered comment: "As for Rennard? I think you're just jealous."

Karigan's snort of laughter was met with several grumbles of "*Quiet!*" and "*Go to sleep!*"

* * *

The cooks woke up before dawn, which meant Karigan and Estral did, too. After a hearty breakfast, they prepared to leave, and with Enver joining them, tacked the horses and loaded Bane the pony with their supplies. Just as a night in a warm, dry building had done Karigan and Estral a world of good, so had a night in a sheltered paddock done for the horses. As they left the paddock area, Captain Treman and Lieutenant Rennard came to see them off.

"The lieutenant and his people will guide you back on course," the captain said, "though I have deep reservations about that course."

He was not, Karigan thought, the only one. "I understand, sir. We will be vigilant and avoid trouble."

Treman nodded, then handed her a sheaf of papers. "A report for the king. I realize you are not heading directly back to Sacor City, but I don't know when we'll see another messenger. Nothing of great import anyway, but perhaps of some use to the king."

Karigan took the sheaf and deposited it in her message satchel.

Treman then turned to Estral. "I hope you locate your father, my lady. We'll keep watch for him, and if we've any sign, we'll send word to Sacor City."

"Thank you."

Someone touched Karigan's sleeve and she turned to find Destarion standing there.

"Rider," he said, "I have a jar of rub for your wrist."

Karigan took the proffered jar. "Thank you, Master Destarion."

"If you think of it," he said, humbly gazing at his feet, "might you put in a good word about me to the king?"

The awkwardness returned. After a thoughtful moment, she replied. "When I see the king next, I will tell him how helpful you've been, and about the good things I've heard about your work with the River Unit."

"Thank you, Rider, thank you. It is more than I deserve." He backed away, head still bowed.

Awkwardness gave way to regret that so gifted a mender

had fallen so far. But he was still alive, which was more than she could say about his fellow conspirators, and, she reminded herself, he was here as a result of his own actions.

Rennard and a half dozen of his scouts led them through the woods. They moved quietly, ever on the alert for enemies. As before, Karigan, Estral, and Enver walked, leading their horses along, until they came to the place where Rennard had found them the day before. While his scouts melted into the woods, he remained for final farewells.

"I will be more courteous to the next messenger who passes through my woods," he told Karigan with a grin. "Safe journeys to you." To Enver, he said, "We enjoyed your singing last night. Not what we expected from the Elt, and perhaps you are not the usual Elt." They shook hands, and finally he turned to Estral. "My lady." He gave her a courtly bow and kissed her hand. "Lord Alton is a very fortunate man to have your devotion, but should you ever have a change of heart, I hope you will remember Rennard of the River Unit. I am ever at your service." He bowed once more, and disappeared into the woods.

Well, Karigan thought. That was that. Estral looked a little . . . troubled? Forlorn? Certainly pink in the cheeks. They mounted, taking up their usual order with Enver in the lead and Karigan bringing up the rear. Some time had passed before she dared say anything.

"Are you pleased to be rid of Rennard?" she asked Estral.

"Rid? Once Miles backed off a little, he actually ended up being quite charming. Dashing, really."

Uh-oh, Karigan thought. Might Alton have some competition, after all? She doubted it. In any case, Estral's attachments would not likely be foremost in either of their minds the closer they got to the Lone Forest.

TEA WITH THE PRINCE

"Are you sure you are up to this?" Connly asked.

Laren sighed. "It doesn't matter if I'm up to it or not."

They walked slowly toward the west wing, the Weapon Willis escorting them. More guards than ever stood sentry along the walls. The castle was on full alert, and ever since the ousting of the aureas slee, Laren had been guarded and trailed by a Weapon. She was certain it had little to do with her own safety, but with the queen's. They wanted to make sure that all who came in direct contact with the queen were not replaced by the changeling elemental as Zachary had been.

Zachary, Zachary, where are you? For all her knocks and injuries, the re-dislocated shoulder, it was her heart that hurt most of all, for she knew not whether he lived or was dead.

Her progress through the castle was painstaking. How she hadn't been killed by the aureas slee, she did not know. Somehow she had avoided broken bones. She'd bumped her poor skull, of course, but she was alive. After the queen had been seen to, Vanlynn ordered Ben to heal her, but in increments so he did not exhaust himself, should the queen need him. For Laren, he'd first taken care of her head, but it was the shoulder he would work on over time. Despite the healing help, she was stiff and exhausted, and she'd been doing poorly enough that Gresia excused her from arms training. For the time being.

When they reached the entrance to the royal wing, they halted. The way was blocked by four Weapons, two of whom were unfamiliar enough that they were likely tomb guards.

"I guess this is where we part," Connly said. "If you need anything at all, if you get tired, send for me."

"Thank you, Connly, I will."

The Weapons permitted her entrance, Willis still trailing her, and she made her way down the corridor and then to a flight of stairs. She halted and gazed at all the climbing she'd have to do.

"Do you require assistance, Captain?" Willis asked.

She was tempted to ask him to carry her, but pride and the ridiculous image of herself being thrown over one of his broad shoulders overcame her exhaustion. "No, thank you. I'll manage."

It seemed to take hours to climb the stairs. When she paused on the top landing, she found the corridor blackened by more Weapons than she had ever seen assembled in one place before. They all looked angry and bristling for a fight, and she found herself relieved to be escorted by one of their brethren so she would not be mistaken for an enemy. They were, she knew, taking the disappearance of their king, and the impersonation of him by the aureas slee, very personally, and had no real way of venting their fury. No one had any idea where Zachary had been spirited to, if he was alive, or where to even begin searching. Someone had suggested going to Eletia to find out if they knew how to reach the slee's domain, but entering Eletia was a problem in itself. No mortal had found a way in for hundreds of years, except Karigan, and even then by means improbable—if not impossible—to duplicate.

There were more Weapons in Estora's apartments. She could feel their intensity as a physical thing. Estora was not on her sofa in the sitting room as had been customary, the burned one having been replaced. Laren was led all the way back to the bed chamber. There she found yet more Weapons, and Estora in bed propped against pillows. She spoke quietly with a moon priest.

"May the blessed ones be with you," the man said, and he made the sign of the crescent moon. "I will make offerings in the king's name during tonight's rituals."

Laren wondered what Zachary would think of that. Following the Clan Wars, his Hillander predecessors had removed the influence of the moon priests as far away from the throne as possible, and limited their powers in other ways, an arrangement Zachary embraced. He did celebrate high days and attended chapel, but he sought no counsel from priests in matters of state, or anything else as far as she knew.

Was that what Estora was doing? Ignoring two hundred years of tradition and seeking counsel? Laren chided herself for jumping to conclusions, recalling where Estora came from. The east coast of Sacoridia tended to be more traditional, parochial. It would be natural for her to seek succor from a priest, under the circumstances.

"Blessings to you, as well, Prime Brynston."

The luin prime? Laren gave the priest a second look as he bowed to Estora, and she kissed his ring. Laren had heard a new priest had recently ascended to prime and been installed in the Sacor City chapel of the moon. He was relatively young, in his late twenties, perhaps, and not difficult to look upon. As he left Estora's bedside, his long ivory robes of silk flowed silently behind him. She watched after him as he exited the chamber and a Weapon closed the door.

"Captain," Estora said, "I am so glad you have come, but may I say you look . . . unwell? Please sit and rest."

Laren bowed. A chair was brought forward and she dropped into it with relief. Estora looked healthy, her cheeks rosy, and she, like the Weapons, emanated energy. Not bad for a woman in her gravid condition whose husband had gone missing, and with a kingdom to run.

"I believe the bed rest is unnecessary," Estora continued, "but Vanlynn insists. I am fine. My children are fine."

Laren, who wouldn't have minded trading her the chair for the bed, replied, "I have found it easiest to acquiesce to that woman's demands, my lady. I've had enough experience of late to know better." She rubbed her shoulder.

Estora's expression softened. "Yes, for all that we know, Vanlynn is in charge around here. I am, however, glad she has been looking after you."

"So that was the new luin prime?" Laren asked.

"Yes, the youngest ever elevated. He is from Coutre." Estora smiled. "I suggested him last year when I heard the old prime was retiring. No doubt the Assembly wished to please me."

No doubt, Laren echoed, they would do the utmost to attain the favor of the throne.

Estora asked her polite questions about how she was doing, but Laren replied, "With respect, Your Majesty, I will mend in time, and I suspect there are more urgent matters on your mind."

"Yes. Once more I find myself responsible for the realm." She gazed down at her hands clasped on her lap. "With my husband missing, the responsibility weighs on me. I have been praying to the gods for his return."

Laren, who normally had little time for the gods or an inclination to pray, had been, as well. "You may rely on your counselors to help in any way possible."

"At least no one is pushing for me to remarry," Estora said with deceptive lightness. "Not yet, anyway, though Javien is advocating for the pretense that all is well so word doesn't get out that Zachary has disappeared."

"I am afraid that with all the guards on high alert, that any illusion of normality has been dispelled."

"Yes, I have heard that Prince Tuandre is alarmed, and he'd already been put off by the behavior of the one who we thought to be Zachary. I have no idea what this is going to do to relations between our two realms."

"Perhaps the best path is forthrightness. Rhovanny is, after all, our friendliest ally."

"I agree," Estora said, "but the others resist."

So that was why she had asked Laren to visit, to see if she would provide counsel that countered the others. "You are the queen, and you can proceed as you wish. As much as this hurts to say aloud, we may never—" and here her voice quavered, "—see Zachary again, and you will be faced with making all sorts of decisions. If you feel it is in Sacoridia's best interest to be forthright with Prince Tuandre, then it overrides anything Javien or the others say."

Estora spread her hands across her quilt. "How am I to

convey this to the prince while in my confinement? Vanlynn will not permit me to even leave this chamber."

"Invite him to tea."

"Tea? Here?"

Laren shrugged, which sent a shock of pain through her bad shoulder. She winced and asked, "Why not? I'm sure your servants can attire you as befits your station, if that's what concerns you. The prince knows your condition. He'd probably deem it a great honor to be summoned to see you, and it might go far to mend any affront he has felt by how his visit has transpired thus far."

"Yes . . ."

Laren could see Estora latching on to the idea, but Donal stepped forward. "Your Majesty?"

"What is it, Donal?"

"I protest bringing outsiders into your chambers."

"This is a royal prince we are talking about," Estora replied.

"He is still an outsider, a foreigner, and a possible danger to your person."

"I will not be ruled by fear, Donal. I realize it is your task to protect me, but to give in to fear is to lose the battle before it is even engaged."

"If it helps," Laren said, "I can use my ability to read the prince."

"Yes," Estora said fiercely. "I say we do it. I think Zachary would approve."

The next day, the prince arrived for tea at the appointed hour. As predicted, Javien had protested vigorously against the scheme, and Les Tallman had expressed his misgivings, but their queen overruled them.

As the prince and two select counselors entered Estora's bed chamber, it was to a room lined with Weapons and several of Estora's ladies in attendance. Two Hillander terriers panted beside the bed under the watchful eye of the kennel master. Her personal staff, including Anna, Laren was pleased to see, were at hand. She was less pleased to see

Prime Brynston, but tried not to let her personal feelings about moon priests prejudice herself against the man. Ben was also present, which Vanlynn had insisted on, should Estora experience any distress. Laren, and counselors Javien and Tallman, completed the Sacoridian complement.

Laren had to hand it to Estora. Not only had she corralled an impressive retinue to be present for the prince's visit, but she and her chamber were outfitted in regal adornment. She wore her royal raiment, her crown and jewels, and bore her scepter. Gone from the canopied bed were the feminine drapes of fabric. They were replaced by material ornamented with clan heraldry in brocade, silk, velvet, and silver thread. The top quilt featured a meeting of the Hillander terrier with the cormorant of Coutre. These, Estora explained, had all been meant for her marriage bed, but had arrived well after she had wed Zachary following the assassination attempt, more in line with the original wedding date.

As if this was not enough, Zachary's swords had been brought in and prominently displayed on the wall, as if to represent him in his absence.

Prince Tuandre and his counselors bowed deeply to Estora.

"We welcome you, cousin," she said.

"Most gracious queen," Tuandre replied, "I am honored to meet you at long last, and that you have permitted me entrance to your most private sanctum during your confinement."

"Please be at your ease," Estora said with a sweeping gesture.

Servants brought forth cushioned chairs for Tuandre and his counselors, and a sumptuous tea of cakes and candied fruit was laid out and served. At first the conversation was of a cautious, polite nature of inconsequentialities, but Laren, peering at Tuandre over the rim of her teacup, sensed the prince gathering his courage to broach topics of greater import. His mind felt open, if wary, and absent of ill intent.

"Madam," he said at last, "I would ask after the welfare of His Majesty the King. One hears the strangest rumors."

"What you have heard likely has an element of truth in it," Estora replied. Javien's pained expression at this admission was of no surprise, but it was as Estora and Laren had discussed.

"But it is so utterly fantastical," the prince replied. "Too difficult to believe."

"Rhovanny clearly has not been as affected by magical irregularities as Sacoridia has been," Estora said. "It grieves me to tell you that this castle, my home, was breached by an entity the Eletians call aureas slee, an elemental being. It abducted my husband and then took on his form and pretended to be him. The Zachary you met was this changeling creature, not His Majesty."

Tuandre's counselors leaped to their feet as though to protest this misuse of safety on the prince's behalf, but he waved them back to their seats. Laren sensed only honest concern and alarm from him.

"This is most extraordinary, my lady. Overwhelming. I offer my fullest desire that he be returned." He paused, then added, "Do you not fear that if word of this gets out that your enemies will view this as some victory and think Sacoridia weak?"

"My husband has managed this realm for strength, and it is his will that guides me. Sacoridia has never been stronger. As for the aureas slee, it is a force of nature beyond mortal ken. It deceived us all for but a time, and it has been ousted."

"What of His Majesty?"

"We do not know."

"It is grave and unsettling news," Tuandre replied.

"Yes. Unsettling and upsetting in the extreme that the father of my children, this realm's sovereign, has vanished. We do not know where to even begin our search for him. However, it was his desire," she continued, with a slight shift in her voice, "that Sacoridia and its neighbor, Rhovanny, rekindle their alliance of old in the face of the rising of ancient adversaries. Prince Tuandre, I have told you the truth of my husband's disappearance, so you may know the reality of what we are facing. The aureas slee, the elemental, was likely bespelled by a magic user of Second Empire to wound Sacoridia and its king. We were attacked, and if we could be so attacked, then Rhovanny may also be in danger."

"We have had no direct grievance with Second Empire," Tuandre replied. "My father has been skeptical of the claims of imminent danger that have come from King Zachary."

"Blackveil Forest does not border King Thergood's land," Estora countered. "My husband has shared with the king the awakening of that dark place and its master. The rising of Second Empire is in response to the forest's restlessness. Does King Thergood believe King Zachary has been inventing these matters?"

A blush bloomed on Tuandre's cheeks. "No, madam." He bowed in his chair. "No insult was intended. But there has been little evidence of danger in Rhovanny."

"Counselor Tallman," Estora said, "would you please share with His Royal Highness what we know of Second Empire?"

Les Tallman stood and recounted the intelligence and confessions that had been collected regarding Second Empire's activities, finishing with, "Second Empire will have mixed into your population, pretending to be Rhovan citizens. Some will probably hold rank within your military and governing bodies."

"It is known to me," the prince replied, "that King Zachary had communicated as much to my father. Some preliminary investigations have been conducted into the matter, but I will advise my father that we must go deeper."

Though Laren's ability was to detect honesty, it sometimes amplified her ability to read other aspects of a person. Tuandre might appear calm on the surface, but she could tell he was deeply troubled by all he'd heard. She was certain he'd convey his concerns to his father, but as the youngest of seven sons, she had doubts about how seriously he'd be taken.

She turned her gaze to one of the counselors who had accompanied him, an older gentleman of quiet but attentive demeanor. On occasion, he spoke softly in Rhovan to Tuandre. This gentleman exuded years of wisdom, and she sensed his judgment might carry weight with King Thergood.

The other counselor was average in appearance in every way, and she nearly dismissed him, but when her ability rippled against his mind, she recoiled. His thoughts seethed dark as pitch, and full of ill intent. She stood.

"Captain?" the queen asked, drawn from her conversation with the prince.

The man stared at her and it brought to mind a viper about to strike.

"Donal!" she cried as the man lunged from his chair, a stiletto drawn from his sleeve.

A CALLING, OF A SORT

The man whirled on Tuandre to the sound of screaming servants. The terriers barked and strained at their leashes. He raised his stiletto to plunge into the prince's chest. In a blur of motion, Donal tackled him to the floor, wrenched his arms behind him, and knelt on the small of his back.

The prince stood. It had all happened so quickly that everyone else, including Laren herself, had frozen in place. Then chattering broke out among those present. Weapons made a barrier of themselves around Estora's bed while Ellen assisted Donal with lifting the assassin to his feet and restraining him.

"Garmell," Tuandre demanded, "what is this?"

The assassin replied acidly in Rhovan and spat at him. Donal and Ellen dragged him out, but as they did, he shouted in the common, "We will defeat you vermin! The empire rises!"

Estora's bed chamber fell into shocked silence before a babble erupted once more, Prime Brynston muttering a prayer and making the sign of the crescent moon.

"I told you this was a terrible idea!" Javien jabbed an accusatory finger at Laren. "This is your fault."

Exhausted and head throbbing, Laren sank into her chair. She hadn't the energy to argue, and perhaps Javien was right.

"I beg your pardon, sir," the prince said to Javien, "but I say nonsense. This messenger flushed the assassin out, which would not have happened had we not met. You should be praising her as I intend."

"She is our Green Rider captain," Les Tallman said, "Laren Mapstone."

To Laren's astonishment, the prince bowed to her. "I thank

you, Captain. I had no idea we harbored a snake among us. Garmell had always been exceedingly loyal, but now we know it to be a sham."

"I cannot see!" Estora was complaining. It took some convincing, but the Weapons parted so her field of vision extended beyond her bed and they could see her in turn. "You are unscathed, Prince Tuandre?"

Now he bowed to Estora. "Yes, madam, with thanks to your Green Rider captain and Weapons."

"Your Majesty," Javien said, "this is exactly why I discouraged this meeting—it exposed your person to treachery."

"Javien, I wished this meeting to proceed even knowing there was some risk. I am thinking that perhaps it has been made all the more successful for now, in the prince's regard, the threat from Second Empire is made even more real."

"Indeed it is," Prince Tuandre said. "Indeed it is."

Estora insisted the talks continue. Zachary, Laren thought, would be proud of Estora for how she was carrying on despite the scare. She once more touched the minds of Prince Tuandre and his remaining counselor, but sensed no treachery from them.

Ben sidled over to her and leaned down to whisper in her ear, "How are you holding up?"

"Well enough," she murmured.

He touched her shoulder and she felt a mild warming sensation. She glanced sharply at him and shook her head. He should not use his healing ability in a room with so many watching eyes.

He whispered, "It was not enough for anyone to see." Then he backed away.

Her shoulder did feel easier, but her whole body ached, as it often did after using her own ability, and especially in addition to having been flung into a stone wall by the aureas slee just days ago. The meeting dragged on covering not just topics of alliance and security, but broaching trade once more. Estora, for all that her bed was her throne, presided with dignity and authority, speaking always in the realm's best interest. Yes, Zachary would not only be proud, but well pleased. She made a fine queen.

For an odd moment, a vision of Karigan in Estora's place came into her mind. Would Karigan do so well under such conditions? Laren was sure she would, but she had a hard time imagining her Rider confined to bed like this and not out in the world. It was not suited to her, but for all that Estora disliked the confinement, she was disposed to make the best of it.

It was to Laren's great relief when the meeting came to a close. They all stood when the prince rose, she grimacing at her creaking joints. Tallman and Javien went immediately to speak informally with the prince, and Estora beckoned Laren over.

"Captain," she said in a hushed voice, her eyes bright, "I think it went well."

"Yes, I agree, and may I say that I don't think Zachary could have done any better."

A sadness shadowed Estora's features. "I have no wish to dishonor his rule. I wish to reign in a manner that would honor his . . ."

His memory? Laren wondered when Estora did not finish her sentence. Now that they had admitted to Prince Tuandre that Zachary had disappeared, word would spread to the general population, and no doubt to their enemies. It would be a blow to morale, no matter they had Estora. There was much work to do on that end to bolster their people.

"If I may?" Ben stepped forward. "I am to check Her Majesty for strain, as Master Vanlynn has ordered. And Captain, I am ordering *you* back to quarters to rest."

Laren scowled at him, but he was right. She'd had in mind to return to her quarters and put her feet up anyway. Maybe go over reports and—

"Rest," Ben said sternly as if he could read her mind.

"I'll send Anna with her to make sure she follows orders," Estora said. "Now, now, Laren, do not frown. You are highly valued and I need you in good form for all that may come."

Estora had called her "Laren" instead of "Captain" for the first time she could recall, as Zachary always had during times of informality. Was this another indication of Estora's increasing confidence in her role as monarch?

"Anna," Estora called. The girl came to her bedside and curtsied. "See that Captain Mapstone returns to her quarters. She is to go and rest."

"Yes, Your Majesty."

Before Laren was dismissed, Estora said, "That was well done with the assassin. If you had not recognized his ill intent, he could have gone straight to Second Empire to report on all he heard here, or maybe even succeeded in assassinating the prince."

Laren nodded. There was nothing more to say, so she and Anna left Estora's bed chamber, Willis following closely behind. The outer rooms were crowded with Weapons, and the discussion between the prince, Javien, and Tallman had moved out there, the luin prime insinuating himself into the conversation. Les Tallman glanced at her as though to invite her to join them, but she shook her head and continued on her way.

In the corridor outside were more members of the prince's retinue, blocked from entering the queen's apartments by a line of forbidding Weapons. Among those who awaited their prince's return were more counselors and aides, secretaries and body servants, the prince's personal mender, and some military officers in red. There was also a pair of messengers. The entire retinue was male, for the women in Rhovanny played a much more limited role in their society. It had been heartening to Laren that Tuandre had responded so well to Estora, when not every Rhovan male would have. Of course, she was head of state and this was her realm, so it was required of him to show respect, but Laren also thought he had showed a natural respect.

One of the messengers stepped forward and said, "Green Rider?"

She halted, Anna stopping beside her. The man bore the rank of lieutenant on his shoulders. His gray uniform was ornamented with far more brass and piping than a Green Rider's, the Rhovan messengers being more tied to the military. Fancier, perhaps, but not as practical. His mustache was also quite grand with curling ends. How did he keep it groomed while on an errand?

"Tell us," he said in his thick Rhovan accent, his tone haughty, "what occurred within. Why was Counselor Garmell taken away?"

"I believe, Lieutenant, that is for your prince to tell you." Not caring for his tone, she started to move on, but he stomped in front of her and blocked her.

"I asked you a question," he snapped.

The other messenger, a corporal, murmured in Rhovan to the lieutenant. The lieutenant barked in Rhovan at him in what could easily be translated to: "Shut up!" The corporal shrugged. The lieutenant then muttered at Laren in Rhovan and she knew enough of the language to recognize that what he was saying about her was unflattering, and that he thought very little of women in uniform.

"I order you to tell me what transpired, woman."

Order her, did he? She was not going to waste time on the fool, and was about to move on, when Prince Tuandre emerged into the corridor and made straight for her. The two Rhovan messengers straightened to attention.

"Captain!" Prince Tuandre said. The lieutenant glanced around trying to see who his prince addressed.

Laren bowed her head. "Your Highness."

"I wish to thank you again, Captain, for saving us from disaster. I am going to go see the traitor now. We could use more like you in Randann."

"Your Renhald is a good man," she replied. The lieutenant, she saw, was looking dismayed. "I am sure he and the messengers he commands serve you and King Thergood to the utmost." The lieutenant's dismay increased. She was, of course, acquainted with her counterpart in Rhovanny, and he would not tolerate, she was sure, the lieutenant's comportment, especially as a visitor in another realm.

"Yes, yes. Captain Renhald is excellent. But you are always welcome." The prince actually shook her hand before turning away to speak with his aides.

The corporal spoke again to the lieutenant. She made out that he was explaining the gold knot on her shoulder and the rank it denoted. The corporal looked smug as he spoke, then he straightened and saluted her. The lieutenant, now looking both embarrassed and displeased, executed a precise salute, as well.

"As you were," Laren said mildly in Rhovan.

Now the lieutenant paled realizing she had understood his unflattering remarks.

"Please give Captain Renhald my kindest regards," she told him. She smiled inwardly. If the lieutenant worried that she was going to report him to his captain, it was well deserved. She would not, of course, waste her time. How that man had gotten the rank of lieutenant without knowing what her gold knot represented, and his poor behavior as a guest in a foreign kingdom, she could not guess. Renhald was indeed a good captain, and she couldn't imagine him being pleased with such behavior from one of his officers, but then, things were different in Rhovanny.

Before she could be forestalled by any further idiocy, she strode rapidly down the corridor, Anna hurrying to keep up with her. Once she was down the stairs into the main castle hall, she slowed down. Willis kept at a discreet distance.

"I heard you helped expel the aureas slee," she said to her young companion. "That was very brave. You prevented it from taking our queen."

Anna looked down at the floor as they walked. "He-*it*-didn't like fire. And I fainted after."

"Well," Laren replied, "you remained conscious longer than I did."

"But you didn't faint."

Laren looked at her in surprise. She appeared genuinely upset.

"You or Sir Karigan wouldn't have fainted," Anna said fiercely.

Laren halted in the middle of the busy hall and let people flow around her and Anna. "Young lady, most people would have run away and hidden rather than face the aureas slee, even if it meant sacrificing their queen. Do you know what that means? No? It means you are not most people. Look, Karigan and I have a few more years of experience. Be easy on yourself. You've done the realm a great service even when no one would have blamed you had you run and hidden instead."

They set off again, Anna looking only slightly less downcast. Why, Laren wondered, couldn't this girl, who was earnest, a good worker, and quick thinking, not come into an ability so she could be a Green Rider? But maybe it was for the best for her if she never heard the call and didn't have to face all the dangers that being a king's messenger entailed.

Yet, Anna had come to Laren wanting to join of her own free will. Wasn't that, she wondered yet again, a calling of a sort?

TRADING FOR MEAT

Grandmother concentrated on her footing as she made her way through the twilight woods. The weather had turned the snow into a glaze of ice and was treacherous. Two of the men walked beside her to assist her so she would not fall. Despite nearing winter's end, the air had a bite to it and was harsh to breathe. As always, she yearned for summer warmth to melt the ice in her old bones. She sighed thinking of gentle sunsets, not the cold light that dimmed in the woods now.

As they approached the edge of the guarded perimeter, several of her people had their arrows trained on a small group of groundmites.

Captain Terrik turned at her approach. "Grandmother, I am glad you are here."

"It looks like Skarrl and his group. Have they come to trade again?"

"It appears so."

When the groundmites had first been spotted near their perimeter months ago, she had ordered her people not to kill them outright unless directly threatened. Her experiences in Blackveil had taught her that the creatures could be useful. They were not without intelligence, and this group had managed to evade all their traps in the forest.

In time, the groundmites made plain their desire to trade for meat, though all they had to offer were bone necklaces, rotting hides, and rusted tools and weapons they had scavenged from who-knew-where. Grandmother carefully encouraged these encounters, trading a chicken or pig for whatever rubbish the groundmites had to offer. The creatures were skinny and flea-bitten, but not as badly off, she suspected, as other groups. It had been a hard winter.

The one known as Skarrl shambled forward. He was the most decorated of the groundmites she had seen, with bone jewelry and the best furs to cover his body. She took him to be the chief of his group, or tribe, or clan, or however they organized themselves. His necklaces of bones and teeth clicked around his neck as he approached.

He halted before Grandmother, seemingly oblivious to the arrows trained on him. He launched into an avalanche of groundmitish gibberish interspersed with grunts and occasionally recognizable words of the common tongue: trade, meat, want.

"What trade, Skarrl?" she asked. "What have you got?"

Skarrl grunted, then turned toward his companions. He issued a stream of more unintelligible chatter and gestured at them. They rose from crouched positions, the arrows of Terrik's archers following every move they made. They dragged a litter behind them as they approached. When they halted before Grandmother, Skarrl pointed a crooked claw at the litter. "Trade. Meat, want."

A lantern hissed to life and the groundmites leaped back in dismay, then calmed when they saw the light would not harm them. Grandmother peered down at the litter. The light revealed a man bound into it beneath a rough fur. She could tell little about him, except that his face was mottled by bruises and crusted with blood. Beneath the bruises he was pale. He looked dead. She removed her mitten and placed her hand on his forehead. He was warm, not yet a corpse.

"Who is he?" Captain Terrik asked. "If the 'mites are hungry, why didn't they just eat him?"

"As for your first question, I do not know, but some lost soul to be out this far in the wilderness. As for your second question, perhaps they thought bringing us this man would please us and they could get better meat from us. I do believe they've developed a taste for mutton and chicken. Skarrl, where did you find this man?"

But Skarrl only answered in his groundmitish babble that

seemed to simply signify that he did not understand the question.

"I guess we'll not know," Grandmother said. "At least not from the groundmites."

"You aren't going to trade our good food for this half-dead man, are you?" Captain Terrik asked.

"Captain, where is your curiosity? I am going to trade, and if this man regains consciousness, we might discover he's perhaps a trapper, or a wayward wanderer, or maybe even a spy. If he is a spy, it would be good to know, yes?"

"Yes, Grandmother."

She turned to the soldiers who had escorted her and said, "Bring the oldest ewe we have. There is the black-faced one that is lame and has little life left in her. Also, the sack of grain we discovered today that is moldering. Hmm, perhaps a couple loaves of bread to seal the transaction."

She turned to the groundmite chief and said, "Yes, Skarrl, we trade."

He grunted in understanding.

Grandmother sensed the captain's disapproving gaze on her, but she ignored him. He was just concerned, and justifiably so, about the welfare of their people. She believed they would make it to spring. They'd set aside a healthy amount of stores for the winter, and her people had either brought their own livestock or acquired other animals from villages and farms Second Empire had raided.

After the soldiers returned and the trade was made, Captain Terrik said of the groundmites, "We can still kill them and get our ewe back."

"No, Captain," Grandmother replied. "It would serve little purpose. We traded in good faith. You never know where a positive relationship with our neighbors might lead."

"Trouble, most like," he grumbled.

She *tsked*. "There is no telling how many creatures belong with this small group that comes to us. Better to not invite trouble by killing their chief. After all, we already have an enemy to the south. We do not need another here in the north. Now if some of your men would help me back and drag this litter home . . ."

* * *

She trudged toward the overgrown ruins of the ancient keep that was home. A few of the walls still stood to a certain degree. One among them who was a mason had, with the help of others, spent the warm months making repairs and stabilizing what remained, while others rebuilt the roof to keep the weather off. The keep was surrounded by a crumbling curtain wall. The complex was situated upon a hillock within the forest. It must have once stood prominent over agricultural lands before they were deserted and the forest closed in.

Rough shacks and cabins had gone up against both the curtain wall and the keep proper, a shanty village erected by both soldiers and civilians of Second Empire, the refugees who had fled Sacoridia, her people. This far north in the Lone Forest, beyond the boundaries of Sacoridia, the winter was especially harsh. Frigid winds rushed down from the arctic ice, and each day saw the loss of the weak and infirm. It meant fewer mouths to feed, but to Grandmother, it felt terribly unfair that her people should suffer while her enemy, King Zachary, stayed warm and well-fed in his grand castle.

The air smelled of smoke. Bonfires, torches, and lanterns offered a golden welcome as she approached the keep. Luckily, they did not lack for wood.

"Where do you want the litter to go?" one of the soldiers asked her.

"To the great hall," she replied. "There we shall get a closer look at our trade."

Dogs barked at their arrival, and people called out greetings to her as they warmed themselves by the fires. They cast curious glances at the litter.

Soldiers saluted as they passed through the gap in the curtain wall where there had once been a gate. Little remained of the original, but carpenters were working on a new one. Its utility would be questionable until other gaps in the wall were repaired. Currently, an army could swarm through at will.

Inside the wall were more shacks and pens for sheep, pigs, and a few cows. Chickens roamed where they wished. She crossed the courtyard, and a soldier pulled aside an old wool blanket that served as the keep's door so she could enter.

Inside the keep it wasn't much warmer, but the walls cut the wind. The air was dank and smoky. Roiling torch flames cast erratic shadows that slithered across stone. The great hall was the most repaired chamber in the keep with a roaring fire in the massive hearth. Some great clan chief of old would have feasted his vassals in this chamber. When they found it, it had been filled with the detritus of hundreds of years of neglect, and whatever had drifted through the broken roof from the forest. But for the new rafters and roof, one would have little idea the level of disrepair the place had been in. It had taken substantial effort to make it habitable for people rather than rodents. Luckily, they'd captives to do the hard labor.

The litter had been dragged over by the hearth, and a group of her people were peering down at its occupant, including Lala and her tutor.

"Now, now," Grandmother said as she approached. "Give us some space to see what we've got."

The group parted and let her in. The heat of the fire was a relief, though she did not think her toes would thaw out completely until summer. She gazed down at the man, and if anything, his face looked more ghastly than it had by lantern light out in the woods. Swollen and bruised and cut, and who knew what his beard hid. What would they find when they removed the fur that covered him? She reached down and peeled his eyelids back. Brown eyes, with pupils unevenly dilated. Concussion, but not surprising.

"Who is he?" Lala asked.

"I do not know, child. The groundmites found him."

"Groundmites . . ." Arvyn, the tutor, murmured. He stared down at the man in disbelief.

"Yes, we traded some things for him. Now all of you, back to work so Min and Varius can have a look at the fellow."

Varius was a skilled mender, and Min very capable, as well. She left them to tend the man, whoever he was. If they needed help, they would call on her. If the man survived his wounds, whatever they were, they would learn his name and how he came into the clutches of Skarrl and his people. If he were no one of particular interest, she could always put him to work on the excavation. If he did not survive? She shrugged. He would die a mystery.

She headed back toward the chamber they had set up as a kitchen. The broken walls had been patched with timbers and tarps, but the hearth was fully repaired and kept the area warm. Sarat and a few others fussed around her, getting her seated by the fire with a cup of tea to warm her hands, and entertaining her with the day's gossip of who had shirked their chores, which young man was stealing kisses from which young woman, what the children were up to. It was all very domestic and cozy, and she could almost forget she was in some abandoned keep in the wilderness preparing her people to battle the Sacoridians and their allies. She left most of the military strategy to Birch, now a general rather than a colonel, and he was spending the winter ensconced with his troops at one of their bases a day's ride to the east. Soon, winter would fade and conflict would reignite.

As Grandmother relaxed, another woman entered the kitchen. She was a stocky person with a mop of curling hair. She was bundled in a cloak, her cheeks red as if she'd just been outside.

"Hello, Grandmother," the woman said, ignoring Sarat who looked displeased to see her.

"Ah, Nyssa, dear," Grandmother replied. "How goes your latest project?"

Nyssa dropped onto a bench. Her cloak fell open revealing trousers and a tunic flecked with blood. Not her own. "Forty strokes was too much for him," she said with a shrug. "His heart stopped. He was old, anyway."

Sarat frowned in disapproval from across the chamber. It was clear how she felt about Nyssa and her work, but to Grandmother's mind, Nyssa took a disagreeable but necessary task and turned it into an artform. She clearly loved her work as much as it disgusted Sarat.

"He was no longer productive," Nyssa added, "so no great loss. But I saw that we may have a replacement. Varius told me how you traded with the groundmites for that fellow. It's an odd thing."

"Yes, it is," Grandmother replied. "If he survives, then perhaps he'll be suitable for the labor. I should like to find out how he came to be in the hands of groundmites in the first place."

A tight smile formed on Nyssa's face. "If he does not tell you, then I will get the answers for you."

SONG OF THE STARRY CROSSING

In the dream, he drew the bowstring taut and aimed down the shaft of the arrow. He'd found the doe standing in a meadow at the edge of a wood, flicking her tail as she grazed, the golden sunshine of spring falling softly on her russet-brown back. She was a beautiful creature with a delicate face and limbs, every movement mesmerizing in its grace, but he was a hunter, and finally, in a moment of stillness, she was in range. If he was successful, she would be his. He let fly the arrow.

It arced through the air, its shadow flickering over meadow grasses, the sun stroking the shaft as it flew. The doe looked up, gazed across the meadow at him and tensed as though to flee, but it was too late. The arrow struck.

The doe flung herself into the woods, and he pursued, running across the meadow into the shade of leaf and limb. Her trail was obvious—broken branches, hoofprints, smears of blood on vegetation. He followed her trail over peat and duff and came upon her in a clearing as she took faltering steps, the arrow jutting from her ribs, blood darkening her side.

Her legs gave out, and she went down onto her chest on a deep bed of velvet green moss. He approached carefully. Now on her side, she thrust her legs out weakly, still fighting, still trying to flee. He knelt down and placed his hand gently upon her head. Her breaths came in raspy gusts and she looked up at him, but her right eye was not the brown of a deer, but the silver gleam of a mirror.

He realized in horror his mistake. *No! No! No!*

The arrow had rammed through Karigan's ribs just below

her heart. He held her in his arms as she took her last breaths and her mirror eye dulled to pewter, a single tear gliding down her cheek.

"NO!" He thrashed, fought against hands that pressed him back. "No! No! No!" How could he kill her? How? Pain clamped his skull, a terrible headache, and with it he realized he had been dreaming. No, he would not have killed her. Just a dream, just a dream. Then he said it aloud, his words slurring: "Jussst a dream."

"Must have been some nightmare," someone muttered.

Zachary opened his eyes to slits and jerked in surprise at a blurry face nose-to-nose with him. The vision made him feel sick, so he closed his eyes.

"Not quite with us yet," a man said.

"Give him a little time."

Zachary realized he was warm, wrapped in blankets. A fire radiated heat against his cheek. He was among people, so he had made it out of the cave somehow, unless the cave, too, had been a dream.

"Bruises both old and recent," one of the men was saying, "and healing ribs. Looks like he's been in a bad fight or two, and like someone tried to strangle him for good measure."

"Keep an eye on him then," said a woman. The resonant quality of her voice, like well-worn wood that has known years, suggested an older person. "We don't need him starting brawls here."

Had Zachary the energy, he'd laugh at the notion of himself as a brawler.

"Another thing that's odd," the man said, "is his clothing."

The blanket peeled away, and Zachary shivered with the inrush of cold air. After a moment, the blanket was dropped back over him.

"I have not seen that style since my grandfather's time," the woman said. "Once fine garb, but very old. This one must have a very curious story. Let me know when he is ready to talk."

"Yes, Grandmother."

Grandmother. Zachary stilled. What were the chances? No, there were grandmothers everywhere. This could not be his enemy, the leader of Second Empire. He, of course, did not ask, but he squinted once again, fighting the nausea. A man stood nearby staring down at him. Tall with golden hair, he was familiar to Zachary. He blinked trying to clear the blurriness from his eyes, trying to get the man to resolve in his vision. In a moment of clarity, he jerked up and almost spoke Fiori's name.

Aaron Fiori shook his head and drew his finger to his lips. Then said, "I am called Arvyn. Mender Varius thinks you should rest for now." He then glanced about as though to make sure he was not being observed and mouthed, *Danger*.

Zachary closed his eyes for a moment, and when he looked again, Fiori was gone. The pain in his head reinforced that this was not an extension of his dream.

Fiori had given him a false name, let him know he was not among friends. Perhaps he'd managed to fall into the clutches of Second Empire, after all. Even if it were not Second Empire, he knew enough not to reveal his true identity to strangers without good cause. Even the most well-meaning folk could be a danger, should they learn who he was. There was a reason he was guarded by Weapons. Unless any of these people had seen him in person, or his portrait in the castle, they would not recognize him. He was not pictured on the realm's currency, nor were there statues of him. There was a wax mannequin of him in the Sacor City War Museum, but it was, to his mind, a poor likeness.

As for his bruised and swollen face? All the better for concealing his identity. And because there was always the possibility of him finding himself in such a situation, he and his spymasters had put protocols in place, stories, that would further obscure who he truly was.

He tried to relax. Perhaps this was a singular opportunity to deal a blow to Second Empire. In order for that to happen, he would have to play his part well.

As he drifted off, he wondered what had happened to Nari and Magged. Had they escaped the aureas slee? He remembered little past an icy hand gripping his throat, strangling him, and the cold. He remembered nothing of how he left the cave, or how he ended up here, wherever here was. It was not Nari, or Magged, or the aureas slee he dreamed about, however.

Her blood on his hands, the arrow jutting at an admonitory angle from her ribs. *No, no, no* . . . Her hair lay in a brown wave across his arm as he held her in the dappled sunshine of the wood.

He surfaced enough to realize that yes, her blood was on his hands, as was that of every individual who served him. Every drop of blood they shed in service to the realm bloodied his hands. But he loved *her.*

Cannot lose her. He had come close to losing her too many times. As his awareness dimmed, he thought she did not deserve all she suffered, and the gods take him if he be responsible for it.

The next time he came to, it was to the sound of music, a lullaby his nurse once sang for him, a gentle tune of stepping from star to star as if they were stepping stones in a stream. The song was called "The Starry Crossing." The voice singing it was female and, to his ear, perfectly pitched and melodious. It belonged to a person of exceeding vocal talent. She was accompanied by a lute.

Come to sleep, my little one
Come to rest, my little one

Drift into the starry dream
Step across the night sky stream

Follow the crossing, little one
The starry crossing, little one

The hound, the hawk, the grayling dove
The horse, the fish, the ladle, too
All await beyond the dawn
All await to cradle you

Come to sleep, my little one
Come to rest, my little one

Step into the starry dream
Step across the night sky stream

Follow the crossing, little one
The starry crossing, little one

He of the great wings beckons you
Your spirit he has now unbound
For the Earth is but a mew
The heavens aloft you have found

Come to sleep, my little one
Come to rest, my little one

The music almost drew him back into sleep until it was interrupted by irritating voices.

"Teaching her that Sacoridian heathen rubbish again, Arvyn?" A woman, whose tone was mocking.

"It's just a lullaby," Fiori replied.

"Oh? What do you think the starry crossing means?"

Fiori mumbled something in response. Of course, he would know the stars represented the gods, and that traversing the heavens meant death, but he wasn't supposed to be Fiori. He was playing the part of one called Arvyn.

"It is a perversion, all those gods," the woman said, "and you shouldn't be teaching Lala such trash. There is only one god."

"Now, now, Nyssa," came the voice Zachary recognized as Grandmother's. "Arvyn does not know our ways, yet. I am sure we could teach him some Arcosian lullabies."

"I would like that, Grandmother," Fiori said. "Are they as dark as 'The Starry Crossing'?"

"I should say so. It would seem that portraying dark themes in the guise of children's songs and rhyme is universal."

Zachary experimented with opening his eyes. His vision was still blurry but perhaps not quite as bad as before. High above the rafters was a ceiling made of new wood. Heavy stone walls rose up around him. Parts of the walls looked recently mortared, but the structure had the feel of great age about it. To his side was the large hearth that kept him comfortably warm. To the other side of it, a couple people sat on a crude bench to warm their hands. One, a bespectacled fellow of middling years, observed him looking around.

"You're waking up again, eh?" The man stood and came to Zachary's side. "I am Varius. I do some of the mending around here. How are you feeling?"

"Thirsty." The word came out as a croak.

"That's a good sign." Varius turned and spoke to someone, and Zachary heard retreating footsteps.

An elderly woman stepped into view and also looked down at him. She wore a cloak wrapped around her like a blanket.

"So, our mysterious stranger has reawakened. I must say I am quite interested to hear your story, young man. You are lucky the groundmites preferred to trade you for livestock rather than eat you."

"Thank you," he replied in a hoarse whisper.

"Oh," she said, "don't be thanking me yet."

She smiled as she looked down on him, and he might have thought her kindly but for the ominous quality of her words and the shrewd gleam in her eye.

"Do you have a name?" she asked.

"Perhaps we should wait till he has had a drink," Varius said.

"Of course."

"Here is Min now with some water."

A woman handed Varius a cup and the mender knelt beside Zachary.

"Let me help you drink," he said, "and take it slowly."

Varius helped tilt Zachary's head forward and pressed the

cup to his lips. The movement hurt his head all the more, but he drank eagerly.

"Easy," Varius reminded him.

When he finished, he lay back, wanting more water even while his stomach churned.

"Better?" Grandmother asked.

Zachary sensed Fiori and the others hovering nearby. A woman with curly hair gazed over Grandmother's shoulder. He cleared his throat. "A little." His voice was still hoarse. "Where am I? What happened?"

"For the first," Grandmother replied, "you are in the Lone Forest. As for the second, that is what *we* would like to know."

"The knock to his head may impair his memory," Varius said.

"I know, Varius," she replied, giving the mender a testy look. "You may recall I have some experience in mending, myself."

Varius blushed and bowed his head. "I am sorry."

Grandmother ignored him and said to Zachary, "Perhaps, young man, we can start simply. What is your name?"

PLAYING THE PART

Fiori hovered behind Grandmother, and though Zachary's vision remained somewhat blurred, he could see the anxiety in his eyes.

"Dav," Zachary replied barely above a whisper. He had no idea if Grandmother could detect honesty the way Laren could, but he thought it best to keep an element of truth to what he told her. He closed his eyes, once again feeling the pull of sleep.

"Dav? Is that your first name, or your last?"

"Dav Hill," he murmured as he sank into darkness.

"At least we've got a name," he heard Grandmother say as if from far away.

"We'd best let him rest a while longer," Varius said, "so he can answer more questions later."

Zachary did not hear Grandmother's reply. He heard instead "The Starry Crossing" as though it was being hummed to him by his nurse, at once soothing and disquieting. Some small part of his mind reflected the song must have been created because so many babes never made it beyond infancy, much less to adulthood, which led him to a vision of Estora humming the tune to their children in their cradles. They were lifeless.

He writhed in his blankets and groaned, the pain in his head agony. He was dimly aware of Varius putting a cup to his lips.

"Easy, Dav," the mender said. "This draught will help the pain."

Zachary gulped convulsively of the herbal concoction. He

then relaxed, and headed once more toward slumber, the words of the lullaby once again coming to him. *Come to sleep, my little one. Come to rest . . .*

Zachary next awoke with the headache subdued. His vision was clearer, and the light in the chamber was different. A hint of daylight crept in from somewhere, though on the whole, the dark and shadows claimed the chamber.

Grandmother, he recalled, had said he was in the Lone Forest, which was not surprising because the last intelligence he'd received was that a group of Second Empire was spending the winter in the Lone Forest. He knew there were ruins there, a keep from the time of the First Age, at the very least, and this must be it. From the little he could see, Second Empire had done an admirable job of making it habitable.

It was quiet but for the pop of the fire. People must be out working on whatever chores were required, but he was under no illusion that he was not watched. He took time to assess his condition. Everything hurt, but nothing seemed broken or torn that he could detect. He touched his face and winced. Still swollen and tender. His stomach did not feel poorly, a major improvement. In fact, he was hungry.

Someone's shadow drifted over him, and he looked up to find a woman staring down at him. He dimly remembered her from last night.

"You're awake then, eh?" she asked.

Zachary nodded, rose to his elbows. He'd have to face whatever was to come sooner or later.

"Don't move," the woman said. "I will fetch Varius."

As moving seemed exhausting at the moment, he decided to obey. He ended up dozing until Varius arrived and shook his shoulder.

"Min said you were awake a little bit ago. Do you want to try to sit up?"

"I think so."

Varius helped him. His head pounded, then eased, and he did not feel an immediate need to vomit. Min brought him broth and a slice of toasted bread. He took his time eating. It did feel good to have something warm in his belly.

"You slept hard," Varius told him. "There are many who sleep here in the great hall at night, then we have our meals here, and you lay as one dead. It was a healing sleep, I think."

Zachary did feel noticeably better for it. Varius then helped him to a chamber where he relieved himself and splashed cold water on his face. Gray cave dust runneled off his face and hands into the basin. He gazed at his hands. His nails were jagged and dirt ingrained in the creases of his knuckles. They did not look like the hands of a king, and he was glad. Since there was no mirror, he could not see how the rest of him looked.

When he stepped back out into the great hall, Varius handed him a heavy cloak. "The man this belonged to doesn't need it anymore, but as you've none, you should have it."

Zachary flung the cloak around his shoulders and was glad to have its warmth. "Many thanks," he said. Varius seemed like a good fellow, and it was hard to believe he was Second Empire.

"Grandmother will want to talk to you," the mender said. "I don't think I can hold her off any longer."

"Some reason I should be worried?" Zachary asked. He had to pretend he did not know with whom he was dealing.

"Grandmother is protective of her people is all. While we wait for her, let's get you another cup of broth. You look like you haven't had a good meal in some while."

Zachary thought back to the fungus he, Nari, and Magged had subsisted on in the cave. "No, I haven't."

He awaited Grandmother, wrapped in his cloak by the fire. As he did so, he watched people come and go across the great hall intent on their own business. There were those he identified as soldiers, though they wore no uniform or insignia. They lingered in the great hall keeping watch on him. Their regard was not friendly, and when Varius was called away to tend someone else, he was sorry to lose the one friendly person he'd met, thus far. Min, who seemed to be Varius' assistant, always had a sour expression on her face when she looked in his direction.

When Grandmother arrived, she was flanked by the curly-haired woman and a man who was clearly an officer, for the other soldiers saluted him. Zachary stood, a little unsteadily, at their approach.

"Good morning to you, Dav," Grandmother said, looking him over with a critical eye. "So, you have not died on us. This is Captain Terrik, and Nyssa. They will be listening while you and I talk."

Zachary bowed his head to them, and they all sat on benches before the hearth.

"From where do you hail?" Grandmother asked him.

"Duck Harbor," he replied. "Coast of L'Petrie." It was on the border of Hillander and would explain his slight accent.

"Are you a fisherman?"

"Nah," Zachary replied, trying his best to stay in character. "My da ran the mercantile in the village." Which would explain why his manner of speaking wasn't more rustic.

"What on Earth are you doing up north?" Grandmother looked incredulous.

"I was in North, the town, looking after lumber interests. Y'see, my da supplies the local shipwrights. I was up to do some negotiating with sellers." The next part would strain their credulity, and he was no Fiori when it came to telling stories. He took a deep breath and said, "I was staying at the Full Moon, playing cards, maybe drinking a little."

"That's probably one of the roughest taverns in North," Captain Terrik remarked.

Zachary nodded sagely. He'd certainly heard enough reports about it, and other establishments in North, as well. "The fellows there, the lumbermen, they didn't like that I was winning."

"I think I can see where this is going," Nyssa said, looking amused.

"Probably you can," Zachary said. "A little too much drink, and me winning too much. They, three of them, beat me up, took me out to the middle of nowhere, beat me some more. I woke up stripped of my winnings and my clothes. It was freezing." His listeners, even Grandmother, appeared to be enjoying the tale. If they believed him, he could not tell, but at least his bruises would give credence to the idea he'd been in a fight. He continued to play the part by trying to look aggrieved. "Those fellows just as soon I died out in the woods with no one the wiser. They didn't care."

"Tell us, Dav," Grandmother broke in, "how you did not die."

Zachary coughed. He was still hoarse. "Maybe I could have another drink?"

Grandmother called to Min to fetch more water. An uneasy silence followed as they waited. Nyssa examined her fingernails. Captain Terrik seemed to fall into deep thought. Grandmother gazed speculatively at him from beneath hooded eyes. As a king, he would have met her gaze. As Dav Hill, he did not. He fidgeted, looked anywhere other than at Grandmother. He showed that he was nervous. Meanwhile, he wondered where Fiori was, wondered what magic Grandmother was capable of. He knew some of it, but largely she was a mystery to him and his spymasters. If he could find a way to eliminate her, he could possibly slow Second Empire's rise. If they did not believe his story, he would have to act immediately. If that were the case, the odds were not in his favor.

Min finally returned with a cup of water that was icy cold. He drank it down, but when he was ready to resume his story and tell them how he'd come upon a hermit's cave in the woods, his listeners were distracted by the entrance of others into the great hall. Five men strode in, three of whom were dressed in ordinary woodsmen's attire like the soldiers of the encampment. Two were dressed in the black and silver uniforms of his Sacoridian soldiers. Zachary almost jumped to his feet until he realized who it was.

Grandmother and Captain Terrik did rise to greet the newcomers, Nyssa following. Zachary pulled his cloak up about his shoulders and bowed his head, allowing his hair, which had grown some during his time at the cave, to fall over his face.

"Captain Immerez!" Grandmother exclaimed. "I am ever so glad to see you."

If anyone could identify him, Zachary thought, it was Immerez.

FROM KING TO THRALL

"Terrik!" Immerez exclaimed. "You've been promoted—my condolences."

Good-natured banter accompanied the greetings as though Immerez were a hero returned. Zachary watched from the corner of his eye as the Mirwellian was patted on the back by those who came to see him. Along with his freedom, he'd obtained the hook that replaced his missing hand, the hand Karigan had cut off, Zachary thought with grim satisfaction. He wondered about the soldiers he'd sent in pursuit of Immerez after his escape, and he was soon answered.

"Need we be on the lookout for king's men on your trail?" Terrik asked.

Immerez laughed his gravelly laugh. "The few we didn't kill we left in the dust weeks ago. They'll return home with their tails tucked between their legs."

Zachary frowned. He would not have wanted his soldiers to blunder into Second Empire's base, but it was unsettling that they'd been thwarted. That some had been killed caused his shoulders to sag. He thought perhaps he'd been forgotten until Grandmother and Terrik looked toward him, speaking to one another. Then Grandmother returned to Immerez, and Terrik motioned a couple of his guards forward. Zachary tensed.

"All right, Dav," Terrik said, "Grandmother will finish up with you some other time, but if you are well enough to sit up, you are well enough to work."

"Work?"

"Didn't think we were just going to let you lie around all day, did you?"

The two guards grabbed Zachary's arms and lifted him to his feet. The world spun too much for him to put up much of a fight. He was dragged outside, the cold like a slap to his face. Wood smoke was heavy on the air, and he saw a blur of shacks and people as he was pushed and shoved and pulled.

"Let me go," he said, struggling to release himself from their grasp. "You've no right—"

He was smacked behind the head and all went briefly black and suddenly he was on his knees. They kicked him to get up and he staggered to his feet.

"Keep your mouth shut," one said. "Whatever you were before, you belong to Second Empire now."

They dragged him through a gap in the curtain wall and into the woods. Were they going to kill him? But then he saw people ahead who seemed to be working, carrying baskets filled with rocks and dirt, which they dumped in piles. There were other armed guards here. Zachary was thrown to the ground at the feet of a man with a spiked cudgel.

"Got you a new worker," Terrik said. "His name's Dav. Be careful, he's a brawler."

The man gazed down at Zachary. "Looks a little worse for wear."

"That's the way he came in. Grandmother figures he can still move rocks."

Cudgel man grunted in what sounded like some kind of assent. "Git up, then."

Zachary was grabbed by the collar and thrust toward the other workers, gaunt, half-starved souls who moved as though dead on their feet. They were silent but for gasps and grunts as they shifted heavy loads. He was put to work in a tunnel that burrowed into an earthen mound, with timber supports to keep the ceiling from collapse. He was directed to remove rocks and scrape up dirt and debris. If he did not move fast enough, one of the guards whipped a caning rod across his back, as if he were no more than a mule.

He was so in shock, his head still not right, that he stumbled about and dropped as much as he carried. How his fortunes had reversed. He'd gone from king to thrall, for thrall was what he'd become. He'd known hard work, had even known battle, but forced labor was different, and if this was how Second Empire would treat his people should they claim victory? No, he would not have it. When he paused to catch his breath, the cane whooshed down on him. He pivoted and caught it in his hand. The guard's eyes widened.

Zachary raised his fist to smash it into the man's face, but his feet were kicked out from beneath him. He hit the ground hard and boots kicked and kicked him. The caning rod came down on his side and ribs. He threw his arms over his head to protect it. The blows rained down hard and furiously until he felt he must be reduced to pulp. And then it stopped. He lay there panting, on the edge of darkness, unable to move.

"Your technique is lacking, Cole," said a woman, whose voice Zachary recognized to be Nyssa's. "You're still more cobbler than soldier, aren't you."

Zachary gazed up through blurry eyes to see her looking down at him.

"Maybe that's so," Cole replied, "but these grunts don't need technique. I reckon we'll have him trained up just fine. *Your* training leaves strong workers useless or dead, and Grandmother wants the passage cleaned out."

Zachary was not sure what passed for a time until he was roughly hoisted to his feet, his whole body screaming from the pummeling he had received.

"Get back to work," the one called Cole ordered, and he pushed Zachary back toward the tunnel, or mine, or whatever it was.

He could barely move, barely remain upright when he bent to pick up rocks. He bumped into the walls, and when he stumbled into other workers, they pushed him away. The guards did not beat him if he moved too slowly. Not mercy, he supposed, but pragmatism that further beating would render him unconscious and useless.

He leaned against the mine's wall to regain his balance. He rubbed his aching head. Deep breaths hurt. The other workers just trudged around him as though they were revenants out of some nightmare. It did not help that he'd only had some broth and no real food in who knew how long.

It was as he leaned against the wall that he realized it was, in fact, a wall, not just rough, natural stone, but blocks of granite shaped by tools. He did not linger, for Cole was fingering his caning rod, looking eager for a chance to use it again.

At midday they were allowed to take a break. Zachary eased himself down onto the floor of the passage and leaned back against the wall, and closed his eyes.

"Here," someone said, placing a bowl into his hands. It was warm. He forced his eyes open to discover it was gruel with a chunk of pan bread in it. His appetite was uncertain at best.

"You'd better eat it," his benefactor said. "Still got a long day ahead."

He looked up. The woman had a Rhovan accent, and was as covered in dirt and rock dust as everyone else. He had not distinguished her from the others at first because everyone had looked pretty much the same.

She handed him a tin of ale. "My name is Lorilie."

"Dav," he said, barely above a whisper. "Thank you." He sipped the ale. It was flat as piss, but it helped return moisture to his parched mouth.

"Looks like you've had a hard day," Lorilie said.

Much more than a day, he thought. How long since the aureas slee had snatched him from the castle?

"Do the best you can," she continued, "and they won't beat on you. Trying to fight them is not worth it. Trust me, I know."

She left him then, to take her own bowl and cup to sit elsewhere in the passage. He watched after her as she limped away. It was hard to tell much about her, except for her Rhovan accent. He felt as though he were missing something, something that he should know, but he'd been so beaten his mind was not working well. He would worry about it later. He forced himself to eat.

Lorilie had been correct. There was still a lot of day left to move rocks. Even if he had not been in such terrible condition, it would have been backbreaking work. He tried to get through it by counting his steps back and forth, then by counting the rocks he loaded into his basket. When that palled, he thought about swordfighting forms, imagining each movement in his mind. Perhaps this was how the other workers got through their day, by immersing their minds in something other than their current reality.

After dusk, they were herded into a rough-hewn building with a firepit in its center, the smoke spiraling up through a hole in the roof. The packed dirt floor was strewn with old rushes.

One of the thralls doled out stew from a cookpot over the fire. There was some pushing and shoving among the workers, now suddenly come to life. Zachary was too tired to fight, and so he ended up at the rear of the line with some of the older workers. There was barely any left for them.

He could hardly hold his bowl in his bruised and bleeding hands, but once he found a place to sit, he ate his pittance, scooping it out with a piece of greasy pan bread. At least he was keeping his food down.

Lorilie, he noticed, sat across the room in a circle with others as though holding court. No one else paid him any mind, and he figured it was just as well. He almost fell asleep with his face in his bowl, when someone came to collect it. Others were wrapped in blankets or cloaks and lay down to sleep. Several lay close to one another for warmth. Zachary blessed Varius for the gift of the cloak and fell into the slumber of the grave.

Sometime during the night, he dreamed he was a stag crowned with branching antlers, but he was not free. He was surrounded by snarling wolves. Karigan entered the vision though not the Karigan he had hunted and slain with an arrow, nor was she Karigan the Green Rider. Rather, she was clad in strange armor that gleamed with the light of stars. Unknown symbols crawled across the surface of it changing shape and form. Somehow he knew the armor to be made of star steel, a substance of legend. She wore a winged helm upon her head and carried a lance. Upon her shield, the device of the crescent moon shone with ethereal luminescence. She was not herself, but more a supernatural being filled with the power of the heavens. She casually swept away a few of the wolves by merely pointing her lance at them.

"Think," she commanded him in a voice that was more than her own. She flicked more of the wolves away as if they were nothing. *"Observe."* The rest of the wolves fled before her and she stood above him. *"Protect."*

Then she left, astride a great black steed.

When Zachary awakened at dawn, he remembered only a sensation of the dream, as if he'd been under some spell. It ebbed away in the reality of a body barely able to move for all the pain, and a day ahead of hard physical labor and deprivation.

THINK, OBSERVE, PROTECT

The work was again mind-numbing. An older man fell, and his basket of rocks spilled across the passage floor. He curled up where he lay and would not move. The other workers just walked around or stepped over him. Zachary glanced over his shoulder. The guards, deep in some conversation, had not yet reacted. He knelt beside the man.

"Are you sick?" Zachary asked. "Hurt?"

"I am so tired," the man murmured.

Another worker paused beside them. It was Lorilie. "Get up, Binning, or they will beat you."

"They can drag me off into the woods and kill me," the man said. "I can't take it anymore."

"Let me help," Zachary said. He started refilling Binning's basket.

"Hurry," Lorilie said. "They're coming." She left them, carrying away her own burden.

"Let me help you stand," Zachary whispered.

"Leave me be," Binning said. "I'm too tired."

"What's this?" asked Cole, slapping his rod against the palm of his hand. The guard with the spiked cudgel stood square beside him. "Are we going to have to make you move?"

"He tripped and fell," Zachary said. "He'll be up in a moment."

"A moment too long." Down came the rod.

Protect.

Zachary shifted to shield Binning, and the rod lashed across his shoulders. Before he could be struck again, he grabbed Binning's arm and raised him to his feet.

"We are working," Zachary said fiercely.

"Then get on about it."

He put Binning's arm around his smarting shoulders. "Think you can hold your basket?"

Tears streamed down the man's cheeks, cutting runnels through the stone dust. Zachary gave him the lighter basket, and hoisted the heavier to his own hip.

"You shouldn't have done it, lad," Binning said. "Should've just let them finish me."

Protect. The word had struck Zachary as a lightning bolt and given him the strength to overcome his own injuries and weakness to help Binning. Wasn't this the duty of a king, after all? To protect his people?

Zachary gave him encouraging words all the way out to the pile to empty their baskets, then guided Binning back into the passage beneath the smirking gazes of the guards. They were like vultures looking upon carrion.

"Think I can shuffle along on my own now," Binning said. "Had a weak moment back there."

"I'll keep close," Zachary replied.

"My thanks. You are wearing Skinner's old cloak."

"Skinner?"

"Aye. They took him away to the one called Nyssa because he mouthed off at the guards. He never came back. He was an old farmer, like me."

At the end of the passage came the clack of metal on stone as workers swung picks at the earth and stone that blocked the way.

As Zachary knelt to collect rocks into his basket, he asked, "Where did you farm?"

"On the border. A little northwest of North. It wasn't much of a farmstead, mostly rocks." He tossed one into his basket in disgust. "But it was mine. I was no tenant, didn't owe no one nothing. Not even the king. But then Second Empire came and took the little I had."

"Life on the border is not easy," Zachary said. He knew the stories of those who braved groundmites and rugged living conditions there. As Binning had indicated, it was not good farmland, but having a place of one's own was something. It was freedom, a way of bettering oneself and not being under the thumb of a landowner, or the king's taxes. He smiled to himself. He admired the border folk for their ambition and courage despite the fact most of them despised him as their king. And now they'd been hit hard by Second Empire.

He helped Binning lift his load, then hefted his own, and they continued down the passage. Before they could be accused of moving too slowly by the guards, the midday meal was called. Binning dropped where he stood.

"Wait here," Zachary said. "I'll get you something to eat."

It was the same as the day before, gruel and pan bread. Zachary found Binning with his back against a tree and handed him the food and a cup of ale.

At first they ate in companionable silence; then Binning asked, "Where you from, lad? Sounds like the coast to me."

Zachary smiled. "Good ear. I hail from Duck Harbor, in L'Petrie."

"I've never been to the big water, never been south of Sacor City."

"It is well worth seeing."

"Don't think I ever will," Binning replied. "Not in this life."

"Don't say that."

"Look at us, lad. What are these people gonna do with us when there are no more rocks to move?"

Zachary did not have an answer for him. When they returned to work, Binning appeared better for the meal, such as it was, but Zachary stayed by his side. On one of their trips into the passage, they discovered the workers with the picks had uncovered something in one of the walls. As Cole raised his lantern to look, Zachary glimpsed what appeared to be a lintel. He could not linger, for he was threatened by the cudgel-bearing guard to keep moving. On subsequent trips into the passage, more and more was revealed of what looked to be a stone door. On his final trip of the day, ancient glyphs of the gods carved into the stone were exposed. Most prominent was that of Westrion, god of the dead, and his steed, Salvistar. They'd been burrowing into a tomb.

Binning sat with Zachary that evening for their supper. Stew again. He was absorbed in wondering what Grandmother was after in the tombs.

"Bad business," Binning said, "breaking into tombs."

Yes, it was.

Soon after eating, Zachary lay down to sleep. Binning stretched out beside him, sharing his body heat. He clenched and unclenched his aching hands with their shredded skin and broken, bloody fingernails. If Grandmother's goal was reaching that tomb, then perhaps his rock-carrying days were over. Perhaps his life would be over. He fisted his hands, ignoring the pain. He could not allow Grandmother to succeed in obtaining whatever it was that she wanted in the passage. He would not allow Second Empire to overcome his realm. He would not die a thrall.

Think! came the command, but he was too exhausted in body and spirit, and he fell into a hard sleep.

The next day, he was surprised when they kept digging downward past the tomb entrance. No one bothered to open it. What was Grandmother after?

Binning held his own, but Zachary helped others if they stumbled or tired. He began to learn the names of his fellow captives and from where they hailed. Most were from the northern boundary, but Pitkin, a hapless merchant from Penburn, had been taken from the North Road. Then there was Lorilie, with her Rhovan accent. He helped her lift her basket when they both ended up at the end of the passage at the same time.

"I do not need help," she said.

"Of course," he replied. "I will not help again unless requested." There were enough fierce women in his life that he knew when not to argue.

She gave him an aggravated look and hurried along with her burden as best she could. Zachary did not tarry, for the guard with the spiked cudgel watched him closely. Too closely. He followed Lorilie up the passage, nodding to others as they headed back down with empty baskets.

Lorilie, Rhovan. *Think.* And then it came to him. Lorilie

Dorran, the leader of the Anti-Monarchy Society. Of course. She and her followers had inhabited the area around the Lone Forest, perhaps planning to create their own community free of the tyranny of kings, like many of the other border folk. At one time she'd been very active trying to turn his people against him. She had retreated north after his brother's coup attempt, and little had been heard from the Anti-Monarchists since then. How, he wondered, would Lorilie react if she found out who he was? It was a diverting thought as he emerged into sunshine and dumped his basket of rocks.

That night during supper, Lorilie invited him to sit with her group. Binning, though uninvited but now seemingly attached to him, came, too. The others grudgingly made space for him. Zachary, considering his earlier revelation about *who* Lorilie was, was both amused and intrigued to be so favored.

She quietly asked how each person was faring. Pitkin nodded toward Zachary. "Thanks to Dav here, I probably avoided a caning."

"Good," Lorilie said, "we must help one another to stay strong, take care of one another, because no one else is going to. The imperialists will work us to death. Those of us who survive the dig? When it's done, we'll be put to use at some other slave labor, or be slaughtered outright." She spoke as a leader, one who naturally exuded charisma. It was no wonder she had been the head of the Anti-Monarchy Society.

"King might send soldiers," Pitkin said. "Before I was captured, he'd led skirmishes against Second Empire on the border."

Lorilie gave him a long look, but she did not lash out at him. "Even if the king's forces assault this place, what do you think our captors would do to us?"

Zachary knew the answer, and so did the others. Now that he was aware of the captives, he could formulate a plan that might prevent their slaughter. That was, if he were free and leading the assault against Second Empire. Since he, too, was a captive, the notion was not going to get very far.

"I take it," he said, "there have been escape attempts."

The others nodded. "They do not end well," Lorilie said.

"The few who have tried were quickly captured and flogged by the Nyssa woman in front of us as an example of what will happen to any of us who would try. There are many guards who watch us. In the unlikely event someone got by them, there are traps set out in the woods."

"What can you tell me about this place?" Zachary asked. "I've seen very little beyond the great hall of the keep, this building, and the excavation. And does anyone know what Grandmother is trying to dig up?"

No one knew the answer to the last, but they offered what they could about the layout of the keep and its grounds. He would have to try to escape eventually, once he regained his full strength, and the more he knew about Second Empire's base, the better chance he had of navigating his way out. And when he was out? He would have inside knowledge of it for when he returned with a force to destroy it.

THE BRAWLER

The passage pitched sharply downward, which added to the strenuous work of removing debris. Zachary still had no idea what it was Grandmother sought underground, but though they uncovered no more entrances to burial chambers, more glyphs appeared on the walls. He could not pause to examine them closely with the guards watching, so what he got were fleeting glimpses, impressions of figures and symbols that gave him a sense of foreboding. He saw Westrion, wings spread, and his raptor's countenance fierce, and Salvistar rearing. There were few other gods depicted, but several skeletal figures being faced down by a mounted knight carrying a lance. The horse looked as though it, too, could be Salvistar, but the knight was not Westrion.

The atmosphere of the passage was oppressive, and he was always relieved to reach the sunshine without when he made the trip to dump his basket, but he'd have to turn around and reenter the gloom. In the downward shaft, the sensation of oppression intensified. Those who labored with him, and even the guards, seemed to feel it, too, if their grim expressions were any indication.

It did not help that he worried about what was happening back home, how Estora and their children fared. How did she govern in his stead? He tried to remind himself that she had good counselors to help her, not least of all, Laren, who had advised him longest. Did they search for him, or did they assume he was dead? He couldn't even imagine where they'd begin . . . As a captive of Second Empire, he felt helpless, unable to do anything about these great concerns.

At midday, work halted, much to Zachary's surprise, but apparently no one else's. They were led through the gap in the curtain wall and into the great hall of the keep where they were instructed to sit on the floor. Zachary looked, but neither Grandmother nor Immerez were anywhere in sight.

"What's going on?" he asked Binning.

"Once a week they talk to us about their god, offer us a chance to convert or be damned for all eternity. Mostly they damn us."

Ah, Zachary thought. The one god of Arcosia. He had nothing against any god. It was those who would push their particular set of beliefs on others that he detested. Maybe a sermon would take his mind off his concerns about his wife and realm.

Guards stationed themselves around the chamber, and an older man in robes shambled out and stood in front of them. He gazed down his beaky nose at them like an angry gull. Zachary thought this task might have been under the purview of Grandmother as spiritual leader, but she was nowhere to be seen. The lay priest, known as Elder Smurn, ranted against the heathen gods that the Sacoridians venerated.

"They are false! Superstition! Abominations! At the time of judgment, your souls will be cast into the blackest pit of damnation and will cease to exist."

The ranting continued on, but just seemed to bounce off Zachary and his fellow laborers. They were exhausted, and used the time to rest with heads bowed. Some nodded off.

::Dav.::

It came to him as a whisper in his ear. He straightened his posture and carefully looked about himself. Was he just hearing things?

::I am sitting behind you.::

He did not dare look while under the scrutiny of the guards. He did not have to, to know it was Fiori using some kind of speech-throwing trick. He gave a subtle nod to indicate he heard and understood, even as Elder Smurn railed on.

::I am trying to figure out how to free you from here. I have not been able to find a way for myself, however. Too many guards. One day I will want to know the whole story of how you came to be here.::

Zachary smiled to himself and wished he could respond. He had many questions for the minstrel, himself.

"God favors Arcosia and her descendants above all others," Smurn exhorted.

::You may remember from your history,:: Fiori continued in Zachary's ear, ::that this keep is Ifel Aeon. It was a seat of power of the northern lords in ancient times.::

Of course, Zachary thought. Perhaps if he had not been hit on the head so many times, he would have figured it out himself. There were ruins all over the north, but this one was prominent in Lone Forest lore.

::Grandmother has sought not only shelter for her people here, but she searches for some sort of relic . . .:: Fiori paused, sounding uncertain. ::I have heard her mention a 'seal.' There are old parchments in Selium that describe the keep standing sentinel over a portal to—::

"Your eternal damnation!" The edges of Smurn's mouth were foaming. "Repent! Repent!"

Binning snored softly beside Zachary.

::—and it can't mean anything good.::

Zachary had missed a portion of Fiori's explanation due to Smurn's thunderous sermon. There was enough damnation to go around, he thought bitterly.

::He's almost done,:: Fiori said. ::Try to lie low, keep safe, for all our sakes.::

The sermon ended abruptly with Smurn looking contemptuously at the dirty, exhausted slave laborers at his feet. Having done his duty, he whirled and stalked off. The guards came forward to prod their charges back to work. Zachary glanced behind himself, but Fiori was nowhere to be seen.

"Had the strangest dream," Binning said as they filed from the great hall to the outdoors. "A man was whispering to me." He screwed his finger in his ear as if to clear it.

"Oh?" Zachary said carefully. "What did he say?"

Binning's brow became furrowed. "To keep watch over you."

"That *is* strange," Zachary replied, trying to sound surprised.

Back at the dig, he noticed two of the guards watching him and whispering to one another. He did not think it boded well. He wondered if they had somehow detected Fiori talking to him. He hastened into the passage with his basket so as not to draw any additional attention. Fiori was right that his safety lay in remaining beneath notice. Whatever those guards had already seen couldn't be helped. They hadn't recognized him somehow, had they?

As he worked and passed by the glyph-covered walls, he forgot the guards and thought about what Fiori had said, that Grandmother sought a seal or relic of some sort, and that the keep had stood over a portal.

Think.

One of the workers stumbled and fell to her knees in front of him. He hurried to help her rise. She was one of Lorilie's folk.

"Thank you, Dav," she said.

"Your knees are bleeding."

"That won't be all if we don't get moving."

He went back to work and as he trudged along with his burdens, he recalled what it was about portals and this old keep that stirred his memory. There were legends about how there were Earthly passages into the hells, where dark spirits and demons dwelled, and that once, far beyond human ken, these evil entities ran rampant across the lands. In the more obscure sections of the *Book of the Moon,* the religious text kept by the moon priests, it was written that the gods waged war on the dark ones and rounded them up. It fell to Westrion to confine them for all time. Guardians were appointed to keep watch over the prisons, ensuring the seals that blocked them remained strong. The *Book of the Moon* went so far as to suggest that these guardians were actually mortal avatars of Westrion, his representatives on Earth.

Zachary, down on his knee, tossed rocks into his basket and glanced over his shoulder where other workers heaved pickaxes at the blocked passage. Did it lead to the hells, or at least to one of the prisons that contained dark spirits? Or, was it all pure legend? Grandmother seemed to think there was something back there, or why else have them digging out the passage? If she thought one of these seals lay beyond, did she intend to break it to release the entities? She was a necromancer. Perhaps she believed she'd have some power over them, but if it had taken a war with the gods to subdue them, he was not sure any human, necromancer or not, could control them.

Let it be legend, he thought. Many of the stories in the *Book of the Moon* were, after all, metaphorical, or even pure fantasy. Even in pure fantasy, however, could be found some kernel of truth.

There was not much he could do about it at the moment, but *observe.* Observe and plan.

That evening after supper, he sat by himself to work on the planning part when guards burst into the building. Other prisoners scuttled out of the way.

"This is never good," Binning told Zachary.

"Why? What are they—?"

"Where's Dav?" one of the guards shouted. "Dav Hill, where are you?"

All the other prisoners, even Binning, moved away from him as though he were infected with the pox. He climbed to his feet. "I am here."

The guards grabbed him and dragged him out. He wondered if Grandmother finally wanted to hear the rest of his story about how he'd been caught by groundmites, but they didn't take him into the keep. They pushed and shoved him through the woods to a clearing lit by lanterns with a bonfire in the center. A number of soldier types stood around the clearing's perimeter, drinking. Binning was right. This could not be good. The circle opened, and he was kicked into the clearing from behind.

One of the guards from the dig, the one that carried the spiked cudgel, joined him in the clearing. "You are gonna entertain us, Dav," he said. "Strong fellow like you, always helping the others carry their rocks, surely you can put a good show on for us."

There was boisterous shouting, and the circle opened to admit a large and heavily muscled man. Zachary had a very good idea of where this was leading.

"This is Mace," the guard said, indicating the big man. "One of our own looking for a workout. Poor lad hasn't had anyone to pound in a while. Dav, you are going to fight him. Wagers, anyone?"

Zachary stared at Mace, while the soldiers made their wagers all around him. He knew how to take down big men. His arms training, after all, had not consisted solely of learning the sword. He could use his hands as well as any warrior. The problem was, if he put to use too many of the techniques he'd been taught, he'd be identified as more than the son of a lumber merchant, even more so if he won. They expected him to fight as a brawler, not as a well-trained warrior.

"Just in case you are thinking about throwing the fight," the guard said, "we'll cane your friend here real good."

Zachary's heart sank as they dragged Binning to the edge of the circle. The older man's face had gone pale. Zachary did not think the farmer was in any condition to survive a harsh caning. He'd have to fight convincingly, but as a brawler, in order to spare Binning. He sighed in resignation.

PORTALS, AVATARS, AND KNITTING

It was not difficult to give the audience a "show," for Mace proved to be a skilled fighter. It was all Zachary could do to dodge the hammerlike blows from Mace's fists. The soldier was both large and quick, a bad combination. It was hard for Zachary to hold back on the finer techniques he'd been taught in order to retain his brawler persona. He jabbed his own fists at his opponent, his feet moving lightly over the ground. If he hadn't been half-starved and worked so hard, he might have been able to land a couple meaningful blows, but his poor condition left him slow.

Do you think you have time to be tired in battle? he imagined Drent yelling at him. *Do you think the enemy will take a break so you can nap?*

Had Drent ever been in a situation like this? Zachary didn't think so, and he told his imagination to silence itself.

Mace's fist rammed straight for his face. Zachary hopped aside, but the blow clipped his ear. It felt like it had been ripped off. He backed away and touched it, and though it was still attached to his head, his fingers came away bloody. Then he noticed the dull gleam of metal on Mace's fingers. Iron knuckles. It figured.

The audience yelled and cursed at them. They wanted action. They wanted more blood. Zachary switched his stance and drove his fist under Mace's guard. It slammed into a gut seemingly made of steel. Mace shoved him back and followed up with a punch that glanced off the side of his head. If it had been more than a glance, he would have been down.

Then he got lucky and scored a hit across Mace's jaw, but

it crunched his fingers. He shook his hand out. Unfortunately, the lucky punch roused the big man, and he was on Zachary like a rabid wolf. The last thing Zachary saw was the iron knuckles flashing in front of his eyes.

Zachary could not see. He did not want to see, really, if the crackling in his head was any indication. Something cold covered his eyes and brow, and had an herby scent, which eased him. He seemed to be lying on a pallet and was covered by a blanket. The fire snapped nearby. It took him a while to remember the fight, though he couldn't place exactly what had happened. He guessed he'd gotten hit good and was now back in the keep's great hall for mending.

Just as he did not want to see, he did not wish to move. He lay still, fading in and out. Someone changed the compress over his eyes, the blessed coolness, the serenity of the herbs. He was surprised they hadn't just thrown him back with the other slaves to suffer as he would, but maybe they valued good workers.

Presences came and went around him, and voices murmured in the background and faded. At some point, a pair of voices did catch his attention, though he was not sure if they were real or part of a dream.

"How is the knitting coming along?" Immerez asked.

"It is complicated," Grandmother replied. "I have never made anything like this before."

Was she knitting a sweater? Zachary wondered.

"So you do not know if it will work?" Immerez asked.

"Rarely do I know, especially when dealing with unknown powers. If all goes as I hope, this will be like the web of a spider that traps its prey."

It must have been a dream, for spiders crawled through Zachary's mind and wove fine strands in the eye sockets of his aching skull.

"—really exists?" Immerez was asking.

"There are sources that suggest that this being does exist, chosen by one of your gods."

Immerez laughed. "They're not my gods, not anymore now that I am sworn to the one God."

"Yes, my friend, of course. Let me say one of your *former* gods then. The aspect of death called Westrion. It is said he chooses one, a human, to be his voice and presence on Earth when in need, to keep the dead in check, and dark beings, in particular, trapped beyond the portal. The avatar can communicate with and command the dead. I think I saw her once in a vision. I was in Blackveil, gazing into the fire, when she appeared clad in strange armor and a winged helm. She rode as a dark angel astride the death god's stallion."

The description created an image in Zachary's mind, recalling something from a dream. He was caught in the vision for some time and missed a portion of conversation between Immerez and Grandmother.

"So, when you reach the seal . . ." Immerez mused.

"Westrion's avatar, if the sources are correct, will have no choice but to appear."

"Thus your knitting."

"Thus my knitting."

Portals and gods and avatars and knitting . . . Dreams, or just his hurt, foggy head trying to make sense of words? He faded out again, and when he briefly resurfaced, heard Grandmother say, "—tomorrow to go meet with General Birch."

"I look forward to it," Immerez replied. "I will see you in the morning."

"How are we doing?"

Zachary blinked against gray light as the compress was pulled away from his eyes. Everything was a blur. "I feel like I've been buried in an avalanche."

Varius, the mender, chuckled. "Not surprising. I'll give you a minute, and then let's see if you can drink a little."

As Zachary thought about it, he did not feel as bad as he might have, and he was soon able to focus on Varius. The mender helped him sip water.

"Grandmother was furious last night when she heard about the fight," Varius said. "It was a breach of discipline and not the sort of thing she tolerates. She was not pleased one of her best workers got damaged. For punishment, the organizers of the fight, including Mace, are being made to move rocks today." He sounded amused, and Zachary had to admit that he was, too.

He tentatively touched the bridge of his nose and his temple. There was swelling and pain.

"You were bad enough that Grandmother used a healing spell," Varius said. "Mace's iron knuckles cracked bone. It should be mended, but the rest of the healing will have to be done the conventional way."

"Why would she heal a slave?" Zachary asked, genuinely surprised.

"She needs good workers, and you are one. When a slave is seriously hurt or sick, she will do what she can. She is determined to get that passage dug out."

Zachary was glad to know he had not been singled out. It meant she had not guessed his true identity.

"She never heard the rest of my story," he said, "of how I ended up with the groundmites."

Varius shrugged. "She has had other things on her mind of late."

"She's going someplace . . ."

"Went," Varius replied. "You rest while you can. They'll want you back hauling stone before you're ready."

The keep's great hall remained quiet through the day, with no sign of Fiori or Immerez about. He took advantage of the opportunity to rest, receiving a bite to eat at midday, and a cooling compress for his head. It was miraculous he was not feeling worse, and he enjoyed the dark irony of having received healing from his arch enemy.

As the shadows deepened with dusk, Varius came to him again. "I am sorry to say, for your sake, that it is time for you to return to the workers quarters."

Zachary had expected this and rose from his pallet with Varius' assistance. He walked unsteadily from the keep to the building that housed his fellow slaves, escorted by a sullen guard. When he stepped inside, he was met with silence. Everyone stared at him.

Finally, Binning rose to his feet and said, "You're alive. We thought you was dead for sure. You look like all five hells, lad, but you're alive."

Binning brought him over to where Lorilie's group sat, and helped him down. "Glad to see you're all right, too," Zachary told him.

"After that Mace clobbered you, the chief guard found out what was going on and lit into the others over it."

"We heard Grandmother was displeased," Lorilie said, a small smile on her lips. "There were guards carrying rocks with us all day."

Mockery of the guards followed, for they had been hardly able to keep up with the work without passing out. When the evening soup was ready, Binning fetched Zachary a bowl. It grew quiet as people ate, and Zachary considered telling Lorilie what Grandmother was after, or what he thought she was after. He figured there was no reason to withhold the information and so told the little group all about it.

"She is after a portal to the hells?" Lorilie asked.

"That seems to be what she has us trying to dig up," he replied.

"She doesn't even believe in our gods," Pitkin protested.

Binning said, "Don't mean they don't exist. Lotsa strange stuff has been happening the last few years."

"Wouldn't releasing these demons hurt her own people, too?" someone asked.

"Grandmother has powers," Zachary said. "Maybe she thinks she can control the demons." Was her motive really to release them, or just to lure and ensnare Westrion's avatar? Or, both? If she had some way of controlling the dark entities, they could devastate his people. By ensnaring the avatar, she would prevent the avatar from interfering with her plans.

He contributed nothing more to the group's speculation about the portal, and he was beginning to think that escape was not the best of ideas. If only he could get his hands on Grandmother, or at least prevent the opening of the portal, and should those efforts fail, somehow warn Westrion's avatar. Unfortunately, Grandmother was away, and being significantly outnumbered by guards, he could not see how to disrupt the dig. Besides, how did one find a god's avatar? Just thinking about it seemed beyond reason.

"Dav," Lorilie said.

He looked up from his musings to see that the group had broken up. Lorilie knelt beside him.

"Yes?"

She gazed at him, assessing. Quietly she said, "I am a good judge of people, and you are no merchant's son."

He stiffened. "What makes you say that?"

"You don't sound like one, and you don't carry yourself like one. You are too, hmm, thoughtful to be the careless brawler you want Grandmother and her people to think you are."

He started to protest, but she cut him off with a curt shake of her head.

Even more quietly, she continued, "I won't say anything to the others. You might be an agent of the king, or someone more important. A noble, even. I hope, whoever you are, that you'll find a way to put an end to all this." She touched him lightly on the wrist and gave him an earnest look, then rose to go to her customary sleeping spot.

He would have to be more careful, forget that he was Zachary. Even if the other workers and guards didn't see as Lorilie saw, he knew Grandmother would.

THE CAPTAIN'S RUNNER

Anna shifted her burden on her shoulder, saddlebags stuffed with supplies. Gil, likewise burdened, walked beside her as they trekked across castle grounds toward Rider stables.

"What about a Green Foot runner?" Gil asked, picking up on an earlier conversation.

"I'm just about too old," Anna said. "Plus, I don't want to be a runner."

"Nay? What're you doin' now?"

Gil, Anna had learned, was the newest Rider to hear the call. He arrived in late fall just as the first snowflakes began to swirl in the air. He hailed from Arey Province, way up in the northeast coast of Sacoridia, and came from a fishing family. His journey to Sacor City was an adventure tale of stowing away on a ship, being caught and pressed into service as a deckhand, and his eventual escape by diving overboard into the freezing waters off Hillander Province. Fortunately, he knew how to swim and made it to shore shivering and numb. With his thick Arey accent and all, he was right. She'd become something like Captain Mapstone's personal runner, sent on errands all over castle grounds.

They parted to avoid walking through a slushy mud puddle and came back together on the other side.

"I just don't understand why," Anna said, "I am being asked to do these things if I can't be a Green Rider." It wasn't that she didn't want to help and be around Green Riders—she did!—but it was confusing and a little hurtful. She was still, of course, tending the hearths in the royal apartments, except those of the king's. They'd been left cold since his disappearance.

They hastened off the path into a crusty, dirty snowbank as a unit of infantry in formation trotted by at a good clip, splashing right through the puddles without a flinch. Castle grounds had become very busy with the general muster of troops for the forthcoming trouble with Second Empire. The fields outside the city had become a major encampment, and the city itself and castle were filled with uniformed men and women. Provincial militias were being summoned to their own capitals, as well. From Sacor City, the troops would move out to wherever their generals wanted them. It was all beyond Anna, but she did her best to stay out of everyone's way.

When finally they reached Rider stables, they found Mara and Brandall waiting for them, and Sophina just leading her horse outside.

"Good," Mara said, "the provisions are here."

They helped strap the saddlebags to each horse's saddle, while Mara gave Brandall and Sophina instructions. When Anna finished with her saddlebag, she patted Brandall's mare, Eagle, on the neck. She'd grown much more at ease around the horses, thanks to her riding lessons.

"And here come your traveling companions now," Mara said.

Anna glanced up as the two Weapons rode their black horses toward them. Actually, only one, Willis, was a full Weapon. The young woman beside him, dressed in charcoal gray, was a Weapon-in-training, but she looked just as grim as any full Weapon. Trainees and instructors alike had been summoned from the Forge to aid in the search for King Zachary, and to make sure there was no shortfall in protection for the queen. Parties of four had been going out to search for the past few weeks, consisting of a pair of Riders, a Weapon, and a Weapon trainee.

Gil sidled over to Anna and nudged her shoulder. "Mebbe you can become one of them." He nodded toward Willis and the trainee.

The trainee appeared to overhear and watched Anna to see what she would say. Inside, she shrieked, *No! Not for nothing!* The idea of standing silently in the shadows did not appeal. Their ways were mysterious and they seemed unreal to her.

Aloud, she said, "It is a worthy profession, but I'd make a poor Weapon."

When the party rode away and the Weapon trainee was no longer in earshot, Anna turned and socked Gil in the shoulder.

"Ow!" he exclaimed. "What'd that be for, eh?"

"For asking me that question in front of Weapons."

He rubbed his shoulder. "You afraid they'd stick you with their swords? It was a good question."

"Do I look like a Weapon to you? Can you see me like that?"

"Weeell, I s'pose not."

She noticed, abashed, that Mara was watching their exchange with her hands on her hips.

"If you two are done," the Chief Rider said, "Hep could use Gil's help inventorying and cleaning tack." When Gil groaned, she pointed toward the stables. *"Now."*

"Aye, Chief." He flashed Anna a smile and trotted toward the stables.

Anna then found Mara's attention entirely on her. She swallowed hard.

"You don't have hearth duty till this evening, right?" Mara asked.

"Yes'm."

Mara looked relieved. "I am running all out and someone needs to check on the captain. Sometimes she works too hard and forgets meals. Think you could look in on her for me?"

"Yes'm."

Mara smiled. "Good. And make sure she's resting her shoulder, or Vanlynn will have my hide."

Instead of going directly to officers quarters, Anna set off for the castle and its kitchens. She figured that even if the captain had remembered her midday meal, a snack would not be remiss. The cooks gave her a full basket to lug back to officers quarters. Apparently they were aware of the captain's habit of missing meals.

She tapped softly on the captain's door, and entered at the sound of a weary, "Come." She found the captain crouched over her work table, brow creased in concentration. She barely noticed Anna. Anna carried the basket in, using her skill as a servant to move as silently and unobtrusively as she could. There was a small table that could be used for dining, but presently it was covered with ledgers, papers, and an old glove. On top was what appeared to be a personal letter, its blue seal broken. Her reading skills were still nascent, but she was able to make out the name "G'ladheon" in the signature, and she realized it must be from Sir Karigan's father. She did not dare try to read it. She moved the items aside into a neat pile, the glove splayed on top, and started unpacking the food.

When she turned to announce that the meal was ready, she observed the captain gazing into space, her expression decidedly sad. She was worried about King Zachary, Anna guessed. She had been around the Riders long enough to know that the captain and king were very close.

"Captain?" she said quietly.

Captain Mapstone sat up in her chair and blinked at Anna as if startled to find her there.

"I've brought something for you to eat." Anna lifted the lid off chicken soup and uncovered freshly baked meat rolls. Steam plumed from the food.

The captain smiled. "That smells good. Thank you, Anna. Is it midday already?"

"About an hour past," Anna replied.

"I am always losing track of time."

The captain rose to take in the food and Anna noticed she was not using her sling. It hung slack across her shoulder. Anna did not want to have to say something. She didn't want to annoy or anger the captain, but Mara had instructed her to say something. She cleared her throat.

"Yes?" The captain held a spoonful of soup before her lips, and gave Anna a sideways glance.

Anna quailed, at least inwardly, and said, "Chief Rider Mara asked me to remind you to use your sling, or . . ."

The captain crooked an eyebrow. "Or?"

Anna held herself steady under the regard of those sharp

hazel eyes. "Or else Master Mender Vanlynn will have her hide."

The captain's mouth twitched. Was she trying not to laugh? She set the spoon back in the bowl, the soup untasted, and straightened. "Be easy, Anna. You have done your duty by Mara." She did not put her arm in her sling. "All is healed."

Anna bit her lip. She did not want Mara angry with her, or for Master Mender Vanlynn to be angry with Mara. She cleared her throat again.

"Yes, Anna?"

"It—it would be best if you rested your shoulder properly."

The captain's mouth twitched again, but this time she obeyed. "Very well, but my shoulder is fine. Really."

Anna, not sure what to say, just stood there.

"Are you returning to the castle?" the captain asked. "I have some papers that need to go to—"

A pounding came upon the door, which made them both jump.

"Come," the captain called.

A Green Foot runner poked her head in. "Captain, Counselor Tallman requests your presence in the queen's apartments immediately."

"Did he say why?"

"No, ma'am, but he's also summoning Master Mender Vanlynn."

"Oh, no," the captain murmured.

Anna helped her with her coat.

"Come along," the captain said. "I don't know what this is about, and Mistress Evans might need all the royal household staff at hand."

Anna rushed out the door after her, the food she had brought left to grow cold on the captain's table.

TWO STARS AND A CROWN

When they reached the west wing, Laren sent Anna to report to Mistress Evans, and continued up the stairs toward the royal apartments. She dreaded every step, dreaded what she would find out about the queen's condition.

The corridor outside the royal apartments was clogged with Weapons, officers, administrators, and their aides. She spotted a few lord-governors, and representatives of absent lord-governors. Estora had been meeting with various parties concerning the upcoming campaign season, and Laren had been due to report later in the afternoon.

She scanned the crowd looking for a friendly face, and found an unexpected one. Seeing Dakrias Brown outside the records room took some adjustment, for it seemed out of context. He usually handed over meetings and the like to his deputy, and rarely left the records room if he could help it. She grabbed his arm, and he gazed at her in surprise.

"Captain?"

"What's going on?"

"Oh, Captain, it is good to see you. I haven't the faintest. We were waiting to be admitted to meet with the queen when there was a bit of an uproar. They admitted the chief mender and some of her assistants a little while ago." He leaned forward and confided, "There are many rumors afoot."

Laren could believe it, and she doubted any of them were good. Just then she heard someone call out to her.

"Captain Mapstone?" It was Fastion, peering over the heads of the crowd, searching for her. When he spotted her, he shouldered his way to her. "This way, please."

"I'll talk to you later," she told Dakrias, and she fell in step behind Fastion as he cleared a path to the entry of Estora's apartments. Angry muttering followed her, that she, a mere messenger captain, should be allowed access when more senior officers and nobles were not. It was a relief when she crossed the threshold and Fastion closed the door to the hubbub outside.

"The queen—how is she?" she asked him.

"The queen was having some pains. Master Vanlynn is in with her now."

There were other Weapons in the entry area, some from the tombs whose names she did not know, and a trainee from the Forge in dark gray. Fastion led her to the queen's sitting room, where others waited, a much smaller group that included Les Tallman and Castellan Javien. They spoke in hushed voices, and a wave of unease rolled over her as though she were reliving that terrible day almost a year ago in which they thought Zachary was dying from the assassin's arrow. She'd been standing next door in his rooms back then, waiting for word of his death.

"Captain? Captain?" Les Tallman gently tapped her good shoulder, and she shook herself back to the present.

"Les," she said, "do you know how the queen is?"

"I haven't heard anything," he said quietly. "I was sitting in on her fourth meeting of the day when suddenly she started having pains. I am sure Vanlynn will tell us when she knows more. I am guessing it is false labor, or . . ."

"Or?"

"Something worse. Sometimes twins want to come too early."

Much too early, Laren thought fretfully. Like four months too early.

"And, of course, there can be other complications, as well," he added.

He wasn't helping to calm her worry. Recalling, however, that Ben was now stationed in the royal apartments day and night did help. Surely his true healing ability could avert disaster. After all, it was his use of his ability that had revealed the queen was carrying twins in the first place.

She seated herself near the fire, and again the sensation of reliving the day of the assassination attempt on Zachary crept over her as she overheard snippets of conversation about what was next, should the queen perish. She at least did not pick up on any conspiratorial plans to marry Estora off as she lay on her deathbed, but if anyone offered her tea, she was refusing.

They needed Zachary back. *Where are you, Moonling? Come back to us. Your wife needs you, your people need you, and* I *need you.*

Estora had been working hard to govern the realm and prepare it for what must come. She worked too hard, to Laren's mind, hosting meetings all day in her bed chamber, and defying Vanlynn's instructions to rest. Laren had known pregnant women to be tough, working in the fields as labor came on, walking miles to reach a midwife, hauling fish from the sea. But with their queen carrying royal progeny? No chances could be taken.

When Vanlynn emerged into the sitting room, those awaiting word crowded around her. Laren, stuck in the back, stood on her tiptoes to see over shoulders.

"The queen is fine," Vanlynn announced. The sigh of relief that accompanied her announcement was unanimous. "It was false labor, and she is in need of rest and *quiet.* I want all of you to leave except Counselor Tallman, Castellan Javien, General Washburn, and . . . Captain Mapstone? Are you there?"

"Yes," Laren called.

"The rest of you *scat.*"

Only Vanlynn could get away with such irreverence. There were protests and grumbles from the others, but once the Weapons closed in to remove them, they quickly cleared out.

Vanlynn gave Laren a hard look up and down. "I am astonished," she said.

"Astonished?"

"You're using the sling as I instructed. I'd have expected you to have tossed it away days ago."

"I did think about burning it, but my Riders look after me." Even though Anna was not a Rider, Laren could not help but think of her as one.

Vanlynn looked them all over with an unhappy expression on her face. "You have not been taking care of your queen. She has been working much too hard and I am of a mind to forbid anyone at all into her chamber on business."

General Washburn, who had replaced Harborough as the commander of all the military, said, "In the king's absence, it is crucial she—"

"Enough," Vanlynn said. "Your queen has many duties on behalf of the realm, and right now the most important is to carry and birth two healthy children. You should be ashamed of yourselves for letting these strategic planning meetings get out of hand, as if the strain of having her husband taken from her was not enough, not to mention the horror of having lived with that elemental creature who impersonated him. From now on, *no more meetings*, no more bringing problems to the queen."

"But—" Javien began.

Vanlynn turned her frosty gaze on him. "*No more.* In fact, I am going to limit how much any of you can see her. The four of you will have to do the hard work. And that's how it's going to be."

Laren applauded Vanlynn's fierce stance. The queen and her children were too precious to the realm to endanger unnecessarily.

"Now, she does insist on seeing you lot," Vanlynn continued, "but we're keeping it short. You will not annoy her with the problems of the realm, understood?"

They allowed that they did, and Washburn even threw his shoulders back and clicked his heels. They filed after Vanlynn into Estora's bed chamber. Laren spotted Ben immediately at Estora's bedside, but he retreated to a corner to stay out of the way. Jaid set a tea tray on the bedside table, nodded to the newcomers, and exited the room. The Weapon, Ellen, stood discreetly in a corner, and Estora's secretary, Ulf, attended nearby. The queen herself looked well-ensconced in her bed, none the worse for what must have been panic at the premature sensation of labor. In fact, she looked healthier than ever with her cheeks rosy, her face and breasts full.

"Good afternoon," she said.

As one, Laren and her fellow counselors bowed.

"I am sure that Master Vanlynn has given you her commandments?" Estora said.

"Indeed, she has, my lady," Les Tallman replied, "and I think that I speak for all of us when I say how relieved and pleased I am that you are well. Also, know that you may rest easy, for the realm's business will be in competent hands."

She reached for her teacup, took a sip, and peered at them over the rim. "I certainly expect so. Master Vanlynn will allow *brief* visits from each of you so that I may receive daily reports of what is happening in the realm. Ulf will schedule your appointments accordingly. Master Vanlynn says I have done enough today already, but there is one thing I must have done before you leave. Ulf? Please bring me the coffer."

The secretary hastened to her side with a cherrywood coffer. She set her teacup aside and placed the box on her lap.

"Laren Mapstone, please approach," Estora said.

Laren raised her eyebrows. Her fellow advisors looked as surprised as she felt. She obeyed and stepped up to Estora's bedside.

"It occurs to me," Estora said, "that this is long overdue for you have served this realm faithfully, and with courage and professionalism, for many years. I can only guess it was not done before because of tradition. The Green Riders have only ever had a captain to lead them since the founding days. It makes sense—the messenger service is a fairly small, independent unit. However, the times are growing more turbulent, and I wish to show my personal gratitude to you, as well as demonstrate the throne's support for the leader of the Green Riders. I want you, Laren Mapstone, to be endowed with greater authority to accomplish your work."

Was this, Laren wondered, what she thought it was? Another glance at her fellow advisors revealed Les Tallman grinning, Javien remaining as inscrutable as ever, and Washburn scowling. She returned her attention to Estora, who was lifting the lid of the coffer. Inside, seated on green velvet, was gold-braided cord. A lot of it. The kind that officers of high rank wore on their shoulders. Laren's eyes went wide. She had to clamp her mouth shut.

"I have found your captain's knot," Estora said, "inadequate for the challenges ahead."

Along with the copious gold cord were nested two sets of rank badges—two north stars and a crown each, designating the rank of colonel—to go on her shoulders. Ulf, the secretary, took the coffer from Estora and presented it to Laren with a bow.

She accepted it into trembling hands. "I . . . I don't know what to say."

"Thank you generally works," Les Tallman said.

"Yes, yes, thank you."

"Congratulations, Colonel Mapstone," Estora said. "I would have liked to have conferred your new rank in front of your Riders, but Master Vanlynn would not have it."

Ben, from his place in the corner, grinned and saluted, and to Laren's astonishment, so did Ellen.

"Colonel?" Washburn demanded. "There are no Rider colonels."

"There seems to be one now," Javien said in his characteristically droll manner.

"But one cannot skip ranks. You cannot—"

"General," the queen said, "Colonel Mapstone has been doing the duty of a general longer than you have served in the king's military. The Riders are the king's own messengers, and the queen's. We will promote Our Riders as We see fit. We do not have to explain Ourselves."

"But—"

"General," Les Tallman said mildly, "remember whom you address. The queen decrees as she wills."

The general, chastened and cheeks glowing red, clicked his heels together and bowed to Estora. "Forgive me, madam."

"We forgive you this one time, General. Do know that Colonel Mapstone is under royal command, answerable only to Our royal selves as the commanders of the messenger service have been since its founding. She will also now be Our eyes, ears, and voice concerning military matters and is to be fully accommodated. Is this clear?"

"Yes, madam. Perfectly."

Laren was relieved. With Estora's words, she would not be

caught in the inevitable power struggles of the military hierarchy, at least not directly. While the Green Riders had always been answerable to the king, the high general also held an organizational command position of sorts over them, but mostly, the Riders, seen as lesser in the eyes of the rest of the military, were left to function autonomously. Now Estora had made it official, and Laren was proud of her for not being cowed by the intimidating general when some lesser gentlewoman might have been. She had assumed the crown quite naturally, and now she was, in essence, Laren's direct commander in Zachary's absence.

"In the short time we've been working together," Les Tallman said, "I have found Laren Mapstone more than equal to the task of performing the duties required of a colonel. As our queen says, she has been doing the duty of a general for years."

Laren thought her face must match Washburn's for redness.

"The papers for your new commission," Estora told her, "should arrive at your office by the end of the day."

"Well, then, I think that is quite enough," Vanlynn said. "I want everyone out."

"I would like to speak privately with Colonel Mapstone for a few minutes," Estora said.

Tallman, Javien, and Washburn all shook Laren's hand and congratulated her on their way out, though she suspected there would be some blustering on Washburn's part once he was out of the queen's presence. Vanlynn, Ben, and Ellen were also commanded to leave.

"Have a seat, Colonel," Estora said.

There was a chair near the bedside and Laren obeyed. "I admit, it's going to take some getting used to."

"Hearing yourself called 'colonel'?"

Laren nodded. "It will take a while for others, like General Washburn, to accept it, as well."

"It is a break with tradition. I noticed long ago that the messenger service was undervalued by the other services, and it has not helped the Riders that they have not had a voice in the upper echelons. You've always been by Zachary's side as advisor, and that is a very important role, but now you have direct entry with other top officers."

Laren had plenty of experience tangling with those at her own level, but the prospect of moving up was daunting.

"I believe," Estora continued, "that if Zachary had thought of it, he'd have broken tradition and promoted you himself a long time ago. I'd have raised you even higher, but there would have been considerable backlash from the likes of General Washburn. So, colonel it is, at least for the time being."

The time being? Laren had never expected to be around long enough to achieve rank as a colonel, much less a general, even had the messenger service traditionally had ranks above captain.

"I do not expect your duties to change overmuch," Estora said, "except that you will be interacting with higher level officers. You may want to consider promoting a few of your Riders to absorb some of your old duties. At your discretion, of course."

Laren forced back an irrational fit of laughter at the absurdity of it all. She wondered what Stevic would have to say about it.

"I will still expect you to serve as my advisor as before."

Laren finally found her voice. "Of course, Your Majesty."

They spoke some more about how Laren could claim larger quarters if she wished, and of the other benefits of her new position.

An ebb came to their conversation, and Laren asked, "You are truly well? And the children?"

"Yes." Estora smoothed her hand over her rounded belly. "Master Vanlynn and Ben have both determined all is well. But I must tell you, I would be much better if Zachary were here. You've had no word? None of your Riders have returned?"

"No, my lady. I'm afraid not. It is still very early, and the country is large. There is no telling where the elemental took him."

Estora's expression grew decidedly downcast. "I will miss the meetings and conferences, for they took my mind off his disappearance, and my loneliness."

"I think about him, miss him, in quiet moments, as well. You have done an exceptional job in his absence."

"With a great deal of help." Estora shook her head. "I ask the gods every day to bring him back." Then she lifted her gaze to Laren, her eyes haunted. "What if he never comes back? My children will never know their father, and I—I will be alone."

"I try not to consider that possibility." Laren, of course, had thought about it a lot, but she did not want Estora to lose hope. "But should it come to that, my lady, you will not be alone. I will see to it personally."

"Thank you, Laren, your words comfort me. And now, I should probably release you to your work, or Vanlynn will never let me hear the end of it."

"I understand." Laren stood, the coffer tucked beneath her arm, and bowed. She started to leave.

"One more thing," Estora said.

Laren paused. "Yes, my lady?"

"I meant what I said earlier. You are to be my eyes, ears, and voice when it comes to military matters. I think those officers believe me a witless woman with nothing useful to offer, and I would rather be sure I was being well informed."

"Then they'd be more than wrong." Laren feared, however, they'd have much the same opinion of her, no matter her rank.

"Yes, well, they would not willingly admit they were wrong."

No, they wouldn't, Laren thought. "I will be sure that they do not make that mistake."

"I am depending on you, Colonel."

"Yes, Your Majesty." Laren bowed once more and left Estora gazing out her window. She paused outside the queen's bed chamber, wondering just what in the name of the gods she was in for.

SPIRIT

Karigan parted the branches of evergreens, and driven by a curiosity that had built during all their days of travel to follow Enver from their campsite and into the woods, she peered into the clearing. The light of the waxing moon puddled on a ledge of smooth granite softened by clumps of snowy deer moss. Enver stood in the center of the clearing, his back to her, the moonlight gilding his hair. He gazed into the sky, his muna'riel cupped in his hands.

She shouldn't be watching, she thought, this thing that Enver was doing. It was private, but she couldn't help herself. Was he praying? To whom would an Eletian pray? They did not worship her gods, though she could not say she actively worshipped her own gods, either. Feeling guilty for spying, she decided she ought to return to their campsite. She'd left Estral there writing in her journal. She turned to leave.

"Galadheon," Enver said, "will you not join me?"

She froze and squeezed her eyes shut in even greater shame that she had been caught. She turned around and stepped hesitantly into the clearing to stand with him in the moonlight. The way the moon's glow lit his face, he looked a mystic.

"I'm—I'm sorry," she said. "I shouldn't have followed you, spied on you, but I was curious."

"I am pleased," he said to her surprise, "by your curiosity."

"You are?"

He nodded. "I have long hoped that you might take an interest."

"In listening to the voice of the world? It's what you're doing right now, isn't it?"

"Yes," he replied. "It is always there as an undercurrent singing in every living thing like water that travels from the roots of a tree all the way to its leaves." He made a graceful gesture toward the night sky with its expanse of stars. "But when I still myself, that is when I hear it ever clearer."

"Sounds peaceful," Karigan said.

"It is. Listening helps me maintain balance in a time of unfolding. It promotes discipline over other more primal instincts."

A time of unfolding? she wondered. *Primal instincts?* What sort of primal instincts? But before she could ask, he continued, "Sometimes I receive insight to a problem when I listen, or my *aithen,* which resides within the *aithen'a,* will offer me wisdom or counsel in some way." Her expression must have looked perplexed, because he added, "The aithen is a guide and usually appears as an animal, or in an animal-like guise. The aithen'a is the realm of spirit."

"You get advice from an . . . animal, in the realm of spirit?"

There was laughter in Enver's eyes. "It is perhaps more involved than that, but on an elemental level, yes."

She shifted her stance, her feet sinking into soft moss. "Dare I ask what animal guides you?"

"Most Eletians' guides are magnificent creatures—bears, lions, porpoises, even dragons and gryphons. You will recall Graelelea? She had an affinity for the winter owl that transcended the aithen'a into our world."

Karigan remembered Graelelea very well. She had led the Blackveil expedition with skill, but had not survived, her body left to rest within the tarnished walls of Castle Argenthyne, the snowy feathers of the winter owl braided into her hair.

"My aithan is humble by comparison." He looked very proud. "It is a turtle."

Intrigued though she was by this rare insight into Eletian spirituality, she was also skeptical. And yet, she wondered, who was *she* to judge when she had come face-to-face with the steed of the god of death? She suspected, however, this was not in any way similar. There was no equivalent to an aithen that she knew of in the religion or philosophies of her people.

"The wise find many meanings for the turtle, but for me, it is its dual nature, its ability to live in water and on land, that resonates with me. I am half-Eletian, half your kind. I may exist in either realm."

An owl hooted, and in the distance came an answering call.

"Would you like to try?" he asked her.

"Er, try? Try what?"

"Listening to the voice of the world. Perhaps you would find your aithen."

"I'm sorry, Enver. I do not think it's for me. I've never been religious, anyway. I don't leave offerings for the gods, pray, or go to chapel, or anything like that."

"It is not about rituals or worship or gods, though your gods could be perceived as part of the energy in nature, the world."

"The priests," she said, "would maintain that the gods created nature and the world."

"Perhaps it is so, I do not know, but this hearing the voice of the world is more about finding accord with the universe. Harmony."

"I'm sorry," she said, and she turned to leave.

He placed his hand on her arm. "I am making this too complicated. Think of it as feeling the sun on your shoulders and being fully conscious of it."

She shook her head and walked on, leaving Enver in the clearing. If she wanted to feel the sun on her shoulders, she had but to stand in the sun. Doing so, she thought, was safer than communing with forces beyond her ken, forces that might take an interest in her as others already had. She had no desire to invite new ones in.

Estral looked up from her journal as Karigan entered their camp. "Where did you go?"

"A walk." Karigan tossed a piece of wood onto the campfire, which sent a galaxy of orange sparks hissing up into the branches of trees. She stood there, gazing into the flames. What had she sought when she followed Enver to the clearing? She had been curious, but there was more to it, like an itch she could not satisfy, and an emptiness of sorts. She was about that which was real and in front of her, what she could see and touch, not illusory phantasms of the air.

Enver returned shortly after her. With a sideways glance, she noted Estral looking back and forth between the two of them as if trying to figure out what it meant that they had both returned from the same place in the woods just moments apart. Karigan knew exactly what conclusion she would draw.

Enver halted a few yards from her. "Galadheon, it was not my intention to offend you."

"I am not offended. I just don't think that stuff is for me." She could almost *feel* Estral dying to ask questions.

Enver took a step closer, and then a second. "The path of spirit is not for all. There have always been warriors who are of the physical world only. To travel the path is to divert their energies from the task at hand."

Was he calling her a warrior? If so, she liked it.

"And yet," he continued, "there are warriors who embrace the path, for it sharpens their focus, allows them to surpass ordinary skills. Your Black Shields were once of this nature."

She turned to him in surprise. "What?"

He nodded. "It is so. The forms you learn as a swordmaster are not only moves you use to combat an opponent, but embodiments of focus, and communion with spirit, a joining of the inner and outer worlds."

"How in the hells do you know this?"

"While at the castle, I had some conversations with the one called Fastion. He has an interest in history, particularly that of his vocation. Many Black Shield traditions are descended from such thought, not just the swordfighting. Alas, they have lost, through time, their spiritual connection."

Fastion. Karigan sat hard on a stump. She was going to have to have a talk with Fastion. It made sense, the association between the forms and spirit, though clearly it was not taught as such. At least, not to first order swordmasters.

"There were various schools at one time that emphasized the connection between body and spirit," Estral said, "but they faded from existence centuries ago."

Karigan turned to face her. "You know about this, too?"

"Daughter of the Golden Guardian here, if you'll recall, with access to all the histories." She shrugged. "I just remember mentions of it, though. Nothing specific. Had I known you were interested, I could have done some research for you."

"I don't think I'm interested." Karigan kind of was, but didn't want to be.

"Hmm." Enver gazed at her through the flames and smoke of the fire, then shook his head as though to himself. He strode to his tent.

Hmm, what? she wondered. Then she stood and headed for the tent she shared with Estral. She would forget all this stuff about aithen and aithen'a, spirit and animal guides. There was enough else in the world that was real and troubling to worry about without adding superstition into it.

The next day, with the sun shining brightly, all talk of spirit was far away and inconsequential. Before they left camp, Karigan pored over a map of the north she had brought along and tried to ascertain where they were so they did not end up blundering into Second Empire. However, because they were following Eletian ways, it was more difficult to pinpoint their specific location.

"Enver," she said, "can you help me out here?"

He gazed over her shoulder, then peered into the sky as though making some mental calculation. Then he turned round, facing in each direction. She was beginning to get annoyed when finally he returned to her, peered thoughtfully at the map, and pointed.

"We shall be outside the Green Cloak by the end of the day."

That meant they were indeed getting closer to the Lone Forest and Second Empire territory. The lumber camp Captain Treman had mentioned as a place in which Lord Fiori had expressed interest was not so far off. They would try to find it so she could satisfy Estral's need to investigate for a sign of her father; then they'd launch into the more perilous part of their journey, following the Eletian ways that passed near the Lone Forest.

As she mounted Condor, she thought that if she were more attuned to the nonphysical world, she'd find that other forces were inevitably leading them to the Lone Forest. Her own inner voice was silently screaming against it.

PYRE OF THE DEAD

Karigan insisted on scouting ahead on foot, while Enver and Estral waited with the horses. She moved carefully through the woods, the ground half-frozen and half-sodden with slushy snowmelt. There were even a few early biters circling over puddles, too dull-witted and slow to be a bother.

The woods she traveled through, here on the northern edge of the Green Cloak, consisted not of evergreens, but the pale gray bark of younger deciduous trees, their fallen leaves decaying underfoot in the mud adding to the earthy, fecund scent of approaching spring. This patch of woods had been logged maybe some fifteen years ago, and it would be decades before the mighty pines and firs once more reigned over the land.

A brightening appeared ahead, where the sun fell unimpeded into a cleared area, and she continued her careful progress forward. When she reached the edge, she saw that she had come upon the lumber camp they'd been looking for. There were a few log buildings—bunkhouses, a main lodge, kitchen, and work pavilion, crude stables. Something about it looked wrong.

She skirted the clearing, and as she did so, the changing view revealed that a couple of the buildings had burned. One of the bunkhouses was a shell. Little stirred in the clearing but squirrels and birds. What had happened here?

She tripped over a tree root but caught herself before she fell headlong into a pool of mud. When she turned to give the root a piece of her mind, she realized it wasn't a root at all, but a human arm protruding from a half-melted snowdrift.

She leaped back clamping down on a scream. She attempted to calm her racing heart and catch her breath as she processed the sight. An arrow also protruded from the snowdrift. It was an ordinary arrow with goose feather fletching that looked as if it had been exposed to the weather for some time.

She gathered her courage and scooped away snow. Beneath, she found a man in woodsman's garb lying face down, the arrow deep in his back as though he had been trying to run away. It was hard to tell how long dead he was for the snow and cold would have slowed down decomposition.

She found no more corpses on the perimeter, and when she was convinced there were no threats lurking about, she searched the camp's grounds. She found five more corpses, but as they were more exposed, their bodies were more decayed, and in some cases, partially eaten and torn apart by scavengers. One had a couple arrows stuck about its ribs. It was harder to tell what had killed the others. Blades?

She hastened back to Enver and Estral, trying to dispel the images of her gruesome discoveries from her mind. Condor whickered at her approach. She went to him and hugged his neck.

"What is it?" Estral asked. She had found a boulder in the sun on which to sit, and now stood.

Karigan faced her and Enver. "I found the camp." After a drink from her waterskin, she explained, finishing with, "There was no one there. No one alive."

"My father?" Estral asked in a quavering voice.

"I—I don't think any of them were your father." After a pause, she added, "I think we should go there, put those men to rest." Not that she wanted that grim task, but it was the right thing to do. "And maybe we can find some clue about who attacked them." The arrows hadn't looked like crude groundmite arrows, though groundmites were known to use stolen weapons, but she was already pretty sure the men must have been cut down by Second Empire.

They rode in silence to the camp. When they reached the clearing, Karigan directed Estral to care for the horses, and she and Enver started collecting wood for a pyre. The ground was too frozen for digging, and the job of raising a cairn too great. Karigan sacrificed a tarp for the carrying of remains. Fighting her revulsion, she searched the corpses for anything that might identify them or the attackers, but found only one ring, some dice, and a couple pipes. As she worked, Estral joined them, and to her surprise, gazed hard at the bodies. Karigan had sent her to take care of the horses to spare her the gruesome sight.

"None of them are my father," Estral said.

"I didn't think so," Karigan replied. None had had his stature or golden hair.

"I had to make sure."

Karigan nodded in understanding. She searched the nearby woods to make sure she hadn't missed any other corpses. She could find no more, and when she returned, they covered the dead as much as possible with the one tarp, piled more wood on top, and lit the pyre as Estral sang a mournful song of leave-taking.

When all was done, they retreated into the main lodge of the camp to escape the smoke and stench of the pyre, and to regroup. Taking care of the dead men had occupied most of their afternoon, so it was decided they would spend the night there.

"I think we should keep a watch tonight," Karigan said. The dead lumbermen were, to her, a warning. "And no more fires." She was beginning to regret the pyre—no doubt the smoke could be seen for miles. Would it draw those who had attacked the camp to investigate? The Lone Forest was still a day's ride away, but what if there was a Second Empire patrol somewhere in the vicinity?

"The pyre will be burning into the night," Enver said. "I do not think another small fire in the hearth will be of further harm."

"It *is* damp in here," Estral added.

"Very well," Karigan said, "one last fire."

She set about righting chairs along a heavy table. The main lodge was pretty empty, the supplies likely stolen, or already sent south with other lumbermen who'd been done for the season. Enver went out to tend the pyre and check the remains of the other buildings once more, while Estral prepared to build a fire from the supply of wood stacked beside the hearth.

"What is this?" Estral exclaimed. She was tugging something out from between sticks of wood.

Karigan joined her by the hearth. "What did you find?"

Estral held a leather pouch. She opened it and shook out the contents. Two gold, glistening objects fell onto her hand. "I know these," she whispered. "My father was here." She held a gold signet ring, and a brooch in the shape of a harp that was the badge of a Selium minstrel. "The ring has been passed down through generations of Fioris."

Karigan could not dispute the evidence. Lord Fiori had been there, but where was he now? Did his body lie somewhere out in the forest where they couldn't find it? She dared not say it aloud.

"He had to have a reason for concealing these," Estral said. "He needed to hide the fact he was the Lord Fiori."

"Might someone have stolen them from him and concealed them here?" Karigan asked. Estral gave her such a look that she did not pursue that line of inquiry. The idea of someone trying to steal from Lord Fiori, who was a big man and an able swordfighter, was difficult to conceive.

Estral continued to cradle the objects in her hand. "Got to find him," she said with determination. "Whoever attacked this place could have taken him. Or, he's hiding out there somewhere." She swept her arm out to indicate the world. She started pacing back and forth. Just as suddenly, she swung around to face Karigan, her fingers now closed around the ring and brooch. "Second Empire," she said fiercely. "Second Empire must have him."

"Let's not jump to—"

"Who else would have attacked this camp?" Estral demanded. "It wasn't groundmites, even I can see that."

"Well—"

"It had to be Second Empire. They attacked this place. They took my father."

"Bandits? Maybe?" Karigan suggested, though Second Empire had been her first thought, as well. She had never seen her friend quite so wound up.

"Bandits? What in the hells would they want in a lumber camp?"

"Er, lumber?" Karigan said in a small voice. There was such a thing as timber poaching, but probably not this far north.

"You think this is a joke?"

"No, but—"

"Karigan, this is my father. He could be close by. He could be in the Lone Forest."

"Estral, please, just calm—"

"Don't you tell me to calm down. I know you don't want to go anywhere near the Lone Forest. You've made it abundantly clear. Whatever happened to the Karigan who would confront danger, no matter the odds?"

Karigan was too dumbfounded to respond. She had never been that person, had she? Ready to just throw herself into one perilous situation after another? Maybe there were a few times, but they had been with good cause and it wasn't like she'd *wanted* to. There'd been circumstances. Yes, circumstances.

Estral gave her a look of disgust and strode down the length of the room. Karigan watched her in astonishment, then ran to catch up. She grabbed Estral's shoulder. "Where are you going?"

Estral pulled away. "To go look for my father." She strode off again.

Karigan sprinted ahead to block the door. "Listen to me. I might not seem like the person you want me to be at the moment, but you aren't being yourself, either." Before Estral could protest, she continued, "You found a clue today that your father was here. Let's talk it out, go over all the possibilities. You know Enver said we'd be traveling near the Lone Forest. But it doesn't make sense to go blundering in there, right? Getting caught ourselves won't help your father. Plus, it'll be dark soon. You won't make it there before nightfall."

Estral stared at her, her eyes still a stormy sea green. Then she shifted subtly, her stance and expression relaxing.

"All right," she said warily, "going off tonight is not sensible. But I *will* go."

Karigan sighed. The door bumped into her back. "Huh?"

"Galadheon?" Enver called from outside. "Something is blocking the door."

They talked in front of the fire over cups of tea. Enver supported Karigan, saying that it wouldn't be prudent to ride off on a search without due planning. They tried to offer alternatives as to where Lord Fiori might be and how his ring and brooch ended up stashed among the sticks of firewood, but Estral would have none of it, though she agreed not to run off without them. For the time being.

When it came time to retire, Enver went out to stand beneath the eaves of the wood and commune with the voice of the world. Estral took first watch and sat on the front step of the lodge. That left Karigan to try to sleep. She tossed and turned in her blankets, however, worrying that despite Estral's assurances, she would ride off without them. No, Karigan did not want to go to the Lone Forest. No, she was not so ready to face such peril without good cause. Was Estral right that she'd become too cautious?

"Damnation."

She decided she wasn't going to get any sleep, so she rose, slipped on her boots, and grabbed her coat, longsword, and bonewood staff, and headed outside. She found Estral sitting placidly on the front step, looking out into the night. The pyre had died down a little, and the air was still so that the smoke and the worst of the stench drifted skyward, carrying the souls of the dead into the heavens.

"You might as well head in and try to sleep," Karigan told her. "At least one of us should be rested tomorrow."

Estral did not argue and stood. Before she went in, she said, "I'm sorry I got so hot earlier. I wasn't thinking clearly."

"You are worried about your father. If I were in your shoes, I'd be the same."

Estral smiled sadly. "I have been worried for a long time, and I guess it just built up." She turned to go in, then halted. "Also, I'm sorry for what I said about you and danger. You've grown a lot, and after all you've been through, leaping headlong into danger would have meant you had not learned from your experiences."

"Thank you. I think." It didn't make her younger, inexperienced self sound very good.

Estral smiled again and went inside, leaving Karigan alone to contemplate the blanket of stars above, and the glowing orange embers of the pyre of the dead below.

SPIRITS IN THE SMOKE

Karigan's chin slipped off her hand as she nodded off. She shook her head in an attempt to wake up.

"This won't do," she muttered groggily.

She stood to stretch her back. Movement near the embers of the pyre made her catch her breath. She stilled to listen, but at first heard only the restlessness of tree branches in a breath of air. As her sight sharpened, she noticed the smoke from the pyre winding in sinuous ribbons along the ground, where before it had been drifting straight up into the sky.

The smoke then billowed and reformed into humanlike shapes, six of them. Gooseflesh rose on her arms. The smoke apparitions drifted toward her.

Ssseee . . . their voices hissed. *Ssseee* . . .

She backed away until she was pressed up against the door. Condor whinnied from the paddock.

Ssseee . . .

"See what?" she demanded.

The smoke figures elongated and twined together. Before she knew what was happening, the smoke gusted into her face, forced its way into her mouth and nose, burned down her windpipe. She was held there, her back arched and eyes watering, unable to breathe with smoke filling her lungs, and then the visions came.

It was the lumber camp in daylight, and snow flurried down. She saw as if from multiple pairs of eyes, which was confusing. Arrows whizzed by. Men scattered. They ran for the woods. Armed warriors entered the camp, hunting each man down. She caught the flash of a tattoo on the wrist of one of the assailants—the dead tree of Second Empire. One by one, each viewpoint vanished as the life of each man was snuffed out. As the last faded, she saw an old woman walk out of the woods, snowflakes alighting on her gray hair. *Grandmother.*

Then all went dark and she exhaled smoke. She fell to her knees, retching and choking, her lungs burning. She could not stop.

"Galadheon, let me help," came a gentle voice. Enver helped her into the lodge.

Estral sat up from her bedroll. "What's going on?"

"Please boil some water," Enver instructed. He eased Karigan down onto a chair. "Better that you are sitting up for the moment."

Karigan could only cough. It was not as severe as it had been outside, but she could not get in an easy breath. While Estral moved about the hearth, Enver rummaged through his packs and . . . She was too busy coughing and her eyes too runny to see what he was doing exactly.

An interminable time elapsed. Her chest felt tight, hurt, and all she tasted was smoke. Enver stood before her and placed his hands on her head. His touch was soothing. He began to sing though she was not aware of the words. His voice resonated through her like cool, clean air into her lungs. It made her easier, made breathing less of a challenge.

Without breaking off his song, he accepted a pot from Estral and crumpled leaves into it. He held the pot before her and said, "Breathe deep of the steam."

She obeyed and an herbal fragrance penetrated through the stench of smoke, cooled and calmed her irritated throat and lungs. The coughing quieted.

"What happened?" Estral demanded.

"Smoke," Enver said. "Unnatural smoke."

"Second Empire," Karigan said in a hoarse whisper.

"They're here?" Estral asked in alarm.

Karigan shook her head. "Killed the men." She started coughing again.

"Don't talk," Enver told her. "Just inhale the steam."

She obeyed and he started singing again. She was doing much better, but the stinging of her airways persisted. She actually started to doze off, or so it seemed, but a need came upon her to finish what had been left incomplete. She stood and, like a sleepwalker, left Enver and Estral and headed for the door.

"Karigan?" Estral called. Her voice was a far-off dream, and Karigan paid it no heed. She was only peripherally aware of them as they followed her outside. She strode purposefully toward the pyre. The smoke hazed along the ground.

"Karigan," Estral called again, "what are you doing?"

"Let her go," Enver said.

Smoke apparitions formed before the fire, billowing and wavering, waiting. A voice rose up inside her.

"Sleep," she commanded. "It has been witnessed. You will be avenged."

The figures of smoke melted away until there were just normal wisps of it lifting from the remains of the pyre. She exhaled, and more smoke was expelled upon her breath.

She lay upon her bedroll. It had all been a dream after all, but then she coughed and tasted smoke. The steaming pot sat near her head.

"What in the hells?" she said, her voice ragged.

"That is the question," Estral replied, kneeling beside her. "How are you feeling?"

"Tired. Smoky."

"Then you'd best sleep. We've still got a couple hours till daylight."

"Enver?"

"He's keeping watch outside. Do you need me to get him?"

"No."

"Would you like a drink? Are you warm enough?"

At the suggestion of a drink, Karigan felt as parched as the pyre's flames. "Water, please."

Estral brought her a skin. "Enver says you are to take it slowly."

Karigan did, and when she had her fill, she lay back down, exhausted. "What happened, exactly? It's all a little confusing."

"There were spirits in the smoke. That's what Enver said, and that somehow you had inhaled them." There was an edge of incredulity to Estral's voice.

It came back to her now. "The smoke, it—it was forced on me, and I saw through their eyes, the lumbermen, being attacked by Second Empire."

"Did you see my father?"

"No." She closed her eyes.

"After that," Estral continued, "Enver brought you in and tried to calm your coughing."

"I think I remember that."

"Then you probably remember going back outside and talking to the smoke."

"What?" Karigan rose on her elbows. "Wait . . ." That had seemed all part of a dream. "That really happened?"

"Yes." Estral gazed at her with a strange look in her eye. "I am not exactly sure what you did. You sort of changed your voice . . ."

"What did I say?"

"You told the smoke, the apparitions, I guess, to sleep."

Karigan eased back down into her blankets. "I don't remember."

In the flickering light of the fire, Estral watched her friend drift back to sleep, her breathing easier. This time she did not writhe and mutter, but rested peacefully. Estral had heard, of course, about Karigan's various adventures since that day long ago when she'd run away from Selium. Hearing was incredible enough, but watching her fight off groundmites, or commanding smoke apparitions to sleep? That was something else entirely.

She recalled the scene of Karigan standing out by the pyre, surrounded by smoke. There was a faint shimmer about her. Estral had not been able to see her clearly, whether it was the smoke or—or what? Karigan had ordered the ghosts to sleep in a voice that was overlain with the authority of the heavens.

She tried to recall Karigan the schoolgirl, the troublemaker. Much had happened to her since those days in Selium, and although the girl Estral had once known reappeared at unexpected moments, she wasn't sure what to make of this other Karigan, this Karigan who crossed through time and faced Mornhavon the Black and talked to ghosts. She only knew that she must write it all down, and in doing so, maybe better understand. But even Karigan did not appear to understand, herself.

Enver entered the building. When he reached her, he said, "How is the Galadheon doing?"

"She drank some water."

"Ah, that is good. Tomorrow she should have some chocolate." He knelt beside Karigan and placed his hand on her brow. "Yes, she is easier."

"Enver, do you know what happened out there?"

"She put the spirits to rest."

"Yes, but . . ." Estral tried not to think about how outrageous it sounded. "How can she do that?"

He now sat cross-legged on the floor. He gazed down at Karigan before speaking. "You know that her special ability allows her to cross thresholds, yes?"

"Like going into the future?"

"When there are extraordinary forces at work, yes. But otherwise, she can fade out, turn invisible, as it were. What is really happening is that she is stepping onto a threshold. These thresholds cross the layers of the world. It allows her to detect and communicate with the shades of the mortal dead."

"And tell them to sleep."

"Yes. Because of her ability, there is another entity who speaks through her. She acts on his behalf, whether she is aware of it or not."

"Who?"

He glanced at Karigan who slept peacefully and innocently beside him. When he turned his gaze back to Estral, he looked uncertain about what to say. "It is said among the Eletians that a couple years ago, by working on this entity's behalf, she rescued the living world from a great calamity."

"And the entity is?" Estral demanded in exasperation.

"Your god of death."

GHOSTS

"You have the command of them," the ghostly Rider said. "You must not let them into you."

She had walked out of a smoky mist into the Painted Turtle, only the inn was larger and built at exaggerated angles. An enormous butter cream pie almost covered the whole tabletop. The edges of the common room fell into shadows through the murk of smoke. The Rider joined her at the table. He wore ancient garb, and carried with him a bow and quiver of arrows. The horn of the captain was slung over his shoulder.

"You cannot let them control you," the Rider said, his eyes the deep wells of the heavens. "You must control *them*. There will be those of a dark nature who will try to trick you, to take advantage, they who have no wish to be contained or subjugated."

"How do I do that?" she asked.

"You can will it, just as you will yourself to fade out when you use your ability. Remember also, the gods are capricious. Westrion will use you, but he will not always help you. He will only help you if there is some advantage to himself."

It all made sense in the way only a dream would, she thought.

The Rider stood. "It is time I left."

"Wait," she said, "what is your name?"

He smiled. "We have met before." He turned and his winged horse brooch flashed gold as he disappeared into the smoke.

Another man stepped out of shadow and gazed down at her. She knew him immediately.

"Cade!" she tried to rise so she could fling her arms around him, but she could not leave her chair. She was dead weight.

He did not look right. His eyes were burning coals of orange. His skin was slashed and scorched. Blood oozed from open wounds.

"Cade?"

"You left me behind."

"No, you told me to—"

He pointed a bloody finger at her. "You left me to suffer! *You left me!*"

LEAVING THE GREEN CLOAK

"NO!" Karigan flung herself into a sitting position. "No!" she cried again, and then she doubled over hacking uncontrollably and weeping.

Gentle hands held her and bathed her face with a damp cloth fragrant with soothing herbs. When she calmed and the coughing subsided, she found it was Enver who held her. Estral knelt before her, her face a mask of concern.

"That must have been some dream," Estral said.

"I left him," Karigan said in a hoarse whisper, tears flowing anew. "I left him to suffer."

There was no questioning of who the "he" was that she spoke of, just comforting words. Enver tried to get her to take a drink, which she discovered was not water, but a cooling cordial. It soothed her throat, which had become so raw from smoke and coughing.

"He let *you* go, remember?" Estral said. "He wanted you to come home."

As the dream lost its immediacy, Estral's words made more sense. The real Cade would not accuse her of leaving him to suffer. *Remember*, came words into her mind, *those of a dark nature will try to trick you and take advantage.*

She shook herself, trying to find some equilibrium after so wrenching an awakening. Who was tricking her? Ghosts, she vaguely recalled.

You cannot let them control you.

Now she knew she could have prevented the smoke ghosts from trespassing on her. By using her will. She placed her head in her hands. *My life is so strange.*

Estral squeezed her shoulder. "You should try to eat some breakfast. I have it warming over the fire. Some tea, too."

Karigan readied herself for the day. She still coughed from time to time as she went about her ablutions, but it was not as hard as the racking cough of before. Finally she sat down to the very welcome tea, but had little appetite for the porridge Estral had prepared. Enver offered her a Dragon Dropping, but even chocolate did not appeal.

"I am thinking perhaps we should stay here another day so that you can rest," he said.

"No."

Enver and Estral exchanged glances.

"I don't want to stay here another night," Karigan said.

"You are in rough shape, if I may say so," Estral said.

"I am all right. I can travel."

"Then we should discuss our path," Enver said.

"I intend to take the path that leads to my father," Estral said with determination. "Even if it leads to Second Empire."

"I do not think—" Enver began.

"Estral is right," Karigan said in her raspy voice. They both looked at her in surprise. "They were here—Second Empire. The ghosts showed me. They killed the lumbermen. Second Empire would know Lord Fiori's fate." She looked steadily at Estral. "You must be prepared for whatever that fate may be."

Estral looked down at the tabletop.

"What of the p'ehdrose?" Enver asked.

"We haven't had contact with the p'ehdrose for a thousand years. A few more days won't hurt anything. I believe King Zachary would want to know what became of Lord Fiori."

She also knew the king and Captain Mapstone would not be happy about her coming to this decision. She was supposed to use caution when it came to Second Empire, but that was before they had known Lord Fiori was involved. Sacor City was too far away to seek instructions, and if Lord Fiori was in Grandmother's clutches, time was of the essence.

Across the table from her, tears glistened on Estral's cheeks. "Thank you."

"Do not mistake me. I am not suggesting that we go rushing into the Lone Forest on a rescue mission."

"What *are* you suggesting?"

"That I scout ahead and see if Second Empire is indeed in the Lone Forest, and see if I can detect any sign of Lord Fiori *from a safe distance*. If the answer is yes to either, then we fall back, return to the River Unit and get help."

Estral did not look happy. "That would take too long."

"There are three of us," Karigan said, "and possibly hundreds of them. It won't help your father if we act rashly and get caught ourselves." Her statement was followed by a coughing fit bad enough that it made her eyes water. She sipped tea, which helped.

"Enver," she said, "this is not part of your mission. I don't blame you if you wish to go on to the p'ehdrose without us."

"Galadheon, I am your guide and tessari, so it is my mission, too."

His words were of an immense relief to her.

"I would feel better, however," he said, "if you would eat some chocolate."

She smiled, but demurred. "We will have to establish a secure camp outside the forest. We need to go slow, and keep alert. If they see us first, we'll be in trouble."

On that portentous note, they set to packing their gear and readying the horses. As they rode out, Karigan took one last glance at the remains of the pyre. A fitful breeze lifted ash and whirled it into the air, then settled.

Some aspect of the men who had died here remained in her rough throat and irritated lungs, but they were at rest now. She knew it to be true, by whatever odd circumstance. She had told their restless spirits to sleep, and for some reason, they listened to her.

By midday, they left the heavy eaves of the northern Green Cloak behind and entered a land of scrub and icy bogs and stunted, wind-sculpted trees. The wind howled sharp and hard with so little to break it. A hare, in its winter white coat, dashed across their trail. In the distance, Karigan espied a pair of coyotes loping across the bog. She kept as alert as she could, more interested in spotting people than wildlife, but as the wind hissed through the brush, none were to be seen.

Soon they picked their way up onto a ridge, its spine scoured of snow except in patches protected by boulders and squat bushes.

"There is the Lone Forest," Enver said, pointing into the distance.

Down beneath the ridge lay an expanse of evergreen amid the bleak gray and brown of the rocky plain. Karigan wished she had a spyglass to get a closer look.

"Perhaps we should get off the ridge," she said, feeling uneasy. "We could be visible for miles."

"And maybe get out of this wind," Estral muttered.

The bitter air irritated Karigan's lungs, and she pulled the scarf her aunts had made over her mouth and nose.

They picked their way down the ridge into a fold of land through which an ice-rimed stream flowed. It blunted the wind, and they paused to rest the horses and eat. Karigan picked at a piece of dried meat and hardtack, still not interested in food, but determined to keep up her strength.

"Are we still following the Eletian ways?" she asked.

"Yes," Enver replied, "but they veer off from the Lone Forest, north northwest, and then . . ."

"And then?"

"I am not certain."

"Right," Karigan murmured. "The way to the p'ehdrose is not found on maps." She doubled over, seized by another fit of coughing.

"Perhaps," Enver said, "we should consider spending the night here."

Karigan stood. "We still have half a day left. Let's use it."

"You should have chocolate first," Enver said.

This time she accepted a Dragon Dropping and tried to enjoy it. She was too tired to argue.

They rode through the afternoon, Karigan muffling the occasional coughing spell with her scarf. Condor's ears swiveled, and he even glanced back at her, as if in concern. She patted his neck and assured him all was well, though it was not. The smoke had hurt her worse than she thought and she did not know what kind of scout she was going to be if the hacking kept up.

Finally they halted in a copse of spruce that helped block the wind. There was a depression in the rocky ledge like a small natural amphitheater that offered further shelter.

"I am going to place wards around our campsite," Enver said, "since we are so close to the Lone Forest."

As he went about doing just that, Karigan and Estral tended the horses. When they finished, Karigan dropped her gear and lowered herself to the ground beside it. Staying at the lodge would have been warmer, but she was just as glad to be away from the remains of the pyre. She pulled her hood over her head and huddled out of the wind.

"I think we should chance a fire," Enver said.

Karigan opened her eyes to find him standing before her. Had she dropped off for a few minutes? Estral was struggling with their tent. Karigan knew she should help her, but she just couldn't make herself move.

"No fire," she said. Speaking tickled her airway and she coughed again.

"I need to brew you a tea," he said. "I will limit the smoke. I would rather you did not inhale anymore, anyway."

Me, too, she thought.

Enver was as good as his word, building a small, warming fire. The depression they sat in protected it so that the smoke did not blow into their faces. Karigan was glad of the tea and being able to inhale the herb steam that Enver prepared for her. He watched her from across the fire.

"Galadheon, did you intend to do this scouting of the Lone Forest tomorrow?"

She nodded.

"Hmm."

"Hmm, what?"

"I believe you should wait a day to rest your lungs."

Estral stiffened beside her.

"Maybe more steam would help," Karigan said.

Estral moved to put the pot back over the fire.

"Perhaps, but I believe both of us would prefer that you did not aggravate your condition into lung sickness."

No, she did not need to be sick. "I hate to delay, but if I coughed at an inopportune moment, I'd give myself away."

"Perhaps Enver could go," Estral said.

"No," Karigan replied. "This is outside his responsibility." He started to speak, but she cut him off. "My decision."

"I could try," Estral said, resolve shining in her eyes.

Karigan had a feeling this conversation was going to exhaust her more than the actual scouting. "I know you are worried about your father, but you haven't been trained as I have been for this sort of thing."

Estral did not argue, but glared at the fire.

Karigan sighed, not sure she was getting through to her friend. "Riders have died on scouting missions looking for Second Empire." She shuddered, remembering how they'd returned the corpse of poor Osric M'Grew to the king as a "message." "And you remember what Captain Treman said about losing his own people to Second Empire? The River Unit is one of the most highly trained units that serves the king."

"I understand," Estral said, her gaze downcast.

Karigan was not sure that she did. The reminder of those who had perished in pursuit of intelligence about Second Empire only served to cause Karigan to doubt the course she had chosen.

"We'll see how I'm doing in the morning," she said. "Then we'll decide when I go."

A WORTHY SACRIFICE

Grandmother eased her aching bones beside the fire. The chair was hard, but at least it had a backrest, unlike the benches that Birch and his officers sat upon. This was one of several meetings they were having regarding the forthcoming campaign season, strategy and the like. She'd left Terrik in charge of the keep, and Immerez had already returned to assist. More likely, she thought, to keep Nyssa company.

She knitted while they talked, with undyed woolen yarn, what looked like a deranged blanket, or a clotted, sickly web. Birch's maid, a girl of maybe thirteen or fourteen forced to serve him, brought them cups of weak wine. Her family had been killed when Birch's troops took the settlement. The men had spared some of the folk for work, mostly females to cook and perform other services. The girl's face was marked with bruises, both old and new, and she kept glancing at Grandmother with imploring eyes, as if she hoped Grandmother would help her.

Grandmother ignored her as Birch recounted the losses they'd experienced over the winter, from exposure, accident, and illness. She was pleased by the low number. Undoubtedly, occupying the settlement, with its existing buildings and stored foodstuffs and livestock, had proven an advantage. Some of the other encampments had not been so lucky.

He also revealed he'd engaged in negotiations with raiders in an effort to form an alliance. It was true that Second Empire needed help where it could get it, but she didn't exactly approve of dealing with cutthroats and degenerates.

"They will terrorize the common folk," Birch explained,

"keep the king and his folk busy and second-guessing, while we make our own moves."

"And what do these raiders get out of an alliance?"

"Whatever they can steal, and autonomy when the empire prevails. Revenge also plays into it after what was done to them years ago."

Grandmother had misgivings, but she must show confidence in Birch's leadership in front of his officers. "Be very careful in your dealings with them," she warned him. "Men of that ilk are not to be trusted."

"I know, Grandmother. I will keep them in line."

She certainly hoped so.

The girl approached with a cup and stumbled. Wine spilled on one of the officers, and Birch jumped to his feet and backhanded her. She sprawled onto the dirt floor with a cry and curled up to protect herself when he started kicking her.

"Get up!" he roared. He kicked her again. "Get up, you stupid wretch!"

"She will not get up if you keep kicking her," Grandmother said as she tied off a knot.

Birch stepped back, his face red. He was a controlled, disciplined military man, but that meant he must find release in other ways, such as the occasional violent outburst. No doubt the girl received the brunt of it.

He straightened his coat and pointed a finger at the girl, and said in a tight voice, "Bring another cup for the lieutenant."

The girl crawled away. Birch seated himself once more. "The little bitch is in heat for the first time, and it has made her exceedingly stupid and clumsy."

The girl hauled herself to her feet at the table in the center of the cabin and poured wine. More spilled than went into the cup with the trembling of her hands. She returned to the lieutenant carrying the cup with great care. Her lower lip bled; her face was smeared with tears. She gave Grandmother an imploring look.

Grandmother paid her little heed. She had no pity for Sacoridians, but she was practical. Beating up a servant and rendering her useless was *not* practical. At least the girl would get some peace from the men while she was unclean.

"About those ice creatures," Birch said, "that Immerez told us about. Does this mean your spell worked, Grandmother? I thought you were of the opinion it had not."

"It was a most difficult spell," she replied, "and I'd seen no evidence that it had." Immerez's report of the attack, which had allowed him to escape prison, had brought her great pleasure.

"What of the king and queen?" Birch asked. "Did they survive?"

"There is no way to know. I've had no visions, but with winter waning, one of our people will come with news of the city. In the meantime, we can only pray to God that the elemental reached the king and queen and killed them."

"That would leave Sacoridia in chaos and make it very easy for us."

"Yes," Grandmother replied, "but we cannot count on it."

"You have *seen* nothing?"

"My visions have been few, and God has not spoken directly to me since I left the accursed forest." Something had happened in Blackveil to take His voice from her. "My faith is such that God will speak to me once more when He sees fit, and perhaps when I ensnare the avatar of one of the false gods." She raised the spellwork to show them. Even unfinished, it radiated malignancy, such was the intent she put into each stitch and snag, each loop, each precisely knotted snarl. The men did not laugh or ridicule her art, for they knew well what she could do with even just an inch of yarn. "A worthy sacrifice to please God, don't you think?"

The men nodded and made affirmative noises. They were, she could tell, in awe. It did not take one gifted with the art to see what a monstrous thing she was creating.

Their talk shifted to strategy once more, Grandmother's knitting needles clacking in the background. Birch already had his troops preparing for war, training and stocking up on weaponry. They discussed supplies and logistics and communication among their different bases. Birch moved stones and twigs on a rough map he had scored into the dirt floor. Ready or not, war was coming to them.

By the time they had finished for the night, Grandmother

was spent. Just traveling to Birch's encampment in the cold had been exhausting; then there was her spellwork as they talked, which took its own toll. Now as she reckoned things, it was quite late. Birch had given his cabin over to her, with its rush-filled pallet drawn up to the fire, and blankets and furs to cover herself. Like most of the northern settlers, the one who had lived here had done many things to subsist, including the hunting and trapping of furbearers.

She folded her knitting into its basket. The slave girl lay in a heap in the corner with only a tattered cloak to keep her warm. Indeed, the men had left her alone in her unclean state this night.

Grandmother uttered a short prayer and made a sign of warding, and hunkered down to sleep.

At some point, she was awakened by a scuffling sound. She blinked, trying to clear the sleep from her eyes. The fire was down to low, lazy flames and embers, and the orange light glowed against the figure of the girl hunched over the yarn basket.

"What are you doing?" Grandmother demanded.

The girl glanced up, then grabbed a knitting needle and flung herself at Grandmother. Grandmother cried out and threw her arm up to block the dagger blows of her own knitting needle. The girl was quick and strong and desperate, and with the light shining in the whites of her eyes, insane.

But Grandmother had not lived as long as she had, had not gone into Blackveil and survived, without having a certain amount of strength of her own, not to mention a good dose of common sense. She always carried her knife attached to her belt—even when she slept—and grabbed it now. She pulled it out from beneath the covers and stabbed up into the girl's ribs. The girl made a throttled cry and rolled off onto the floor and curled into herself.

On inspiration, Grandmother dragged herself off the pallet. She could not tell if the blood on her front was the girl's, or her own from the shallow puncture wounds made by the knitting needle.

The girl was still alive and writhed on the floor. Grandmother grabbed her spellwork from the basket and flung it over the girl like a blanket. She screamed for surely it must burn, even though the spellwork had not yet been primed. Grandmother had simply inured herself to it as she worked on it. She had woven enough spells into it that she could feel its receptivity, its hunger. She leaped onto the girl and stabbed through the yarn. She thrust the knife again and again, even after the screams died and the girl lay limp.

By the time Birch and some of his guards burst into the cabin, Grandmother was standing over the girl, breathing hard. Her shift was saturated with blood.

"Grandmother, what have you done to my slave?" Birch demanded.

The undyed yarn of the spellwork greedily absorbed the girl's blood. The fact that she'd been experiencing her first courses would imbue it with even more life energy, power. Spells were nearly living things, and they'd find the taste of her succulent.

"Your slave," Grandmother said, "has made herself useful."

ESTRAL'S DECISION

"Are you telling me I should be listening to the voice of the world?" Karigan demanded. She was situated in the tent, wrapped in her blankets and using her saddlebags to support her upper body. It was easier on her chest that way. A bowl of steaming water was placed next to her.

"All I am suggesting," Enver said patiently from the tent opening, "is that you try the visualization. It might relax you, ease your lungs for a good night of sleep."

At this point she was almost willing to try anything. "You believe it will really work?"

"I believe it will help."

She stared hard at him for a moment, then relented with a sigh. "All right. Let's give it a try."

"Close your eyes," he replied, "and imagine a clear blue sky . . ."

He led her through calming visions of gently lapping waves along the shore, leaves rustling in the woods. She followed along, relaxing as he guided her down a forest path lined with ferns, and dappled with sunlight and shade. He told her to imagine the smoke and irritation leaving her lungs, that her lungs were as clear as the sky, that her breath moved as easily as the breeze through the trees.

She lost track of where his images left off and her dreams carried on.

"How bad is it?" Estral asked as Enver emerged from the tent.

"All will be well with reasonable rest. The trespass of the smoke apparitions was not gentle."

"What is 'reasonable'?" Estral did not think she was going to like the answer.

"A week would be ideal."

"A *week*?"

"Quietly, please, little cousin. Do not wake her. A week would be cautious and best, but we do not, I know, have that luxury. I suggest we let her rest tomorrow and see how she does. Had she not been so eager to leave the lumber camp, I would have preferred we stayed there another night, but alas, here we are. I will sing the healing. Will you join me?"

Estral thumped down onto a rock beside the fire. "You had better handle it. I'm not up to it."

Enver nodded, and sitting before the fire, he began his song of healing, a song without words. It soothed her some, but she couldn't help feeling desolate. Her father was likely dead or a captive of Second Empire. He could be very close, and she couldn't seem to do a thing about it. The one person who could was not well.

She gazed at the tent she shared with Karigan. As unreasonable as it was, she was angry at Karigan for being sick. She blamed Karigan for her inability to reach her father. She was angry that Karigan had become the focus of supernatural events. Was it true what Enver had said about Westrion? So strange. What had she become? Did Estral even know her anymore?

She lowered her chin onto her hands and watched the flames flickering in the fire ring. Individual flames seemed to dance and bend with Enver's music, and for a while she lost herself in it until she became aware of hot tears of frustration and guilt trailing down her cheeks. Guilt over her angry thoughts about Karigan. How could she be angry after all that Karigan had sacrificed for Sacoridia? And for being sick? Maybe what she was really mad about was her own inability to take action.

* * *

In the morning, Enver woke them both up. "How are you feeling, Galadheon? You were quieter during the night."

"All better," she said in her hoarse voice; then she started coughing.

"Hmm. I will make some tea." He left them.

"You don't sound all better," Estral said.

"First thing in the morning is always hard. Ick. I keep coughing up soot."

Ick, indeed. It was clear to Estral that Karigan should not attempt her scouting mission, and it was in fact what Enver suggested when he returned with tea.

"You should rest today," he told Karigan.

That she did not argue was telling.

"I plan to do some scouting of my own today," Enver said. Estral felt Karigan tense beside her to protest, but Enver continued before she could speak. "I intend to follow the ways to get a sense of where our path to the p'ehdrose may lead when we are done with the Lone Forest. Do not worry, I will be vigilant and keep well away from the forest itself. The two of you should stay here within the wards. They will conceal you."

"Damnation," Karigan muttered when he was gone. "I'm sorry, Estral, but I can't go into the Lone Forest hacking my head off. Maybe this afternoon . . ." She coughed again and spilled tea on herself. "Ow! Damnation. I'm not good for anything."

Estral's guilt intensified after her uncharitable thoughts of the previous evening. Despite the many strange things that occurred to and around Karigan, she sounded very human at the moment.

"Don't worry," Estral said. "Just rest and feel better. I'll be outside if you need me."

Karigan had set her cup aside and was already snuggling beneath her blankets. "You are my best friend," she murmured.

Feeling even worse, Estral crawled out of the tent to greet the day. Enver had already ridden off on Mist. He'd left a pot of water warming over the fire, and it appeared he'd fed and watered Coda, Condor, and Bane. Talk about not being good for anything! She hadn't been this whole journey. She was just a problem for Karigan and Enver to drag along—excess baggage. The gray bleakness of the morning sky and landscape did not improve her frame of mind.

She crawled up atop the higher rocks and looked out toward the Lone Forest. At this hour, it was a dark blotch on the horizon. How long would it take to reach on foot? Distances could be deceiving.

She returned to the campfire and sat with her blanket wrapped around her. She winced at the sound of racking coughs coming from the tent.

My father is my *problem,* she thought.

She made herself some tea and settled in to consider her options.

When Karigan awoke again, the cough wasn't as bad. It felt good to just rest, to linger beneath the warmth of her blankets and not move. The Lone Forest, however, loomed large in her mind, and she thought she'd like to get her scouting mission over with.

Tomorrow will be soon enough.

She drowsed until the state of her bladder became unbearable. She pulled on her boots and stepped out of the tent, wrapped in her greatcoat. Their camp appeared to be deserted, their little fire cold. She approved of the dead campfire—if they could see the Lone Forest, the Lone Forest could see their smoke.

"Estral," she called. There was no reply. She took care of her need, then started looking around their campsite and called for Estral. When there was no sign of her friend, her heart started to pound in alarm.

She gazed critically at their campsite. There were no signs of struggle, and she certainly had not been attacked as she slept peacefully. Perhaps Estral had just gone for a walk or something, but Enver had instructed them to stay within his wards. Then she noticed that not only was Mist gone, but so was Coda.

"Oh, Estral," Karigan murmured. Then to Condor she demanded, "Why didn't you tell me she was leaving?" He blinked at her with soulful eyes.

She returned to their tent and discovered a note on Estral's bedding. *Please don't follow me,* it read. *My father is my problem. I'll be back before nightfall.*

"Damnation." Estral didn't know the first thing about scouting. And did Estral actually think she would just sit around and wait for her return? When had Estral left? To Karigan's calculation, it was only mid-morning. Could she catch up? Their fire was cold, which meant Estral had been gone for a while.

She hurriedly readied herself and, in doing so, discovered her saber was missing. She was more pleased than annoyed that Estral had thought to arm herself, though she was pretty sure Drent would remind her of her incompetence at protecting her weapons. In her own defense, she hadn't expected her best friend to take her saber. She must have been deeply asleep to have been so unaware.

She still had her longsword, and she strapped the bonewood across her back. She left a note for Enver, weighted with a rock, by the firepit, telling him she was hoping to intercept Estral. Then she tacked Condor. She hated to approach the Lone Forest on horseback because it would make her all the more visible, and surely Second Empire had sentries watching all approaches, but if she had any hope of catching up with Estral before she did anything stupid, she had to.

She mounted up and coughed. Eyes watering, she looked to Bane. "Keep an eye on things here, will you?"

He stomped a hoof in response. Karigan reined Condor around and rode toward the Lone Forest.

She tried to keep as close as possible to the copses of trees that made small islands of themselves on the rocky plain. She either trotted or cantered Condor in the spaces between, hoping speed would reduce the chance of watchers spying her approach. Of course, speed potentially made her more visible if watchers happened to be looking her way at just the right moment, but Estral had perhaps hours on her and she had to make up for it. If luck was with her, Estral had ridden at a much more sedate pace.

In one copse, she spotted hoofprints in the thin, gravelly soil that had accumulated between rocks. She could not say for sure if they belonged to Coda, but they looked fresh. She also found a pile of fresh droppings.

Her apprehension grew the closer she got to the forest. She tried to detect Estral ahead, but could not. It was when she reached a thicket of spruce and scrub within what she figured to be a half mile of the forest that she found Coda. He nickered at their approach. He was haltered and hobbled, his girth loosened, Estral nowhere in sight. She patted Coda's neck. He seemed content enough, nibbling on sparse grasses.

She could, she surmised, always ride to the edge of the wood. If Estral was on foot, she could maybe still catch up. Or, she could return to their campsite and wait for Enver; then the two of them could decide what to do. But she had come this far, and much could happen between then and now.

Reluctantly, she haltered and hobbled Condor. She would walk into the Lone Forest, scout as she had intended originally, and return to their campsite whether or not she found Estral. When she did find Estral, she intended to give her a piece of her mind.

"Be ready for my return," she told Condor. "We may need to ride fast to get out of here."

He nibbled at her sleeve as though to hold her back. She kissed his nose, and left the cover of the thicket for whatever awaited her in the forest.

THE LONE FOREST

The stretch between the spruce thicket and the forest proper was more lush with thatches of tall, yellow grass and scraggy trees. Karigan ran, bent low, stopping now and then to hack and catch her breath. All the good her morning's rest had done was quickly fading away.

She splashed through a stream and clambered over boulders, and when at last she reached the edge of the forest, she threw herself to the ground gasping, and coughed into her arm in an attempt to muffle the sound. It would be a great way to announce herself to Second Empire. When the fit passed, she saw that a sooty residue speckled her sleeve. The next ghost who tried that again . . . Maybe, she thought, trying to keep positive, all the running would help expel the last of the smoke from her lungs.

When she caught her breath, she sat up to take her bearing. Beneath the eaves of the forest, the light dimmed, the air felt closer, all sound muted. It had an age to it that rivaled the oldest parts of the Green Cloak. She peered into the shadows, past deadfalls, and through matted, low-hanging branches bearded with stringy lichens, but she saw no one. She glanced back the way she had come, across the gray land, back toward the thicket where Condor and Coda waited. It seemed so very far away.

With a sigh, she stood, adjusted her swordbelt, and walked into the woods. It was dark enough that she could more than half fade if she needed to use her ability, and that provided a certain level of comfort.

She hunted for any sign of Estral and soon found a partial

footprint in deep moss. The woods were tangled enough with deadfalls and brush that she figured Estral would have taken the path of least resistance, and she was rewarded with another footprint. Farther along, she found a fresh gouge in a decaying log that lay on the forest floor. She guessed Estral had stepped on it to get to the other side, as she did now.

She continued on her path and began to think it was all a little too easy. She recalled how following a deer path had once brought her face-to-face with a monster out of Blackveil. But what choice had she but to go forward if she wished to find Estral? The feeling of being funneled into the center of a spider's web, however, was strong. She paused and drew the bonewood before continuing, looking warily around herself.

She came to a clearing where there was still snow and found more footprints. She followed them through the clearing, squinting in the sudden light, until she was once more shadowed by overarching boughs. She made little rock cairns to mark her trail the deeper she went. She needed to be able to find her way out. It would be a dead giveaway to a Second Empire tracker, but she felt she had little choice in the matter.

Something Captain Treman had warned her about began to niggle in the back of her mind about the dangers of the Lone Forest. Something about—

"Karigan!"

She looked up, startled, and there high above, balled up in a rope net strung from a tree, was Estral.

"Estral?" She took a step forward.

"No!" Estral cried. "Don't—"

SNAP!

Steel clamped Karigan's ankle and she fell from surprise and pain. It was a bear trap.

"Fekking hells!" she cried. *Traps.* That was what Captain Treman had warned her about.

The bear trap was bolted into a huge rock by a length of heavy chain. Fortunately, it wasn't the kind with teeth, which would have pierced right through the leather of her boot and into her flesh. As it was, she was relieved it hadn't snapped bone.

"Are you all right?" Estral asked.

"Do I look all right?"

Karigan searched for a mechanism that would release the trap, but couldn't find one. Somehow it had been modified from what she knew of such contraptions.

"I left a note telling you not to follow me," Estral said.

Karigan glanced up at her. "If that's not like an invitation to me, I don't know what is. What did you think I was going to do? Sip tea and eat Dragon Droppings by the fire until your return?"

"Whose fault is that? At least I told you where I was going."

"Just like you did for Alton," Karigan muttered.

"Oh, as if you'd ever bother to pick up a pen to write *me* once in a while."

Karigan muttered an oath and jammed the bonewood into the trap beside her foot in an attempt to leverage it open, but it would not give. Those who had set it did not want their human quarry to escape.

"I just wanted to find my father," Estral said.

"Next time, leave it to the professional."

"Oh, you mean the one stuck in a trap?"

Karigan growled and tried to pull her foot out of her boot, but she could not get her ankle past the steel clamped above it, and her foot would not budge. Trying to force it was painful.

"You can't free your foot?" Estral asked quietly.

"Maybe if I chop it off." Animals were known to chew their paws off to escape such traps. A coughing spell sent her sprawling.

"I'm sorry," Estral said.

"We can worry about that later. Can't you cut yourself out of that net?"

"I can't move an inch. It's got me bound up like swine in a corset."

"Swine in a—?" Karigan laughed despite herself and went back to work trying to release her foot. Whoever had contrived the traps had been clever. There had to be a way to free herself. Or maybe, those who had set the trap in fact expected to cut off the feet of the trespassers caught in it. It was not a comforting thought.

Sweat dripped off her brow as she continued to struggle. She even tried smashing the steel with a rock, but to no avail. She only succeeded in striking her foot. She stilled to catch her breath and gather her thoughts. Her foot had grown numb in the trap.

"What about Enver?" Estral asked.

"I left him a note, which I hope he'll see sooner rather than later."

"Hah! I guess I am not the only note leaver."

Karigan scowled at her. Since she could not free herself, she decided to see what she could do for Estral. Using the bonewood, she pushed herself up to stand on her free foot. She hopped as close to Estral's tree as she could, the chain clinking as she went until it tautened and almost yanked her back down. Using the bonewood for balance, she drew her sword and reached as high as she could, but the tip came up short of the net, no matter how she strained to reach it. Enver, she thought, had better hurry, but who knew how long he'd planned to scout? If only she had an ax, she'd chop down the tree.

"Someone is coming," Estral whispered.

The hunters, Karigan thought, to check their traps. She was not wrong. Four men and a woman in woodland garb broke through the brush and came face-to-face with her. She raised her sword.

"Look at what we've got," one of the men said.

"Don't get too close," the woman warned him. "That's a swordmaster's band on the blade."

"Now what would a swordmaster Greenie be doing in our woods, eh?"

"We were lost," Karigan said. "Let us go."

They laughed at her.

"Truly," Estral said, "we were just looking for a—a friend. He's tall, middle-aged, sings . . ."

"We've got a bunch like that," the first man said. "There is no way this Greenie doesn't know what forest this is. I suggest she drop her weapons."

"Release us," Karigan countered.

"No way that's happening, is there. If you drop your weapons, it'll go much easier for you."

Karigan shifted her stance to improve her balance. She did not lower her sword.

"Get the one in the tree down first; then we'll deal with the other."

They worked out of her reach. When the net came down, it opened like the strings of a purse and Estral spilled out. She looked like she could barely move from her cramped position. One of the men quickly retrieved the saber and her knife, and prodded her with his own sword. Karigan took a futile swipe at him, but only upset her balance. She struggled to remain upright.

The man and woman disregarded Estral's protests and hauled her to her feet. She cried out as they whipped her hands behind her back and bound her wrists.

A droplet of sweat slowly rolled down Karigan's temple and cheek, and splattered onto her sleeve. The soldiers, and she deemed that that's what these people were by their manner regardless of their garb, gazed at her speculatively as she held her defensive position.

"I guess you want this the hard way," the first man said. "Very well."

In one quick motion, he drew his sword and came for her. She met his blade soundly, but she floundered hopping on one foot, the chain dragging on her. The bonewood kept her upright, but she also used it in concert with her sword to block blows and return them.

The man was a swordsman and a good one, and he stepped out of reach as if to mock her.

"I never fought a swordmaster before," he said, "and I can't say I'm impressed."

Having a foot ensnared in a bear trap was one scenario for which Drent had never trained her. It was a disadvantage, to be sure. Otherwise, it wouldn't have even been a contest.

He dove back in, his companions cheering him on, and she tried to adapt the forms of her training to her circumstances.

She fought aggressively, pushing him back, and when he was once more out of her reach, she almost fell on her face.

"C'mon, Darren," said the woman, "get it over with already. It's time for us to get back to camp."

The man, Darren, grinned at Karigan, and then, instead of attacking, he just reached down and yanked the chain, pulling her leg right out from under her. She fell onto her back. When the soldiers came for her, she rose to her knees and held them off at first with her sword and bonewood, but they surrounded her. She was grabbed from behind, and the others pried the weapons out of her hands.

She punched and kicked to the last, but there were too many of them. When she got kneed in the gut, she curled up on her side, coughing and retching. They bound her hands behind her and released her foot from the trap using a key-like mechanism, then hauled her to her feet. She almost fell at the pain that shot through her ankle, but they held her up. Her ankle was probably just bruised to the bone, but at the moment it hurt like all five hells.

"Let's go," Darren said. "We'll take the Greenie to Captain Terrik. The other one can go to Nyssa's workshop until the cap decides what to do with 'em."

Karigan was shoved forward and she almost fell headlong, but somehow she kept to her feet. She limped along behind Estral. An annoying strand of hair had come loose from her braid and hung in her face. She tried blowing it aside, but it just fell back.

"Don't think about running off into the forest," Darren warned her. "There are worse traps for you to step in."

"Wouldn't think of it," she muttered. Not with her own sword being jabbed into her back. No, Drent would not be pleased. Not at all.

THE BURNING FIRE

::Grandmother's true granddaughter has Estral's voice.::

Zachary nodded subtly to acknowledge Fiori's words. He knew the story of how Estral had lost her voice, but he could not say so aloud. He and his fellow slaves had been herded into the great hall to be proselytized by Smurn, and once again, Fiori had sat behind him, doing his whisper-throwing trick.

::You could not imagine my shock at hearing my daughter's voice from another girl. They used some magic, some spell, to steal it from Estral. I have been at my wit's end trying to figure out how to steal it back.::

Binning once again snored softly next to Zachary as Smurn droned on. Fiori had told him that he'd been captured in one of the northern lumber camps. He'd changed his name and hidden his affiliation with Selium, but when the intruders discovered he'd a talent for music and was educated, Grandmother decided not to kill him, but kept him as a tutor for her granddaughter. He was teaching her music, reading, writing, and figuring.

::I don't even know how this has affected Estral,:: Fiori continued. ::I don't know how it has hurt her or if . . .::

Zachary could hear the pain in Fiori's voice and desperately wished he could tell him that Estral was fine and searching for him.

A sudden disturbance interrupted their "conversation." A soldier strode across the great hall to one of the guards. "Get Captain Terrik."

The guard ran off. There was the sound of others approaching, and distracted slaves gazed across the hall to see what was going on. Smurn did not look pleased to have his sermon interrupted.

"Listen to me, you heathen sinners!" he cried.

Two more soldiers entered with a captive held between them, her hands bound behind her back. It took a moment for it to sink in that the captive wore Rider green, had brown hair and a patch over her eye.

"Karigan . . ." he murmured in shock. He started to rise.

::No!:: Fiori came up alongside him and grabbed his arm. ::Do not reveal yourself!::

Zachary was strung taut. Karigan's gaze fell in their direction, then wandered off as though taking in all her surroundings, then whipped back to them, her expression registering recognition.

"Uh-oh," Fiori murmured.

When one of the soldiers started to follow her gaze, she looked straight ahead and lunged. The two soldiers gripping her arms yanked her back. She recoiled, and using their hold on her as leverage, sprang and kicked both feet forward into the lead soldier, who sprawled headlong. She then pivoted and kneed one of the soldiers holding her, and rammed her shoulder into the other.

Zachary was ready to jump to his feet, his fists clenched.

::Steady!:: Fiori told him. ::You will not help her by running to her. She is doing this to cover up her recognition of you. Let her do what she needs to!::

A growl rumbled from Zachary's chest and Binning shook himself awake. "What's goin' on?"

Other onlookers and slaves laughed at the hapless soldiers who cried out in pain and swore as Karigan planted a swift kick or crunched toes or butted heads. Even bound as she was, she was a mad whirlwind that spun and lunged and charged. She laid waste to any who got in her way. Other guards, finally taking pity on their fellows, closed in.

"No," Zachary whispered.

When one of the soldiers raised the pommel of a very familiar sword to strike her head, he opened his mouth to shout a warning, but Fiori's fist slammed into his gut. He doubled over and gasped for air.

::I am sorry,:: Fiori said, ::but you must not reveal yourself.::

When Zachary regained his breath and looked up, Karigan and her captors had disappeared and his fellow slaves had erupted into fist fights with the remaining guards. A big man named Merth punched Smurn in the jaw, and the lay priest flew onto his back and skidded across the floor, robes billowing about his legs.

Zachary looked for Fiori, but he, too, had vanished. He rose to his feet to make a run for it when Binning grabbed his arm.

"What you doing, Dav?"

Zachary didn't answer. A couple dozen soldiers ran into the great hall straight toward the fighting slaves. His chance to run now quashed, he dragged Binning against a wall to lie low while the soldiers dove in among the fighters swinging their cudgels with merciless ferocity.

"Keep calm and put your hands over your head," Zachary told Binning. He hoped the soldiers would see that they were not participating in the fight and spare them the beating the others were receiving.

"Why'd that fellow slug you?" Binning asked.

Zachary shrugged and winced as a cudgel cracked against Merth's skull. The big man fell hard.

"And why aren't you fighting?" Binning asked.

"Look at Merth," he replied. "Don't need that." No, if he was going to free himself so he could help Karigan, he would not risk injury.

The thralls were soon subdued and Zachary's plan had worked for the most part. A cudgel had grazed his shoulders, but it was a minor blow compared to what had happened to Merth and a few of the others.

Those who could work were sent back to the passage. Zachary moved stones, cursing himself for not having acted more quickly to help Karigan. Then he reminded himself he could not have gotten far, which would not have helped either of them. His rational mind warred with his need to protect, and he was so agitated that he slammed rocks into his basket and hurried up and down the passage in record time.

Where were they holding her? What would they do to her? How was it she had been caught? He emptied his basket of rocks and made the return trip into the passage. He had sent her north to find the p'ehdrose, guided by the Eletian and accompanied by Estral Andovian. Where were Estral and Enver? Were they, too, being held by Second Empire? Had they come to the Lone Forest because they had traced Fiori here?

At the end of the passage, he knelt on one knee and hurled the rocks into his basket. A hand grabbed his wrist and he nearly flung a rock at whoever it was, but stopped himself. It was Lorilie Dorran.

"What's eating you, Dav?" she demanded. "The guards are noticing. You might want to calm down."

How could he? But he took a deep breath and instead of hurling the next rock into the basket, he let it roll off his hand.

"That's better," Lorilie said. She picked up a stone for her own basket. "Save your strength for when you truly need it."

When would that be? He felt so helpless.

"Is it the Greenie who has you so riled up?" Lorilie asked in a low voice. "Heard they were taking her to Nyssa."

Nyssa. The name chilled him. He forced himself to shake his head and rise calmly with his full basket. Inside he raged, raged as hot as the firebrand the Eletians named him. He'd learned enough to know that Nyssa was the resident torturer, that she took delight in her role. Having a Green Rider in her clutches would please her. He wore the cloak of one she had flogged to death.

If she hurt Karigan, he would destroy her. Her, and all of Second Empire, and he'd do it single-handedly if he had to. But alas, for all his plotting, he could not yet see a clear path. He had to calm himself again when he dumped his rocks.

Slow down, slow down.

He could not help it. It infuriated him that the woman he loved was at the mercy of one such as Nyssa, and he a captive, too, and so impotent. He paused before reentering the passage. Plotting and planning were not what were needed, perhaps . . .

"Keep moving, idiot," a nearby guard said.

Zachary trembled, the rage rising to the surface. *I cannot bear it. I cannot bear the thought of her being hurt.* He closed his eyes, recalling the scene of the sword's pommel coming down on her head.

The guard closed in with his cudgel. "I said, keep moving."

Zachary dropped his basket and launched at the guard, who gaped in surprise before he was knocked down. Zachary pummeled him, loosed himself upon his captor. While some guards menaced the watching slaves and pushed them back into the passage to prevent them from joining the fray, others rushed to the aid of their comrade. Zachary met them, taking fierce joy in releasing his rage. Bones crunched beneath his fists. He did not hold back this time. He used his training to its full extent, disarming a guard and using his cudgel as though it were a sword. He was wild; he was the burning fire.

He smashed skulls and sent guards flying, but in the end, there were many of them and just one of him, and they all had cudgels, too.

NYSSA'S WORKSHOP

The guards flung Karigan onto the straw-strewn floor, at Estral's feet. She was barely conscious, and Estral thought the cords binding Karigan's hands behind her back excessive, for she looked far from capable of doing much harm at the moment.

Estral dropped to her knees beside her. "Karigan," she whispered, and shook her shoulder. "Wake up. *Please.*"

Karigan did not respond.

At some point, the guards had parted Karigan from her greatcoat and waistcoat, and now searched through the pockets. They turned up wadded handkerchiefs, a few coppers, some hair ribbons, and a hoofpick.

"Nothing of importance," one of the guards said in disgust as he tossed Karigan's greatcoat onto a table next to her weapons.

They were in a simple wood building with low beams, few windows, and a brazier at the opposite end. The wood looked light and smelled relatively new. The structure had been recently built, unlike the ancient keep Estral had spotted through the trees before she'd been separated from Karigan and locked up.

"What's a Greenie doing without a message satchel?" the other guard asked.

"Spying, that's what."

"And the other girl?"

"Who knows. Another spy, probably. Nyssa will find out."

Since Estral's hands were not bound, she started to work on loosening the cords around Karigan's wrists. One of the guards poked the bonewood through the slats of the pen and jabbed her shoulder.

"Ow!"

"You leave those, or we'll hurt you," the guard said.

"What is she going to do in her condition?" Estral demanded.

"She's done plenty already."

Estral rubbed her shoulder and decided she would try later, when they were not so attentive. She could only imagine what "plenty" Karigan had done. It must have been impressive considering the bump on her head. Blood matted her hair.

"Please wake up," Estral whispered.

Karigan groaned. Her foot twitched.

"Karigan?"

"What the hells . . . ?" she murmured.

"We're being held. You must have put up a fight. They won't let me untie you."

Karigan gave a raspy laugh, then fell silent and still. Estral feared she'd fallen unconscious again, but then she suddenly said, "It started out . . . a promising day."

Estral could have cheered to hear her friend speak. "I know. I ruined it for you. I'm sorry."

Karigan quieted, looking for all the world like she had fallen asleep. Estral grew anxious again.

"Karigan?"

"What?" She sounded beyond tired.

"Just wanted to make sure you were still with me."

Karigan expelled a long breath, and then started wrestling with her bindings, twisting and writhing her wrists. They had already looked chafed and raw, and now she was only making it worse by causing the cords to cut deeper into her skin.

"Ow. Damnation," she snarled, but she kept struggling.

"Stop," Estral told her, "you're bleeding."

"Get these off me."

Estral licked her lips. "I told you, they won't let me. They'll hurt me if I do." A quick glance revealed the guards were indeed still keeping a watchful eye on her.

Karigan gave up and slumped, seeming to rest. Then, just as suddenly, she fought to sit up. Estral helped her.

"Shouldn't you stay down? Take it easy?"

"Probably," Karigan said, grimacing. "Why is there a herd of horses galloping through my head?"

"I'm sorry," Estral said again, overcome by a fresh wave of remorse. "If I hadn't— "

"We can discuss that later." Karigan closed her eye for a few moments, then with a deep breath and a grunt of effort, forced herself to her feet and lurched across the pen to peer through the slats. Estral stood, as well, and followed her gaze to the two guards talking over her coat and weapons. One puffed on a pipe. Karigan's gaze moved on, seeming to scrutinize the rest of the building.

"What are you looking for?"

"A way out." A coughing fit took her, and she reeled away from the slats to lean against the wall. "Oh, that hurts my head," she said hoarsely when the fit passed. "I think I'm going to be sick." She heaved, but little came up.

"Why don't you sit?" Estral suggested.

Just then, a door opened with a flash of daylight before it was securely closed again. Karigan returned to the slats to view the newcomer.

"Who is that?" she whispered.

Estral shuddered. "They call her Nyssa. I don't think she is a very nice person."

Karigan snorted softly. "She's Second Empire."

Nyssa spoke quietly with her guards, and then all three turned to gaze at their captives.

"Well, well," Nyssa said. "The Greenie is awake and standing. Do you realize the ruckus you started in the keep?"

Karigan did not answer, but a smile formed on her lips.

"In any case," Nyssa continued, "Captain Terrik has left it to me to ask you some questions. Bring the Greenie out."

Karigan turned to Estral and hastily whispered, "No matter what they threaten, no matter what they do, tell them nothing." She stared hard and beseechingly at her as if to ensure her words penetrated.

She sounded brave, but there was the fear in the tightness of her jaw, in the intensity of her eye. Estral, whose legs shook, could not even imagine how scared she must be.

The guards unlocked the pen and threw Estral into the back wall. She slid to the floor and shook her head. Her good ear was ringing from the impact. By the time she had gotten over the shock, the guards had already dragged Karigan out and relocked the door. One held Karigan from behind with his cudgel pressed firmly across her throat in a choke hold. The second stood ready to beat her with his own cudgel, should she make a wrong move. Just what damage had she wrought in the keep?

Nyssa stood before her, looking her over. "I bet you think you are clever and strong, the way you fought those soldiers. You can fight me if you like, which I'd enjoy, or you can answer my questions straight away. Either way, I'll get what I want."

Estral, pressed up against the slats once more to watch, shuddered. *Please, Karigan, don't be stubborn for once in your life. Tell her something, anything.*

She knew, however, that a king's messenger would not divulge information to the enemy, not willingly, and must resist even under duress. Karigan, with her sense of honor and sheer obstinacy, certainly would not give in without a fight. Estral could see only too clearly where it would all lead. *Just this once, Karigan, please, tell her anything.*

Nyssa stepped over to the table and drew Karigan's longsword. She pointed it at Karigan's midsection. "You're not just a Greenie, but a swordmaster. How very unusual." The swordtip then swept to the insignia on Karigan's right shirtsleeve. "And you wear the sign of the Black Shield on your uniform. Even more unusual. You must be a very special Greenie, indeed. It makes one wonder what a Black Shield Greenie is doing prowling around this forest."

Karigan said nothing.

"Not going to talk? I should warn you from the outset that I am very passionate about my work and quite happy to engage in it, but I am also fair. All you have to do is tell me what your purpose is here, and what your king is planning. So very simple."

"We were just looking for a friend!" Estral cried.

Nyssa glanced her way and gave her a withering look. "I

did not ask you, and this will be your only warning. If I hear another outburst, I will take it out on this Greenie."

Estral bit her bottom lip.

"Now," Nyssa said, returning her attention to Karigan, "I could work on your companion, and maybe she would tell all."

"No." Karigan's voice came choked from the pressure of the cudgel against her throat. "Leave her out of this. She doesn't know anything."

Estral's knees almost gave out at the mere thought of Nyssa coming anywhere near her, and yet, Karigan remained defiant before that terrifying woman. She was, as always, Estral's steadfast champion. What, Estral wondered, had she done to deserve such a friend?

"Protecting your friend?" Nyssa said. "How sweet. She doesn't look sturdy enough, anyway. I doubt she would hold up long under questioning, which would be disappointing for me, to say the least, and it is why *you,* a Green Rider and swordmaster, are standing here. I suspect you are made of sterner stuff. You see, for me, it's not just about getting answers to my questions, but *how* I get them. I prefer a little challenge—it keeps life interesting. You know who Grandmother is? Yes, I can see by your expression that you do. Well, even Grandmother calls me a sadist. With love, of course. She has her way of questioning, and I have mine. She isn't here at the moment, so I get to work on you. But because I am fair, I am offering you a chance to have your say, to tell me your purpose here. As charming as looking for a friend sounds, I find it unlikely."

"I have nothing to say."

"Bravely said." Nyssa smiled and set the longsword aside. "And I am not disappointed." She ordered the guards to move Karigan forward and clasp irons around her ankles, which were bolted to the floor. "I will not tolerate the footwork you used on the others in the keep."

Estral, who was terrified just watching, could not imagine how it must be for Karigan.

Karigan's wrists were then untied and shackled to a beam overhead and hoisted so that she hung almost suspended by her wrists, her toes barely touching the floor, the chains of the ankle irons taut. Nyssa circled her to inspect her guards' handiwork.

"This will do," she said. Her attention turned to implements hanging on a nearby wall. She took her time examining them, touching and caressing individual items. Though Estral could not identify them from where she was, she knew they could not be anything good.

Karigan coughed and Nyssa spun on her. "Are you sick?" When Karigan did not reply, she said, "It is a simple question, and if I do not receive an answer, there will be pain. Are you sick? Yes or no."

Karigan cleared her throat. "No."

"Excellent," Nyssa replied. "That is a positive sign you answered, and it is good to know you are not sick. It would not stop me from my work, but it is, you know, very bad for stamina and would force me to adjust how I proceed." She picked up a thin knife, polished the blade, and checked it front and back. Estral tensed even as she saw Karigan's posture grow more rigid.

"Since you answered me about your health," Nyssa continued, "I am going to give you one more chance to tell me what I want to know, and by answering, you will be spared some pain. What is your purpose in the Lone Forest, and what is your king planning?"

Karigan, please tell her, Estral thought. *Tell her anything, please . . .*

Time and silence stretched to excruciating lengths. All of Estral's muscles were taut with anxiety as Nyssa gazed at Karigan, rolling the knife across the palm of one hand to the other.

After an interminable wait, Nyssa shrugged. "I guess I will be making you answer. I am pleased."

"Wait!" Estral cried. "I can tell you!"

Nyssa plunged the knife into Karigan. Karigan gasped and writhed in her shackles. Estral screamed. Nyssa left the knife lodged in place and stalked up to the pen. She reached in and grabbed Estral by the throat, and pulled her into the slats.

Estral cried out, tried to pry Nyssa's fingers loose, to no avail. The woman was insanely strong.

"I told you," Nyssa said, "that another outburst from you would be bad for your friend. The stabbing is *your* doing. Now, will you keep your mouth shut? This time was just through muscle—I know how to avoid the organs—but if you open your mouth again, it'll be much worse."

Estral nodded as best she could with Nyssa's hand strangling her.

"Good." Nyssa let her go, and she fell to her knees, gagging. Blood dripped from her nose and mixed with tears. She wiped it away with the back of her hand. Yes, this was all her doing, her fault.

"Never fear," Nyssa said, "I will get to you eventually." She then returned to Karigan and gazed at the hilt jutting out of her midsection. "Reed, get me an iron."

One of the guards hastened to the brazier and returned with a long iron, its tip glowing orange. Nyssa yanked the knife out and Karigan gasped. Blood pattered onto the floor. Nyssa then tugged Karigan's shirt up to expose the wound.

"I see this is not the first time you've been stabbed. I have heard that being a Greenie can be dangerous work." Nyssa took the iron from the guard, Reed. "Now, I'm going to close your wound. I don't want blood loss to cut our session short."

Estral buried her head in her arms and squeezed her eyes shut as the glowing tip of the iron was pressed against Karigan's flesh.

HIS LITTLE STARLING

Estral rocked herself on the floor of the pen, not sure if the scream was hers or Karigan's. Tears and snot smeared her face. *My fault, my fault . . .*

Then there was silence. She opened her eyes and dared peek out. Nyssa was just standing there, talking to Karigan. The hot iron was gone, but she still held the knife and was wiping the blood off its blade with a rag.

"Would it surprise you to know I trained to be a mender?" Nyssa asked. "I apprenticed in Mirwellton. The knowledge is very useful in my work. I know how the body functions, what pleasures it, and what pains it, how much it will bleed. While I can perform useful tasks like setting bones, I am more interested in breaking them." She glanced at Estral. "Burson, make sure the other one watches."

"Yes, Nyssa."

The guard came toward the pen and Estral scuttled to the back wall. He entered, grabbed her by the collar, and bashed her into the slats. He pressed his cudgel against the nape of her neck so she could not move her head.

"I also have a knife," Burson said. "Nyssa is not the only one who knows how to use one. If I catch you closing your eyes and not watching, I'll make you bleed, too."

With little choice but to watch, Estral observed Nyssa walk behind Karigan with her knife poised. She stood there for some time, and the agony of waiting made Estral feel as though she must burst. Then, in one swift motion, Nyssa slit Karigan's shirt up the back. She draped the cloth to the sides to expose Karigan's shoulders and the curve of her spine. Nyssa took it all in, staring long and hard at the bared flesh.

"Excellent," she said. "Smooth and unblemished, a blank page. I can tell from your musculature that you do indeed work with a sword. Well done, but you may not be able to do so ever again by the time we are finished." She tenderly, almost lovingly, trailed her fingers down the bumps and depressions of Karigan's spine. Karigan flinched at her touch, and Nyssa chuckled. "If you are reacting so to such a light touch now, just wait until you feel what comes next."

There was more gentle examination of Karigan's back, as though Nyssa were trying to memorize all the contours, the underlying structure and sinew.

"A pity, in a way," Nyssa murmured. "Such a well-formed back. But also exciting to leave my exclusive mark upon it."

Without warning, she grabbed Karigan's braid and jerked her head back, exposing her throat.

Estral shrieked.

"Shut up," Burson said, jamming his cudgel harder into the back of her neck.

Instead of cutting Karigan's throat, however, Nyssa caressed it, her fingers tracing it from jaw to collar bone. "Admit it," she said, her lips very close to Karigan's ear, "you like me touching you."

"Go to the hells," Karigan gasped.

Nyssa smiled indulgently and tapped her on the nose. Then she sawed off Karigan's braid.

Estral, shaken and exhausted, exhaled a long trembling breath.

Nyssa stood before Karigan and held the braid before her face. "Your lovely hair. It was in the way. Think you'll miss it?" She tickled Karigan under the chin with it. "Or, will some man, some lover of yours, miss running his hands through it?" She trailed the end of the braid along Karigan's throat, down her front. Karigan shivered, and Nyssa laughed. "Perhaps you like me just a little, hmm?"

Karigan averted her face when Nyssa caressed her cheek, but Nyssa forced her to look at her, and kissed her long and hard on the lips. Karigan jerked in her chains and tore away.

"No? Not even a little? More's the pity." Nyssa tossed the braid aside on the table.

Gods, Estral thought, her stomach churning in revulsion.

Nyssa returned to her wall of implements and took her time examining what hung there. "Work well done cannot be rushed," she murmured, "it just requires the correct tool to achieve the finest effect."

She fingered a couple of the implements, and finally decided on one. She removed from its hook a whip of multiple braided and knotted leather thongs. She showed it to Karigan, taking her time to ensure it was seen from one end to the other.

"This is one of my favorites," she said. "I made it myself, a beautiful tool to do beautiful work. The handle is made of horn, and in the knots of the thongs, I have wound wire into barbs, which add weight to the lash and will allow me to etch the most pleasing designs into your back. You will bear them for the rest of your life, however long or short that may be, and every time you feel the scars pulling at your back, feel some pain or stiffness, every time you touch them or glimpse them in a mirror, you will think of me, their creator." She smiled. "And this one will be the hardest of all to forget, for it will not be so easy to hide." She grasped one of the barbed knots and pressed it against Karigan's cheek, and ripped down. Karigan jerked, her shackles ringing. Nyssa stepped back as though to assess the effect. She nodded in satisfaction at the result, absently stroking the tendrils of her whip.

"I am going to give you one more chance, Greenie," Nyssa said. "Is there anything you would like to tell me? What is your king planning?"

Please answer, Estral thought. *Tell her anything.* She dared not speak up herself after what had happened the last time.

Then Karigan did speak, her voice hoarse. "I am just a messenger. The king doesn't tell me his plans."

"Wrong answer," Nyssa said, "but I am delighted." She stepped behind Karigan as if to size up her subject once more.

No, no, no, Estral thought. *Please, dear gods, no.*

Karigan glanced over her shoulder as if to see what Nyssa

was up to. The gash down her cheek dripped blood onto her shirt.

Nyssa paced and rolled her shoulders, taking her time to limber up. Maybe, Estral thought, it was all for show. She was drawing it all out in the expectation Karigan would crack just waiting for the lash to fall.

Then, without preamble, swiftly and with the same deft precision Nyssa had exhibited with the knife, she struck. Karigan's body spasmed and she gasped, but she did not cry out. Estral sobbed as though she was the one who'd been lashed. The first stroke had raised welts and drawn blood across Karigan's back. It was no longer a "blank page." The wire barbs in the knots would savage her.

"One!" Reed called out.

Nyssa prepared to deliver another stroke, and Estral squeezed her eyes shut.

"Don't you be closing your eyes," Burson growled in her ear. "Nyssa wants you to watch." When Estral didn't obey, he jabbed the tip of his knife into the small of her back. "Open your eyes and *watch*." He jabbed again and she cried out, and obeyed.

"Do you know that my left hand is as strong and as accurate as my right?" Nyssa asked. "I can write with both, do tasks with one or the other with equal ability. It is truly a rare gift. It means I can switch hands to alternate the lashes across your back to create an artistic, but excruciating, pattern."

"Two!" Reed called as the lash fell again.

Estral screamed even as Karigan did not. Tears blurred her vision of red.

"Three!"

She welcomed the blurring, choked on tears.

"Four!"

She tried not to see the blood. She tried not to hear the sound of the thongs rushing through the air and smacking Karigan's back. She tried not to hear Reed's count, now up to eight, then eleven, and relentlessly on. How could Karigan bear it?

My fault, my fault... If Estral hadn't been so set on finding her father right away, if she had only listened to Karigan.

"Thirteen!"

"It's going beautifully, Greenie," Nyssa said, her cheeks flushed from exertion and her eyes sparkling. "Soon you will scream for me."

Estral went into a sort of stupor, pressed up against the slats, tears runneling down her face, snot dripping from her nose. Her breaths came in ragged gasps as the litany of *My fault, my fault, my fault . . .* continued to stream through her mind. She lost focus, went numb.

When Karigan finally did scream, Estral jolted back to herself and the stench of blood filled her nostrils. There was a look of ecstasy on Nyssa's face.

The count continued. "Twenty-six!" And so did Karigan's weakening screams. On, and on.

Estral was not sure how much time had passed when she realized the cudgel was gone from the back of her neck and Burson was stepping out of the pen and locking the door behind him. Her knees gave out and she sank to the floor. The flogging had stopped, and there was another man speaking with Nyssa. They blocked her view of Karigan, but she could see the blood spatter on Nyssa's tunic, her hands, across the wall, staining the floorboards beneath Karigan's feet.

"I've missed you," Nyssa was saying.

"And I, you," the man replied. He was bald, wore a patch over his eye. His right hand was a hook.

Immerez, Estral thought. She'd never met him, but knew his description well enough. He had escaped the day the ice creatures had attacked the castle, and this was where he'd come. He and Karigan had a history, and this could only make things worse. The pair turned to examine Nyssa's handiwork.

"Terrik told me how the Greenie got caught in one of the traps," Immerez said, "and her companion." He glanced back at Estral. "It's very odd. Greenies usually travel alone. I wonder . . ." He moved around to look at Karigan from the front.

No, no, no. His moving revealed Karigan's shredded back to Estral, the strips of bloody skin hanging off it. She reeled, and heaved up whatever remained of her breakfast.

Immerez laughed.

She wiped her mouth and looked again, trying not to see Karigan's back by focusing on Immerez. He lifted Karigan's chin with his hook to gaze into her face.

"It's her," he told Nyssa.

"The one who cut off your hand?"

"Yes, and I was denied retribution, but here she is, like a gift."

No, no, no, Estral thought.

Nyssa glanced from Immerez to Karigan, and back. "You two are a matching pair."

"Yes, the eyepatch. That's curious. I wonder what happened to her eye. I tried to take hers out once, but missed my chance. Greenie, what happened to your eye?"

In response, Karigan, who somehow remained conscious, or had just regained awareness, spat at him.

Immerez calmly wiped his cheek. "You will pay for that, of course, but first . . ." He reached up to look under her eyepatch. She flinched away, but then sagged in what must have been deep exhaustion.

Immerez hastily replaced the patch and stepped back.

"What is it?" Nyssa asked.

He wiped his hand across his brow. "What are your intentions for her?"

Nyssa shrugged. "More lashes. I want to hear her scream some more. Terrik wanted answers, and I aim to get them, and will keep going until she gives them or passes out entirely."

"I believe you should hold off."

"What? Why?"

"Grandmother needs to see her."

"But Grandmother—"

"She'll be back in another day or two. I am telling you, Nyssa, leave this one alone for now."

"What? Not even one more lash?" Nyssa placed her fingertip, coated in Karigan's blood, on Immerez's lips and smeared them. His tongue darted out to taste it, and he and Nyssa kissed long and deep. Her hands delved down the front of his trousers. Soon she had his belt and fly undone and she knelt before him, right there beside Karigan's tortured body. Reed and Burson watched on in bored fascination, but Estral turned away in revulsion, unable to entirely block out the sounds of Immerez's pleasure.

When Nyssa finished, she said, "One more lash? I'll even let you administer it."

"How can I refuse?"

He was buckling his belt by the time Estral dared look again. He accepted Nyssa's whip.

"If Grandmother lets me," he said, "I'll have her hand."

This time, without Burson pressuring her to watch, Estral could turn away, but Karigan's scream curdled into the center of her being.

"You got her side and ribs," Nyssa complained.

"I thought you liked blood and pain."

"I am accustomed to making my subjects last by controlling the blood loss—the ribs bleed too much." Then she added more brightly, "Though they do tend to be more painful. I suppose it's all right since we are doing no more tonight."

"There are other things we can do tonight," Immerez said.

"Yes, and I will train you next time to be more precise. Reed, Burson, see to the prisoner. We're done with her for now."

"You and I," Immerez told Nyssa, "are just beginning, my little bird, my dark Starling."

A STORY

They simply dragged Karigan into the pen and dropped her facedown, her shredded back exposed and oozing.

"She needs help," Estral told the guards. "At least something to clean her wounds."

The guards merely shrugged as they stepped outside and locked the door.

"Please!" Estral pleaded, but they ambled away, removing their pipes from belt pouches and heading outside.

She stood there trembling for a moment, unable to look at Karigan. She closed her eyes and tried to bear up. Studying the remains of those unknown men at the lumber camp had been one thing. Seeing the abused, bloodied body of her friend was another. She steeled herself and looked. The barbs of the whip had carved into the muscles of Karigan's back and left her skin in ribbons. Estral's stomach churned and she fought the bile that rose in her throat. She must be strong. For Karigan.

She licked her lips and knelt beside her. She stroked back the loose, shorn hair from her face, a face that was uncharacteristically pale but for the lurid gash down her cheek.

Reed unexpectedly reappeared with two buckets and some blankets. He opened the pen's door and placed them inside. He pointed at the buckets. "One's for slops, other's for water."

"Thank you. Do you have a mender? Could I at least have bandages?"

He shrugged, locked the door of the pen, and left her, pipe smoke trailing behind him as he stepped outdoors once more.

Estral took the first blanket and covered Karigan from the hips down, leaving her back uncovered for fear that anything that touched it would irritate and adhere to her wounds. The second blanket she folded and, gently lifting Karigan's head, placed it beneath as a pillow. She then nested straw around the rest of her, except where Immerez had scored her side. This bled worst of all.

She removed her shirt from beneath her sweater and wadded it against Karigan's side and held it there to staunch the bleeding.

Karigan stirred, murmured.

"Karigan? Can you hear me?"

"Ears work," she said barely above a whisper. It clearly took effort for her to speak. "As for the rest . . ."

"Yes? Yes?"

"Not so good. Terrible day."

"Yes, it is. I am so sorry. I—I wish I could do something for you." Why didn't they send in a mender? "How can I help?"

After a time, Karigan said, "Story. Tell me . . . story. Take my mind off . . . this."

Estral rubbed tears from her face, tried to control herself for Karigan's sake. If only she'd not made so terrible a decision that morning to enter the Lone Forest. She would never forgive herself.

"Story." Karigan coughed weakly.

Estral took a rattling breath, feeling as if it were the last thing she wanted to do, but for Karigan, who had endured far more, it was such a small request. "All right. I'm trying to think of a good one."

"Make it up."

"What? Make it up?"

"Mmm."

"Uh, all right." She recalled that Karigan had always enjoyed *The Journeys of Gilan Wylloland,* rather light but colorful adventure tales. Making up something similar might work. She cleared her throat. "There once was a sorceress named Myrene who worked for the good of her realm and the order of Givean. A protector named Tiphane was assigned to her as she went about doing her good works, but

Tiphane had a slight problem when it came to Myrene's magic—she was allergic to it."

Karigan gave a breathy laugh.

As Estral went on detailing the adventures of Tiphane and Myrene, she warmed to the telling of how the two friends, chained together in a coracle on the Lake of Souls by the villain, Sedir, attempted to save themselves. The worse their predicament grew as they drifted toward a waterfall, the more they bickered. Finally they managed to resolve their differences and work together to escape and restore their friendship. Sedir came to a satisfying end, as well, in the hands of the souls that haunted the lake's depths.

When Estral concluded, she found Karigan to be asleep and breathing deeply. She pressed her hand to Karigan's brow and frowned. Cool and clammy. Before long she was shivering. Nyssa's workshop wasn't freezing, but it wasn't exactly warm. She decided it would be worse for Karigan to freeze than to have her wounds irritated, so she pulled the blanket to her shoulders, and hoped it would be bearable. She lay down against Karigan, thinking perhaps her body heat would help.

She dozed off, only to be awakened by Karigan mumbling beside her. She turned over to see how she was doing. It was dark; no lamp or candle had been left behind for her to see by. There was only the ambient light of the brazier. She put her hand against Karigan's cheek. Now she was hot, her forehead beaded with sweat.

"Damn."

She scooped some water into her hand and patted Karigan's brow, trying to cool her.

"Why?" Karigan demanded.

"Karigan?"

"Why did he do this to me?"

"You mean Nyssa?"

"The professor. Why . . ." Then she quieted, falling back into her fretful slumber.

The professor. She was remembering something of her sojourn in the future. Estral sat with her knees pulled up to her chest, not sure she could bear much more. Once again she wished she had never left their campsite that morning. She wished she was in Alton's arms, that she had never left him even if it meant never regaining her voice. If she hadn't, Karigan would be all right.

"Dear gods, don't let her die, don't let her die." It became a mantra, a prayer, murmured over and over until she slumped in exhaustion. How would the gods answer? With help, or with silence?

The dark filled every corner, every rafter and crevice of Nyssa's workshop, except where the brazier glowed orange and cast monstrous shadows across the far wall and ceiling. Wind gusted against the building, causing timbers to creak and groan and settle. Karigan murmured incoherently beside her. Emptiness weighed on her, the sense of how hopeless their situation.

She swallowed hard and clasped Karigan's limp, too-warm hand in her own, fighting against the surge of despair and the panic. She was not alone, she told herself fiercely. She must remain strong for Karigan. Must remain calm. But she shook, the despair bearing down on her. The gods had spoken with silence. They had abandoned her, and Karigan, too.

"Meep?"

She looked up and was met by the golden glow of cat eyes. "Mister Whiskers?" Maybe *she* was the one suffering from delirium. "Is that you?"

He came to her purring, his tail crooked.

"How is it you came to be here?" she asked.

A shadow slipped through the slats of the pen behind him, but stayed at a cautious distance, a pair of green eyes gazing at her. A black cat?

"Did you find a mate?" she asked Mister Whiskers.

"Prrrt." He rubbed against her hand.

"Good kitty," she said, running her fingers down the silky fur of his back. "Can you help us? Karigan isn't doing well."

Karigan had grown fitful again beneath the blanket. Mister Whiskers sniffed her head and licked her nose. Then he curled up beside her shoulder and purred.

"Can you become a gryphon and help us escape?" Estral asked.

"Meep."

But he didn't transform. How had he found them? She tried to temper her hope that Mister Whiskers could somehow help. He did not appear about to turn into a gryphon, and even if he did, what then? Could he break the pen open and protect them from the guards? Even if he could, how was she to get Karigan out? She couldn't carry her, and then there were all the other guards and the traps in the forest. Her hope plummeted once more.

"Such a nightmare," she muttered.

"Morphia," Karigan muttered. "Why did the professor . . . ?"

Estral gazed in despair at her friend trapped in nightmares within and without. The black cat, who'd been crouched near Karigan's feet, crept cautiously alongside her body, and up to Mister Whiskers, then extended a paw and smacked him on the head.

"Prrrt?" He backed away, eyes large.

She smacked him again.

Mister Whiskers, getting some message, moved away while his mate curled up in his place. It was clear who was in charge. He then settled on Karigan's other side and transformed. There was barely enough room for the four of them with him in gryphon form, but somehow he squeezed himself between Karigan and the wall, and to Estral's wonder, he extended one of his wings so that it sheltered Karigan.

"Thank you," Estral whispered, deeply moved. She was not as alone as she had been. She wondered what the guards would think when they found a gryphon in the pen with their prisoners.

GHOSTS

Karigan moved through dark dreams and memories of an underground passage, saw a blurred glimpse of Cade's face.

Then it all shifted, and she was standing beside a river. On the opposite bank stood imperious brick mill buildings that were much taller, more imposing, than she remembered. She was talking again to the Rider who wore ancient garb, or rather, he was doing all the talking, as usual.

"I once had to quell the Aeon Iire, myself," he said. "That is a dangerous one and you must be vigilant. The dark ones are very aggressive."

She could not see him quite right, and she realized it was because she was wearing a gauzy veil. It made her feel too hot, but she could not seem to gather the strength to lift it away from her face.

The Rider gazed hard at her. "I see you are not well. This is not good, for the necromancer could have control of the Aeon Iire soon. You must be ready."

So hot. Flames reflected on the surface of the river. The mill buildings were engulfed in fire. The river bank burned, as well, surrounded her and the Rider.

"You really are unwell, aren't you." The Rider produced a cloth and knelt by the water. He dipped it in, and the rings that drifted outward along the surface rippled flame. He wrung it out and then returned to her and lifted her veil, and dabbed her face with the cloth. It was cooling, and the intensity of the fire moderated.

He shook his head. "And, of course, no help from Westrion."

What did the death god have to do with it?

"You need to be well, be strong," the Rider said, dabbing her neck with the cooling cloth. "The living world, and yes, even the spirit world, are depending on you. If the Aeon Iire is broken and the dark ones escape, we are all doomed."

PAST MIDNIGHT

"Doomed."

Estral shuddered out of an uneasy sleep. "What?" she asked Karigan. "What did you say?"

But Karigan did not answer. Then, out of silence, Mister Whiskers and his mate started to emit low growls. Given Mister Whiskers' size, his growl rumbled like an earthquake. Estral looked out to see what could possibly be perturbing them, and in the shadowy dark, discerned a girl standing outside the pen, but little of her features.

"Who are you?" Estral demanded.

"I have your voice," the girl replied.

Estral leaped up and jammed her arm through an opening in the slats to grab at the girl who hopped back and stuck her tongue out.

"Come here!" Estral cried. "Give it back!" If only she could lay her hands on the girl, then she could say the word that Idris had given her.

"It's mine now. You can't have it back. Besides, you get to have kitties, so why shouldn't I have something?" The girl started to skip away, then paused. "And your friend is gonna die. Especially if Nyssa works on her again. Nyssa likes blood." Then she was gone, giggles trailing after her.

Estral banged her hands against the slats and screamed her rage; then she dropped down onto the straw, ready to weep.

"Water . . ."

Estral looked up. "Karigan?"

"Water . . ." came the hoarse whisper.

"Yes, yes, of course."

She filled the ladle with water, but by the time she brought it to Karigan, she was once more asleep or unconscious. Estral placed her wrist against Karigan's brow. Definitely fevered. She patted the water on her face.

When she was done, she said to Mister Whiskers, "Can't you do anything more than provide a protective wing?"

"Meep?"

She sat again ready to give in to her helplessness. *What can I do? Nothing, nothing at all. I am no mender, and Karigan is paying for my mistake. I am worse than useless.*

It then occurred to her maybe there *was* something she could do. It's what Enver would do: sing the healing. He had taught her a little of it as they traveled. Song without words, a resonance and harmony. Feeling the earth beneath her, letting the music rise through her, and then releasing it to the sky and into the burning fire of the stars. She did not know if it actually helped the injured and ill, but it could not hurt, and so she began.

Perhaps it was the influence of the gift Idris had given her seemingly ages ago, but the music swelled within her, filled the pen, and, it seemed to her, escaped to the heavens. Was it her imagination, or did Karigan rest easier? Mister Whiskers and his mate purred. If it had no other effect, perhaps she herself was healing, at least a little.

She was about to begin again when she sensed another presence in the building. If it was that girl—

"Little cousin?" Silver moonlight blossomed from Enver's cupped hands where he stood outside the pen.

"Enver!" Now tears did fall.

"I heard your song," he said. "You have done well."

"Thank the gods you are here. Karigan—it's unspeakable what they did to her."

He unlocked the door, having somehow acquired the key. He knelt beside Karigan, and Mister Whiskers withdrew his wing. He peeled back the blanket. Flaps of skin stuck to rough wool, which caused crusted wounds to bleed again. The moonstone revealed Karigan's back in all its raw detail. Estral glanced away.

"I will never understand," Enver said, "the cruelty your people inflict on one another."

"I don't understand it either, except that it has always been so. Can we move her? Can we—can we leave?"

"What must be done, will be," he replied. He wrapped the blanket around Karigan as he gently lifted her and placed her over his shoulder.

"No carry," she muttered.

"Shh, Galadheon," Enver said. "There is no carrying. It is just a dream."

She quieted.

"Come, little cousin. The gryphons will be our escort."

Estral followed Enver out of the pen, reveling at the sense of freedom she now felt. But they were not really free, not by a long way. She had the presence of mind to grab her coat, and Karigan's, off the table, along with their weapons. She put her coat on and slung Karigan's bonewood over her shoulder. She girded herself with the saber just to make the carrying of everything easier.

Before they stepped outside, Enver extinguished his moonstone, and then they were out the door. The night felt silent, clear and cold. Mister Whiskers and his mate padded alongside them. At some point, she had changed into her gryphon form, a panther with raven wings that shone sleek and glossy in the moonlight. She needed a name. Midnight, Estral thought, would suit.

She wondered how Enver had gotten through the guards to reach Nyssa's workshop, then spied the bodies of Reed and Burson, their throats cut. Smoke still wisped from the bowl of Reed's pipe cupped in his lifeless hand. Enver came across as mild and naive at times, but it was deceptive. She wondered how many more bodies lay in the encampment and woods.

Nyssa's workshop was outside the keep's wall, away from the shacks the people lived in. Perhaps the encampment's inhabitants did not want to hear the screams of her victims. Whatever the case, it worked in their favor.

Enver stepped into the woods, Karigan limp over his shoulder, and there was a shimmer among the trunks of trees—Mist! The mare trotted up to them, moving as silently and sinuously as her name.

"Little cousin," Enver said, "you will ride with the Galadheon. I have arranged a new camp that will show no evidence of our presence."

"What about you?"

"I will follow behind. Mister Whiskers will escort you. His mate will stay with me."

"Midnight."

"It is past midnight."

"I mean, her name. Mister Whiskers' mate. She needs a name."

"Ah, yes. Midnight and I will follow. We must hurry now. It will not be long before your escape is discovered."

He bade Estral mount, and placed Karigan before her. "Do not worry about the reins. Mist knows where to go and where the traps are. Just hold on to the Galadheon. Mist will not let you fall."

Shouting erupted from the vicinity of Nyssa's workshop.

"There will be one awaiting you at the campsite, who will aid you. You must go now."

Before Estral could ask "one what?" Mister Whiskers launched into the air, his great wings carrying him aloft above the trees, and Mist moved off at a trot, then a canter, gliding effortlessly through the woods, so smoothly that Estral hardly felt she was on a horse, at all. While it could have been a struggle to hold on to the dead weight that was Karigan, Mist's subtle adjustments of stride and balance made it less difficult for her.

Like following the Eletian ways, Mist avoided underbrush and low-hanging branches. She ran swiftly, and unhindered, and so Estral was surprised at how quickly they left the forest for the plain beyond. Mist put on a new burst of speed as she navigated the rocky and hummocky terrain with ease.

Estral glanced up and saw the dark shape of Mister Whiskers against a field of stars. Had she been less exhausted from her ordeal and not holding onto her terribly injured friend, her awe would have been far greater. She held Karigan close and prayed she wasn't hurting her badly.

Mist's gait was so gentle that after a time, Estral caught herself dozing off. She shook herself and tightened her hold on Karigan. She had no idea how much time had passed when Mist finally slowed to a trot, then a walk. To her dismay, Mist walked right into a rock—and through it! She felt nothing at all at the passage, just air, and decided it must be an illusion. Both tents were set up in a bowl-like depression in the bedrock, and the horses were hobbled nearby. Condor neighed shrilly as if sensing Karigan's condition, and Mist whickered back. He quieted. Mister Whiskers glided into a graceful, feline landing.

Mist halted, and just as Estral wondered how she was going to get Karigan off without dropping her, Mist knelt onto the ground.

"Let me help," said a woman appearing seemingly out of nowhere. She supported Karigan while Estral dismounted. The two of them, holding Karigan between them, lifted her. "To Enver's tent," the woman said.

They carried Karigan into Enver's tent, which was softly lit with another moonstone. It seemed much bigger inside than it appeared from outside. The woman started to lay Karigan on her back.

"No," Estral said. "She is hurt on her back."

"I see blood on her front."

The stab wound. Estral hoped it had not reopened, but assumed Nyssa had been more than thorough with the iron. "It is worse on her back."

They settled her on soft bedding. In the light, her face was flushed and glistened with sweat. The woman, Estral saw now that she had a moment to breathe, was Eletian.

"I am Nari," the woman said. She carefully pried the blanket from Karigan's wounds, and spoke sharply in Eltish.

Estral could not bear to look again. She had already seen too much. Mister Whiskers, now in his cat form, crouched at Karigan's feet, watching with large eyes. Estral glanced at Nari, who was busy with a bowl of water and cloth, and began to clean the wounds. Estral told her all that had been done to Karigan at the hands of Nyssa so she would know what needed tending.

Nari was silent at first, as if taking it all in; then she said, "I will care for your friend, all her hurts, until Enver returns." She glanced at Estral. "You have been through much, too. Perhaps you will wish to rest? Your tent is ready for you."

Estral nodded, and feeling more weary than she remembered ever having felt before, she stumbled across the campsite and crawled into the tent. Her bedroll had been laid out for her. She removed Karigan's bonewood from her back and unbuckled the swordbelt and placed the saber aside. She crumpled onto her blankets and wept. Wept as she had not since she was a child, wept for what she had done to cause her friend so much harm, wept knowing that she did not deserve forgiveness.

HILLANDER EYES

Immerez did not envy Terrik, who had received the "honor" of explaining to Grandmother, upon her return from Birch's camp, just how two captives had escaped in the night, and about the unrest among her slaves. The three of them walked together toward the curtain wall of the keep.

"What did you say?" Grandmother asked, halting. "Flying cats?"

"Two of my men swear they saw it," Terrik said, looking a little red around his ears. "But it was dark. Some of our sentries, though, looked like they'd been mauled by a catamount."

"But flying?" Grandmother persisted.

No, Immerez did not envy Terrik.

"As for the captives," she said, "Green Riders can touch etherea. The one could have used it to escape."

"No," Immerez replied. "I saw her. She was in no condition. Nyssa had already worked on her. They had to have had outside help."

Grandmother raised her eyebrow at him. "Flying cats?"

He shrugged, and they resumed their slow walk toward the wall's gate. Many more guards were on duty after the previous night's excitement. When it had all happened, he'd been with Nyssa in her chambers. He smiled, thinking of his time with her. Torturer she may be, but when it came to the bed chamber, she preferred to play a submissive role, an arrangement he found more than tolerable.

A gaggle of children came to mob Grandmother and tug on her skirt. They laughed and talked in high-pitched voices, vying for her attention. She patted them on their heads and urged them to go play. They ran off in a pack as though they had not a care in the world.

"About the Greenie," Immerez said as they passed through the gate and into the keep's courtyard, "you met her once in Teligmar. She was the one who deceived us by taking Lady Estora's place. Name's G'ladheon."

"Yes, I recall. She was brave or foolish, that one. She also went on to steal the Silverwood book from us, for all the good it did her king."

It had, Immerez reflected, kept it out of Grandmother's hands, preventing her from doing whatever it was she had intended. "There is something more you should know about the Greenie." They paused in the sunny courtyard, and he told her about the girl's strange mirror eye. It made him shudder to think of it, it was so inhuman, and it did not help that Grandmother looked disturbed.

"Are you sure it was not a false eye of some sort?"

"I don't know what to think," he replied. "I could almost swear images started to form in it. It startled me so much I stopped looking and figured you'd know what it was."

Grandmother gave Terrik a sidelong look. "And we won't find out now, will we."

"We have teams out searching," Terrik said. "They can't have gotten far."

"I hope not for your sake, Captain," Grandmother replied. "There is no telling what that Green Rider saw of our position here, and she'll take it back to her king. Now, about the uprising of my slaves . . ."

They walked in a leisurely way around the exterior of the keep, scattering chickens. People called out greetings to Grandmother. She was much loved by them, and feared. They should fear her, Immerez thought. She would not think twice about sacrificing any one of them, not even the children, if it meant furthering Second Empire's goals.

Terrik told her about the fight that had broken out during Smurn's weekly sermon. "The Greenie started it, really," he said. "She resisted the guards, and it inspired the slaves to rise."

On the backside of the keep, they came to the broken part of the curtain wall and stepped through. Terrik explained how the worst perpetrators had been dealt with, and the rest put back to work.

"It was later," he said, "when one just went absolutely berserk."

They continued on to the dig, where the slaves filed in and out of the underground passage, lugging their baskets. They looked like sleepwalkers to Immerez, uncaring of the world around them, their only goal to simply make it through another day. One had been singled out to stand by the rock pile, burdened with a heavy log borne on his shoulders, his wrists shackled to it. He shifted to keep his balance, his teeth gritted and whole body trembling. His battered face gleamed with sweat.

"If he falls or drops the log before time is up," Terrik told Grandmother, "we'll pull one of the others out of the passage to beat on. He'd been helping some of the weaker ones. Now he'll see where that got him, and teach the others a lesson, too."

"Why didn't you just give him to Nyssa?"

Terrik shrugged. "He's one of the best workers. He wouldn't be of much use after a session with Nyssa. Plus, this way he is a very visible example."

"I approve." She stepped closer to the man. The entirety of his focus appeared to be on staying upright. "He is beat up, Captain, but he looks familiar."

"The guards had to subdue him after he went berserk. No cause that we could figure out, but he sure has some good training."

Immerez looked sharply at Terrik. "What do you mean he has training?"

"He's not just a brawler like we thought, but has some real warrior training. He put three of my men totally out of commission and wounded a pack of others. I can only imagine what he's like on the battlefield."

Immerez gazed more intently at the man. Shaggy hair, a full beard, and bruises and welts on his face partially obscured his features.

"You remember him, Grandmother," Terrik said, "that fellow, Dav Hill."

"Who?"

"The man you got from the groundmites."

"Oh, now I remember. He looks even worse than when he came in. We never did hear his whole story. We should make a point of it now, perhaps."

Immerez stepped right up to the man, grabbed his forelock and lifted to see his face. He looked familiar. Immerez tried to see beyond the grime, the cuts and bruises, the eye swollen shut.

The eyes . . .

Immerez took a step back. The almond-shaped eyes. "He has Hillander eyes."

"He said he was from L'Petrie, on the border with Hillander."

"No," Immerez said. "I mean he has *Hillander* eyes. Grandmother, do you realize who you have here?"

"What are you talking about?"

Immerez laughed. He'd been in chains the last time he'd seen King Zachary. Oh, the irony. The beautiful irony. It took some imagining to see beyond the ravages of captivity, but he knew that face. There was no mistaking it. And Terrik's description of his fighting skill? Only further evidence.

"Grandmother," Immerez said, "this is why that Greenie was poking around here. It has to be. This man is her king."

He'd never seen her look so aghast. "Are you certain?"

"Very certain. He questioned me when they took me prisoner. I also saw quite a lot of his brother when he was hiding out with old Lord Mirwell. Amilton was sharper-featured, but the resemblance is unmistakable."

"This is fortuitous," Grandmother said calmly, though he could see the excitement in her eyes.

"Where . . ." the prisoner began in a voice much weaker than Immerez remembered from when he'd stood before that stern, unbending king. *Look at him now.*

"Where what?" Terrik demanded.

"Where is she? What have you done with her?"

"He means the Greenie," Immerez said.

"Yes," Terrik mused, "he would have seen her brought into the keep yesterday."

"Where is she?"

"She is not your concern," Immerez said. "Nyssa made her bleed. Painfully."

They did not expect the roar from this diminished man, or for him to charge with the log on his shoulders and spin. Terrik had been right—the man was a berserker, and it was Immerez's last thought as the log smashed into him.

Aaron Fiori, known as Arvyn the Bard to his Second Empire captors, sat before the fire in the great hall giving Lala her daily music lesson. It was not easy to concentrate on it, for he'd heard that prisoners had escaped during the night—the "Greenie" and someone else. He knew little more than that, but for rumors of flying cats. He could only guess there had to have been some kind of outside help. From what he'd overheard, Karigan wouldn't have been in any condition to escape under her own power.

He closed his eyes remembering the schoolgirl he'd known, of age with Estral. They were best friends. He was horrified to hear what had been done to her and thanked the gods she had gotten out, however it had happened. He prayed for her recovery, and hoped that someone would come back for him and the king.

He attempted to focus once more on the lesson. He was trying to teach Lala chords to a ballad on his lute. She'd a natural sense of musicality, but she had not yet acquired the dexterity and strength to easily form the chords. Her singing, in contrast, was of the heavens, but of course it was Estral's voice, her nuances of tone and style, with which Lala sang. If he closed his eyes, he would not have been able to tell the two apart. It chilled him every time he heard Lala speak or sing.

Sadly, he was no closer to learning how she had acquired Estral's voice than when he first arrived, and thus could not know how to return it. There was a spell involved, of that he was certain.

"That's very good, Lala," he said when she finished singing and playing a simple lute tune. "It was lovely."

Lala smiled in that odd way of hers and cocked her head as she gazed at him. "I saw the lady whose voice I've got."

Fiori just sat there, digesting her words. As they sank in, he trembled with the effort to remain calm. "What do you mean?"

"Last night. She was with the Greenie Nyssa striped, but she had a new voice, and kitties, too."

It took all he had not to reach out and shake her for more information. Estral had been with Karigan? Why? What had they been doing in the Lone Forest? With terrible clarity, he realized that Karigan had probably been looking for the king, but Estral would have been looking for *him*.

Dear gods, what could she have been thinking?

Worse were the other questions that occurred to him: Was she hurt? Had Nyssa touched her? Had she been the one who escaped with Karigan? He wanted to ask Lala all these questions and more, but a disturbance came into the hall.

"I want him! Let me have him!" Nyssa cried. "I will flay the flesh from him!"

Fiori had never heard her so worked up.

"No, my dear," Grandmother replied in a soothing tone. "He is too great a prize for rash retribution."

No, Fiori thought, guessing who "he" was.

"Varius will mend our dear Immerez, have no fear," Grandmother continued. "I will see to him personally and help as needed. There *will* be punishment, but we must use this opportunity to the fullest."

"What will you do then?"

"There are so many glorious possibilities. I need to meditate on it."

"Arvyn," Lala said, "you aren't paying attention."

He tore his gaze from the two women and gave her some semblance of a smile, a very false smile, and continued the lesson though his mind reeled. Estral had been captured and he knew not her fate, and now they had discovered the king's identity. Now all was lost.

GHOSTS

She stood in a clearing of Blackveil Forest near the remains of Telavalieth, a village once inhabited by Eletians when the land was still Argenthyne. The dark forest crowded in, crushed the ruins beneath root and branch, and mist oozed between tree trunks and formed a low ceiling over the clearing. Tendrils of vegetation hissed as they snaked through the forest, seeking, seeking . . . They had lost Hana to the forest this way, the second member of the expedition to perish, when roots reached out like tentacles and snatched her away.

Blackveil. Why was she in Blackveil again?

The Rider in ancient garb stood with her, cloaked in billowing mist. His gaze wandered around the clearing. "You choose such strange places to meet," he said.

Had she chosen it, or had it chosen her?

Something screeched in the distance. The heavy air dampened her hair and uniform. The forest leaned in, menacing, aggressive, the hiss of seeking roots louder, insistent.

"Still not doing well, are you," the Rider said, peering closely at her. "Well, this cannot wait. None of it can. I wanted to tell you about the marks on the armor and the seals. The marks are the aegis of Westrion, symbols of protection and shielding. And in the case of the seals, of exile and confinement. It is not known to me if the marks are living entities, or if they just seem alive. These things I do not know. They are strong, but not impervious to enemies. Just because you are armored with star steel marked under the aegis of Westrion, doesn't mean you are impervious to harm. You must always be watchful, be on your guard. If the marks die, you will become vulnerable. And of course if the marks on the seals degrade, the danger is to us all."

A long tendril of vegetation slithered across the clearing. She stepped back and more mist wafted into the space between them.

"You must ensure the seals are whole," the Rider continued. "If they fail? The dark ones will be freed, and they can harm the living, and even the dead. This is why you are avatar, to stand in the way of such devastation."

"Siris," she murmured. His name came to her from some lost memory. "Siris Kiltyre."

"That is Captain Kiltyre to you, Rider." There was a hint of a smile on his face.

The mist rolled in thicker than ever and obscured him. The tendrils of vegetation reached for her, wrapped around her ankles, and yanked her off her feet. She fell hard onto her back. She screamed.

FALLING TO PIECES

At Karigan's scream, Estral sat bolt upright from a dead sleep, her heart pounding. She tried to remember where she was, had flashes of a terrible nightmare where she and Karigan had been held captive by Second Empire. She closed her eyes and forced her breathing to calm. When she opened them, she found the woman, Nari, with her head stuck through the tent flaps. Estral blinked at the influx of sunlight.

"Ah, I thought perhaps that last scream might have awakened you," Nari said.

Last scream? Then she remembered what had been done to Karigan. She rubbed eyes crusted with dried tears. Almost afraid to know the answer, she asked, "How is Karigan? Why did she scream?"

"Enver has been tending her. As for the scream? I do not know. Pain and fever alter the mind. But Enver asked me to look in on you. It is not only the Galadheon who was hurt."

"Just bruises," Estral replied. "Nothing like . . . Nothing like Karigan."

In a graceful gesture, Nari put her hand to her heart. Her fingers were long and tapered. "It is not the wounds of the flesh, but the hurt within that injures you. Remember, torture comes in many forms. But here, Enver has instructed that you take a sip of his cordial, and that you eat a . . . a . . . I believe he called it a Dragon Dropping."

Estral smiled despite herself. "Yes."

"He gave me one to eat, and at first I was repulsed by the notion, but the scent intoxicated me, and the taste! I have not been so enlivened in centuries, but perhaps after so long eating cave fungus, it is not a surprise. I do not understand, however, how it is your people, and not Eletians, who have created these Dragon Droppings. That is, if they are truly made by people and not the dragons."

"The cocoa for the chocolate," Estral replied, wondering about Nari's diet of cave fungus, "comes from the very south of the Under Kingdoms. It is grown and harvested there, and turned into chocolate elsewhere."

"Ah. But perhaps you should have these now, or I will talk and ask endless questions and you will not receive succor."

She passed in a flask, of which Estral sniffed the contents. The warmth of spring sunshine seemed to melt over her shoulders, and she smelled the sweetness of balsam needles on the forest floor. The taste on her tongue was cooling, like the breeze off a lake. It sent calming waves down to her toes and to the tips of her fingers.

She took the chocolate though she knew it would not affect her the way it had "enlivened" Nari, but it comforted her anyway. When she was done, she said, "I would like to see Karigan."

Nari nodded. "When you are ready, but do not expect her to be wakeful, or to know you if she is."

Estral frowned. That sounded ominous. When she was ready to face the day, she crawled out of her tent. The sun was high and warm—she had slept into the afternoon. After the horror of the previous night, she was not surprised.

Mister Whiskers lay on his back in the sun, in housecat form, with his paws in the air. Midnight lay decorously curled on a rock, her intense green eyes half-lidded, watching Estral as she walked across the campsite.

Nari beckoned her to Enver's tent, and he met her at the opening. He looked her over as though to ensure she was all right.

"I know you wish to see the Galadheon," he said, "but Nari has prepared you breakfast for after."

"I don't think I could eat," she said. Her stomach was in turmoil.

"You are in need of sustenance to keep up your strength, for the Galadheon's sake, if not your own."

She knew he was right.

"Please be welcome," he said, gesturing to his tent. "The Galadheon walks the dreams of one who is fevered, and may not be aware of your presence. The healing will take time. Nari and I will await you outside."

She nodded, and taking a deep breath, ducked into the tent. It appeared to be larger on the inside than she remembered, the interior a soothing blue. The air was not stuffy, not too warm or too cool. An herby aroma suffused the tent from a steaming bowl of water with unknown leaves steeping in it.

Karigan lay on her stomach with a blanket drawn up to her hips, her back exposed to the air. It had been cleaned up, but for all that, it looked worse with the weals darkened into bruises, and the gaping wounds of scored flesh clearly visible. Estral closed her eyes to steady herself, breathed deeply. When she was ready, she knelt beside Karigan.

"Karigan?" she said softly.

Sweat beaded and dripped down Karigan's face. She did not respond. Estral sat beside her. How had it all gone wrong? All the self-accusations rose up again. She was so tired, too tired for tears.

"Not without you," Karigan murmured.

"What?"

But Karigan did not seem to hear her. She muttered and twitched, caught in some dream ". . . will not leave you. No . . . no . . . *Cade . . .*"

Oh, gods, Estral thought. If she hadn't felt miserable enough for having been the cause of Karigan's hurts, it now appeared Karigan was reliving her loss of Cade.

"Why . . . ?" Karigan whispered. "Why do you do this to me? Let me go back . . . let me go . . ."

Estral could only guess at who the "you" was. Karigan's body tensed, trembled so violently, that Estral took a cloth from the bowl of herby water, wrung it out, and bathed Karigan's face. After a moment, Karigan stopped trembling, though her muscles remained tense.

Estral called on her own childhood, remembering how her mother had sung to her when she was sick, and so now she softly sang a lullaby—not one of the creepy ones that were actually about death or dark creatures coming for naughty children, but a gentle nonsensical tune about a mouse, a cow, and stardust. Karigan's taut muscles relaxed, and as Estral continued to sing, her breathing eased.

From the lullaby, she went into a quiet ballad about the vineyards of Rhovanny and the love between two who harvested the grapes. She sang other songs of a soothing nature, all the ones she could think of until her voice grew hoarse. When she could sing no more, she sat exhausted with her head bowed, her friend still obviously fevered, but peaceful.

Enver entered the tent. "You sing the healing in your own way, little cousin. It was well done, but now you must see to your own strength. Nari awaits you by the fire. I will keep watch over the Galadheon."

"She is going to be all right, isn't she?"

"She is strong."

His answer was not, she thought, as reassuring as it could have been. She left the tent feeling lightheaded. She sat hard before the fire and stared into the flames. Apparently Enver was not concerned about smoke the way Karigan would have been. She was barely aware of Nari placing a warm bowl of porridge in her hand.

"You must eat," Nari said, "so your weakness does not distract Enver from the healing of the Galadheon. You will feel better for some nourishment."

Estral obeyed, eating mechanically. Nuts and dried fruit had been added to the porridge, which proved heartening, and before she knew it, she'd eaten it all. She'd had no food since the previous morning.

Nari held a muffin out to her. "I found this among the food stores. There was but the one. Perhaps you would eat it?"

It was the last cranberry nut muffin from the wife of the innkeeper in the village of Red Rock. It was hard, but she resolved that problem by dunking it in her tea. When she finished eating, she did feel better. Mister Whiskers sauntered over and flopped across her feet. She stroked his cheek, and his purr relaxed her.

Nari watched her from across the fire, and it occurred to Estral to introduce herself properly and ask questions.

"I am Estral Andovian," she said. "I don't think I introduced myself last night. It was a difficult night."

"Yes," Nari said with a nod.

"Thank you for your help, though I was surprised Enver found another Eletian in this territory. How did you come to be here?"

"It is a long story, but just as Enver found the gryphons soaring above as he scouted the land, he found me as I hunted."

"Hunted?"

"Yes. I hunt the aureas slee."

Nari then told her the incredible tale of how she'd been taken from Argenthyne so long ago and held captive by the aureas slee. She only knew the passage of time and the changes in the world from other adult captives the elemental had imprisoned with her.

"The most recent," Nari said, "was the king of your people."

"Who?"

Enver emerged from his tent. "King Zachary. It appears he was taken by the aureas slee shortly after we left Sacor City."

"*What?* How in the hells? Where is he?"

"I do not know," Nari said. "The slee battled the gryphons and carried him off."

Estral half-stood, sat back down, assailed by dozens of thoughts all at once, and none of them good. What would they do? Return to Sacor City? Would that do King Zachary any good? Was he alive? Then she thanked the gods they'd a queen, but how would Estora handle the responsibility of the realm? And she in the precarious position of carrying twins . . . They *needed* King Zachary in this time of unrest, with Second Empire exerting itself.

"Little cousin?" Enver said.

She shook herself. "Yes?"

"It is ill news. I believe it should be withheld from the Galadheon for the time being. I mean, until after she regains her full senses. The blow could be a detriment to her healing."

"Yes, yes, of course." It occurred to her to wonder if he

knew of the feelings between Karigan and Zachary, or if he believed that just the fact it was her king who had been taken by the aureas slee would cause Karigan a setback.

"It was clear," Nari said, as if reading her mind, "that he possessed strong affection for the Galadheon. It was in his demeanor, if not his words."

"Yes," Enver agreed, his expression inscrutable.

Estral looked from Nari to Enver. Eletians *were* perceptive . . . "So, what now? Where do we go from here?" She still had not found her father, and the one who had stolen her voice was in the middle of Second Empire's encampment. And speaking of her voice, it remained hoarse. Was Idris' gift waning?

"I believe it will be for the Galadheon to ascertain," Enver replied, "once she is well enough to receive the news."

"Are we just going to hide until then?"

"We are well hidden. Nari helped put in place an illusion in addition to my wards. It will give us the time we need to regroup and make decisions. And, of course, the Galadheon should not be moved until she is well enough to do so on her own."

Everything, it seemed, had fallen to pieces. She stood and headed back to her tent and crawled beneath her blankets. Sometimes sleeping and forgetting was the best way to cope.

THE SPIRIT AND SOUL OF THE REALM

In the courtyard between the curtain wall and the keep, a platform was erected with a stout post at its center. To this, Second Empire had tied King Zachary. Fiori shifted nervously from one foot to the other. He stood assembled with the other slaves to view their king, he assumed, being humiliated. A larger group of Second Empire's citizenry thronged before the platform like vultures ready to spring on carrion.

Captain Terrik stood on the platform identifying the king, though by now, all knew who he was. Word had spread more rapidly than a Coutre clipper that the slave known as Dav Hill was actually Zachary Davriel Hillander, king of Sacoridia. Oh, how Grandmother had exulted at the discovery.

Zachary did not look very kingly at the moment, but beaten and starved, the ropes all that held him up. His clothing, of some earlier era, was turning to rags, and was stained with blood and grime. His hair hung lank and shaggy, his beard untrimmed. His work digging out Grandmother's special passage, the beatings he'd received, and, Fiori thought, whatever had happened to him before he ever came into Grandmother's clutches, had taken their toll on him.

"I know you are keen to see this man executed," Terrik was saying, "torn to pieces. I am, too, but Grandmother has grander designs for him, so he will not die this day." His pronouncement was met with grumbling. "Be assured," the captain continued, "of what a great blow his capture will be to his people, one which Grandmother means to exploit for the glory of God and the empire."

He was answered with shouts of "God and empire!" and applause.

"Grandmother knows your hatred for this man and all he stands for, and so she is offering you this opportunity to express yourselves. Remember, throw nothing too hard—Grandmother wants him alive." Terrik then jumped off the platform.

The people of Second Empire had come prepared: from toddlers to the elderly, they carried refuse, rotten eggs, entrails, slops, mud. All of these were hurled at the king. He averted his face, but it was the only sign he was conscious of the proceedings. The people jeered, cursed him, and laughed when a particularly well-aimed missile slapped against his body.

Fiori grimaced. Most of the slaves looked away. A few maybe wished they could join in. An older man, the one the king had befriended, grew red in the face and practically quivered with rage. Binning, Fiori recalled, was his name.

Inevitably, someone threw a rock despite the orders not to, and it hit the king's chest with an audible *thunk*.

Oh, no, Fiori thought.

There was a pause, and then like a wave, more rocks were flung at the king.

"Hold!" Terrik cried, but a madness gripped the assembled, and people cast about themselves for rocks and stones. Someone lobbed a large block from the crumbling wall, which, thankfully, fell well short of the king.

Fiori looked desperately about for some miracle, for a flying cat to arrive and rescue the king as Karigan was rumored to have been rescued, but he saw only the bloodlust of the crowd. A stone clipped the king's shoulder.

"No, no, no," Fiori murmured.

But then, to his wonder, Binning broke from the group of slaves and ran—he ran for the platform and jumped up before the guards could stop him, and wrapped his arms around the king to shield him. He was hit in the back with projectiles.

Then, Lorilie Dorran, who had stood fuming beside him, ran. She had been the leader of the Anti-Monarchy Society, otherwise known as the King-Haters, but now she leaped onto the platform to help Binning protect King Zachary. Perhaps she had learned there were worse leaders than he. A moment later, several of her followers among the slaves ran after her to also use their bodies as shields. One by one, the slaves braved the anger of the crowd and their projectiles, creating a veritable wall around the king. When Fiori recovered from his incredulity, he, too, sprinted forward. He was not the last, but he was ashamed not to have been among the first.

A rock grazed his cheek, but he held steady before the platform in the face of the mob, his height making him an excellent target. A mud ball slapped against his chest.

By now, Terrik and his guards were pushing their own people away, forcing them to disperse. If the slaves were expecting to be thanked for preserving Grandmother's special prisoner, they were to be disappointed, for when the crowd was sent away, the guards turned their attention to tearing the slaves away from the king. They were none too gentle, and Binning in particular had to be pried off him.

"You, too, Arvyn," Terrik said. "I expected better of you."

Why? Because as Lala's tutor they treated him better than the other slaves? He shrugged. "He had no way of defending himself and it seemed unfair." Then, with daring, he added, "And he is still my king."

Terrik shoved him hard in the direction of the keep before turning back to the platform. Fiori glanced over his shoulder to see the king slumped at the post, fresh blood dripping from his face onto his shirt. Fiori wondered if there'd been one miracle, might there be another? He would send prayers to the gods, fervent prayers.

His only hope was that Karigan could somehow bring help. He'd heard something of what had been done to her, so she could not be in much of a condition to do anything herself. Still, she had escaped. Had been rescued. If they, whoever they were, including a flying cat, apparently, could rescue her, surely they could help the king. He feared that if King Zachary remained in Second Empire's clutches much longer, if he was subjected to whatever twisted designs

Grandmother intended, it would be a greater blow than Sacoridia could withstand, for the king was the realm's spirit and its soul.

"You are disgusting."

Nyssa's voice came distantly to Zachary, through a gray haze. He'd ceased caring about his surroundings, how he smelled, so caught in the miasma of pain and exhaustion was he. Until the shock of frigid water hit him. It stole his breath.

"Again," Nyssa said.

He opened his one eye that was not swollen shut just in time for another bucketful of water to splash over him. He shivered uncontrollably. There'd been a crowd watching, he recalled, but the courtyard was now quiet, any onlookers pushed well back.

"Cut the rags off," Nyssa ordered.

Guards came at him with bared knives and did just that. Trussed to the post, there was little he could do. The frigid air prickled his skin.

"Another bucket," Nyssa said.

He braced himself, but gasped as the icy water cascaded over him. When he regained his breath, he saw Nyssa giving him a thorough look over.

"You've seen better days, haven't you, King Zachary. Your ribs are jutting out." Her gaze dropped. "By all accounts, your wife must be pleased with what you bring to the bed chamber. I bet she misses it. Too bad you are not the sort of man I am interested in." Her gaze lingered downward, and he was aware of mockery and hooting coming from the remaining onlookers. "I'd be more interested in cutting off what you've got, but Grandmother says no."

"Cut him! Cut him!" the onlookers cried.

She smiled, made some joke, then told him, "I suppose Grandmother has her reasons why I can't, and it is not my place to question her."

He fought the chills, but they were such a force they could not be repressed. They came out in a large shudder.

Nyssa laughed. "A little cold, eh? Well, we're not finished. I won't have you stinking up my workshop."

She made some signal with her hand, and guards came forward with more buckets full of sudsy water, scrub brushes in hand. They were not gentle. He was thoroughly washed and rinsed, no doubt to the great entertainment of Nyssa and the watchers. There was nothing he could do to combat it, so he endured the humiliation.

When the guards dumped a final rinse on him, Nyssa stepped up again. "Much better. All rosy and pink all over. Well, where you aren't black and blue."

At her order, the guards untied him from the post and threw a blanket over his shoulders. He thanked the gods and wrapped himself in it. They marched him beyond the curtain wall, a ways into the woods, to a simple wooden building he presumed to be Nyssa's "workshop."

They unceremoniously forced him onto a table where he was strapped down with leather bindings, even his head. He struggled, but the leather was snug. To his relief, they covered him with the blanket.

Nyssa leaned over him so that they were nearly nose-to-nose. He tried to turn his face away, but the strap around his forehead prevented him. "Wouldn't want you to freeze before Grandmother gets here, would we?" she said. "Sadly, I am not to touch you until she says so. I look forward to cutting you, which will sorely disappoint your wife and whoever else you lie with. That Greenie, perhaps? That was quite a reaction you had for so lowly a servant as a messenger. That's why you acted up, isn't it? Because of her?"

He fisted his hands. Refused to speak. He would not let her get to him.

She chuckled. "So determined you are not to give me satisfaction. How admirable. You are an honorable man, King Zachary. I like honorable men—they are so much more pleasing to break. You see, I *will* get satisfaction, even if I must wait. In the meantime, Grandmother will not begrudge me a little blood."

She peeled his blanket away to reveal his chest. "I see your old arrow wound healed well enough. Yes, I heard about that. By the time all is well and done, you will be wishing that assassin had proved successful." She then walked away, humming. He could not see what she was up to. When she returned, she showed him a whip with multiple thongs. She separated one from the others. The leather appeared to be stiff with crusted blood. She showed him the knot at the end of the thing, twisted with wire so the ends created sharp barbs. Barbs that had clots of skin adhering to them.

"This has tasted the blood of your Greenie."

He started to bellow his rage, but it turned to a sharp cry of surprise and pain as she jabbed the barb into his chest and ripped it across and through his nipple. She stepped back to admire her handiwork, then to his revulsion, dipped her finger in the blood that welled up from the wound, and tasted it.

"This pleases me," she said. "Is it not interesting how closely aligned pain and pleasure are? I cannot say I have tasted royal blood before. Your Greenie's was fine, too."

He strained against the straps.

"Yes, she is more than a mere messenger to you, isn't she. Grandmother will find that interesting. Too bad your Greenie is gone."

"Gone?" he whispered.

She nodded and dropped something on his chest. "Something for you to remember her by."

It looked like . . . Looked like brown braided hair. Karigan's? What had they done to her? The rumors he'd heard of an intrusion on the encampment must have been a wishful dream—he'd been beaten into a stupor, then made to carry that log on his shoulders, and there was no accounting of what was real and what was not. Had they killed her?

"No . . ."

"No, what?"

"What did you do with her? Where is she?"

Nyssa shrugged. "Does it matter? Grandmother will be here soon and you won't care about anything, not even your Greenie. Now, I am going to go check on my guards. You are a special prize, and there is no way anyone is going to get past our safeguards. No one will rescue you. You are ours to do with as we wish. You may be a king, but here you have no power. You are nothing."

She turned and left him then, and as far as he knew, he was alone inside the building. The sting of the wound across his chest was nothing compared to the other abuses he'd received, but he didn't care about himself. They could do whatever they wanted to him. What burned him inside was his rage, rage for whatever had been done to Karigan.

He fought his restraints anew, but they only seemed to tighten with his struggles. He sighed and relaxed. Karigan's braid, if it was really hers, and he saw no reason for Nyssa to have lied about it, rose and fell on his chest with his breaths. How often had he wanted to stroke that long, brown hair . . . He closed his eyes, pictured himself doing just that, drawing her to him in a kiss . . . The pleasant vision gave way to imagining the many ways he'd murder Nyssa, how he'd defeat Second Empire, how he'd obliterate not only this encampment, but all of them so his realm could remain at peace.

Currently he was in no position to do anything. He would preserve his thwarted rage, use it when opportunity presented itself. If it ever did.

Voices talked over him. He must have drifted off, exhausted as he was in spirit and body. He did not open his eyes or move. Let them believe he was still asleep.

"Why didn't you tell me about the braid?" Grandmother asked.

"I forgot about it," Nyssa replied, "after everything happened."

"You know I find such things useful when I work with etherea. Do not forget again."

"I'm sorry, Grandmother. I won't."

"Of course you won't, dear."

How would Grandmother find Karigan's braid useful? Did it mean that Karigan had escaped, after all? If she were dead, what use could the braid possibly be? No, she had to be alive. He must cling to that hope.

"He is feigning sleep," Grandmother said. "I can tell. Young man, open your eyes."

He looked up at the women who stood on either side of the table.

"Well, well," Grandmother said. "The great king of Sacoridia, the warrior who has fought us on the border, does not look so impressive at the moment. No armor, no guards, no sword. You are just flesh and blood, after all, aren't you."

"He doesn't talk much," Nyssa said.

"That will change over time," Grandmother replied. "Do you know I had to undo the entire scarf I made for Lala in the fall just so I had enough yarn to work on him?"

Scarf? Yarn? Then Zachary remembered that Grandmother somehow worked her magic into yarn, made spells of the knots she tied. The opening and closing of a door announced the arrival of someone else.

"There you are, Lala," Grandmother said. "You will help me with the knots."

A girl appeared in his peripheral vision, her expression neutral. Grandmother let this girl help with—with whatever she was going to do to him?

"Young man, I recommend you open your mouth."

He did not.

"Now don't be ridiculous and fight us on this. It is for your own good so you don't bite off your tongue, and so we don't have to listen to your screams all night."

"I wouldn't mind it," Nyssa said.

"I know, dear, but other people like to get their sleep."

When he failed to obey, Nyssa, who seemed unnaturally strong for her size, forced his jaw open. Grandmother dropped a thick strip of leather between his teeth to bite on. When she swept his blanket off and she and the girl started tying knots and placing them on his body, he understood why.

A VISION OF THE AVATAR

As Grandmother walked away from the king, his body arched in pain—as much as the restraints permitted, at any rate—she reflected it was a job well done. Lala's work was nearly the equal of her own. Nyssa had retired for the evening to sit with Immerez, who was still recovering from the blow he'd received from the king, and now Grandmother would go to her supper. She barely nodded to the guards who surrounded the workshop. They would check on the king periodically through the night to ensure his heart had not stopped, or he'd gone into shock, always a danger with spells of this strength.

She walked absently toward the keep with the braid grasped in her hand. Lala, who'd been following her, ran off to play with some children. The king would suffer this night, and she acknowledged it was all little more than retribution for the pain he had caused her people. In the morning, she would rearrange the knots, which would alter the intensity and location of the sensation that his blood was burning through his body. There were other things she had in mind for him, as well, but for the moment, seeing him in excruciating pain was quite satisfying.

Now the braid, that might help her answer a question about the Greenie and her eye. A mirror, Immerez had described it. She was curious, very curious, but that could all wait until she had some food in her stomach.

The previous night, upon learning they'd the king in their midst, they'd slain a bull for a celebratory feast. Some of the leftover meat and preserved vegetables had been served in a fine stew this evening. Grandmother, her stomach warm and full, sat before the hearth thinking in pleasure how it was *she* who was comfortable and well-fed this time, and not the king. The guards brought her periodic updates. Yes, he was still in the throes of agonizing pain. No savory stew for him tonight, no soft bed, only pain. Retribution was a fine thing.

She now studied the braid of hair in her hand, tied off at both ends so it would not unravel. It was really a rich gold-brown, she now saw, depending on the light. She pried out a few strands, carefully so they did not snap. Then she removed a length of undyed yarn from her pouch and started tying knots around the hair, knots of seeking, knots of learning.

Karigan G'ladheon. That was the Greenie's name, according to Immerez, and she had been a concern to Weldon Spurlock, Grandmother's predecessor. "G'ladheon," derived from the Arcosian word for "betrayer," *galadheon.* Hadriax el Fex, who had been Mornhavon the Great's best friend and right hand, had taken the word as his name after he betrayed the empire by giving himself up to the Sacoridians during the Long War. Had Mornhavon's servants killed Hadriax before he gave away the empire's secrets, they would not be contending with his descendent now, and Sacoridia would be a much different place.

Likewise, they could have dealt with Karigan G'ladheon back at Teligmar, but Immerez's camp had been attacked by a phalanx of king's Weapons seeking Lady Estora, and the Greenie went on to prevent Second Empire from using the book of Theanduris Silverwood to destroy the D'Yer Wall. It seemed they were thwarted at every turn.

Where was Karigan G'ladheon now? Why did she have a mirror eye? What did it mean?

The others had been ordered to stay away so she could pour all her focus into the spell. When she was done, she gazed at her handiwork. The knots were misshapen, ungainly things, and rough compared to the delicate hairs. With one more request for the information she desired, she tossed it into the fire. The flames flared as they consumed the yarn, and she waited.

* * *

Very rarely did the visions come instantly, and this case was no different, but she remained patient. The fire kept her warm, and she sipped a cup of tea Sarat had set beside her. Soon, her patience was rewarded.

An image formed among the flames, of a young woman lying on her stomach, her back bare and ravaged. Grandmother viewed Nyssa's work with admiration. Sweat glistened on the young woman's skin. She appeared to be asleep or unconscious, neither unexpected from the trauma she'd endured. What Grandmother really wanted to see, however, was her eye, but she could only see one eye, and it was closed.

The vision rippled away into another and she found herself in an unusual setting, and she became cool as though someone blocked the fire. The lighting was sepulchral and glanced off hard stone and marble surfaces. As the vision clarified, she realized she was surrounded by sarcophagi. She was in a tomb, and by the statuary and other adornment, she knew this had to be the *royal* tombs, which lay beneath the castle in Sacor City.

Oddly, Karigan G'ladheon stood in an empty sarcophagus. Her form was . . . ghostly, and it appeared she was listening to something or someone Grandmother could not see or hear. She willed the vision to close in on the Green Rider. Such intention took great force of concentration, and even then, the power behind the spell could very well refuse her.

Her will prevailed, however, and the image of the Greenie grew closer, and Grandmother tried to steer around so she could see her face. The Rider was still ghostly, and her eye, the one Grandmother wanted to see, was covered by a patch. It was a disappointment, but it confirmed there was *something* about the eye that required concealment.

As she gazed at the Rider's face, such a young face, she thought, it suddenly transformed. The young woman who stood before Grandmother was no longer a Green Rider, but a knight clad in gleaming armor, with a winged helm, and a lance and shield in her hands. Symbols moved across the steel as though alive. Grandmother had seen a version of this image before. It was the dark angel, the avatar of the god of death. The figure raised the helm's visor, and there was the face of the Green Rider, her visage cold and dispassionate, her mirror eye revealed. It flashed, blinding Grandmother, and then the vision was gone.

Grandmother rocked back in her chair in surprise, and rubbed her eyes. When she recovered, she clapped and laughed.

Her people gathered around her, alarmed. "What is it, Grandmother?" Min asked.

Casting spells and seeking visions could be taxing, but Grandmother only felt elated. She stood as though she were a much younger woman and clapped again.

"Not only do we have the king," she said, "but I know who the death god's avatar is!"

"It's a *who*?" Min asked. "And not a *what*?"

"My dear, it has to be a who to function on the Earthly plane. We had her here, and we will have her back."

"The Greenie or her friend?"

"The Greenie, Min, the Greenie."

Grandmother could have danced. The Green Rider would be compelled to come back, drawn by two separate, but potent, forces. The first was her king. As soon as she was able, she would attempt to rescue him again no matter the peril, just as she had the Lady Estora back in Teligmar. If that was not enough, there was the second compulsion, the Aeon Iire. She would have to come in her avatar form. Either way, Grandmother and Second Empire would have her, her and that curious mirror eye.

She stooped and picked up the braid that had slipped from her lap when she stood. Nyssa had not known how fortuitous it was that she cut off Karigan G'ladheon's braid. Not only had it given Grandmother the vision, but she had another use for it.

"Lala!" she called.

The girl ran to her from the kitchen.

"Where is my basket? Would you bring it to me, please?"

"Yes'm."

Grandmother sat while Lala ran off, jubilant, almost giddy. Everything was falling into place for her people. She had the Sacoridian king, and soon she'd control the death god's avatar, hence the dead. Lala soon skipped back into the great hall with the basket and set it at Grandmother's feet.

Grandmother pulled out her great working. Not only had she allowed it to absorb the blood of Birch's slave girl, but it seemed to have taken years from Grandmother, as well, just in its making. Her hair had grown whiter, her hips and hands more arthritic. She had slowed down perceptibly.

But it was all worth it, she thought, as she began to weave strands of Karigan G'ladheon's hair into the net that would trap her.

GHOSTS

She gazed at the high king's tomb. Lamplight glowed on the marble features of the effigy of King Zachary carved on the lid of the sarcophagus. She stood in its companion, the queen's sarcophagus. It had no lid.

The sculptural effigy of the king was even more lifelike than she remembered, almost as though if she touched it, she would feel his skin and not cold marble. There was something about the king, something she knew, and though she wrestled with herself in an attempt to remember it, she could not. She was so tired.

I just want to go to bed.

"This is familiar," a man said.

She turned to find Siris Kiltyre leaning against a column. Shadows shrank and enlarged in an exaggerated dance against the walls and ceiling. It *was* familiar.

"You acted as Westrion's avatar for the first time in these tombs," he said. "Reluctantly, of course, though I can't say I blame you. You did come around and do a great service for the realm of the living."

She shook her head at memories that buzzed around it like flies. Salvistar appearing, she riding him, sending spirits of the dead to rest. How could the memories be real? They were . . . ridiculous.

"Overwhelming, isn't it? Your memory of it was put out of reach. It is not an easy concept for any living mortal to assimilate, but now it must be made more accessible to you."

She'd ridden Salvistar into a deep pit and, in its very

depths, mended a seal that kept dark entities at bay. Had they escaped, the chaos would have destroyed the living world.

"Yes," Siris Kiltyre said, "in these tombs there is an access point to a realm beyond death, to the darkest realms of existence, and the iire, the seal, imprisons the dark entities. The Aeon Iire is now in danger. If it is broken, all hells will break loose, and this is no euphemism."

She wiped her hand across her brow. These dreams, they were so tiring. Something bad had happened to her in the waking world. When she was sick, her dreams became stranger than usual, more real somehow.

Siris Kiltyre took a step toward her. "You are still unwell, I know, but this is no mere dream. You must remember. You must remember what I've said about the armor, and about how spirits will try to trick you."

It took everything she had to speak. "What if *you* are tricking me?"

"Ah," he said, brightening, "now you are thinking. That is good."

Then he vanished, and all fell into darkness.

STUBBORN

Estral had slept through to the next morning. Nari, she learned, had gone to soak in a nearby hot spring. Estral was eager to make use of it herself, to wash away the darkness of her captivity, but first, Enver wished to speak to her.

"Is it Karigan?" she asked anxiously. "Is she worse?"

A line of concern creased his brow. "Her cough has subsided, which is good, but she is not well. There may be some corruption of one or more of the wounds, but I am watching closely. Of course, I speak only of the physical wounds."

"Just the physical . . ." Estral murmured. She closed her eyes to steady herself. If what she had experienced in Nyssa's workshop had so traumatized her, she could only guess how it would be for Karigan, who had been the object of the physical torture.

"The wounds of her body, and those of the mind, will take time to heal, and both will leave scars."

"That does not sound good."

"No, it is not good, which is why I am reassessing how we should proceed."

"I thought you didn't wish to move her."

"I do not plan to." He gazed steadily at her. "I intend that you ride Mist to the encampment of Captain Treman and report to him what we know of the Lone Forest, and of our predicament, and what Nari told us about the king. It may be he can send some aid, maybe even the mender who may have different herb lore that will help the Galadheon."

"I won't leave her," Estral said. "I can't. Even on Mist, that journey would take over a week."

"It is best that Captain Treman hears from one of his own people who is also held with esteem for her status in her realm. Nari and I will keep watch on the Galadheon. My healing skills are more developed than Nari's, but I believe hers exceed yours."

Estral scowled. It was all very logical, but her feelings about the situation were not. "I—" she began; then they both glanced in the same direction at the same time. Karigan, wrapped in a blanket, was dragging herself out of Enver's tent and across the ground.

"Galadheon!" Enver cried.

"Karigan!"

Karigan ignored them and kept crawling. Enver was beside her before Estral could even react.

"Galadheon," he said, "you will reopen your wounds."

She kept crawling forward with single-minded intent until he grasped her shoulder.

"Karigan," Estral demanded, "what in the hells are you doing?"

It was unclear whether Karigan was really aware of them. Her feverish gaze was focused straight ahead. "I need to . . ." she murmured.

Estral and Enver exchanged glances.

"Need to go back," Karigan said.

Estral knelt in front of her. "What are you talking about?"

Sweat dripped down Karigan's brow, and she looked up at Estral, registering recognition. "Back to the forest. I need to go back."

"Why?" Estral asked. "You need to rest."

Karigan tried to struggle out of Enver's grasp and looked almost angry. "I need to get the king."

Estral glanced at Enver. "She's clearly delirious."

"Galadheon, you must return to the tent, recuperate," Enver said in his gentle voice.

"No." She struggled against the hold he had on her, then lay on her stomach, exhausted. "No, no, no. I am not delirious." Her eye started to close. She blinked, fighting the exhaustion.

Enver gathered her into his arms, handling her delicately as if she were very fragile.

"No, no, no," she murmured. She pounded on his chest, but it was more like a feeble pat. Then she cried out in pain as he shifted her.

"I am sorry," he said.

Estral followed him into the tent and watched as he settled Karigan back onto her bedding. When she lay on her stomach once again, she fell limp as one dead. The helpless feeling washed over Estral again, and she wanted to weep.

"I am not delirious," Karigan insisted in a weak voice. "They have the king. I saw him, and Lord Fiori, too."

Stricken, Estral could only gape.

"Must free the king," Karigan murmured.

"Galadheon, you must rest; then we can discuss it, yes?"

With a surge of strength that defied rationality, Karigan pushed herself up. "Don't placate me. Must get him out of there." Then she collapsed into the blankets and whispered, "I can't leave him, too."

Estral stumbled outside. Her father *and* the king in Second Empire's hands? And Karigan injured and feverish, thinking she could crawl into the Lone Forest and rescue them. In her mind, she'd left Cade behind and she could not do it again. Estral slowly sat down by the fire. Mister Whiskers came over and rubbed against her elbow.

Nari soon appeared, took one look at her, and asked, "What is wrong?"

"Karigan says Second Empire has the king and my father."

Nari looked off into the distance and murmured, "He is no longer with Slee, then."

Enver emerged from his tent. Estral twisted around to face him. "She wasn't delirious, was she? She really saw my father. And the king."

"No, not delirious," Enver said.

She didn't tell me they were there while we were being held, Estral thought, *so Nyssa couldn't get it out of me in case Second Empire was ignorant of who they had.* She shuddered.

"What are we going to do? We can't just leave them there in the hands of Second Empire."

"I think not," Enver agreed.

Estral was relieved. As an Eletian, Enver had no allegiance to Sacoridia's king. He could say it was not part of his mission, that he was not required to get involved. He could have abandoned Estral to do as she would, and continued on his journey to find the p'ehdrose.

"Thank you," she said, with a quaver in her voice.

"I would not leave you and the Galadheon to face this alone," he replied, "nor would my prince wish it of me."

"Nor my queen of me," Nari said, "were she still of this Earth. She showed the Galadheon favor."

Laurelyn the Moondreamer, Estral thought with a thrill, despite the circumstances.

"We must deliberate," Enver said. "Make a plan."

"Not without me!" Karigan cried from the tent.

Enver raised his eyebrows, said something in Eltish, then added in consternation, "She was asleep when I left her."

"It is *Karigan*," Estral said. "Too stubborn for her own good."

"Yes. I see that very clearly."

"I'll crawl back out there if I have to," Karigan said.

Deciding that it was better to accede to her demand rather than risk her reopening her wounds, Estral, Enver, and Nari filed into the tent, followed by Mister Whiskers and Midnight, so they could plan in Karigan's presence. The tent seemed to expand to accommodate them all as they sat beside her.

"The question is," Estral said, "does Second Empire know who they've got? And if so, do they realize we know, too?"

"When I saw them," Karigan murmured tiredly, "they were not in immediate duress. Neither of them. If Second Empire had known who either of them were, they'd have been treating them much differently."

"But what if they *do* know?" Estral said. "They would expect a rescue attempt."

"We should err on the side of caution," Enver said, "and assume they are expecting our return."

"Yes," Karigan agreed, "on guard. Hunting us."

"Even if they do not expect us," Enver continued, "they will not be pleased someone got through their defenses and successfully effected a rescue. They will have already bolstered their guard."

"So what do we do?" Estral asked. "Fly in on winged cats?" Mister Whiskers and Midnight gazed at her with big eyes. "I'm kidding," she told them.

"I go," Karigan said.

They all glanced at her.

"What—?" Estral began.

"My ability."

"Galadheon," Enver said, "your condition."

"You have a better idea?" she demanded.

"What is the Galadheon's ability?" Nari asked.

When Enver did not answer immediately, Karigan said, "I can fade out, sneak in there, in the dark."

"You cannot even walk," Enver said.

"Not today," she conceded. "Tomorrow."

Enver once again raised his eyebrows.

"Stubborn, remember?" Estral said.

"Even if you can walk tomorrow," Enver said, "your strength and stamina will be depleted from the fever alone. Your wounds could reopen. We must consider another way."

"The king is more important than me, than my . . . comfort," Karigan replied. "What Second Empire would do to him if they found out who he was . . . ?" She shuddered.

"It is not just your comfort," Enver replied, "but your ability to do this thing."

"I will do what I have to. The king in Second Empire's hands would be devastating to the realm. We need him. We could be defeated without him."

"I understand that, Galadheon, but I think you fail to understand your own importance."

"Not important." Her voice sounded as though she was beginning to drift off.

Estral gazed down at her friend, not at the raw wounds on her back, but at her flushed face, the one long tendril of hair trailing down her cheek. Karigan had spoken of what the king meant to the realm, but how much of it was what he meant to her? No, Estral was sure she would be thinking mostly of the realm, and in that regard, she was absolutely right. If Second Empire knew what it had, it would thoroughly capitalize on it to demoralize its enemy and further its chances of defeating Sacoridia. Estral, more than anything, wanted to rescue her father, but Karigan was in no condition to stand, much less go on such a mission.

"Karigan," she said, "under normal circumstances, when you are well, your ability drains you. I don't mean to be cruel, but right now, you'd be a liability to any rescue attempt."

A ponderous silence fell over them once again. There was only the rustle of the tent walls as a breeze caressed them, and the anxious purr of Mister Whiskers. She thought, perhaps, Karigan had finally fallen asleep. When Karigan spoke, it startled her.

"Then you had better come up with a way to help me recover. And fast."

Enver and Nari glanced at one another, and Midnight walked up to Karigan's face and swatted her head.

She cracked her eye open at the cat. "What was that for?"

"I believe," Enver said, "that Midnight has spoken for us all."

Karigan sighed. "Please, just help me."

"We are doing our best," Enver said, "both Nari and me. Neither of us are what you would call a true healer like your Rider Ben, or even my father. The etherea does not work in that way for us."

"Please . . ." Karigan said softly, and this time she did seem to drift off for real, her breaths deepening, her muscles relaxing.

Estral, Enver, and Nari retreated from the tent and stood by the campfire.

"I knew the Galadheon was a determined person," Enver said. "Lhean told me as much, but he may have understated it."

"Short of tying her down," Estral said, "she won't give up." All of Karigan's adventures, it seemed, had only conspired to make her more headstrong, rather than less.

"Then we must do what we are able for her," Nari said.

"Or come up with a better plan in the meantime," Enver said.

SINGING THE HEALING

Monsters, tombs, a Rider in ancient garb, torture, and Blackveil cycled through Karigan's dreams. Her brief interludes of waking were no less nightmarish, her consciousness overlain by shadows and dominated by pain. In bouts of panic, she felt that she must get up, get up and—and do *something. King Zachary.* She had to get him away from Second Empire. Then she'd fall into a restless sleep again with dreams full of blood and disaster, Nyssa and her whip of vipers.

Periodically, songs of peace would roll over her, and all the troubling visions, and even the pain, would dissipate for a time. She was quite certain the words were Eltish, and yet she seemed to understand, or perhaps she merely dreamed it all.

From the bones of the earth beneath,
Along the rivers that flow
through root, branch, and leaf,
Rising into the air of the sky,
Into the cleansing fire of the stars . . .

She imagined some power of the Earth rising through her, building as it rushed through her blood and continued onward into the heavens. It made her feel lighter, until Nyssa reappeared and the lash fell once again.

She cried out and jerked awake. As before, everything was a hazy veil around her. The pain washed over her anew. What was the hour? The tent walls were bright enough that it was daytime. The same day as her earlier awakening? Or, a day later? The thought that it could be a day later brought on the panic and she tried to rise.

"Easy, Galadheon," Enver said. He was sitting beside her.

"How much time have I lost? Since my last awakening?"

"It has been only a few hours."

Could he be lying? Telling her that just to placate her?

He placed his hand against her forehead, and then her cheek. His touch was cool and the tension went out of her muscles.

"You should drink," he said, "especially with the fever."

He helped her sip from his flask of cordial, which cooled her without chilling her; then he switched to water. It was not easy to drink, she just did not feel like it. He encouraged her with quiet words.

"I need to go to the Lone Forest," she said.

"I know. Resupplying your body with fluids is important for you to be able to do so."

The urgency was building within her once again. "Yes, but—"

"Galadheon, it has not even been two full turnings of the Earth." He described how he'd been treating her with oils, herbs, and salves to fight corruption of the wounds, and to ease her pain. He said, "We have been singing the healing, even Lady Estral, whose voice has begun to deteriorate."

"Oh, no," Karigan murmured.

"You must come to an accord with the healing of your body. You will be weak for a time, and it may be that, due to the deep injuries to your back, you will find it difficult to do all you did before."

Her sword work. "Permanently?"

"I do not know. You are young and in otherwise good health. It could be you will find new ways of completing old tasks."

He was being very careful in his wording, which made it all somehow worse. The darkness in her mind only grew deeper, and the only piece of sanity she could cling to, to keep herself from going under, was her need to return to the Lone Forest and retrieve both King Zachary and Lord Fiori. She would do it if it was the last thing she ever did.

She must have dozed off, for Enver was suddenly gone. The heaviness, the darkness, descended on her once again. All seemed so bleak and gray, but then soft footfalls padded alongside her and a soft furry body plopped beside her face and started purring.

"Hello, Whiskers," she murmured.

His fur smelled of the cold air and a sunny rock, and of an indefinable cat spice. It hurt to lift her hand and reach up to pet him, but when she did so, she was rewarded with even louder purrs.

She'd been hurt before, injuries inflicted during clashes with enemies, but never had they been so systematically applied. She'd been made to feel as helpless as possible, unable to defend herself. Nyssa ensured she'd had no control over the situation. Though Nyssa had demanded information, Karigan knew it was only a pretense. She'd seen the look in Nyssa's eyes, that she enjoyed the torture for the power she held over others. She liked inflicting pain just for the sake of it.

I did not give away the king's presence, Karigan tried to tell herself, but Nyssa's voice came into her head, *I did not care.* Any illusion that Karigan had maintained some vestige of control by withholding information evaporated. A small cry passed her lips, and Mister Whiskers' purrs grew louder, more resonant. He licked the sweat from her brow with his rough tongue, then settled down again next to her face. More soft footfalls entered the tent, and a small warm body snuggled against her leg. Midnight added her purr to Mister Whiskers', and perhaps it was their own form of singing the healing. While they were with her, she did not lapse into dreadful memories of Nyssa and her whip.

When Nyssa did return to Karigan's dreams, it was King Zachary who was chained to the beam. Only, King Zachary was Cade. She tried to reach for him, crawl to him, but he was always too far away and she was held back by a web of knotted yarn that burned where it touched her. She had nothing with which to slash it.

King Zachary, with Cade's face, turned to look at her. "You left me behind."

Nyssa's lash fell.

She awakened with a gasp. Sweat dripped into her eye and stung.

"Karigan?" This time it was Estral who sat beside her, her journal and pen in hand. Enver's muna'riel emitted a gentle glow for her to see by. It was night. "Bad dream, eh?"

"One of many. Sometimes I can't tell what's real and what's not."

"How are you feeling otherwise?" Estral asked. "Any, er, improvement?"

"Hard to say." Her whole body was still blanketed by pain, but she did feel slightly more clear-headed.

"Well, Enver is out doing whatever it is that he does, and he instructed me to make sure you drink, and to offer you some broth. Do you think you could handle that?"

"Don't know."

Estral gave her a skin of water to drink from, and stepped out to retrieve the broth. When she returned, she said, "Enver thinks this will help you regain your strength."

Karigan sniffed the contents of the mug Estral presented. It did not smell disagreeable.

"The gryphons went hunting and brought back a wild goose. They shared."

A sign of spring, Karigan thought, if geese were to be found in the north. She raised herself on her elbows and stirred the broth with the spoon Estral provided. Chunks of meat swirled in the liquid. When a spoonful cooled enough to be tasted, she determined that, under different circumstances, she'd probably drink it right down. After a few spoonfuls, she pushed the mug aside and rested.

"Can't you please try to eat more?" Estral asked.

"Not right now."

"If you don't try, you won't regain your strength to help the king and my father."

"I'll try again later." When she gazed up at her friend, she saw that her eyes had dark circles beneath them and that there were bruises on her face. Her expression was drawn with worry. "Truly, I'll try again."

Estral nodded slowly. "Do you promise?"

"Yes." It was tiring just to talk, but she asked, "Are you doing all right?"

Estral blinked in surprise. "You're asking *me*?"

"Yes."

Estral placed her face in her hands as if to weep, but then she looked back up and folded them on her lap. "I am out of tears, completely dried up."

"Perhaps you need broth, as well."

"Karigan G'ladheon, I wish, sometimes, you'd stop being so damnably *you*."

Estral did not swear often, which lent more weight to her words.

"I'm sorry?"

"Even when we were in school, you were like this, standing up to the bullies. Now it's—it's—" She waved her arms about in futile explanation. "More extreme. You just do these things, and now that I've actually seen you do what you do, I wish you'd just stop it."

Karigan closed her eyes. In her condition, it was difficult enough to make sense of straightforward sentences. "You don't want me to tell off bullies?"

"Oh, Karigan, you have no idea, do you?"

"About what? I'm having trouble following. So tired." Her words were met with silence. She opened her eye to see that Estral still sat beside her with head bowed.

"You do know, don't you," Estral said, "that not just anyone would go running after me into the Lone Forest?"

"You're my friend," Karigan said. "Of course I would."

"You knew it was dangerous, but you went anyway. You were hurt horribly as a result. You should have left me."

"I would never—"

"And you still want to go back."

"The king and your father are—"

"Most people," Estral said, "after what you've been through, would leave such a rescue to someone else." She then listed several of Karigan's acts—her rescue of the then

Lady Estora, jumping into a river to save Fergal Duff, going into Blackveil. She finished with, "It's—it's just too much."

"Well, when you list it all like that, it does sound rather mad." Karigan started to drowse, the waking world becoming a distant twilight. "I'm sorry," she murmured.

"And now you're the one apologizing when I owe you everything. Why do you have to be the hero all the time? I am not sure I know who you are anymore . . . or *what* you are."

Karigan tried to shake herself awake for Estral was clearly agitated. It took great effort. "I know it's not normal, but I'm still me."

After several moments of silence, Estral said, "Oh, gods. I'm sorry. That was a terrible thing for me to say. It came out all wrong. I just can't believe . . . It's hard. Your back, and all of it. Why must it always be you? I hate that these things happen to you, especially when the latest is all my fault."

"Nyssa's fault," Karigan muttered. She was too tired to offer further comfort.

"I hope you can forgive me, and I'm sorry for carrying on like this. It's not what you need." Estral paused. "I did want to tell you that I am probably leaving in the morning."

This woke Karigan up enough to ask, "What? Where?"

"Enver wants me to ride Mist to the River Unit for reinforcements."

"That'll take too long," Karigan replied.

"I know, and my father is so close. I don't want to go."

An image came unsummoned to Karigan of a pale cat sitting beside her with a message tube attached to its collar. Was this some fancy, some whimsical detail out of one of the novels she liked to read? Or, was it memory?

"Send a cat," she told Estral, and finally she let go, slipping into a deep slumber.

DETERMINATION

During one of Karigan's awakenings, she heard Enver humming softly. When she looked, he was seated beside her, his back erect, and his eyes closed. The quiet glow of the moonstone revealed his peaceful expression. For all that they had traveled so far together, she really hadn't learned a whole lot about him, his history. He liked to sing, he was keen on spiritual matters, he was as good an archer as any Eletian she'd ever met, and he'd always seemed interested in the ways of Sacoridians, which she had found at once annoying and endearing. All of that was on the surface, but there had to be more depth than his seemingly simple nature revealed.

"Galadheon," he said without opening his eyes, "how is your pain?"

For how long had he perceived her studying him? "It hurts."

Now he opened his eyes and looked down at her. "More, or less than before?"

"I don't know. More bearable, I guess. Could be getting used to it."

He checked her for fever. "Ah, not as fierce. That is an improvement. Here is some water to drink."

She accepted the skin he passed her and drank without complaint.

"We sent Mister Whiskers to Captain Treman," Enver told her, "thanks to your suggestion."

"Why? What suggestion?"

"I was going to send Lady Estral to inform him of the situation here, which, of course, would take time. When Lady Estral told you this earlier, you suggested we send the cat."

She had? It sounded familiar . . .

"It will take much less time for a gryphon to fly there, though we instructed Mister Whiskers to approach the encampment in his small cat form. Should he arrive as a gryphon, well, there is no telling how the soldiers might receive him."

They'd find a house cat strange enough, she thought, but whether or not she remembered making the suggestion, she was glad she had. It would cut down on the time getting word to Captain Treman.

"Lady Estral, of course, wrote the missive. She borrowed your sealing wax and pressed it with her father's signet ring."

That would be another surprise for Captain Treman—the Golden Guardian's sigil in messenger green wax. She was sure Estral explained all in her message to him.

"What time is it?" she asked.

"An hour after midnight."

She felt oddly restless, but perhaps it was because her head was clearer. "Enver, this Eletian woman who is here . . . Nari? How did you come upon her? I seem to have missed a few things since the Lone Forest."

"I was searching for the way to the p'ehdrose when I spotted her from afar, walking across the rocky plain. When I investigated, I found it was Nari of Argenthyne."

"Argenthyne," Karigan murmured. "But Argenthyne is gone."

"Yes," Enver said. "She was abducted by the aureas slee well before the fall of Argenthyne and held captive all this time. I sang to you of her back when we were at Eli Creek waystation."

"Wait . . . Narivanine?"

"Yes, but she prefers Nari now, for it represents that she has lost much."

"Hadwyr," Karigan said.

"She tells me she knew in her heart he was gone. Eletians have a way of knowing such things, and perhaps she is more perceptive than most, for she was an attendant of the Sleeper's Grove by Castle Argenthyne. But, it was still grievous for her to hear it confirmed. Now she hunts the aureas slee in vengeance, though she has paused her search to help us and, I think, to speak with me, an Eletian. She has not seen another of our kind in many a year. Not only that, but she feels indebted to you for helping the Sleepers who were trapped in Blackveil."

"She knows about that?"

He recounted to her the conditions of Nari's captivity and how King Zachary had also been imprisoned by the aureas slee. "He told her of what you had done." He went on to explain that somehow, following the aureas slee's battle with the gryphons, King Zachary ended up in the Lone Forest among Grandmother's people. Karigan couldn't wait to find out how *that* happened.

"We must get him out," Karigan said with determination.

"Then you must regain your strength. You must eat even if you do not wish to, and rest; then as time passes—"

"Enver, we can't let time pass. Every moment the king is there in the Lone Forest?" She bit her bottom lip.

To her surprise, he did not argue. "Then rest, Galadheon. We will see what daytime brings."

Karigan exhaled a long breath, and as she drifted off once more, she thought of Nari and her lost love, Hadwyr. She thought she could understand how that felt, but to carry it for centuries? That, she thought, would be worse punishment than bearing the lash of any whip.

She awoke at mid-morning, determined to get up, and demanded her clothes. Enver lent her one of his shirts, telling her it would be less abrasive to her back than her own. It was lighter and smoother than silk, and she thought her father could make an entirely new fortune if he could get his hands on the fabric. It was a blue as pale as the winter sky, and the motion of putting it on hurt more than to have it touching her back. It was a little large, but she rolled up the sleeves and pinned her brooch to it.

Estral brought her socks, boots, and breeches. Karigan could not bend to pull on the socks, so Estral helped.

As for the breeches, Estral said, "I tried to wash these out best as I could. They were stained."

With blood. They were still dark around the waist, but Estral had done a good job of washing them out.

"Thank you," Karigan said. "That could not have been pleasant to do."

Estral shook her head. "I burned what was left of your shirt. It was . . . very bad."

Karigan could only imagine. She was glad it was gone and that she didn't have to see it. Just thinking of it brought Nyssa's leering face into her mind. She shuddered.

"It is cold outside," Estral said. "Do you think you can bear your greatcoat over your shoulders?"

"I don't know. Let's try without first."

Estral helped her stand, and she wavered.

"Do you need to sit back down?" Estral asked.

"Forward. Forward motion," Karigan murmured.

"You aren't going to faint on me, are you?"

"Keep moving."

Lightheaded and with a fog filling her vision, she held on to Estral and exited the tent. The cold air was invigorating, and her vision resolved. She found Enver, Nari, and Midnight awaiting her by the fire. Condor neighed to her and would have, she knew, come running to her if he hadn't been hobbled.

"Condor. Take me to Condor."

Estral helped her. He was not too far away, but it felt like miles. When she reached him, she pressed her forehead against his neck. He stood still as if afraid any movement might break her.

"I'm all right, I'm all right," she told him.

When she stepped back, he gave her a gentle whuff of air that stirred the one long strand of hair hanging in her face. She pushed it away and patted Condor's nose. Then they returned to the fire.

"I need a knife," she said.

"What for?" Estral asked.

Karigan held out her hand, and it was Enver who handed her his knife. The blade had a graceful, deadly curve to it, unornamented but for some characters in Eltish. The blade seemed to collect the light, as though it were white steel. She grabbed the long lock of hair and cut it off in one easy slash so that it was even with the rest. Just that simple movement pulled painfully at her back. She returned to Enver his knife, hilt first, even as the lock of hair drifted to the ground.

"Thank you," she said.

They'd arranged seating out of logs and rocks. She dropped onto a log with a saddle blanket over it. Sweat glided down her temple and cheek. Curiously, her borrowed shirt kept her comfortable, but for the occasional chill breeze that snaked beneath her collar.

"It is good to see you up," Enver said. "Would you have some broth now? It might help dispel any lightheadedness."

Karigan consented to having broth brought to her. Her stomach still wasn't sure about accepting much into it, but if it meant regaining her strength, she would try.

"Nari and I have spied the enemy searching," Enver said, "but they are some distance away, and far off the trail. I made several false trails, but they haven't even found those."

Karigan nodded, sipping the broth slowly. Just sitting strained her back and the stab wound. She was tiring very quickly.

"Nighttime," she said, "is when I go." When her pronouncement was met with silence, she looked up from her broth to see the three exchanging glances. "What?"

"You can barely sit up," Estral said. "The gods know I am anxious to get my father out of there, but I don't want a rescue to fail because you are not well."

Karigan gazed into the broth. To her surprise, she'd consumed almost the whole mugful. Rationally, she knew Estral was right. She was weak. Using her ability to slip into the encampment would be a drain on her energy she'd be unable to sustain.

"I know," she said finally, though it pained her to admit it aloud, "but I don't dare leave the king there, or Lord Fiori, and I certainly don't dare await Captain Treman."

"We understand this," Enver said. "Perhaps we will not go this night, but tomorrow night may be another story, yes? If you continue to eat and drink, and accept my ministrations, we may be able to do what is necessary."

"There is no 'may,'" she said. "There is no other choice." If she weren't half falling off her seat, she'd go right then.

"We have not been idle during your rest," Enver said. "All will be ready when it is time."

When exhaustion claimed her, Enver helped her back to the tent. She nearly collapsed onto her bedding, wondering how in the hells she was ever going to be of any use in a rescue attempt.

"May I suggest," Enver said, "that putting yourself into a state of tranquility would promote healing and energy? You can focus with your breathing."

This sounded suspiciously like listening to the voice of the world again, but she followed his instructions to clear her mind, breathe deeply, and imagine herself in the green depths of a summer forest. And promptly fell asleep.

THE DOMAIN OF GRANDMOTHER

Karigan spent the next day resting, eating the little bits of food Enver offered, and drinking his herbal concoctions. He also slathered her wounds with salves and wrapped her in bandages against the coming exertions of the planned rescue attempt. Her fever remained low, if not broken, and she felt better than she had in days. That was not to say she was herself yet.

While she rested, she wrestled with Estral's words of the other night, the list of all the situations she'd found herself in. Why did she always step in to help? Why did it have to be her? Why didn't she wait for someone else to do what was necessary?

In her case, she thought, there usually wasn't anyone else around, and if she didn't take action, what might be lost? For instance, Fergal Duff might have drowned in the Grandgent. Yes, there had been others on the ferry with her when he went over, but none of them made a move to rescue him until *after* she dove into the water. What might have become of Estora in the Teligmar Hills had she not intervened? Grandmother would have possessed Sacoridia's future queen, and claimed a major victory.

There were consequences to not helping. Even if there were an army of potential rescuers, what if none of them stepped in? If not her, then *who*?

Estral entered the tent and sat beside her. "I guess my part will be staying here," she said.

"What? You aren't going with us?"

"Enver says someone needs to stay here. I volunteered."

Karigan was surprised. "I thought you wanted to—"

"Help rescue my father? Of course, but I also realize I am not *you.* I am not even my father. I haven't the skills or the resilience. Often I wonder what kind of Golden Guardian I'm going to be if I can't do these things." She laughed derisively. "My thing is teaching music to children, not this—this adventuring. Besides, Enver thinks that the fewer who go into the Lone Forest, the better. You will have a better chance of getting my father and the king out without me in the way."

"What about your voice? You said the thief was there."

"It is more important to get the king and my father out. I can live without my voice, I know that now, but I am not sure how I could stand life without my father."

Estral's voice had gotten scratchier. There was no telling how long Idris' gift would last. For Estral, staying behind would be more courageous than going.

"We'll bring Lord Fiori back," Karigan said.

"Just keep yourself in one piece, and if you see that nasty Nyssa?" Estral made a cutting motion across her throat.

Karigan hoped not to see Nyssa at all, and if she did, she very much doubted she'd be in any condition to engage in a fight. Her part would be in stealth.

As daylight waned, she dressed. The weight of her greatcoat proved painful against her back, so she carried it as a bundle under her arm. Enver's shirt had a quality to it that kept her warm, despite its thin fabric. She made her way out of the tent with Estral's assistance. Enver and Nari stood by with Condor, Mist, and Coda. Karigan looked Condor over and was pleased to see her saber strapped to the saddle. With her back so damaged, she could not use it, but she figured the king or Lord Fiori could. She did not even arm herself with the bonewood. She just could not use her wounded back muscles to wield it. The only weapon she took was her longknife.

"You will ride Mist," Enver said.

"But Condor—" Before she could finish, she saw why. Mist knelt down on the ground, waiting for her to mount. It would be easier than trying to climb up into Condor's saddle.

"You were not aware at the time to know how smooth Mist's gaits were when last you rode her."

She kissed Condor's nose and, feeling guilty, sat upon Mist's saddle. The mare rose with nary a jolt to her back. Nari mounted Coda, and Enver, Condor. Midnight leaped up behind him. It was strange seeing someone else, plus a black cat, riding her horse.

"Hurry back," Estral said, by way of farewell.

Karigan glanced over her shoulder as they rode away, Estral a solitary, unmoving figure. "I'll bring him back," she murmured.

Enver and Nari watched for trouble with their sharp vision as dusk settled in. The Lone Forest was still quite a distance away. Smooth as Mist's gaits were, Karigan's back and stab wound felt the ride.

It was full dark, and they were much closer to the forest when they approached what appeared to be a wide, deep crevice through the landscape. Instead of altering their course to avoid it, Enver guided Condor over its edge.

"No—" Karigan began, but then Enver and Condor did not fall, but simply vanished from existence.

"It is illusion," Nari said, "like the one around our other campsite." Then she and Coda vanished as they stepped into the "crevice."

Mist followed, and though Karigan braced herself, there wasn't even a slight sensation of falling, only the tingle of wards. It was clever, she thought, to create an illusion that appeared more as an obstacle to be avoided than, say, a thicket of trees that would look like an obvious hiding place.

"Nari made this illusion yesterday," Enver explained. "A place to leave the horses and to which we can retreat and hide. But come now. We will wait until the hour of night's end, and you must rest until then."

"Galadheon," Enver said.

Karigan blinked her eyes open. Hadn't she just lain down?

"It is nearing the time," he said. "You should take some food and water."

She grimaced as she sat up, pain rippling through her back. Even with the illusion, they had not dared light a fire, so she forced down some hardtack and the Dragon Dropping Enver gave her. Then he handed her his flask of cordial.

"Drink all that is left," he instructed her.

"All of it? Are you sure?"

"You will need it."

There was about a third of a flask left, and when she drank, this time it tasted of the deepest, coolest of mountain springs. Exhaustion slipped away, and she was filled with a sense of peace and well-being. The pain ebbed. She wondered how long it would last.

The plan was for Karigan and Enver to ride into the Lone Forest on Mist, accompanied by Midnight, while Nari waited for them at this temporary campsite with Coda and Condor.

Karigan rode behind Enver, the belt of her saber looped around the saddle's pommel. She had left her greatcoat behind as too painful to wear and a hindrance to what must be accomplished. Midnight vanished into the dark as she padded somewhere alongside them. Enver had told Karigan that he and Mist would be able to sense traps and avoid them. Human guards would be dealt with. The bare glint of the fingernail of a moon allowed them to melt into the concealment of the dark. It was agreed that Karigan would not use her ability until they reached the encampment proper, unless some necessity required it before then. He did not wish for her to drain her energy unless she had to.

He rode with bow and arrow at the ready, his quiver strapped to his hip. Mist traveled at a jog, her hooves light on the rocky terrain. Anxiety knotted Karigan's insides, her tension worsening the pain in her back, especially when they entered the subdued world beneath the eaves of the forest. Enver did not speak, and if he saw traps, he did not point them out. She certainly could not see any. Sometimes she was aware of Midnight, darker than shadow, slipping through the underbrush.

She lost all sense of time. Sweat dampened her brow, whether from fever or anxiety, she could not tell. At one point she was sure Midnight transformed into her larger form and darted off in a different direction. Enver turning to look confirmed it. Farther on, Mist picked up her pace, and Enver raised his bow with arrow nocked. He loosed two arrows in quick succession. Karigan could not see a thing, but she heard the cracking of foliage as bodies fell to the ground.

Mist veered in a new direction, Karigan wrapping her arms around Enver's waist to keep from flying off the mare's back. Doing so wrenched the wounds of her back, even as she felt the muscles of Enver's own back tense and flex as he drew the bowstring taut and released another arrow. The white arrow soared silently into the dark as though its quarrels were the flight feathers of an owl.

Elsewhere, she heard a snarl and a man's scream cut short. Midnight.

"They are expecting us," Enver said, "as we believed they would. There are more armed guards in the woods, and new traps."

"Do you need my ability?" she asked.

"Not yet."

Mist ran on without falter, careening through the woods. Whether her erratic path was to evade traps or guards, Karigan could not tell. All her focus was tied to hanging on to Enver and trying not to think about how much her back hurt. After an interminable passage of time, Mist slowed to a walk, then a halt.

"From here we will continue on foot," Enver said.

Releasing Enver hurt just as much as holding on to him had. He slid to the ground, then Mist obligingly knelt to make it easier for Karigan to dismount. When this was done, the mare rose to her feet and Enver pressed his hand to her forehead and whispered softly in Eltish to her. Her ears flickered; then she turned on her haunches and trotted off, melting into the dark like the mist that was her name.

"She will come when we need her," Enver said. "Are you ready, Galadheon? Are you able to continue?"

She nodded. Enver's cordial was holding her in good stead.

"The keep is not far. We will need the use of your ability."

The plan was to infiltrate the keep because that was where

she had seen the king and Lord Fiori. It was a place to start. She held out her hand, and he took it. Reassured by the strength and warmth of his grip, she called on her ability and they faded into the dark even more thoroughly than Mist.

They walked through the woods, Midnight padding somewhere behind them. When they reached the edge of the woods, they halted. The keep, and its wall, stood in a clearing. Fires, torches, and lanterns flickered here and there among the shanties, and even in an arrowloop of a tower. The light was gray to Karigan, not bright.

"We must stay away from the light," she reminded Enver.

The encampment appeared quiet. Most of the civilians must be asleep, but she saw guards on watch, some nearby. There were also a few dogs prowling about.

"What about the dogs?" Karigan whispered.

"Not to fear," he told her.

They walked across the clearing, steering away from the guards and light. When a dog seemed to catch wind of them, Enver . . . She wasn't sure what he did, if he sang, gave a command, or whistled; it was beneath her hearing. The dog lay down and rolled onto its back.

They edged past darkened shanties toward the gate opening. This would be the most lighted space outside the keep. Enver found the deepest shadows as they slipped past yawning guards. It seemed to her that he also enhanced her ability, making them fade more completely, and alleviating the drain on her.

They crossed the courtyard and around another guard who stood sentry before the keep's entrance. They slipped behind the blanket that served as a door. They'd made it into the keep, the domain of Grandmother.

RETURN TO NYSSA'S WORKSHOP

The keep was still and dark. It was a simple structure of ancient days with few rooms. It was not difficult to locate the great hall. A fire glowed in the hearth, dimly illuminating the sleeping forms on the floor huddled beneath cloaks and blankets. Karigan hoped Grandmother was not one of them.

They carefully picked their way among the sleepers, she peering at the faces and seeing none that resembled King Zachary or Lord Fiori. A woman stirred at their passing. Karigan froze, her heart pounding, but the woman just murmured in her sleep and rolled over.

When they had inspected just about everyone, Enver pointed to a dark corner where a man lay bundled in a blanket next to a lute case. They stepped carefully over to him and Karigan tried to discern his shadowed features. Firelight glinted on gold strands of hair, and he looked the right size, tall man that he was.

"It is Lord Fiori," Enver whispered. "I sense his Eletian blood." He let go her hand and knelt by the sleeping man, visible to any who happened to look. Karigan glanced apprehensively behind them, but all remained quiet.

Enver placed his hand against Lord Fiori's temple and spoke almost inaudibly. Lord Fiori's eyes opened and slowly focused. He sat up, his eyebrows raised.

Enver continued to speak inaudibly, and Lord Fiori nodded. He then looked about, and Karigan realized he was searching for her. She reached out and touched his shoulder and he jumped. He looked older and more haggard to her than she had ever seen. There had always been a timeless quality to him that she put down to his Eletian blood, but not now. Clearly captivity had been harsh on him.

::The king is not here.:: His lips moved, but his words were delivered in a whisper right into her ear. Estral had once mentioned he could do this trick of throwing his voice. Useful, that.

"Where?" Enver whispered.

::Nyssa's workshop,:: Lord Fiori replied.

A chill of fear shuddered through Karigan. She glanced around again, and dropped her fading.

::Disconcerting,:: Lord Fiori said. He shed his blanket and rose. Karigan wordlessly handed him her sword. He accepted it with questions in his eyes, then buckled it on.

Enver spoke to him some more, explaining what needed to be done, and he nodded and stretched his hand out. Karigan took it, and Enver's, and they faded out. Enver led them through the great hall, away from the sleepers.

::I regret leaving my travel lute behind,:: Lord Fiori said in her ear. ::It has gone many a mile with me.::

She squeezed his hand in acknowledgment. Preserving his life was more important at the moment than an instrument that could be replaced.

They left the keep without incident, but Karigan felt a growing unease. She glanced up at the tower, but the light that had glimmered in the arrowloop had been extinguished. Was that where Grandmother dwelled? Yet it was not the tower from which the uneasiness emanated. It was not in the direction of Nyssa's workshop that she felt it either, but from somewhere on the far side of the keep. Something ancient, something hidden, something, or many somethings, scratching at that which contained them in a—in a prison?

As though roused by the dread sensation, filmy figures ranged about the clearing around the keep. Many appeared to her agitated and beseeching, while others drifted aimlessly, some vanishing among the trees in the woods. Her skin felt clammy, and she realized that Enver and Lord Fiori were pulling on her as they moved back into the woods toward the building that was Nyssa's workshop. She shook her head, focused on where she was, and the apparitions vanished from her vision.

Several guards ranged around Nyssa's workshop, and to her surprise, Enver let go of her and swiftly drew his knife. He placed his hand over the mouth of the first guard they encountered and cut his throat. Enver eased him to the ground so that he made no noise falling. He looked fierce, almost feral, as he hunted, far different from the man who had so gently tended her and listened to the voice of the world, whose spirit guide was a turtle.

He swiftly struck one guard after another. When one, puffing on a pipe, came around the corner of the building and saw a fallen comrade, Enver blurred out of the shadows. The man's pipe dropped out of his mouth, and Enver took him to the ground, his knife jammed in the guard's throat.

For all that they were quiet, more guards arrived, having found the slain.

"Galadheon," Enver said, "go see to your king. Lord Fiori and I will hold off these guards."

She let go of Lord Fiori and, without hesitation, ran to the door of Nyssa's workshop, maintaining her fading as she went. She threw the door open. The interior was dimly lit by a lamp at low glow. She stood on the threshold waiting for her eyes to adjust, then shut the door behind her and dropped her fading. That no guard leaped out of the shadows to kill her was a relief, but being back in that place made her skin crawl.

She saw the pen where she and Estral had been held, but it was empty. Her gaze was then magnetically drawn to the beam to which she'd been manacled for the flogging. The cuffs hung open and empty, as if awaiting her return. She took a step back, tried to calm her breathing. She wanted to run as far away from the building as she could, but then, in the soft orange glow of the brazier, she saw *him*, on the table that dominated the center of the room. She rushed to him, took in his bruised, abraded face, his full beard. She almost did not recognize him.

She placed her hand on his chest to feel its rise and fall. "My lord?"

He took a rumbling breath.

Thank the gods.

She saw that he was strapped down and that there were

knots of yarn across his face. Peeling back the blanket that covered him revealed more. She drew her knife and started slashing at the yarn, the knots stinging her hands, and threw the pieces to the floor as she went. As she pulled the blanket down farther, she realized he was entirely unclothed. A fleeting warmth rushed to her face as she worked to destroy the yarn, and then she covered him back up. She flexed her stinging hands and then sawed through the strap that bound his head down, and then that of his wrist.

His eyes fluttered open.

"My lord?" she said. "Can you hear me?"

"Karigan?" he whispered. He raised a trembling hand to her face. His fingers brushed across her cheek. "Are you real, or another vision sent to torment me?"

She pressed his hand against her cheek. "I am real. We've come to get you out."

His eyes focused then, and gleamed with tears. "I think you are sent from the heavens."

Taken aback, she gently placed his hand on his chest. "Let me undo these straps and we'll see if we can get you up."

She moved along the table to his feet. She raised the knife to cut through the strap that bound his ankle when leather thongs lashed out of the dark and wrapped around her forearm. Her knife clattered to the tabletop, and she cried out as barbs ripped her sleeve and bit into her skin. She grabbed onto the whip beneath the handle. Holding the handle, of course, was Nyssa, her face distorted in the dim light and as nasty as any nightmare wrought by Karigan's imagination.

"I did not think you would be up and about so soon," Nyssa said. "Clearly you deserved a few more lashes. No matter, we will remedy that. Grandmother will not be pleased you cut up her knotwork."

Karigan hauled at the whip, trying to loosen its hold on her, but there was only weakness and pain where once there had been muscle strength. Nyssa was as strong as ever, and she started to reel Karigan in.

"We were waiting for you," she said. "We knew you would come back for your king."

Resistance only strained Karigan's back all the more, and

the barbs only dug deeper into the flesh of her forearm. When she was face-to-face with Nyssa, the torturer grinned, drew back her fist, and slammed it into Karigan's stab wound. Everything melted away into a gray fog. When it settled, she found herself curled on the floor, her wound screaming.

"Where is the tough Greenie I've heard about?" Nyssa demanded from behind her. "The swordmaster and avatar?"

Ava-*what*? Karigan thought numbly.

"Such a disappointment," Nyssa said.

Karigan started to push herself up, but Nyssa kicked her in the back. She screamed and collapsed to her side and was kicked again, and again, and flipped over so that she faced Nyssa. So overwhelmed by pain was she that she could only stare up at her tormentor. Tears blurred her vision turning Nyssa into a monster that loomed above, her whip swinging at her side like a prehensile extension of her arm. She knelt beside Karigan, grabbed her chin in a vicelike grip. She filled Karigan's vision.

"I'd finish you off Greenie, but that's no fun. Besides, Grandmother wants you. And I have a friend who wants *a piece of you*, as well." She chuckled. "If you are still alive when they are done with you, I'll have my turn, and I will make you my slave. Don't think it can be done? Think again."

Nyssa threw her head back to laugh, but stopped short, a quizzical expression on her face. Then she simply collapsed in a heap. Karigan was not sure if it was her own state of mind, or some other force in the universe, but the world seemed to shift beneath her, a thread among the stars changing course. When the sensation passed and her vision cleared, she saw her king standing there, her own knife in his hand, and blood dripping off the blade.

She must have passed out briefly because Enver was shaking her awake. She wanted to go back to sleep. Everything hurt. She tried to push him away, but felt too feeble to lift a finger.

"Galadheon," he said, "you must go."

"Go where?" she asked wearily.

"Out of the forest. You and the king must leave."

King? And then she remembered. She tried to rise, but

pain ripped through her back, and she slumped onto the floor. "Where is he?"

Enver glanced over his shoulder, then returned his gaze to her. "Dressing."

"Dressing?"

"Yes."

Karigan's gaze wandered and fell on the corpse of Nyssa very close by, her eyes rolled back. Karigan looked away. Dead or not, that woman was going to haunt her dreams.

The door creaked open.

"Hurry," said Lord Fiori. "The keep is waking up."

"Stand, Galadheon," Enver said. He more or less lifted her to her feet, and she cried out in pain and almost fainted away. "I am sorry, but there is little time. You and your king will ride Mist to Nari. Mist will know the way, but you must use your ability. Do you understand?"

"Yes, I . . ."

"I am ready." The voice belonged to King Zachary.

Karigan looked over Enver's shoulder. The king was dressed in buckskin and looked a different man, a rugged woodsman, and the effect was not displeasing. A dead man, relieved of his clothes, lay on the table. Apparently he'd been the source of the king's new attire. The king gazed back at her, his expression unreadable, and then Enver started to drag her outside.

"Wait," she said. She went over to the brazier and tried to kick it over, but even that was too much for her. The king, seeing what she was about, finished the job for her. Coals spilled across the rough-hewn floor and slammed into the wall. She watched in satisfaction as flames licked at the wood.

Enver drew her away and outside into the dark. The woods were filled with shouts of alarm and barking dogs.

"Your ability, Galadheon," he said.

She held out her hands. The king took her left, his grip warm and reassuring. Enver took her right, and Lord Fiori grabbed Enver's arm. She had never tried to fade so many people at once, but she did it. Perhaps Enver's influence helped. They moved awkwardly through the forest, pausing if anyone came too close. People converged on Nyssa's workshop. Karigan glanced over her shoulder, and firelight shone through the open door. Grandmother, she thought, was not going to be pleased. Despite the pain and exhaustion, she smiled.

The clamor fell behind as they traveled more deeply into the forest. She was having trouble remaining on her feet, and both the king and Enver practically carried her. After a time, Enver halted.

"Muna'reyes," he whispered.

Karigan, focused on maintaining invisibility, was not even aware of Mist's approach. She only realized the mare was there when Enver and the king broke contact with her—the king so he could mount, and Enver so he could lift her up onto Mist's back behind him.

"Your ability," Enver said. "Make you, your king, and Mist vanish."

"What about you? And Lord Fiori?"

"Muna'reyes! *Tesh, tesh!*" Enver cried.

The mare bounded off, and Karigan grabbed King Zachary around his waist so she did not tumble off. Remembering herself, she called on her fading ability once more and became aware of little else than keeping them invisible, and clinging to the warmth that was her king.

FLAMES ENTWINED

Zachary could not see the horse, he could not see himself, and he could not see what lay in the woods around him. He could feel the mare surge beneath him, that her stride was sure and effortless, and considering the natural terrain, smooth. He felt Karigan pressed up against his back, her arms around him in a death grip. Of anything, she was the most real, but doubt that any of it was real remained strong, for whatever Grandmother's knots had done to him made him question everything.

The invisibility of the horse, of him, was Karigan's doing, he tried to tell himself, not some spell of Grandmother's. It was night, so the dark of the woods was natural. Still, he doubted. Perhaps it was all a ploy to make him *think* he was free, and at any moment, the truth would be revealed that he was still in Nyssa's workshop and the torment of pain would begin again. And yet, it all felt so real.

The horse suddenly burst out of the woods—the world opened up and stars appeared above. Cold air rushed over him. Karigan leaned more heavily against his back, and he placed his hand over hers, which were clasped around his waist. They were icy.

He glanced toward the sky and detected a large, winged form gliding against the stars. Enver had told him a gryphon would be escorting them. Had he not witnessed the gryphons fighting the aureas slee, he'd be more certain this was all a deception of Grandmother's.

His very soul exhausted from being so long a slave and captive, his body beaten and tortured, he was slumped over the mare's neck by the time she slowed to a walk. Before he could rouse himself to stop her from stepping into a wide crevice, she went forward. They did not fall and ended up on an ordinary flat, rocky area. A woman stood there looking about.

"I know you are there," she said, "though I cannot see you. Galadheon? You can cease your fading." The gryphon alighted next to her, folded its wings, and sat. "Galadheon?"

The horse once more became visible beneath him. He could see his hands. "Nari? Is that you?"

Karigan groaned behind him, her hands slipping away from him. He did not turn in time to catch her as she fell from the horse.

"Karigan!" he cried.

Nari rushed over and half-caught her before her head hit the ground. Zachary dismounted. He'd seen Nyssa kick Karigan, but did not know how badly she was hurt. He knew the use of her ability also took much out of her.

"Help me get her to the blankets," Nari said.

They carried Karigan between them, and when they reached a bedroll spread on the ground, Nari said, "Let us lay her down on her belly."

"Her belly?"

"It is best."

When they did so, he saw that a darkness stained the back of her shirt, or perhaps it was shadow. Then he gazed at his hands. "Nari," he said, a quaver in his voice. They were sticky with blood.

"There is not much we can do for her until Enver returns."

"But she's bleeding—she could be badly wounded."

Nari placed her hand on his wrist. "She was wounded a few days ago, yes. The lacerations must have reopened. She needs Enver's skills. Our meddling will only make it worse."

"But—"

"Peace, Zachary." She went to the mare, placed her hands beneath her forelock, and spoke softly to her in Eltish. The mare then turned on her haunches and bolted back toward the forest. Zachary half-sat, half-fell beside Karigan. She was shivering and he pulled a blanket over her. He took her icy hand into his.

"She is freezing," he told Nari. "We need a fire."

"We are too close to the forest." She knelt beside Karigan and touched her forehead in much the way she had the mare's.

Zachary started to remove the cloak he'd taken from the dead guard to spread over Karigan.

"No," Nari said. "You, too, need warmth. Food and drink, as well, it appears. We've other than cave fungus here." She removed her own cloak and placed it over Karigan. "Rest while I fetch a waterskin and food for you."

"What was done to her?" Zachary asked. He knew she'd been caught in Nyssa's clutches for a time, but could only guess at what she might have endured.

Nari gazed down at saddlebags piled on the ground. "It is not pleasant."

Zachary swallowed hard. "Please tell me."

He expected the worst, and what she told him was bad enough. She explained why Karigan had gone into the forest, how she was captured, and what Nyssa had done to her. A flame blazed in his chest.

"Gods," he muttered. The death he'd given Nyssa had been too kind. He gazed at Karigan. Her hair had fallen across her face, and he remembered the severed braid and Grandmother wanting it for something. He brushed her hair away and traced the long cut down her cheek. Why her? Why must *she* endure so much?

Nari knelt beside him with a waterskin and what appeared to be . . . chocolate? The scent came to him in an alluring wave, and his stomach churned. He was not sure when last he'd eaten. He had a hazy memory of Nyssa's guards making him drink.

"There is chocolate, and what some of your people call hardtack, and—" she frowned in distaste "—dried meat."

He drank more than ate, unsure of what his body would accept. Nari left him to watch for the return of Enver. Unable to keep his head up, he wrapped himself in his cloak and lay down beside Karigan so she might share his heat. She shifted against him, seemingly by instinct, and he placed his arm around her so she could use his shoulder as a pillow. Something stirred within him, with her so close, and he took a quavering breath and gazed at the stars. He guessed the horror of what had been done to him, and to her, was still too fresh for it all to sink in. Of course, he could not remember much of his own torment, but his imagination allowed him to vividly picture hers.

A falling star whisked across the sky and was just as quickly gone.

Nari gazed down at Zachary and the Galadheon. Enver picked his way over to her while Lord Fiori sat apart pressing a bandage to his wounded leg. They had sent Midnight on to Lady Estral with a note informing her of the success of the mission. The Galadheon, at some point, had nestled her head on Zachary's shoulder, her body tucked up against his side as though the two had always fit together as water to the shore. They were both deeply asleep.

"Her wounds need tending," Enver said.

"It can wait, I think," Nari replied.

"I am a healer," he said. "I must tend her, and the Firebrand, as well."

When he started forward, Nari placed her hand against his chest to stay him and said, "Leave them be. When they awaken will be soon enough. They need rest, and their being together is a different kind of healing." Despite her words, she still felt his resistance.

"I disagree."

"If you want to help, sing."

He looked rebellious.

"I see what is in your eyes, Enver of Eletia, and it is not just the watchfulness of the tessari. What was the council of the Alluvium thinking when they sent you out into the world alone?"

"I do not need others." His tone was defensive. "My discipline, my control, is sound. I have mastered my instincts."

"You are entering your first age of unfolding. You've no idea the power of *accendu'melos.* Discipline is not enough. You need others around you to help you control your urges."

"I can master my own urges."

It was an arrogant statement, Nari thought. She glanced down at the Galadheon sleeping so innocently, so peacefully. "You hear the song of her spirit. It calls out to you. Her scent fills you and you must be near her. Is this not true?"

Enver did not answer.

"Hear me now, Enver of Eletia, this one is not for you, and perhaps for none of this Earth. You know as do I, her god of death has claim of her. A claim greater than even that of her king. You see it, don't you? She is marked, and by more than just her god."

"She is used."

"Are not we all in some way? With her, however, it is by the hands of greater powers."

Enver turned. "Very well, I will wait."

She watched as he walked over to where Lord Fiori sat. He had not liked her words. She still did not understand why the council of the Alluvium would send him out alone, especially when he was so young and close to his first unfolding. It was dangerous. Dangerous for him, and even more dangerous for the object of his desire. And, dangerous to the one who might be considered a rival. Her gaze fell on Zachary.

Humans, in her experience, only saw Eletians as peaceful and balanced. They did not see the more primal side of the Eletian nature, especially when one scented another in the deepest sense, heard that other's song. The drive to bond and mate was fierce, the act often savage, wanton, especially among the young who possessed less control, and it could last for days. For Eletians, it was not just the melding of bodies, but an empathic joining of emotions and thoughts, as well. If Enver should undergo his first unfolding in the presence of the Galadheon and she was unwilling? It did not even bear imagining, especially with her in her weakened state.

Nari was old enough to have attained great control long ago and no longer succumbed to such drives. Life in the cave of the aureas slee had only enhanced her discipline.

Enver did show signs of remarkable control now, but in time? He had a gentle nature, but that would not restrain him during his unfolding. She shook her head once more at the poor decision of the council to send him out alone, then caught herself. Eletians were nothing but deliberate in their decisions, even if their motives were opaque, their intrigues more convoluted than an epic ballad celebrating the disparate lineages and extended families of the Great Houses. With their eternal lives, those Eletians who engaged in intrigues played a very long game, as had her sister. It occurred to her that this "mistake" was intentional, whatever the consequences. Intrigues and machinations, signs and portents, wove the fabric of Eletian custom and polity.

If Enver losing his discipline in the presence of the Galadheon was the intent of the council, to whatever end they desired, then she could only agree with Enver that the Galadheon was being used, and so was he. Nari could tell the Galadheon did not hear the song of Enver's spirit as he heard hers, which would make his unfolding all the worse, for she'd be an unwilling participant.

The one whose song she did hear was Zachary's. Nari could see the bond between them as a fusing of her living light with his, with no room for Enver. Zachary's shone in a range of blues that revealed coolness and peace, but could easily give way to fire. Hers was an appropriate green, though tinged with brown and a sickly yellow, indicating her wounding. Her green, not surprisingly, was also disposed to fire. As for the dark wings that shadowed her, they were *other*, and separated her from all who walked the Earth, including the one with whom she'd bonded. It was no wonder, Nari began to think, the council of the Alluvium had taken an interest in the Galadheon, and no doubt it was something of the powers that surrounded her that called out to Enver.

Nari started away, but glanced back when she heard a stirring. Zachary's eyes fluttered open, and he looked as if to ensure the Galadheon was still there with her head on his shoulder. Her hand rested on his chest, and he placed his over it; then he closed his eyes and sighed with contentment. Peace as Nari had not seen before settled over his features.

Yes, she thought, their bond shone brightly as two flames entwined.

GHOSTS

"Kendroa Mor," Siris Kiltyre said with a low whistle. He was a black silhouette with the flames of a pyre roiling behind him. The smoke plumed into the night sky, clouding the stars. The granite summit of the mor spilled off into the concealing cloak of the dark. "Lil Ambriodhe's ride down this mor was already an established legend by the time I became a Rider. By some miracle she survived that ride, right through Varadgrim's forces, and despite an arrow in her back. Somehow she reached King Jonaeus' host. Because of her actions that night, most of her Riders survived when they'd have otherwise been massacred, and turned a prized prisoner over to the king, Mornhavon's best friend and right hand."

Karigan had known all this, of course, for she had been there, a ghost from the future forced to visit the past. She'd helped Lil reach King Jonaeus. The prized prisoner was her own ancestor, Hadriax el Fex.

The wind shifted, sending the smoke streaming through Siris and toward her. She turned away, not wishing to be touched by the smoke of a pyre, whether this was a dream or not.

"Ah, you are learning," Siris said.

When the wind shifted yet again and the smoke cleared, she gazed at him once more. It was just them, the pyre, and the windswept summit of Kendroa Mor, which in her time was called Watch Hill.

"There are similarities of character between you and the First Rider," Siris continued, "that have nothing to do with the fact that you share the same brooch. She was a very determined, driven person, Lil was, as are you, both of you willing to do the hard work, the dangerous work. There is the courage you have both exhibited, and the stubbornness. Lil thought she could solve most problems on the end of a sword, and in those days? Well, it was usually the only way. She was brash, and fearsome to even those who loved her." He laughed. "The stories of the rows she and the king used to have! They were both hard-headed people, and tempestuous lovers."

During her visit to the past, Karigan had last seen the First Rider on what appeared to be her death bed, suffering from the arrow wound that had also caused her to prematurely birth a child who had not survived. Karigan wanted to ask if Lil had lived beyond that point, for the history was clouded and no one seemed to know, though theories were argued back and forth. Karigan was so tired, however, that she could not summon the energy to ask.

"While there is much in common between you and Lil, there is much that is not. Your approach is quieter, more thoughtful. Perhaps, under the same conditions Lil faced, you might have turned out as brash as she. Alas, her lack of subtlety made her unsuitable to be Westrion's avatar. She was a cunning strategist in battle, yes, but the mind has to find a deeper place in order to traverse the veil of death. There have only been a handful of us."

The smoke of the pyre spiraled, and she was certain she could see grayed faces within it, shapes, ascending into the heavens.

"Go deep into your thoughts," Siris said, "for wit will serve you when strength fails." He glanced up at the sky. "And perhaps, do as the half-Eletian who travels with you does and listen to the voice of the world."

The scene faded away, and she was aware of lying on the ground beneath a blanket, of the pain of her wounds. She reached out beside her but felt only the grainy surface of granite. She thought she recalled someone warm beside her. Cade? The king? How odd.

She opened her eyes to a gray morning, or maybe it was dusk, and silence, not even the sounds of birds. She shivered with a chill, thinking her companions had deserted her. Fog filled her vision, and when it cleared, she saw that she was not, in fact, alone. He lay on his side next to her, his head propped on his hand as he gazed back at her.

"Cade," she said, gladness filling her heart.

But his eyes were dead. "You left me behind."

"No, I—I love you. I wanted to go back, but I couldn't."

Nyssa's whip appeared in his hand, and then he was not Cade, but Nyssa.

"No . . ." Karigan murmured.

"Yes," Nyssa said, "you will learn to love me as a slave loves her master. What? You thought that because I am dead you would no longer see me?" She shook her head. "We have only just begun."

WOUNDS LAID BARE

Karigan's cry made Zachary's hair stand on end, and he saw Fiori go pale. He and Enver leaped up at the same time.

"She must be quieted," Nari said. "The enemy might hear."

Zachary hurried to Karigan's side. She reached out as though struggling with a phantom. He tried to grab her wrist, but she hit his hand away.

"Karigan!" he said.

Enver also knelt beside her. "Galadheon, peace."

"It's Nyssa!" she cried, still struggling.

"She will start bleeding anew if she continues this," Enver told him.

Zachary captured her hands in his. "She is dead," he told her. "Nyssa is dead."

"The whip—"

"She's dead, Karigan," he said. "I killed her myself. *She's dead.*"

Seemingly exhausted, she slumped into her bedding with a groan, and then looked up at him. "Hells . . . What was I thinking?"

"It must have been quite a dream."

"I thought she was here," she said, "real."

"You should continue to rest, Galadheon," Enver said. "When the dark comes, we will move to the other campsite."

"I don't want to close my eyes again," she murmured.

"I will be here to keep watch so nothing troubles you," Zachary said.

"But you could change into her."

"I will not change," he said. It must have been part of her dream. The fever had returned, and it was difficult to say if she were awake or still moving in a dream world. He squeezed her hands. "I promise I will not change. I will stay here beside you. Enver, Nari, and Lord Fiori are here, too."

She did not respond, and her breathing deepened. He sat intending to make himself comfortable so he could keep his promise. If it helped, it was a small thing.

Enver glanced at the afternoon sun. "The sooner we return to our campsite, the better. I have more supplies there to properly tend her."

He had cleaned and bandaged the gouges to Karigan's forearm. For the time being, the bandages she already had on her back, and even the shirt she wore, staunched the bleeding, and he had decided that attempting to inspect those wounds before they reached the other campsite would only cause more problems.

As for Zachary's own wounds, Enver had cleaned and applied salve to his lacerations, but they didn't dare build a fire to brew a tea that would be soothing for his pain. He had slept until late morning, his back and neck stiff from the cold and unforgiving ground, on top of the aches of injuries from his time with Second Empire. Awakening to the open sky above and not the rafters of Nyssa's workshop had confused him at first; then relief washed over him. Any remaining darkness had faded when he'd found Karigan still tucked up against him, her head on his shoulder. He just lay there reveling in the closeness.

When he rose, he had spoken with the others about his experiences, about how he'd fallen into the hands of Second Empire. They already knew some of it, thanks to Nari. He in turn learned of Magged's passing and Nari's search for the aureas slee. They, of course, had no news of Sacor City and his queen, for they had been out of contact with the city for longer than he. Afterward, he sat and wondered how his wife fared, how her pregnancy proceeded, and he brooded over the loss of Magged, and about his subjects who remained enslaved by Grandmother. It galled him that he'd been unable to do anything for them, especially after how they had shielded him from the rocks flung by the people of Second Empire. He did not think Grandmother would allow yet another incursion onto her grounds. The Lone Forest would be more intensely guarded than ever, and she would now know what to look for. The one person capable of slipping back into the forest undetected lay twitching and mumbling in fevered dreams beside him. Even were she well and robust, he would not ask it of her.

There was also the problem of the seal that Grandmother wanted to open. Did they just wait and hope that she failed, or was there something they could actually do to stop her?

Enver had told him a message had been sent to the River Unit, a wise move, and good thinking to use a gryphon as a courier, though he did wonder about its reliability. He needed to get word back to the castle, to Estora.

Fiori limped over and settled on a rock opposite him and nodded toward Karigan. "How is she doing?"

"I don't really know. Quieter, now."

"And you?"

"I am fine."

"You were not treated well. Grandmother and Nyssa, that whole lot, they are insane."

"To be honest, I have little memory of any of it after they figured out my identity."

"Perhaps that is for the good."

Zachary gazed off into the distance. The day was fine with milder breezes from the south that riffled through his hair. Then he looked at Fiori dead on. "I do not know what happened during those blank spaces in my memory. I do not . . . I do not know if I passed on critical information." When Fiori did not respond, he demanded, "Don't you understand? They could know all the plans for this season's campaign. Not only that, but the complement of my troops, their locations, supply routes, weaponry, any number of secrets."

"I understand, Your Majesty. Then you will have to alter your plans."

Zachary stared at him in disbelief. "Alter my plans? Just like that? Plans that were in the making for more than a year?"

"I am not saying that you should scrap everything, but make adjustments that will throw Second Empire some surprises. Obviously, they will be expecting changes, now that you are free of them, but anything you do, stay the course or alter your plans, will leave them unsure."

It was a rather optimistic view that Zachary did not share. "I need to return to Sacor City, or at least get some word there, but I can't just leave my people enslaved in the Lone Forest." He glanced at Karigan once more. "My Green Rider is in no condition for a message errand."

"I could go," Fiori said. "At least I could intercept Treman's folk and have one of them continue on to Sacor City with a message written in your own hand."

Zachary rubbed his upper lip. "Yes, that is a possibility, unless the gryphons would consent to carrying a message."

As the day dragged on, he mulled over the possibilities of what a message might contain. He observed Enver and Nari keeping watch, and stayed by Karigan's side as he had promised. Now and then he caught a few words of her otherwise incoherent mumbling. Cade came up more than once. Zachary reached over and took her hand into his.

"Shh, it's all right," he murmured. "You are safe, you are safe. I will not let anyone hurt you." He continued on in this vein for a while even after she quieted.

When dusk set in, they prepared to move to their other campsite under cover of dark. Enver said he'd seen pairs of the enemy searching across the rocky plain, but none had come close enough to their illusion-concealed location to be of much worry.

Enver tried to wake up Karigan. "Come, Galadheon, it is time to ride."

"No, don't wanna," she muttered.

After fruitless, gentle cajoling, Zachary told Enver, "Allow me." He leaned close to her ear and said in a sharp voice, "Mount up, Rider."

"Yes, Your Majesty." She attempted to rise, but crumpled with a cry of pain.

Zachary and Enver lifted her to her feet.

"We aren't staying at the Golden Rudder, are we?" she asked in a drowsy voice.

"What is this Golden Rudder?" Enver asked.

"An inn," Zachary replied. It was a well-known brothel in certain circles, but he wondered how Karigan knew of it. There was a story there, and he thought it would be amusing to ask her about it when she was more coherent. He told her, "No, Sir Karigan, we are not going to the Golden Rudder."

"Where—where am I?"

Enver explained.

"Oh," she said. "I remember now."

"You will ride Mist with me," Enver told her.

Zachary wanted to protest, wanted her to ride with *him*. Had he not sat by her side all day to offer comfort? But he caught himself and merely nodded. Mist was Enver's horse, and smoothly gaited for carrying one who was injured.

It was decided that he and Nari would double-up on Condor, and Fiori would ride Coda. Enver, with Karigan wrapped in a blanket and sitting slumped before him, led the way into the dark. Zachary had, of course, never ridden Condor before and was impressed by the gelding's confident strides and alert demeanor. He stuck close to Mist as though wanting to keep an eye on his Green Rider.

Nari remained silent behind Zachary. No one spoke. There was just the wind and the clip-clop of hooves on stone. Despite his day of rest, he was still weary after his ordeal with Second Empire, and he dozed in the saddle. He was unsure of how much time had passed when Nari placed her hand on his shoulder.

"We are here, Zachary."

He awoke just in time to experience walking through a wall of stone, which was just air, another of Nari's illusions. Beyond, a pony whickered in greeting, and there were two tents and a small campfire. He would have never guessed the campsite's existence from the other side of the illusion.

A figure emerged from the smaller tent and launched at Fiori just as he touched ground beside Coda.

"Father!" Estral Andovian cried, throwing herself into his arms. "They got you out!"

"Yes, yes they did," Fiori murmured.

"Family," Nari said before she slipped off Condor's back, an echo of Magged.

"Yes," Zachary replied softly.

Estral did not seem to know which direction to go, torn between a hasty bow to her king and checking on Karigan, or returning to her father.

"No formalities with me," he told her.

She nodded and hastened to help Enver walk Karigan into the larger tent. Zachary busied himself with tending the horses, and when he was done, he paused at the large tent's entrance just as Enver stepped out.

"Is Karigan all right?" he asked.

"She is weak and in pain, but with some rest she will heal."

"I would like to see her."

Enver glanced over his shoulder at the tent, then gazed back at Zachary. "She requests that you do not."

Zachary was taken aback. "Why?"

Enver shrugged. "She does not wish for you to see her in her present condition."

"But I have." Zachary raked his hair out of his face. "I sat with her all day, and last night . . ."

"It is her wounds laid bare," Enver said. "She does not wish you to see her that way."

Oh, Karigan. Did she think he would judge her in some way, besides thinking how brave and resilient she was, because of how she appeared?

"Firebrand," Enver said, "it would be well for you to rest, too. Know that you are safe and you can truly sleep after all you have endured."

Safe. He sat before the welcome fire, not sure if he could ever sleep well again. He glanced at the tent, the silken fabric that stood as solid as any stone wall between him and Karigan. If he did sleep, it would be, to his sorrow, without her by his side.

SEEKING COMPLETION

Zachary slept soundly through the night and deeply into the day. He awoke to a fair afternoon. At first he saw no one about, and the only movement was laundry hanging from branches to dry, namely the light blue shirt Karigan had been wearing. The blood stain on the back had not come completely clean, and the right sleeve was punctured and torn. Strips of stained cloth also fluttered from the branches.

Bandages.

Estral arrived into the campsite with her arms filled with wood. "Good afternoon, Your Majesty. I hope you are feeling a little rested?"

"I am. Stiff, but a bit better."

She set her wood aside and moved a kettle over the fire. "I'll get some tea and porridge heated up for you then."

"Where is everyone?" he asked.

"Well, my father is bathing. There's a hot spring a short distance from here. Nari is—I don't know where Nari is. Enver is in his tent checking on Karigan. The gryphons? I don't know where they are, either."

"How is she? Karigan?"

Estral found a mug and spooned tea leaves into it. "As well as can be expected. I am thankful that Nyssa is dead. What she did . . ." She shook herself and poured hot water into the mug and handed it to him.

"Thank you." He cupped his abraded hands around the mug to absorb the heat. As he sipped the tea, it tasted like the best thing he'd ever had. The porridge proved heartening as well, topped with nuts, and wrinkled winter berries the birds hadn't gotten. Nari, he was told, had scavenged them. By the time he finished, he was feeling much better than he had in a long while.

Estral then presented him with a message tube.

"What is this?" he asked.

"Mister Whiskers arrived with it this morning."

He opened the tube and drew out a rolled piece of paper, its seal cracked. Someone had already seen its contents. It was from Captain Treman saying that he was preparing the River Unit to march on the Lone Forest in order to rescue Sacoridia's sovereign.

"He must be apprised of developments," he murmured.

"Would you like to write a return message?" Estral asked.

"Yes, I would. But I also need to send a message to the queen. Do you think the gryphons would convey both?"

"I don't know. I guess we'll find out when they come back."

Estral brought him Karigan's message satchel. It had a hole in it as if it had been punctured by an arrow. He frowned, then looked inside and found the letter he had written himself to be presented to the p'ehdrose, documents from Captain Treman, paper, a pen, ink, sealing wax, and the seal of the Green Riders. Using a pen and writing out a message made him feel more civilized than he had in months. He wrote Captain Treman first and told him to stay the River Unit's approach, to hang back beneath the fringes of the Green Cloak and send forth only a few riders so that they could consult. He was free of Second Empire, he told Captain Treman, but there were other Sacoridians who were not.

He then wrote a brief letter to Estora outlining the situation. When it came to signing the message, he hesitated. He could always sign it in some official way, but that would be rather cold. Still, he could not bring himself to assign a sentiment he did not, in his heart, feel. It was dishonest. What *did* he feel? Admiration, concern, fondness, respect, and something akin to love . . . Would expressing love actually be dishonest?

He mulled it over and decided that she, being the intelligent woman she was, would detect any falsehood. He finally settled on, *With deepest admiration and affection.* It was not perfect, but it *was* honest.

He did not have a royal seal, so he used the Green Rider seal for both.

When Fiori appeared looking refreshed and scoured clean, Zachary explained about the messages.

"I'd be happy to take them," Fiori said. "I can leave tomorrow morning."

"I thought the gryphons might take them."

"Not sure they're coming back." Fiori squinted at the empty sky. "Saw them fly off early this morning. The way they circled and made a beeline south, it looked like they were leaving for good."

Zachary sighed. It was unfortunate to lose their winged messengers, but he *had* wondered about their reliability. "Then you shall be our courier, unless the gryphons return before morning."

Fiori bowed. "It is my honor. I'll give Treman both messages, and one of his folk can convey the queen's to Sacor City."

The message situation settled, Zachary decided to take a turn at the hot spring himself.

"Take this with you," Fiori said, handing him a pouch. "Some sort of Eletian lathering grains."

Zachary accepted the pouch and took along the woodsman's knife he had lifted off the guard who had also supplied his buckskin attire. He followed the path through a patch of woods to where steam rose from the mossy, rock-rimmed pool. Enver had promised him the pool was warded and concealed from the enemy.

Sinking into the hot spring proved not only restorative to his abused body, but now he could cleanse away his captivity. Nyssa might have had him doused with freezing bucketfuls of water, but that had been as her prisoner, and unpleasant. Now he could soak away both the physical and psychic soiling of his captivity.

The cut across his chest stung at first, but soon his muscles began to unknot and relax, the toil and cares, the hardships, all fading away. Before long, however, he made use of the "lathering grains" Fiori had given him, and applied the knife.

Scoured and clean-shaven, he returned to the camp feeling more himself than he had in months, but for the buckskin he wore. He was greeted by Fiori at the fire.

"I almost do not recognize you without whiskers, my lord," Fiori said.

Zachary smiled. It felt strange to have air caressing his bare cheeks. "It will grow back, but I felt a need to remove what was there."

As the day went on, he sat by the fire trying to relax. Nari soon joined him.

"I will be leaving in the morning," she said, "to resume my hunt for Slee. With winter melting away, Slee will dissipate and be more difficult to find."

Zachary wondered about the wisdom of hunting down the elemental and asked, "What will you do if you find it?"

She turned her stormy gaze on him. He found it unsettling.

"Slee already senses my wrath," she said.

Seeking vengeance seemed very unEletianlike to Zachary, but then he knew too little of the Eletians to offer judgment. He had known Nari long enough to be surprised, however, for she'd always been so calm and level. But then again, it was not always easy to discern what turbulence existed beneath the serene surface of a lake.

"I also seek friends," she said in a distracted voice, and then she drifted away.

Friends? Zachary wondered. What friends?

"Nari is one of the very old ones," Enver told him as he watched after her, "and of another time. Most her age Sleep."

"She once told me she tended the grove by Castle Argenthyne."

"Yes, but much that she once knew has changed in the world while she was captive and away from her people. Much was lost. I believe she seeks not vengeance, not even justice."

"What, then?"

"Completion."

"Completion?"

"Yes, of her story."

That sounded so very final to Zachary.

Enver gazed steadily at him and said, "Do not underestimate one such as Nari. If the aureas slee is wounded, as she suspects, then as one of the old ones, she is its match."

Zachary wished her well then, but was sorry that she'd be leaving them.

Later, when Estral came to sit by the fire, he asked, "Now that you have found your father, will you be returning south?"

"Not yet, Your Majesty." She glanced toward Enver's tent. "I feel responsible for what was done to Karigan. If I hadn't . . ." She swallowed hard and shuddered as though to shake away bad memories. "I think I should stay to help her in what little way I can. I will return south when she does."

Zachary nodded. She had told him earlier how she and Karigan had been captured by Second Empire. Though Estral was not to blame for the cruelty Nyssa had inflicted, she would live with the guilt for her own part in Karigan's capture and torture for a long time to come. Ironically, had she not run off into the Lone Forest in search of her father, Karigan might have never found him and Fiori in the keep, and the two of them could still be there enduring who-knew-what. However, he'd have endured *anything* if it meant sparing Karigan.

In the night, Nari spelled Enver and sat with the Galadheon. The young woman slept peacefully, though Nari knew this was not usually the case. Even when she was away from the Galadheon, she could sense the dark turbulence of her dreams and memories, and not all of them were rooted in her recent experience with the Nyssa woman. She was haunted.

Nari also detected a shimmer about her that was a mark of favor from her sister. It was the light of Laurelyn, the lingering phosphorescence of some ancient silver moon that had once shone over Argenthyne. The glow had faded, and it would continue to fade, but would not, she thought, extinguish entirely.

Zachary had told her something of how Laurelyn had

drawn the Galadheon to her to aid the Sleepers, and Enver had told her more. Laurelyn had always possessed the gift of seeing long and manipulating events to a purpose. But she had not been able to see all, certainly not Nari's abduction by the aureas slee.

Nari was certain her love, Hadwyr, had searched relentlessly for her, and Laurelyn had, too, but even Hadwyr, with his lore of the wild, and Laurelyn, with all her sight and power, had not been able to find her. It had taken the arrival of Zachary and the gryphons to liberate her.

She considered the Galadheon, her wounded back, its rise and fall with each of her breaths. She'd adversaries, it was clear, and other entities used her, as Enver had put it, who were not necessarily her allies. The ability to cross thresholds, to walk the liminal line, was rare, and these others, even Nari's sister, took advantage where they could: the god of death, the Mirari, her own people. The Galadheon's adversaries would also take advantage if they became aware of what she was able to do.

I have not the power of my sister, nor am I a healer, but I am thankful to the Galadheon for what she has done for my people, especially those I once tended in the grove. It had taken courage and sacrifice.

She decided to give the Galadheon a gift in return. Nari had her own journey to complete, and that which she had carried within during her captivity, that which had sustained her, was no longer needed. It would only end when she did. Better to pass it on as a gift.

She laid her hand on the Galadheon's head. The young woman's eyelashes fluttered, but she did not awaken. Nari summoned the gift, her own piece of Argenthyne that she'd hidden deep inside, away from Slee's prying, away from all those who'd been imprisoned with her. Even Enver had been unable, as far as she could tell, to detect it.

It shone as an emerald glow about her hand, the essence of the living forest, which coalesced and melted into the Galadheon's temple. It had sustained Nari in the cold, barren environs of the cave for all those years, and now, she hoped, it would sustain the Galadheon in need.

Nari watched in satisfaction as her piece of Argenthyne bolstered Laurelyn's mark of favor. Silver-green flared all around the Galadheon before finally fading.

She had, she thought, given the gift well, for she sensed the Galadheon had a part to play not only in the preservation of her own realm, but also in the fate of the world.

In the end, Nari did not feel emptiness as she thought she might. Only peace and satisfaction.

AUREAS SLEE

Slee had drifted to the arctic north after its fight with the gryphons. Wounded, it was a frosty haze that floated among the clouds. The milder weather of the changing season made it difficult for Slee to heal, to reconstitute itself, and it feared it would take another winter to do so, which meant a very long summer even in the arctic, and its revenge delayed.

It drifted for an unknowable time, dreaming of vengeance. If the gryphons were anywhere to be found, they'd be frozen and broken. There was the girl who had thrown fire at it, and the Weapons who had forced it to leave without the Beautiful One. They would be dealt with, as well. It reserved its greatest fury for the Zachary, and revenge against him would also allow Slee to deal with the one who had cut off its arm the first time it sought the Beautiful One. Afterward, it would return to the castle and claim what was Slee's.

But first it must heal. When it did, it would be stronger than ever, and nothing would get in its way. Not even Narivanine, who, it sensed, sought her own vengeance.

FIREBRAND

The next morning, Nari was gone before Zachary awoke, and Fiori had ridden out on Coda with the messages not long after. He was still exhausted from his captivity and had slept hard, but he was restless, too, so he hiked out some distance from their camp to look upon the Lone Forest from afar. He kept low to the ground, should there be watchers, but little stirred on the rocky plain between him and the forest.

He recalled something of a dream or notion that had told him to *think, observe, protect*. He could not recall the source of those words, but they had been wise, and he'd done his best to memorize what he could of the keep and its surroundings. Those memories would help in an offensive against Second Empire. They would have to overcome the traps set in the forest first, but the advance scouts of the River Unit could eliminate that threat. He was certain the keep would not stand up to a siege. Its walls were ruins, and Second Empire's people mostly exposed. He would, of course, discuss strategy with Captain Treman and his officers to come up with a plan that would preserve the lives of his people while securing their freedom.

How far had they gotten with the dig? he wondered as he stepped back through the wards of their campsite. Was it actually possible for Grandmother to break the seal and lure the avatar of Westrion?

"Ah, Firebrand," Enver said. "I was growing concerned and was about to go search for you."

"I took a look around," Zachary replied. "Back toward the forest."

"Not too closely, I hope."

"Trust me, I did not dare."

There was a hint of a smile on Enver's lips. "That is good. I do not think we would be able to mount another rescue."

"How is Karigan this morning?"

"Still sleeping," Enver replied. "Her dreams are quieter for the moment. Lady Estral sits with her now." Zachary thought that was going to be all, but Enver said, "One moment, if you please." He ducked into the tent and returned with Karigan's longsword. "The Galadheon wished for me to give you this."

"She did?"

Enver nodded. "She cannot use it until her back heals, so, as she says, you might as well have the use of it."

Zachary took it into his hands, the sword he had secretly given her when she obtained swordmastery.

"I fear it will be some time before she can properly wield it again," Enver said, "or any other sword."

"Her injuries—they're that bad?"

"Yes, Firebrand. It will take time and work for her to re-strengthen that which was hurt. But to my thinking, the greater challenge may be overcoming what is in her mind."

"Is there anything I can do that will aid her?"

"You are in a position to understand what can haunt the mind after one has been cruelly treated. Tortured. Use that understanding with her."

"I will," Zachary said. "I would, that is, if she'd let me see her."

Enver glanced at the tent. "Seeing is not everything, and she is not surrounded by stone walls."

Now Enver did start to walk away, but Zachary called him back.

"Yes, Firebrand?"

"I want to thank you for all you have done. It has been beyond any duty required of you by Prince Jametari."

"It is not duty that compelled me. Would you not render aid were our roles reversed?"

Zachary nodded. "Still, you have performed a great service for me and mine. If there is anything you wish of me, you need but name it."

Enver bowed his head. "It was not done for reward, and you are welcome all the same."

"There is one other thing . . ."

Enver gazed at him curiously. "Yes?"

"You and your people call me 'Firebrand.' I realize the firebrand, the burning torch, is one of Sacoridia's sigils, but I still find it curious you should call me that."

"Yes, it is the symbol of the realm you lead, and you are the light-bearer of your people in a time of darkness. Not just the light, but the burning flame that is the spirit of a realm. Our own King Santanara called your first high king such."

King Jonaeus. Zachary shuddered with the weight of history. Did the Eletians expect too much of him? Jonaeus had not only been a warrior king fighting Mornhavon the Black for decades and, against all odds, leading Sacoridia to victory, but he was also a uniter. He brought the disparate Sacor Clans together to war against Mornhavon instead of one another, and helped form the alliance between Sacoridia, Rhovanny, and Eletia, and the other peoples who had stood against Mornhavon. Whatever the Eletians expected of Zachary, he was dedicated to leading his people to a peaceful existence so they might prosper, but it meant they'd have to weather dark times. A light in the darkness, Enver had said. He shook his head and watched after the Eletian, who strode along the path that led to the hot spring.

Estral then appeared out of the tent shaking her head.

"What's wrong?" he asked.

She dropped wearily to a rock beside him. "Your Green Rider is impatient to heal, and a bit angry. I think she's been having really bad dreams, but she won't talk to me about it."

He could see it was taking a toll on Estral. "Perhaps I can talk to her."

"Yes please. She will talk to *you*."

He wasn't sure about that, but he set the sword aside and made his way to the tent. Karigan had asked that he not enter, and though he sorely wished to, he honored her request. He sat beside the tent instead.

"Karigan?" he asked. Met with silence, he continued, "How are you doing?"

When she did not immediately answer, he thought she must be asleep. But then she did speak.

"I'm tired. I just want to be my old self *now*."

He feared, after what Enver had said, that it would be a long road for her to be back to her old self. "You have been through an ordeal, and recovery will take some time."

The tent rippled between them and he was not sure if it was her sigh he heard, or the breeze against the silken wall that separated them.

"I want you to be well, too," he continued. "After my arrow wound, I felt the same as you. I was weak, tired, and, I'll add, a most uncooperative patient, but the menders were right that I would once more be myself in time."

There was silence again from within the tent, as though she was considering his words. Then, "I'm—I'm sorry. I must sound like a whiny child."

"After what you've been through, you have every right to 'whine.' In fact, I encourage it. During my convalescence, I learned that it is best not to bottle up frustration. It just makes the healing take longer."

"It does?" she asked with a suspicious edge to her voice.

He smiled to himself. "If your captain were here, she'd say I spoke truth."

"I think you must be making that up."

"I am your king. I do not make things up. I leave that to minstrels and politicians." This elicited a surprised laugh from her, which made his smile broaden. "Estral says you've been having bad dreams."

She did not speak for a time, and when finally she did, she said, "Tell me a story."

Startled by the change of topic, he replied, "Wouldn't Estral be better for telling stories?"

"Estral has already told me stories."

"I'm not sure I can think of any."

"Tell me about when you were a boy."

He was so taken aback that he did not reply for some time. She was, of course, trying to change the subject from herself.

"Please," she said. In her voice was not just the desire to hear some tale told, but a pleading tone and pain. She was, he

realized, desperate to have her mind taken off her wounds and dreams, not to have him reminding her of them. He would help if he could, but he was not accustomed to storytelling, especially stories of a personal nature.

"Of course," he replied. "I am trying to think of something suitable." He delved back into his boyhood wondering what might prove amusing. Sadly, his training as a young prince had been far from amusing, but then a memory came to him that made him smile. "I will tell you how your captain and I became friends."

"Good," came her muffled reply.

"It happened," he began, "one day when I was hiding from my brother." He'd often hidden from his brother. "I chose to conceal myself in Rider stables. Most of the Riders, I recall, were out on errands with the fine summer weather. I must have been seven or so." He crinkled his brow trying to remember, and nodded to himself. "Besides my brother, I also managed to evade the Weapon who was assigned to me. His name was Joss, and I am certain I was responsible for turning him prematurely gray." Poor Joss, he thought.

"At any rate, I was hiding and sulking, wishing I could be back home in Hillander looking for crabs along the shoreline, or stuffing my mouth full of blueberries instead of being stuck in Sacor City all summer. I hid up in the hayloft and watched as this red-haired Rider walked slowly and unsteadily down the aisle between the stalls. Her arm was in a sling."

"A sling?"

"Why, yes. She had a dislocated shoulder, cracked ribs, and a concussion, but I'll get to that in a minute. I remember being fascinated as she halted in front of the stall of a blue roan gelding. He poked his nose out to look at her, and I could swear the two of them were locked in some mental battle. The gelding, who I soon came to learn was named Bluebird, stepped backward, his head drooping.

"Next thing I know, she's haltering him and hooking him to the crossties in the aisle. All of this one-handed, of course. After brushing him, she brought out his tack. I think she must have heard the floorboards of the loft creak as I shifted my weight, because she looked up and demanded, 'Who's there?' I replied, 'No one.' 'Well, No One,' she said, 'why don't you come down here and show yourself.' I remember thinking her rather frightful with her red hair and sharp voice. She could not have been more than seventeen at the time, but she seemed very old to me. I had been taught, of course, to be respectful of elders, so I obeyed and climbed down from the loft.

"She was a fairly new Rider then and did not know me on sight. Royal princes don't normally spend time in common stables. I think she probably thought I was one of the other castle children. 'Well, No One,' she said, 'what are you doing here?' 'Nothing,' I replied. 'Nothing, eh? Then you can help me put a bridle on this horse.' And so I did. We saddled Bluebird, and she led him out to the pasture with me opening gates for her.

"She stood there, staring at Bluebird, then prepared to mount. I told her she couldn't do that, not with her arm in a sling. 'Whether I can or can't,' she said, 'I have to try.' You probably won't be surprised to know that she made it onto Bluebird's back."

"No," Karigan murmured, "not at all."

"She managed the reins one-handed and rode about the pasture, crouched over in pain. You see, Bluebird was green, hardly gentled, and Laren was green, as well. You know that she's from Penburn?"

"Yes."

"From a family of river drivers, many generations counting. She knew boats on unsteady river currents, but not horses. I learned later that two days previous, Bluebird had thrown her off into the paddock fence. She smashed a whole section of it. The hazards Green Riders face are numerous, and horses are just the beginning."

"When did she realize who you were?" Karigan asked.

Zachary smiled. His story had engaged her. He hoped it distracted her from the pain, at least a little. "Joss found me watching her ride. She overheard him address me as 'Your Royal Highness.' I think her face blushed as red as her hair." He chuckled. "As you can imagine, she had made quite an impression on me, and I think I fell a little in love with her the way a young boy might. I kept turning up at Rider stables to look for her and help with Bluebird—against my grandmother's wishes, of course. Laren was soon called to the throne room to explain herself. I would have loved to have seen those two formidable women in that face-to-face encounter, but I was not invited. They must have come to some accord, for after that, Laren became a strong presence in my life—not as a tutor, not as a mentor, exactly, but as an elder companion who looked out for me when she wasn't on a message errand. Because of her, I learned at an early age the stern stuff of which Riders are made."

After a quiet moment, Karigan said, "Thank you."

He touched the tent wall as if doing so would bring her closer to him, almost like a caress.

Telling the story had helped him, too. It took his mind away from what had been done to him, away from worries about Second Empire, and it brought other memories to the fore, of Laren reading to him when he was sick or feeling sad, going riding with her, playing games, the countless ways in which she had made his childhood much brighter.

He closed his eyes and almost imagined that Karigan pressed her hand against his from the other side of the tent wall.

BROKEN

Nyssa came into Karigan's mind whenever she was most vulnerable, when the pain was intolerable and she felt weak and useless and endlessly tired. Nyssa came in dreams, too, or in the gray haze between sleep and waking and, of late, even when Karigan was fully awake and lying prone in Enver's tent. She came flailing the thongs of her whip.

"You are broken," Nyssa said.

Broken, broken, broken . . .

The words burrowed deeply into Karigan's soul, worse than barbs into her flesh, and she knew Nyssa spoke truth.

Nyssa made her relive not only the flogging, but she brought the shadow of Cade to her, as well. He told her yet again how she had failed him. "It is all your fault," he told her, "that I suffer."

"No, no, no," she murmured. She crushed bedding in her clenched hands.

"Karigan," Estral said, "wake up. You're having bad dreams again."

Karigan gazed up at her. "Was . . . was I loud?"

"Not particularly. I was just looking in on you." Estral placed her wrist against Karigan's forehead. "Your fever doesn't seem to be back. That's good."

Karigan realized she was dripping with sweat.

"Do you want to talk about it?" Estral asked.

Her voice, Karigan noted, seemed to be eroding by the slightest amounts. "No," she replied.

Estral's lips formed a narrow line.

"I'm fine." Karigan wiped sweat from her brow.

Estral shook her head. "If you are fine, maybe you would feel even better getting cleaned up in the hot spring. It's quite wonderful, and Enver says it has minerals with healing qualities."

It did sound enticing.

Go ahead, Nyssa murmured in her mind. *Try it. But you won't feel any better.*

Go away, Karigan thought back at the apparition.

You are not strong enough to send me away.

"Think about it," Estral said. "I'll be back in a few minutes."

When she was gone, Karigan tried to summon her voice of command. "Sleep," she ordered Nyssa.

Nyssa simply watched her with an air of amusement.

"Sleep," Karigan tried again, but she heard only her own weak voice. And she tried yet again, putting her will into it, but still nothing.

Nyssa laughed. "I told you you were broken. You are not nearly as strong as everyone thinks you are. Give up, Greenie. What is the point of fighting?"

"Won't let you win," Karigan muttered.

"You've already lost," Nyssa said.

"Let who win?" Estral asked as she entered the tent.

"No one."

"How about the hot spring? Enver is scouting and the king is still sleeping, so it's all ours."

Karigan scowled at Nyssa. "Yes."

Nyssa remained silent, but Karigan didn't think it was because she'd "won."

"It'll probably be too much to submerge your wounds," Estral said as she helped Karigan rise, "but you can wade and wash up."

Karigan shivered as she stepped outside into the chill morning air, where Nyssa stood waiting, the everpresent smirk on her face.

When Zachary awakened, he felt the need to cleanse himself again, for something of his recent captivity clung to him still. Their camp was quiet in the dusky light, but for the morning chatter of birds. Thinking himself the first one to rise, he walked to the hot spring, only to find it occupied.

He backed silently into the trees and observed Karigan, facing away from him, shadowed and hip deep in the morning-gray pool where twists of steam rose around her in an ephemeral fairy dance. His joy at seeing her up and about was tempered by how stiffly and slowly she moved, as though in great pain, when he was accustomed to seeing only her strength and grace. Estral sat on a rock, knees drawn to her chest, keeping watch.

Not wishing to be a voyeur, he started to turn away to retreat to their camp, but Karigan stepped into a shaft of sunlight that slanted down through the trees, and he could not look away. He saw, in full brilliance, her back, its slender contours ravaged, her flesh in tatters. All that was not blood-crusted scabs was still-angry welts and bruises.

Dear gods.

He reeled away and stumbled down the path, only to pause and lean against the trunk of a tall pine to catch his breath. Nari had told him what had been done to her and hearing about it had been bad enough, but seeing it was all that much worse.

I am so sorry, Karigan.

If he hadn't already slain Nyssa, he'd do it again, but more slowly this time. He'd make her suffer as she'd made Karigan suffer. Alas, that retribution was denied him, and he could only hope that her soul, if she had one, was delivered to the deepest, darkest, and cruelest of hells.

Back at the campsite, he sat by the fire and stared into the flickering flames. He tried to still himself, but he could not get the image of Karigan's back out of his mind. He stood once more and paced. He thought back to when she had first arrived in Sacor City. Had she been sixteen? Seventeen? Young, at any rate, and already she had faced villains and monsters, and, against the odds, survived the journey to bring him a message for which another Rider had been killed. He'd known she was an extraordinary person then, but even so, he never suspected all she would do and accomplish in the following years.

I never wished this for you, Karigan, he thought. *You would have been much better off staying a merchant, perhaps marrying someone to help carry on the work of your clan. Having a family.* However, he knew the call to be a Green Rider could not be ignored, but oh, how she had tried. He shook his head at the memory. She had held out far longer than he and Laren had expected.

He was grateful when she'd finally answered the call, not just because of what she had done for his realm, but for his own selfish reasons. If only rank and status did not matter . . . He sighed. There was no use in stewing over what could not be.

A cry for help came faintly, but urgently, from the direction of the hot spring. He sprinted down the path. About halfway, he found Estral trying to support a sagging Karigan.

"We overdid," Estral said.

"I'm fine," Karigan said in a slightly slurred voice. She was in Enver's oversized shirt and wrapped in a blanket.

"You keep saying that," Estral said, "and yet here I am holding you up."

Zachary helped lift her to her feet, careful not to hurt her back; then he took her into his arms and carried her back toward camp. She did not protest, which he thought of as a bad sign.

Once they were back in Enver's tent, he helped her down onto her bedding. She lay on her stomach, and he nested the blankets around her. Estral tugged slippers from her feet that looked distinctly Eletian. Enver had been tending her in *his* tent, she was wearing *his* shirt and slippers . . . Zachary let go an irrational swell of jealousy before it could overcome him. Enver had also rescued her, and was mending her. For those two things, Zachary was most grateful.

Karigan looked tiredly up at him. "You lost your beard."

It took a moment for her words to make sense. He scraped his stubbled chin with his hand. "Yes, do you like it?"

"It is better than the beard you had when we found you," she replied, "but I miss your old beard."

"Very well. Then I will grow it back as it was before."

She plucked at a length of her own wet hair. "It grows back. Hair. A good thing."

"Would you like another story?" he asked, but she did not answer. Her eye was closed and she breathed deeply as though she were already asleep. He drew a blanket over her.

Estral motioned that they should step outside. When they did so, she said, "Thank you for the rescue."

"I was going to bathe," he told her. "I didn't realize the two of you were there. I saw—I saw her back." Estral remained silent, so he continued, "I never wanted, never meant for her to be hurt. Not any of my people, but especially not her."

"She is a Green Rider," Estral said, as if it explained all, and in a way it did.

The rage he always held at bay made him tremble. "Green Riders ride into danger. I know that." He shook his head. "I have witnessed floggings before, and it is an unpleasant punishment, but what was done to her was not just flogging, not even just torture. It was the work of a sadist." He clenched his hands, the cheerful song of the birds counterpoint to the darkness that welled up within him.

"I know," Estral said after a time. "I saw Nyssa's pleasure as she hurt Karigan. Karigan was strong during it all. She never told Nyssa a thing, not even to make her stop." She took a shaking breath. "Do you know that when we were imprisoned in Nyssa's workshop, Karigan didn't tell me she'd seen you and my father in the keep? She knew I would not be able to withstand torture, or even witnessing her being tortured, so she kept the information to herself with the hope that Second Empire didn't know who you really were. I did not find out you were there until after Enver rescued us and she regained consciousness and told us."

Even under those circumstances, he thought, she'd been protecting him. Her honorary Weapon status had been well bestowed.

"I was so eager to find my father." Estral squeezed her eyes shut, obviously still racked by guilt. "If Karigan hadn't followed me into the Lone Forest, we would not have known you and he were there. Thank the gods you are both now safe, but I keep asking myself, would I run off into the forest again knowing what would happen to Karigan? Do I prefer to have Karigan safe, but my father in the hands of Second Empire?

Or to have my father safe and my best friend savaged by Nyssa?"

"It is an impossible choice," Zachary replied.

"Yes. You cannot win when playing such games with the universe." She shuddered. "Her screams, I can still hear them."

He'd been assailed by what-ifs, as well, but no matter how dire his situation, he would have dealt with it if it meant sparing Karigan. If he entered his realm into the equation, and how Grandmother might have used him against it, the question grew murkier for the situation became much greater than the fate of two individuals. Estral was wise, he decided, not to play that game.

"I know that Karigan asked that you not see her," Estral said. "She did not want you to see her wounds, because of how it would make you feel."

"She should not be ashamed by how her injuries look," he whispered.

"No, my lord, it is more than that." Her sea green eyes were earnest.

"What do you mean?"

"She thought it would make you angry, and she knows you have more than enough to worry about than just her."

How fortunate for Cade Harlowe, he thought, to have had her love.

Estral continued to gaze at him with a tilt to her head. "Your Majesty, she didn't want you to see her because she cares about you. More than cares, and she didn't want to cause you pain."

He stared at her, hope surging.

"She loved Cade Harlowe, yes, but she loved you first." Estral took his hand and squeezed it, then let it go. "Perhaps you would sit with her a while? I am going to go watch for Enver."

"Of course," he said more calmly than he felt. He slipped back into the tent and sat beside Karigan.

He had always been certain of his own feelings for her, but he'd never known hers for sure. Until now. Estral had provided confirmation, and he trusted her word as Karigan's best friend. With the thrill of confirmation, however, came severe disappointment, the disappointment he could not act on it. He had tried a few years ago, and had failed miserably. He'd made the choice to marry Estora for the good of the realm, but had tried to have it both ways. Karigan had rejected him then, as well she should have. He'd been foolish. The irony of being king, the most powerful person in the land, was that he had so little power over his own life to do with as he wished.

Karigan awoke, cracked her eye open to see, to her surprise, her king sitting beside her. He was gazing off into the distance, his expression, in profile, pensive. There must be a thousand things on his mind, she thought, not least of which was what to do with Second Empire.

Was he really sitting there, she wondered, or was it just another false dream? At times, it was difficult to separate the dreams from reality. She thought to reach out to touch him to see if he was, in fact, real, for what king would sit with one of his lowly servants?

He would.

She resisted the temptation, content to study his profile, his strong jawline that had been concealed by his beard since first she'd met him. It took years off him, the removal of his beard, but she knew that if she looked into his eyes, it would be there, the years and all he'd witnessed, the depth of his thinking and concerns. His eyes made him older than his years.

Cade, whose life certainly hadn't been easy, had not had the weight of a realm on his shoulders, and had been some years younger than the king. That level of responsibility had not been upon him, though if he survived to carry on the work of the opposition against the empire of his time, it would not take long.

The two men were different and, yet, alike, each intense and prepared to fight for their people. She had loved them both, but with Cade, there had been no barriers between them as there were between king and messenger.

Not going to touch him? Nyssa said. *Your great unrequited love? What does it matter? You've already betrayed Cade, what's a little more betrayal?*

Go away. Karigan just wanted to sleep and forget the world for a while, but Nyssa only insinuated herself deeper into her mind, cloaking every thought in shadow, obscuring even the king beside her, until only darkness filled her vision.

You are broken, Nyssa told her, and the lash fell again.

SEEING THROUGH THE GREENIE'S EYES

Grandmother sat before the fire in the great hall knotting red yarn around a single strand of brown hair. She'd been so infuriated by the escape of King Zachary and the deaths of so many of her people in the process, that she'd dared not use the art until now. It had been bad enough the Greenie and her friend had managed to escape. And then the king? Her great prize? Working with the art while enraged would have led to disaster, but now that her strong emotions had settled, she could focus and work her intentions into the knots.

Since looking in on Karigan G'ladheon had worked well the last time she had done it, she decided to try this time looking *through* her eyes. The red yarn represented intensity, her strong desire for the spell to work.

Lala dropped onto the bench beside her and kicked her feet back and forth so that they scuffed the floor. She'd been moody since the escape of Arvyn, whoever *he* really was. Someone more important than an itinerant musician, it would seem. Lala knew only that Arvyn had been kind and patient with her, and she liked the music. After his departure, she had smashed the lute he left behind and fed the pieces to the fire.

"Quiet, child," Grandmother said. "You know I must focus or the spell will go awry. Either sit and watch quietly, or go out and play with the other children."

"They don't want me around anymore."

"What? Why not?"

Lala shrugged.

Grandmother could guess. Lala wasn't like other children. She had never really fit in. Among other things, she had a talent for the art, which could make others uncomfortable. Perhaps they actually feared her. Grandmother knew that feeling well, for all that her people respected her.

"What are you doing?" Lala asked.

"I want to see through the Greenie's eyes, to see what I can learn."

"You think she's still alive?"

"I do."

"Damn. I told her friend she'd die."

"Lala, language, please."

"Sorry, Mum."

Grandmother nodded. Just as well Lala did not play with the other children if she was picking up bad habits like swearing. "We don't want the Greenie dead just yet, so it is good she did not die of her wounds." Nyssa had been very good at what she did, and would have taken the Greenie to the edge, had Immerez not intervened. That was another sore point—Nyssa had been taken from them, she with her skills that were so difficult to replace. Grandmother grieved her death anew.

Lala, as if detecting her sorrow, touched her wrist. Grandmother patted her hand. The responsibility for all the failures—the escapes and deaths—rested on Terrik's shoulders. How could he have permitted the king to escape when they'd just experienced the escape of the Greenie and her friend? The loss of so high profile a prisoner as the king was a blow. She had intended him to be the symbol she would use to crush the spirit of the Sacoridians.

Terrik was now imprisoned in an underground box where he'd have time to consider his failures and pray, and he'd be further punished when she was ready, in a way that he would do the most good for his people and God.

She'd replaced Terrik with Immerez, who had a much stronger military background. He'd already enhanced their defenses and improved discipline, which was very important, he told her, because the escaped prisoners now had inside intelligence about the keep's complement and layout. They'd know its vulnerabilities and exploit them. There were Sacoridian troops in the north, he said, that the king could mobilize relatively quickly, as such things went.

She knew he was right. It was maddening how little information she'd gleaned from the king while he'd been wrapped in her knots, but she'd seen enough of his mind to know that Immerez was correct. The king would attack simply to release her slaves and deal a blow to Second Empire. That one was strong-minded, had resisted her. If only she'd had more time, but she hadn't wanted to rush it. She had not been, however, entirely unsuccessful in her efforts. She'd learned, for instance, the very interesting information that his wife was carrying twins.

Perhaps I'll knit them baby blankets, she thought with no small amount of amusement.

She had also had the foresight to set a few spells upon him that would, in time, bring him much grief, no matter how far away from her immediate influence he might be.

She needed to put aside thoughts of the king to concentrate on her project with the Aeon Iire, this current working of the art a diversion. The brown hair was almost completely wound into the bulky knots of yarn.

"Put another log on the fire," she instructed Lala. "Let us have the fire hot and bright."

As Lala obeyed, Grandmother tied the final knot. The hair was barely a glimmer amid the yarn. Using more than one hair would give her a better connection, but she'd used most of what had been taken for her great working. She wanted to keep the few that remained for any unforeseen need that might arise.

Lala did a good job with the fire, stoking it up to inferno proportions. The heat it generated almost pushed Grandmother back as she approached.

"Well done," she told her granddaughter. In the Arcosian tongue, as taught to her by her mother and grandmother, she said, "Let me see as Karigan G'ladheon sees." She tossed the working into the fire, then seated herself back on her bench and settled in for the duration.

As the fire died down, Grandmother, her back aching from sitting so long, was about to give up when a darkness appeared amid the languid flames. A very complete darkness. Had the Greenie died, after all? No, then there'd be nothing, no connection at all. Perhaps she simply slept. Grandmother bemoaned her poor back and hoped the Greenie woke up soon, and that she did so before the fire turned to ashes.

However, much sooner than she believed possible, an image resolved in the dark space and drew her in. To her surprise, she saw Nyssa. A ghost? A dream? The Greenie saw her as huge, the thongs of her whip extra long, the tendrils like vipers, and the barbs dripping blood into a puddle. Nyssa's face was half-shadowed, her expression a leer of delight.

"You are broken," Nyssa said.

Grandmother flinched with the Greenie when the whip came down, the barbs burrowing into her flesh.

The vision evaporated, but she heard, *Broken, broken, broken . . .* as an echo, the words carrying their own cutting strength.

She was shaking when the world around her became real again with the pop of dying flames and her people moving about the keep, their chatter and footsteps. She took a trembling breath.

Lala sat beside her again and took her hand. Her grip was warm and Grandmother was grateful.

"What did you see?" Lala asked.

"Nyssa."

Nyssa who was dead, but in the mind of the Greenie, she was a larger presence than ever, carrying on her work through the veil of death. Dream or ghost, it did not matter, for she'd broken the Greenie. Dear Nyssa, how Grandmother missed her.

"I want to be like Nyssa when I grow up," Lala said.

"You do?" Grandmother asked in surprise.

Lala nodded.

Lala, Grandmother thought, with her talent for the art, could be far more than a mere torturer, but obtaining additional skills would not hurt.

"I would that Nyssa were here to train you herself. You do know she studied mending first? Hers was a long training."

Lala practically bounced beside her. "I want to learn!"

"Then I must send you to the man who trained Nyssa." Grandmother was not sure she wished to part with her true granddaughter. It meant postponing her work with the art, but perhaps there was a way to do both. "He is in Mirwell Province. Would you be able to live away from me?"

Lala's young face became serious. There was a sharp quality to her eyes. "I would miss you, but I want to be like Nyssa."

Grandmother nodded. "Very well. It will be arranged, but we will communicate often and I will expect you to continue your studies with the art regardless of how much training you do with Nyssa's master."

Lala threw her arms around her. "Thank you! I will be good and learn lots!"

Grandmother chuckled and patted her back. "I know, child, I know you will."

THE TORMENT OF KARIGAN

"You left me behind so you could return to *him*," Cade said, destruction all around him.

"No, no, I love you . . . wanted to go back."

His eyes burned in accusation from where he stood amid the rubble and fog of dust. Even now she stretched her hand out, tried to reach him, but more debris fell and he was lost from sight.

Lost . . .

"Galadheon, Galadheon," Enver said. "You are dreaming." He gently shook her shoulder.

She was clenching her bedding again. Her hair stuck to her sweaty brow.

"Perhaps you would try to listen to the voice of the world with me," he said. "It would bring you ease and—"

"No." It came out harsher than she intended. He'd had her try calming teas, and placed steaming bowls of water and lavender oil near her pillow. He'd tried singing soothing songs, and, she believed, blown some of his magic sleeping dust on her—she'd awakened with some suspicious gold glitter scattered on her blankets. Still the dreams tormented her. She could not see how "listening to the voice of the world" could help, but only make everything worse by opening herself up to attack. She could not see beyond the shadows that clung to her.

"Very well," Enver said. "I would like to look at your back before you begin the day."

Begin the day? That was a laugh. The days were as bad as the nights. Nyssa dogged her, stood just outside her peripheral vision, was an unrelenting presence. Karigan was so tired she could barely force herself to carry on a conversation.

Enver was quiet as he examined her back and applied the evaleoren, then dabbed it over the burn that sealed her stab wound. The salve helped, but the pain and weakness, like Nyssa, were constant companions. He bandaged her wounds without breaking his silence. She was well beyond modesty when it came to his ministrations.

When he finished, he asked, "Should I send in Lady Estral?"

"No," she replied. She could, with some difficulty, dress herself, though she didn't think there was much point to it.

Enver rose and left her, and she sighed, not wishing to move, not wishing to leave the tent and face the others and their concern. After she forced herself to dress, she simply slumped back into her bedding.

"Yes, you are broken," Nyssa said. "The old you would have gotten up long ago and faced the world, no matter what."

Karigan closed her eyes, but Nyssa was there in her mind, as well. There was no escape, no relief.

"As for your companions," Nyssa continued, "they are getting sick of you, having to wait on your every need and listen to your whining." She played with her whip, twirling it through the air so that it sent droplets of blood spiraling in every direction.

Karigan loathed herself, her weakness and dependence, so it was no surprise that her caretakers would loathe her, as well.

"Right now they are huddled together talking about what to do with you," Nyssa said. "More than likely, they just want to get rid of you. Go ahead, take a look if you don't believe me."

Karigan crawled on her belly to the tent opening and peered out. Standing by the fire and speaking in hushed tones were the three: Estral, the king, and Enver. They did not look happy.

"I think your king is very disappointed in you," Nyssa said, "the weak and self-pitying whiner that you've become."

"I am not," Karigan whispered. She crawled back to her bedding. "I am not." But she could only imagine what he thought of her.

Nyssa simply shrugged, for she didn't have to say anything.

"I am not." But Karigan no longer believed herself.

"I am concerned," Enver said, "that the Galadheon's wounds are not healing as quickly as I would like."

The three of them stood by the fire. Zachary looked from Enver to Estral, their faces full of concern.

"Are her wounds festering?" he asked.

"The physical wounds, no," Enver replied. "Her spirit is another matter."

"She won't eat," Estral said, "and just wants to sleep, but whatever sleep she gets is very poor. She is no longer interested in songs or stories, and she doesn't even get angry anymore."

"That is so," Enver agreed, "and if she won't eat and her sleep does not improve, it won't matter if her wounds are festering or not."

Estral looked near tears. A sense of helplessness pervaded the air.

"What can we do?" Zachary asked.

"I have tried everything I know, Firebrand, as has Lady Estral."

They looked at him as if he might have the answer, but he was no mender. Clearly they thought he could do *something*. He was a king—he should know what to do, but he felt wholly inadequate.

"I will talk to her," he said. It was all he knew to do. Talk, and lend comfort and support.

He poured a cup of tea and paused at the tent's entrance. "Karigan," he said, "I am coming in." He didn't give her a chance to protest, just pushed his way in.

He found her as he'd last seen her, lying unmoving on her stomach, but her face looked more pale and lacked animation. He sat down beside her.

"I brought you some tea."

"Thank you," she murmured, but she didn't even flick her eye open.

This was not, he thought, like her at all. "Can you talk to me? Tell me what is wrong? Enver says your wounds are healing, but . . ." He didn't know what else to say.

"Broken," she murmured.

"What's that?"

"Broken."

"What do you mean? What is broken?"

"*I'm* broken."

"Oh, gods, Karigan, no you are not. Why would you say such a thing?"

"Because it is true. I am sorry to be such a burden to you. You don't have to—"

"You are no burden," he said softly. How could she even think it?

"But—"

"Rider," he said sharply, "you are no burden. I will do as I wish. If I am sitting here beside you, it is because I choose to. Now, you will drink this tea."

"But—"

"It is an order."

Her eye widened at that.

"Let me help you up," he said more gently.

He assisted her into a sitting position, hoping he did not cause her additional pain.

"You—you shouldn't," she whispered. "Just let me be."

"Why should I let you be?"

"You are the king."

He pressed the cup of tea into her hands. "Ah, you think I should be off doing other kingly things, like sitting on a throne and ordering people about. My dearest Karigan, taking care of my subjects *is* one of my kingly duties."

She sipped her tea, then gazed up at him. She looked so sad and haggard. "I can't imagine you bringing tea to *all* of your subjects."

"Perhaps not." He smiled. "There would not be time for anything else. And I must admit, you are a special case."

She looked away. "Please, you mustn't think of me as special. This thing between us . . ." She shook her head. "Estora is your wife, and she is a good person, whole."

"What? What do you mean whole?"

"Look at me," she said. "Useless. I can't even sit up on my own. So weak, my back . . ."

"Karigan, Karigan," he murmured, "strength and stamina can be regained. You are the strongest person I know, even now. Not many could endure what you have. You and Estora, well, you are two very different people." He paused, searching for the right words. "If I could change it all for you, if it were in my power to spare you, I would do so. If I could trade places with you, I would. But I can only be here with you, and I will tell you this: you are *not* broken, and every inch of you is dear to me and whole." He took a long breath before continuing. "I once told you how I felt about you. It was a couple years ago atop the castle roof."

"I remember," she whispered, looking away.

He placed his finger under her chin and turned her gaze toward him. "My feelings have not changed since then, not even wavered. If anything, they have only grown. Karigan, I—"

"No! Please don't." And she looked away again.

He cursed himself. His desire to express himself only made her hurt worse. At this time, of all times, he should be able to say all he longed in his heart to say, but a wall still stood between them, a wall that could not be breached.

"I will crush Second Empire for the harm they've caused you," he said, instead of what he really wanted to say. Words made such poor tools at times. "Now, drink your tea, and that is an order." He sat there as she drank it down. The intake of fluid could only help her, but the shaking hands that held the cup disturbed him.

When she finished, she gave him a tentative smile and lay back down. He stood to leave, but just before he stepped outside, she said, "My lord? Zachary?"

Startled to hear her use his name, he halted abruptly. "Yes?"

"I do, too."

It took him a moment to understand what she meant, and

when he did, he nearly rushed to her side again, but he saw she had already surrendered to sleep. Instead, he stepped outside, stunned and thrilled, and in mourning for what could not be. Enver was nowhere in sight, but Estral came to him.

"Well?" she asked.

"She drank the tea," he replied.

"That's more than I've been able to get her to do."

"She is in a dark place," he said. "She says she is broken. I don't know what to do to reach her."

Estral shook her head sadly and went to her own tent, as though in defeat.

He stood by the fire and threw a log on it. He watched the flames waver, then flare and roil as they ate into the dry wood. There had to be something he could do to lead Karigan from her place of darkness. He could continue to show her his love, but even love might not be enough. His gaze drifted across the campsite where the horses were picketed. Condor lifted his head and seemed to meet his gaze. He smiled. He would let her rest for a while; then he would try again.

Karigan drifted. Someone else wanted into her dreams, someone who had been there before and offered guidance, the Rider of ancient times, she thought, but Nyssa would not let him pass. She could not fight Nyssa, heard only the voice that told her she was broken, of no use, selfish and cruel. She stewed in a haze of deprecations, thinking it better her companions just leave her. She was no good to them at all.

Strangely, the clip-clop of hooves entered her awareness. She shook herself awake, and the horse came to a halt just outside the tent.

What? she wondered.

The next thing she knew, Condor stuck his head through the tent flaps and whickered.

"Condor? What?"

He stretched his nose as far as he could and lipped her feet. Even Enver's accommodating tent could not enlarge enough to fit an entire horse. With some effort, she maneuvered around so she could pet his velvety muzzle. His breath smelled of sweet grain.

"How did you get here, boy?" she asked.

Her king, *Zachary,* for he was more to her than just her king, poked his head in, then worked his way around Condor to sit beside her. "He misses you," he said.

And she missed him, but now she was torn—wanted to turn away, isolate herself, but also have the comfort of their company.

"Thank you," she said.

Zachary came closer and her urge to turn away grew more urgent. She regretted having indicated her feelings to him, for what couldn't be. She focused on Condor. Mercifully, Zachary did not try to engage her in conversation. He just sat quietly while she petted Condor's nose. Sometimes, silence comforted better than anything anyone could say, but now it only allowed Nyssa's voice to be louder.

He just pities you, you know. It's not because he really cares.

Tears streaked down her cheeks, and he moved even closer as though he intended to take her in his arms, but she shook her head.

"Please leave," she whispered, and she turned her back on him and Condor, and lay down once more in her bedding. She was empty and exhausted, and truly broken.

CAPTAIN TREMAN ARRIVES

Zachary led Condor back to his picket. He was alarmed by Karigan's dejection, didn't know what to do. The sense of helplessness washed over him again. He was a king. He was supposed to have the power to make things better, and it ate at him that he could not even help one whom he loved.

He decided he could use the company of a horse himself, so he cast about for Condor's grooming kit. When he found it, he set to Condor's hide with a curry comb. He raised clumps of winter coat that tumbled away in the breeze.

"Thought you, of anyone, would have drawn her out," he murmured to the gelding.

Zachary had some familiarity with despair due to his own wounding. There had been dark times when he wondered if he'd ever return to his old strength. The betrayals of his then-counselors and the situation with Estora had not helped, and it all only worsened when Karigan did not come back from Blackveil.

He leaned into the currying, and Condor grunted with pleasure and flicked his tail.

"You missed her, too, didn't you, boy."

Only Zachary's duty, and conflict with Second Empire, had brought him back, and there was always that fine thread of hope he'd held on to that Karigan would, in fact, return. He always felt he'd have sensed it if she'd perished, and so he never gave up, though he did come close more than once. When she did return, he finally healed fully. Sadly, it seemed his own experience with despair failed to help him with Karigan's.

He ducked under Condor's neck to work on his other side, and Zachary reminded himself that if it took him so long to recover from the arrow wound—both mentally and physically—he could not expect Karigan to be all better in so short a time. She hadn't even the benefit of Ben Simeon's true healing ability to help her.

He had been tortured himself at the hands of Grandmother, but with no obvious lasting wounds. He remembered pain, but no longer felt it. He could not recall much about what was done to him during that time. Perhaps one day he'd know if he'd given up any information. There was no evidence of torture upon his body. Not like Karigan, who would bear the scars for the rest of her life.

Estral wandered over and surveyed the clumps of chestnut horse hair snagging on grasses and brush. "You make a fine groom, Your Majesty."

He smiled. "Spring shedding, a sure sign of winter in retreat, at last."

"Poor Bane looks like he wants a little love, too."

"I will work on him next. We could stuff a mattress with *his* hair." A glance revealed that Mist looked as pristine as ever as she daintily cropped at the coarse grass.

Estral chuckled, then sobered. "I saw what you did with Condor earlier, taking him to see Karigan. Did it help at all? Did she respond?"

Zachary paused and picked hair off the curry comb. "Not much, I'm afraid. I—I fear that perhaps I am pushing too hard. I have never seen her so despondent. But you have known her longer . . ."

Estral slowly shook her head. "I haven't either. I've seen her angry, upset, grieving. Nothing like this, but then I don't know how one is supposed to be after having been hurt like she was. That on top of all that happened to her in the future time."

Her loss of Cade, Zachary thought. He slowly worked the curry comb over Condor's hind end.

"I can't help thinking," Estral said, "that she has some battle going on inside, and it is taking all she has."

Zachary stopped. "That is an apt description. I have tried

to help, but I am afraid I am more of a hindrance. She feels . . . she is scrupulous about not wanting to interfere with my marriage, and I am afraid my own desire to help only hurts her, makes it all the worse." He was not afraid to speak of such things to Estral for she had shown she already very clearly knew there were feelings between him and Karigan.

"I can see it is difficult," Estral replied. "She must be torn, both wanting to be comforted by you, and to be distant."

"I do not know what to do, if helping is hurting her." Facing an army of Second Empire seemed easier. It was concrete, he knew what to do, it was a problem he could solve.

"It may be," Estral said, "it is a battle she must fight on her own."

Zachary thought back to his own struggles after the arrow wound. Karigan may *want* to be left alone, but she shouldn't be. She may have to fight her inner battle on her own, but she needed friends to lend support. But maybe he shouldn't be one of them.

"I must admit," Estral said, "she has me a bit perplexed this time around. She's pretty resilient, but maybe it gets harder to rebound after a while."

"So, you've no advice for me?"

"I know what I'd tell you if you were not married to someone else," Estral said, "but since you are? It's a little harder. Still, I don't think love is ever misplaced."

He watched after her as she wandered away; then he exchanged the curry comb for a stiff brush, planning to work Condor from nose to tail. Before he started, however, the gelding rested his chin on Zachary's shoulder and heaved the longest, deepest, most heartfelt sigh ever.

Zachary patted his neck. "I know exactly how you feel, boy."

By the time Zachary finished with both Condor and Bane, he was overcome with a sense of accomplishment he hadn't felt in far too long. He was also covered in horse and pony hair, but the two gleamed in the sun and had seemed to bask in the attention. He'd combed and pulled Condor's mane and tail, as well, and now wound some of the coarse tail hair into a circle and inserted it into his belt pouch.

He was trying to brush the hair off his clothes when he heard some commotion in the campsite. He left the horses at a jog, his hand on the hilt of his sword. Or, rather, Karigan's sword.

To his relief, Captain Treman had finally arrived, accompanied by one of his officers, as well as Fiori, and, to Zachary's surprise, Rider-Lieutenant Connly and a pair of Weapons. Actually, one of the Weapons was a trainee in dark gray. The other, the full Weapon, was Donal. Estral and Enver had already gone forward to greet them.

When he approached, the Weapons dismounted and bowed before him. The others followed their example. The formality felt odd after so long away from court.

"Your Majesty," Donal said, "we are pleased to see that you are safe. Your message, which Lord Fiori bore, has been sent on to the castle with Rider Oldbrine. Lieutenant Connly is at your disposal, should you like to send any others."

He glanced at Connly, who was, at the moment, speaking softly with Estral and Enver. He followed them into Enver's tent. *Good,* Zachary thought. Perhaps the presence of another Green Rider would help Karigan.

Zachary, the captain, his lieutenant, and Fiori sat beside the campfire. The Weapons stood off some distance taking up their customary watchful stances, which was a familiar feeling, and not unwelcome. Perhaps he could now put much of his ordeal as a captive behind him.

"Lord Fiori explained to us a good deal of what happened to you," Captain Treman said, "and how you were freed from Second Empire. It would seem the realm owes a great deal to Enver of Eletia and Rider G'ladheon."

"Yes," Zachary replied. "More than you know."

He learned how, before Fiori had arrived at the River Unit's encampment, the Weapons and Green Riders had shown up in search of him.

"It was the queen's idea to send such configurations of searchers throughout the realm looking for you," Treman explained.

"And she did so without leaving herself or the royal tombs unguarded," Donal added. "As an additional benefit, our trainees are receiving some real world experience."

He also learned how the aureas slee had been overcome at the castle.

"The ash girl?" he asked.

"Yes, sire," Donal said from where he kept watch. "Captain Mapstone says the girl has been training with Green Riders, though she has no special ability. Something of the Riders, especially Sir Karigan's quick thinking, seems to have rubbed off on her."

The girl, he thought, deserved some commendation. If all his servants were so brave, Second Empire would not stand a chance. He thanked the gods, also, for Laren identifying the elemental.

"The ash girl also helped the captain after her accident, running errands and the like," Donal said.

"Accident? What accident?"

Donal explained.

"Good gods." Zachary shook his head. "I thought she would have learned the first time she was thrown into a fence." He was relieved she had not been hurt worse.

"The queen managed to salvage talks with the Rhovans," Treman told him.

The Rhovans. In all the crises, Zachary had forgotten about the Rhovans, and as they talked, his pride in his queen swelled, and he was humbled by her abilities and accomplishments in a time of duress.

Connly soon emerged from Enver's tent and joined them by the fire; his expression was disturbed.

"How did Rider G'ladheon look to you?" Zachary asked.

"I did not see her wounds," Connly replied, "though Lord Fiori told us what happened."

"I am not speaking, precisely, of her wounds," Zachary said.

"She is not well," Connly replied. "Dark, like I have not seen her before."

Captain Treman, who had been listening, asked, "Should I have our mender come?"

Zachary knew who that mender was since he had assigned him to the River Unit himself. His immediate inclination was negative, to not let a traitor near Karigan, but that mender had been one of the finest in the realm. Still, Enver had done very well by Karigan.

"Firebrand," the Eletian said, "I have done all I can for the Galadheon. Perhaps the mender has lore that I do not that will help her."

"Very well," Zachary said.

The captain nodded. "Lieutenant Connly, head back to our intermediate position and bring Destarion to us." Most of Treman's complement had hung back in the cover of the Green Cloak as Zachary had wished, but he'd also set up a small intermediate camp about halfway from there.

Connly rode out immediately. Zachary was relieved that the River Unit had arrived at last and he could takc action—no more waiting or wondering. He turned back to Captain Treman to talk strategy.

EXTRACT OF POPPY

When Destarion arrived in the evening, Zachary hardly recognized him. In Destarion's time with the River Unit in the northern wilds, he'd become trim, and his face was stubbled with beard growth. Rough attire had replaced his mender's smock and tailored city garb.

"Your Majesty," Destarion said, going to his knee. "It is good to see you and learn that you are well."

Zachary, still not past his anger at those who had betrayed him, answered coldly. "Rise."

Destarion obeyed, could not look him in the eye.

"Rider G'ladheon has not been well. You have heard what has befallen her?"

"Yes, Your Majesty."

"Enver thought it would be beneficial to have another set of eyes on the situation."

"I will do whatever I can to help."

Destarion looked like he had more he wanted to say, but Zachary turned away to resume talks with Captain Treman. From the corner of his eye, he watched Destarion pick up his mender's satchel and follow Enver into the tent. He tried to concentrate on what the captain was saying, but his attention kept straying toward the tent.

Estral, who had been sitting with them and adding any details about Second Empire's encampment that she could think of, said, "I believe, Captain, it is perhaps past time to start preparing that brace of grouse you so kindly brought us."

"Ah, yes—we were lucky on that count," the captain said.

"The birds are just starting to thrum with the season, and Lieutenant Rennard here has an excellent eye with bow and arrow."

Rennard rose to help Estral with the grouse, and Fiori engaged the captain and Connly in conversation, leaving Zachary to rise and pace. While the young Weapon trainee, Rye, kept watch somewhere on the perimeter of the campsite, Donal stood near the entrance to Enver's tent, which was a little odd. Did Donal not trust Destarion? As much as Zachary was still angry with Destarion, he did not believe he would do anything to worsen Karigan's condition, much less actively harm her. Besides, Enver was there with her. But, then, the Weapons had a very curious relationship with Karigan, and he couldn't say he entirely understood it himself.

"Do you know what's going on in there?" he asked Donal, indicating the tent.

"Master Destarion has expressed approval for Enver's work, and they've been discussing herbs and remedies. Sir Karigan has remained largely quiet."

Zachary listened for a moment, and indeed, Destarion was describing the efficacy of something-foil versus the many healing qualities of lavender.

"Sire," Donal said, "if you wish a change of garb, I've spare uniforms with me, though your buckskin *is* fitting in this setting."

"I would give you my kingdom for a change of clothes," Zachary replied.

"No, thank you, sire," Donal replied, as stoic as ever. "No kingdom necessary. I'd rather leave *that* in your hands."

It turned out that Donal's uniform fit Zachary rather well. By the time he had changed, Enver and Destarion had emerged from the tent.

"Well?" Zachary asked.

Destarion was decidedly solemn. "I have tended flogging wounds before, administered to wayward soldiers and the like, but nothing like this. Nothing so purposely brutal. More lashes and Rider G'ladheon might have bled to death or been crippled. As it is, no sane person would cause such mutilation, and I do not know if she will ever recover the full range of her back muscles."

Zachary felt the blood drain from his head. He'd known, of course, from his own brief glance at her back, that even she would not have withstood much more, but to hear it so stated?

"Enver has done remarkable work with the wounds," Destarion continued. "Rider G'ladheon is otherwise physically healthy, though very weak. Enver tells me that at first she fought against the pain and weakness, but now she has given up."

"Her spirit," Enver said, "of which we've spoken."

"So there is nothing new you can tell me?" Zachary asked.

"She is unable to sleep well," Destarion said. "If one cannot sleep, the mind is not able to rest and the body regenerate, and as a result, the spirit, as Enver calls it, can fall very low. The patient's dolor then becomes a detriment to the healing process. Enver has tried various remedies to aid Rider G'ladheon's sleep, but none have worked sufficiently. So I am going to administer a soporific of my own concocting."

Zachary crossed his arms. "Like you gave Laren Mapstone the night you and your fellow conspirators decided I required a deathbed wedding?" He couldn't help his rancor.

Destarion bowed his head. "I deserve punishment, my lord. I wronged you, and I wronged Laren, who was my friend. The soporific I, er, gave Laren was more basic. The one I've readied for Rider G'ladheon is more complex and healthful. I call it 'Morphia.' It is infused with extract of poppy seed."

"Then do it," Zachary said gruffly.

"Yes, my lord." Destarion reentered the tent.

"Do you agree with Destarion's conclusions and treatments?" Zachary asked Enver.

Enver nodded. "His lore is sound, and he is skilled in the healing arts."

"It would reassure me if you would watch over what he does."

"I will, Firebrand."

Nyssa had beaten her. She was broken and useless and weak, everything Nyssa said she was. It had gotten to a point that all she heard was Nyssa's voice in her head, even when Connly came to see her, even when Master Destarion examined her back. She replied to their questions with a simple "yes" or "no," if she answered at all.

And then, Master Destarion returned and showed her the vial of fluid. "This will help you sleep, Rider," he said. "It is potent, so I am going to give you only a quarter of the contents."

Karigan gazed blearily at the vial. "What is it?"

"I call it Morphia," he replied. "Extract of poppy seed can be very efficacious for pain and sleeplessness."

"Morphia" sparked some memory of the future time. She remembered drifting in peaceful nothingness. Yes, she thought, it would help her sleep and forget.

You think you can escape me? Nyssa goaded. *Then drink it. Drink the whole thing.*

Karigan peered up at her, that vicious smile on her face, the blood dripping infinitely from the barbs on the thongs of her whip. Yes, drinking the Morphia would be the only way to silence Nyssa.

Destarion removed the stopper to pour her dose into a small cup with measurements etched on its side.

What's the point of fighting? Nyssa said. *Drink it all and you can rest.*

There was no point, Karigan thought. None at all. She simply wanted to rest. She snatched the vial right out of Destarion's grasp.

"What?" He gazed at his empty hand in surprise.

Karigan tossed her head back and started drinking.

"Rider! No!" Destarion cried. He grabbed for the vial, but she rocked away from him and swallowed more.

That's it, Nyssa told her. *Soon you will have peace.*

Liquid dripped down Karigan's chin and spilled on the tent floor. When she observed Nyssa gloating, she paused. Some small part of her mind that was still her own stopped, resisted.

Drink it! Nyssa said. *Finish it.*

But Karigan resisted, and Destarion pried her fingers from around the vial. She drifted toward darkness, and at some point she heard the king calling to her, shaking her.

"Had to make her shut up," she murmured, and then there was nothing.

BEING THE KING AGAIN

"Rider! No!" Destarion cried.

Zachary needed no more than that to charge into the tent after Enver, with Donal on his heels. He grabbed Destarion by the front of his shirt.

"What have you done?" he demanded.

"I didn't—she—she drank the extract—too much of it! I couldn't stop her."

Zachary stared down at Karigan. To all appearances, she was peacefully asleep.

"Don't you understand?" Destarion said. "Drinking too much of it could cause her to stop breathing; her heart could fail."

Zachary shoved Destarion out of the way and knelt beside Karigan and started shaking her. "Wake up, wake up," he pleaded.

"She grabbed the vial right out of my hand," Destarion said, then he muttered something about her taking her own life.

Zachary would not have it. "Karigan G'ladheon, wake up. Wake up *now*!"

"Had to make her shut up," Karigan murmured sleepily.

"What? Who?" He shook her harder, but she was as limp as one dead.

"We must force her to bring it up," Destarion said.

"Firebrand, a moment," Enver said calmly.

He took the vial from Destarion and examined it. There was still a small amount of fluid in it. "She did not drink it all," he said. He then felt around the tent floor near her, then brought his hand to his nose for a sniff. "Some of it was spilled, as well."

"Did she drink enough to kill her?" Zachary asked.

"I do not know this extract," Enver replied.

They turned to Destarion, who looked relieved.

"I—I panicked," he said. "I thought she drank it all—didn't realized she spilled so much. No, it is not enough to kill her, but she will sleep hard and be groggy for a day or two upon awakening, with, perhaps, a headache. I do not think she took enough to stop her heart."

Zachary stood and thrust the vial at Destarion. "I do not want you near her again. Do you understand?"

"But—but she did this to herself."

Thunderous silence. Then, in a voice flat with anger, Zachary said, "Do you understand?"

"Yes, Your Majesty."

Enver handed Destarion his satchel, and he left the tent, escorted by Donal.

Zachary took a moment to contain his fury. Enver knelt again at Karigan's side, listened to her breathing and peeled back her eyelid to check her eye.

"Well?" Zachary asked. "Is she going to be all right?"

Enver did not answer immediately, and the wait was interminable.

Finally, he replied, "Her body is not distressed. In fact, it may be just what she needed, and she instinctively knew it would provide her with deep sleep."

Zachary exhaled. "That is a relief to hear." Karigan G'ladheon was, he thought, taking years off his own life. She did look more peaceful than he had seen since his rescue. Before, even in her sleep, there had been a tautness to her. It was gone now.

"I will sit with her to ensure all is well," Enver said.

Zachary hesitated, wanted to sit with her himself.

As though understanding, Enver said, "You've Captain Treman to speak with, and after, perhaps, you will sit with her for a while. In the meantime, if there is any change, I will alert you."

"If she changes for the worse?"

"I've my own healing skills. Be easy, Firebrand, I feel she'll be well, and even better when she awakens."

"Thank you. I am reassured."

He took one last look at Karigan. She breathed deeply and regularly, and he stepped outside the tent to find Connly and Estral waiting anxiously.

"Karigan?" Connly asked quietly.

"Enver says she'll be fine."

Both of them looked relieved.

"I don't think my heart can take much more of all the trouble she gets into," Estral said.

Zachary understood the feeling well. He saw Destarion standing apart clutching his satchel and staring at the ground. He should have maintained control over the situation, but then again, Karigan was not the usual patient. Maybe Zachary could forgive him one day, but it wouldn't be tonight.

"Lieutenant," he said, "please escort Destarion to the River Unit's camp."

"Yes, sire," Connly replied. He bowed and set off.

Zachary was about to return to the fire to continue talking with Captain Treman and Fiori, but Estral touched his sleeve.

"One moment, if you please," she said.

"Yes?"

She spoke quietly so no one else would hear. "Your reaction just now to Karigan—it was very strong, and it was noted by the captain and Lieutenant Rennard."

"Yes, what of it?" he asked, sensing what she was going to say.

She lowered her voice even more. "Rennard asked if Karigan was your . . ."

"Mistress?"

She nodded.

"What did you tell him?"

"The truth—that she is not. I explained that you care deeply about all your people, those enslaved by Second Empire, as an example. I also said you worked closely with your messengers and that Captain Mapstone was your close friend."

"And what did he think of your explanation?"

She shrugged. "We minstrels are pretty persuasive, and he seemed to accept it at face value, though he may come to his own conclusions."

"Thank you, Lady Estral." She would, he thought, make a fine Golden Guardian one day.

"I bring it up," she said, "for Karigan's sake. Rumors could prove damaging to her."

She left him then, and he mulled over her words. Many nobles kept mistresses—they were open secrets. Many kings before him had, as well. The idea of mistresses never reflected poorly on the man, but there was always a different standard for the woman, and yes, rumors could damage Karigan's effectiveness as a Green Rider and make life very difficult for her. They would also hurt Estora. But it was true, Karigan—no matter how he felt about her—was most definitely *not* his mistress, and he had no wish for her to be regarded as such.

The Weapons would maintain silence as was their wont, and which was expected of them by the oaths they took. Estral would not hurt her friend by spreading rumors, either. Lord Fiori, who must guess at his feelings, was a master of discretion. Of the Riders, he did not believe rumor would spread beyond their ranks. They had guarded Estora's secret affair with F'ryan Coblebay well enough, after all. The soldiers of the River Unit? That was an entirely different situation.

He must conduct himself with great care for his sake, Estora's sake, and especially for Karigan's sake. They were no longer on their own in the wilderness. The River Unit had arrived, and he had to be king again.

GHOSTS

She felt Nyssa trying to scratch at her mind even in the depths, pursuing her, trying to fill her with venom. Karigan tried to escape, but Nyssa surrounded her, closed in, suffocated her.

"You cannot escape me, Greenie."

No, it seemed she could not.

But even as Nyssa moved in, the clarion notes of a horn rang out through the darkness and roused Karigan. It was the Rider call, and she must answer. Nyssa hesitated, and Karigan took the opportunity to hurtle right past her and toward the sound, toward light. The light grew and grew until she was within it, and she found herself standing beneath a tree looking down into a valley. The silence was beautiful.

"Indura Luin," Siris Kiltyre said beside her, his hand resting on the twisted horn of the Green Riders that hung over his shoulder. "Or rather, what remains after Mornhavon the Black drained it."

Indura Luin was the name, in the old tongue, of a lake that once existed there, Mirror of the Moon, in the common. It had been of spiritual importance to the Sacor Clans, which was why Mornhavon had drained it. Now the valley was simply known as the Lost Lake.

Karigan remembered the tree she was standing beneath. She and Alton had picnicked beneath it five years ago. It had turned into an eventful day, for Shawdell the Eletian had lain in wait on the opposite ridge to ambush the king as he and his party hunted in the valley.

"We are holding the torturer at bay," Siris said.

We? A haze formed around them, and then resolved into

the ghostly figures of Green Riders, some mounted on phantom steeds, others afoot, their uniforms and weaponry of ages past and present. It was apt, she thought, for on that day five years ago, ghosts had helped her and Alton fight off Shawdell.

A few of the ghosts grew more solid in her vision than others—Joy Overway, Osric M'Grew, Yates Cardell, Ereal M'Farthon, and others she had known. F'ryan Coblebay stood more distant. She looked for one face in particular among the misty shifting mass, but could not find it.

Siris seemed to know whom she sought. "The First Rider is still answering for her transgressions and is not allowed."

Transgressions she had committed on Karigan's behalf.

"You must fight the torturer with all your power," Siris said. "You are the avatar of Westrion."

"She is everywhere."

"She is not *here*."

Not here, not here, not here . . . the ghosts murmured.

"You were hurt," Siris said, "and tormented, but there is no time to waste feeling sorry for yourself."

"Feeling sorry—?"

"As I've told you before, listen to the half-Eletian, let him guide you so you may strengthen your mind and resolve yourself to be rid of the torturer."

"But—"

"Rider, you are an avatar of Westrion. I have tried to impart wisdom that may aid you in that capacity. Always remember it is you who must command the ghosts, not the other way around. Remember that some will attempt to mislead you. Remember that the gods do not always have your best interests at heart, only their own."

He stepped forward, placed his hand on her shoulder. It was cold.

"We will watch over you while you recover," he said, "but after that, you are on your own."

The Rider ghosts closed around her, touched her hands, her shoulders, her back. Yates caressed her cheek and gave her a long, unfathomable gaze, and then they were gone. It was not so much that *they* vanished, but that she was absorbed into a dark, peaceful slumber.

THE DAY HORSE

Karigan accepted the cup of tea from Estral. She was still groggy and had a dull headache, but the long, deep sleep made her feel stronger. Estral told her she'd slept for two solid days. Nyssa was still there trying to scratch her way back in, but the blockade of Rider ghosts held strong.

Had they actually been real? Those dreams with Siris Kiltyre? He had called her "avatar," and there was something she had to do. Something to do with ghosts. The strange fragments of dream images made no sense.

"You do look better." Estral's voice wasn't hushed because she was trying to be quiet, but because the gift of Idris was fading. "More color in your cheeks. Feel up to eating some eggs?"

"Eggs? Where did you get eggs?"

"Connly brought them from the River Unit."

Karigan was already salivating. It was the supper hour and not breakfast, but she didn't care. She was too weak to sit outside, so she waited in the tent, listening to the sound of Estral banging pots and pans around out by the fire. She did not know where Enver was, but Estral said the king, his Weapons, and Connly had gone to where the River Unit had established an intermediate encampment about halfway to the Green Cloak. The fewer who moved back and forth, she explained, the better chance they had of remaining undetected by Second Empire, and the king wanted to meet with all the officers and survey the troops. So it was, once again, just the three of them. Karigan missed the king and wished he could be there beside her, but it was also a relief that the temptation of him was out of reach.

When Estral returned with eggs and sausage and panbread, Karigan's eyes went wide. "They gave us sausage, too?"

Estral smiled and nodded.

For the first time in a long while, Karigan was hungry and willing to eat. She ate as much as she could, but left a good portion untouched. Estral, however, looked pleased.

"Enver was right," she said.

"About what?"

"That you drinking so much of Destarion's soporific might in fact help you. We were afraid you'd had too much, that . . . that you would not wake up."

Karigan remembered Nyssa's nagging, but she had resisted, had just wanted to sleep. She then told Estral all about her torment.

"She's a ghost?" Estral asked.

"I am not sure exactly. She appears to me like one, but she is also in my head."

She then explained what she remembered of her dream of Siris Kiltyre and the Riders.

"If it was anyone other than you," Estral said, "I would have a hard time believing it, but I know you've become accustomed to dealing with ghosts."

"I am not sure 'accustomed' is what I am, but I certainly seem to deal with them an awful lot."

"It is good to hear you able to talk about it." Estral reached over and squeezed her hand. "We've all been very worried about you. The king, especially."

Karigan felt her cheeks warm. "I—I wish he wouldn't."

"It is difficult for both of you, I know. The heart does not always obey the head. Which reminds me . . . The king asked me to give you something." She produced a bracelet of braided horse hair made from Condor's own tail.

"*He* made this?" Karigan asked, running it through her fingers.

"He said Captain Mapstone taught him how to make them when he was a child. He and Condor, by the way, seem to be getting on famously. He thought that if you had something of Condor close by, it might make you feel better."

"I am so sorry," Karigan murmured, "that I worried everyone so much. I was lost."

"You were badly hurt. Still are, and we know this. With Nyssa haunting you, it is not surprising you were having an impossible time of it. Even had you not been haunted, the trauma of it . . . *I* have been having nightmares."

Estral tied the bracelet around Karigan's wrist for her, collected the dishes, and left to let her rest some more. She stroked the bracelet and smiled. She had once rejected a fine brush, comb, and mirror set he'd tried to give her. This, she would keep. So simple, so telling. And yes, having something of Condor close to her was a comfort.

She rested some more, in peace. When Enver returned and checked on her, he was pleased to learn she had eaten and was feeling better. She explained to him the torment of Nyssa, and then about the dream.

"Siris Kiltyre was," she said, "the third captain of the Green Riders, and he wore the same brooch I now wear, which is why, I guess, he and I have a connection." She told Enver how the ghosts of Riders past buffered her from Nyssa. "Siris said I should seek your help. I realize it all sounds incredible, but I have had dealings with ghosts before, including that of the First Rider."

"I know this about you, Galadheon, and saw it when you breathed in the smoke spirits."

Of course. With everything that had happened, she'd forgotten about that incident at the old lumber camp.

"You are wise to acknowledge the truth of these dreams and heed them," Enver said. "In what way did Siris think I should help you?"

Karigan thought back. "He said to strengthen my mind against Nyssa. To give me the resolve to get rid of her. He wants you to show me how to listen to the voice of the world. I know I have not been very receptive." She was still not enthused at the prospect, but she'd do anything to be free of Nyssa.

"The last time we attempted it," he replied, and not without humor, "you fell asleep."

"I remember."

"Your Siris Kiltyre is wise. This Nyssa has found a way through your natural defenses, and despite your ability to command the spirits of the dead, you have been too weak to fend her off. Siris Kiltyre and the Riders beyond the veil are giving us a chance to strengthen your defenses; then you may do with the torturer what you must."

What must I do with her? Karigan wanted to ask, but Enver was already bustling about, digging through his packs. He produced, to her surprise, two tiny teapots and an equally tiny cup. They were made with simple clay and glazed to a natural finish, and inscribed with intricate, swirling decoration.

"We're having tea?" she asked.

He produced a pouch and sprinkled dry leaves into one of the teapots. "Yes, Galadheon."

"We didn't do this last time," she said, with mounting suspicion. "Is it going to do something to me?"

He looked at her with amusement in his eyes. "We did not do this before because of your condition after inhaling the smoke spirits. The tea will help you clear your mind and find focus, but it is also the manner in which it is served that is important."

A ritual, she thought.

He took one of the teapots outside, and when he returned, it was filled with steaming water. He sat beside her and placed it on a tiny trivet of metal birch leaves.

"We use all the elements," he said. "The fire to boil the water. Water, which steams into the air. The clay pot is of the earth. The tea leaves, too, are of the earth, but also need water, the fire of the sun, and air to grow."

As the tea leaves steeped, an herby scent pervaded the air. He then poured the tea into the other teapot. He used that teapot to pour into the cup. The tea was a light amber color speckled with tea leaves. He bowed over it, spoke softly in Eltish, and then handed it to her.

"As you drink, remember the elements that have gone into the tea's making. Feel the heat of the fire, the moisture that has rained from the sky. Taste the earth of the leaves and clay, and feel the steam on your face."

It was, indeed, hot, so she took care in sipping it, and tried to do as Enver said without her own skeptical thoughts intruding. The tea had a nutty tang, but mostly tasted like stewed grass. Or, at least, what she thought stewed grass would taste like. Again, she tried to focus on the elements that created the tea and not her own sardonic thoughts.

It took only a few sips to empty the tiny cup, and he gave her instructions to relax and lie down on her stomach as usual, since sitting for any length of time would strain her back.

"When you are stronger, we will do this outside," he told her, "closer to the wind, to leaf and petal, the living rock. For now, if you fall asleep, it is all right. We will try again another time."

She was determined not to fall asleep, and she tried to visualize the peaceful scenes he described as he led her along a mind path. Breathing deep was also important to the process. At times he chanted quietly in Eltish. She tried to stay with it, but her nose itched, she had to yawn, her head ached.

The aching, however, soon dissipated with Enver's soothing tones, or maybe it was the effect of the tea setting in, but the visualizations came easier with startling clarity. Finally, he led her into a starry meadow of dew-laden grasses.

"Listen," he said, "to the breeze rustle the grasses."

She did.

"Feel the cool damp of a summer evening."

She did.

"Hear the chirping of crickets pass in waves through the meadow."

She did.

He gave her more sensory details, the spongy earth beneath her feet, the sweet scent of grasses on the air, and on until she felt she was truly there.

"You are hearing the voice of the world," Enver said.

She was?

"You will hear it more clearly with practice. Do you sense the Nyssa spirit there?"

"No." Karigan's voice felt disembodied, as though she spoke in her sleep.

"Is there anyone else there with you?"

"There is a horse," she said with some surprise.

"Ah, that is very appropriate. Tell me about this horse."

"A mare. She is white, so white that she radiates light in the dark. She is walking across the meadow to—to meet me. I am offering her a handful of grass, and she is . . . a little taken aback, I think. All right, she is going to try it. I think she is doing so just to humor me. Oh, dear."

"What is happening?" Enver asked.

"She doesn't like the grass and is spitting it out." It was actually quite comical to see the beautiful horse with such a look of distaste on her face, and working her lips and tongue to expel the grass. "She does not eat grass, apparently. She is gorgeous, and I think made more of light than horseflesh, though she is so soft to the touch. She tells me her name is Seastaria, and she is telling me not to be afraid."

Seastaria permitted Karigan to stroke her graceful neck, and it was like warmth and goodness and strength, and most of all, love flowed out from her.

"Her eyes are the sky in daytime," she told Enver. "I can see clouds drifting in them. She says she is my balance."

The mare then turned away and trotted off across the meadow, her tail flowing behind her. She vanished, and Karigan felt the weight of night in her absence.

It was some while before Enver spoke again. She thought she must have fallen asleep for his voice sounded very far off.

"This meadow is a safe place for you, Galadheon. Come to the meadow if you need to escape the Nyssa spirit."

He guided her out of the meadow, reversing the path he'd used to get her there. When she was back to herself, she felt peaceful.

"That wasn't too bad," she said.

When Enver did not reply, she rolled to her side to look up at him. He stared incredulously at her.

"What?" she asked.

"Seventy-five years or more it took me to meet my aithen," he said. "It took you less than an hour. And that was no ordinary aithen," he continued. "A very powerful one. Seastaria is the day horse."

"The day horse? What does that mean?"

Enver shook his head as if he couldn't believe her. "She is deep in Eletian lore, and even in that of your people. She is what you told me, balance. The light to the dark, the feminine to the masculine, peace to strife, day to night. She is life. Your balance, Galadheon, has weighed too much toward the night."

Salvistar's opposite, Karigan thought, but she had never heard of Seastaria.

"She has come to you as aithen, a protective spirit and guide." Enver still appeared to be incredulous. "You are truly favored. And," he added, "cursed."

"Cursed?"

"Great powers interfering in your life."

Oh, she thought. That was nothing new. But if the day horse could help protect her from Nyssa, it was an interference she could tolerate.

THE AEON IIRE

"The bad air should have cleared by now," Cole said.

"Let us go see, then," Grandmother replied.

At last, the excavation had been completed. The massive seal stone had been removed from the chamber of the Aeon Iire, and now she could go see the iire for herself. As she, Cole, and Immerez walked down the passage, their lanterns sent shadows jumping across stone walls.

"I've sent a messenger off to Birch," Immerez said, "requesting reinforcements."

"That's fine," she replied.

Slaves passed in the opposite direction, burdened with the last baskets of rock and soil to be removed, ushered up the passage by guards. Lantern light fell upon the sealed entrances to tombs with their ridiculous iconography of the death god warning away trespassers. Even if Grandmother had wished to gain access to those old burials, she'd no fear of false gods. Westrion held no power over her. In fact, she intended to demonstrate the power *she* wielded over *him*.

The passage sloped sharply downward, and Grandmother had the sense of walking toward the center of the Earth. The air grew stuffier, damper, smelled strongly of soil and wet rock. Cole had made the slaves clear the floor so that it was smooth to make the walking easier.

As they approached the chamber, she felt uneasy as she neared the living dark, or rather a dead dark that was yet animate. It wanted to feed on the mind, to steal one's life force, to destroy and bring suffering into the world. The chronicles of her people, it appeared, had been right about the existence of the portal, the Aeon Iire.

At last they came to a stone archway with the boulder that had blocked it pushed aside. It was not high, nor grand, but roughly hewn of solid granite and incised with more of the glyphs and pictures made by the Sacor Clans of old. Like the high wall that bordered Blackveil Forest, the Sacoridians had neglected other ancient sites such as this one to their peril.

Grandmother and her companions stepped into the chamber beyond the arch, and on the walls of bedrock, the glyphs became more alarming and forbidding, as though they were yelling at her to turn away, to go back. In fact, there was some residue of etherea present in the glyphs that must have once been wards.

The ceiling was low, made also from natural bedrock. She could not imagine what it had taken to carve the chamber. The work of her slaves was nothing in comparison. Staring down from the ceiling was a huge, crudely rendered, but well-preserved image of Westrion, the god of death, his wings spread, his hawk's eyes sharp. He looked wrathful and ready to slay with his sword any who approached the iire, the supposed portal to one of the underworlds of the heathen Sacoridians.

In the very center of the chamber beneath the image of Westrion was the iire. It was circular in shape, a shield of metal that rested on the ground, but not just any metal, *star steel.* Forged, it was said, by the god Belasser, who made the stars his furnace. Heathenish legend, of course, but even so, it was a creation of untold magic. Symbols more ancient than even Old Sacoridian, and of some otherworldly tongue, moved fluidly across its shining surface. She could not say precisely what they meant or represented, but she assumed they were protective glyphs of some kind that strengthened the already impregnable seal.

Immerez bent over to look at it, reached out to touch it.

"No!" Grandmother cried. He jumped back. "Do not touch it. There is no telling what would happen to you if you did." Instant death, she guessed.

She approached the seal herself, feeling its warning like a high-pitched whistle just above her hearing, a pressure in her head. There was also the sensation of dread, of the malfeasance it imprisoned beneath. Demons and dark spirits clawed at it for escape, shrieked for release, hungered for the living. She shuddered. Only a great magic could restrain such wild evil, but there was nothing that couldn't be broken.

She studied the smooth steel, tried to make sense of the symbols, but they folded and coiled and tangled as they swam across the seal's surface. They looked alive, if such things could live. There was not a speck of dust on it, no rust, no tarnish, no pitting, or deterioration. Had it weakened, the world would have been endangered, according to the chronicles. She could feel the truth of it.

Though the seal appeared intact and in perfect condition, she observed that a few of the symbols moved sluggishly, as though tired. Or dying. That was very interesting. Very.

On impulse, she produced a brown hair from her pocket, taken from the Green Rider who was the avatar, the avatar who should be protecting the seal. She dropped the hair onto one of the sickly symbols. It curled around the hair, and there was the most subtle of gleams, and the hair was gone. Was it her imagination, or did that one symbol grow just a little more lively? Only a very tiny bit, but still . . .

"Now what?" Immerez asked. "Now that you've found this iire thing, what are you going to do?"

"You leave that to me," she replied. "You worry about our readiness."

She was so entranced by the symbols swimming across the seal that she was barely aware of Immerez's departure. Cole had stationed himself at the entrance to the passageway. No one else came or went.

The sluggish symbols, she thought, were the weak point, and she'd have to find a way to exploit it. The longer she stared at the seal, the more she sensed the dark spirits clawing at its underside. They seemed to know she was there, and they were ravenous. Ravenous for flesh, ravenous for souls.

She smiled. There was no time like the present to begin.

"Cole, could you please send for my basket with the great working in it?"

"Yes, Grandmother." He turned up the passage and left her alone.

Once she had the trap set in place, she would bait it by weakening the Aeon Iire. She would need Terrik, and others, for that task.

PREPARING FOR BATTLE

Events were in motion. The best scouts of the River Unit had already been monitoring movements around the Lone Forest. They'd taken out some of Second Empire's own scouts and messengers who either fought to the death or killed themselves rather than face capture. It meant, Zachary thought with displeasure, that Second Empire was aware of them, expecting them. No matter, it was the new moon, and in the deep of night they would advance, and strike.

He decided he'd wait at the campsite where he'd already spent so much time with Karigan, Estral, and Enver, and use it as their command position. So he rode forth on a sturdy horse of the River Unit, with a borrowed helm and light breastplate, and accompanied by his Weapons, Fiori, Connly, Captain Treman, and Lieutenant Rennard. They left behind a few officers and soldiers to coordinate the advance. It was all carefully done to prevent Second Empire from knowing exactly how or when the Sacoridians would attack.

They rode through the illusion that guarded the campsite, which was dappled with gentle morning light, and Condor whickered a greeting. Zachary gazed apprehensively at the blue tent. Even though he'd poured all his energy into strategy sessions, concern about Karigan still chafed in the back of his mind. Had Enver been right that Karigan would benefit from the soporific she had swallowed? Or, had she . . . ? No, he dared not think it. The campsite was quiet, but for the arrival of him and his companions. Condor had not sounded distressed, and nothing seemed out of place. He dismounted and Connly took his reins.

Enver emerged from his tent and greeted the arrivals. He looked unperturbed, but he always looked so.

Zachary tried not to sound too anxious. "How is Rider G'ladheon?" After his quick conversation with Estral the other night, he was determined not to sound overly familiar with Karigan in the presence of others.

Enver's neutral expression could have been read in many different ways, and Zachary's apprehension only intensified.

"You may see for yourself, Firebrand." Enver gestured toward the path that led to the hot spring.

Estral, and then Karigan, stepped from the trees and into the campsite. Karigan's hair was wet, her cheeks flushed. She no longer wore Enver's shirt and slippers, but her own Rider garb, her greatcoat draped around her shoulders. Relief flowed over Zachary, and he watched her move stiffly and slowly, with Estral at her side to help, but she was alive and up, and the despair that had all but emanated from her appeared to be absent. They stared across the campsite at one another. Her one eye was bright and animated in a way he had not seen in so long. He wished to go right over to her, but he restrained himself.

Horses were led between them, and when once again he could see her, her vibrant gaze was turned away as she and Estral spoke with Fiori, Enver joining them. Zachary removed his helm, and Donal came to help him unbuckle and remove his breastplate. By the time this was done, Karigan was sitting on a log by the fire, and Enver was talking with her. She nodded at some question.

Zachary was on his way to speak to her when Treman intercepted him and said, "You should probably get some rest while you can, Majesty. We had a long night of planning, and will have a longer night, tonight. Of course, if the rest of us had our way, you'd be traveling to Sacor City already."

"We've been over this," Zachary replied.

"I know, I know, and I saw you in action last summer. You are an able warrior and leader, but we shouldn't take chances."

"I have made my decision, Captain. I have promised to stay out of the thick of it, and I'll have two Weapons with me."

"No offense to the trainee, but that is *one* Weapon, not two."

"A well-trained trainee. Now, if you will excuse me."

Treman bowed.

Zachary resumed his course. Karigan was now sitting alone, and at his approach, she started to rise.

"No, Rider, stay seated," he said. "I am very glad to see you up and about." It was an understatement, but he was too aware of listeners and how they would construe his words.

"Thank you, Your Majesty," she replied. There was an actual glint of humor in her eye. She no longer looked haunted, and he saw, with pleasure, that she wore the horsehair bracelet he'd made for her.

"I would return your sword to you," he said, "as I have been offered another by the River Unit."

"I think you should keep it for now," she replied, "as I am still unable to use it. I'd be honored if you did. Perhaps it will bring you luck."

"I thank you. I will use it then, and return it to your keeping when you are ready." He cleared his throat. "There is another matter we should discuss, and Enver and Lady Estral should be part of this."

When requested, Estral and Enver joined them.

"Tonight we attack Second Empire," he told them. "It is my desire that the three of you retreat south, behind the River Unit's intermediate camp. There is no telling how this will go, and I'd rather the three of you were out of harm's way." His words were meant mainly for Karigan, but he hoped she'd find them more palatable if she didn't feel singled out. Enver looked thoughtful, Estral was impossible to read, and Karigan stared at the ground. To his surprise, it was Enver who spoke up first.

"Firebrand, your scouts are very good, but perhaps I will find the traps of Second Empire more easily."

"This is not your fight, Enver of Eletia."

"Is it not? These people claim themselves to be the descendants of the Arcosian Empire, and adhere to its ways. Should they gain the upper hand, will they destroy Eletia as their ancestors destroyed Argenthyne? I would rather not find out."

"Then we are honored to have your help."

"I go where Karigan goes," Estral said. "I'm of no use in a fight."

Zachary gazed at Karigan. "Then perhaps the two of you should prepare to leave."

Karigan shook her head. "I'm sorry, Your Majesty. I realize I'm not much good to anyone right now, but I'm not sure I could ride even a short distance."

It was something that she admitted her limitations. Zachary glanced at Enver for his confirmation as a mender.

"It would be better for the Galadheon to not undo the healing to her back. This place is protected by wards and illusions. They should be safe."

"Besides," Karigan said, "Enver and I haven't found the p'ehdrose yet. I haven't completed my mission."

He stared in disbelief at her. "Karigan—*Rider*, I don't expect you to seek the p'ehdrose at this point. Not after what happened to you."

"I would like to continue. I can't imagine it would hurt to have more allies."

"We will discuss it later, after we take the Lone Forest. In the meantime, I won't ask you and Lady Estral to move. I *will* ask Captain Treman to post guards to this site to ensure your safety."

Again, Karigan did not argue when he expected her to. But then, she was intelligent, and even with her stubborn nature, common sense prevailed. He hoped that was what it was and that she wasn't giving up. But she smiled and there was that spark in her eye. Much relieved, he nodded to her and the others, and turned to resume preparations.

The black the king wore transformed him, and it startled Karigan. From rugged man in buckskin, to stern king in black. She watched him now as he consulted with Captain Treman, his intensity, the barely contained energy. If she were not such a liability in her weakened state, she would go with him into the Lone Forest, make sure he came out alive. But she could barely sit up for any length of time. The soak in the hot spring had been wonderful, but exhausting.

Lieutenant Rennard approached Estral almost shyly. "My lady," he said, "this may be a bit forward of me, but seeing as no one knows how a battle may turn, I was—I was wondering if I might have some token of your kind regard to carry with me. For luck, of course."

Estral's cheeks grew red. "Uh . . ."

"I'm sorry," he said hastily. "It was wrong of me to ask. Please, forgive me." He started to turn away.

Karigan shot Estral a significant look. "He's going into battle," she whispered.

"Wait!" Estral cried. He paused, a hopeful look on his face. "You took me off guard. Of course I'll give you a token. I, er, just have to find one."

Rennard gave her a most gentlemanly bow and turned to attend the captain, a broad smile on his face and a certain bounce to his step.

Estral sat beside Karigan and groaned. "What am I getting into?"

"You are putting him in a good frame of mind for battle," Karigan replied. "You can put him off after, *if* he returns."

"If? I hadn't considered that he might not."

"There is always the risk that no matter how well trained, no matter how strong, or how much experience a soldier has, he may not come back." It was not Rennard whom Karigan watched as she spoke, but her king.

Estral followed her gaze. "They'll come back. They have to. Even my foolish father, who insists he must go."

Karigan had lost enough Rider friends to know they did not always return.

"I asked Connly if he'd been in communication with Trace at all," Estral said. "If he had news of Alton and the wall."

"And?"

"Days before he and the River Unit found us, Trace told him all the Riders, except Alton, had been ordered to return to Sacor City. Trace and the others had already left the wall and were on their way. Trace guessed they were needed to supplement the search for the king."

"Even Dale?"

Estral nodded.

"Oh, dear," Karigan said. "That can't have made Alton happy."

"Apparently he was furious." Estral frowned. "First me being gone, then his losing the little help he had? I hope he does not become angry again like he was."

Karigan knew exactly what she was talking about. The wall had changed Alton, made him volatile, obsessed with its repair. But when Estral had entered his life, he had changed again. She eased his fury. Estral had told her that sometimes the old anger simmered, but it dissipated quickly.

"I am sure he misses you very much," she told Estral.

"You don't know how much I've wished to have him here." Estral shook herself. "Now I need to find something for Rennard. Any suggestions?"

"Usually a handkerchief will do."

"Just like the old ballads." Estral grimaced. "I don't think he'll want one of mine. They're all rather . . . used."

Karigan smiled. "You'll come up with something. I am worn out now. Going to go rest."

"Do you need help?"

"No, I'll be fine. You find something for Rennard."

Karigan marked the king's gaze following her as she rose and trudged toward Enver's tent, until Treman drew his attention back to the map they had been examining. She would be sure to get up and see them off, if nothing more. In the meantime, she would seek a white mare in a starry meadow.

TOKENS OF ESTEEM

Estral pinned her harp brooch to Rennard's tunic. "There, that should do it."

"You honor me," he said with a bow. "But is it not too much?"

The brooch represented her affiliation with Selium as a minstrel. It was all she had, but she would not tell him that. "May it bring you success."

He bowed again, this time with a kiss to her hand, and when he turned to prepare for departure, his back was maybe a little straighter, his chin up. Karigan had been right—who was she to deny a soldier going off to battle some small token of esteem? When he came back safe and sound, that would be soon enough to break his heart.

From the corner of her eye, she saw the king slip into Enver's tent. Karigan had not awakened to see him off, so he must be making a farewell of his own. When this was all over and they returned to Sacor City, it would also be a return to reality, and she grieved for her friend. Grieved for both of them.

Her father came to her, and she helped clasp the gray and green cloak the River Unit had given him over his shoulder. Under a matching tunic he wore a breastplate. He bore a helm beneath his arm.

"You will give Karigan her saber back when she awakens, won't you?" he asked. "The longsword Captain Treman has lent me is much more suitable for what lies ahead."

She placed her hands on her hips. "I'd find it much more *suitable* if you weren't going with them."

He tugged gloves on and flexed his fingers. "I should not

worry. I will be in the rear, with the king and his guard. I aim to get my hands on Lala and bring her back so you can regain your voice."

"I'd rather have you. We've only just found you. Besides, didn't Captain Treman say it appeared there was an exodus of civilians from the forest?"

"For the first, you will have both. For the second, even on the off-chance that Lala is there, I am going."

Despite his brave words and outward lack of fear, she was afraid. No matter how many times he had left on his far-ranging wanderings, no matter how many dangers he'd faced before, this was different. This was purposely walking into a situation where the object was to kill or be killed.

"I would be content to live without my voice if only you would stay," she said.

"When you have your voice back," he replied, "you can berate me, call me names if you like, tell me how angry you are about this mess I got caught up in. We must not forget this is bigger than the both of us. Didn't you just tell me a little while ago that your singing was helping with the mending of the D'Yer Wall?"

She nodded. How selfish she must sound.

"For now," he continued, "I am doing my part, just as the king is, just as young Rennard and so many others are."

"You've already done your part," she whispered, tears threatening.

He held her close. "I am very proud of the woman you have become, first traveling to the D'Yer Wall to help there, and then coming north to find me. I know it is not your natural inclination to do such things, but you've been very brave." He stepped back, his hands on her shoulders. "In fact, Rider Oldbrine is riding not just with messages for the queen from the king, but with one from me to go to Selium, to Dean Crosley and your masters. In my message, I have explained to them that you have exceeded the requirements for your master's knot."

Estral's mouth dropped open. "I—I haven't even been thinking about that."

"I know, which makes it all the more deserving. You had

passed all your tests and just needed the travel portion of the requirements to achieve master. I believe the experiences you've had, true life experiences, have more than met expectations. I am proud of you, and love you, daughter mine. You are a true Fiori."

They hugged again, she now overwhelmed by the significance of what he had done. Being raised to master would be life changing. She could be the teacher she'd always wanted to be. But first, there was the wall . . .

"Thank you," she said.

He grinned. "It is the best part of my position, you know, raising journeymen to masters. But now, as your father, I must ask what is this between you and Rennard? He is wearing your brooch. I thought you were rather serious with Alton D'Yer."

He'd heard? Of course he had.

She glanced at Rennard who was in deep conversation with some of his soldiers.

"I, uh . . . Alton and I . . ." This was, it turned out, awkward to explain to her father. "I love Alton," she said finally. "But Rennard seems to like me, and he wanted a token. Karigan said I should give him something since he is going into battle."

"Ah. Karigan has grown very wise, and that was kind of you. Either man would be a fine match for you, and I think your mother would agree."

"Father . . ." Her cheeks warmed.

He grinned again. "Now that all is settled, it appears it is time to go—they are waiting for me. I'll be back soon."

He turned and strode toward those who awaited him, and she watched as they departed, stepping through the illusion that protected the campsite. As dusk deepened, she realized she had failed to tell him that she loved him, too.

Into the evening dark, Zachary trotted with the others over the uncertain terrain, relying on perceptions other than sight to sense his footing. They had departed the campsite at dusk to allow their vision to adjust to nightfall, but without moonlight, it was impossible to make out all the details of the rocky plain. The soldiers were forbidden to use light of any kind since this was to be a mission of stealth. Any armor was shrouded beneath tunics, and bucklers held only dull finishes. This was not the River Unit's first night raid, and its soldiers moved with catlike assurance through the dark.

Fiori breathed hard beside him, but his long legs helped him keep up. Zachary, while not breathing as hard, was pressed to maintain his position, for he had not quite recovered from all he had endured as a captive. The soldiers were younger than he and Fiori, as well, but Treman, who was of an age, did not labor at all and, in fact, had increased his speed to move among the ranks.

Donal ran a few yards ahead, and Rye took up the rear. Rennard held a position to his right. The soldiers were spread out and silent, so it was difficult to make out their positions. Zachary knew he was somewhere in the hindmost ranks—Treman, his Weapons, and Fiori had insisted. Enver, in contrast, had been enjoined by the captain to move with the forward scouts to help pick out and disable traps.

The order to walk came down the line. After a time, they'd pick up the pace again. It would go on like this until they entered the forest. It was impressive that no one had turned an ankle or worse on the uneven landscape.

He caught his breath as they trudged on, his hand wrapped around the hilt of Karigan's sword, reassured by its weight at his hip. He considered it a token, much as that of the harp brooch Estral had given Rennard to wear. He was sorry Karigan had not awakened in time to see them off, though it might be for the better. Such partings were not easy. He had not dared interrupt her slumber. She was, Enver had told him, making up for the poor rest she'd endured until now, which she dearly needed if her wounds were to heal properly. When he thought no one was paying attention, he had stolen into the tent and knelt beside her. In the dim glow of a moonstone, he saw her face was peaceful, her breathing deep and regular. She looked much more herself, but he was not deceived, for he had seen her wounds.

Brave lady, he had once called her, and it was still apt, a thousand times over. How much could she give of herself? He would do her sacrifices honor in battle. He had kissed her cheek light as a feather so as not to disturb her. She did not stir, and he backed out of the tent in silence.

Stars winked in a vast array over the plain, though was that a cloud bank rolling in from the north? The night had turned sharp and biting, as though winter threatened to make a resurgence—not uncommon for the north in the early spring. As he gazed at the stars, he wondered, as he often did, if the gods resided among them, or if the stars were simply gaseous bodies as the star masters said. In any case, he would not rely on the unknowable, but on the leadership and skill of the River Unit and the steel of their blades.

"I should have listened to my daughter," Fiori said in an almost-whisper, though unnecessary chatter was forbidden.

"How so?"

"She asked me not to do this. Said she'd only just found me." He chuckled. "She was onto something—I'm getting too old for such adventures."

Fiori was considerably older than he appeared, and it was said that his unnatural appearance of youth was due to his Eletian blood.

"You could head back," he replied.

He perceived, more than saw, Fiori shaking his head. "I've come too far. Got to see it through. Most of all, I've got to find Lala so Estral can have her voice back."

The order was passed back to pick up the pace once more. As they ran, the darkness of the Lone Forest ahead blotted out the stars on the forward horizon. Their approach went on like this, walking, then running, and then taking short rests to drink water or to eat some small provision to maintain their stamina. When the Lone Forest loomed just ahead and its verdant scent drifted to them, they halted and a runner came back to confer with Rennard, then hurried back the way he had come, disappearing into the dark.

"What is it?" Zachary asked.

"Our lead scouts have been clearing the way, and first ranks have entered the wood and engaged the enemy," Rennard explained. "Second Empire's soldiers have helped to makc targets of themselves for our archers by keeping watch fires. We will advance after second and third ranks."

There would not be much left for him to do, Zachary thought in disappointment, but then he recalled how wily their enemy was. Outside the forest, it was difficult to believe there was a battle going on, for the night remained quiet, but for the scuff of boots on stone, and someone coughing in the distance. He paced in impatience, waiting for the order to move. When finally he entered the forest, he would take on Second Empire however he could, and cut off its head.

THE UNCERTAINTY OF THE WAIT

Karigan was disappointed to discover she had missed seeing Zachary and Enver off, and was rather surprised to find it full dark when she rose and stepped out of the tent. She breathed deep of the chill air, feeling rested and peaceful. She had found her way to the starry meadow that Enver had shown her, even without his special tea ceremony, but the day horse, Seastaria, had not appeared. It had been a good exercise nonetheless, and she had slept well after.

She pushed her hands into her pockets and walked over to the fire where she was greeted by Connly and Estral. Estral ladled out some sausage and gravy over biscuits for her.

"More food from the River Unit?" Karigan asked, sniffing the fine aroma.

"Yes," Estral replied. "They do know how to keep their soldiers well fed."

"A well-fed army," Connly said, "is a fighting army."

Karigan sat with her bowl, once again surprised by her own desire to eat. She spied one of their guards beyond the light of the campfire. The others remained unseen. She learned Zachary and his forces had departed for the Lone Forest about an hour previous.

As she ate, Connly caught her up about the doings in Sacor City following her departure, about Captain Mapstone's shoulder, the aureas slee, and how Anna had begun taking riding lessons and other classes with the Riders.

Karigan was pleased. "She'd make a good Rider, if only she'd hear the call."

"Yes," Connly said, an odd look on his face. "The captain has certainly felt the same."

He then told her about the arrival of the Rhovan delegation and how the captain revealed an assassin who had been one of Prince Tuandre's advisors. Karigan listened raptly and was surprised when her fork hit the bottom of her bowl.

"It sounds like I've missed a lot of excitement," she said.

Connly and Estral exchanged looks of disbelief.

"I guess," she conceded, "it's been a little exciting here, too."

Estral's expression was particularly pained.

"All right," Karigan said, "*more* than a little."

Connly was about to take a sip of tea when he paused. His eyes grew distant, glassy. He set the mug aside without looking, stood, and walked off without saying a word to stare into the dark.

"What's that about?" Estral asked.

"Trace," Karigan said.

"Ah." Estral, who had spent so much time down at the wall with the Riders, was well acquainted with the ability that Trace and Connly shared. "Useful."

"Yes."

Connly laughed suddenly at something they could not hear.

"And a bit disconcerting," Estral added.

"Very," Karigan agreed. It had been disconcerting back when she and Trace had shared a tent. Trace would go into rapport with Connly and laugh and smile, seemingly at nothing. Karigan, of course, could only guess at what was transpiring between the two, but didn't really want to know. "It's very cold tonight," she said. She could see her breath upon the air.

"Feels like winter is coming back."

"What did you end up giving Rennard to take?"

"My harp brooch."

"Your *what?*" That brooch was the badge of a minstrel, just as the winged horse was that of a Green Rider.

Estral shrugged. "It was the only thing that wasn't a well-used handkerchief or dirty socks."

Karigan laughed at the idea of Rennard going off to battle with Estral's dirty socks, but neither of them spoke of the impending battle. She stood to ease her back.

"You all right?" Estral asked.

"Fine. Or what passes for fine these days." She might not speak of the battle, but her thoughts were there. She wished to be with the king, to help as she could, but even with her ability she'd be a hindrance. She was still so weak and useless. She stopped herself when she realized the downward spiral of her thoughts. They sounded too like Nyssa.

Connly returned and warmed his hands over the fire. "They've been riding hard for Sacor City," he said of Trace and the other Riders who had been assigned to the wall. "Trace says Dale is whining a lot."

"About what?" Estral asked. "Being separated from Captain Wallace?"

Connly chuckled. "Not even. If you think about it, she's been at the wall for close to two years. Without any regular message errands. She's feeling the ride."

Karigan smiled. Poor Dale. Had it really been that long? "Where are they?"

"They've stopped for the night in Cloverville."

They'd still days to go before they reached Sacor City.

"It'll be a race to see who reaches Sacor City first," he said. "Trace and her group from the south, or Tegan from the north. Though, really, coming from the north is the longer ride. The sooner the queen gets word of the king, the better."

Estral smiled.

"What is it?" Karigan asked.

"Huh?"

"That big smile."

"Oh, when Connly mentioned Tegan. My father gave her messages for the dean and my masters, telling them that I am to be raised to master."

Karigan and Connly congratulated her. Rising in the ranks of Selium took serious study, ability, and true life experience. Estral had likely surpassed all the requirements, but as her smile slowly died, Karigan said, "You don't look as happy about it now."

“I didn’t want him to go off with the others,” she replied.

Karigan could have spoken words of comfort, but words would not ensure the survival of Lord Fiori, or any of them. The words would only be false assurances, palliatives. There was no telling how it would all fall out, and she worried about the outcome for one man in particular. So, instead of words, she reached over and clasped Estral’s hand, and squeezed it.

“It is always hardest for those left behind,” Connly said, “those who must endure the uncertainty of the wait.”

Karigan shivered and pulled her collar up. It was going to be a long, cold night.

SETTING THE TRAP

A bound and gagged Terrik knelt before the seal, still alive, his eyes wide as blood leaked out of his neck from the artery Grandmother had nicked. Meanwhile, she wrestled with a length of brown yarn, the color of earth, for they were underground. She knotted frantically, desiring to finish the spell, a variation of one she had tried before, but this time she exerted better control over it, would not let it master her.

The knots resisted being tied, forced her hands apart, stung her fingers. Sweat beaded on her brow as she concentrated. She made the yarn go under and over and through. She tightened the knot and felt the pressure within the chamber quicken.

She spoke the words of power in a precise cadence. She tried not to gag as she spoke these words of shadows and death. The things beneath the seal boiled and clamored all the more. The symbols on the seal writhed and glowed as though to increase its protection. The sluggish ones did not change. She rocked back and forth as she chanted and felt the burgeoning power build. Had she made a mistake doing this at night? When entities of the dark were strongest? Could she control it, dark within dark?

An end of the yarn started to untwine, separate into individual strands. Hastily she commanded it to cease, and then tied a knot for *awakening*.

Before the yarn defied her again, she tied a knot to *call*.

The last time she had tried this spell, it had failed to awaken the dead in the royal tombs, or at least she had not heard that it had. She thought she would've if it had proven successful. Perhaps it would have worked if she had been at the source commanding the spell herself, as she did now.

Terrik made a gurgling sound and collapsed to his side. Swiftly, she tied a knot to *rise*.

Her fingers stung, stung with the sensation of burning needles. Wind howled through the passage into the chamber, tossing her cloak about her shoulders. It bit her cheeks and caused the flame in her lantern to flicker. The shadows were preternaturally deep, her lantern light so feeble.

She must finish the sequence and use all her strength to do so. The wind now roared, an unnatural wind that felt not refreshing, but foul. As it careened around the chamber, it seemed to carry voices of another world, from the land of the dead, voices of the past, of those begging her not to kill them, voices of her sacrifices, the wail of a baby.

She spoke words of power, and the knotted yarn bulged and contracted and contorted. She felt the power she loosed rush out into the forest, seeking life, feeding as it went. It fed on greenery, even that which had yet to sprout from the earth, and the small lives of forest creatures. She directed it with single-minded purpose outward, seeking, seeking. It must not feed on the soldiers of Second Empire, no, and not even that of the enemy. She must be precise, control how much the power consumed, or it would become utterly unstoppable and destroy all, which was not her goal. She diverted it, and it flushed out sleeping birds, took foxes in their dens, caught a doe and day-old fawn even as they tried to run away. Coyotes in a pack . . .

It hungered, seeking with greedy fingers till it found the groundmites—Skarrl and his group—where her people had trapped them. It sucked the life from them, all eight of them, and when her control slipped for a panicked moment, it took those of her people who guarded them, as well.

She called the power back, lured it back with the promise of fresh blood. It surrounded her, a restive breeze that tapped her cheek. It pressed in on her as if to crush her. She caught her breath. Would her personal shields hold?

She used everything she had and drew the power into the knots. They bulged and expanded, the strands of yarn worming as though alive, then melding into one another and darkening until a black sphere hovered above her blistered and oozing hand. It lowered until it sat on her palm as smooth and cold as the first one she had ever made. Now she must bind it.

Blood pooled beneath Terrik's throat. She touched his forehead. His eyelids flickered. He was barely conscious. The sphere quivered on her hand in anticipation.

"You are doing your duty for the empire," she told Terrik. She had actually attended his birth all those years ago, assisting his mother's midwife. He had always been a good boy, but he'd failed as a captain. "I now absolve you of your sins and failures," she told him, "as you provide this one final service for your people and empire." She did not know if he heard her, but in the afterlife he would know. She was certain, with her blessing, he would find paradise, and they would remember him as a martyr. Yes, that's how she would explain it to his mother—he was a martyr for the cause.

She placed the sphere in the pool of blood beside his throat, and it drank. When it was sated, Terrik's corpse was drained of blood and the sphere was a dull silver that pulsated. Grandmother dared not pick it up.

"Cole!" she called.

It took a few minutes for him to reach the chamber. He looked around warily, his gaze settling on Terrik and the sphere, and then her. He looked rattled.

"Are you all right, Grandmother? That was some wind that tore through, shrubs dying before my eyes, birds dropping dead out of trees."

"Yes, Cole, I am fine." Truth was, she was exhausted and her hands, with their blistered and open sores, pained her. She wished Lala was there to coat them with ointment, but she'd been evacuated with the others. "Please bring the slaves. I am ready for them."

"Yes, Grandmother." He gave the chamber one more look before heading back up the passage.

All was ready. The time had come. She glanced at the sphere and sensed an eagerness about it. It wanted to fulfill its purpose. She was sad about Terrik, but proud of him, too.

Perhaps he'd been a poor choice for captain, but he'd faced sacrifice without fear.

She then glanced up at the chamber's ceiling where her great working hung like a canopy of knots, twined with the Greenie's hair. It obscured the painting of Westrion. The strands and knots crawled with restless energy. All the elements were in place, and once Cole returned with the slaves, the trap would be set.

"Soon," she told the unquiet ones beyond the seal. "Soon."

THE BERSERKER

Zachary spun round and drove the sword through his opponent's midsection. The soldier's mouth fell open as if to scream, but only blood gushed out. Zachary tilted the sword, and the man slid off it and crumpled to the ground. He wiped the blade clean on the man's tunic, then paused, panting hard, but alert, his senses heightened. Sounds of clashes came to him through the woods, the clang of metal, shouts and cries, the crack of branches. He glanced skyward and through the spaces between the limbs of evergreens he saw that clouds encroached on the stars. He wiped chill sweat from his brow.

The fighting around him waned as his companions subdued the enemy, but there was the sound of more clashes deeper in the forest, so he and his group ran again, leaping logs, thrashing through deadfall, and weaving between tree trunks. Now and again they came across bodies, either that of their foe wearing buckskin, or of their own. They found traps that had been tripped—nets hanging limp from trees, bear traps that clasped stout limbs, and pits with their camouflage of branches removed. They ran past watch fires guarded by only the dead.

Zachary's Weapons stayed right with him. Rennard ranged farther out, and Fiori disappeared in and out of the shadows. Other members of the River Unit blended into the night wood and were all but silent. He wondered how Enver fared when he stumbled across a Second Empire corpse with a white Eletian arrow in one eye.

They came upon another knot of fighting. The Weapons

cleared the path ahead with swift and deadly strikes, but not to be left out, Zachary rammed his buckler into the face of one foe and engaged another with his sword. The warriors of Second Empire had not the prowess with a blade that a swordmaster possessed, but some were better than others. This one was not. Zachary did not play at showing his superior skill, but killed expediently and moved on to the next.

Swordplay in the thick of the forest was not always easy. The sword or his arm got caught up in grasping branches. Maintaining solid footing proved a challenge on the uneven terrain, and tree roots were apt to trip one at a crucial moment. The darkness sent some thrusts askew, lending a dangerous unpredictability to bouts. He rounded on an assailant creeping up on him and bashed the pommel of his sword into the man's gut.

When they quashed this knot of the enemy, they paused again to catch their breath, the air thick with the foul stench of blood and rent bowels, and the cold cutting edge of winter. The eaves of the forest groaned in an unruly prelude to a storm.

"Weather moving in," Donal muttered.

"How far to the keep?" Zachary asked.

"I have lost track," Fiori said. "Lieutenant?"

Rennard was about to answer when a wild gust of wind bent and whipped the trees around and almost knocked Zachary off his feet. Pine cones and branches pelted them. The wind grasped his breath, and he felt the air being drawn from his lungs. The wind *hungered*, sought sustenance. Undergrowth shriveled right before his eyes and birds fell dead from their perches in the trees. The wind died as suddenly as it had surged, and pine needles drifted softly down on them.

"What in the name of the gods?" Rennard said.

"That was no natural wind," Zachary said.

"You're right," Fiori replied. "Not natural. I wonder what Grandmother is up to. She was devising some major spell during my time at the keep. She called it her 'great working.'"

"I remember. The Aeon Iire, the seal. She must have found it."

The others had heard of this aspect of Grandmother's pursuits during their strategy meetings, so they were not surprised, but they looked disturbed.

"There can't really be a portal to the hells, can there?" Rennard asked.

"It is in our lore," Fiori replied. "If it is real, one can see how it would be of interest to Grandmother. As for her use of magic, it is known."

"Yes, we will proceed with this in mind," Zachary said, "though I don't know what we can do to counter the magic. It could all be a big trap, and not just for Westrion's avatar."

"It's all very strange," Rennard muttered.

Zachary understood. Though he had become accustomed to the concept of magic actively affecting his world, he had also been exposed to it more than most, and not just around his Green Riders. The average Sacoridian was less likely to have encountered magic even as it became more present in the world. As for an avatar of the death god? Even he had a hard time swallowing that bit.

"With respect, sire," Donal said, "I think we should return you to—"

"We will do no such thing," he interrupted. "Captain Treman needs all the swords he can muster. Now, we had better move on before the rear guard runs into us."

Donal looked ready to protest, but Zachary strode off. The others hurried so they would not be left behind.

"What's that?" Fiori asked. He gestured toward a flickering light some distance off to their side.

"Let us see," Zachary replied.

Donal put his hand up to stop him. "Let us investigate first."

Donal and Rye moved through the underbrush, and in their black uniforms, they vanished into the night. Only the rustling of branches minutes later announced the return of one of them.

"Donal says for you to come," Rye said.

They followed him toward the light, which turned out to be a lantern sitting on a rock, its flame weak in the heaviness of the dark. Bodies of half a dozen Second Empire soldiers lay about on the ground.

"We've a mystery," Donal said.

Zachary saw what he meant soon enough. The bodies lay unmarked by any violence, not a drop of blood on them, but their faces were contorted in some agony.

"There is more," Donal said. He took the lantern and passed it over a hole in the ground. "It's a Second Empire trap."

The lantern light gleamed off the eyes and fangs of groundmites crumpled at the bottom of the hole, a deep pit. There was no evidence of obvious violence upon them, either, other than the fact that they had fallen into the pit. It was not deep enough to have killed them, just to contain them. In the tangle of limbs was one who looked more prominent than the others with finer furs and necklaces of teeth. On the whole, these 'mites looked better fed than one would expect after so long and hard a winter.

"A mystery, truly," Zachary said, wondering if these were the same ones that had brought him to Grandmother, "but one we cannot solve right now, for we must go on."

They left the lantern to mark the pit so others would not fall in it, and before they left, he noticed that much of the vegetation surrounding the bodies and pit appeared to be dead—no needles on the evergreens, the underbrush dry and brittle.

They caught up with the fighting and found, with dismay, the River Unit was being pushed back. Two soldiers rushed toward them with a wounded man between them. Zachary realized with a start that it was Treman, blood staining the front of his tunic.

"Stop, stop," the captain told his soldiers. "Put me down."

"Captain," Zachary said, striding up to him as he was lowered to the ground.

"Sire . . . Met a stronger defense than expected. Our front rank . . . falling apart. Rennard, you must . . ." His head lolled to the side. Either he'd fallen unconscious, or was dead. Rennard blanched.

Zachary wasted no time. He grabbed Rennard's shoulder. "Come, we must reverse the situation."

Donal tried to convince him to stay back, but he did not

listen. Rennard looked shaken, and he practically dragged the young man with him. Donal and Rye helped form a wedge, with Fiori falling in behind, to force their way through melees in an attempt to reach the front. Even with his eyes well-adjusted to the night, it was not easy to distinguish between friend and foe.

Metal rang against metal, there was the splash of blood, the cries of the wounded and dying, but as Zachary surged forward, he became singularly focused on reaching the front. His sword took on a life of its own, a scythe to reap a bloody harvest. The killing joy came upon him. There were no politics to restrain him, no betrayals to feed doubt. He harnessed all the unexpressed rage that had built up over the years, at the helplessness he'd felt during his captivity, and used it against the enemy.

Second Empire had little in the way of armor, and he threw himself against its warriors. They were too easy to kill, like bugs to be squashed. A thrust to the gut here, the razor's edge hewing off a head there. He gloried in the spray of their life's blood upon him.

His Weapons fought to keep up with him. He'd lost track of Rennard and Fiori, somewhere behind him, but felt the troops rallying around him, following his example, pressing back the enemy.

A spiked cudgel descended toward him and he sheared off the arm of the warrior who wielded it. He did not pause to provide the killing blow, but moved on to the next, and the next, stepping on and over bodies to reach the enemy. No longer a man governed by reason or empathy, he was a force of skill, strength, and bloodlust. If any steel touched him, he did not feel it. If anyone stepped in his path, he cut them down.

He soon broke into a clearing, his nostrils flared, and he searched vainly for another enemy to slay. The soldiers of the River Unit flooded in around him, and he raised his sword high above his head.

"Forward! Forward till the enemy falls!"

His words were greeted with a great shout from his soldiers, and they surged after him.

He paused when he felt a cold pinprick upon the heat of his cheek. And then another. He blinked and turned his face up toward the sky as snowflakes sifted between the limbs of trees, drifting this way and that as air currents carried them on their wayward course. For a brief moment, Zachary Hillander came back to himself, remembering how, as a small boy, he took joy at first snowfalls, at the games he would play, his cheeks ruddy and mittens soaked through from building armies of snow soldiers. It was a brief moment only, before he once more scented death on the air and the fury took him again.

BREAKING THE IIRE

The slaves were in place, about fifty of them chained together in the chamber they had worked so hard to dig out. It would most likely become their tomb. Leg irons were bolted to the floor so they could not escape. They were dirty, hunched and beaten. One or two coughed, someone sobbed, most looked resigned, and there was the one who looked fierce. Beneath the dirt caked on her face and the tangle of hair that hung over it, Grandmother recognized her, the agitator, the one who would have no kings. No emperors, either. Lorilie Dorran.

"Are you going to slaughter us now that you're done with us?" Lorilie demanded.

"Not precisely, dear," Grandmother replied, "though you may wish it before long. In fact, you may survive, but it depends."

"On what?"

"On how much one of your gods is interested in the welfare of you and your people."

The chamber felt very full with all the slaves in there at once, almost suffocating with its low ceiling. Cole and his second hung back by the entry to the passage. The silver sphere still floated by Terrik's corpse and drifted a bit toward the slaves. It wanted more blood, but there were other entities that needed to be sated.

Scrape, scrape. Scratch. Scrape, scrape.

She could feel them massed beneath the seal. When she glanced at Lorilie, she saw that the woman had blanched beneath the dirt of her face. She must sense the dark denizens of the underworld, as well. How could she not? Dread permeated the chamber. Perhaps Grandmother had more faith in Westrion than Lorilie, whose god he was.

"Your empire will never rise," Lorilie said.

Grandmother was impressed by her conviction. "Oh, it will rise. Sacoridia is dead." She chuckled at her own joke, but it was a weary sound. It was too much for a woman her age to contend with, and soon she must step back for the younger generation to take over. She just had to see her people through the fall of Sacoridia, and then she could live out the rest of her days resting and teaching the art to any with the talent who would learn it.

But now, the time had come to lure the avatar. She stepped over Terrik's body and scooped up the sphere into her sore hands. It pulsated more wildly, and she felt it sucking on her blisters, trying to reach the blood beneath.

"Oh, no you don't," she told it in a mild tone. "You've another purpose."

She gazed down at the seal, at the sluggish symbols. She stooped and lowered the sphere and felt the attraction between it and the seal like a magnetic force. The scratching beneath the seal grew furious. She gently placed the sphere over the dying symbols. It clicked when it touched the steel of the iire, and she stepped away.

"Come," she told her guards. "We do not want to be here when the spell erupts."

"Grandmother, I don't think you should be here at all," Cole said as they hastened out of the chamber and up the steep rise in the torchlit passage. She heard crying from the slaves behind them. Some were pleading with her to release them.

"If I am not here," she replied, "then I cannot finish what I've worked so long and hard to achieve."

She did not speak again until they stepped into the open air. She shivered and was astonished to see snow cascading down. A layer of powder already covered the ground.

"It appears winter has come for another visit."

In the distance came the sounds of battle, the shouts, the clash of blades. Somewhere through the wall of falling snow was the keep, empty of civilians, but guarded. The assault by the king's forces was not unexpected, and though Immerez had requested reinforcements from Birch, none had come. Had Birch refused, or had their messenger been slain enroute to his encampment? She would find out in time, and if the former, she would express her displeasure with Birch in no uncertain terms.

"Go now," Grandmother told her guards. "Go to Captain Immerez to help in our defense."

"But—" Cole began.

"You will not wish to be nearby when the spell begins."

"What about—"

"Go."

Her tone brooked no argument, and they left her alone in the snow. She stood there in silence for a moment, then removed a length of yarn from her coat pocket. It was crusty with Terrik's dry blood. It was time.

She tied the knot, a complicated chain, more by feel than sight in the dark. The lantern Cole left at the mouth of the passage offered scant light. She felt the power pulling at her as she worked, connecting her to the sphere, felt its pulsations through the yarn. When she tied off the last knot, she unsheathed her knife and cut the length of yarn in half. She checked the wards she had put in place behind a large rock near the entrance to the passage, and hid. Now she would see what came of her great working.

Lorilie Dorran had never liked the feeling of the passage as she and the other slaves cleared it out. The closer they had gotten to the chamber she and the others now stood in, the darker and more oppressive it felt. When Grandmother had placed the sphere on the round metal object she called a seal, the sensation grew even worse.

"I just wanna die, I just wanna die," Binning said.

Others prayed.

Pitkin said, "The king will come for us. He was with us here. He wouldn't just abandon us."

Lorilie was less certain. Royals were more likely to preserve their own hides than risk themselves for someone else, but King Zachary, who they'd known as Dav, had surprised her. He'd helped his fellow slaves if one weakened or needed assistance. It was not for nothing that she and the others had shielded him that day when Second Empire started stoning him. They were not absolutely sure what had become of him after Nyssa's workshop burned down. They were told he'd burned within, but most believed he had been rescued, and it was because of this rescue that Terrik lay dead at their feet. He'd allowed the king to go free. There was also something else happening—the civilians of Second Empire had left the encampment, along with their belongings and livestock, and the guards had been particularly alert of late. It meant, she believed, that Grandmother was anticipating an attack. Was the king coming back for them as Pitkin suggested?

"Let me out! I can't stand it. Let me out!"

Lorilie couldn't turn all the way around to see who was shouting, but she thought it sounded like Em. "Let us be calm, my friends," she said in an effort to prevent full-blown panic.

It was not easy to convince them, chained together as they were, and anchored in this malignant chamber waiting for who-knew-what to happen.

"We have already endured so much," Lorilie said. "We can endure anything Grandmother puts before us."

Binning kept muttering to himself. There were sniffles and more sobbing, but no more panicked outbursts. A *hiss* drew her attention back to the seal in time to witness Grandmother's sphere dissolving upon it. Some of the odd symbols moved more frantically, racing across the metal surface. A black viscous fluid began to ooze from the remains of the sphere and across the shining steel, swallowing the symbols. She could hear howls emanating from beneath the seal that turned her cold. Inhuman, they were. The panic started to build again, the weight of the earthen chamber closing in around her. Her own breath grew ragged.

The fluid now engulfed the top surface of the seal. It seeped over its edges, translucent with the hue of dried blood. A twisting, tortured groan arose from the metal, and the sound of hammer blows came from beneath it. A crack formed across the blackened seal and widened. It was as though all the world had gone still, silent, waiting. Lorilie heard not a breath, not the faintest flick of an eyelash.

She was not sure if her eyes were playing tricks on her, but dark mist appeared to rise through the crack. Her fellow captives shifted, cried. Binning struggled, yanking on the chains that bound them.

"Be brave, friends," Lorilie wanted to shout, but it came only as a whisper, for at that moment, a clawed, scaled hand reached up through the seal's crack, and a wave of despair crashed so violently into her she thought she would drown.

Zachary's forces had broken through the ranks of Second Empire to face those who guarded the keep. They were sorely outnumbered, but he led the charge into the clearing. Gore clung to his sword as he raised it above his head for his soldiers to rally around and follow, and follow him they did, roaring all the way.

Arrows descended in the dark from guards on the curtain wall loosing at will, and blindly through the snow and dark. Zachary's soldiers fell around him. He rushed heedlessly toward the wall and the enemy that loomed in the squall.

Donal and Rye tried to race before him, but they labored to keep up. Zachary caught the smashing blow of an enemy sword on his buckler, and deftly maneuvered his sword beneath the man's guard and disemboweled him.

He did not pause, but moved on to the next defender, who was armed with only a cudgel. Down he went. The joy still burned in Zachary, and he laughed as his sword swept across the neck of another. There was only the snow and the killing, until he heard a familiar voice, a distinctive gravelly voice, shouting orders from near the wall. He angled his attack in that direction, thrusting his sword into a soldier engaged with Rye and then stepping over the body. He went on to the next, and the next after that. He had turned feral, as untamed as the wind that rushed around him.

He glimpsed the shape of Immerez urging his soldiers on, but there were so many swords cutting through the falling snow between them. Instead of being deterred, the fire in his blood rekindled, and with a savage cry, he charged sword first, slashing and knocking soldiers out of his way with his buckler.

And then, he halted. Everything, everyone, heaved to a stop, fell silent. Even the snow slowed as though each snowflake was suspended in motion. A darkening dread spread through the air. His steamy breaths blew flurries swirling away.

The pressure of the air split, and shapes darker than night blackened the veil of snow. Their screams pierced beyond the range of hearing. The sky was full of flapping, drifting terror that changed the pattern of the snowfall. The spaces around the combatants filled with a darkling mist, and creatures—entities of some kind—scuttled by, perceived if not seen. Soldiers cried out in terror on both sides.

What the hells? Zachary wondered.

Rye turned to him. "Sire, I think we should—" Some clawed thing ripped off the young man's face, exposing jawbone and eye socket, before he could finish his sentence. He fell to the ground, and dark entities converged on him, jerking and tugging at his body. They slurped and gnawed in a frenzy of gluttonous feeding.

Zachary stabbed at the shadows, hit something that resisted the point of his sword, but he threw his weight into it and plunged the blade until it touched ground. The thing gurgled. He loosed his sword and plunged again and again until it stopped moving. He did so to the others that had clustered around Rye's body.

When he finished, he saw Donal's back to him, defending him from demons of the air. Yes, demons they had to be. Grandmother must have succeeded in opening the Aeon Iire, for what else could explain this?

The combatants no longer fought one another, but the dark beings that clawed and bit and feasted. A man dropped dead beside Zachary after he'd walked into a black mist. Zachary tried cutting at it, but it just continued drifting along and leaving corpses in its wake. How could they overcome mist?

He slashed through something skeletal, scattering bones, and fouled his blade in a winged creature that dove at him. A claw raked his shoulder, and only his breastplate saved him from worse. Fire lanced through the wound. Donal pivoted and killed the entity that scored him.

"I must get you away," Donal said.

"How do you get away from this?" Zachary demanded. "They are everywhere."

Shadows slithered by his feet. Others moved quickly among them, growling and snarling. They were horned and tailed and scaled, and stank of decay when stabbed. They flapped just above the heads of the soldiers, and some made chuckling, chittering noises before sinking serrated teeth into an unprotected arm or leg.

The Aeon Iire was broken, and now their only hope was that the avatar of Westrion truly existed and would come to their aid.

AUREAS SLEE

Slee continued to drift in its insubstantial form. Its time in the arctic had helped heal it some, and during its drifting time, it had plotted and planned, and found it had not the patience to wait until winter to take its revenge. So, it hunted, and brought with it snow.

It searched for the one who had hurt it most, the Zachary, and then it would hunt the others who had injured it, and take the Beautiful One with her offspring to its new domain, an ice cave in the far, far north. There they would live together. The Beautiful One would grow to love Slee. It would make her.

Slee had caught the tang of the Zachary upon the wind. He was still in the north region. It then whiffed the scent of the other that was dear to the Zachary, the Karigan. She was not far off.

Slee moved against the air currents to investigate. It roiled across tundra, over treetops and boglands. More woods and a stretch of rocky terrain. The air was milder here, but Slee persisted and found the Zachary below, in the wood. He smelled of metal and intent, as did the many other humans who moved with him.

A little farther south, Slee located the one it sought. The Karigan sat before a fire with another woman. Others kept watch nearby, but they were of no concern. She smelled of blood and wounds, and a darkness surrounded her. The guards carried the accursed steel, but *she* did not. She was weak. Slee was pleased.

The air felt potent, crackled with energy. Slee collected

itself as it prepared to take revenge. Hurting the Karigan would hurt the Zachary in a most pleasing way. Slee prepared to descend. It would snatch the Karigan, torture her, turn the snow beneath her red. Slee imagined the Zachary's anguish with much anticipation. It began to drift down, but the atmosphere abruptly changed, and Slee paused. The air currents of the north carried to it a foulness that it could not ignore, a sensation of great impending horror.

Down below, its prey stood. Slee roiled into itself when it sensed a god-being approaching her. The Karigan, it now saw, served the gods, and Slee would not interfere. Doing so would only end badly. So it would wait and observe, investigate the foulness on the air. After the Karigan had attended to her duty for the gods would be soon enough for Slee to satisfy its thirst for revenge.

THE DEATH GOD'S OWN

Karigan was up and down in an attempt to ease her back. She'd taken to leaning on the bonewood to steady herself. The muscles in her back were just too injured, and she was not accustomed to being up and about for such a long stretch. Estral, she observed, tried to write by the fire, but mostly she stared into the flames. Connly periodically paced out to check on their guards.

"Don't you think you should go lie down?" Estral asked.

Karigan was exhausted. She knew she should, but how could she? "Maybe in a little while."

It was past midnight, and it would be hours before they had any word of the assault on the Lone Forest. The night was deceptively quiet but for the restive moan of the wind. She thrust her hands into her pockets against the cold. Yes, she should try to sleep, but she knew anxiety would leave her unable to even close her eyes.

Clouds had moved across the field of stars like a low, oppressive ceiling. It reminded her of winter, the night gravid with uncertainty. More than that, the world felt thin, as though it chafed against others, other layers. Ghostly presences stepped through the thin places to make themselves known.

It began to snow.

Estral shut her book with a thump and hastily slipped it into its oilskin cover. "I can't believe it's snowing."

Snowflakes tapped on Karigan's shoulders like a drumbeat, lightly at first, then harder, thicker.

"This is just what they need for battle," Estral said, her voice despairing.

Karigan put her hand out and caught snowflakes on her palm. The flurries showered down harder and harder, walling them off, confining them to the glow and hiss of their fire. Did she hear voices in the wind?

Her gaze was drawn across the campsite as she detected the approach of . . . She peered through the snow. A large dark shape advanced through the curtain of white, becoming darker and blacker as it neared them. Estral was oblivious to it, and Karigan said nothing, just waited, for a knowing came upon her. She knew who sought her as though she'd been expecting him all along. The shape solidified into a horse as she knew it would, an impossible black like a horse-shaped hole to the heavens. No snow alighted on him. He halted before her and gazed at her from beneath his long forelock. Firelight did not touch his liquid black eyes.

"Karigan?" Estral said. "What do you see?"

Death and gods and duty, she thought.

Salvistar, god-being, the harbinger of strife and battle, and steed of the death god, blew gently through his nostrils, and there was memory. Memory of herself as Westrion's avatar.

"You need me," she murmured. She could not demur. Westrion had already laid his claim on her.

"Who are you talking to?" Estral asked.

Karigan did not acknowledge her. "I cannot ride," she told the stallion. "I am injured, weak."

Ride, Green Rider, breathy ghost voices told her. *Ride.*

With the knowing that had come upon her, she understood she would not feel the pain, the weakness, the exhaustion while she worked on Westrion's behalf. She knew his steed would not have come to her without great need. It was her duty as avatar. He knelt before her.

Ride, ride, ride, came the ghost voices.

Karigan sat upon Salvistar's back. By the time he rose, she was armored in star steel, a winged helm upon her head. She held a shining lance and a shield with the device of the crescent moon glowing in an ethereal pearlescence. She was cradled in a war horse's saddle, and though a chafron of star steel protected his face, he wore no bridle, for no bit would he tolerate.

"Karigan!" Estral cried, but her voice was lost upon the wind as Salvistar turned on his haunches and sprang into the shroud of snow.

"Karigan, what do you see?" Estral asked.

Her friend stared intently into space, standing stock still, snow crowned on her head and blanketed her shoulders.

"You need me," Karigan murmured to someone whom Estral could not see.

What in damnation? "Who are you talking to?" Estral demanded.

"I cannot ride," Karigan said. "I am injured, weak."

And hallucinating? Estral stood, took a step forward, but suddenly Karigan was gone and in her place was a knight clad in gleaming armor, sitting atop an astonishing horse. Estral rubbed her eyes to make sure she was not the one hallucinating.

"Karigan?" she whispered.

The stallion pawed the ground with a massive hoof. He gazed at her, and she knew she'd met death.

"Karigan!" she cried, but then they were gone.

Estral dropped to her knees, and snow soaked through her trousers. "Oh, gods, oh, gods . . ."

Connly dashed into the campsite, his hair gone gray with the snow. "Lady Estral, what is it?"

"Karigan. She's gone."

"What? What do you mean she's gone?"

"I—she . . ." Estral's memory of a conversation with Enver came back to her. Karigan had inhaled the spirits of the dead from the pyre they'd burned at the old lumber camp. He had explained that because of Karigan's ability to step across the thresholds of other worlds, she was able to communicate with the dead, and that there was an entity that acted through her. "*Who is this entity?*" Estral had asked. "*Your god of death,*" he replied. It had been too incredible to believe, but Estral had seen her command the ghosts of the lumber camp. There was so much about her friend she did not understand, and now this, the truth before her, incredible or not.

She rose and crossed over to where she'd last seen Karigan standing. Already her footprints were filling in with snow. Estral reached down and picked up Karigan's bonewood staff. It was like she had vanished from all existence.

Connly stood beside her and touched her arm. "Lady Estral, what do you mean she is gone?"

"She is the death god's own."

STELLAR FIRE

The landscape blurred by as the stallion ran like an arrow driving through the falling snow. In a leap, they were across the rocky plain and into the woods, his hoofbeats silent upon the ground. New spirits rose from fresh corpses along the way, and she might have paused to aid them on their journey beyond the living world, but as avatar, she knew the Aeon Iire was broken and that there was no time to waste.

The stallion flew through the woods. Mundane concerns of everyday existence, of who she was and what her life meant, were as nothing. She was only the avatar, Westrion's servant. The rest did not matter and remained some forgotten memory.

Deeper into the forest were more corpses and more spirits. Some swung swords as though they were still in the midst of combat and did not realize they were dead. The number of corpses half-buried in the snow increased as they went on. To the avatar, it did not matter which side the spirits had fought on, or why they fought, or even that they had died. The matters of the living were of no interest. However, the darkness that threatened the dead—their corpses *and* their souls—did.

The avatar encountered the first of the escaped hovering over corpses of those who looked to have been fleeing. The dark spirits balked at her arrival, and the stallion trampled them. There were many more throughout the woods. Some attacked, but she repelled them with her shield or ran them through with her lance.

"Come," she called to them. "You must return to your prison."

The dark ones, whether winged, scaled, or incorporeal, resisted, but hers was the voice of command overlain by that of a god, and she drew them along with her, willing or not.

She arrived at the edge of the forest where there was a clearing around the Ifel Aeon, collecting more of the demons as she went. The clearing was full of the living combating the dark spirits, and they were losing badly.

Zachary's inner fire turned to desperation. He screamed at his soldiers to hold their ground, to focus on killing the entities. He raised his sword, now coated in black gore, to slay a scaled creature, when there was a break in the onslaught, an easing. He sensed the creatures recoiling, like an inhalation.

The snowfall changed course again, away from another who came from the woods. He blinked sweat or blood from his eyes in an attempt to see clearly. There was nothing, but *something* . . . The demons scattered before it.

Again the world slowed, individual snowflakes of intricate design and prismatic dimension hovering in space. For a moment that stretched infinitely, everything else vanished from existence except for the snow and an armored figure on a magnificent stallion. The stallion was black, but not the black coal of the burning hells that were the demons. No, the stallion encompassed the cosmos, the brilliant light of stars, the amorphous tints of celestial clouds and colorful planetary bodies. Like his rider, he was armored, a chafron upon his face. His mane and tail flowed in no natural breeze, and snow did not touch him.

The knight sat erect, slender, the form of a woman, he thought. The armor was some strange steel he'd never seen before, and its surface rippled in his vision. She held a lance, which changed into a greatsword in her hands. She dispatched demon beings in effortless, sweeping blows. The stallion reared to crush others under its front hooves. With one hand she seemed to beckon, *command,* the rest of the entities as they trailed reluctantly behind, as if caught in some invisible net.

Westrion's avatar, Zachary thought. She had come, and she was saving them. Then he remembered that it was what Grandmother wanted. Grandmother intended to trap the avatar. He must warn her.

His movements, however, were sluggish as if he were mired in deep mud. He was barely able to take a single step forward. He tried to shout his warning, but she had vanished. He had blinked and she was just gone. Battle surged and he was once more aware of all those around him. They were still hacking and stabbing at demon creatures, but there were fewer now and they appeared to be drawing away.

The avatar saw that one of the living stood out from all the others. A bright flame, was he, like stellar fire. He stared back at her, and some distant memory that came from the part of her that was human sparked recognition. The flame of him warmed her. And he could see her? Not many could.

She changed her lance into a greatsword and continued on her mission to end the invasion of the dark ones, the image of the stellar fire lingering pleasantly in her mind.

She rode the stallion toward the entrance of the passage that led to the chamber of the Aeon Iire. An old woman concealed herself nearby, behind a rock, shielded by etherea to protect herself from the dark ones. It was plain she could not see the avatar. She was the one who had broken the iire, the avatar knew, but the star steel sword was not for touching the living, and so she rode on.

The dark ones tried to disgorge themselves from the passage into the open, but the avatar raised her shield and pushed them back. Claws scrabbled at her armor. The ones she had dragged along with her continued to resist, but they could not escape.

"You will return to the deep," she commanded, and her sword's blade easily cut through a clump of them. Their bodies leaked black rot and steamed in the snow.

Some retreated, others attacked. She cleaved into them,

the stallion trampling those before him, and slowly they forced their way into the torchlit passage. Healing the iire and stemming the tide of the dark was the only way to halt their invasion.

More claws scraped at her. Some dripped with an acidic venom on her. Her armor shielded her, but she felt the protections of it straining. As they made their way, she left mounds of their corpses behind her.

At last they reached the chamber and she dismounted, for the chamber held some barrier to the stallion. She could not feel it, she did not know what it was, but *he* knew and would go no farther. Within, a group of the living stood chained together. Many others were dead. She swept away the dark ones that threatened those still alive and feasted on the corpses. She ignored the screams and sobs of the living and went to the iire. It had been cracked and twisted and torn. Great magic had been used in its mutilation.

Dark ones swarmed at the breach trying to gain freedom, but she pushed them back, commanded those she had pulled in with her to return to the hell they had crawled out of. She slew those who disobeyed; then she touched the tip of the sword to the iire.

"Steel of the stars, the fire of Belasser, heal. Be whole."

The torn edges of the iire uncurled with fluid ease. Burred edges joined one another, melded together until the iire was once more whole and uncorrupted, and gleamed with renewed strength. She brought the protections back to life until they flowed across the steel with vigor. The dark ones howled and shrieked in frustration from their prison.

The avatar had cleansed the living realm of the dark ones, and the iire would not be easily broken again. She turned at the stallion's sharp whinny of warning. Had she missed something?

Living, burning, constricting tendrils of magic woven into a net fell from above and trapped her.

AUREAS SLEE

Slee had watched the dread denizens of the hells issuing out of the maw of a hill, and streaming among the mortals in their battle. It marked the Zachary's presence, and Slee found itself impressed by his prowess against human enemies and dark ones alike. Slee would get back to the Zachary later, providing he survived the onslaught, for Slee scented magic that carried a familiar tang that it could not ignore.

The avatar, it found, had entered the passage from which the dark ones had emanated, leaving a trail of carnage behind her. A mortal who had hidden herself near the entrance appeared and took mincing steps down the passage. Slee *knew* her, *knew* her scent of magic. This was the necromancer that had forced Slee from its domain, had roused it from its slumber. This wielder of magic had brought great woe upon Slee. Slee would make this person suffer for its many wounds and all it had lost—its cave palace, its collections, its pets.

Slee drifted quickly down the passage in pursuit of the necromancer, the necromancer who had summoned it and forced it to serve, the source of its great misery.

DARK ANGEL

The avatar had not been visible to Grandmother, but when the outpouring of the dark ones stopped, and in fact reversed, she knew it could only be the avatar's work. She'd remained safe within her magical shielding, or perhaps the bloodshed of battle had proven more alluring to the ravening dead than one boney old woman. In any case, she'd been left alone, and now she abandoned her hiding place and entered the passageway.

She stepped carefully among the splattered remains of the dark ones the avatar had left in her wake. Suppurating flesh and gelatinous entrails lay in thick puddles of black blood that boiled and hissed, and produced a caustic steam that burned her nostrils and made her eyes water. She hastened her step.

Near the entrance to the chamber, she detected an indistinct blur of motion, an otherworldly presence that worried back and forth. Salvistar, she thought, well pleased. There were the barely perceived hoofbeats, the ripple upon the air like a horse tossing its head in agitation, the angry squeal of a stallion. Her spell had succeeded in holding him in check.

As she approached, her perception of motion at the chamber's mouth ceased. Did the stallion watch her?

"I know you are there," she told him. "What is wrong? Is your avatar in trouble?"

A distant whinny of rage.

She clucked her tongue at him. "You do not frighten me, Salvistar. You cannot hurt me, for I honor the one true God. You are just an aberration."

She continued past him and entered the chamber as erratic air currents—not those of the passage, but those coming from the heavens—buffeted her, though they could do her no harm. The chamber was strewn with more destroyed demons. More than half the slaves, she observed, were dead, the others wounded and moaning. She caught those details in swift glimpses, for her attention was only for the figure kneeling in the center of the chamber beside the seal. Unlike the stallion, her spells had rendered the avatar visible, or mostly visible. She faded in and out, was translucent on the edges.

Grandmother was elated. Her great work draped and entangled the avatar like a net. It writhed across the armor, the knots seeking to burrow into it, and sparks flew where the knots fell across symbols of protection. The avatar struggled to throw the net off her, but the strands only shrank and tightened.

Grandmother stood before the avatar, almost giddy with anticipation. "I have you," she said. "You may be favored by one of your gods, but you are only human."

The avatar stopped struggling and seemed to gaze up at her through slits in the visor of the winged helm. More sparks erupted as the knots rubbed against the protections. The symbols appeared to be wounded, slowing their glide across steel. Some of the knots were successfully seeping into the armor, and the avatar shuddered.

"Yes," Grandmother continued, "I know who you are. When I am through with you, you will loose an army of the dead upon the lands at my command, and it won't be only the realm of Sacoridia that falls to the empire, but all of them."

Another knot sank into the armor and the avatar spasmed.

Grandmother was delighted. "And, with you, there is something else that has come into my possession."

She bent and pried yarn away from the avatar's helm. The yarn had turned pliant, sticky. She jerked her hand back when a knot sparked. She was not sure if she should touch the armor, but her spell should have neutralized its power enough to prevent her harm. In the end, she was too curious not to. She lifted the visor. But for some burning of her fingers, the steel did not injure her, and she stepped back to get a better view.

"Well, Karigan G'ladheon," she murmured, "we meet again."

A soft glow shone from around the avatar's face. Starlight, moonlight, Grandmother did not know, for the avatar moved partly in the realm of the living, and partly in the heavens, or so the chronicles of her people claimed, and she felt the truth of it in her bones. A patch of fine star steel mesh covered the mirror eye. The avatar's normal eye wasn't quite . . . normal. It was a dark, dusky blue, and fixed Grandmother with a raptor's cutting gaze, Westrion watching through the avatar's eye.

So this was her dark angel, trapped in strands of yarn, and now hers to control. There were more sparks, more knots burrowing into the armor, the avatar's face showing strain.

"Now, let us see your other eye."

Was it her imagination, or did the avatar's lips tighten with the hint of a smile? Undeterred, Grandmother tore the patch off and beheld the mirror eye. It was not just the iris or pupil that had turned silver, but the whole of the eye that gleamed and reflected, exactly as Immerez had described. Grandmother stared at the reflection of her own face with its wrinkled skin, the drooping eyelids, and sunken cheeks.

"The Mirari truly exist," she murmured, "and you are one. I have never seen the like."

She wanted the eye for herself, and her fingers twitched by her belt knife. But if she cut it out, would it still allow her to look across time? To envision the weaving of the world?

Even now, an image formed in the eye, and Grandmother bent closer. She gazed into a tumult of flurries, flurries cascading down in dizzying patterns. Snow, and nothing more. She stepped back, disappointed as the eye returned to its cold, silver gleam.

"Is that all? Snow? If I want to see snow, I just have to step outside."

The avatar smiled her tight smile.

In the chamber, it began to snow.

"What is this?" she demanded.

The wind pushed her back and back until she hit the wall. Through the blizzard she discerned a figure striding toward her. It was blocky, humanlike, but not fully formed. It was made of ice and had only vague features.

"Aureas slee," she murmured in realization. The elemental she had summoned to her service so long ago.

"You are the one," it said. It pointed an icicle finger at her. "You are the one that forced me out into the world, subjected me to pain, humiliation, and defeat. *You.*"

Grandmother put her hands up, palms outward, as though to stem its advance. "I simply called you, requested aid."

"You forced me from my domain, witch, and it has been the ruin of me. And now I will break the binding."

"No, no. Please, let us come to some accommodation." She fumbled in her pouch for any stray bit of yarn she could lay her fingers on, but another fierce gust blew it out of her hands. "We can help one another!" Her lips were numb, her cheeks burning from the cold.

"Enough!" The chamber seemed to shake with the aureas slee's voice. Its hand grew into a long sword of ice, and it thrust the blade into her gut, and twisted.

Grandmother looked down at herself as the ice blade, smeared with her own blood, was withdrawn from her midsection. She was more aghast than anything that it should all end this way. She had been so close to using the avatar's command of the dead and mirror eye to defeat the lands for Second Empire. As everything went cold inside her and she spilled to the chamber's floor, she wondered how her people would go on without her, who would make sure Lala buttoned up her coat on cold winter days, who would lead her people?

Blood, hot in contrast to everything else, flowed over her fingers splayed over her wound. She could not hold in the blood. She saw only melting puddles of snow, and that the aureas slee had already left.

Help, she tried to say, but no word came out. She tried reaching for the slaves across the chamber, but she could not lift her hand.

As her sight dimmed, she saw that her descent into death had weakened the spell that bound the avatar. The avatar forced herself to her feet and shredded the strands of magic, and freed herself. She regained her sword, pushed her visor back in place, and staggered to where Grandmother lay and stared down at her.

"You cannot hurt me," Grandmother whispered.

The avatar did not speak, but even as Grandmother's world faded away, she heard the unmistakable downbeats of Westrion's wings.

No! You are not my god!

When her spirit left her body, the avatar loomed large and bright and winged before her, beautiful and terrible, truly the dark angel. The sword of silver fire pointed at the Aeon Iire, the seal that covered the portal to the deepest, most malignant of hells in the theology of the Sacoridians, reserved for the worst of the worst.

"That is not my hell," Grandmother the spirit said. "I deserve paradise for all I have done for my people. I do not believe in your—"

"Go."

The avatar's voice was both terrifying and majestic, and its power forced Grandmother toward the seal. Her will was no longer her own.

"Go," the avatar commanded once more. "You are judged. May that which you inflicted upon others be visited upon you with no end. I sentence you to an eternity of torment for your crimes. *Go.*"

Grandmother felt her incorporeal self dragged and sucked through the iire. Darkness scrabbled around her and shrieked its shrill delight.

RAGE

After the attack of the demons, Zachary observed that something had changed in the attitude of Second Empire's forces. Despite having the advantage of cover in the keep, their defense crumbled. Now that the demons harried them no longer, the soldiers of the River Unit swarmed through breaks in the curtain wall, Fiori with them. Other combatants fought in small clutches before the main entrance of the curtain wall, Zachary among them. He eagerly traded blows with one of the better swordsmen.

"I know you," his opponent said breathlessly. "You're the—"

Zachary slashed through his neck before he could say more, almost beheading him. He turned to take on another enemy, but they were few, and they were engaged. He stood there in the snow squall, his heart pounding, his blood singing in readiness for more slaughter, but all else—the din of battle, the storm, the stench of blood—fell away, grew remote, slowed down. Snowflakes hung in the air.

The avatar and her stallion reappeared. They gleamed of starshine and silver fire, the stallion's muscles rippling like ebon silk as he tossed his head and pawed at the snow. Flurries gyred gently around them, did not touch them.

And then, as though Zachary lost time, the stallion was simply no longer there, and the avatar stood upon the ground. Her armor, he saw, had been breached and silver-green luminescence bled through perforations in the steel. She tilted her head back and shed radiance—pure and cold and searing—as first her helm disintegrated in a cloud of coruscating particles, and then her armor, leaving behind his Green Rider.

Karigan? Karigan was the avatar? But *of course* she was.

The brilliant light faded at last, and normal time resumed, the snow falling furiously, and she stood there unarmed and wavering. He started to go to her, but someone launched out of the dark and grabbed her, held a weapon against her throat. Zachary ran forward, his sword ready in his hand.

"No closer!" Immerez shouted. It was his hook, sharpened to a cruel point, that he dug into Karigan's flesh. "If you come any closer, I'll rip her throat out."

The rage surged through Zachary so that he trembled in the effort to control himself, to keep himself from leaping across the space between them. Normally, he knew, Karigan would have defended herself if she could, but she was still weak from her wounds, and who knew what being the avatar might have done to her.

"You can't escape," Zachary shouted.

"I can and I will." Immerez jerked Karigan along as he backed away. Her soft cry made Zachary's heart pound harder. He was only peripherally aware of another standing by his side. "I will take her and—"

There was the softest whisper of an arrow being loosed. It carved through the squall, flurries swirling in eddies behind the trailing edges of its feathers. White against white, an Eletian arrow.

Immerez fell into the snow with the arrow lodged in his chest, and Karigan staggered away. Zachary launched across the space between them. Immerez's mouth worked as though he tried to speak, but Zachary's blood roared in his ears and his vision narrowed. He held his sword hilt in both hands and drove the blade down into Immerez again and again and again, venting the full of his fury, all the anger and fear and hatred he'd held inside during his captivity and torment, and for all that had been done to Karigan, too.

"Enough! He's dead!" The words came as though from a distance. He raised his sword to impale Immerez yet again when someone grabbed his arm to stop him. He whirled sword first.

"Sire—!"

The blade careened toward her neck.

"Zachary!"

Karigan. He cried out and let go the hilt before the blade could strike and it spun through the air landing somewhere well beyond her. All at once the fury drained from him. The force that had maddened him, that had made his blood run hot, faded and now he shivered with the cold. He sank to his knees in the snow before her, a supplicant, and she knelt with him. He labored to catch his breath. He trembled, and trembled more when she placed her hands on either side of his face. Her touch warmed him, but not with fury as before, only peace. The sound of battle faded.

"Are you all right?" she asked.

"I almost killed you," he said in a hoarse voice.

"But you did not."

"So close . . . I was—I was not myself. My rage, it blinded me. I am so sorry."

She pressed his head to her shoulder, put her arms around him.

"So sorry," he murmured into her coat. "Not myself."

"I know," she said.

They stayed like that for a time, as if by some grace they were separate from the rest of the world and its battles, snow falling softly on them. He reveled at their closeness, she holding him, he calmed by her scent and warmth, while guilt and fear of what could have been cut him up inside.

"Sometimes I don't know who I am anymore."

She shook with quiet laughter. "Believe it or not, I can kind of understand."

He raised his head from her shoulder so he could gaze at her, so close. Snowflakes melted on her cheeks, caught in her eyelashes, and he realized the patch was gone and he could see himself in the silver of her mirror eye. Images began to unfold so rapidly he could not follow. He glimpsed a child—was it himself, or one of his own? A man he somehow knew to be Cade Harlowe appeared. He was . . . he was making love to Karigan, her hair splayed across a pillow. There were brief images of Estora and Laren, a blur of battle and arrows in flight, and . . . The images layered over so quickly he was not sure what he saw, only that he could not stop looking until Karigan gasped and turned away, her hand clasped over her eye.

"Oh, gods," he murmured. "I'm sorry. I didn't mean to . . ."

"I'm all right, it'll pass."

He helped her to her feet. She was unsteady. "Your back, is it—? Are you—?"

"I'll live," she replied. "You?"

"I am all right, because of you." Then, "We need to get you to some shelter."

She brushed snow off the crown of her head and drew her hood up. The storm resurged in intensity, and ice now pelted them. He turned to look for Enver and Donal, and he barely saw their shapes through the wind-driven squall. There was a third person with them who looked neither like Rennard nor Fiori, but was female in form. It appeared they'd kept their distance to allow him a moment with Karigan.

A whirling cone of snow kicked up in the space between them. Karigan grabbed his arm. "The elemental!"

His sword—where was it? He'd tossed it and now? And now it was buried somewhere in the snow. He kicked at drifts trying to find it. When the whirl loomed into a rough human shape, he threw himself in front of Karigan.

HEART OF ICE

Nari had walked the northlands seeking the aureas slee. It had hidden among the clouds, mending its wounds, out of reach. She thought, perhaps, it would retreat until next winter, but clearly it could not let go of the vengeance it felt it needed to wreak upon Zachary.

She'd followed it back to the rocky plain between the campsite and the Lone Forest, and she sensed it stalking the soldiers approaching the forest in the night. Zachary, she deduced, was among them.

Her careful entry into the forest followed, through the snowstorm generated by the Slee. She could move as silently and unobtrusively as any Eletian, and so she remained undetected by the combatants. She tracked Zachary's clutch of fighters and followed them as they worked their way through the forest.

She marveled at how brightly Zachary shone as he led his soldiers, how he fought to the front lines. If there was beauty in death, he created it, his gleaming sword arcing with grace through the night, its movement the rhythm of music, the blade a living extension of his arm. He was a burning flame and, in truth, the "firebrand" of his people.

Then came the attack of the dark ones, and she took up the sword of one of the fallen to defend herself. She could sense the abyss they'd spewed from, a gouting wound in the Earth. The dark ones had preceded the existence of even the Eletians in this world, but an ancient conflict, ancient to even the Eletian people, had cast them into their prisons.

She was quick, quicker than they, and when the avatar

rode by, she was able to pause and look, and see that the great stallion carrying the avatar was so much more than a horse, and immediately she recognized the Galadheon as the vessel of the death god. She'd seen the dark wings about her when they met, and now she knew what they represented.

The avatar went on to draw away or destroy the dark ones as she passed. Nari had lost track of the slee while she fought, and so looked for Zachary, and found him as bright as ever, once again fighting human foes. She watched and waited, knowing Slee would come for him.

She found Enver nearby, who also appeared to be keeping watch, but not for Zachary or Slee, she guessed.

"Nari," he said, "what are you doing here?"

"I have followed Slee," she replied.

Soon the avatar reappeared, her armor damaged and bleeding silver-green moonlight. It pleased Nari that her sister's gift, and her own, helped shield the Galadheon even as the armor of the gods failed.

The stallion vanished, and the Galadheon was once more herself, and when the hook-handed man threatened her, Enver was already in motion, his arrow sailing with a whisper just over the Galadheon's shoulder and into its mark.

When Zachary and the Galadheon knelt in the snow in one another's arms, Enver started to move forward, but she stopped him.

"Let them be," she murmured. "Remember your discipline, control."

He stiffened beside her and she sensed his unhappiness, but she could once again see Zachary's aura meshing harmoniously with the Galadheon's.

Why do they not kiss? she wondered, but then she remembered Zachary was married and the barriers mortals put between themselves, the artificial walls that kept them apart. Of all the strange rules of mortals was the one that dictated with whom they could bond despite what their inner natures craved. So occupied with their bloodlines were the mortals, she thought with distaste. As Zachary and the Galadheon leaned into one another, their feelings clear, she mourned for them, but not for long, for Slee had arrived.

It grew out of snow and ice and loomed over Zachary and the Galadheon. Zachary placed himself in front of her as a shield.

"Both of you together," Slee said. "You will know true pain."

"I've spent all my arrows," Enver told Nari.

Zachary's guard emerged from the shadows and rushed forward brandishing his sword, but Slee just knocked him aside. Other fighters in the area backed away, unsure of this new threat in their midst. A giant hand formed out of the snow behind the Galadheon and grasped her, lifted her high.

"No!" Zachary cried, battering at the base of the hand.

"First you watch this one die," the slee said. Its own hand grew into a sword of ice.

Enver ran toward it, unsheathing his sword as he did so, but he, too, was flung aside.

The ice sword started sliding toward the Galadheon, and Zachary attempted to wrestle it away from the slee, but the slee just knocked him down.

"Slee!" Nari cried. She was of an elder time, which gave her voice authority.

Slee paused, turned to look upon her. "Narivanine."

"I have been following and watching you," she said.

"I know."

"You have gone too far. It is not yours to take lives in this manner."

"You cannot tell me what I can or cannot do. I AM SLEE!"

A tremendous wind thrashed through the trees. Snow and ice pelted Nari, but she did not waver.

"You are an elemental," she said, "that is all. No god to take life."

"No? Then watch." He turned his attention back to the Galadheon, still held in the fist of snow.

Nari flew across the snow and put herself before the blade's tip. "*Slee!* You have overstepped. When I was freed, I made some friends, such as the Galadheon and Zachary. Others are less corporeal."

"You will die first," Slee said.

"I think not." She pressed her hands together and closed her eyes. She imagined one friend in particular. When she looked upon Slee once more, an icy swordtip was pressed against her throat, sharp and painful when she swallowed. Slee gazed at her with eyes like hailstones. "You are out of season," she told it.

Slee cocked its head as if trying to comprehend her statement.

"I call upon the *ventos strallis!*" she cried.

Slee looked incredulous, then threw its head back and laughed. "You cannot—"

But she could. The winds reversed the slee's, coming from the south, pushing back the cold that the slee emanated. Slee stopped laughing, turned to face the oncoming mild wind even as snowflakes turned into raindrops, and raindrops turned into a downpour.

The giant hand gripping the Galadheon crumbled and she fell to the ground. Zachary helped her to her feet and they scrambled from the center of the maelstrom.

Slee whipped back to Nari, fighting to retain its shape as its snowstorm failed and became a gale of rain and wind. "How did you do this?" it demanded. The more it attempted to push back with the north wind, the more it failed.

"I told you," Nari said, "I made friends. One such is the ventos strallis."

Slee wailed as water gushed off it in freshets. Ventos strallis, the south wind, dominated the season they were entering. Slee had no power over it.

Slee shrank, began to lose definition as any snowdrift in a spring rain. Its arms fell off and Nari stepped right up to it, stared into its melting face. "You will never harm another," she said. "You will never steal someone away from their loved ones again. Not ever."

The aureas slee's mouth had melted so it could not reply, only make a pitiful moaning sound. Its hailstone eyes also shrank within their sockets, and rolled out.

Nari plunged her hand into the slush of its chest, and she groped and searched for the slee's cold heart. When she found it, she yanked it out, triumphant. The heart of ice sat upon her hand, and what remained of the aureas slee collapsed and melted into a puddle that was washed away by the rain.

"Nari," said Enver, his eyes wide as he looked upon her and her prize. He was soaked, his hair stuck to his face. He looked otherwise unharmed from his encounter with the slee. "You have called the south wind. How?"

"One can make friends anywhere," she replied. It had taken effort, but had been worth it. Now she could take vengeance.

"What will you do now?" he asked.

She gazed at the ice heart. It pulsated with the life of contained winter. It would not melt, and Slee would reform next winter to torment others unless she ended it.

"I must destroy it," she said.

"Nooo," came the disembodied voice of the ventos strallis. "There must be balance. Nature must have its ice." Its words flowed around Nari and caressed her cheek.

"But I do not want Slee to return," she said.

"Ice must return, but it does not have to be in the guise of the elemental now melted," the ventos strallis replied.

"What do you mean? How can this be accomplished?"

"You," the ventos strallis said, "may draw the heart of ice into yourself. *You* may bring balance."

Nari weighed the heart in her hand. Long had she lived, and so much had changed since Slee had taken her captive. Her love, Hadwyr, was long dead, but that loss stung her as new as the spring wind. Her sister was gone from the world, and Argenthyne destroyed. Little of what she had once known remained.

"Nari," Enver said, "you are not truly considering this, are you?"

"I have no one, and nowhere to go," she replied, "and I grow weary."

"You would be welcomed in the Elt Wood. There are those of Argenthyne who would greet you."

She shook her head. "My time is past. I would just take the Great Sleep. Or, I could do some good in the world."

Enver nodded and touched her arm. "I will look for you when autumn freezes into winter."

Nari smiled. She pressed the heart of ice against her chest, first feeling how cold it was, but then it sent a welcoming warmth tingling through her body. She took a deep breath and pushed it into herself and was Nari no longer, substantial no longer, but the element that was of the ice. She turned to vapor and drifted to the clouds, and whispered, "I am the aureas narivannis." She had sought, and at last found, completion.

AFTERMATH

When the giant hand of snow had crumbled apart and Karigan tumbled out, Zachary had helped her to her feet, thrown his arm around her shoulders, and run her to safety against the curtain wall, where they stood hidden in deep shadow. He drew her against him, wished that his breastplate was not between them so he could feel her heart beat against his chest.

"Thank the gods," he murmured over and over. "Thank the gods you are all right." Overcome by having nearly lost her yet again, and by equal measures of relief that he had not, he kissed her hair, her eyes, her face, her lips, but she gasped and wrenched herself free of his embrace.

"I am sorry," he said. "I presume too much." His urgent need to be physically close to her had caused him to trespass.

"I—" It was hard to see her expression in the dark. "My back—your embrace and the breastplate—it hurt. That is all."

"Oh gods, Karigan, I'm sorry!" The last thing he'd wanted to do was cause her pain, but he'd been so caught up in the moment. He glanced over his shoulder through the slackening rain and saw that the aureas slee was no more, and when he reassured himself that the fighting had not reignited, he returned his attention to Karigan. "In my relief, I forgot. I'm so sorry." But was her reason for pulling away true, or was she just trying to spare his feelings?

He was answered when she took his hands into hers and leaned in for a sweet, lingering kiss, of which he had only dreamed until now. He discovered the reality was, in fact, far better than the dream. This time, when she moved in closer to him, he held her gently, placing no pressure against her back. Then he forgot all else, even the rain soaking them.

When finally they parted, there was some shyness between them, and he imagined a radiance expanded between them, engulfed and bound them. Imagined? No, *felt* it. She had stolen his heart long ago, and gave to him, in return, an intrinsic part of herself. He held her, their foreheads touching.

After a time, Karigan said, "I think you need to see to your people. Your people who were slaves. They're in the chamber of the Aeon Iire and need their king."

"Yes, of course."

"Do not let anyone touch the iire," she warned him. "It is not meant for the living."

"I understand." He could not resist brushing her lips with another kiss. Reluctantly he let her go, turned, and nearly plowed into Enver. As disconcerting as Zachary found it, Enver's expression showed little emotion, though his eyes told the truth of what he'd seen. There was sorrow, and something steely cold in their depths.

Enver told them what had become of Nari and the aureas slee, and then promised to keep Karigan safe as Zachary attended to his people.

The battle for the keep of Ifel Aeon and the Lone Forest had wound down quickly after the loss of Immerez. The River Unit squelched the defenders and rounded up those who survived and held them prisoner in the old slave quarters. Zachary freed the slaves from the chamber of the Aeon Iire, keeping in mind Karigan's admonishment that no one touch the strange silver metal of the iire itself. To his sorrow, Binning and many others had not made it. Lorilie Dorran had, and she flung her arms around him when she was freed of her chains.

"This does not mean I think there should be kings," she told him, "but thank you for coming back for us."

Zachary only wished he had been able to come back sooner. He felt as though he had failed her and the others, but he hugged Lorilie in return.

"Whether or not you think there should be kings," he said, "I am pleased you are all right." Most of the surviving slaves had suffered wounds of some kind.

She shuddered. "I think it will be some time before any of us are truly all right. We saw some strange things tonight, demons and . . . I don't know, a ghost of a knight? Then there was the strange creature of ice that killed Grandmother. And of course there is what we suffered in our captivity, as you well know."

So, it was the aureas slee, and not the avatar, who had killed Grandmother. He would have to find out what Karigan recalled of it.

The able-bodied among the slaves helped their injured fellows. There was a guard barracks where they could shelter. Destarion and his assistants had been summoned to help with all the wounded.

The corpses of demonkind smoldered away until they left behind only a black mark to show they had existed at all. He ordered the corpse of Grandmother to be displayed for the enemy prisoners so that they would know in truth that their leader was dead. For all his fury, he would have liked her alive for questioning. The head of the serpent had been taken, but he was not so naive as to believe that some other wouldn't rise to lead Second Empire. Birch came to mind first and foremost.

The bodies of the former slaves would be removed from the chamber of the Aeon Iire, and he ordered the chamber and its passage blocked off. Should the avatar need reentry, he did not think an earthen blockade would be a barrier to her.

He still marveled that it was his Karigan who was the avatar. Could she have ever imagined, when she was a runaway schoolgirl, that one day she would be the chosen one of a god? Before he left, he found a small piece of leather on the chamber floor, her eyepatch, and pocketed it.

Outside, it had stopped raining altogether, and for that he was grateful. He and Donal headed back toward the keep. He was exhausted and sore, his shoulder wound burning. The battle seemed to have laid waste to his fury. His brief moments with Karigan in his arms, her lips upon his, had restored his humanity and equilibrium. Now he was just a tired man wanting nothing more than his bed, but he knew that all the soldiers of the River Unit were just as tired, and if they couldn't rest yet, neither could he.

When they entered the courtyard, they found soldiers lining up the dead, mostly those of Second Empire who had defended the keep. Inside, a mender tended the wounded under the watchful gaze of guards.

"Varius?" Zachary said in surprise.

Varius gave him a harried glance. "Not now, Dav, unless you are dying."

Zachary nodded and did not reprimand him for disrespect. He knew that focused look as Varius tended the wounded of both sides.

He spotted Karigan across the great hall, her back to him, head bent into her hand. Enver stood beside her with his arm around her to support her. Zachary thought that if he was weary, then she must be doubly so. Rennard stood with them, and he realized they were looking down at a body. He approached with foreboding, and when he stood beside Karigan, he realized she was crying. When he looked down, he saw why. Stretched out on his back with his hands crossed on his chest, was Lord Aaron Fiori, the Golden Guardian of Selium, and the father of Karigan's best friend.

"Gods, no," he murmured.

"One of my men said he charged into the keep looking for someone called Lala," Rennard told him. "The civilians were all gone. No Lala here."

Fiori looked as though he slept, his golden hair glinting in the lamplight. Only the stab wound that had found its way beneath the edge of his breastplate indicated he was not just asleep. Beside Zachary, Karigan made a strange motion with her hand toward Fiori and softly whispered, "Sleep well."

"He will need an honor guard for his return to Selium," Zachary told Rennard.

"Yes, sire, I will arrange it." The lieutenant then shrouded the body with a cloak.

Zachary turned to Karigan, placed his hand on her shoulder. "You should get some rest."

She wiped her eyes with the heel of her hand, kept her

right eye covered. "I should go be with Estral. She'll need to know."

"Mist is coming," Enver said. "She will carry the Galadheon and me back to the campsite."

Zachary struggled with himself, not wanting her to leave, but knowing it was for the best. This was a dark place, filled with death and dying. Even if she was Westrion's avatar, she need not be in death's constant presence. In any case, he was certain she would rest better at the campsite and there Enver could more easily tend her. Her cheeks were hollowed and her expression exhausted. She tried to conceal her pain, but it only told him how much she hurt. He longed to hold her once more, to comfort her. Would onlookers care, or even notice?

Enver glanced over his shoulder. "Ah, I believe Mist has just arrived and awaits us."

The moment passed, and Zachary simply squeezed Karigan's shoulder and let his hand drop to his side. "Oh," he said, "I found something of yours." He pulled the eyepatch out of his pocket and pressed it into her hand.

"Thank you," she said in relief. Hastily she put it over her eye and tied it in place, but not before he caught a glint of silver. She turned away, but then paused to look at him. "You need rest, too, and you should get your shoulder looked at." Then she made her painstaking way across the hall, leaning on Enver.

He glanced at his shoulder, at the torn fabric and the bloody grooves demon claws had cut into his flesh. It hadn't bothered him much at the time, but now with the battle over and the energy that had sustained him draining away, the burning pain was even worse.

"Sir Karigan is correct," Donal said. "That should be looked at." He made Zachary sit on a rough bench while he collected supplies.

Zachary leaned back against the cold stone wall and shivered with a sudden chill. When it passed, he gazed around the torchlit great hall, watching as more injured streamed in and more corpses were carried out. Varius worked feverishly to help those he could with the assistance of a couple of soldiers. Moans and cries came from that end of the hall. On the opposite end, where he recalled the kitchen to be, other soldiers bustled about boiling water and perhaps finding some food to make for their weary comrades that would sustain them better than the simple rations they carried with them.

Donal soon returned with a bowl of water, a bar of soap, and a cloth and bottle. He started to cleanse the wound and Zachary hissed at the sting.

"Have you no wounds?" he demanded.

"No, sire," Donal replied.

"I am sorry about Rye."

"As am I. He was young and did not have his full training, but he did very well. He would have made a fine Weapon."

"I agree. Had he family?"

"Yes. Poor farmers in D'Yer Province."

"Then I will recommend to the council of Black Shields to confer status posthumously so that his family will receive a stipend. He, and they, are deserving."

"That is most generous, sire."

Zachary winced as Donal probed into his rent flesh. "You did not seem very surprised to see Sir Karigan here."

"Little surprises me where Sir Karigan is concerned."

Zachary laughed. No truer words had ever been spoken.

"If she was here," Donal continued, "it was meant to be."

It was a very curious statement, Zachary thought, but though he had been surrounded by Weapons his entire life, he knew he would never completely understand their ways. There were already enough mysteries for one night—the demons of the Aeon Iire, Grandmother's spellcasting, the avatar, and the aureas slee. He had a better grasp of it all than most, and he could only imagine what everyone else thought. Unlike Donal, they'd find Karigan's sudden appearance among them odd.

Donal uncorked the bottle he had found.

"Is that whiskey?" Zachary asked, sniffing the air.

"Yes, sire. Someone kept a small stash here." Donal grimaced at the scent. "Not a very fine grade, however."

Well, it would still be a fine— "Ow! Damnation, Donal!"

he exclaimed as the Weapon poured the contents over his wound.

"Sorry, sire, but it was the only medicament I could find. The mender might have something else, but he is overwhelmed at the moment. Thought this would work in a pinch."

"All the fires of hell . . ."

Donal bent down and searched his eyes. Was that a line of concern across his brow? "I suggest you sleep if you can, sire," he said, bandaging the wound. "Once the urgent matters of caring for the wounded and so forth are sorted, decisions will have to be made, and you'll be needed."

The gray light of dawn was already showing through cracks and windows. "What about you?"

"I am your shield. I will keep watch."

Zachary had not expected any other answer. "You need to get some rest, too."

"Soon, sire, after you have had yours. If Sir Karigan had been in better condition, she and I could have taken turns, but I will be fine."

So, Donal considered her Weapon enough to guard him when no other was available. He wondered what the Weapons would think if her back never fully recovered enough for her to withstand the rigors of being a swordmaster. He decided he would not even consider the possibility. She *must* recover fully.

He wrapped his cloak around himself against another episode of chills, and then found a likely spot on the floor in a quiet corner to lie down and rest. His last vision before he fell asleep was of Donal standing sentry, his arms crossed and stance ready for a fight.

THE GOLDEN GUARDIAN

Scouts of the River Unit waved them through another checkpoint, and Mist went on at a gentle trot. Even as seamless as Mist's gaits were, Karigan clenched her teeth trying not to cry out at the slightest bump. Her back felt like it had been ripped apart all over again. It may not have hurt while she was the avatar, but the stress and exertion she had placed on it while she was the avatar assailed her in full after, and she didn't want Enver to know so he would not stop or turn back. Estral needed to have the news of her father, and it must come from a friend.

As they rode, the sky lightened subtly as night gave in to dawn, and Karigan concentrated on staying seated behind Enver and not sliding off in pain or exhaustion. Thankfully, the wind and rain had stopped, though she still felt soggy and, in turn, chilled. To take her mind off her discomfort, she reflected on the night's events. Since she had been preoccupied with escaping the aureas slee at the time, she little understood how Nari happened to be there, or what had become of her and the ice elemental. Enver's cursory explanation that Nari was the new ice elemental failed to satisfy her, but the news that the old slee was gone and would never come after her or Zachary again was welcome.

Yes, the old slee was gone, and so were Grandmother and Immerez. She could hardly believe it, and while it brought relief, she knew it would not be the end of their troubles with Second Empire. Perhaps she'd feel more optimistic once she got some rest.

They left the woods, at last, just as the first fingers of sunrise crept over the eastern horizon. If she had managed this far, she could make it all the way to the campsite.

She continued reflecting on her experiences of the night, of being an avatar. This time, her memory of it had not been taken away, though much of it felt like a dream, of having that power flow through her, and not just to contain the dark ones. The keep and its surrounds had been full of the newly dead as well as those of a more ancient time. It had been overwhelming. Most spirits, she knew, would pass on in their own time to whatever the afterlife held for them. Others would continue fighting, unaware they were dead. She had helped as many as she could with a whisper as she rode by.

She couldn't resist dwelling for some time on the kissing, which made her cheeks warm and filled her with a keen thrill that made her shiver. But there was also much remorse. She shouldn't have let it happen, and yet another part of her could not help but give over to desire. How would it play out, she wondered, when they were back home, out of the wilderness and away from battle, and sharing the same roof as Estora? Estora did not deserve this. It *should not* have happened, and *could not* happen again. Yet, every time she tried to prevent her feelings for Zachary from growing, they only deepened.

The hardest part of the night had been looking upon the body of Lord Fiori, and then seeing his spirit form also gazing at it. His expression had been grave, but when he glanced up at her, he looked confused at first, perhaps recognizing that she was not just Karigan.

Look after my daughter, he had told her.

She'd promised she would with a whisper, then wished him sleep, but it was unnecessary for he'd become surrounded by starshine. A look of joy crossed his translucent face. *There is music!* he exclaimed. Then he'd turned and vanished forever into the light.

Why her? she wondered. Why was it she who could do this thing, this seeing of ghosts and commanding them? Intellectually, she knew it was because of her special ability to cross thresholds, but still, why *her*? Why did *her* life have to be so strange? She did not wish to contemplate the possibility of

Westrion calling on her again to perform the role of avatar. She hoped he did not.

In the distance, they spotted support troops of the River Unit moving in the direction of the Lone Forest with pack mules. Karigan did not know if they intended to hold the keep, but it was looking that way.

By the time they encountered the guards at the campsite, she was slumped against Enver's back and barely aware when they passed through the wards and into the camp itself. Connly came to help her dismount, and she could not keep to her feet when she did. Connly placed his arm around her to support her.

"Are you injured?" he asked. "New injuries, I mean."

"She needs rest," Enver said. "A great deal has happened."

"Estral," Karigan murmured. "Need to see Estral."

Estral appeared out of her tent, rubbing her eyes. "Karigan? You're back!" She rushed over and looked as though she wanted to hug her, but held back. "Are you all right? What happened?"

"Estral," Karigan said. She was so tired that just speaking was difficult. "Must tell you . . ."

"Did we win?"

"Yes," Karigan replied, "but, I'm sorry . . ."

"You're sorry? For what?" Then Estral's face clouded. "My father?"

"I'm so sorry. He was killed."

"No," Estral said, "that can't be right. No . . ."

Karigan tried to reach for her so she could provide comfort, but she was assailed by dizziness and all went dark.

When Karigan stirred again, she was in Enver's tent lying on her stomach on her bedding, her back bare.

"Ah, Galadheon," Enver said, "you are with us once more."

"Estral," she said, trying to gather her strength to rise.

Enver placed his warm hand on her shoulder and eased her back down. "Connly is looking after her. Please remain still for now. Your deeper wounds have taken longer to heal and were not fully knitted back together when your god sent you to the forest. Some have reopened yet again."

She groaned in frustration, frustration at her injuries, frustration that she hadn't been able to break the news more gently to Estral and be there for her.

"There are marks on you," he continued, "like mild burns in different places. Do you know what caused these?"

It took Karigan a moment to remember. "Grandmother's knots. They breached the avatar's armor, but something protected me, I think."

"Yes, something did. When you appeared outside after imprisoning the dark ones, silver-green light shone through the breaches of your armor."

"Laurelyn?"

"Yes, and Nari."

"Nari?"

"It appears she left you a gift, to strengthen whatever was left of Laurelyn's."

"I would thank her if I could."

"Do so when winter comes and the north wind blows. She will hear you."

It was like living in some sort of fairy tale, where the elements were personified and a merchant's daughter could command the dead.

"I would like to see Estral, see if she needs me," Karigan said.

"You will rest. As soon as I finish with your back, I will stay with her myself. She will not be alone."

Sometime after Enver left, she slipped into sleep. She dreamed she walked among the dew-laden grasses of the starry meadow. She did not see the day horse, but she found Siris Kiltyre walking with her.

"You did well, Rider," he told her, "despite the challenges. The Aeon Iire should remain secure for many a century to come, so long as no other powerful necromancer tries to break it. By then, it will be someone else's responsibility."

"I am no longer the avatar?"

"Oh, I did not say that, but we are mortal and do not live forever. One day, your existence will slip into oblivion, and other generations will come and go, like the turnings of the pages of a book. Nothing stays the same."

This was not a cheery thought.

They paused by a stream that gurgled and sang around the rocks that studded its surface. Fireflies blinked around them.

Siris laughed, and she realized he was laughing at *her*. "The look on your face," he said. "Be not so morose, for you are not likely to pass to the heavens today, or even tomorrow. You have more pages yet to turn, but how many, even Westrion cannot say. Use what you've learned and it will hold you in good stead."

He bounded across stepping stones to the opposite bank of the stream, and somehow she knew she was not allowed to follow.

"The protections we placed around you," he said, "against the intrusions of the Nyssa spirit, will soon weaken. You must learn to shield yourself and oust her." He began to fade, the forest beyond showing through his luminous form. "I do not know if we will meet again, Rider G'ladheon, but it has been an honor." He bowed and vanished.

Karigan slept until a commotion outside woke her up. She dressed as quickly as her hurts allowed in time to see Lieutenant Rennard arrive with a squad of soldiers bearing a shrouded figure on a bier.

Rennard went to his knee before Estral, his head bowed. Estral swayed as though the slightest wind would knock her over. Karigan took a few steps toward her, and Rennard held out his hands, gold shimmering on his palms in the glint of the late afternoon sun.

"Lady Fiori," Rennard said.

Karigan almost reeled to hear Estral addressed as such, but it was true that as Aaron Fiori's heir, she was now *the* Lady Fiori, the Golden Guardian, her father's title and responsibilities now passed on to her.

Estral accepted her father's signet ring, and his harp brooch—Rennard still wore hers.

"The king has commanded that I lead these others as an honor guard for Lord Fiori's final journey home to Selium. If we may help you prepare for departure, we will go as far as the Green Cloak today."

A deep sob arose from Estral, and Karigan, her own eyes wet with tears, went to comfort her friend.

Karigan helped Estral pack as much as she could. Enver had ordered her not to lift anything, so she folded clothes and blankets. Connly, meanwhile, readied Coda.

"I would like to go with you," Karigan said as she rolled up Estral's bedding in their tent.

"I know you can't." Estral's voice was fading, had become wispy, and not just from the crying.

"I will come as soon as I am able to. I promise."

Estral turned to her. "Don't make promises you can't keep." Karigan was about to protest, but Estral grasped her wrist. "You still need to recuperate, and you've duties. I know this. You *could* write me a real letter now and then, though."

Karigan grimaced. She was ever the abysmal correspondent, but she'd make an extra effort in Estral's case.

"I will come when I can," she said firmly.

"Enver explained to us what went on at the keep, what you did, what you faced. Who you are. Can you . . . can you see my father?"

"I already did. Back at the keep. He asked me to look after you. He heard music, and when he left, he walked into starshine. He looked . . . joyful." And when she thought about it, she knew it to be true.

Estral broke into racking sobs and Karigan did what she could to comfort her.

"I don't know what I'm going to do without him," Estral said, sniffing. "I can't be the Golden Guardian."

"Your father knew you could," Karigan said, "and I know you can. You were practically running Selium anyway when he was off on his travels."

"But Karigan, how can I be without my voice? It's going away. The Golden Guardian must have a voice."

"I don't know, but it seems to me you are capable of quite a lot. And didn't you tell me you'd found another voice with your writing?"

Estral hugged her journal. "That was before my father—" She swallowed hard. "That was before my father passed away.

What is the Golden Guardian without a voice? So much to do. Without my voice I won't be able to— "

"Estral, you just need to think about mourning right now, getting your father home. You need to take care of yourself. I'll make sure that the king permits a message to go to your mother so she knows what you're up against. And Alton. Alton needs to know."

"You'll take care of that for me?"

"Even if I am the worst letter writer ever, yes, I will see it done. Your friends are many and we love you."

Estral looked forlorn as she rode Coda out of camp, Lieutenant Rennard walking at her stirrup, and the honor guard following with their sad burden.

Karigan felt forlorn herself, having to say good-bye, and especially the reason for it. In time, she was certain Estral would become comfortable in her role as Golden Guardian, and she would make the office her own. In the meantime? It would be damnably tough, and she hoped all the staff at Selium would do their utmost to support her. Karigan thought that, in addition to letters to Alton and Estral's mother, she'd write Master Rendle and Melry, and others, to ensure Estral had friends around her.

Once Estral and her escorts vanished from sight, Karigan found herself trembling from fatigue and emotion.

"Perhaps you should sit down and have something to eat," Connly suggested.

"In a little bit."

First she needed to go hug her horse.

MISTER WHISKERS RETURNS

Everything was falling apart, Alton thought. Estral had left him, King Zachary was missing, and his Green Rider helpers had been recalled to Sacor City. Even Dale. No one else was able to enter the towers, and not for lack of trying. Though the tower mages to the east of the breach could communicate with him, it was not the same as having his fellow Riders, his friends, to assist and keep watch. He guessed he'd keep trying to bring in members of his clan to see if any of the old stoneworking magic remained in the blood of his family and allowed them entry to the towers. So far he'd met with no success.

Now he stood in Tower of the Heavens in a passage beneath the west arch that put him in direct contact with the wall. His hands were pressed against the cool, grainy texture of solid granite, and his consciousness drifted among the sparkling flecks of feldspar and hornblende, and the crystalline structures of quartz. He heard the voices of the wall guardians in song, those disembodied, magical stoneworkers of old whose sacrifices had made the wall strong enough to withstand the ages.

Their song held the wall together, which in turn held the evil of Blackveil at bay. Periodically, Alton communed with the wall and its guardians to help maintain the song and its magic. The guardians accepted him, did not begrudge his presence, but it was clear they missed Estral. Her music and voice had done so much more than strengthen the wall, and in fact, they reduced the cracks that radiated from the breach. Much more than he had done or could do. He sensed the disappointment of the guardians when he made contact and it was just him. He tried to not let it affect his mood as he worked with them, but they only reflected what he truly felt himself.

He came back to himself and dropped contact. Out in the main chamber he found Merdigen sitting in a chair combing out his long, ivory beard.

"The wall has not yet fallen, I see," the great mage said.

"No, it hasn't."

"I wish Lady Estral would return. You've been so sulky since she left. Especially since the other Riders departed for the city. I still can't imagine what is more important than the wall that they had to be recalled."

"The king, remember? They're supposed to help look for the king."

Merdigen shrugged. "Why the urgency to find the king? You have a queen, after all."

Merdigen's priorities tended to be rather skewed at times.

"I need some fresh air," Alton said.

"Sure, sure, leave me alone. Me and my beard."

Alton shook his head. Just before he stepped through the tower wall to the outside world, he heard Merdigen mutter, "I wish *I* could go out and have some fresh air."

The weather was fine, so Alton saddled up Night Hawk for a ride down to the main encampment at the breach. Hawk tossed his head and pranced, and Alton was assailed by guilt that he did not pay his horse nearly enough attention.

At the main encampment he examined the cracks around the breach, made measurements, and recorded his findings in his logbook. He took reports from the officers on duty there. They kept watch over the breach and into Blackveil Forest. All was quiet, they said. They saw little but the undulating mist on the other side of the wall, and heard little but the occasional scream of some creature within.

"Would you like to take a look, sir?" Corporal Mannis asked. She'd just descended the ladder that leaned against the repairwork of the breach where she'd been keeping watch.

Alton stiffened. It was something he avoided after having been pushed over the side and left to perish in Blackveil. Not that anyone here would do that to him again, but the mere thought of climbing the ladder made him sweat.

"Look!" someone shouted, and pointed to the sky.

Two large shapes circled overhead. Soldiers nocked arrows and aimed crossbows.

"No, wait!" Alton ordered. He shielded his eyes against the sun, wishing he had thought to bring along his spyglass. Were the two circling creatures what he thought they were? Or, were they monsters from Blackveil?

They descended toward the earth in lazy spirals, one tawny, the other black with raven wings. Not monsters of Blackveil, he decided. Mister Whiskers had succeeded in his mission, unless this was just a friend of his and not a mate.

"Put your weapons away," he ordered the soldiers. "Mister Whiskers has come home." Merdigen would be pleased. If Alton had been sulky since the departure of his friends, Merdigen had been sullen since the departure of his cat.

The two gryphons landed atop the repairwork of the breach and changed shape into ordinary cats.

Corporal Mannis gasped. "Did I really just see that?"

"I'm afraid so," Alton replied with a smile.

The cats sat on their roost looking down upon the human beings who assembled to gape at them.

"Welcome back, Mister Whiskers," Alton said. "Who is your friend?"

"Meep."

She was a shiny black short-haired feline with a regal demeanor.

"I wish you could speak the common tongue so you could tell us all about your travels."

Mister Whiskers simply groomed his paw and otherwise ignored him. Just looking at them now, even considering their gryphon forms, he wondered if they'd be of any real use in defending the towers, or just provide Merdigen with amusement. It was rather remarkable that Mister Whiskers had returned at all.

The two appeared content to sun themselves on their roost, the newcomer crouched and gazing into the forest, and Mister Whiskers sprawled on his side working on his other paw. Alton decided he would join them and take a look into Blackveil, after all.

He climbed the ladder, feeling a little shaky as he always did. The man who had pushed him into the forest, an operative of Second Empire, was long dead, but the betrayal, and memory of waking in the forest, still loomed large.

The repairwork of the breach stood only ten feet high. The rest of the wall to either side appeared to soar to the heavens. It looked and felt as solid as the granite base of the wall, but it was magic, the lost art of the D'Yers.

When he was up far enough to look over the side into Blackveil, he stopped. No need to climb atop it. The incessant mist wafted on the other side, and he could see little but the ghostly shapes of spindly, black tree branches beyond.

The new cat had tensed when he climbed up, but Mister Whiskers stretched and sauntered over to him to butt his face with his head. Alton sneezed. The allergy had not miraculously gone away during Mister Whiskers' absence.

The forest was as calm and quiet as ever, but Alton didn't like it. It was too quiet, he thought. The kind of quiet that presaged storms. There was no telling what was going on in the rotten heart of the forest. What if the spirit of Mornhavon had recovered from whatever injury Karigan had caused him when she broke the looking mask? What if he was preparing an all-out assault?

Both of the cats stared into the mist with him, and suddenly, Mister Whiskers started chattering as though he watched a bird. The black cat looked intently in the same direction, her hackles raised.

"What is it?" Alton asked.

A fetid stench preceded a black shadow that hurtled toward him on great wings. He fell back off the ladder as an enormous creature brushed over him. He hit the ground hard, maybe blacked out for a moment, his breath slammed out of him. Shouts went up from the encampment.

A huge avian creature circled above. It had a long reptilian neck, and black oily wings, and cruel talons clenched beneath its body. Alton knew such creatures well. One had killed a young noble lady in this very encampment, and another had wounded Dale. The Eletians called such creatures *anteshey.*

Arrows were loosed skyward, but the avian veered on a wingtip away from them and screeched. Two other winged creatures pursued, one tawny and one raven black. They pumped their wings aggressively to catch up with their quarry. The avian craned its head around and screeched its defiance at the gryphon pair.

"Hold your arrows!" someone shouted. Alton thought it might be Corporal Mannis who gave the order, and he approved. Arrows might hit the gryphons instead of the intended target.

Mister Whiskers roared and he flapped his wings harder, his mate right behind him. They skimmed the canopy of the woods beyond the encampment, tearing off treetops and scattering birds as they went. They ascended higher into the sky and stooped into dives. The aerial maneuvers were incredible, and the gryphons did not waver in their pursuit. He watched mesmerized, still lying on his back as the gryphons closed the gap, stretched out their forepaws, and grabbed the avian.

The creature screamed, dove and rolled, and reached back with its fearsome beak to snap at its assailants, but the gryphons pursued undeterred. The black one simply caught the creature's head in her jaw and twisted. After that, the gryphons played with their prey, tossing it back and forth between them through the air.

When they started to tear the creature apart, Alton climbed to his feet and ran for cover beneath the awning of a tent. First, oversized blue-black feathers drifted down; then bigger pieces, hunks of meat, a stray talon, fell to the ground. When it began to rain entrails, other wall personnel ran for cover, as well.

Mister Whiskers swept low and dropped the avian's head at Alton's feet. A present? Maybe Merdigen had been onto something, Alton thought, when he had suggested so long ago that they needed kittens to help protect the towers. He smiled, hoping for large litters.

TO NOT LEAVE

Nightmares clawed at Zachary in black shapeless forms. He kept fighting, kept striking with his sword, but he could not kill the entities, he could not quell the dark.

An awakening. He was surrounded by blurry stone walls, and he shook uncontrollably. "What's wrong with me?" he asked between chattering teeth.

Donal's head seemed to float over him. "You are ill, sire, your wound poisoned. So it has been for others of our warriors and prisoners who were wounded by the dark ones."

"Am I dying?"

Donal did not reply immediately. "Destarion and Varius are doing everything they can. We've also sent for Enver."

The nightmares returned in the shape of ice fists wielding ice daggers. Karigan was clutched in the grip of a giant slee. Zachary tried running through hip-deep snow to reach her, but he could not seem to fight his way through to cross the ever-expanding distance between them.

Between nightmares, people talked around him, tried to get him to swallow water. He saw Destarion and Varius with their heads together.

"Definitely leeches to suck out the poison," Destarion said.

"There is a moss that grows in the forest that can be used in a poultice to help draw it out, too," Varius replied.

Zachary was not sure if they were real or part of a dream, but he soon had nightmares of being buried in thick layers of moss, and he could not breathe. These gave way to giant, bloated leeches stuck to his body and sucking all his blood.

When he was on fire, cool, wet cloths were placed on his brow. Someone spoke to him in soothing tones, rinsed the cloth, replaced it. A familiar voice . . . Karigan? It must be a dream, and a much better one than the others.

". . . and don't you dare die on me," he heard her say. "I can't lose you, too."

He sensed her rising to leave, and he flung his hand out and caught her wrist. "Don't leave me."

Her expression stricken, she eased back down beside him and took his hand in hers. "I'm not, and I won't. I just needed to stand a minute for my back."

"Don't leave me," he whispered.

Her eyes filled with tears. "I will not leave you."

His last awareness as he slid back into darkness was of her sitting close beside him and holding his hand. This time as he slept, the hellish nightmares stayed away. A guardian seemed to keep watch over him, she in the gleaming armor of the heavens. Had he died? But when he awoke sometime later, he felt clearer, his vision steady. He made out in the flickering lantern light that he lay on a pallet in a circular chamber. Nearby, Karigan lay prone on her bedroll, breathing deeply with sleep. He was about to speak when another stepped between them and knelt beside him.

"Quietly now," Enver said in a soft voice. "The Galadheon has only just fallen asleep and you do not want to wake her. She has been up long hours. Would you try some water?"

Zachary nodded, and found that he needed to slake a great thirst. Enver made sure he took it slowly. He asked questions between sips.

"What happened? Why am I sick?"

"The claws of the dark one that injured you were poisonous and caused corruption of the wound. Others have been likewise made ill and not all have survived."

Zachary remembered now, having been told this.

"Destarion and Varius have done very good work," Enver continued, "but sent for me to see if I could help." He smiled. "The poisons of the dark ones retreat before the evaleoren of the Eletians."

"How long . . . sick?"

"A few turns of sun and moon."

"You mean a few days?"

Enver nodded.

Zachary tried to sit up, his head pounding, but Enver pushed him back down.

"You must rest, and not awaken the Galadheon. She has her own healing to accomplish, which has been delayed by circumstances. She insisted on coming when she heard you had been taken ill, and has been by your side almost constantly, no matter her own injuries."

Zachary glanced at her, at her peaceful expression. "She stayed . . ."

"Yes, Firebrand, she stayed."

He saw a flash of something in Enver's gaze then, something feral, that coldness he had seen before. Was it jealousy?

It was a relief when Enver stepped back out. Zachary reached for Karigan's hand, but she was not close enough. He contented himself with studying the curl of her fingers, the way her shortened hair fell across her cheek, and he fell asleep with her image in his mind, and this time it was a deep, restful slumber.

His next awakening was to a shaft of sunshine beaming through an arrowloop in the stone wall. To his pleasure, Karigan sat at the table writing, the light a nimbus glow around her, while all else in the room fell into shadow. He watched her for a while, her concentration as she dipped her pen in ink and wrote, the nib scratching on paper. After a time, she looked up and stared into space. Then, as if perceiving his gaze, she turned to him. Her expression changed entirely, rippling with emotion.

"You're awake," she said barely above a whisper, "thank the gods."

Before he could speak, she sprinted across the chamber and pushed a blanket aside that hung over the doorway. "Donal, he's awake."

Donal replied softly, and Zachary heard footsteps on the flagstone floor hurrying away. Karigan returned and knelt awkwardly by his side.

"How are you feeling?" she asked.

"Better to see you."

She smiled tentatively. "Not half as glad as I am to see you awake. You were truly and deeply out for the last couple days, and I—we were worried."

He could see it in her eye, and in the line that furrowed her brow. "It would take much more than a scratch from some demon to kill me." He reached across his chest to touch his shoulder, but felt a bulging poultice instead.

"I should have known . . ." Karigan swallowed hard. "I should have known the touch of the dark ones would fester so."

He grabbed her hand. "How could you have?"

She looked away.

"You may be Westrion's avatar," he said, "but that does not mean you know all there is about the spawn of the hells." He squeezed her hand, but she continued to look away. She would be beating herself up over this for a while, he knew.

"I want to thank you for staying with me," he told her. "It helped more than you can know."

She turned back to him, smiling again, a smile like he had not seen since they had come together in the north, the dimples he loved so much deepening on her cheeks. At that moment, Donal stepped in, followed by Destarion, Varius, and Enver. Karigan reclaimed her hand and stood, and backed away. He closed his fingers wishing to retain something of her touch. As the two menders chattered at him and Enver looked coolly on, he followed Karigan with his gaze as she collected her writing materials and left the chamber.

Zachary learned he was occupying Grandmother's old chamber in the keep's tower. He was not sure how he felt about that, but Donal had wanted to keep him separate from the other injured. Destarion and Varius poked and prodded him, chatting in delight with one another over the efficacy of their treatments and Enver's evaleoren salve. They pushed water and soup on him, and when Donal helped him rise, he felt like a newborn colt who couldn't get his legs under him. As the day passed and he ingested more food and drink, he began to feel much improved.

He learned from Donal that Captain Treman had not survived and that Dannyn was now captain of the River Unit. Dannyn came to his chamber and gave him a rather dry recitation of numbers of casualties, and of those imprisoned. He explained how his people were working to secure both the keep and the forest.

"Any sign of Birch retaliating?" Zachary asked.

"No, Your Excellency. Our scouts have seen nothing to suggest he's making a move, except to absorb the civilians that had occupied this keep. In the meantime, a message to the Lake Unit has been dispatched requesting reinforcements. It's unlikely we'd be able to hold the Lone Forest ourselves in the advent of a full scale assault."

Zachary nodded. It was as he'd have ordered them to do himself.

Connly reported next, and after a deep bow he said, "I am pleased to inform you that Trace and the other Riders from the wall have reached Sacor City and informed the queen that you have been found. Something of all that has befallen you has been conveyed."

"What of the queen? Is she well?"

"Yes, sire. She remains on bed rest under the watchful gazes of Master Vanlynn and Ben Simeon. Very few are allowed to approach her regarding the business of the realm. Master Vanlynn says the pregnancy is doing well, thus far, despite the stresses."

Zachary let go an anxious breath he had not realized he'd been holding. *Thank the gods.* She'd been left with far too great a burden in his absence, and when Connly relayed news of troop readiness and the results of diplomatic missions, he could not believe how much she had accomplished.

Connly got the faraway look in his eyes that meant he was in rapport with Trace. "The queen has asked Trace to relay that she has made some organizational changes to the messenger service, as well." He looked perplexed as he said it. "To be honest, sire, I haven't the faintest what she's talking about."

"It sounds to me like your captain has been up to something in my absence."

Connly, his gaze still distant, raised his eyebrows as if in disbelief. "Apparently she's not the captain anymore."

"What?" Zachary sat up, seized by sudden panic. The call had abandoned Laren? After all these years? It couldn't be! What would he do without her?

Connly smiled. "She's not captain anymore, but colonel. The queen promoted her."

Zachary laughed out loud. Why hadn't he thought of it? It was long overdue, no matter that the Green Riders had only ever had a captain to lead them.

"Please have Trace convey my compliments to the queen for her wisdom."

After a moment, Connly replied, "The queen thanks you and wishes me to express her great joy that you've been found and are regaining your health. She looks forward to seeing you soon."

"And I, her." And he did. He was concerned for her well-being, and for that of the twins she carried. He longed to be home despite all the pressures that accompanied his position. He did regret, however, what it would mean for him and Karigan.

The communication with the queen complete, Connly paused. "There is one more thing, sire."

"Yes?"

"Karigan has asked for several messages to go out to the family and friends of the Golden Guardian in regard to Lord Fiori's death."

It took Zachary a moment to make sense of the statement, for wasn't Lord Fiori the Golden Guardian? But memory of Fiori's corpse lying on the floor came back to him, a shadow on his mind. Estral was now the Golden Guardian, the Lady Fiori.

"Karigan hopes the messages will encourage others to offer Lady Fiori support while she makes the transition to her new office during so difficult a time."

"Yes, yes, of course. My court must also have a major presence for his funeral."

Connly bowed. "I will then assign the messages when we return to Sacor City."

After Connly departed, Zachary was left alone to rest and ponder how surreal the idea of returning home to his former life felt after being so long away. Captive, slave, warrior, he'd been. It was time to once more be king.

ZACHARY DEPARTS

As one day turned into the next, Zachary saw little of Karigan, and when he asked Enver where she was, the Eletian's reply was enigmatic: "Regaining her strength."

What Zachary didn't see of her by day, he made up for in his dreams. He did not see the avatar in her gleaming armor, or even the Rider in green, but the woman in his arms, entwined with him. He could feel the softness of her skin against his, her lips on his, the thrill and release of joining. The dreams were so real he woke up with his heart pounding, his back arched, and an ache in his loins.

"Gods," he muttered, passing his hand over his sweaty brow.

To his embarrassment, he was not alone. Donal stood by the entry, and Varius at the foot of his pallet, looking over a journal and squinting down at him through specs perched on the tip of his nose.

"Weeell," Varius drolled, "you seem to be feeling much better."

Heat warmed Zachary's face.

"No need to feel ashamed. It is a natural part of being a man."

Donal's expression, as usual, was neutral. Zachary hoped he'd not spoken in his sleep, had not called out, for his sake and Karigan's. The dream had been so very real.

Varius checked beneath his poultice and deemed his wound was doing well enough that it required only a light bandage. "After you have some porridge, I don't see why you can't get out of bed and take in some fresh air outside."

That was very good news. "Thank you, Varius, I know this can't be easy for you."

"It would be easier if you'd stop hurting yourself."

"I believe you know what I mean."

Varius let out a breath and nodded. "Because I am descended from Arcosia and was with Second Empire." He walked over to the table and dropped into the chair. "There are many descendants of Arcosia across the lands, and not all are aligned with Second Empire. Your Rider G'ladheon is one such. How can it be helped? Arcosia's people, all men, were abandoned here by the emperor. Naturally, the men took wives from the populace and otherwise spread their seed. Second Empire will not admit it, but they are more Sacoridian or Rhovan than Arcosian, despite their ancestors and inbreeding."

"Yes, of course, but you were still here with Grandmother, part of Second Empire."

"Second Empire monitors its own. Should any knowingly betray them, or do anything to offend its leader, they are dealt with. They disappear. Grandmother took great store in punishing intransigence. I am from Penburn, got my training there. I was aware of my heritage, but didn't think much of it, didn't attend meetings or engage with my local sect. I was content with my life as a Sacoridian practicing his calling. Alas, Grandmother and the others value menders, especially with war coming, and I was not given a choice as to whether or not to uproot and spend a miserable winter in this keep.

"When I received my mastery in mending, I took an oath to do no harm. I practice my skills, my gifts, not for a political entity, or because I was forced to be here, but because I value life."

Zachary had liked Varius from the outset and now liked him even more, but his position was difficult. "You do realize I can't just set you free."

"I do. All I ask is to be of service in some way, to be able to use my skills."

Zachary thought he knew how. "There will be prisoner camps out on some of the islands. They will need menders."

Varius bowed his head in acceptance.

* * *

Once Zachary finished his porridge, he dressed in his borrowed Black Shield uniform, now cleaned and mended. He threw a cloak on, and he and Donal went outside as Varius had suggested. He found members of the River Unit and some of his fellow, former slaves repairing walls and doors, and bracing existing, precarious walls. Out where he had spent so long carrying rocks and debris, he found prisoners, under the watchful gaze of guards, blocking the passage to the Aeon Iire and building cairns over their dead. Grandmother's corpse, he was told, was simply tossed in with the rest of Second Empire's dead with no special consideration.

Out by the pickets, he found Karigan brushing Condor. She still moved slowly and with great stiffness.

He cleared his throat so as not to startle her as he approached. "Good morning."

"Good morning," she replied with a half bow.

Of a sudden, his dream came flooding back to him and he grew hot, felt a tightening of his loins. He cleared his throat again. "Condor is looking grand."

She smiled. "It is good to see you back on your feet."

He returned her smile, an awkward silence falling between them.

"I am thinking we can begin the journey back to Sacor City in a day or two," he said, "if you are ready for it."

She swiped the brush over Condor's hindquarters a couple times before turning back to him. "I will not be returning just yet, unless you command otherwise."

"If it's your back, we can wait longer, but I don't want to delay too much."

"You must return," she said. "The realm needs you, but my mission is not complete."

"The p'ehdrose? You still mean to seek them out?"

"Enver says the entrance to their valley is not far from here. This whole time, even before . . . even before what happened to me, he was searching."

Zachary could not tell her to abandon a mission he'd assigned her, and she had that determined look on her face he'd grown to know so well.

"I need to do this," she said.

"May I ask why you are so set on this? Besides the fact I gave you the mission?"

She looked at the ground, then back at him. "After what Nyssa did to me, I have been unable to do much. Enver will not allow me to pick up or carry even small loads. I don't know if I can return to being a swordmaster, or handle a sword at all. The avatar you saw was not me, really, but the power of Westrion. Without that, I am physically weak, not useful for much of anything."

"Karigan—" he protested.

"Please, let me finish. As bad as what Nyssa did to my body was, it's nothing compared to what she did in here." She tapped her head. "I do not have . . . Nyssa stripped my confidence. I am unsure of myself, of what I can do. If I go to the p'ehdrose, that is something I *can* do."

"Oh, Karigan," he murmured. He felt her pain as his own, as he had often questioned his competence as he healed from the assassin's arrow. "If you only knew how I see you. When your wounds were so fresh, you rescued me from Grandmother, and that took unbelievable strength. And *I* will not discount your role as avatar, either, for not just anyone could fill it and keep a sane mind. Connly told me of the messages you are having sent out in support of Estral. These are not small things. You are more than useful—you are essential, and I would have it no other way. Seek out the p'ehdrose if you must—I will not deny you. If anyone can make them our allies, it is you." He was disappointed, however, they would not be riding back together.

"Thank you," she replied.

"I know words won't change what you feel inside," he said, "but I hope they bring you some peace. Recovering from what you went through, it will take time. When you finish with the p'ehdrose, hurry home to us. I suspect your colonel will be just as happy to see you as I."

Karigan's smile indicated she had heard the news about Laren's promotion. "My poor father," she said.

"Your father?"

"Uh, they've become friends, he and the captain. My father seems fated to be surrounded by commanding women."

"Ah, your aunts." *And you,* he thought. He knew how Stevic G'ladheon must feel.

"Exactly," she replied.

He wished there was more to be said, wished he could demonstrate to her how he felt, but there was no privacy, too many eyes and ears near the horse pickets. Perhaps before they parted ways?

Unfortunately, he did not see her again until the morning of his departure when many of the River Unit and the former slaves came to see him off. He shook hands with Destarion and Varius.

"You have both done good work here," he told them. "You saved many lives, including my own. For that, I thank you."

Destarion looked particularly pleased by his words. "It is my honor to serve, and I will continue to do well by the River Unit."

Down the line, Captain Dannyn clicked his heels together and bowed to him. Zachary complimented him on how well and how quickly the old keep was being organized and fortified.

When he reached Lorilie Dorran, he asked, "What will you do now?"

"Rest for a time, I think," she said. "I've friends in North whom I'll stay with for a while, then who knows? If you are ever in need of a good book on equitable governance, I recommend *Beyond Monarchy: A Republic for the People,* by Edwin Grommer, who—"

"I have read all of Grommer's work," Zachary replied. He found the look of profound surprise on Lorilie's face gratifying.

"Uh, well then, if you ever need an advisor on alternate governments, seek me out."

"I will do that." He couldn't help but grin when her eyes went wide.

Down the line he went, speaking some personal words of

farewell to each of the assembled. When he reached Enver, he extended his hand for a shake.

"Thank you for all you have done," he told the Eletian. "You are welcome to my home in Sacor City any time. When next I see Prince Jametari, I intend to extend my high regard of you to him."

"Thank you, Firebrand." There was a flash of that coldness again in Enver's eyes.

Zachary leaned closely and said in a soft voice, "Please continue to watch over Karigan, and return her home as soon as you may."

"I will." Enver glanced toward Karigan and Zachary sensed a . . . possessiveness?

Was it a mistake to allow the two to travel together? But when he looked back at Enver, the Eletian seemed as good-natured as ever, almost as if Zachary had imagined anything else. Was it his own jealousy making him misread the situation? He shook his head and continued down the line.

At the end stood Karigan. She gave him her stiff half-bow.

"Stay safe," he said, "and good wishes to you in coaxing the p'ehdrose to our cause."

"Thank you, sire."

Because there were so many watching and listening, he kept his words careful. "I would be much too ill-humored were you to delay your return home by too long, Rider. We cannot do without you." Let the others try to figure out if "we" meant everyone in general back at the castle, or if he was using the royal "we" to indicate only himself. He hoped Karigan could tell.

She gave him a barely perceptible smile. "I will be home before you know it."

He nodded, pleased, but thought how much more complicated it would be when she did return. He'd become no better than a cad, he thought, who dishonored both Karigan and Estora. He did not deserve either of them. He was about to turn away, but paused. "I hope you do not mind if I hold on to your sword for a while longer." He patted the hilt.

"Of course not," she said.

"My thanks." He smiled and continued to where Donal

held the reins to his horse borrowed from the River Unit. After the battle, the sword had been found half-buried in the melting snow. He did not intend to return it to Karigan, for it was soiled by his use of it, by his madness and rage during the battle, and from all the killing. He intended she have another when she returned, one that was unsullied, and which she could use to regain her strength. He was determined that she train once more as a swordmaster.

He mounted his horse and, accompanied by Donal, Connly, and a dozen guards, departed. He glanced over his shoulder before the keep and clearing were lost to sight, and saw that she alone lingered to watch him leave.

RIDER ASH

Elgin used a horsehair brush to remove lint and dust from Laren's formal longcoat. It tickled in some spots, and she, someone who did *not* giggle, couldn't help but giggle.

"Not very dignified," Elgin muttered.

She'd never had an orderly before, and now Elgin seemed to take to the job, and voluntarily, like he was born to it.

"I'll brush you off and see how you like it," she said.

Much had changed since her promotion. She now occupied the largest rooms in officers quarters. The bed chamber was separate from the public room. There were even a small office and separate bathing room. The trade-off, of course, was having to take on greater responsibilities and deal with the other colonels and high officers. They'd looked askance at her infringing on their meetings. She could read their disdain for her just by looking at their faces—she didn't need her ability for that. It was clear in their manner that they did not believe she deserved to be among them, even though General Washburn had informed them she was there by royal command.

It was not unlike when she had become Rider captain years ago, but the other captains and lieutenants were accustomed to there being Rider captains, male or female, among them. Eventually they got used to her. The higher officers would get used to her, as well. They'd little choice. Their copious amounts of gold braid and medals did not intimidate her at all. She now had some nice gold braid herself.

Elgin set aside his brush and retrieved her sash of blue-green plaid. He started to wind it around her waist.

"I can do that," she said, snatching it from him.

"All the other colonels have orderlies to dress 'em."

"You are *not* dressing me." She took the sash and knotted it around her waist.

He gazed at her work in disapproval. "Can't even tie a decent sash knot."

"Elgin."

He waited with his hand held out. She untied the sash in resignation and handed it over. He straightened it out, carefully wound it twice around her waist, and tied a far neater knot. He then handed her her swordbelt, and this he let her buckle on herself.

She looked in the mirror to see the effect of the gold braid and new insignia, and the flourishes Estora insisted be added to her dress coats. Around her collar were embroidered gold wings, the tips nearly touching at the nape of her neck. Her cuffs featured gold embroidered feathers. She laughed at herself. Elgin looked indignant.

"Finally you get what you deserve and you laugh?"

It only made her laugh harder. "I've gotten what I deserve all right. Maybe those other officers will like me better with all the gold thread, but I doubt it."

"Hmph. I do think there is something missing."

"Oh, please don't bring *that* up. You know I prefer not to remember."

"Did you stop to think you dishonor their memory by not wearing what was given you?"

"Elgin, I can't."

"It was a long time ago and we all hurt, but now it is time for your Riders to see their captain, their new colonel, in a different light." He went into her office and opened a drawer—she had an actual desk now—and withdrew a flat box. How in the hells did he know where she kept it? He brought it out and flipped the lid back, and metal glinted. "I even polished them for you."

"Elgin, I don't—"

"If you can't wear 'em for yourself, wear 'em for your Riders, the ones here now, and the ones who are not."

She looked away, closed her eyes. All that the medals in that box represented to her was blood. Not valor, but blood.

"Make them proud, Red," Elgin said.

"Queen Isen used to hand out medals like calling cards."

"She did not, and saying so devalues the sacrifices of many. Those were dangerous times. I bet none of those baby-faced generals you've got to deal with were even out of nappies during the time of the Darrow Raiders. You should wear these when you meet with them and remind them that these aren't the only dangerous times, and that you're not just a nobody the queen picked." When she hesitated, he added, "The Riders did most of the hard, dangerous work against the Raiders. They need to remember. We need to remember the sacrifices, and you are being selfish."

Selfish, was she? She shook her head and relented because it was easier than arguing with Elgin. Three medals for valor during the Darrow Raiders, one for the mission that had caused her to be almost split in half by a knife, which had left its own prominent mark on her. Several lesser medals for actions in combat, and several colorful campaign ribbons.

She gazed in the mirror once again, sobered by difficult memories. But making light of it, she said, "I am not sure I can stand the glare of all the shiny stuff."

Elgin laughed, as she had hoped he would, and the city bell tolled three hour.

"Better get going," he said. "Your Riders will be waiting for you."

She'd told them they'd be meeting in the records room beneath the stained glass dome of the First Rider—not to mourn this time, but to go over matters of organization and to celebrate King Zachary's victory in the Lone Forest against Second Empire, as well as the demise of Grandmother and Immerez. Many of the details were unclear, like how Zachary had ended up there in the first place, what had happened to the aureas slee, and how Karigan and her companions had come into the picture.

Connly tried to feed Trace as much as he knew, but he seemed to be withholding some details until they were able to speak in person. He had sent the news about Lord Fiori, which was a huge blow, not only to Selium, but to the entire realm. He had always been such a grand presence, had been wise and generous, and he'd be missed. Laren had sent up a prayer for Estral to be able to cope with all that she must now endure with his passing.

When she arrived at the records room, her Riders were waiting for her, the stained glass dome alight from above, with its richly colored panels celebrating the heroics of the First Rider and the end of the Long War. There were only about thirty Riders in residence at the moment. Most were still out looking for Zachary. She could not wait for them all to return.

When her Riders noticed her and saw her regalia, they all stiffened to attention.

Well, she thought. That didn't happen often. The Green Riders rarely stood on formality.

"Be at ease," she told them.

They all gazed expectantly at her. It was good to have Riders there whom she hadn't seen in a while: Dale, Fergal, Trace, and others. She'd made sure Anna had come, too, and there was Mara, poor, frazzled Mara, who was now trying to do Connly's job, as well as her own.

"As you have no doubt heard," Laren said, clasping her hands behind her back, "the king has been found after unknown adventures, has waged battle against Second Empire and won, and is now on his way home."

Shouts of "hurrah" echoed around the chamber. Laren had shouted her own happiness in the privacy of her new quarters.

She spoke a little about Lord Fiori and others who had lost their lives—her friend, Captain Treman, a Weapon trainee named Rye, among numerous others. Her Riders regarded her with solemnity during this part. Most would not have met Lord Fiori, but many had known Estral.

"Finally, there are organizational matters to be addressed," she said. "It may have come to your attention that I've been promoted." Laughter followed this statement. "That means I've had to reconsider the structure of our command staff."

She felt Mara stiffen beside her. Most of those whom her announcement was going to directly affect were absent, but all the Riders needed to know and grow accustomed to the changes.

"Beryl Spencer, who has served at the level of major in the Mirwellian militia, will assume that position for the Green Riders." Unfortunately, Beryl was too often away on spy business to be an effective second. Laren had been informed recently that Beryl was currently somewhere on the east coast. Unlike the queen, Laren could not skip ranks and promote Connly to major. "Your new captain is Connly." No one expressed any surprise at these changes. "This means that Mara Brennyn moves to lieutenant." Again, no surprise, but poor Mara sighed mournfully. All she had ever wanted to be was Chief Rider, though she'd already been performing at a higher rank. The Riders cheered for Mara, even if Mara did not cheer for herself.

"Congratulations, Lieutenant," Laren said.

"Thank you," Mara mumbled.

"This brings us to the position of Chief Rider." It had taken a good deal of consideration, and she'd discussed the issue extensively with Mara, but there had really been only one choice. "Karigan G'ladheon will assume the role of Chief Rider." The job of chief was the direct supervision of the noncommissioned Riders, seeing to their everyday needs, scheduling, assigning message errands, and taking care of Rider accounts, all of which Karigan had done before. Zachary would be pleased because it would limit how often Karigan would be sent out on errands, thus into danger. The Chief Rider needed to be on castle grounds to accomplish her duties. It could be a grievous mistake, Laren reflected, to have Zachary and Karigan in such close proximity all the time, but she'd genuinely believed Karigan was the best person for the job.

The Riders seemed to think this was the extent of her announcements and chatted among themselves. She cleared her throat, but they did not hear her.

"Listen up!" Mara shouted. That silenced them.

"There may be more adjustments in time," Laren said,

"but there is one more thing that needs doing now before I dismiss you. Anna, would you please step forward?"

Anna had been warned ahead of time this was coming, but she still looked a little shocked.

"You've all met Anna. She's kept your hearths, and has been joining some of you for your studies and lessons. She has been a member of the queen's personal household staff, and she in fact helped save the queen when the aureas slee threatened to spirit her away. Anna was also helpful to me after I broke the paddock fence." More laughter here. "She has expressed interest in becoming a Green Rider, but she has not heard the call. At least, not the call that the rest of us are familiar with. She's answered a different sort of call, one that does not require magic. Being a Rider has always been a matter of spirit, anyway, not just of magic. Therefore, after much consultation with the queen, I present to you the newest member of our Green Rider family, Anna Ash."

The reaction was startled, with some scattered applause. Laren had warned Anna it would take all of them a while to get used to the idea. As for Anna's last name, it was what she had used to sign her papers. She'd said it suited her more than the one that came from her family, who'd given her away to the castle to do drudge work.

Laren's Riders, she knew, liked Anna and would get used to the idea of a non-magical Rider among them. At least, she hoped so. She considered it something of an experiment. If Anna worked out well, Laren would be able, perhaps, to fill out their ranks with those lacking magical abilities so she could realize her dream of establishing messenger relay stations throughout the realm. First, she thought, they'd all have to survive whatever Second Empire threw at them, and the reawakening of Mornhavon the Black.

It was not easy being singled out in front of the others, but Anna had stepped into the middle of their circle on shaky legs, thinking she had better get used to scary things if she was to become a Rider. And a Rider she was to be. She had signed her papers the day before. The queen said she was sorry to lose her, but was also happy for her. Since Anna didn't have a brooch to dictate how long she stayed a messenger, the capt—colonel—said they'd try it for a year, and if everything worked out, she could stay on longer.

When the announcement was made, there was some clapping, surprise, and bemusement among the other Riders. Gil clapped the loudest. Afterward, most came to congratulate and welcome her, and wish her good luck, even the ones whom she hadn't met before. It was hard to tell exactly what they thought. They were a special group, the Riders, magically called to serve, and they had abilities that, though kept secret, separated them from ordinary folk like her. Most Sacoridians hated and feared magic, which made the Riders even more tightly bound to one another, and she, lacking any magic whatsoever, was an interloper, an outsider.

"You see," Gil told her, "it all worked out!"

"I see," she said.

What she *saw* at the moment were the captain's medals, Mara's burn scars, and the glass overhead depicting the First Rider at war. Even Gil had had his share of excitement just in the process of answering the call. Did she have courage enough to be one among them? Would she faint in the face of danger as she had with the aureas slee? She felt lightheaded just thinking about it.

"Why don't you look happy?" Gil asked. "Second thoughts?"

She nodded. "What have I got myself into?"

He leaned close and whispered, "Know what you mean. I try not to think about it much." He glanced toward Mara. "Some pretty nasty things can happen to a Rider, but same for anyone else, really. A fisherman, for instance, can face a lot of danger. Did I ever tell you about the time I got this huge hook stuck through my hand? It happened while we was long-lining for saberfish."

In that moment, as Gil showed her his scar and told her the details of his injury, she realized that danger came in many forms, and not just to Green Riders. As Gil continued to tell her more grisly tales of his time at sea, she thought maybe it was better to be a Green Rider than a fisherman.

She looked around at the assembled Riders, observed their ease with one another, their camaraderie. She could rely on these people, she thought, for anything. The colonel had described them as a "family," and Anna realized that despite the possibility of danger, she had truly come home.

OATHBREAKERS

"This does not seem like an especially auspicious start," Karigan said. Condor pawed the ground beneath her.

"You have an uncanny knack for understatement, Galadheon," Enver replied.

The two of them were surrounded by shining bronze speartips wielded by rather angry-looking p'ehdrose. Some of the speartips were just inches from her heart and throat. She and Enver had used a hidden entrance to the valley of the p'ehdrose, hidden similarly to the Eletian ways, but it required her special ability to allow them to pass.

When they crossed the threshold, the lush valley opened up before them, bisected by a lake and a chain of ponds and wetlands that were segmented by beaver dams and dotted with the piles of sticks that were the beavers' lodges. Onshore were clusters of longhouses and other signs of civilization. They had not gotten far when this group of p'ehdrose appeared. They were males and females, and large, forbidding, and silent. They towered over even mounted riders. They wore loose woolen garments over their upper, muscular, human halves. It appeared to Karigan that their human hips melded into moose shoulders. One could not say, however, that their upper halves were entirely human. Some had moose ears that swiveled to catch every sound, and brown hide that encroached as far as their necks and into their faces. Some of those faces were decidedly long with wide, flat noses. A dewlap hung beneath the jaw of one male, and nubs of antlers grew from the skulls of others.

They gazed at the intruders with large brown eyes that

were fierce in their regard. At first they had looked more curious and cautious than hostile, but then one had pointed at the Black Shield insignia on Karigan's sleeve, and that was when their attitude had changed.

She decided to try again. She raised her empty hands and said, "My name is Sir Karigan G'ladheon. I am a Green Rider from the realm of Sacoridia. My companion is Enver of Eletia. We come in friendship with greetings from our leaders. We wish to speak with your chieftain, Ghallos." Only because of her travel into the future did she know his name.

There was movement among the p'ehdrose, and suddenly they rushed in, crowding Condor and Mist. They removed Karigan's saber from her saddle sheath and disarmed Enver. One of the p'ehdrose placed a curly horn to his lips, much like the horn of the Green Riders, and blew three sharp notes that rang out and echoed among the hills that cradled the valley. They bumped and pushed Condor and Mist into a headlong gallop down into the valley, packed in their midst. The pounding was excruciating to Karigan's back, and her balance was not what it had once been, but she held on, gritting her teeth all the way.

When they reached the valley floor, they were pulled back to a walk and taken into the habitation she had seen from above, a primitive village of tall huts and longhouses. More p'ehdrose, young and old, emerged to watch. Off in the distance, woolly horned creatures she believed to be komara beasts grazed on marsh grass.

The group halted. Without warning, Karigan was shoved out of the saddle and she fell to the ground with a startled cry. Enver, who had dismounted before they could force him, stepped toward her, but speartips were thrust to his throat.

Karigan perceived that the p'ehdrose valued strength and would look down upon weakness, so she rose to her feet as quickly and steadily as she could, trying to conceal signs of stiffness and pain. She and Enver were then prodded into a circular hut.

"Galadheon," Enver said, stepping over to her. "Did they hurt you?"

"I'll be all right," she said, brushing dirt off her sleeve.

She'd worn her dress longcoat and sash since this was supposed to be a diplomatic occasion. "Do they even understand my words?"

"I do not know. Contact with the p'ehdrose was cut off so long ago that they may have lost the common tongue."

Karigan pried the hanging away from the door just enough to peer outside. Mostly she saw the rear haunches of their guard, but beyond she could make out guttural voices in conversation. She let the hanging fall back into place.

"My Black Shield insignia seems to be what set them off."

"Yes," Enver agreed.

"Do you know why?"

"I have guesses."

When he said no more, she placed her hands on her hips. "Do you care to enlighten me?"

"They do not care for the Black Shields."

"Well, thank you very much. That's very illuminating."

She paced about the hut. The ceiling, like the doorway, was quite tall, and to call it a hut was to diminish it, for it was quite spacious, large enough to admit a few adult p'ehdrose at one time in comfort. Enver sat on a rush mat on the floor, his legs crossed and eyes closed. So, he was going to retreat. It was a good way to pass the time for an Eletian, she supposed, but also a good way to avoid talking to her. She paced, which helped stretch her back after the ride. No p'ehdrose came to them, and so were clearly in no rush to deal with their visitors.

No, not visitors, she thought, but prisoners.

She kept walking, following the contours of the walls, round and round. She would have liked to have begun the journey home the previous day with the king's party, but her back was not ready for extended riding and . . . It would have been difficult. Difficult to be with him among all those watchers as he made his way back to his wife.

She also had to prove to herself that she could complete her mission. Her loss of confidence had cut more deeply than the thongs of Nyssa's whip. She must not hesitate, must not be fearful, but even as she thought it, she felt Nyssa scratching at her mind again, trying to find her way in.

Karigan could not say how much time passed, but the sunlight that bled beneath the door hanging retreated and she grew weary. Enver remained in his meditative state, his expression suffused with peace.

She shrugged, knelt on one of the rush mats, and lay on her stomach. She thought back to Zachary abed with fever. After all he'd endured, he'd lost much weight. The wound on his shoulder had been red and angry with black striations radiating from it. It had made her feel totally helpless as he writhed and muttered in dreams that she could do so little for him. Destarion intimated that had he not turned when he did, they would have lost him, and she would not have been able to do anything about it. Her last thought before she drifted off was to wonder why it was that she could help the dead, but not the living.

The entrance of a pair of p'ehdrose startled her out of a dream, some nonsense of being a gryphon merchant trying to sell winged kittens. A speartip was shoved in her face, while the other p'ehdrose held Enver at bay.

"Stand," she was ordered. So, at least one of the p'ehdrose had something of the common tongue.

She obeyed, again trying to show that it was no difficulty to do so. The two p'ehdrose grabbed her under her arms and lifted her off her feet. They carried her outside between them, while a third blocked the doorway so Enver couldn't dart out after her.

She was dropped before a bonfire, and she gave a throttled cry at the pain that ripped through her back. Many p'ehdrose crowded in around her. They smelled of the earth, and a strange mixture of animal musk and human odor. The westering sun had cast the valley in shadow, and firelight limned the grim faces that surrounded her. Once again, she climbed to her feet, trying to retain some semblance of dignity.

She turned to the one who had ordered her to stand in the hut. "I demand to see your chief. This is no way to treat a king's envoy."

At first there was no reaction, then an old, grizzled p'ehdrose stepped forward. "The only reason you are not dead yet," he said, "is that you wear the green of Lil Ambriodhe's

Riders." He took another step forward. "I am Yannuf, chief of the Fforstald Clan, and your trespass into this valley carries the death penalty. You broke an oath by coming here."

"I do not know of any such oath."

"It was made by Lil Ambriodhe, King Santanara, and our great chief, Braaga, long ago. It allowed the p'ehdrose to vanish into obscurity for their services rendered during the Long War."

A long time ago, indeed, Karigan thought. Clearly no one in Sacoridia had remembered it, just one more detail lost from that ancient time. She fumed, thinking that the Eletians would have remembered it. What of Enver? Had he known?

"We let you live because we owe a debt to Lil Ambriodhe," Yannuf continued. "She aided us in a time of persecution."

"The Scourge," Karigan murmured.

"It was called that by some, yes. The Black Shield on your sleeve represents a great darkness that occurred after the Long War, when there were those who would stop at nothing to eliminate magic from the lands and exterminate those who were different. Like my people."

Karigan had gathered hints that the Weapons had been an instrument of those who sought to destroy magic following the Long War, but this was the most concrete statement she'd had of it. She thought about the Chamber of Proving, which had dampened her ability. Brienne had said it was used after the Long War during the Scourge. Had the Weapons of ancient times used it to suppress those with magical abilities as a form of punishment, or for some other purpose?

"It was not my intention to break any oath," Karigan said. "Many, many years have passed since the Long War, and much has been forgotten. Likewise, many generations of Black Shields have come and gone, and whatever their roots in the old days, they no longer suppress magic." If they did, she certainly knew nothing about it. They had done nothing to persecute the modern Green Riders.

"We thought it curious," Yannuf said, "that a Green Rider would bear the symbol of the Black Shields, unless the Black Shields had successfully eliminated magic from the Green Riders."

So, Yannuf put the blame for the persecution of magic users directly on the Weapons. That was interesting. "The Black Shields have made me an honorary member of their order," she said. She did not dare address the question of Rider magic directly. "They have caused the Riders no harm. They accept me, and they have my respect."

"It is long since any of my folk have ventured into the outside world. I agree the Long War was many generations ago. Perhaps you can give us news of the lands."

"Yes, but my king—"

"News first, Green Rider; then we will discuss what has brought you here." He clapped his hands. "We need food and wine for our guest." Several of the p'ehdrose peeled off to obey.

This, Karigan thought, appeared to be a positive change of attitude on their behalf. "My companion should be present as well, so you may have the Eletian side of things."

Yannuf studied her with his dark brown eyes, and smiled. "Your Eletian friend should have known of the oath. But no matter, we will hear him, too."

A mat was produced for her and Enver to sit on since the p'ehdrosians had no use for chairs or stools, and earthenware pitchers of wine, and platters of food that contained tubers, watercress, cheese, cold-smoked salmon, and flatbread were brought out to them. The wine was good. It had a wild flavor to it she could not place, and between sips she tried to answer Yannuf's questions about the past to present. Enver helped fill in some gaps. She espied young, leggy p'ehdrosians peeking beneath the bellies of their mothers to get a look at her and Enver. She could only guess that having two-legged people in their midst was a very strange sight to them.

"And so you say Mornhavon has reawakened," Yannuf said.

She was surprised to realize it had grown full dark. The stars were slightly different here, as if the valley wasn't just hidden, but slightly askew from her own world.

"Yes," she replied, and she and Enver described Mornhavon's return and the rise of Second Empire.

"I assume," Yannuf said, "it is why you have come here seeking us. You remembered your old allies."

"An image of the p'ehdrose was recently found in a panel of stained glass depicting the Long War."

Yannuf turned his gaze to Enver. "You mean the Eletians did not tell you?"

"Our people knew yours had gone into seclusion," Enver replied. "We did not know if you persisted."

Yannuf squinted his eyes as if he didn't quite believe him. "Your people should have remembered, even if hers didn't, not to break the oath. Especially your king."

Karigan saw that Enver looked disturbed. Had he even known? It would be like the Eletians to send them into a situation even if they knew better.

"King Santanara Sleeps," was all Enver would say.

One of the p'ehdrose whispered into Yannuf's ear. Now he turned his sharp gaze back on Karigan. "How is it you know of Ghallos?"

There was some pushing and shoving among the onlookers as a p'ehdrose burst to the front. Karigan recognized him immediately.

"Yes," Ghallos said, "I would like to know, too."

GHALLOS

Karigan stared wide-eyed at Ghallos. He was large even among the p'ehdrose, and so *alive.* She'd last seen him as a stuffed specimen on display in a museum in the future. His moose half had been well-preserved, but his human half had been poorly executed. She shuddered as she remembered someone telling her how difficult it was to preserve human flesh. His skin had appeared old parchment, puckered and yellowed, his hair and beard like dry straw. The living Ghallos radiated energy and looked nothing like old parchment.

"Well?" he demanded. "How do you know my name?"

"It's, uh, a long story," Karigan said. "My pardon, Chief Ghallos." She bowed.

There were murmurs among the assembled, and when Karigan looked up, the p'ehdrose was staring hard at her.

"I am not the chief," he said. "Yannuf is, and any of my kind would be punished severely for suggesting otherwise."

"Again, my pardon." The sudden appearance of Ghallos had shaken her, and she should have guessed that some of the things she had understood in the future to be true might not have yet come to pass in the present.

"I have been listening in the back, Uncle," Ghallos told Yannuf. "I think these creatures should be put back in their pen while we have a talk."

"Agreed," Yannuf said.

Before Karigan could protest, she was picked up beneath her arms again by a pair of p'ehdrose and carried back into the hut, where they dropped her. They brought Enver right behind her, but he landed neatly on his feet.

Karigan crawled over to a mat and sat. "Damnation."

"Did they hurt you?" Enver asked.

"No worse than last time."

"I should look at your back."

"No." She did not want to be caught unprepared should the p'ehdrose return for them. Besides, what could Enver do? The p'ehdrose had all of his belongings, including his herbs and medicaments. She'd also grown reluctant to let him care for her on so intimate a level. She'd the feeling of late that his desire to help came less from a place of healing than his own personal need to be near her. "This is not going the way I hoped."

"They are a primitive race, Galadheon. They always have been."

"Did you know about the oath?" she asked.

Enver sat fluidly onto his own mat. "Believe me, I did not. When I was given my orders, that information was left out."

Eletians. Prince Jametari apparently thought them expendable. "They may kill us, you know. They will not want the secret of their valley to get out."

"I am sorry, Galadheon. I did not know of this oath."

She sighed. "It's not your fault. It doesn't help that I'm not much of a diplomat." She wondered if there was any way to evoke the friendship of Lil Ambrioth. During the Long War, a p'ehdrose named Maultin had given the First Rider a horn of the komara beast. It was used to summon Green Riders and was supposed to be passed down from one Rider captain to the next. Karigan hadn't thought to bring it along as a reminder of old friendships because she was *not* captain, and now she silently berated herself.

She sat for a while, then got up and paced, and then sat again, while Enver remained in his meditative posture.

"What will you do," he asked suddenly, "when you return home?"

Karigan looked at him in surprise. "Home? That's if we aren't killed . . ."

"I prefer to believe all will be well."

As if to counter his words, voices were raised in argument outside.

"*If* I get home, I guess it will be a return to the usual." She paused, looked down at her hands. "Of course, I will have to get my back working properly first."

"You will practice listening to the world." It was not a question.

"I—yes, I guess I will."

"What else, Galadheon?"

"I haven't really thought about it. It depends on what duties I'm assigned."

"Not just your duties," Enver said. "What else?"

What was he driving at? "I don't know."

"What of your king?"

"What about my king?" she asked in a sharp voice. Unconsciously, she toyed with the bracelet he had made her.

"You will return to him."

"Yes, of course I will. I am his messenger. I will return to resume my duty in Sacor City."

"There is more to it than that," he said, "between you." He actually sounded angry.

She stood, not pleased with the direction in which this conversation was going. She paced some more, and then turned on him. "It is nothing. It can be nothing. It never could have been anything."

"Are you just saying that to appease me, or do you believe it?"

"Why are you bringing this up?"

"I've an interest," he said.

She stared at him, and he stared right back. His eyes took her in hungrily and there was no question of his "interest." She stepped back, then shook herself and started pacing again. When she paused once more, she said in a low, intense voice, "I do not want to talk about this again, not about the king or—or your interest." She turned away, but not before she saw the stung expression on his face.

It might have been a couple hours before the p'ehdrose returned for them. This time, before Karigan could be carried out, she shouted at her escorts, "I can walk! Leave your hands off me." She was far beyond being diplomatic at this point, especially after having to sit in such pained silence with Enver for so long.

Ghallos and Yannuf stood foremost at the bonfire, waiting for them. Karigan and Enver were shoved in front of them as if in judgment.

"We have discussed long and hard what to do with a pair of oathbreakers," Yannuf said. "Oathbreakers of peoples with whom we once had friendly ties."

"We hear your plea for help," Ghallos said, "as an old dark revives, but though we are sympathetic, it is not our world and not our care. We will go on as we always have."

Karigan was about to protest when Yannuf said, "No interruptions. Your lives have been very much at stake here. There will be justice."

She balled her fists. She wouldn't get far against these brawny, armed p'ehdrose, but she would not die without a fight.

"Because of the friendship between our peoples of long ago," Yannuf continued, "because of the high regard one of our greatest heroes, Maultin, held for the First Rider and King Santanara, we will spare your lives."

She exhaled in relief and relaxed her tense muscles. Her back was killing her.

"*However,* we cannot allow you to leave our valley ever again."

"What?" Karigan cried. "Why not?"

"You have seen too much. You know our secret. We cannot have outsiders entering our valley."

"You don't think our people won't come looking for us?" she demanded.

"If they do, they won't find you," Ghallos said, his arms crossed upon his chest.

"*We* found you."

"The entrance to our valley will be changed," Yannuf said.

She looked from one to the other, from youngster to elder. "You expect me to accept this?"

"We offer you our hospitality," Yannuf replied. "If you choose not to accept, you will be dealt with accordingly."

"Killed."

Yannuf nodded.

Karigan began to tremble with rage. She stepped boldly up to the two p'ehdrose. Enver tried grabbing her arm, but she shook him off.

He whispered an urgent, "Galadheon, they are already angry!"

She ignored him. "You think changing the entry to your valley will keep searchers out?" she demanded of Yannuf and Ghallos. "You think the rising darkness will not affect you? That the tainted wild magic of Blackveil will not reach you? You think Mornhavon won't remember you? Then I suggest you think again."

"I'll not hear this—" Yannuf began.

"You ignore me at your peril!" she shouted. "You look to the past, but what about the future? Let me show you the future." And she ripped off her eyepatch and stared up at Ghallos. There were intakes of breath from those who caught the gleam of her mirror eye.

"Mirare," one or two whispered.

Ghallos bent toward her as though her gaze drew him inescapably in. She saw nothing out of her mirror eye. Until she did. Through it she viewed the universe with myriad stars and the interweaving of threads, past, present, future. Some threads ran their course unbroken, twined with others, but moving so rapidly like a comet that she could make no sense of it. Others frayed and threatened to snap. And then there were those that had snapped, the severed ends dangling, wispy, reaching out to rejoin, but it was too late for them. Of one of those she got an impression of Nyssa on one end, and on the other, of a man named Starling, one who would have been born in the future had Nyssa not been killed.

Ghallos seemed to stare into her eye for what felt like forever—she'd never revealed it for so long before. Daggerlike pain stabbed her eye, and she fell back with a cry into Enver's arms.

"It is all right, Galadheon," he whispered in soothing tones. "I have you. It is all right." He cradled her while she caught her breath, while her heartbeat steadied, while she tried to make sense of who she was, where she was.

When she came to her senses and her vision cleared, she saw that Ghallos was pale. He knelt down before her, his legs shaking. "You are Mirare," he said.

"So I have been told."

He shivered. "One such as you has not been seen among our people since Maultin's time. What I saw in your eye . . . You were telling us truth. We are not safe, not even here. Nothing we could do would guarantee our safety." He stood once more, looked at his uncle and all the p'ehdrose assembled. "If we do nothing, we will be hunted down and slaughtered, every last one of us, until we are no more. Mornhavon the Black is rising, and he has not forgotten us. Now is not the time to hide, but to strike before we are destroyed."

Voices rose and raged around him in the guttural language of the p'ehdrose. Karigan remained reclined in Enver's arms, feeling rather muddled. One voice stood out from the others—Ghallos. He paced among the other p'ehdrose, his tone by turns cajoling, argumentative, authoritative. She did not know how much time elapsed for she seemed to fall in and out of awareness, the fire flickering against the faces of the p'ehdrose, dreamlike. Enver carried her back to their hut.

"Ghallos looked in your eye a very long time," he told her. "The effect on him was profound."

"Have they decided?" Karigan asked.

In the hut, Enver gently set her down and wrapped her in his cloak. "No, Galadheon. I think they will be arguing much of the night."

As she drifted off, she was vaguely aware of him seated so close beside her that they touched. She thought, perhaps, she should move away, but she hadn't the energy, and the dark of sleep descended.

In the morning she awoke with a headache. One of the p'ehdrose brought them a tray of food and drink. There was more of the cold-smoked salmon, cheese, and a stout bread dripping with honey.

Karigan tried to shake off the grogginess and sipped tea. "Have they come to a decision?" she asked Enver. She peered through the doorway and found the outer world quiet but for the morning song of birds and a few p'ehdrose moving about, attending to chores. The bonfire from the previous night was nothing but ashes.

"I believe they have," Enver said, "but I am not sure which way it has gone."

Breakfast was long finished, and Karigan pacing with anxiety and impatience, by the time Yannuf came to see them, his expression grim.

"Tell your kings," he said, "that the p'ehdrose will honor its alliance of old. We will once more go to war."

While Karigan no longer saw the heavens with its many threads, she *felt* one snap, and decisively. Her body actually jerked with it and Enver hastened to steady her. She had done it. She had turned the p'ehdrose to their cause. And now she could return home to whatever uncertainty awaited her there.

SOLITUDE

Ghallos led Karigan and Enver from the valley. Before they parted, Ghallos told Karigan, "I keep expecting you to, I don't know, change into a bird or something incredible. You are Mirare, but all I see is an ordinary woman, or, at least, as ordinary as one with only two legs can be."

She smiled, pleased, for once, to be considered ordinary.

He then took her aside and bent down to whisper, "Just a warning about Eletians. You may think you know them, but they are not always what they seem. This one smells of . . . danger."

She glanced at Enver, who watched them without expression. She did not doubt his keen hearing had picked up all that Ghallos said.

"In what way?"

"I am not sure," Ghallos replied, "but be wary, and keep in mind that though they may have only two legs like you, they are very different creatures and, in some ways, much less civilized."

Karigan smiled weakly and bade Ghallos farewell. Because he helped show them the path out of the valley, the use of her ability was not required. She had considered asking him about Odessa before they left, the p'ehdrose who, she'd learned in the future time, was his mate, but she decided that if he wasn't yet chieftain of the p'ehdrose as she had believed, perhaps Odessa was not yet his mate, and she did not wish to disrupt the natural course of whatever might lie between the two.

* * *

It was a pleasant day for a ride in the sunshine, and Karigan was feeling much better thanks to the deep sleep she'd gotten after the long exposure of her mirror eye the previous night. She had succeeded in reforging the alliance with the p'eh-drose, even if by unconventional means, and had in her satchel a document of agreement marked by Yannuf's bloody thumb-print to represent his signature. She and Enver had not been killed or forced to live in the valley. She considered the en-deavor to have been a great success.

As they rode, however, she was already thinking about the journey home, about what Nyssa had done to her confi-dence, and about Enver. She gave him a quick sideways glance. His gaze was fixed on the terrain ahead, but too often she'd felt that gaze fixed on her, and that his regard of her had intensified. She could not pinpoint exactly when it had happened, but he seemed to have need of being near her constantly, always having to have some physical contact with her. No matter how harmless the touch, it had begun to feel proprietary, as though he held some claim to her that others were not permitted. It had gotten to the point where, not only had she declined having him tend her wounds, but she had refused to let him help her mount Condor. Then there was the exchange they had had in the hut of the p'ehdrose when he'd expressed his "interest" and had seemed jealous of Zachary. It all made her feel uneasy and she kept what distance she could.

When they halted for a break, she dismounted and paced to relax her back, and she came to a decision. When she saw Enver following her every move, she knew it was the right one.

"Enver," she said, "back in the valley you asked me what I was going to do when I returned home."

"I did."

"Well, what are *you* going to do?"

"I will ride with you to Sacor City," he replied.

"What then? You must need to get word back to Prince Jametari about the p'ehdrose."

"Word will reach the Alluvium."

He'd grown stolid. She collected herself before she spoke

again. She just needed to say it. "I don't want you to go to Sacor City with me."

A wildness filled his eyes. "Why?" He took a step toward her, and she felt his aggression as a physical thing.

She remained warily by Condor's side, patted his shoulder. "I have not been very strong since Nyssa hurt me," she said. "I mean, inside me, not just the outside. I need to go it alone from here, for my own sake, and try to find my confidence again. Face the world on my own. Do you understand?"

Such an expression of . . . anger? Desperation? Despair? fell over his face that she was not sure what he intended to do.

"You don't want me?" he asked.

"It's not about *wanting you*," she said, "or not wanting you. I just need to be on my own now."

"But *me*," he said, that wildness flaring in his eyes. "Your spirit sings to me, calls to me. Does mine not call to you?"

She tensed. This was not a conversation she wanted to have. "We are friends."

"No," he snarled. "I do not mean just friends. Does my spirit call to you?"

There was no gentle way of saying it, so she didn't even try. "No."

He turned away, shaking.

"Enver?" She took a step after him.

"Do not approach," he warned her. "Do not come near. It is not safe. You should go."

"I'm sorry, I—"

"Do not speak!"

Had her answer meant so much to him? Matters of the heart could cause anguish, and she had sensed for a time he'd been attracted to her more than just a little, though it wasn't always easy to tell with an Eletian. And of late, there'd been that intensification of his regard of her.

He struggled with himself, she saw, quaking, and clenching and unclenching his hands. He writhed as if in pain and she wished to help him, but he'd ordered her not to.

"Do you not see?" he demanded of her. "I am a danger to you. *Go.*"

"What— "

"My unfolding is upon me. Nari was right—I am young and a fool, and I have been too arrogant to see the truth. Please go before I— " He emitted a strangled, growling sound, his body tightly drawn and contorted in some agony. "Go before I force myself upon you. I do not wish to destroy that which I love."

He would force himself on her? She backed away, put Condor between them, and climbed on a rock to aid in mounting. She fumbled for the stirrup.

"The council must have wished this upon me, us," he continued in a tight voice. "They must have known I would lose control in your presence. What end they wish to accomplish by pairing us, I do not know, though they would value one with your ability to transcend thresholds, and have you bound to Eletia by your—*our*—young."

What the hells? She shook herself and at last managed to get her toe in the stirrup. She painfully hauled herself into the saddle. "You will explain this to me later?"

He made a growling sound. "Go!"

"You'll be all right?"

"I will be when you are away from me. Mist will prevent me from following. You will go on to Sacor City without me as you wish. Now go, *please*, before I lose all control and attack. *Go!*"

She clucked Condor away, but when Enver howled—a gut-wrenching, wild howl—she glanced over her shoulder and saw him on his knees, his head thrown back and fists clenched. Mist lipped his shoulder.

Karigan rode on, soon entering the Lone Forest in a state of lingering bewilderment and feeling utterly depleted. She was unsure of exactly what had happened, except that Enver had come very close to— No, she did not wish to even think about it, what could have happened.

What was this "unfolding" of his? She swallowed hard. The council of the Alluvium had some audacity. Did they not know Green Riders could not conceive while they heard the call? Or, in their arrogance, did they believe an Eletian could overcome even that? Regardless, had Enver not sent her away . . . The danger she had been in was only just sinking in. She was under no illusion that she would have been able to stop him, had he lost control.

She was trembling hard by the time she reached the clearing of the keep. She halted Condor beneath the fringe of the woods, her gaze taking in, but not really seeing, all the soldiers on the grounds going about their work.

Her general lack of trust for Eletians, it appeared, was well-founded. She did not include Enver in that assessment. She still trusted *him,* and perhaps even more so now, but those who ruled, this council of theirs, they'd sent her and Enver to the p'ehdrose knowing they'd be breaking an oath, which could have resulted in their deaths, or at the very least, never being allowed to leave the valley again. The Eletians had also paired her with Enver, not just because they were familiar with her from past collaborations, or because she had the ability to cross over into the valley of the p'ehdrose, but for other reasons, an as-yet-to-be-determined endgame. They must have known that, as Enver put it, her spirit called to him. One day, she would put an end to their meddling in her life. Prince Jametari and his councilors would be made to atone for their interference, and the apparent agony that now assailed Enver.

When she returned to Sacor City and reported it all . . . She shook her head, not sure she should make mention of this particular manipulation. She could not guess how Zachary would react, and she had no wish to be the cause of a rift between Sacoridia and Eletia at so crucial a time.

She dismounted and led Condor onto the keep grounds, bewilderment and anger giving way to acute loneliness. Estral had departed for Selium, Zachary was on his way home, and now Enver would be going his own way, as well. There were many people here at the keep, but most were strangers. She might as well be alone.

Captain Dannyn spotted her, and she halted as he picked his way across the clearing toward her. "Rider," he said when he reached her, "welcome back. Was your mission to the p'ehdrose a success?"

"Yes," she replied.

He brightened. "That is very good news. And Enver? Is he with you?"

"No, sir. I don't know if he'll stop back here. I believe we'll be traveling our separate ways at this point."

Dannyn nodded. "Well, go ahead and get some rest and food while you can. You've earned it."

She took his advice and napped in the tower chamber. Later, when Master Destarion examined her back one final time, he told her that Enver had returned briefly. He'd collected his gear and departed immediately. Tears welled in her eyes, which she hastily wiped away.

"Did he seem all right when you saw him?" she asked.

"Yes, Rider. Shouldn't he have?"

She did not answer.

"He left me what remained of his evaleoren," Destarion said, as he rubbed the aromatic salve into her wounds. "Miraculous stuff. But you are not to strain yourself on the ride home. Take it easy, go slow, take plenty of breaks. When you reach the castle will be soon enough. No sense to hurry."

The next morning, Karigan readied herself for her journey, and after a hearty breakfast prepared by the indefatigable cooks of the River Unit, she rode Condor out of the Lone Forest, her saddlebags bulging with provisions. She'd left Bane behind, figuring the River Unit would have much greater need of him than she.

She halted Condor on the rocky plain, a heavy, leaden sky hanging low over the landscape. She stretched out her hand and felt sprinkles patter on her upturned palm. Behind her was the forest wafting in morning mists, with the darkness of battle and torture hidden beneath its eaves. Ahead lay home and many days on the road where she'd be alone with her thoughts. Difficult thoughts and memories. Should she run into trouble, she still was not able to wield a sword. Weakness remained. And what if the Nyssa spirit returned to torment her? Well, she had the command of ghosts, didn't she? And there was always retreat to the starry meadow.

This journey would be, she realized with some surprise, her first time on her own since before her travel into the future, since before even her mission into Blackveil. But the solitude was as she wished. She would face her journey all alone, and on her own terms.

I will regain my strength. I will and I must.

Condor danced beneath her, anxious to run, and she laughed. No, she was not really alone, and he'd have her home before she knew it.

MIDHAVEN HARBOR, COUTRE PROVINCE

Rider Ty Newland, sitting at a scarred table in the Whale's Tooth Tavern with a tankard of ale before him, watched the young man enter from the street. His baggy trousers and striped shirt indicated he was a sailor, and his dusky skin suggested he was also Tallitrean. Unlike most sailors, his features were not gruff or weathered, but fine, almost delicate, and his body one of whipcord strength. Ty couldn't take his eyes off him. When he caught the young man's gaze, he smiled.

"Ahem."

Another sailor dropped into the empty chair across the table from him, but this one he knew. He tried to see around her, but the young man had disappeared into another of the tavern's rooms.

"Admiring the pretty scenery?" Beryl Spencer asked.

"Was," he said, "until you came along."

A knowing smile crossed Beryl's face, and it was not a particularly friendly one. She was not the usual Green Rider, but a spy that King Zachary often sent on secretive missions. Currently, she was attired as a sailor to blend in with the harbor folk. He could not remember the last time he had seen her in a Rider uniform.

"I have a lead," she said.

Finally, he thought. She'd been hunting for Lord Amberhill most of the winter as a result of the information Karigan had brought back from the future.

"Met a shipmaster of a sealing vessel who took Lord Amberhill on as a passenger last year, along with his manservant. They disembarked near an archipelago off Bairdly."

"What in the hells does he want with an island? Or an archipelago?" Ty asked.

"Good question. The archipelago is uninhabited and has a bad reputation among sailors for being uncanny. Lots of stories of lost mariners and the like, and of late, sea monsters." She waved her hand dismissively. "Tall tales, legends. Sailors are very superstitious."

"So, now what?"

"I am going to take ship with this captain, and she will leave me off where she left off Amberhill. I need to buy my own skiff or sailing dory, apparently. I am sure the king won't mind the expense." Again, that smile. "I will investigate the islands for sign of Lord Amberhill, and if I find him?"

"You will drag him back to Sacor City," Ty concluded.

"That would be optimal," she replied, "though not expedient."

He could only guess what she'd consider expedient. Beryl had many skills, and he would not have been surprised if assassin was one of them.

"What do you want me to do?" he asked.

"I want you to return to Sacor City and tell the king and captain what I just told you, and that I will endeavor to bring his cousin back, tied hand and foot, or otherwise."

That, Ty thought, would solve many of their problems before they even began. He took a final sip of his ale, and when he set his tankard back down, Beryl was gone just like that. He sighed, dropped a couple coppers on the table, and left with a look of regret over his shoulder toward the room into which the Tallitrean had disappeared. Outside, a southerly breeze mixed with the harbor's briny sea scent and hinted at a fine spring day.

He strode toward the stables where he had boarded his horse, Crane. They were going home, back to Sacor City.

Kristen Britain is the author of the best selling Green Rider series. She lives in an adobe house in the high desert of the American Southwest beneath the big sky, and among lizards and hummingbirds and tumbleweeds.